The Graveyard Book

Also by Neil Gaiman from Bloomsbury

Novels

Coraline
Odd and the Frost Giants

Picture Books

The Dangerous Alphabet
The Day I Swapped My Dad for Two Goldfish
The Wolves in the Walls

Graphic Novels

Mirrormask
Signal to Noise
The Tragical Comedy or Comical Tragedy of Mr Punch

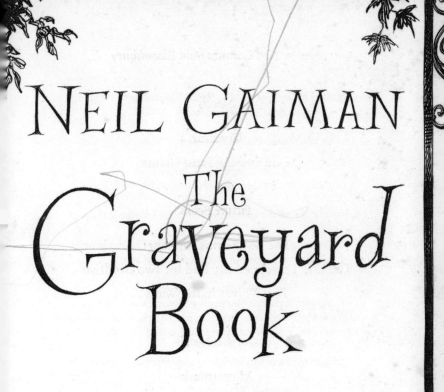

NEIL GAIMAN

The Graveyard Book

ILLUSTRATED BY Chris Riddell

BLOOMSBURY

LONDON BERLIN NEW YORK

First published in Great Britain in 2008 by Bloomsbury Publishing Plc
36 Soho Square, London, W1D 3QY

Text first published in the US by HarperCollins Publishers.

Text copyright © Neil Gaiman 2008
Illustrations copyright © Chris Riddell 2008

The moral rights of the author and illustrator have been asserted

'Graveyard' lyrics by Tori Amos, Copyright © 2001, Used by permission,
Courtesy of Sword & Stone, Inc. (ASCAP)

A CIP catalogue record of this book is available from the British Library

Hardback ISBN 978 0 7475 6901 5
Export ISBN 978 0 745 9884 8

The paper this book is printed on is certified by the
© Forest Stewardship Council 1996 A.C. (FSC). It is ancient-forest
friendly. The printer holds FSC chain of custody SGS-COC-2061.

FSC
Mixed Sources
Product group from well-managed
forests and other controlled sources
Cert no. SGS-COC-2061
www.fsc.org
© 1996 Forest Stewardship Council

Typeset by Dorchester Typesetting
Printed in Great Britain by Clays Ltd, St Ives Plc

3 5 7 9 10 8 6 4

www.bloomsbury.com

Rattle his bones
Over the stones
It's only a pauper
Who nobody owns

Traditional Nursery Rhyme

The man Jack paused on the landing.

CHAPTER 1

How Nobody Came to the Graveyard

There was a hand in the darkness, and it held a knife. The knife had a handle of polished black bone, and a blade finer and sharper than any razor. If it sliced you, you might not even know you had been cut, not immediately.

The knife had done almost everything it was brought to that house to do, and both the blade and the handle were wet.

The street door was still open, just a little, where the knife and the man who held it had slipped in, and wisps of night-time mist slithered and twined into the house through the open door.

The man Jack paused on the landing. With his left hand he pulled a large white handkerchief from the pocket of his black coat, and with it he wiped off the knife and his gloved right hand which had been holding it; then he put the handkerchief away. The hunt was almost over. He had left the woman in her bed, the man on the bedroom floor, the older child in her brightly coloured bedroom, surrounded by toys and half-finished models. That only left the little one, a baby barely a toddler, to take care of. One more and his task would be done.

He flexed his fingers. The man Jack was, above all things, a professional, or so he told himself, and he would not allow himself to smile until the job was completed.

His hair was dark and his eyes were dark and he wore black leather gloves of the thinnest lambskin.

The toddler's room was at the very top of the house. The man Jack walked up the stairs, his feet silent on the carpeting. Then he pushed open the attic door, and he walked in. His shoes were black leather, and they were polished to such a shine that they looked like dark mirrors: you could see the moon reflected in them, tiny and half full.

The real moon shone through the casement window. Its light was not bright, and it was diffused by the mist, but the man Jack would not need much light. The moonlight was enough. It would do.

He could make out the shape of the child in the cot, head and limbs and torso.

The cot had high, slatted sides, to prevent the child from getting out. Jack leaned over, raised his right hand, the one holding the knife, and he aimed for the chest . . .

. . . and then he lowered his hand. The shape in the cot was a teddy bear. There was no child.

The man Jack's eyes were accustomed to the dim moonlight, so he had no desire to turn on an electric light. And light was not that important, after all. He had other skills.

The man Jack sniffed the air. He ignored the scents that had come into the room with him, dismissed the

4

scents that he could safely ignore, honed in on the smell of the thing he had come to find. He could smell the child: a milky smell, like chocolate chip cookies, and the sour tang of a wet, disposable, night-time nappy. He could smell the baby shampoo in its hair, and something small and rubbery – *a toy*, he thought, and then, *no, something to suck* – that the child had been carrying.

The child had been here. It was here no longer. The man Jack followed his nose down the stairs through the middle of the tall, thin house. He inspected the bathroom, the kitchen, the airing cupboard, and, finally, the downstairs hall, in which there was nothing to be seen but the family's bicycles, a pile of empty shopping bags, a fallen nappy and the stray tendrils of fog that had insinuated themselves into the hall from the open door to the street.

The man Jack made a small noise then, a grunt that contained in it both frustration and also satisfaction. He slipped the knife into its sheath in the inside pocket of his long coat, and he stepped out into the street. There was moonlight, and there were street lights, but the fog stifled everything, muted light and muffled sound and made the night shadowy and treacherous. He looked down the hill towards the light of the closed shops, then up the street, where the last high houses wound up the hill on their way to the darkness of the old graveyard.

The man Jack sniffed the air. Then, without hurrying, he began to walk up the hill.

Ever since the child had learned to walk he had been his mother and father's despair and delight, for there never was such a boy for wandering, for climbing up things, for getting into and out of things. That night, he had been woken by the sound of something on the floor beneath him falling with a crash. Awake, he soon became bored, and had begun looking for a way out of his cot. It had high sides, like the walls of his playpen downstairs, but he was convinced that he could scale it. All he needed was a step . . .

He pulled his large, golden teddy bear into the corner of the cot, then, holding the railings in his tiny hands, he put his foot on to the bear's lap, the other foot up on the bear's head and he pulled himself up into a standing position, and then he half climbed, half toppled over the railing and out of the cot.

He landed with a muffled thump on a small mound of furry, fuzzy toys, some of them presents from relations from his first birthday, not six months gone, some of them inherited from his older sister. He was surprised when he hit the floor, but he did not cry out: if you cried they came and put you back in your cot.

He crawled out of the room.

Stairs that went up were tricky things, and he had not yet entirely mastered them. Stairs that went down however, he had discovered, were fairly simple. He did them sitting down, bumping from step to step on his well-padded bottom.

He sucked on his dummy, which his mother had just begun to tell him that he was getting too old for.

His nappy had worked itself loose on his journey on his bottom down the stairs, and when he reached the last step, when he reached the little hall and stood up, the nappy fell off. He stepped out of it. He was only wearing a child's nightshirt. The stairs that led back up to his room and his family were steep and forbidding, but the door to the street was open and inviting . . .

The child stepped out of the house a little hesitantly. The fog wreathed around him like a long-lost friend. And, uncertainly at first, then with increasing speed and confidence, the boy tottered up the hill.

The fog was thinner as you approached the top of the hill. The half-moon shone, not as bright as day, not by any means, but enough to see the graveyard, enough for that.

Look.

You could see the abandoned funeral chapel, iron doors padlocked, ivy on the sides of the spire, a small tree growing out of the guttering at roof level.

You could see stones and tombs and vaults and memorial plaques. You could see the occasional dash or scuttle of a rabbit or a vole or a weasel as it slipped out of the undergrowth and across the path.

You would have seen these things, in the moonlight, if you had been there that night.

You might not have seen a pale, plump woman, who walked the path near the front gates, and if you had seen her, with a second, more careful glance you would have realised that she was only moonlight, mist and shadow. The plump, pale woman was there, though. She walked the path that led through a clutch of half-fallen tombstones towards the front gates.

The gates were locked. They were always locked at

four in the afternoon in winter, at eight at night in summer. A spike-topped iron railing ran around part of the cemetery, a high brick wall around the rest of it. The bars of the gates were closely spaced: they would have stopped a grown man from getting through, even stopped a ten-year-old child . . .

'Owens!' called the pale woman, in a voice that might have been the rustle of the wind through the long grass. 'Owens! Come and look at this!'

She crouched down and peered at something on the ground, as a patch of shadow moved into the moonlight, revealing itself to be a grizzled man in his mid-forties. He looked down at his wife, and then looked at what she was looking at, and he scratched his head.

'Mistress Owens?' he said, for he came from a more formal age than our own. 'Is that what I think it is?'

And at that moment the thing he was inspecting seemed to catch sight of Mrs Owens, for it opened its mouth, letting the rubber nipple it was sucking fall to the ground, and it reached out a small, chubby fist, as if it were trying for all the world to hold on to Mrs Owens' pale finger.

'Strike me silly,' said Mr Owens, 'if that isn't a baby.'

'Of course it's a baby,' said his wife. 'And the question is, what is to be done with it?'

'I dare say that is a question, Mistress Owens,' said her husband. 'And yet, it is not *our* question. For this here baby is unquestionably alive, and as such is nothing to do with us, and is no part of our world.'

'Look at him smile!' said Mrs Owens. 'He has the

sweetest of smiles,' and with one insubstantial hand she stroked the child's sparse blond hair. The little boy giggled with delight.

A chilly breeze blew across the graveyard, scattering the fog in the lower slopes of the place (for the graveyard covered the whole of the top of the hill, and its paths wound up the hill and down and back upon themselves). A rattling: someone at the main gate of the graveyard was pulling and shaking it, rattling the old gates and the heavy padlock and chain that held them.

'There now,' said Owens, 'it's the babe's family, come to bring him back to the loving bosom. Leave the little man be,' he added, because Mrs Owens was putting her insubstantial arms around the toddler, smoothing, stroking.

Mrs Owens said, 'He dun't look like nobody's family, that one.' The man in the dark coat had given up on rattling the main gates and was now examining the smaller side gate. It, too, was well locked. There had been some vandalism in the graveyard the previous year, and the council had Taken Steps.

'Come on, Mistress Owens. Leave it be. There's a dear,' said Mr Owens, when he saw a ghost, and his mouth dropped open, and he found himself unable to think of anything to say.

You might think – and if you did, you would be right – that Mr Owens should not have taken on so at seeing a ghost, given that Mr and Mrs Owens were themselves dead and had been for a few hundred years now, and given that the entirety of their social life, or very nearly, was spent with those who were also dead. But there was a difference between the folk of the graveyard and *this*: a raw, flickering, startling shape the grey colour of television static, all panic and naked emotion which flooded the Owenses as if it were their own. Three figures, two large, one smaller, but only one of them was in focus, was more than an outline or a shimmer. And the figure said, *My baby! He is trying to harm my baby!*

A clattering. The man outside was hauling a heavy metal rubbish bin across the alley to the high brick wall that ran around that part of the graveyard.

'Protect my son!' said the ghost, and Mrs Owens thought it was a woman. Of course, the babe's mother.

'What did he do to you?' asked Mrs Owens, but she was not certain that the ghost could hear her. Recently dead, poor love, she thought. It's always easier to die gently, to wake in due time in the place you were buried, to come to terms with your death and to get acquainted with the other inhabitants. This creature was nothing but alarm and fear for her child, and her panic, which felt to the Owenses like a low-pitched screaming, was now attracting attention, for other pale figures were coming from all over the graveyard.

'Who are you?' Caius Pompeius asked the figure. His headstone was now only a weathered lump of rock, but two thousand years earlier he had asked to be laid to rest on the mound beside the marble shrine, rather than to have his body sent back to Rome, and he was one of the most senior citizens of the graveyard. He took his responsibilities extremely seriously. 'Are you buried here?'

'Of course she's not! Freshly dead by the look of her.'

Mrs Owens put an arm around the woman-shape and spoke to it privately, in a low voice, calm and sensible.

There was a thump and a crash from the high wall beside the alley. The rubbish bin had fallen. A man clambered up on to the top of the wall, a dark outline against the mist-smudged street lights. He paused for a moment, then climbed down the other side, holding on to the top of the wall, legs dangling, then let himself fall the last few feet, down into the graveyard.

'But my dear,' Mrs Owens said to the shape, now all that was left of the three shapes that had appeared in the graveyard. 'He's living. We're not. Can you imagine . . .'

The child was looking up at them, puzzled. It reached for one of them, then the other, finding nothing but air. The woman-shape was fading fast.

'Yes,' said Mrs Owens, in response to something that no one else had heard. 'If we can, then we will.' Then she turned to the man beside her. 'And you, Owens? Will you be a father to this little lad?'

'Will I what?' said Owens, his brow crinkling.

'We never had a child,' said his wife. 'And his mother wants us to protect him. Will you say yes?'

The man in the black coat had tripped in the tangle of ivy and half-broken headstones. Now he got to his feet and walked forward more carefully, startling an owl, which rose on silent wings. He could see the baby and there was triumph in his eyes.

Owens knew what his wife was thinking when she used that tone of voice. They had not, in life and in death, been married for over two hundred and fifty years for nothing. 'Are you certain?' he asked. 'Are you sure?'

'Sure as I ever have been of anything,' said Mrs Owens.

'Then yes. If you'll be its mother, I'll be its father.'

'Did you hear that?' Mrs Owens asked the flickering shape in the graveyard, now little more than an outline, like distant summer lightning in the shape of a woman. It said something to her that no one else could hear, and then it was gone.

'She'll not come here again,' said Mr Owens. 'Next time she wakes it'll be in her own graveyard, or wherever it is she's going.'

Mrs Owens bent down to the baby and extended her arms. 'Come now,' she said, warmly. 'Come to mama.'

To the man Jack, walking through the graveyard towards them on a path, his knife already in his hand, it seemed as if a swirl of mist had curled around the child, in the moonlight, and that the boy was no longer there: just damp mist and moonlight and swaying grass.

He blinked and sniffed the air. Something had happened, but he had no idea what it was. He growled in the back of his throat, like a beast of prey, angry and frustrated.

'Hullo?' called the man Jack, wondering if perhaps the child had stepped behind something. His voice was dark and rough, and there was an odd edge to it, as if of surprise or puzzlement at hearing himself speak.

The graveyard kept its secrets.

'Hello?' he called again. He hoped to hear a baby cry or utter a half-word, or to hear it move. He did not expect what he actually heard, a voice, silky smooth, saying:

'Can I help you?'

The man Jack was tall. This man was taller. The man Jack wore dark clothes. This man's clothes were darker. People who noticed the man Jack when he went about his business – and he did not like to be noticed – were troubled, or made uncomfortable, or found themselves unaccountably scared. The man Jack looked up at the stranger, and it was the man Jack who was troubled.

'I was looking for someone,' said the man Jack, slipping his right hand back into his coat pocket, so the knife was hidden, but there if he needed it.

'In a locked graveyard, at night?' said the stranger drily.

'It was just a baby,' said the man Jack. 'I was just passing, when I heard a baby cry, and I looked through the gates and I saw him. Well, what would anyone do?'

'I applaud your public-spiritedness,' said the stranger. 'Yet if you managed to find this child, how were you planning to get out of here with it? You can't climb back over the wall holding a baby.'

'I would have called until someone let me out,' said the man Jack.

A heavy jingling of keys. 'Well, that would have been me, then,' said the stranger. 'I would have had to let you out.' He selected one large key from the key ring, and said, 'Follow me.'

The man Jack walked behind the stranger. He took his knife from his pocket. 'Are you the caretaker, then?'

'Am I? Certainly, in a manner of speaking,' said the

stranger. They were walking towards the gates and, the man Jack was certain, away from the baby. But the caretaker had the keys. A knife in the dark, that was all it would take, and then he could search for the child all through the night, if he needed to.

He raised the knife.

'If there *was* a baby,' said the stranger, without looking back, 'it wouldn't have been here in the graveyard. Perhaps you were mistaken. It's unlikely that a child would have come in here, after all. Much more likely that you heard a nightbird, and saw a cat, perhaps, or a fox. They declared this place an official nature reserve, you know, thirty years ago, around the time of the last funeral. Now think carefully, and tell me you are *certain* that it was a child that you saw.'

The man Jack thought.

The stranger unlocked the side gate. 'A fox,' he said. 'They make the most uncommon noises, not unlike a person crying. No, your visit to this graveyard was a misstep, sir. Somewhere the child you seek awaits you, but he is not here.' And he let the thought sit there, in the man Jack's head for a moment before he opened the gate with a flourish. 'Delighted to have made your acquaintance,' he said. 'And I trust that you will find everything you need out there.'

The man Jack stood outside the gates to the graveyard. The stranger stood inside the gate, and he locked it again, and put the key away.

'Where are you going?' asked the man Jack.

'There are other gates than this,' said the stranger. 'My

car is on the other side of the hill. Don't mind me. You don't even have to remember this conversation.'

'No,' said the man Jack, agreeably. 'I don't.' He remembered wandering up the hill, that what he had thought to be a child had turned out to be a fox, that a helpful caretaker had escorted him back out to the street. He slipped his knife into its sheath. 'Well,' he said. 'Goodnight.'

'A goodnight to you,' said the stranger, whom Jack had taken for a caretaker.

The man Jack set off down the hill, in pursuit of the infant.

From the shadows, the stranger watched Jack until he was out of sight. Then he moved through the night, up and up, to the flat place below the brow of the hill, a place dominated by an obelisk and a flat stone set into the ground dedicated to the memory of Josiah Worthington, local brewer, politician and later baronet, who had, almost three hundred years before, bought the old cemetery and the land around it, and given it to the city in perpetuity. He had reserved himself the best location on the hill – a natural amphitheatre, with a view of the whole city and beyond – and had ensured that the graveyard endured as a graveyard, for which the inhabitants of the graveyard were grateful, although never quite as grateful as Josiah Worthington, Bart, felt they should have been.

There were, all told, some ten thousand souls in the graveyard, but most of them slept deep, or took no interest in the night-to-night affairs of the place, and there were less than three hundred of them up there, in the amphitheatre, in the moonlight.

The stranger reached them as silently as the fog itself, and he watched the proceedings unfold, from the shadows, and he said nothing.

Josiah Worthington was speaking. He said, 'My dear madam. Your obduracy is quite, is . . . well, can't you see how ridiculous this is?'

'No,' said Mrs Owens. 'I can't.'

She was sitting, cross-legged, on the ground, and the living child was sleeping in her lap. She cradled its head with her pale hands.

'What Mistress Owens is trying to say, sir, begging Your Honour's pardon,' said Mr Owens, standing beside her, 'is that she dun't see it that way. She sees it as doing her duty.'

Mr Owens had seen Josiah Worthington in the flesh back when they were both alive, had in fact made several pieces of fine furniture for the Worthingtons' manor house, out near Inglesham, and was still in awe of him.

'Her *duty*?' Josiah Worthington, Bart, shook his head, as if to dislodge a strand of cobweb. 'Your *duty*, ma'am, is to the graveyard, and to the commonality of those who form this population of discarnate spirits, revenants and such-like wights, and your *duty* thus is to return the creature as soon as possible to its natural home – which is not here.'

'His mama gave the boy to me,' said Mrs Owens, as if that was all that needed to be said.

'My dear woman . . .'

'I am not your dear woman,' said Mrs Owens, getting to her feet. 'Truth to tell, I don't even see why I am even here, talking to you fiddle-pated old dunderheads, when this lad is going to wake up hungry soon enough – and where am I going to find food for him in this graveyard, I should like to know?'

'Which,' said Caius Pompeius, stiffly, 'is precisely the point. What *will* you feed him? How *can* you care for him?'

Mrs Owens' eyes burned. 'I can look after him,' she said. 'As well as his own mama. She already gave him to me. Look – I'm holding him, aren't I? I'm touching him.'

'Now, see reason, Betsy,' said Mother Slaughter, a tiny old thing, in the huge bonnet and cape that she had worn in life and been buried wearing. 'Where would he live?'

'Here,' said Mrs Owens. 'We could give him the Freedom of the Graveyard.'

Mother Slaughter's mouth became a tiny 'O'. 'But,' she said. Then she said, 'But I never.'

'Well, why not? It en't the first time we'd've given the Freedom of the Graveyard to an outsider.'

'That is true,' said Caius Pompeius. 'But *he* wasn't alive.'

And with that, the stranger realised that he was being drawn, like it or not, into the conversation and, reluctantly, he stepped out of the shadows, detaching from them like a patch of darkness. 'No,' he agreed. 'I am not. But I take Mrs Owens' point.'

Josiah Worthington said, 'You do, Silas?'

'I do. For good or for evil – and I firmly believe that it is for good – Mrs Owens and her husband have taken this child under their protection. It is going to take more than just a couple of good-hearted souls to raise this child. It will,' said Silas, 'take a graveyard.'

'And what of food, and the rest of it?'

17

'I can leave the graveyard and return. I can bring him food,' said Silas.

'That's all very well you saying that,' said Mother Slaughter. 'But you comes and you goes and nobody keeps track of you. If you went off for a week, the boy could die.'

'You are a wise woman,' said Silas. 'I see why they speak so highly of you.' He couldn't push the minds of the dead as he could the living, but he could use all the tools of flattery and persuasion he possessed, for the dead are not immune to either. Then he came to a decision. 'Very well. If Mr and Mrs Owens will be his parents, I shall be his guardian. I shall remain here, and if I need to leave I shall ensure that someone takes my place, bringing the child food and looking after him. We can use the crypt of the chapel,' he added.

'But,' expostulated Josiah Worthington. 'But... A human child. A living child. I mean. I mean, I *mean*. This is a graveyard, not a nursery, blast it.'

'Exactly,' said Silas, nodding. 'A very good point, Sir Josiah. I couldn't have put it better myself. And for that reason, if for no other, it is vital that the child be raised with as little disruption as possible to the, if you'll forgive the expression, the *life* of the graveyard.' With that he strolled over to Mrs Owens, and he looked down at the infant asleep in her arms. He raised an eyebrow. 'Does he have a name, Mrs Owens?'

'Not that his mother told me,' she said.

'Well, then,' said Silas. 'His old name won't be of much use to him now, anyway. There are those out there who mean him harm. Suppose we pick a name for him, eh?'

Caius Pompeius stepped over and eyed the child. 'He looks a little like my proconsul, Marcus. We could call him Marcus.'

Josiah Worthington said, 'He looks more like my head gardener, Stebbins. Not that I'm suggesting Stebbins as a name. The man drank like a fish.'

'He looks like my nephew, Harry,' said Mother Slaughter, and it seemed then as if the whole graveyard were about to join in, each inhabitant offering his or her own comparisons between the infant and someone long forgotten, when Mrs Owens broke in.

'He looks like nobody but himself,' said Mrs Owens, firmly. 'He looks like nobody.'

'Then Nobody it is,' said Silas. 'Nobody Owens.'

It was then that, as if responding to the name, the child opened its eyes wide in wakefulness. It stared around it, taking in the faces of the dead, and the mist, and the moon. Then it looked at Silas. Its gaze did not flinch. It looked grave.

'And what kind of a name is Nobody?' asked Mother Slaughter, scandalised.

'His name. And a good name,' Silas told her. 'It will help to keep him safe.'

'I don't want trouble,' said Josiah Worthington. The infant looked up at him and then, hungry or tired or simply missing his home, his family, his world, he screwed up his tiny face and began to cry.

'Leave us,' said Caius Pompeius to Mrs Owens. 'We will discuss this further without you.'

*

Mrs Owens waited outside the chapel. It had been decreed over forty years before that the building, in appearance a small church with a spire, was a listed building of historical interest. The town council had decided that it would cost too much to renovate it, a little chapel in an overgrown graveyard that had already become unfashionable, so they had padlocked it, and waited for it to fall down. Ivy covered it, but it was solidly built, and it would not fall down this century.

The child had fallen asleep in Mrs Owens' arms. She rocked it gently, sang to it an old song, one her mother had sung to her when she was a baby herself, back in the days when men had first started to wear powdered wigs. The song went:

> *Sleep my little babby-oh*
> *Sleep until you waken*
> *When you're grown you'll see the world*
> *If I'm not mistaken.*
> *Kiss a lover,*
> *Dance a measure,*
> *Find your name*
> *and buried treasure ...*

And Mrs Owens sang all that before she discovered that she had forgotten how the song ended. She had a feeling that the final line was something in the way of 'and some hairy bacon', but that might have been another song altogether, so she stopped and instead she sang him the one about the Man in the Moon who came down too soon,

20

and after that she sang, in her warm country voice, a more recent song about a lad who put in his thumb and pulled out a plum, and she had just started a long ballad about a young country gentleman whose girlfriend had, for no particular reason, poisoned him with a dish of spotted eels, when Silas came around the side of the chapel, carrying a cardboard box.

'Here we go, Mistress Owens,' he said. 'Lots of good things for a growing boy. We can keep it in the crypt, eh?'

The padlock fell off in his hand and he pulled open the iron door to the crypt. Mrs Owens walked inside, looking dubiously at the shelves, and at the old wooden pews tipped up against a wall. There were mildewed boxes of old parish records in one corner, and an open door that revealed a Victorian flush toilet and a basin with only a cold tap, in the other.

The infant opened his eyes and stared.

'We can put the food here,' said Silas. 'It's cool, and the food will keep longer.' He reached into the box, pulled out a banana.

'And what would that be when it was at home?' asked Mrs Owens, eyeing the yellow and brown object suspiciously.

'It's a banana. A fruit, from the tropics. I believe you peel off the outer covering,' said Silas. 'Like so.'

The child – Nobody – wriggled in Mrs Owens' arms, and she let it down to the flagstones. It toddled rapidly to Silas, grasped his trouser-leg and held on.

Silas passed it the banana.

Mrs Owens watched the boy eat. 'Ba-na-na,' she said,

dubiously. 'Never heard of them. Never. What's it taste like?'

'I've absolutely no idea,' said Silas, who consumed only one food, and it was not bananas. 'You could make up a bed in here for the boy, you know.'

'I'll do no such thing, with Owens and me having a lovely little tomb over by the daffodil patch. Plenty of room in there for a little one. Anyway,' she added, concerned that Silas might think she was rejecting his hospitality, 'I wouldn't want the lad disturbing you.'

'He wouldn't.'

The boy had finished his banana. What he had not eaten was now smeared over himself. He beamed, messy and apple-cheeked.

''Narna,' he said, happily.

'What a clever little thing he is,' said Mrs Owens. 'And such a mess he's made! Why, attend you little wriggler . . .' and she picked the lumps of banana from his clothes and his hair. And then she said, 'What do you think they'll decide?'

'I don't know.'

'I can't give him up. Not after what I promised his mama.'

'Although I have been a great many things in my time,' said Silas, 'I have never been a mother. And I do not plan to begin now. But I *can* leave this place . . .'

Mrs Owens said simply, 'I cannot. My bones are here. And so are Owens's. I'm never leaving.'

'It must be good,' said Silas, 'to have somewhere that you belong. Somewhere that's home.' There was nothing wistful in the way he said this. His voice was drier than deserts, and he said it as if he were simply stating something unarguable. Mrs Owens did not argue.

'Do you think we will have long to wait?'

'Not long,' said Silas, but he was wrong about that.

Up in the amphitheatre on the side of the hill, the debate continued. That it was the Owenses who had got involved in this nonsense, rather than some flibbertigibbet johnny-come-latelies, counted for a lot, for the Owenses were respectable and respected. That Silas had volunteered to be the boy's guardian had weight – Silas was regarded with a certain wary awe by the graveyard folk, existing as he did on the borderland between their world and the world they had left. But still, but still . . .

A graveyard is not normally a democracy, and yet death is the great democracy, and each of the dead had a voice and an opinion as to whether the living child should be allowed to stay, and they were each determined to be heard, that night.

It was late autumn, when the daybreak was long in coming. Although the sky was still dark, cars could now be heard starting further down the hill, and as the living folk began to drive to work through the misty nightblack morning, the graveyard folk talked about the child that had come to them, and what was to be done. Three hundred voices. Three hundred opinions. Nehemiah Trot, the Poet, from the tumbled north-western side of the graveyard, had begun to declaim his opinion, although what it was no person listening could have said, when something happened; something to silence each opinionated mouth, something unprecedented in the history of that graveyard.

A huge white horse, of the kind that the people who know horses would call a 'grey', came ambling up the side of the hill. The pounding of its hooves could be heard before it was seen, along with the crashing it made as it pushed through the little bushes and thickets, through the brambles and the ivy and the gorse that had grown up on the side of the hill. The size of a shire horse it was, a full nineteen hands or more. It was a horse that could have carried a knight in full armour into combat, but all it carried on its naked back was a woman, clothed from head to foot in grey. Her long skirt and her shawl might have been spun out of old cobwebs.

Her face was serene, and peaceful.

They knew her, the graveyard folk, for each of us encounters the Lady on the Grey at the end of our days, and there is no forgetting her.

The horse paused beside the obelisk. In the east the sky was lightening gently, a pearlish, predawn lumines-cence that made the people of the graveyard uneasy and made them think about returning to their comfortable homes. Even so, not a one of them moved. They were watching the Lady on the Grey, each of them half-excited, half-scared. The dead are not superstitious, not as a rule, but they watched her as a Roman Augur might have watched the sacred crows circle, seeking wisdom, seeking a clue.

And she spoke to them.

In a voice like the chiming of a hundred tiny silver bells she said only, 'The dead should have charity.' And she smiled.

The horse, which had been contentedly ripping up and masticating a clump of thick grass, stopped then. The Lady touched its neck, and it turned. It took several huge, clattering steps, then it was off the side of the hill and cantering across the sky. Its thunderous hooves became an early rumble of distant thunder, and in moments it was lost to sight.

That, at least, was what the folk of the graveyard who had been on the hillside that night claimed had happened.

The debate was over and ended, and, without so much as a show of hands, had been decided. The child called Nobody Owens would be given the Freedom of the Graveyard.

Mother Slaughter and Josiah Worthington, Bart, accompanied Mr Owens to the crypt of the old chapel, and they told Mrs Owens the news.

She seemed unsurprised by the miracle. 'That's right,' she said. 'Some of them dun't have a ha'p'orth of sense in their heads. But *she* does. Of course she does.'

Before the sun rose on a stormy grey morning the child was fast asleep in the Owenses' fine little tomb (for Master Owens had died the prosperous head of the local cabinet-maker's guild, and the cabinetmakers had wanted to ensure that he was properly honoured).

Silas went out for one final journey before sunrise. He found the tall house on the side of the hill, and he examined the three bodies he found there, and he studied the pattern of the knife-wounds. When he was satisfied, he stepped out into the morning's dark, his head churning with unpleasant possibilities, and he returned to the grave-yard, to the chapel spire where he slept and waited out the days.

In the little town at the bottom of the hill the man Jack was getting increasingly angry. The night had been one that he had been looking forward to for so long, the culmination of months – of years – of work. And the business of the evening had started so promisingly – three people down before any of them had even had a chance to cry out. And then . . .

Then it had all gone so maddeningly wrong. Why on earth had he gone up the hill when the child had so obvi-ously gone *down* the hill? By the time he had reached the bottom of the hill, the trail had gone cold. Someone must have found the child, taken it in, hidden it. There was no other explanation.

A crack of thunder rang out, loud and sudden as a gunshot, and the rain began in earnest. The man Jack was methodical, and he began to plan his next move – the calls he would need to pay on certain of the townsfolk, people who would be his eyes and ears in the town.

He did not need to tell the Convocation he had failed.

Anyway, he told himself, edging under a shopfront as the morning rain came down like tears, he had not failed. Not yet. Not for years to come. There was plenty of time. Time to tie up this last piece of unfinished business. Time to cut the final thread.

It was not until the police sirens sounded and first a police car, then an ambulance, then an unmarked police car with a siren blaring, sped past him on their way up the hill that, reluctantly, the man Jack turned up the collar of his coat, put his head down and walked off into the morning. His knife was in his pocket, safe and dry inside its sheath, protected from the misery of the elements.

'I am the master of this place!'

CHAPTER 2

The New Friend

Bod was a quiet child with sober grey eyes and a mop of tousled, mouse-coloured hair. He was, for the most part, obedient. He learned how to talk, and, once he had learned, he would pester the graveyard folk with questions. 'Why amn't I allowed out of the graveyard?' he would ask, or 'How do I do what *he* just did?' or 'Who lives in here?' The adults would do their best to answer his questions, but their answers were often vague, or confusing, or contradictory, and then Bod would walk down to the old chapel and talk to Silas.

He would be there waiting at sunset, just before Silas awakened.

His guardian could always be counted upon to explain matters clearly and lucidly and as simply as Bod needed in order to understand.

'You aren't allowed out of the graveyard – it's *aren't*, by the way, not *amn't*, not these days – because it's only in the graveyard that we can keep you safe. This is where you live and this is where those who love you can be found. Outside would not be safe for you. Not yet.'

'*You* go outside. You go outside every night.'

'I am infinitely older than you, lad. And I am safe wherever I am.'

'I'm safe there too.'

'I wish that that were true. But as long as you stay here, you *are* safe.'

Or:

'How could you do that? Some skills can be attained by education, and some by practice, and some by time. Those skills will come if you study. Soon enough you will master Fading and Sliding and Dreamwalking. But some skills cannot be mastered by the living, and for those you must wait a little longer. Still, I do not doubt that you will acquire even those, in time.

'You were given the Freedom of the Graveyard, after all,' Silas would tell him. 'So the graveyard is taking care of you. While you are here, you can see in the darkness. You can walk some of the ways that the living should not travel. The eyes of the living will slip from you. I, too, was given the Freedom of the Graveyard, although in my case it comes with nothing but the right of abode.'

'I want to be like you,' said Bod, pushing out his lower lip.

'No,' said Silas firmly, 'you do not.'

Or:

'Who lies there? You know, Bod, in many cases it is written on the stone. Can you read yet? Do you know your alphabet?'

'My what?'

Silas shook his head, but said nothing. Mr and Mrs

Owens had never been much for reading when they were alive, and there were no alphabet books in the graveyard.

The next night, Silas appeared at the front of the Owenses' cosy tomb carrying three large books – two of them brightly coloured alphabet books ('A is for Apple, B is for Ball') and a copy of *The Cat in the Hat*. He also had paper, and a packet of wax crayons. Then he walked Bod around the graveyard, placing the boy's small fingers on the newest and clearest of the headstones and the plaques, and taught Bod how to find the letters of the alphabet when they appeared, beginning with the sharp steeple of the capital A.

Silas gave Bod a quest – to find each of the twenty-six letters in the graveyard – and Bod finished it, proudly, with the discovery of Ezekiel Ulmsley's stone, built into the side of the wall in the old chapel. His guardian was pleased with him.

Every day Bod would take his paper and crayons into the graveyard and he would copy names and words and numbers as best he could, and each night, before Silas would go off into the world, Bod would make Silas explain to him what he had written, and make him translate the snatches of Latin which had, for the most part, baffled the Owenses.

A sunny day: bumblebees explored the wildflowers that grew in the corner of the graveyard, dangling from the gorse and the bluebells, droning their deep, lazy buzz, while Bod lay in the spring sunlight watching a bronze-coloured beetle wandering across the stone of G$^{eo.}$ Reeder, his wife Dorcas and their son Sebastian (*Fidelis ad Mortem*). Bod had copied down their inscription and now he was only thinking about the beetle when somebody said:

'Boy? What're you doing?'

Bod looked up. There was someone on the other side of the gorse bush, watching him.

'Nuffing,' said Bod. He stuck out his tongue.

The face on the other side of the gorse bush crumpled into a gargoyle, tongue sticking out, eyes popping, then returned to girl.

'That was good,' said Bod, impressed.

'I can make really good faces,' said the girl. 'Look at this one.' She pushed her nose up with one finger, creased her mouth into a huge, satisfied smile, squinted her eyes, puffed out her cheeks. 'Do you know what that was?'

'No.'

'It was a pig, silly.'

'Oh.' Bod thought. 'You mean, like P is for Pig?'

'Of course like that. Hang on.'

She came around the gorse bush and stood next to Bod, who got to his feet. She was a little older than he was, a little taller, and was dressed in bright colours, yellow and pink and orange. Bod, in his grey winding sheet, felt dowdy and drab.

'How old are you?' said the girl. 'What are you doing here? Do you live here? What's your name?'

'I don't know,' said Bod.

'You don't know your name?' said the girl. ''Course you do. Everybody knows their own name. Fibber.'

'I know my name,' said Bod. 'And I know what I'm doing here. But I don't know the other thing you said.'

'How old you are?'

Bod nodded.

'Well,' said the girl. 'What was you when you was last birthday?'

'I didn't,' said Bod. 'I never was.'

'Everybody gets birthdays. You mean you never had cake or candles or stuff?'

Bod shook his head. The girl looked sympathetic. 'Poor thing. I'm five. I bet you're five too.'

Bod nodded enthusiastically. He was not going to argue with his new friend. She made him happy.

Her name was Scarlett Amber Perkins she told him, and she lived in a flat with no garden. Her mother was sitting on a bench at the bottom of the hill, reading a magazine, and she had told Scarlett to be back in half an hour, and to get some exercise, and not to get into trouble or talk to strangers.

'I'm a stranger,' pointed out Bod.

'You're not,' she said definitely, 'you're a little boy.' And then she said, 'And you're my friend. So you can't be a stranger.'

Bod smiled rarely, but he smiled then, hugely and with delight. 'I'm your friend,' he said.

'What's your name?'

'Bod. It's short for Nobody.'

She laughed then. 'Funny sort of a name,' she said. 'What are you doing now?'

'ABCs,' said Bod. 'From the stones. I have to write them down.'

'Can I do it with you?'

For a moment Bod felt protective – the gravestones were *his*, weren't they? – and then he realised how foolish he was being, and he thought that there were things that might be more fun done in the sunlight with a friend. He said, 'Yes.'

They copied down names from tombstones, Scarlett helping Bod pronounce unfamiliar names and words, Bod telling Scarlett what the Latin meant, if he already knew, and it seemed much too soon when they heard a voice further down the hill shouting, 'Scarlett!'

The girl thrust the crayons and paper back at Bod. 'I got to go,' she said.

'I'll see you next time,' said Bod. 'Won't I?'

'Where do you live?' she asked.

'Here,' he said. And he stood and watched her as she ran down the hill.

On the way home Scarlett told her mother about the boy called Nobody who lived in the graveyard and had played with her, and that night Scarlett's mother mentioned it to Scarlett's father, who said that he believed that imaginary friends were a common phenomenon at that age, and nothing at all to be concerned about, and that they were fortunate to have a nature reserve so near.

After that initial meeting, Scarlett never saw Bod first. On days when it was not raining one of her parents would bring her to the graveyard. The parent would sit on the bench and read while Scarlett would wander off the path, a splash of fluorescent green or orange or pink, and explore. Then, always sooner rather than later, she would see a small, grave face and grey eyes staring up at her from

36

beneath a mop of mouse-coloured hair, and then Bod and she would play – hide and seek, sometimes, or climbing things, or being quiet and watching the rabbits behind the old chapel.

Bod would introduce Scarlett to some of his other friends. That she could not see them did not seem to matter. She had already been told firmly by her parents that Bod was imaginary and that there was nothing at all wrong with that – her mother had, for a few days, even insisted on laying an extra place at the dinner table for Bod – so it came as no surprise to her that Bod also had imaginary friends. He would pass on their comments to her.

'Bartelmy says that thou dost have a face like unto a squishèd plum,' he would tell her.

'So does he. And why does he talk so funny? Doesn't he mean squashed tomato?'

'I don't think that they had tomatoes when he comes from,' said Bod. 'And that's just how they talk then.'

Scarlett was happy. She was a bright, lonely child, whose mother worked for a distant university teaching people she never met face to face, grading English papers sent to her over the computer and sending messages of advice or encouragement back. Her father taught Particle Physics, but there were, Scarlett told Bod, too many people who wanted to teach Particle Physics and not enough people who wanted to learn it, so Scarlett's family had to keep moving to different university towns, and in each town her father would hope for a permanent teaching position that never came.

'What's Particle Physics?' asked Bod.

Scarlett shrugged. 'Well,' she said. 'There's atoms, which is things that is too small to see, that's what we're all made of. And there's things that's smaller than atoms, and that's Particle Physics.'

Bod nodded and decided that Scarlett's father was probably interested in imaginary things.

Bod and Scarlett wandered the graveyard together every weekday afternoon, tracing names with their fingers, writing them down. Bod would tell Scarlett whatever he knew of the inhabitants of the grave or mausoleum or tomb, and she would tell him stories that she had been read or learned, and sometimes she would tell him about the world outside, about cars and buses and television and aeroplanes (Bod had seen them flying high overhead, had thought them loud silver birds, but had never been curious about them until now). He in his turn would tell her about the days when the people in the graves had been alive – how Sebastian Reeder had been to London Town and had seen the Queen, who had been a fat woman in a fur cap who had glared at everyone and spoke no English. Sebastian Reeder could not remember which queen she had been, but he did not think she had been queen for very long.

'When was this?' Scarlett asked.

'He died in 1583, it says on his tombstone, so before then.'

'Who is the oldest person here. In the whole grave-yard?' asked Scarlett.

Bod frowned. 'Probbly Caius Pompeius. He came here a hundred years after the Romans first got here. He told me about it. He liked the roads.'

'So he's the oldest?'

'I think so.'

'Can we make a little house in one of those stone houses?'

'You can't get in. It's locked. They all are.'

'Can *you* get in?'

'Of course.'

'Why can't I?'

'The graveyard,' he explained. 'I got the Freedom of the Graveyard. It lets me go places.'

'I want to go in the stone house and make little houses.'

'You can't.'

'You're just mean.'

'Not.'

'Meany.'

'Not.'

Scarlett put her hands into the pocket of her anorak and walked down the hill without saying goodbye, convinced that Bod was keeping something from her, and at the same time suspecting that she was being unfair, which made her angrier.

That night, over dinner, she asked her mother and father if there was anyone in the country before the Romans came.

'Where did you hear about the Romans?' asked her father.

'Everybody knows,' said Scarlett, with withering scorn. 'Was there?'

'There were Celts,' said her mother. 'They were here

39

first. They go back before the Romans. They were the people that the Romans conquered.'

On the bench beside the old chapel, Bod was having a similar conversation.

'The oldest?' said Silas. 'Honestly, Bod, I don't know. The oldest in the graveyard that I've encountered is Caius Pompeius. But there were people here before the Romans came. Lots of them, going back a long time. How are your letters coming along?'

'Good, I think. When do I learn joined-up letters?'

Silas paused. 'I have no doubt,' he said, after a moment's reflection, 'that there are, among the many talented individuals interred here, at least a smattering of teachers. I shall make enquiries.'

Bod was thrilled. He imagined a future in which he could read everything, in which all stories could be opened and discovered.

When Silas had left the graveyard to go about his own affairs, Bod walked to the willow tree beside the old chapel, and called Caius Pompeius.

The old Roman came out of his grave with a yawn. 'Ah. Yes. The living boy,' he said. 'How are you, living boy?'

Bod said, 'I do very well, sir.'

'Good. I am pleased to hear it.' The old Roman's hair was pale in the moonlight, and he wore the toga in which he had been buried, with, beneath it, a thick woollen vest and leggings because this was a cold country at the edge of the world, and the only place colder was Caledonia to the north, where the men were more animal than human and covered in orange fur, and were too savage even to be conquered by the Romans, so would soon be walled off in their perpetual winter.

'Are you the oldest?' asked Bod.

'The oldest in the graveyard? I am.'

'So you were the first to be buried here?'

A hesitation. 'Almost the first,' said Caius Pompeius. 'Before the Celts there were other people on this island. One of them was buried here.'

'Oh.' Bod thought for a moment. 'Where's his grave?'

Caius pointed up the hill.

'He's up at the top,' said Bod.

Caius shook his head.

'Then what?'

The old Roman reached down and he ruffled Bod's hair. 'In the hill,' he said. 'Inside it. I was first brought here by my friends, followed in their turn by the local officials and the mimes, who wore the wax faces of my wife, taken by a fever in Camulodonum, and my father, killed in a border skirmish in Gaul. Three hundred years after my death, a farmer, seeking a new place to graze his sheep, discovered the boulder that covered the entrance, and rolled it away, and went down, thinking there might be treasure. He came out a little later, his dark hair now as white as mine . . .'

'What did he see?'

Caius said nothing, then, 'He would not speak of it. Or ever return. They put the boulder back, and in time, they forgot. And then, two hundred years ago, when they were building the Frobisher vault, they found it once more. The young man who found the place dreamed of riches, so he

41

told no one, and he hid the doorway behind Ephraim Pettyfer's coffin, and went down one night, unobserved, or so he thought.'

'Was his hair white when he came up?'

'He did not come up.'

'Um. Oh. So, who is buried down there?'

Caius shook his head. 'I do not know, young Owens. But I felt him, back when this place was empty. I could feel something waiting even then, deep in the hill.'

'What was he waiting for?'

'All I could feel,' said Caius Pompeius, 'was the waiting.'

Scarlett was carrying a large picture book, and she sat next to her mother on the green bench near the gates, and she read her book while her mother inspected an educational supplement. She enjoyed the spring sunshine and she did her best to ignore the small boy who waved at her first from behind an ivy-covered monument, then, when she had resolved to no longer look at the monument, the boy popped up – literally, like a jack-in-the-box – from behind a tombstone (Joji G. Shoji, d. 1921, I *was a stranger and you took me in*). He gestured towards her, frantically. She ignored him.

Eventually she put her book down on the bench.

'Mummy? I'm going for a walk now.'

'Stay on the path, dear.'

She stayed on the path until she was round the corner, and she could see Bod waving at her from further up the hill. She made a face at him.

'I've found things out,' said Scarlett.

'Me too,' said Bod.

'There were people before the Romans,' she said. 'Way back. They lived, I mean, when they died they put them underground in these hills, with treasure and stuff. And they were called barrows.'

'Oh. Right,' said Bod. 'That explains it. Do you want to come and see one?'

'Now?' Scarlett looked doubtful. 'You don't really know where one is, do you? And you know I can't always follow you where you go.' She had seen him slip through walls, like a shadow.

In reply, he held up a large, rusted, iron key. 'This was in the chapel,' he said. 'It should open most of the gates up there. They used the same key for all of them. It was less work.'

Scarlett scrambled up the hillside beside him.

'You're telling the truth?'

He nodded, a pleased smile dancing at the corners of his lips. 'Come on,' he said.

It was a perfect spring day, and the air was alive with birdsong and bee hum. The daffodils bustled in the breeze and here and there on the side of the hill a few early tulips nodded. A blue powdering of forget-me-nots and fine, fat yellow primroses punctuated the green of the slope as the two children walked up the hill toward the Frobishers' little mausoleum.

It was old and simple in design, a small, forgotten stone house with a metal gate for a door. Bod unlocked the gate with his key, and they went in.

'It's a hole,' said Bod. 'Or a door. Behind one of the coffins.'

They found it behind a coffin on the bottom shelf – a simple crawl-space. 'Down there,' said Bod. 'We go down there.'

Scarlett found herself suddenly enjoying the adventure rather less. She said, 'We can't see down there. It's dark.'

'I don't need light,' said Bod. 'Not while I'm in the graveyard.'

'I do,' said Scarlett. 'It's dark.'

Bod thought about the reassuring things that he could say, like 'There's nothing bad down there', but the tales of hair turning white and people never returning meant that he could not have said them with a clear conscience, so he said, 'I'll go down. You wait for me up here.'

Scarlett frowned. 'You shouldn't leave me,' she said.

'I'll go down,' said Bod, 'and I'll see who's there, and I'll come back and tell you all about it.'

He turned to the opening, bent down and clambered through on his hands and knees. He was in a space big enough to stand up in, and he could see steps cut into the stone. 'I'm going down the steps now,' he said.

'Do they go down a long way?'

'I think so.'

'If you held my hand and told me where I was walking,' she said, 'then I could come with you. If you make sure I'm OK.'

'Of course,' said Bod, and before he had finished speaking the girl was coming through the hole on her hands and her knees.

'You can stand up,' Bod told her. He took her hand. 'The steps are just here. If you put a foot forward, you can

44

find it. There. Now I'll go first.'

'Can you really see?' she asked.

'It's dark,' said Bod. 'But I can see.'

He began to lead Scarlett down the steps, deep into the hill, and to describe what he saw to her as they went. 'It's steps down,' he said. 'Made of stone. And there's stone all above us. Someone's made a painting on the wall.'

'What kind of painting?'

'A big hairy C is for Cow, I think. With horns. Then something that's more like a pattern, like a big knot. It's sort of carved in the stone too, not just painted, see?' and he took her fingers and placed them on to the carved knotwork.

'I can feel it!' she said.

'Now the steps are getting bigger. We are coming out into some kind of big round room, now, but the steps are still going. Don't move. OK, now I am between you and the room. Keep your left hand on the wall.'

They kept going down. 'One more step and we are on the rock floor,' said Bod. 'It's a bit uneven.'

The room was small. There was a slab of stone on the ground, and a low ledge in one corner, with some small objects on it. There were bones on the ground, very old bones indeed, although below where the steps entered the room Bod could see a crumpled corpse, dressed in the remains of a long brown coat – the young man who had dreamed of riches, Bod decided. He must have slipped and fallen in the dark.

The noise began all about them, a rustling slither, like

45

a snake twining through dry leaves. Scarlett's grip on Bod's hand was harder.

'What's that? Do you see anything?'

'No.'

Scarlett made a noise that was half gasp and half wail, and Bod saw something, and he knew without asking that she could see it too.

There was a light at the end of the room, and in the light a man came walking, walking through the rock, and Bod heard Scarlett choking back a scream.

The man looked well preserved, but still like something that had been dead for a long while. His skin was painted (Bod thought) or tattooed (Scarlett thought) with purple designs and patterns. Around his neck hung a necklace of sharp, long teeth.

'I am the master of this place!' said the figure, in words so ancient and guttural that they were scarcely words at all. 'I guard this place from all who would harm it!'

His eyes were huge in his head. Bod realised it was because he had circles drawn around them in purple, making his face look like an owl's.

'Who are you?' asked Bod. He squeezed Scarlett's hand as he said it.

The Indigo Man did not seem to have heard the question. He looked at them fiercely.

'Leave this place!' he said in words that Bod heard in his head, words that were also a guttural growl.

'Is he going to hurt us?' asked Scarlett.

'I don't think so,' said Bod. Then, to the Indigo Man, he said, as he had been taught, 'I have the Freedom of the

Graveyard and I may walk where I choose.'

There was no reaction to this from the Indigo Man, which puzzled Bod even more because even the most irritable inhabitants of the graveyard had been calmed by this statement. Bod said, 'Scarlett, can you *see* him?'

'Of course I can see him. He's a big scary tattooey man and he wants to kill us. Bod, make him go away!'

Bod looked at the remains of the gentleman in the brown coat. There was a lamp beside him, broken on the rocky floor. 'He ran away,' said Bod aloud. 'He ran because he was scared. And he slipped or he tripped on the stairs and he fell off.'

'Who did?'

'The man on the floor.'

Scarlett sounded irritated now, as well as puzzled and scared. 'What man on the floor? It's too dark. The only man I can see is the tattooey man.'

And then, as if to make quite sure that they knew that he was there, the Indigo Man threw back his head and let out a series of yodelling screams, a full-throated ululation that made Scarlett grip Bod's hand so tightly that her fingernails pressed into his flesh.

Bod was no longer scared, though.

'I'm sorry I said they were imaginary,' said Scarlett. 'I believe you now. They're real.'

The Indigo Man raised something over his head. It looked like a sharp stone blade. 'All who invade this place will die!' he shouted, in his guttural speech. Bod thought about the man whose hair had turned white after he had discovered the chamber, how he would never return to the graveyard or speak of what he had seen.

'No,' said Bod. 'I think you're right. I think this one is.'

'Is what?'

'Imaginary.'

'Don't be stupid,' said Scarlett. 'I can see it.'

'Yes,' said Bod. 'And *you* can't see dead people.' He looked around the chamber. 'You can stop now,' he said. 'We know it's not real.'

'I will feast on your liver!' screamed the Indigo Man.

'No, you won't,' said Scarlett, with a huge sigh. 'Bod's right.' Then she said, 'I think maybe it's a scarecrow.'

'What's a scarecrow?' asked Bod.

'It's a thing farmers put in fields to scare crows.'

'Why would they do that?' Bod quite liked crows. He thought they were funny, and he liked the way they helped to keep the graveyard tidy.

'I don't know exactly. I'll ask Mummy. But I saw one from a train and I asked what it was. Crows think it's a real person, but it's not. It's just a made-up thing that looks like a person. It's to scare the crows away.'

Bod looked around the chamber. He said, 'Whoever you are, it isn't working. It doesn't scare us. We know it isn't real. Just stop.'

The Indigo Man stopped. It walked over to the rock slab and it lay down on it. Then it was gone.

For Scarlett the chamber was once more swallowed by the darkness. But in the darkness, she could hear the twining sound again, getting louder and louder, as if something were circling the round room.

Something said, WE ARE THE SLEER.

The hairs on the back of Bod's neck began to prickle. The voice in his head was something very old and very dry, like the scraping of a dead twig against the window of the chapel, and it seemed to Bod that there was more than one voice there, that they were talking in unison.

'Did you hear that?' he asked Scarlett.

'I didn't hear anything, just a slithery noise. It made me feel strange. All prickly in my tummy. Like something horrible is going to happen.'

'Nothing horrible is going to happen,' said Bod. Then, to the chamber, he said, 'What are you?'

WE ARE THE SLEER. WE GUARD AND WE PROTECT.

'What do you protect?'

THE RESTING PLACE OF THE MASTER. THIS IS THE HOLIEST OF ALL HOLY PLACES, AND IT IS GUARDED BY THE SLEER.

'You can't touch us,' said Bod. 'All you can do is scare.'

The twining voices sounded petulant. FEAR IS A WEAPON OF THE SLEER.

Bod looked down at the ledge. 'Are those the treasures of your master? An old brooch, a cup and a little stone knife? They don't look like much.'

THE SLEER GUARDS THE TREASURES. THE BROOCH, THE GOBLET, THE KNIFE. WE GUARD THEM FOR THE MASTER, WHEN HE RETURNS. IT COMES BACK. IT ALWAYS COMES BACK.

'How many of you are there?'

But the Sleer said nothing. The inside of Bod's head felt as if it were filled with cobwebs, and he shook it, trying to clear it. Then he squeezed Scarlett's hand. 'We should go,' he said.

He led her past the dead man in the brown coat – *and*

honestly, thought Bod, *if he hadn't got scared and fallen the man would have been disappointed in his hunt for treasure.* The treasures of ten thousand years ago were not the treasures of today. Bod led Scarlett carefully up the steps, through the hill, into the jutting black masonry of the Frobisher mausoleum.

Late spring sunlight shone through the breaks in the masonry and through the barred gate, shocking in its brightness, and Scarlett blinked and covered her eyes at the suddenness of the glare. Birds sang in the bushes, a bumblebee droned past, everything was surprising in its normality.

Bod pushed open the mausoleum gate, and then locked it again behind them.

Scarlett's bright clothes were covered in grime and cobwebs, and her dark brown face and hands were pale with dust.

Further down the hill somebody – quite a few somebodies – was shouting. Shouting loudly. Shouting frantically.

Someone called, 'Scarlett? Scarlett Perkins?' and Scarlett said, 'Yes? Hello?' and before she and Bod had a chance to discuss what they had seen, or to talk about the Indigo Man, there was a woman in a fluorescent yellow jacket with POLICE on the back demanding to know if she was OK, and where she had been, and if someone had tried to kidnap her, and then the woman was talking on a radio, letting them know that the child had been found.

Bod slipped along beside them as they walked down the hill. The door to the chapel was open, and inside both of Scarlett's parents were waiting, her mother in tears, her father worriedly talking to people on a mobile phone, along with another policewoman. No one saw Bod, as he waited in the corner.

The people kept asking Scarlett what had happened to her, and she answered, as honestly as she could, told them about a boy called Nobody who took her deep inside a hill where a purple tattoo man appeared in the dark, but he was really a scarecrow. They gave her a chocolate bar and they wiped her face and asked if the tattooed man had ridden a motorbike, and Scarlett's mother and father, now that they were relieved and not afraid for her any longer, were angry with themselves and with her, and they told each other that it was the other one's fault for letting their little girl play in a cemetery, even if it was a nature reserve, and that the world was a very dangerous place these days, and if you didn't keep your eyes on your children every second you couldn't imagine what awful things they would be plunged into. Especially a child like Scarlett.

Scarlett's mother began sobbing, which made Scarlett cry, and one of the policewomen got into an argument with Scarlett's father, who tried to tell her that he, as a taxpayer, paid her wages, and she told him that she was a taxpayer too and probably paid *his* wages, while Bod sat in the shadows in the corner of the chapel, unseen by anyone, not even Scarlett, and watched and listened until he could take no more.

It was twilight in the graveyard by now, and Silas came and found Bod, up near the amphitheatre, looking out over the town. He stood beside the boy and he said nothing, which was his way.

'It wasn't her fault,' said Bod. 'It was mine. And now she's in trouble.'

'Where did you take her?' asked Silas.

'Into the middle of the hill, to see the oldest grave. Only there isn't anybody in there. Just a snaky thing called a Sleer who scares people.'

'Fascinating.'

They walked back down the hill together, watched as the old chapel was locked up once more and the police and Scarlett and her parents went off into the night.

'Miss Borrows will teach you joined-up letters,' said Silas. 'Have you read The Cat in the Hat, yet?'

'Yes,' said Bod. 'Ages ago. Can you bring me more books?'

'I expect so,' said Silas.

'Do you think I'll ever see her again?'

'The girl? I very much doubt it.'

But Silas was wrong. Three weeks later, on a grey afternoon, Scarlett came to the graveyard, accompanied by both her parents.

They insisted that she remain in sight at all times, although they trailed a little behind her. Scarlett's mother occasionally exclaimed about how morbid this all was and how fine and good it was that they would soon be leaving it behind forever.

When Scarlett's parents began to talk to each other, Bod said, 'Hello.'

'Hi,' said Scarlett, very quietly.

'I didn't think I'd see you again.'

'I told them I wouldn't go with them unless they brought me back here one last time.'

'Go where?'

'Scotland. There's a university there. For dad to teach Particle Physics.'

They walked on the path together, a small girl in a bright orange anorak and a small boy in a grey winding sheet.

'Is Scotland a long way away?'

'Yes,' she said.

'Oh.'

'I hoped you'd be here. To say goodbye.'

'I'm always here.'

'But you aren't dead, are you, Nobody Owens?'

''Course not.'

'Well, you can't stay here all your life, can you? One day you'll grow up and then you will have to go and live in the world outside.'

He shook his head. 'It's not safe for me out there.'

'Who says?'

'Silas. My family. Everybody.'

She was silent.

Her father called, 'Scarlett! Come on, love. Time to go. You've had your last trip to the graveyard. Now let's go home.'

Scarlett said to Bod, 'You're brave. You are the bravest person I know, and you are my friend. I don't care if you *are* imaginary.' Then she fled down the path back the way they had come, to her parents and the world.

Above them in the sour red skies, things were
circling on huge black wings.

CHAPTER 3

The Hounds of God

One grave in every graveyard belongs to the ghouls. Wander any graveyard long enough and you will find it – water-stained and bulging, with cracked or broken stone, scraggly grass or rank weeds about it, and a feeling, when you reach it, of abandonment. It may be colder than the other gravestones, too, and the name on the stone is all too often impossible to read. If there is a statue on the grave, it will be headless or so scabbed with fungus and lichens as to look like a fungus itself. If one grave in a graveyard looks like a target for petty vandals, that is the ghoul-gate. If the grave makes you want to be somewhere else, that is the ghoul-gate.

There was one in Bod's graveyard.

There is one in every graveyard.

Silas was leaving.

Bod had been upset by this when he had first learned about it. He was no longer upset. He was furious.

'But *why*?' said Bod.

'I told you. I need to obtain some information. In

order to do that, I have to travel. To travel, I must leave here. We have already been over all this.'

'What's so important that you have to go away?' Bod's six-year-old mind tried to imagine something that could make Silas want to leave him, and failed. 'It's not fair.'

His guardian was unperturbed. 'It is neither fair nor unfair, Nobody Owens. It simply is.'

Bod was not impressed. 'You're meant to look after me. You *said*.'

'As your guardian I have responsibility for you, yes. Fortunately, I am not the only individual in the world willing to take on this responsibility.'

'Where are you going anyway?'

'Out. Away. There are things I need to uncover that I cannot uncover here.'

Bod snorted and walked off, kicking at imaginary stones. On the north-western side of the graveyard things had become very overgrown and tangled, far beyond the ability of the groundsman or the Friends of the Graveyard to tame, and he ambled over there and woke a family of Victorian children who had all died before their tenth birthdays, and they played at hide-and-go-seek in the moonlight in the ivy-twined jungle. Bod tried to pretend that Silas was not leaving, that nothing was going to change, but when the game was over and he ran back to the old chapel, he saw two things that changed his mind.

The first thing he saw was a bag. It was, Bod knew the moment he laid eyes on it, Silas's bag. It was at least a hundred and fifty years old, a thing of beauty, black leather with brass fittings and a black handle, the kind of bag a

Victorian doctor or undertaker might have carried, containing every implement that might have been needed. Bod had never seen Silas's bag before, he had not even known that Silas had a bag, but it was the sort of bag that could only have belonged to Silas. Bod tried to peek inside it, but it was closed with a large brass padlock. It was too heavy for him to lift.

That was the first thing.

The second thing was sitting on the bench by the chapel.

'Bod,' said Silas. 'This is Miss Lupescu.'

Miss Lupescu was not pretty. Her face was pinched and her expression was disapproving. Her hair was grey, although her face seemed too young for grey hair. Her front teeth were slightly crooked. She wore a bulky mackintosh, and a man's tie around her neck.

'How do you do, Miss Lupescu?' said Bod.

Miss Lupescu said nothing. She sniffed. Then she looked at Silas and said, 'So. This is the boy.' She got up from her seat and walked all around Bod, nostrils flared, as if she were sniffing him. When she had made a complete circuit, she said, 'You will report to me on waking, and before you go to sleep. I have rented a room in a house over there.' She pointed to a roof just visible from where they stood. 'However, I shall spend my time in this graveyard. I am here as a historian, researching the history of old graves. You understand, boy? Da?'

'Bod,' said Bod. 'It's Bod. Not boy.'

'Short for Nobody,' she said. 'A foolish name. Also, Bod is a pet name. A nickname. I do not approve. I will call you "boy". You will call me "Miss Lupescu".'

Bod looked up at Silas, pleadingly, but there was no sympathy on Silas's face. He picked up his bag and said, 'You will be in good hands with Miss Lupescu, Bod. I am sure that the two of you will get on.'

'We won't!' said Bod. 'She's horrible!'

'That,' said Silas, 'was a very rude thing to say. I think you should apologise, don't you?'

Bod didn't, but Silas was looking at him and he was carrying his black bag, and about to leave for no one knew how long, so he said, 'I'm sorry, Miss Lupescu.'

At first she said nothing in reply. She merely sniffed. Then she said, 'I have come a long way to look after you, boy. I hope you are worth it.'

Bod could not imagine hugging Silas, so he held out his hand and Silas bent over and gently shook it, engulfing Bod's small, grubby hand with his huge, pale one. Then, lifting his black leather bag as if it were weightless, he walked down the path and out of the graveyard.

Bod told his parents about it.

'Silas has gone,' he said.

'He'll be back,' said Mr Owens, cheerfully. 'Don't you worry your head about that, Bod. Like a bad penny, as they say.'

Mrs Owens said, 'Back when you were born he promised us that if he had to leave, he would find someone else to bring you food and keep an eye on you, and he has. He's so dependable.'

Silas had brought Bod food, true, and left it in the crypt each night for him to eat, but this was, as far as Bod was concerned, the least of the things that Silas did for him. He gave advice, cool, sensible and unfailingly correct; he knew more than the graveyard folk did, for his nightly excursions into the world outside meant that he was able to describe a world that was current, not hundreds of years out of date; he was unflappable and reliable, and had been there every night of Bod's life, so the idea of the little chapel without its only inhabitant was one that Bod found difficult to conceive of; most of all, he made Bod feel safe.

Miss Lupescu also saw her job as more than bringing Bod food. She did that too, though.

'What is that?' asked Bod, horrified.

'Good food,' said Miss Lupescu. They were in the crypt. She had put two plastic containers on the table-top, and opened the lids. She pointed to the first. 'Is beetroot-barley-stew-soup.' She pointed to the second. 'Is salad. Now, you eat both. I make them for you.'

Bod stared up at her to see if this was a joke. Food from Silas mostly came in packets, purchased from the kind of places that sold food late at night and asked no questions. No one had ever brought him food in a plastic container with a lid before. 'It smells horrible,' he said.

'If you do not eat the stew-soup soon,' she said, 'it will be more horrible. It will be cold. Now eat.'

Bod was hungry. He took a plastic spoon, dipped it into the purple-red stew and he ate. The food was slimy and unfamiliar, but he kept it down.

'Now the salad!' said Miss Lupescu, and she unpopped the top of the second container. It consisted of large lumps of raw onion, beetroot and tomato, all in a thick, vinegary

61

dressing. Bod put a lump of beetroot into his mouth and started to chew. He could feel the saliva gathering, and realised that if he swallowed it, he would throw it back up. He said, 'I can't eat this.'

'Is good for you.'

'I'll be sick.'

They stared at each other: the small boy with tousled, mousy hair; the pinched pale woman with not a silver hair out of place. Miss Lupescu said, 'You eat one more piece.'

'I can't.'

'You eat one more piece now, or you stay here until you have eaten it all.'

Bod picked out a piece of vinegary tomato, chewed it and choked it down. Miss Lupescu put the tops back on the containers and replaced them in the plastic shopping bag. She said, 'Now, lessons.'

It was high summer. It would not get fully dark until almost midnight. There were no lessons in high summer – the time that Bod spent awake he spent in an endless warm twilight in which he would play or explore or climb.

'Lessons?' he said.

'Your guardian felt it would be good for me to teach you things.'

'I have teachers. Letitia Borrows teaches me writing and words, and Mr Pennyworth teaches me his Compleat Educational System for Younger Gentlemen with Additional Material for those Post Mortem. I do Geography and everything. I don't *need* more lessons.'

'You know everything, then, boy? Six years old, and

already you know everything.'

'I didn't say that.'

Miss Lupescu folded her arms. 'Tell me about ghouls,' she said.

Bod tried to remember what Silas had told him about ghouls over the years. 'Keep away from them,' he said.

'And that is all you know? Da? Why do you keep away from them? Where do they come from? Where do they go? Why do you not stand near a ghoul-gate? Eh, boy?'

Bod shrugged and shook his head.

'Name the different kinds of people,' said Miss Lupescu. 'Now.'

Bod thought for a moment. 'The living,' he said. 'Er. The dead.' He stopped. Then, '. . . Cats?' he offered, uncertainly.

'You are ignorant, boy,' said Miss Lupescu. 'This is bad. And you are content to be ignorant, which is worse. Repeat after me, there are the living and the dead, there are day-folk and night-folk, there are ghouls and mist-walkers, there are the high hunters and the Hounds of God. Also, there are solitary types.'

'What are you?' asked Bod.

'I,' she said sternly, 'am Miss Lupescu.'

'And what's Silas?'

She hesitated. Then she said, 'He is a solitary type.'

Bod endured the lesson. When Silas taught him things, it was interesting. Much of the time Bod didn't realise he had been taught anything at all. Miss Lupescu taught in lists, and Bod could not see the point to it. He sat in the crypt, aching to be out in the summer's twilight,

63

under the ghost moon.

When the lesson was over, in the foulest of moods, he fled. He looked for playmates, but found no one and saw nothing but a large grey dog, which prowled the gravestones, always keeping its distance from him, slipping between gravestones and through shadows.

The week got worse.

Miss Lupescu continued to bring Bod things she had cooked for him: dumplings swimming in lard; thick reddish-purple soup with a lump of sour cream in it; small, cold boiled potatoes; cold garlic-heavy sausages; hardboiled eggs in a grey unappetising liquid. He ate as little as he could get away with. The lessons continued: for two days she taught him nothing but ways to call for help in every language in the world, and she would rap his knuckles with her pen if he slipped up or forgot. By the third day she was firing them at him:

'French?'

'*Au secours.*'

'Morse code?'

'S-O-S. Three short dots, three long ones, three short ones again.'

'Night-gaunt?'

'This is stupid. I don't remember what a night-gaunt *is.*'

'They have hairless wings, and they fly low and fast. They do not visit this world, but they fly the red skies above the road to Ghûlheim.'

'I'm never going to need to know this.'

Her mouth pinched in tighter. All she said was,

'Night-gaunt?'

Bod made the noise in the back of his throat that she had taught him – a guttural cry, like an eagle's call. She sniffed. 'Adequate,' she said.

Bod could not wait until the day that Silas would return.

He said, 'There's a big grey dog in the graveyard sometimes. It came when you did. Is it your dog?'

Miss Lupescu straightened her tie. 'No,' she said.

'Are we finished?'

'For today. You will read the list I give you tonight and remember them for tomorrow.'

The lists were printed in pale purple ink on white paper, and they smelled odd. Bod took the new list up on to the side of the hill, and tried to read the words, but his attention kept sliding off it. Eventually he folded it up and placed it beneath a stone.

No one would play with him that night. No one wanted to play or to talk, to run and climb beneath the huge summer moon.

He went down to the Owenses' tomb, to complain to his parents, but Mrs Owens would not hear a word said against Miss Lupescu, on, as far as Bod was concerned, the unfair grounds that Silas had chosen her, while Mr Owens simply shrugged and started telling Bod about his days as a young apprentice cabinetmaker, and how much he would have loved to have learned about all the useful things that Bod was learning, which was, as far as Bod was concerned, even worse.

'Aren't you meant to be studying, anyway?' asked Mrs

Owens, and Bod squeezed his fists together and said nothing.

He stomped off into the graveyard, feeling unloved and under-appreciated.

Bod brooded on the injustice of it all, and wandered through the graveyard kicking at stones. He spotted the dark grey dog, and called to it to see if it would come over and play with him, but it kept its distance, and Bod, frustrated, threw a clump of mud towards it, which broke on a nearby gravestone, and scattered earth everywhere. The big dog gazed at Bod reproachfully then stepped away into the shadows, and was gone.

The boy walked back down the south-west side of the hill, avoiding the old chapel: he did not want to see the place that Silas wasn't. Bod stopped beside a grave that looked the way he felt: it was beneath an oak that had once been struck by lightning, and now was just a black trunk, like a sharp talon coming out of the hill; the grave itself was water-stained and cracked, and above it was a memorial stone on which a headless angel hung, its robes looking like a huge and ugly tree-fungus.

Bod sat down on a clump of grass, and felt sorry for himself, and hated everybody. He even hated Silas, for going away and leaving him. Then he closed his eyes and curled into a ball on the grass, and drifted into a dreamless sleep.

Down the street and up the hill came the Duke of Westminster, the Honourable Archibald Fitzhugh and the Bishop of Bath and Wells, slipping and bounding from shadow to shadow, lean and leathery, all sinews and carti-lage, wearing raggedy clothes all a-tatter, and they bounded and loped and skulked, leapfrogging over dustbins, keeping to the dark side of hedges.

They were small, like full-sized people who had shrunk in the sun; they spoke to each other in undertones, saying things like 'If Your Grace has any more blooming idea of where we is than us do, I'd be grateful if he'd say so. Otherwise, he should keep his big offal-hole shut' and 'All I'm saying, Your Worship, is that I knows there's a grave-yard near to here, I can smell it' and 'If you could smell it, then I should be able to smell it, 'cos I've got a better nose than you have, Your Grace.'

All this as they dodged and wove their way through suburban gardens. They avoided one garden ('Psst!' hissed the Honourable Archibald Fitzhugh. 'Dogs!') and ran along the top of the garden wall, scampering over it like rats the size of children. Down into the high street, and up the road to the top of the hill. And then they were at the graveyard wall, and they went up it like squirrels up a tree, and they sniffed the air.

''Ware dog,' said the Duke of Westminster.

'Where? I dunno. Somewhere around here. Doesn't smell like a proper dog anyway,' said the Bishop of Bath and Wells.

'Somebody couldn't smell this graveyard neither,' said the Honourable Archibald Fitzhugh. 'Remember? It's just a dog.'

The three of them leapt down from the wall to the ground, and they ran, using their arms as much as their legs to propel themselves through the graveyard, to the ghoul-gate by the lightning tree.

And beside the gate, in the moonlight, they paused.

'What's this when it's at home, then?' asked the Bishop of Bath and Wells.

'Lumme,' said the Duke of Westminster.

Bod woke then.

The three faces staring into his could have been those of mummified humans, fleshless and dried, but their features were mobile and interested – mouths that grinned to reveal sharp, stained teeth; bright beady eyes; clawed fingers that moved and tapped.

'Who are you?' Bod asked.

'*We*,' said one of the creatures – they were, Bod realised, only a little bigger than he was – 'is most important folk, we is. This here is the Duke of Westminster.'

The biggest of the creatures gave a bow, saying, 'Charmed, I'm sure.'

'. . . and this is the Bishop of Bath and Wells –'

The creature, which grinned sharp teeth and let a pointed tongue of improbable length waggle between them, did not look like Bod's idea of a bishop: its skin was piebald and it had a large spot across one eye, making it look almost piratical.

'. . . and I 'ave the honour to be ther 'onourable Harchibald Fitzhugh. Hat your service.'

The three creatures bowed as one. The Bishop of Bath and Wells said, 'Now, me lad, what's your story, eh? And don't tell any porkies, remember as how you're talkin' to a bishop.'

'You tell him, Your Worship,' said the other two.

So Bod told them. He told them how no one liked him or wanted to play with him, how no one appreciated him or cared, and how even his guardian had abandoned him.

'Blow me down,' said the Duke of Westminster, scratching his nose (a little dried-up thing that was mostly nostrils). 'What you need is to go somewhere the people would appreciate you.'

'There isn't anywhere,' said Bod. 'And I'm not allowed out of the graveyard.'

'You needs an 'ole world of friends and playfellows,' said the Bishop of Bath and Wells, wiggling his long tongue. 'A city of delights, of fun and magic, where you would be appreciated, not ignored.'

Bod said, 'The lady who's looking after me. She makes horrible food. Hard-boiled egg soup and things.'

'Food!' said the Honourable Archibald Fitzhugh. 'Where *we're* going the food's the best in the whole world. Makes me tum rumble and me mouf water just thinking about it.'

'Can I come with you?' asked Bod.

'Come with us?' said the Duke of Westminster. He sounded shocked.

'Don't be like that, Yer Grace,' said the Bishop of Bath and Wells. ''Ave a blinking 'eart. Look at the little mite. 'Asn't 'ad a decent meal in 'e don't know 'ow long.'

'I vote to take him,' said the Honourable Archibald Fitzhugh. 'There's good grub back at our place.' He patted his stomach to show just how good the food was.

'So. You game for adventure?' asked the Duke of Westminster, won over by the novel idea. 'Or do you want to waste the rest of your life *here*?' and with bony fingers he indicated the graveyard and the night.

Bod thought of Miss Lupescu and her awful food and her lists and her pinched mouth.

'I'm game,' he said.

His three new friends might have been his size, but they were far stronger than any child, and Bod found himself picked up by the Bishop of Bath and Wells and held high above the creature's head, while the Duke of Westminster grabbed a handful of mangy-looking grass, shouted what sounded like '*Skagh! Thegh! Khavagah!*' and pulled. The stone slab that covered the grave swung open like a trapdoor, revealing a darkness beneath.

'Quick now,' said the Duke, and the Bishop of Bath and Wells tossed Bod into the dark opening, then leapt in after him, followed by the Honourable Archibald Fitzhugh and then, with one agile bound, by the Duke of Westminster, who, as soon as he was inside, called out, '*Wegh Khârados!*' to close the ghoul-gate, and the stone crashed down above them.

Bod fell, tumbling through the darkness like a lump of marble, too startled to be scared, wondering how deep the hole beneath that grave could possibly be, when two strong hands caught him beneath the armpits and he found himself swinging forward through the pitch-blackness.

Bod had not experienced total darkness for many years. In the graveyard, he saw as the dead see, and no tomb or grave or crypt was truly dark to him. Now he was in utter darkness, feeling himself being pitched forward in a sequence of jerks and rushes, the wind rushing past him. It was frightening, but it was also exhilarating.

And then there was light, and everything changed.

The sky was red, but not the warm red of a sunset. This was an angry, glowering red, the colour of an infected wound. The sun was small and seemed like it was old and distant. The air was cold and they were descending a wall. Tombstones and statues jutted out of the side of the wall, as if a huge graveyard had been upended, and, like three wizened chimpanzees in tattered black suits that did up in the back, the Duke of Westminster, the Bishop of Bath and Wells and the Honourable Archibald Fitzhugh were swinging from statue to stone, dangling Bod between them as they went, tossing him from one to another, never missing him, always catching him with ease, without even looking.

Bod tried to look up, to see the grave through which they had entered this strange world, but he could see nothing but headstones.

He wondered if each of the graves they were swinging past was a door for the kind of people who were carrying him . . .

'Where are we going?' he asked, but his voice was whipped away by the wind.

They went faster and faster. Up ahead of them Bod saw a statue swing up, and another two creatures came catapulting out into this crimson-skied world, just like the ones that carried Bod. One wore a raggedy silken gown that looked like it had once been white, the other wore a stained grey suit too large for it, the sleeves of which were shredded into shadowy tatters. They spotted Bod and his three new friends and made for them, dropping twenty feet with ease.

The Duke of Westminster gave a guttural squawk and pretended to be scared, and Bod and the three of them swung down the wall of graves with the two new creatures in pursuit. None of them seemed to get tired or out of breath, under that red sky, with the burnt-out sun gazing down at them like a dead eye, but eventually they fetched up on the side of a huge statue of a creature whose whole face seemed to have become a fungoid growth. Bod found himself being introduced to the Thirty-Third President of the United States and the Emperor of China.

'This is Master Bod,' said the Bishop of Bath and Wells. 'He's going to become one of us.'

'He's in search of a good meal,' said the Honourable Archibald Fitzhugh.

'Well, you're guaranteed fine dining when you becomes one of us, young lad,' said the Emperor of China.

'Yup,' said the Thirty-Third President of the United States.

Bod said, 'I become one of you? You mean, I'll turn into you?'

'Smart as a whip, sharp as a tack, you'd have to get up pretty late at night to put anything past this lad,' said the Bishop of Bath and Wells. 'Indeed. One of us. As strong, as fast, as unconquerable.'

'Teeth so strong they can crush any bones, and tongue sharp and long enough to lick the marrow from the deepest marrowbone or flay the flesh from a fat man's face,' said the Emperor of China.

'Able to slip from shadow to shadow, never seen, never suspected. Free as air, fast as thought, cold as frost, hard as nails, dangerous as . . . as *us*,' said the Duke of Westminster.

Bod looked at the creatures. 'But what if I don't *want* to be one of you?' he said.

'Don't *want* to? Of course you *wants* to! What could be finer? I don't think there's a soul in the universe doesn't want to be *just* like us.'

'We've got the best city –'

'Ghûlheim,' said the Thirty-Third President of the United States.

'The best life, the best food –'

'Can you imagine,' interrupted the Bishop of Bath and Wells, 'how fine a drink the black ichor that collects in a leaden coffin can be? Or how it feels to be more important than kings and queens, than presidents or prime ministers or heroes, to be *sure* of it, in the same way that people are more important than Brussels sprouts?'

Bod said, 'What *are* you people?'

'Ghouls,' said the Bishop of Bath and Wells. 'Bless me, somebody wasn't paying attention, was he? We're ghouls.'

'Look!'

Below them, a whole troupe of the little creatures were bouncing and running and leaping, heading for the path below them, and before he could say another word, he was snatched up by a pair of bony hands and was flying through the air in a series of jumps and lurches, as the creatures headed down to meet the others of their kind.

The wall of graves was ending, and now there was a road, and nothing but a road, a much-trodden path across a barren plain, a desert of rocks and bones, that wound towards a city high on a huge red rock hill, many miles away.

Bod looked up at the city, and was horrified: an emotion engulfed him that mingled repulsion and fear, disgust and loathing, all tinged with shock.

Ghouls do not build. They are parasites and scavengers, eaters of carrion. The city they call Ghûlheim is something they found, long ago, but did not make. No one knows (if anyone human ever knew) what kind of creatures it was that made those buildings, who honeycombed the rock with tunnels and towers, but it is certain that no one but the ghoul-folk could have wanted to stay there, or even to approach that place.

Even from the path below Ghûlheim, even from miles away, Bod could see that all of the angles were wrong – that the walls sloped crazily, that it was every nightmare he had ever endured made into a place, like a huge mouth of jutting teeth. It was a city that had been built just to be abandoned, in which all the fears and madnesses and revulsions of the creatures who built it were made into stone. The ghoul-folk had found it and delighted in it and called it home.

Ghouls move fast. They swarmed along the path through the desert more swiftly than a vulture flies and Bod was carried along by them, held high overhead by a pair of strong ghoul arms, tossed from one to another, feeling sick, feeling dread and dismay, feeling stupid.

Above them in the sour red skies, things were circling on huge black wings.

'Careful,' said the Duke of Westminster. 'Tuck him away. Don't want the night-gaunts stealing him. Bloody stealers.'

'Yar! We hates stealers!' shouted the Emperor of China.

Night-gaunts, in the red skies above Ghûlheim... Bod took a deep breath and shouted, just as Miss Lupescu had taught him. He made a call like an eagle's cry, in the back of his throat.

One of the winged beasts dropped towards them, circled lower, and Bod made the call again, until it was stifled by hard hands clamping over his mouth. 'Good idea, calling 'em down,' said the Honourable Archibald Fitzhugh, 'but trust me, they aren't edible until they've been rotting for at least a couple of weeks, and they just causes trouble. No love lost between our side and theirs, eh?'

The night-gaunt rose again in the dry desert air, to rejoin its fellows, and Bod felt all hope vanish.

The ghouls sped on towards the city on the rocks and Bod, now flung unceremoniously over the stinking shoulders of the Duke of Westminster, was carried with them.

The dead sun set, and two moons rose, one huge and pitted and white, which seemed, as it rose, to be taking up half the horizon, although it shrank as it ascended, and a smaller moon, the bluish-green colour of the veins of mould in a cheese, and the arrival of this moon was an occasion of celebration for the ghoul-folk. They stopped marching and made a camp beside the road.

One of the new members of the band – Bod thought it might have been the one he had been introduced to as 'the famous writer Victor Hugo' – produced a sack which turned out to be filled with firewood, several pieces still with the hinges or brass handles attached, along with a metal cigarette lighter, and soon made a fire, around which all the ghoul-folk sat and rested. They stared up at the greenish-blue moon, and scuffled for the best places by the fire, insulting each other, sometimes clawing or biting.

'We'll sleep soon, then set off for Ghûlheim at moonset,' said the Duke of Westminster. 'It's just another nine or ten hours run along the way. We should reach it by next moonrise. Then we'll have a party, eh? Celebrate you being made into one of us!'

'It doesn't hurt,' said the Honourable Archibald Fitzhugh. 'Not so as you'd notice. And after, think how happy you'll be.'

They all started telling stories, then, of how fine and wonderful a thing it was to be a ghoul, of all the things they had crunched up and swallowed down with their powerful teeth. Impervious they were to disease or illness, said one of them. Why, it didn't matter what their dinner had died of, they could just chomp it down. They told of the places they had been, which mostly seemed to be catacombs and plague pits. ('Plague pits is good eatin',' said the Emperor of China, and everyone agreed.) They told Bod how they had got their names and how he, in his turn, once he had become a nameless ghoul, would be named, as they had been, after the main course of his first dinner.

'But I don't want to become one of you,' said Bod.

'One way or another,' said the Bishop of Bath and Wells, cheerily, 'you'll become one of us. The other way is messier, involves being digested, and you're not really around very long to enjoy it.'

'But that's not a good thing to talk about,' said the Emperor of China. 'Best to be a ghoul. We're afraid of nuffink!'

And all the ghouls around the coffin-wood fire howled at this statement, and growled and sang and exclaimed at how wise they were, and how mighty, and how fine it was to be scared of nothing.

There was a noise then, from the desert, from far away, a distant howl, and the ghouls gibbered and they huddled closer to the flames.

'What was that?' asked Bod.

The ghouls shook their heads. 'Just something out there in the desert,' whispered one of them. 'Quiet! It'll hear us!'

And all the ghouls were quiet for a bit, until they forgot about the thing in the desert, and began to sing ghoul-songs, filled with foul words and worse sentiments, the most popular of which were simply lists of which rotting body parts were to be eaten, and in what order.

'I want to go home,' said Bod, when the last of the bits in the song had been consumed. 'I don't want to be here.'

'Don't take on so,' said the Duke of Westminster. 'Why, you little coot, I promise you that as soon as you're one of us, you'll not ever remember as you even *had* a home.'

'I don't remember anything about the days before I was a ghoul,' said the famous writer Victor Hugo.

'Nor I,' said the Emperor of China, proudly.

'Nope,' said the Thirty-Third President of the United States.

'You'll be one of a select band, of the cleverest, strongest, bravest creatures ever,' bragged the Bishop of Bath and Wells.

Bod was unimpressed by the ghouls' bravery or their wisdom. They were strong, though, and inhumanly fast, and he was in the centre of a troupe of them. Making a break for it would have been impossible. They would be able to catch up with him before he could cover a dozen yards.

Far off in the night something howled once more, and the ghouls moved closer to the fire. Bod could hear them sniffling and cursing. He closed his eyes, miserable and homesick: he did not want to become one of the ghouls. He wondered how he would ever be able to sleep when he was this worried and hopeless and then, almost to his surprise, for two or three hours, he slept.

A noise woke him – upset, loud, close. It was someone saying, 'Well, where *is* they? Eh?' He opened his eyes to see the Bishop of Bath and Wells shouting at the Emperor of China. It seemed that a couple of the members of their group had disappeared in the night, just vanished, and no one had an explanation. The rest of the ghouls were on edge. They packed up their camp quickly, and the Thirty-Third President of the United States picked Bod up and bundled him over his shoulder.

The ghouls scrabbled back down the rocky cliffs to the road, beneath a sky the colour of bad blood, and they headed towards Ghûlheim. They seemed significantly less exuberant this morning. Now they seemed – at least to Bod, as he was bounced along – to be running away from something.

Around midday, with the dead-eyed sun high overhead, the ghouls stopped and huddled. Ahead of them, high in the sky, circling on the hot air currents, were the night-gaunts, dozens of them, riding the thermals.

The ghouls divided into two factions: there were those who felt that the vanishing of their friends was meaningless, and those who believed that something, probably the night-gaunts, was out to get them. They came to no agreement, except for a general agreement to arm themselves with rocks to throw at the night-gaunts should they descend, and they filled the pockets of their suits and robes with pebbles from the desert floor.

Something howled, off in the desert to their left, and the ghouls eyed each other. It was louder than the night before, and closer: a deep, wolfish howl.

'Did you hear that?' asked the Lord Mayor of London.

'Nope,' said the Thirty-Third President of the United States.

'Me neither,' said the Honourable Archibald Fitzhugh.

The howl came again.

'We got to get home,' said the Duke of Westminster, hefting a large stone.

The nightmare city of Ghûlheim sat on a high rocky outcrop ahead of them, and the creatures loped down the road towards it.

'Night-gaunts coming!' shouted the Bishop of Bath

79

and Wells. 'Throw stones at the bleeders!'

Bod's view of things was upside down at this point, bouncing up and down on the back of the Thirty-Third President of the United States, gritty sand from the path blown up into his face. But he heard cries, like eagle cries, and once again Bod called for help in Night-gaunt. No one tried to stop him this time, but he was not sure that anyone could have heard him over the cries of the night-gaunts, or the oaths and curses of the ghoul-folk as they pitched and flung their stones into the air.

Bod heard the howling again: now it came from their right.

'There's dozens of the blooming blinkers,' said the Duke of Westminster, gloomily.

The Thirty-Third President of the United States handed Bod over to the famous writer Victor Hugo, who threw the boy into his sack and put it over his shoulder. Bod was just glad the sack smelled of nothing worse than dusty wood.

'They're retreating!' shouted a ghoul. 'Look at 'em go!'

'Don't you worry,' said a voice that sounded to Bod like the Bishop of Bath and Wells, near the sack. 'There won't be any of this nonsense when we get you to Ghûlheim. It's impenetrable, is Ghûlheim.'

Bod could not tell if any of the ghouls had been killed or injured fighting the night-gaunts. He suspected, from the imprecations of the Bishop of Bath and Wells, that several more of the ghouls might have run off.

'Quickly!' shouted someone who was probably the Duke of Westminster, and the ghouls set off at a run. Bod, in the sack, was uncomfortable, being painfully slammed against the famous writer Victor Hugo's back and occasionally banged on the ground. To make his time in the sack even more uncomfortable there were still several lumps of wood, not to mention sharp screws and nails, in there with him, the final remnants of the coffin-based firewood. A screw was just under his hand, digging into him.

Despite being jogged and jounced, jolted and jarred with every one of his captor's steps, Bod managed to grasp the screw in his right hand. He felt the tip of it, sharp to the touch. He hoped, deep inside. Then he pushed the screw into the fabric of the sack behind him, working the sharp end in, then pulling it back, and making another hole a little way below the first.

From behind, he could hear something howl once more and it occurred to him that anything that could terrify the ghoul-folk must itself be even more terrifying than he could imagine, and for a moment he stopped stabbing with the screw – what if he fell from the sack into the jaws of some evil beast? But at least if he died, thought Bod, he would have died as himself, with all his memories, knowing who his parents were, who Silas was, even who Miss Lupescu was.

That was good.

He attacked the sacking with his brass screw again, jabbing and pushing until he'd made another hole in the fabric.

'Come on lads,' shouted the Bishop of Bath and Wells. 'Up the steps and then we're home, all safe in Ghûlheim!'

'Hurrah, Your Worship!' called someone else, probably

the Honourable Archibald Fitzhugh.

Now the motion of his captors had changed. It was no longer a forward motion: now it was a sequence of movements, up and along, up and along.

Bod pushed at the sacking with his hand, to try and make an eyehole. He looked out. Above, the drear red sky, below . . .

. . . he could see the desert floor, but it was now hundreds of feet below him. There were steps stretching out behind them, but steps made for giants, and the ochre rock wall to his right. Ghûlheim, which Bod could not see from where he was, had to be above them. To his left was a sheer drop. He was going to have to fall straight down, he decided, on to the steps, and he would just hope that the ghouls wouldn't notice that he was making his break for it in their desperation to be home and safe. He saw nightgaunts high in the red sky, hanging back, circling.

He was pleased to see there were no other ghouls behind him: the famous writer Victor Hugo was bringing up the rear, and no one was behind him to alert the ghouls to the hole that was growing in the sack. Or to see Bod if he fell out.

But there was something else . . .

Bod was bounced on to his side, away from the hole. But he had seen something huge and grey, on the steps beneath, pursuing them. He could hear an angry growling noise.

Mister Owens had an expression for two things he found equally unpleasant: 'I'm between the Devil and the Deep Blue Sea,' he would say. Bod had wondered what this meant, having seen, in his life in the graveyard, neither the Devil nor the Deep Blue Sea.

I'm between the ghouls and the monster, he thought.

And as he thought it, sharp canine teeth caught at the sacking, pulled at it until the fabric tore along the rips Bod had made, and the boy tumbled down on the rock stairs, where a huge grey animal, like a dog but far larger, growled and drooled, and stood over him, an animal with flaming eyes and white fangs and huge paws. It panted and it stared at Bod.

Ahead of him the ghouls had stopped. 'Bloody Nora!' said the Duke of Westminster. 'That hellhound's got the blinking boy!'

'Let it have him,' said the Emperor of China. 'Run!'

'Yikes!' said the Thirty-Third President of the United States.

The ghouls ran up the steps. Bod was now certain that the steps had been carved by giants, for each step was higher than he was. As they fled, the ghouls paused only to turn and make rude gestures at the beast and possibly also at Bod.

The beast stayed where it was.

It's going to eat me, Bod thought bitterly. *Smart, Bod.* And he thought of his home in the graveyard, and now he could no longer remember why he had ever left. Monster dog or no monster dog, he had to get back home once more. There were people waiting for him.

He pushed past the beast, jumped down to the next step four feet below, fell his height, landed on his ankle, which twisted underneath him, painfully, and he dropped, heavily, on to the rock.

He could hear the beast running, jumping down towards him, and he tried to wriggle away, to pull himself up on to his feet, but his ankle was useless, now, numb and in pain, and before he could stop himself, he fell again. He fell off the step, away from the rock wall, out into space, off the cliff-side, where he dropped – a nightmarish tumble down distances that Bod could not even imagine . . .

And as he fell, he was certain he heard a voice coming from the general direction of the grey beast. And it said, in Miss Lupescu's voice, 'Oh, Bod!'

It was like every dream of falling he had ever had, a scared and frantic drop through space, as he headed towards the ground below. Bod felt as though his mind was only big enough for one huge thought, so *That big dog was actually Miss Lupescu* and *I'm going to hit the rock floor and splat* competed in his head for occupation.

Something wrapped itself about him, falling at the same speed he was falling, and then there was the loud flapping of leathery wings and everything slowed. The ground no longer seemed to be heading towards him at the same speed.

The wings flapped harder. They lifted slightly and now the only thought in Bod's head was *I'm flying!* And he was. He turned his head. Above him was a dark brown head, perfectly bald, with deep eyes that looked as if they were polished slabs of black glass.

Bod made the screeching noise that means 'Help,' in Night-gaunt, and the night-gaunt smiled and made a deep hooting noise in return. It seemed pleased.

A swoop and a slow, and they touched down on the desert floor with a thump. Bod tried to stand up, and his ankle betrayed him once again, sent him stumbling down into the sand. The wind was high, and the sharp desert sand blew hard, stinging Bod's skin.

The night-gaunt crouched beside him, its leathery wings folded on its back. Bod had grown up in a graveyard and was used to images of winged people, but the angels on the headstones looked nothing like this.

And now, bounding toward them across the desert floor in the shadow of Ghûlheim, a huge grey beast, like an enormous dog.

The dog spoke, in Miss Lupescu's voice.

It said, 'This is the third time the night-gaunts have saved your life, Bod. The first was when you called for help, and they heard. They got the message to me, telling me where you were. The second was around the fire last night, when you were asleep: they were circling in the darkness, and heard a couple of the ghouls saying that you were ill-luck for them and that they should beat your brains in with a rock and put you somewhere they could find you again, when you were properly rotted down, and then they would eat you. The night-gaunts dealt with the matter silently. And now this.'

'Miss Lupescu?'

The great dog-like head lowered towards him, and for one mad, fear-filled moment, he thought she was going to take a bite out of him, but her tongue licked the side of his face, affectionately. 'You hurt your ankle?'

'Yes. I can't stand on it.'

'Let's get you on to my back,' said the huge grey beast that was Miss Lupescu.

She said something in the night-gaunts' screeching tongue and it came over, held Bod up while he put his arms around Miss Lupescu's neck.

'Hold my fur,' she said. 'Hold tight. Now, before we go, say . . .' and she made a high screeching noise.

'What does it mean?'

'Thank you. Or goodbye. Both.'

Bod screeched as best as he could, and the night-gaunt made an amused chuckle. Then it made a similar noise, and it spread its great leathery wings, and it ran into the desert wind, flapping hard, and the wind caught it and carried it aloft, like a kite that had begun to fly.

'Now,' said the beast that was Miss Lupescu, 'hold on tightly.' And she began to run.

'Are we going to the wall of graves?'

'To the ghoul-gates? No. Those are for ghouls. I am a Hound of God. I travel my own road, into Hell and out of it.' And it seemed to Bod as if she ran even faster then.

The huge moon rose and the smaller mould-coloured moon and they were joined by a ruby-red moon, and the grey wolf ran at a steady lope beneath them across the desert of bones. She stopped by a broken clay building like an enormous beehive, built beside a small rill of water that came bubbling out of the desert rock, splashed down into a tiny pool and was gone again. The grey wolf put her head down and drank, and Bod scooped water up in his hands, drinking the water in a dozen tiny gulps.

'This is the boundary,' said the grey wolf that was Miss

Lupescu, and Bod looked up. The three moons had gone. Now he could see the Milky Way, see it as he had never seen it before, a glimmering shroud across the arch of the sky. The sky was filled with stars.

'They're beautiful,' said Bod.

'When we get you home,' said Miss Lupescu, 'I teach you the names of the stars and their constellations.'

'I'd like that,' admitted Bod.

Bod clambered on to her huge, grey back once more and he buried his face in her fur and held on tightly, and it seemed only moments later that he was being carried – awkwardly, as a grown woman carries a six-year-old boy – across the graveyard, to the Owenses' tomb.

'He's hurt his ankle,' Miss Lupescu was saying.

'Poor little soul,' said Mistress Owens, taking the boy from her, and cradling him in her capable, if insubstantial arms. 'I can't say I didn't worry, for I did. But he's back now, and that's all that matters.'

And then he was perfectly comfortable, beneath the earth, in a good place, with his head on his own pillow, and a gentle, exhausted darkness took him.

Bod's left ankle was swollen and purple. Doctor Trefusis (1870–1936, *May He Wake To Glory*) inspected it and pronounced it merely sprained. Miss Lupescu returned from a journey to the chemist's with a tight ankle bandage, and Josiah Worthington, Bart, who had been buried with his ebony walking cane, insisted on lending it to Bod, who had too much fun leaning on the stick and pretending to be one hundred years old.

Bod limped up the hill and retrieved a folded piece of paper from beneath a stone.

The Hounds of God

It was printed in a purple ink, and was the first item on a list.

> *Those that men call Werewolves or Lycanthropes call*
> *themselves the Hounds of God, as they claim their*
> *transformation is a gift from their creator, and they repay*
> *the gift with their tenacity, for they will pursue an evil-doer*
> *to the very gates of Hell.*

Bod nodded.

Not just evil-doers, he thought.

He read the rest of the list, committing it to memory as best he could, then went down to the chapel, where Miss Lupescu was waiting for him with a small meat pie and a huge bag of chips she had bought from the fish and chip shop at the bottom of the hill, and another pile of purple-inked duplicated lists.

The two of them shared the chips, and once or twice, Miss Lupescu even smiled.

Silas came back at the the end of the month. He carried his black bag in his left hand and he held his right arm stiffly. But he was Silas, and Bod was happy to see him, and even happier when Silas gave him a present, a little model of the Golden Gate Bridge in San Francisco.

It was almost midnight, and it was still not fully dark.

The three of them sat at the top of the hill, with the lights of the city glimmering beneath them.

'I trust that all went well in my absence,' said Silas.

'I learned a lot,' said Bod, still holding his bridge. He pointed up into the night sky. 'That's Orion the Hunter, up there, with his belt of three stars. That's Taurus the Bull.'

'Very good,' said Silas.

'And you?' asked Bod. 'Did you learn anything, while you were away?'

'Oh yes,' said Silas, but he declined to elaborate.

'I also,' said Miss Lupescu, primly. 'I also learned things.'

'Good,' said Silas. An owl hooted in the branches of an oak tree. 'You know, I heard rumours, while I was away,' said Silas, 'that some weeks ago you both went somewhat further afield than I would have been able to follow. Normally, I would advise caution, but, unlike some, the ghoul-folk have short memories.'

Bod said, 'It's OK. Miss Lupescu looked after me. I was never in any danger.'

Miss Lupescu looked at Bod, and her eyes shone, then she looked at Silas.

'There are so many things to know,' she said. 'Perhaps I come back next year, in high summer also, to teach the boy again.'

Silas looked at Miss Lupescu, and he raised an eyebrow a fraction. Then he looked at Bod.

'I'd like that,' said Bod.

'They say a witch is buried here.'

CHAPTER 4

The Witch's Headstone

There was a witch buried at the edge of the graveyard, it was common knowledge. Bod had been told to keep away from that corner of the world by Mrs Owens as far back as he could remember.

'Why?' he asked.

''Tain't healthy for a living body,' said Mrs Owens. 'There's damp down that end of things. It's practically a marsh. You'll catch your death.'

Mr Owens himself was more evasive and less imaginative. 'It's not a good place,' was all he said.

The graveyard proper ended at the bottom of the west side of the hill, beneath the old apple tree, with a fence of rust-brown iron railings, each topped with a small, rusting spearhead, but there was a wasteland beyond that, a mass of nettles and weeds, of brambles and autumnal rubbish, and Bod, who was, on the whole, obedient, did not push between the railings, but he went down there and looked through. He knew he wasn't being told the whole story, and it irritated him.

Bod went back up the hill, to the little chapel near the

entrance to the graveyard, and he waited until it got dark. As twilight edged from grey to purple there was a noise in the spire, like a fluttering of heavy velvet, and Silas left his resting place in the belfry and clambered headfirst down the spire.

'What's in the far corner of the graveyard?' asked Bod. 'Past Harrison Westwood, Baker of this Parish, and his wives Marion and Joan?'

'Why do you ask?' said his guardian, brushing the dust from his black suit with ivory fingers.

Bod shrugged. 'Just wondered.'

'It's unconsecrated ground,' said Silas. 'Do you know what that means?'

'Not really,' said Bod.

Silas walked across the path without disturbing a fallen leaf, and sat down on the bench, beside Bod. 'There are those,' he said, in his silken voice, 'who believe that all land is sacred. That it is sacred before we come to it, and sacred after. But here, in your land, they blessed the churches and the ground they set aside to bury people in, to make it holy. But they left land unconsecrated beside the sacred ground, potter's fields to bury the criminals and the suicides or those who were not of the faith.'

'So the people buried in the ground on the other side of the fence are bad people?'

Silas raised one perfect eyebrow. 'Mm? Oh, not at all. Let's see, it's been a while since I've been down that way. But I don't remember anyone particularly evil. Remember, in days gone by you could be hanged for stealing a shilling. And there are always people who find their lives have become so unsupportable they believe the best thing they could do would be to hasten their transition to another plane of existence.'

'They kill themselves, you mean?' said Bod. He was about eight years old, wide-eyed and inquisitive, and he was not stupid.

'Indeed.'

'Does it work? Are they happier dead?'

'Sometimes. Mostly, no. It's like the people who believe they'll be happy if they go and live somewhere else, but who learn it doesn't work that way. Wherever you go, you take yourself with you. If you see what I mean.'

'Sort of,' said Bod.

Silas reached down and ruffled the boy's hair.

Bod said, 'What about the witch?'

'Yes. Exactly,' said Silas. 'Suicides, criminals and witches. Those who died unshriven.' He stood up, a midnight shadow in the twilight. 'All this talking,' he said, 'and I have not even had my breakfast. While you will be late for lessons.' In the twilight of the graveyard there was a silent implosion, a flutter of velvet darkness, and Silas was gone.

The moon had begun to rise by the time Bod reached Mr Pennyworth's mausoleum, and Thomes Pennyworth (*here he lyes in the certainty of the moft glorious refurrection*) was already waiting, and was not in the best of moods.

'You are late,' he said.

'Sorry, Mr Pennyworth.'

Pennyworth tutted. The previous week Mr Penny-worth had been teaching Bod about Elements and

95

Humours, and Bod had kept forgetting which was which. He was expecting a test but instead Mr Pennyworth said, 'I think it is time to spend a few days on practical matters. Time is passing, after all.'

'Is it?' asked Bod.

'I am afraid so, young Master Owens. Now, how is your Fading?'

Bod had hoped he would not be asked that question.

'It's all right,' he said. 'I mean. You know.'

'No, Master Owens. I do not know. Why do you not demonstrate for me?'

Bod's heart sank. He took a deep breath, and did his best, squinching up his eyes and trying to fade away.

Mr Pennyworth was not impressed.

'Pah. That's not the kind of thing. Not the kind of thing at all. Slipping and Fading, boy, the way of the dead. Slip through shadows. Fade from awareness. Try again.'

Bod tried harder.

'You're as plain as the nose on your face,' said Mr Pennyworth. 'And your nose is remarkably obvious. As is the rest of your face, young man. As are you. For the sake of all that is holy, empty your mind. Now. You are an empty alleyway. You are a vacant doorway. You are nothing. Eyes will not see you. Minds will not hold you. Where you are is nothing and nobody.'

Bod tried again. He closed his eyes and imagined himself fading into the stained stonework of the mausoleum wall, becoming a shadow of the night and nothing more. He sneezed.

'Dreadful,' said Mr Pennyworth, with a sigh. 'Quite

dreadful. I believe I shall have a word with your guardian about this.' He shook his head. 'So. The humours. List them.'

'Um. Sanguine. Choleric. Phlegmatic. And the other one. Um, Melancholic, I think.'

And so it went, until it was time for Grammar and Composition with Miss Letitia Borrows, Spinster of this Parish (*Who Did No Harm to No Man all the Dais of Her Life. Reader, Can You Say Lykewise?*). Bod liked Miss Borrows, and the cosiness of her little crypt, and that she could all-too-easily be led off the subject.

'They say there's a witch in uncons— unconsecrated ground,' he said.

'Yes, dear. But you don't want to go over there.'

'Why not?'

Miss Borrows smiled the guileless smile of the dead. 'They aren't our sort of people,' she said.

'But it *is* the graveyard, isn't it? I mean, I'm allowed to go there if I want to?'

'That,' said Miss Borrows, 'would not be advisable.'

Bod was obedient, but curious, and so, when lessons were done for the night, he walked past Harrison Westwood, Baker, and family's memorial, a broken-armed angel, but did not climb down the hill to the potter's field. Instead he walked up the side of the hill to where a picnic some thirty years before had left its mark in the shape of a large apple tree.

There were some lessons that Bod had mastered. He had eaten a bellyful of unripe apples, sour and white-pipped, from the tree some years before, and had regretted it for days, his guts cramping and painful while Mrs Owens lectured him on what not to eat. Now he always waited until the apples were ripe before eating them, and never ate more than two or three a night. He had finished the last of the apples the week before, but he liked the apple tree as a place to think.

He edged up the trunk, to his favourite place in the crook of two branches, and looked down at the potter's field below him, a brambly patch of weeds and unmown grass in the moonlight. He wondered whether the witch would be old and iron-toothed and travel in a house on chicken legs, or whether she would be thin and sharp-nosed and carry a broomstick.

Bod's stomach growled and he realised that he was getting hungry. He wished he had not devoured all the apples on the tree. That he had left just one . . .

He glanced up, and thought he saw something. He looked once, looked twice to be certain: an apple, red and ripe.

Bod prided himself on his tree-climbing skills. He swung himself up, branch by branch, and imagined he was Silas, swarming smoothly up a sheer brick wall. The apple, the red of it almost black in the moonlight, hung just out of reach. Bod moved slowly forward along the branch, until he was just below the apple. Then he stretched up, and the tips of his fingers touched the perfect apple.

He was never to taste it.

A snap, loud as a hunter's gun, as the branch gave way beneath him.

A flash of pain woke him, sharp as ice, the colour of slow thunder, down in the weeds that summer's night.

The ground beneath him seemed relatively soft, and oddly warm. He pushed a hand down and felt something like warm fur beneath him. He had landed on the grass-pile, where the graveyard's gardener threw the cuttings from the mower, and it had broken his fall. Still, there was a pain in his chest, and his leg hurt as if he had landed on it first and twisted it.

Bod moaned.

'Hush-a-you-hush-a-boy,' said a voice from behind him. 'Where did you come from? Dropping like a thunder-stone. What way is that to carry on?'

'I was in the apple tree,' said Bod.

'Ah. Let me see your leg. Broken like the tree's limb, I'll be bound.' Cool fingers prodded his left leg. 'Not broken. Twisted, yes, sprained perhaps. You have the Devil's own luck, boy, falling into the compost. 'Tain't the end of the world.'

'Oh, good,' said Bod. 'Hurts, though.'

He turned his head, looked up and behind him. She was older than him, but not a grown-up, and she looked neither friendly nor unfriendly. Wary, mostly. She had a face that was intelligent and not even a little bit beautiful.

'I'm Bod,' he said.

'The live boy?' she asked.

Bod nodded.

'I thought you must be,' she said. 'We've heard of you, even over here, in the potter's field. What do they call you?'

'Owens,' he said. 'Nobody Owens. Bod, for short.'

'How-de-do, young Master Bod.'

Bod looked her up and down. She wore a plain white shift. Her hair was mousy and long, and there was something of the goblin in her face – a sideways hint of a smile that seemed to linger, no matter what the rest of her face was doing.

'Were you a suicide?' he asked. 'Did you steal a shilling?'

'Never stole nuffink,' she said, 'Not even a handkerchief. Anyway,' she said, pertly, 'the suicides is all over there, on the other side of that hawthorn, and the gallowsbirds are in the blackberry-patch, both of them. One was a coiner, t'other a highwayman, or so he says, although if you ask me I doubt he was more than a common footpad and nightwalker.'

'Ah,' said Bod. Then, suspicion forming, tentatively, he said, 'They say a witch is buried here.'

She nodded. 'Drownded and burnded and buried here without as much as a stone to mark the spot.'

'You were drowned *and* burned?'

She settled down on the hill of grass-cuttings beside him, and held his throbbing leg with her chilly hands. 'They come to my little cottage at dawn, before I'm proper awake, and drags me out on to the green. "You're a witch!" they shouts, fat and fresh-scrubbed all pink in the morning, like so many pigwiggins scrubbed clean for market day. One by one they gets up beneath the sky and tells of milk gone sour and horses gone lame, and finally Mistress Jemima gets up, the fattest, pinkest, best-scrubbed of them all, and tells how as Solomon Porritt now cuts her dead and instead hangs around the washhouse like a wasp about a honeypot, and it's all my magic, says she, that made him so and the poor young man must be bespelled. So they strap me to the cucking-stool and forces it under the water of the duckpond, saying if I'm a witch I'll neither drown nor care, but if I am not a witch I'll feel it. And Mistress Jemima's father gives them each a silver groat to hold the stool down under the foul green water for a long time, to see if I'd choke on it.'

'And did you?'

'Oh yes. Got a lungful of water. It done for me.'

'Oh,' said Bod. 'Then you weren't a witch after all.'

The girl fixed him with her beady ghost-eyes and smiled a lopsided smile. She still looked like a goblin, but now she looked like a pretty goblin, and Bod didn't think she would have needed magic to attract Solomon Porritt, not with a smile like that. 'What nonsense. Of course I was a witch. They learned that when they untied me from the cucking-stool and stretched me on the green, nine-parts dead and all covered with duckweed and stinking pond-muck. I rolled my eyes back in my head, and I cursed each and every one of them there on the village green that morning, that none of them would ever rest easily in a grave. I was surprised at how easily it came, the cursing. Like dancing it was, when your feet pick up the steps of a new measure your ears have never heard and your head don't know, and they dance it till dawn.' She stood, and twirled, and kicked, and her bare feet flashed in the moonlight. 'That was how I cursed them, with my last gurgling pond-watery breath. And then I expired. They burned my body on the green until I was nothing but blackened charcoal, and they popped me in a hole in the potter's field without so much as a headstone to mark my name,' and it was only then that she paused, and seemed, for a moment, wistful.

'Are any of them buried in the graveyard, then?' asked Bod.

'Not a one,' said the girl, with a twinkle. 'The Saturday after they drownded and toasted me, a carpet was delivered to Master Porringer, all the way from London Town, and it was a fine carpet. But it turned out there was more in that carpet than strong wool and good weaving, for it carried the plague in its pattern, and by Monday five of them were coughing blood, and their skins were gone as black as mine when they hauled me from the fire. A week later and it had taken most of the village, and they threw the bodies all promiscuous in a plague pit they dug outside of the town, that they filled in after.'

'Was everyone in the village killed?'

She shrugged. 'Everyone who watched me get drownded and burned. How's your leg now?'

'Better,' he said. 'Thanks.'

Bod stood up, slowly, and limped down from the grass-pile. He leaned against the iron railings. 'So were you always a witch?' he asked. 'I mean, before you cursed them all?'

'As if it would take witchcraft,' she said with a sniff, 'to get Solomon Porritt mooning round my cottage.'

Which, Bod thought, but did not say, was not actually

an answer to the question, not at all.

'What's your name?' he asked.

'Got no headstone,' she said, turning down the corners of her mouth. 'Might be anybody. Mightn't I?'

'But you must have a name.'

'Liza Hempstock, if you please,' she said tartly. Then she said, 'It's not that much to ask, is it? Something to mark my grave. I'm just down there, see? With nothing but nettles to show where I rest.' And she looked so sad, just for a moment, that Bod wanted to hug her. And then it came to him, as he squeezed between the railings of the fence. He would find Liza Hempstock a headstone, with her name upon it. He would make her smile.

He turned to wave goodbye as he began to clamber up the hill, but she was already gone.

There were broken lumps of other people's stones and statues in the graveyard, but, Bod knew, that would have been entirely the wrong sort of thing to bring to the grey-eyed witch in the potter's field. It was going to take more than that. He decided not to tell anyone what he was planning, on the not entirely unreasonable basis that they would have told him not to do it.

Over the next few days his mind filled with plans, each more complicated and extravagant than the last. Mr Pennyworth despaired.

'I do believe,' he announced, scratching his dusty moustache, 'that you are getting, if anything, worse. You are not Fading. You are *obvious*, boy. You are difficult to miss. If you came to me in company with a purple lion, a green elephant, and a scarlet unicorn astride which was the King of England in his Royal Robes, I do believe that it is you and you alone that people would stare at, dismissing the others as minor irrelevancies.'

Bod simply stared at him, and said nothing. He was wondering whether there were special shops in the places where the living people gathered that sold only head-stones, and if so how he could go about finding one, and Fading was the least of his problems.

He took advantage of Miss Borrows' willingness to be diverted from the subjects of Grammar and Composition to the subject of anything else at all to ask her about money – how exactly it worked, how one used it to get things one wanted. Bod had a number of coins he had found over the years (he had learned that the best place to find money was to go, afterwards, to wherever courting couples had used the grass of the graveyard as a place to cuddle and snuggle and kiss and roll about. He would often find metal coins on the ground, in the place where they had been) and he thought perhaps he could finally get some use from them.

'How much would a headstone be?' he asked Miss Borrows.

'In my time,' she told him, 'they were fifteen guineas. I do not know what they would be today. More, I imagine. Much, much more.'

Bod had two pounds and fifty-three pence. It would, he was quite certain, not be enough.

It had been four years, almost half a lifetime, since Bod had visited the Indigo Man's tomb, but he still remem-bered the way. He climbed to the top of the hill, until he was above the whole town, above even the top of the apple tree, above even the steeple of the ruined chapel, up where the Frobisher mausoleum stood like a rotten tooth. He slipped down into it, behind the coffin, and down and down and still further down, down to the tiny stone steps cut into the centre of the hill, and those he descended until he reached the stone chamber. It was dark in that tomb, dark as a tin mine, but Bod saw as the dead see and the room gave up its secrets to him.

The Sleer was coiled around the wall of the barrow. He could feel it. It was as he remembered it, an invisible thing, all smoky tendrils and hate and greed. This time, however, he was not afraid of it.

FEAR US, whispered the Sleer. FOR WE GUARD THINGS PRECIOUS AND NEVER-LOST.

'I don't fear you,' said Bod. 'Remember? And I need to take something away from here.'

NOTHING EVER LEAVES, came the reply from the coiled thing in the darkness. THE KNIFE, THE BROOCH, THE GOBLET. THE SLEER GUARDS THEM IN THE DARKNESS. WE WAIT.

'Pardon me for asking,' said Bod. 'But was this your grave?'

MASTER SETS US HERE ON THE PLAIN TO GUARD, BURIES OUR SKULLS BENEATH THIS STONE, LEAVES US HERE KNOWING WHAT WE HAVE TO DO. WE GUARD THE TREASURES UNTIL MASTER COMES BACK.

'I expect that he's forgotten all about you,' pointed out Bod. 'I'm sure he's been dead himself for ages.'

WE ARE THE SLEER. WE GUARD.

Bod wondered just how long ago you had to go back before the deepest tomb inside the hill was on a plain, and he knew it must have been an extremely long time ago. He could feel the Sleer winding its waves of fear around him, like the tendrils of some carnivorous plant. He was beginning to feel cold, and slow, as if he had been bitten in the heart by some arctic viper and it was starting to pump its icy venom through his body.

He took a step forward, so he was standing against the stone slab, and he reached down and closed his fingers around the coldness of the brooch.

HISH! whispered the Sleer. WE GUARD THAT FOR THE MASTER.

'He won't mind,' said Bod. He took a step backward, walking toward the stone steps, avoiding the desiccated remains of people and animals on the floor.

The Sleer writhed angrily, twining around the tiny chamber like ghost-smoke. Then it slowed. IT COMES BACK, said the Sleer, in its tangled triple voice. ALWAYS COMES BACK.

Bod went up the stone steps inside the hill as fast as he could. At one point he imagined that there was something coming after him, but when he broke out of the top, into the Frobisher mausoleum, and he could breathe the cool dawn air, nothing moved or followed.

Bod sat in the open air on the top of the hill and held the brooch. He thought it was all black, at first, but then the sun rose, and he could see that the stone in the centre of the black metal was a swirling red. It was the size of a robin's egg, and Bod stared into the stone wondering if there were things moving in its heart, his eyes and soul deep in the crimson world. If Bod had been smaller, he would have wanted to put it into his mouth.

The stone was held in place by a black metal clasp, by something that looked like claws, with something else crawling around it. The something else looked almost snake-like, but it had too many heads. Bod wondered if that was what the Sleer looked like, in the daylight.

He wandered down the hill, taking all the short cuts he knew, through the ivy tangle that covered the Bartleby family vault (and inside, the sound of the Bartlebys grumbling and readying for sleep) and on and over and through the railings and into the potter's field.

He called, 'Liza! Liza!' and looked around.

'Good morrow, young lummox,' said Liza's voice. Bod could not see her, but there was an extra shadow beneath the hawthorn tree, and, as he approached it, the shadow resolved itself into something pearlescent and translucent in the early morning light. Something girl-like. Something grey-eyed. 'I should be decently sleeping,' she said. 'What kind of carrying on is this?'

'Your headstone,' he said. 'I wanted to know what you want on it.'

'My name,' she said. 'It must have my name on it, with a big E, for Elizabeth, like the old queen that died when I was born, and a big Haitch, for Hempstock. More than that I care not, for I did never master my letters.'

'What about dates?' asked Bod.

'Willyum the Conker ten sixty-six,' she sang, in the whisper of the dawn-wind in the hawthorn bush. 'A big E if you please. And a big Haitch.'

'Did you have a job?' asked Bod. 'I mean, when you weren't being a witch?'

'I done laundry,' said the dead girl, and then the morning sunlight flooded the waste-land, and Bod was alone.

It was nine in the morning, when all the world is sleeping. Bod was determined to stay awake. He was, after all, on a mission. He was eight years old, and the world beyond the graveyard held no terrors for him.

Clothes. He would need clothes. His usual dress, of a grey winding sheet, was, he knew, quite wrong. It was good in the graveyard, the same colour as stone and as shadows. But if he was going to dare the world beyond the graveyard walls, he would need to blend in there.

There were some clothes in the crypt beneath the ruined chapel, but Bod did not want to go down to the crypt, not even in daylight. While Bod was prepared to justify himself to Master and Mistress Owens, he was not about to explain himself to Silas; the very thought of those dark eyes angry, or worse still, disappointed, filled him with shame.

There was a gardener's hut at the far end of the grave-yard, a small green building that smelled like motor oil, and in which the old mower sat and rusted, unused, along with an assortment of ancient garden tools. The hut had been abandoned when the last gardener had retired, before Bod was born, and the task of keeping the graveyard had been shared between the council (who sent in a man to cut the grass and clean the paths, once a month from April to September) and the local volunteers in the Friends of the Graveyard.

A huge padlock on the door protected the contents of the hut, but Bod had long ago discovered the loose wooden board in the back. Sometimes he would go to the gardener's hut, and sit, and think, when he wanted to be by himself.

As long as he had been going to the hut there had been a brown working-man's jacket hanging on the back of the door, forgotten or abandoned years before, along with a green-stained pair of gardening jeans. The jeans were much too big for him, but he rolled up the bottoms until his feet showed, then he made a belt out of brown garden-twine, and tied it around his waist. There were boots in one corner, and he tried putting them on, but they were so big and encrusted with mud and concrete that he could barely shuffle in them, and if he took a step, the boots remained on the floor of the shed. He pushed the jacket out through the space in the loose board, squeezed himself out, then put it on. If he rolled up the sleeves, he decided, it worked quite well. It had big pockets, and he thrust his hands into them, and felt quite the dandy.

Bod walked down to the main gate of the graveyard, and looked out through the bars. A bus rattled past, in the street; there were cars there and noise and shops. Behind him, a cool green shade, overgrown with trees and ivy: home.

His heart pounding, Bod walked out into the world.

Abanazer Bolger had seen some odd types in his time; if you owned a shop like Abanazer's, you'd see them too. The shop, in the warren of streets in the Old Town – a little bit antique shop, a little bit junk shop, a little bit pawnbroker's (and not even Abanazer himself was entirely certain which bit was which) brought odd types and strange people, some of them wanting to buy, some of them needing to sell. Abanazer Bolger traded over the counter, buying and selling, and he did a better trade behind the counter and in the back room, accepting objects that may not have been acquired entirely honestly, and then quietly shifting them on. His business was an iceberg. Only the dusty little shop was visible on the surface. The rest of it was underneath, and that was just how Abanazer Bolger wanted it.

Abanazer Bolger had thick spectacles and a permanent expression of mild distaste, as if he had just realised that the milk in his tea had been on the turn, and he could not get the sour taste of it out of his mouth. The expression served him well when people tried to sell him things. 'Honestly,' he would tell them, sour-faced, 'it's not really worth anything at all. I'll give you what I can, though, as it has sentimental value.' You were lucky to get anything like what you thought you wanted from Abanazer Bolger.

A business like Abanazer Bolger's brought in strange people, but the boy who came in that morning was one of the strangest Abanazer could remember in a lifetime of cheating strange people out of their valuables. He looked about seven years old, and dressed in his grandfather's clothes. He smelled like a shed. His hair was long and shaggy, and he seemed extremely grave. His hands were deep in the pockets of a dusty brown jacket, but even with the hands out of sight, Abanazer could see that something was clutched extremely tightly – protectively – in the boy's right hand.

'Excuse me,' said the boy.

'Aye-aye Sonny-Jim,' said Abanazer Bolger warily. *Kids,* he thought. *Either they've nicked something, or they're trying to sell their toys.* Either way, he usually said no. Buy stolen property from a kid, and next thing you knew you'd an enraged adult accusing you of having given little Johnnie or Matilda a tenner for their wedding ring. More trouble than they was worth, kids.

'I need something for a friend of mine,' said the boy. 'And I thought maybe you could buy something I've got.'

'I don't buy stuff from kids,' said Abanazer Bolger flatly.

Bod took his hand out of his pocket and put the brooch down on the grimy countertop. Bolger glanced down at it, then he looked at it. He removed his spectacles, took an eyepiece from the countertop and he screwed it into his eye. He turned on a little light on the counter and examined the brooch through the eyeglass. 'Snakestone?' he said, to himself, not to the boy. Then he took the eyepiece out, replaced his glasses, and fixed the boy with a sour and suspicious look.

'Where did you get this?' Abanazer Bolger asked.

Bod said, 'Do you want to buy it?'

'You stole it. You've nicked this from a museum or somewhere, didn't you?'

'No,' said Bod flatly. 'Are you going to buy it, or shall I

go and find somebody who will?'

Abanazer Bolger's sour mood changed then. Suddenly he was all affability. He smiled broadly. 'I'm sorry,' he said. 'It's just you don't see many pieces like this. Not in a shop like this. Not outside of a museum. But I would certainly like it. Tell you what. Why don't we sit down over tea and biscuits – I've got a packet of chocolate chip cookies in the back room – and decide how much something like this is worth? Eh?'

Bod was relieved that the man was finally being friendly. 'I need enough to buy a stone,' he said. 'A head-stone for a friend of mine. Well, she's not really my friend. Just someone I know. I think she helped make my leg better, you see.'

Abanazer Bolger, paying little attention to the boy's prattle, led him behind the counter, and opened the door to the storeroom, a windowless little space, every inch of which was crammed high with teetering cardboard boxes, each filled with junk. There was a safe in there, in the corner, a big old one. There was a box filled with violins, an accumulation of stuffed dead animals, chairs without seats, books and prints.

There was a small desk beside the door, and Abanazer Bolger pulled up the only chair, and sat down, letting Bod stand. Abanazer rummaged in a drawer, in which Bod could see a half-empty bottle of whisky, and pulled out an almost-finished packet of chocolate chip cookies, and he offered one to the boy; he turned on the desk light, looked at the brooch again, the swirls of red and orange in the stone, and he examined the black metal band that encircled it, suppressing a little shiver at the expression on the heads of the snake-things. 'This is old,' he said. 'It's –' *priceless*, he thought, 'probably not really worth much, but you never know.' Bod's face fell. Abanazer Bolger tried to look reassuring. 'I just need to know that it's not stolen, though, before I can give you a penny. Did you take it from your mum's dresser? Nick it from a museum? You can tell me. I'll not get you into trouble. I just need to know.'

Bod shook his head. He munched on his cookie.

'Then where did you get it?'

Bod said nothing.

Abanazer Bolger did not want to put down the brooch, but he pushed it across the desk to the boy. 'If you can't tell me,' he said, 'you'd better take it back. There has to be trust on both sides, after all. Nice doing business with you. Sorry it couldn't go any further.'

Bod looked worried. Then he said, 'I found it in an old grave. But I can't say where.' He stopped, because naked greed and excitement had replaced the friendliness on Abanazer Bolger's face.

'And there's more like this there?'

Bod said, 'If you don't want to buy it, I'll find someone else. Thank you for the biscuit.'

Bolger said, 'You're in a hurry, eh? Mum and Dad waiting for you, I expect?'

The boy shook his head, then wished he had nodded.

'Nobody waiting. Good.' Abanazer Bolger closed his hands around the brooch. 'Now, you tell me exactly where you found this. Eh?'

'I don't remember,' said Bod.

'Too late for that,' said Abanazer Bolger. 'Suppose you have a little think for a bit about where it came from. Then, when you've thought, we'll have a little chat, and you'll tell me.'

He got up, and walked out of the room, closing the door behind him. He locked it, with a large metal key.

He opened his hand, and looked at the brooch and smiled, hungrily.

There was a *ding* from the bell above the shop door, to let him know someone had entered, and he looked up, guiltily, but there was no one there. The door was slightly ajar though, and Bolger pushed it shut, and then for good measure he turned around the sign in the window so it said Closed. He pushed the bolt shut. Didn't want any busybodies turning up today.

The autumn day had turned from sunny to grey, and a light patter of rain ran down the grubby shop window.

Abanazer Bolger picked up the telephone from the counter and pushed at the buttons with fingers that barely shook.

'Pay dirt, Tom,' he said. 'Get over here, soon as you can.'

Bod realised that he was trapped when he heard the lock turn in the door. He pulled on the door, but it held fast. He felt stupid for having been lured inside, foolish for not trusting his first impulses, to get as far away from the sour-faced man as possible. He had broken all the rules of the graveyard, and everything had gone wrong. What would Silas say? Or the Owenses? He could feel himself beginning to panic, and he suppressed it, pushing the worry back down inside him. It would all be good. He knew that. Of course, he needed to get out . . .

He examined the room he was trapped in. It was little more than a storeroom with a desk in it. The only entrance was the door.

He opened the desk drawer, finding nothing but small pots of paint (used for brightening up antiques) and a paintbrush. He wondered if he would be able to throw paint in the man's face, and blind him for long enough to escape. He opened the top of a pot of paint and dipped in his finger.

'What're you doin'?' asked a voice close to his ear.

'Nothing,' said Bod, screwing the top on the paint-pot, and dropping it into one of the jacket's enormous pockets.

Liza Hempstock looked at him, unimpressed. 'Why are you in here?' she asked. 'And who's old bag-of-lard out there?'

'It's his shop. I was trying to sell him something.'

'Why?'

'None of your beeswax.'

She sniffed. 'Well,' she said, 'you should get on back to the graveyard.'

'I can't. He's locked me in.'

''Course you can. Just slip through the wall –'

He shook his head. 'I can't. I can only do it at home because they gave me the Freedom of the Graveyard when I was a baby.' He looked up at her, under the electric light. It was hard to see her properly, but Bod had spent his life talking to dead people. 'Anyway, what are you doing

115

here? What are you doing out from the graveyard? It's daytime. And you're not like Silas. You're meant to stay in the graveyard.'

She said, 'There's rules for those in graveyards, but not for those as was buried in unhallowed ground. Nobody tells *me* what to do, or where to go.' She glared at the door. 'I don't like that man,' she said. 'I'm going to see what he's doing.'

A flicker, and Bod was alone in the room once more. He heard a rumble of distant thunder.

In the cluttered darkness of Bolger's Antiquities, Abanazer Bolger looked up suspiciously, certain that someone was watching him, then realised he was being foolish. 'The boy's locked in the room,' he told himself. 'The front door's locked.' He was polishing the metal clasp surrounding the snakestone, as gently and as carefully as an archaeologist on a dig, taking off the black and revealing the glittering silver beneath it.

He was beginning to regret calling Tom Hustings over, although Hustings was big and good for scaring people. He was also beginning to regret that he was going to have to sell the brooch when he was done. It was special. The more it glittered, under the tiny light on his counter, the more he wanted it to be his, and only his.

There was more where this came from, though. The boy would tell him. The boy would lead him to it.

The boy . . .

An idea struck him. He put down the brooch, reluctantly, and opened a drawer behind the counter, taking out a metal biscuit tin filled with envelopes and cards and slips of paper.

He reached in and took out a card, only slightly larger than a business card. It was black-edged. There was no name or address printed on it, though. Only one word, handwritten in the centre in an ink that had faded to brown: *Jack*.

On the back of the card, in pencil, Abanazer Bolger had written instructions to himself, in his tiny, precise handwriting, as a reminder, although he would not have been likely to forget the use of the card, how to use it to summon the man Jack. No, not summon. *Invite*. You did not summon people like him.

A knocking on the outer door of the shop.

Bolger tossed the card down on to the counter, and walked over to the door, peering out into the wet afternoon.

'Hurry up,' called Tom Hustings. 'It's miserable out here. Dismal. I'm getting soaked.'

Bolger unlocked the door and Tom Hustings pushed his way in, his raincoat and hair dripping. 'What's so important that you can't talk about it over the phone, then?'

'Our fortune,' said Abanazer Bolger, with his sour face. 'That's what.'

Hustings took off his raincoat and hung it on the back of the shop door. 'What is it? Something good fell off the back of a lorry?'

'Treasure,' said Abanazer Bolger. 'Two kinds.' He took his friend over to the counter, showed him the brooch under the little light.

'It's old, isn't it?'

'From pagan times,' said Abanazer. 'Before. From Druid times. Before the Romans came. It's called a snakestone. Seen 'em in museums. I've never seen metalwork like that, or one so fine. Must have belonged to a king. The lad who found it says it come from a grave – think of a barrow filled with stuff like this.'

'Might be worth doing it legit,' said Hustings, thoughtfully. 'Declare it as treasure trove. They have to pay us market value for it, and we could make them name it after us. The Hustings-Bolger Bequest.'

'Bolger-Hustings,' said Abanazer, automatically. Then he said, 'There's a few people I know of, people with real money, would pay more than market value, if they could hold it as you are –' for Tom Hustings was fingering the brooch, gently, like a man stroking a kitten – 'and there'd be no questions asked.' He reached out his hand and, reluctantly, Tom Hustings passed him the brooch.

'You said two kinds of treasure,' said Hustings. 'What's t'other?'

Abanazer Bolger picked up the black-edged card, held it out for his friend's inspection. 'Do you know what this is?'

His friend shook his head.

Abanazer put the card down on the counter. 'There's a party is looking for another party.'

'So?'

'The way I heard it,' said Abanazer Bolger. 'The other party is a boy.'

'There's boys everywhere,' said Tom Hustings. 'Running all around. Getting into trouble. I can't abide them. So, there's a party looking for a particular boy?'

'This lad looks to be the right sort of age. He's dressed – well, you'll see how he's dressed. And he found this. It could be him.'

'And if it is him?'

Abanazer Bolger picked up the card again, by the edge, and waved it back and forth, slowly, as if running the edge along an imaginary flame. 'Here comes a candle to light you to bed . . .' he began.

'. . . and here comes a chopper to chop off your head,' concluded Tom Hustings, thoughtfully. 'But look you. If we call the man Jack, we lose the boy. And if we lose the boy, we lose the treasure.'

And the two men went back and forth on it, weighing the merits and disadvantages of reporting the boy or of collecting the treasure, which had grown in their minds to a huge underground cavern filled with precious things, and as they debated Abanazer pulled a bottle of sloe gin from beneath the counter and poured them both a generous tot 'to assist the cerebrations'.

Liza was soon bored with their discussion, which went back and forth and around like a whirligig, getting nowhere, and so she went back into the storeroom, to find Bod standing in the middle of the room with his eyes tightly closed and his fists clenched and his face all screwed up as if he had a toothache, almost purple from holding his breath.

'What you a-doin' of now?' she asked, unimpressed.

He opened his eyes and relaxed. 'Trying to Fade,' he said.

Liza sniffed. 'Try again,' she said.

He did, holding his breath even longer this time.

'Stop that,' she told him. 'Or you'll pop.'

Bod took a deep breath and then sighed. 'It doesn't work,' he said. 'Maybe I could hit him with a rock, and just run for it.' There wasn't a rock, so he picked up a coloured glass paperweight, hefted it in his hand, wondering if he could throw it hard enough to stop Abanazer Bolger in his tracks.

'There's two of them out there now,' said Liza. 'And if the one don't get you, t'other one will. They say they want to get you to show them where you got the brooch, and then dig up the grave and take the treasure.' She did not tell him about the other discussions they were having, nor about the black-edged card. She shook her head. 'Why did you do something as stupid as this anyway? You know the rules about leaving the graveyard. Just asking for trouble, it was.'

Bod felt very insignificant, and very foolish. 'I wanted to get you a headstone,' he admitted, in a small voice. 'And I thought it would cost more money. So I was going to sell him the brooch, to buy you one.'

She didn't say anything.

'Are you angry?'

She shook her head. 'It's the first nice thing anyone's done for me in five hundred years,' she said, with a hint of a goblin smile. 'Why would I be angry?' Then she said, 'What do you do, when you try to Fade?'

'What Mr Pennyworth told me. "I *am an empty doorway, I am a vacant alley, I am nothing. Eyes will not see me, glances slip over me."* But it never works.'

'It's because you're alive,' said Liza, with a sniff. 'There's stuff as works for us, the dead, who have to fight to be noticed at the best of times, that won't never work for you people.'

She hugged herself tightly, moving her body back and forth, as if she were debating something. Then she said, 'It's because of me you got into this... Come here, Nobody Owens.'

He took a step towards her, in that tiny room, and she put her cold hand on his forehead. It felt like a wet silk scarf against his skin.

'Now,' she said. 'Perhaps I can do a good turn for you.'

And with that, she began to mutter to herself, mumbling words that Bod could not make out. Then she said, clear and loud:

> *'Be hole, be dust, be dream, be wind*
> *Be night, be dark, be wish, be mind,*
> *Now slip, now slide, now move unseen,*
> *Above, beneath, betwixt, between.'*

Something huge touched him, brushed him from head to feet, and he shivered. His hair prickled, and his skin was all gooseflesh. Something had changed. 'What did you do?' he asked.

'Just gived you a helping hand,' she said. 'I may be dead, but I'm a dead witch, remember. And we don't forget.'

'But –'

'Hush up,' she said. 'They're coming back.'

The key rattled in the storeroom lock. 'Now then, chummy,' said a voice Bod had not heard clearly before, 'I'm sure we're all going to be great friends,' and with that Tom Hustings pushed open the door. Then he stood in the doorway looking around, looking puzzled. He was a big, big man, with foxy-red hair and a bottle-red nose. 'Here. Abanazer? I thought you said he was in here?'

'I did,' said Bolger, from behind him.

'Well, I can't see hide nor hair of him.'

Bolger's face appeared behind the ruddy man's and he peered into the room. 'Hiding,' he said, staring straight at where Bod was standing. 'No use hiding,' he announced, loudly. 'I can see you there. Come on out.'

The two men walked into the little room, and Bod stood stock still between them and thought of Mr Pennyworth's lessons. He did not react, he did not move. He let the men's glances slide from him without seeing him.

'You're going to wish you'd come out when I called,' said Bolger, and he shut the door. 'Right,' he said to Tom Hustings. 'You block the door, so he can't get past.' And with that he walked around the room, peering behind things, and bending, awkwardly, to look beneath the desk. He walked straight past Bod and opened the cupboard. 'Now I see you!' he shouted. 'Come out!'

Liza giggled.

'What was that?' asked Tom Hustings, spinning round.

'I didn't hear nothing,' said Abanazer Bolger.

Liza giggled again. Then she put her lips together and blew, making a noise that began as a whistling, and then sounded like a distant wind. The electric lights in the little room flickered and buzzed, then they went out.

'Bloody fuses,' said Abanazer Bolger. 'Come on. This is a waste of time.'

The key clicked in the lock, and Liza and Bod were left alone in the room.

'He's got away,' said Abanazer Bolger. Bod could hear him now, through the door. 'Room like that. There wasn't anywhere he could have been hiding. We'd've seen him if he was.'

'The man Jack won't like that.'

'Who's going to tell him?'

A pause.

'Here. Tom Hustings. Where's the brooch gone?'

'Mm? That? Here. I was keeping it safe.'

'Keeping it safe? In your pocket? Funny place to be keeping it safe, if you ask me. More like you were planning to make off with it – like you was planning to keep my brooch for your own.'

'Your brooch, Abanazer? *Your* brooch? Our brooch, you mean.'

'Ours, indeed. I don't remember you being here, when I got it from that boy.'

'That boy that you couldn't even keep safe for the man Jack, you mean? Can you imagine what he'll do, when he finds *you* had the boy he was looking for, and *you* let him go?'

'Probably not the same boy. Lots of boys in the world, what're the odds it was the one he was looking for? Out the back door as soon as my back was turned, I'll bet.' And then

Abanazer Bolger said, in a high, wheedling voice, 'Don't you worry about the man Jack, Tom Hustings. I'm sure that it was a different boy. My old mind playing tricks. And we're almost out of sloe gin – how would you fancy a good Scotch? I've whisky in the back room. You just wait here a moment.'

The storeroom door was unlocked, and Abanazer entered, holding a walking stick and an electric torch, looking even more sour of face than before.

'If you're still in here,' he said, in a sour mutter, 'don't even think of making a run for it. I've called the police on you, that's what I've done.' A rummage in a drawer produced the half-filled bottle of whisky, and then a tiny black bottle. Abanazer poured several drops from the little bottle into the larger, then he pocketed the tiny bottle. 'My brooch, and mine alone,' he muttered, and followed it with a barked, 'Just coming, Tom!'

He glared around the dark room, staring past Bod, then he left the storeroom, carrying the whisky in front of him. He locked the door behind him.

'Here you go,' came Abanazer Bolger's voice through the door. 'Give us your glass then, Tom. Nice drop of Scotch, put hairs on your chest. Say when.'

Silence. 'Cheap muck. Aren't you drinking?'

'That sloe gin's gone to my innards. Give it a minute for my stomach to settle . . .' Then, 'Here – Tom! What have you done with my brooch?'

'*Your* brooch is it now? Whoa – what did you . . . you put something in my drink, you little grub!'

'What if I did? I could read on your face what you was planning, Tom Hustings. Thief.'

And then there was shouting, and several crashes, and loud bangs, as if heavy items of furniture were being over-turned . . .

. . . then silence.

Liza said, 'Quickly now. Let's get you out of here.'

'But the door's locked.' He looked at her. 'Is there something you can do?'

'Me? I don't have any magics will get you out of a locked room, boy.'

Bod crouched, and peered out through the keyhole. It was blocked; the key sat in the keyhole. Bod thought, then he smiled, momentarily, and it lit his face like the flash of a lightbulb. He pulled a crumpled sheet of newspaper from a packing case, flattened it out as best he could, then pushed it underneath the door, leaving only a corner on his side of the doorway.

'What are you playing at?' asked Liza, impatiently.

'I need something like a pencil. Only thinner . . .' he said. 'Here we go.' And he took a thin paintbrush from the top of the desk, and pushed the brushless end into the lock, jiggled it and pushed some more.

There was a muffled clunk as the key was pushed out, as it dropped from the lock on to the newspaper. Bod pulled the paper back under the door, now with the key sitting on it.

Liza laughed, delighted. 'That's wit, young man,' she said. 'That's wisdom.'

Bod put the key in the lock, turned it and pushed open the storeroom door.

There were two men on the floor, in the middle of the

crowded antique shop. Furniture had indeed fallen; the place was a chaos of wrecked clocks and chairs, and in the midst of it the bulk of Tom Hustings lay, fallen on the smaller figure of Abanazer Bolger. Neither of them was moving.

'Are they dead?' asked Bod.

'No such luck,' said Liza.

On the floor beside the men was a brooch of glittering silver; a crimson-orange-banded stone, held in place with claws and with snake-heads, and the expression on the snake-heads was one of triumph and avarice and satisfaction.

Bod dropped the brooch into his pocket, where it sat beside the heavy glass paperweight, the paintbrush and the little pot of paint.

'Take this too,' said Liza.

Bod looked at the black-edged card with the word JACK handwritten on one side. It disturbed him. There was something familiar about it, something that stirred old memories, something dangerous. 'I don't want it.'

'You can't leave it here with them,' said Liza. 'They were going to use it to hurt you.'

'I don't want it,' said Bod. 'It's bad. Burn it.'

'No!' Liza gasped. 'Don't do that. You mustn't do that.'

'Then I'll give it to Silas,' said Bod. And he put the little card into an envelope, so he had to touch it as little as possible, and put the envelope into the inside pocket of his old gardening jacket, beside his heart.

Two hundred miles away, the man Jack woke from his sleep, and sniffed the air. He walked downstairs.

'What is it?' asked his grandmother, stirring the contents of a big iron pot on the stove. 'What's got into you now?'

'I don't know,' he said. 'Something's happening. Something... interesting.' And then he licked his lips. 'Smells tasty,' he said. 'Very tasty.'

Lightning illuminated the cobbled street.

Bod hurried through the rain through the Old Town, always heading up the hill towards the graveyard. The grey day had become an early night while he was inside the storeroom, and it came as no surprise to him when a familiar shadow swirled beneath the street lamps. Bod hesitated, and a flutter of night-black velvet resolved itself into a man-shape.

Silas stood in front of him, arms folded. He strode forward, impatiently.

'Well?' he said.

Bod said, 'I'm sorry, Silas.'

'I'm disappointed in you, Bod,' Silas said, and he shook his head. 'I've been looking for you since I woke. You have the smell of trouble all around you. And you know you're not allowed to come out here, into the living world.'

'I know. I'm sorry.' There was rain on the boy's face, running down like tears.

'First of all, we need to get you back to safety.' Silas reached down, and enfolded the living child inside his cloak, and Bod felt the ground fall away beneath him.

'Silas,' he said.

Silas did not answer.

'I was a bit scared,' he said. 'But I knew you'd come and get me if it got too bad. And Liza was there. She helped a lot.'

'Liza?' Silas's voice was sharp.

'The witch. From the potter's field.'

'And you say she helped you?'

'Yes. She especially helped me with my Fading. I think I can do it now.'

Silas grunted. 'You can tell me all about it when we're home.' And Bod was quiet until they landed beside the chapel. They went inside, into the empty hall, as the rain redoubled, splashing up from the puddles that covered the ground.

Bod produced the envelope containing the black-edged card. 'Um,' he said. 'I thought you should have this. Well, Liza did, really.'

Silas looked at it. Then he opened it, removed the card, stared at it, turned it over, and read Abanazer Bolger's pencilled note to himself, in tiny handwriting, explaining the precise manner of use of the card.

'Tell me everything,' he said.

Bod told him everything he could remember about the day. And at the end, Silas shook his head, slowly, thoughtfully.

'Am I in trouble?' asked Bod.

'Nobody Owens,' said Silas, 'you are indeed in trouble. However, I believe I shall leave it to your parents to administer whatever discipline and reproach they believe to be needed. In the meantime, I need to dispose of this.'

The black-edged card vanished inside the velvet cloak, and then, in the manner of his kind, Silas was gone.

Bod pulled the jacket up over his head, and clambered up the slippery paths to the top of the hill, to the Frobisher mausoleum. He pulled aside Ephraim Pettyfer's coffin, and he went down, and down, and still further down.

He replaced the brooch beside the goblet and the knife.

'Here you go,' he said. 'All polished up. Looking pretty.'

IT COMES BACK, said the Sleer, with satisfaction in its smoke-tendril voice. IT ALWAYS COMES BACK.

It had been a long night.

Bod was walking, sleepily and a little gingerly, past the small tomb of the wonderfully named Miss Liberty Roach (*What she spent is lost, what she gave remains with her always, Reader be Charitable*), past the final resting place of Harrison Westwood, Baker of this Parish, and his wives Marion and Joan, to the potter's field. Mr and Mrs Owens had died several hundred years before it had been decided that beating children was wrong and Mr Owens had, regretfully, that night, done what he saw as his duty, and Bod's bottom stung like anything. Still, the look of worry on Mrs Owens' face had hurt Bod worse than any beating could have done.

He reached the iron railings that bounded the potter's field, and slipped between them.

'Hullo?' he called. There was no answer. Not even an

extra shadow in the hawthorn bush. 'I hope I didn't get you into trouble, too,' he said.

Nothing.

He had replaced the jeans in the gardener's hut – he was more comfortable in just his grey winding sheet – but he had kept the jacket. He liked having the pockets.

When he had gone to the shed to return the jeans, he had taken a small hand-scythe from the wall where it hung, and with it he attacked the nettle patch in the potter's field, sending the nettles flying, slashing and gutting them till there was nothing but stinging stubble on the ground.

From his pocket he took the large glass paperweight, its insides a multitude of bright colours, along with the paint-pot and the paintbrush.

He dipped the brush into the paint and carefully painted, in brown paint, on the surface of the paperweight, the letters

E H

And beneath them he wrote:

WE DON'T FORGET

Dawn was breaking. Bedtime soon, and it would not be wise for him to be late to bed for some time to come.

He put the paperweight down on the ground that had once been a nettle patch, placed it in the place that he estimated her head would have been, and, pausing only to look at his handiwork for a moment, he went through the railings and made his way, rather less gingerly, back up the hill.

'Not bad,' said a pert voice from the potter's field, behind him. 'Not bad at all.'

But when he turned to look, there was no one there.

'Last dance!'

CHAPTER 5

Danse Macabre

Something was going on, Bod was certain of it. It was there in the crisp winter air, the stars, in the wind, in the darkness. It was there in the rhythms of the long nights and the fleeting days.

Mistress Owens pushed him out of the Owenses' little tomb. 'Get along with you,' she said. 'I've got business to attend to.'

Bod looked at his mother. 'But it's cold out there,' he said.

'I should hope so,' she said, 'it being winter. That's as it should be. Now,' she said, more to herself than to Bod, 'shoes. And look at this dress – it needs hemming. And cobwebs – there are cobwebs all over, for heaven's sake. You get along,' this to Bod once more. 'I've plenty to be getting on with, and I don't need you underfoot.'

And then she sang to herself, a little couplet Bod had never heard before.

> 'Rich man, poor man, come away.
> Come to dance the Macabray.'

'What's that?' asked Bod, but it was the wrong thing to have said, for Mistress Owens looked dark as a thundercloud, and Bod hurried out of the tomb before she could express her displeasure more forcefully.

It was cold in the graveyard, cold and dark, and the stars were already out. Bod passed Mother Slaughter in the ivy-covered Egyptian Walk, squinting at the greenery.

'Your eyes are younger than mine, young man,' she said. 'Can you see blossom?'

'Blossom? In winter?'

'Don't you look at me with that face on, young man,' she said. 'Things blossom in their time. They bud and bloom, blossom and fade. Everything in its time.' She huddled deeper into her cloak and bonnet and she said:

> *Time to work and time to play,*
> *Time to dance the Macabray.*

'Eh, boy?'

'I don't know,' said Bod. 'What's the Macabray?'

But Mother Slaughter had pushed into the ivy and was gone from sight.

'How odd,' said Bod, aloud. He sought warmth and company in the bustling Bartleby mausoleum, but the Bartleby family – seven generations of them – had no time for him that night. They were cleaning and tidying, all of them, from the oldest (d. 1831) to the youngest (d. 1690).

Fortinbras Bartleby, ten years old when he had died (of *consumption*, he had told Bod, who had mistakenly believed for several years that Fortinbras had been eaten by lions or bears, and was extremely disappointed to learn it was merely a disease), now apologised to Bod.

'We cannot stop to play, Master Bod. For soon enough, *tomorrow night* comes. And how often can a man say that?'

'Every night,' said Bod. 'Tomorrow night *always* comes.'

'Not *this* one,' said Fortinbras. 'Not once in a blue moon, or a month of Sundays.'

'It's not Guy Fawkes' Night,' said Bod, 'or Hallowe'en. It's not Christmas or New Year's Day.'

Fortinbras smiled, a huge smile that filled his pie-shaped, freckly face with joy.

'None of *them*,' he said. '*This* one's special.'

'What's it called?' asked Bod. 'What happens tomorrow?'

'It's the best day,' said Fortinbras, and Bod was certain he would have continued but his grandmother, Louisa Bartleby (who was only twenty) called him over to her, and said something sharply in his ear.

'Nothing,' said Fortinbras. Then to Bod, 'Sorry. I have to work now.' And he took a rag and began to buff the side of his dusty coffin with it. 'La, la, la, *oomp*,' he sang. 'La la la, *oomp*.' And with each 'oomp', he would do a wild, whole-body flourish with his rag.

'Aren't you going to sing that song?'

'What song?'

'The one everybody's singing?'

'No time for that,' said Fortinbras. 'It's *tomorrow*, tomorrow, after all.'

'No time,' said Louisa, who had died in childbirth,

giving birth to twins. 'Be about your business.'

And in her sweet, clear voice, she sang:

> 'One and all will hear and stay
> Come and dance the Macabray.'

Bod walked down to the crumbling little chapel. He slipped between the stones, and into the crypt, where he sat and waited for Silas to return. He was cold, true, but the cold did not bother Bod, not really: the graveyard embraced him, and the dead do not mind the cold.

His guardian returned in the small hours of the morning; he had a large plastic bag with him.

'What's in there?'

'Clothes. For you. Try them on.' Silas produced a grey sweater the colour of Bod's winding sheet, a pair of jeans, underwear and shoes – pale green trainers.

'What are they for?'

'You mean, apart from wearing? Well, firstly, I think you're old enough now – what are you, ten years old? – and normal, living people's clothes are wise. You'll have to wear them one day, so why not pick up the habit right now? And they could also be camouflage.'

'What's camouflage?'

'When something looks enough like something else that people watching don't know what it is they're looking at.'

'Oh. I see. I think.' Bod put the clothes on. The shoelaces gave him a little trouble and Silas had to teach him how to tie them. It seemed remarkably complicated to Bod, and he had to tie and re-tie his laces several times before he had done it to Silas's satisfaction. Only then did Bod dare to ask his question.

'Silas. What's a Macabray?'

Silas's eyebrows raised and his head tipped to one side. 'Where did you hear about that?'

'Everyone in the graveyard is talking about it. I think it's something that happens tomorrow night. What's a Macabray?'

'It's a dance,' said Silas.

'*All must dance the Macabray,*' said Bod, remembering. 'Have you danced it? What kind of dance is it?'

His guardian looked at him with eyes like black pools and said, 'I do not know. I know many things, Bod, for I have been walking this earth at night for a very long time, but I do not know what it is like to dance the Macabray. You must be alive or you must be dead to dance it – and I am neither.'

Bod shivered. He wanted to embrace his guardian, to hold him and tell him that he would never desert him, but the action was unthinkable. He could no more hug Silas than he could hold a moonbeam, not because his guardian was insubstantial, but because it would be wrong. There were people you could hug, and then there was Silas.

His guardian inspected Bod thoughtfully, a boy in his new clothes. 'You'll do,' he said. 'Now you look like you've lived outside the graveyard all your life.'

Bod smiled proudly. Then the smile stopped and he looked grave once again. He said, 'But you'll always be here, Silas, won't you? And I won't ever have to leave, if I don't want to?'

'Everything in its season,' said Silas, and he said no more that night.

Bod woke early the next day, when the sun was a silver coin high in the grey winter sky. It was too easy to sleep through the hours of daylight, to spend all his winter in one long night and never see the sun, and so each night before he slept he would promise himself that he would wake in daylight, and leave the Owenses' cosy tomb.

There was a strange scent in the air, sharp and floral. Bod followed it up the hill to the Egyptian Walk, where the winter ivy hung in green tumbles, an evergreen tangle that hid the mock-Egyptian walls and statues and hieroglyphs.

The perfume was heaviest there, and for a moment Bod wondered if snow might have fallen, for there were white clusters on the greenery. Bod examined a cluster more closely. It was made of small five-petalled flowers, and he had just put his head in to sniff the perfume when he heard footsteps coming up the path.

Bod Faded into the ivy, and watched. Three men and a woman, all alive, came up the path and into the Egyptian Walk. The woman had an ornate chain around her neck.

'Is this it?' she asked.

'Yes, Mrs Caraway,' said one of the men – chubby and white-haired and short of breath. Like each of the men, he carried a large, empty wicker basket.

She seemed both vague and puzzled. 'Well, if you say so,' she said. 'But I cannot say that I understand it.' She looked up at the flowers. 'What do I do now?'

The smallest of the men reached into his wicker basket and brought out a tarnished pair of silver scissors.

'The scissors, Lady Mayoress,' he said.

She took the scissors from him and began to cut the clumps of blossom and she and the three men started to fill the baskets with the flowers.

'This is,' said Mrs Caraway, the Lady Mayoress, after a little while, 'perfectly ridiculous.'

'It *is*,' said the fat man, 'a *tradition*.'

'Perfectly ridiculous,' said Mrs Caraway, but she continued to cut the white blossoms and drop them into the wicker baskets. When they had filled the first basket, she asked, 'Isn't that enough?'

'We need to fill all four baskets,' said the smaller man, 'and then distribute a flower to everyone in the Old Town.'

'And what kind of tradition is that?' said Mrs Caraway. 'I asked the Lord Mayor before me, and he said he'd never heard of it.' Then she said, 'Do you get a feeling someone's watching us?'

'What?' said the third man, who had not spoken until now. He had a beard and a turban. 'Ghosts, you mean? I do not believe in ghosts.'

'Not ghosts,' said Mrs Caraway. 'Just a feeling like someone's looking.'

Bod fought the urge to push further back into the ivy.

'It's not surprising that the previous Lord Mayor did not know about this tradition,' said the chubby man, whose basket was almost full. 'It's the first time the winter blossoms have bloomed in eighty years.'

The man with the beard and the turban, who did not believe in ghosts, was looking around him nervously.

'Everyone in the Old Town gets a flower,' said the

small man. 'Man, woman and child.' Then he said, slowly, as if he were trying to remember something he had learned a very long time ago, 'One to leave and one to stay and all to dance the Macabray.'

Mrs Caraway sniffed. 'Stuff and nonsense,' she said, and kept on snipping the blossoms.

Dusk fell early in the afternoon, and it was night by half past four. Bod wandered the paths of the graveyard, looking for someone to talk to, but there was no one about. He walked down to the potter's field to see if Liza Hempstock was about, but found no one there. He went back to the Owenses' tomb, but found it also deserted: neither his father nor Mistress Owens were anywhere to be seen.

Panic started then, a low-level panic. It was the first time in his ten years that Bod could remember feeling abandoned in the place he had always thought of as his home: he ran down the hill to the old chapel, where he waited for Silas.

Silas did not come.

'Perhaps I missed him,' thought Bod, but he did not believe this. He walked up the hill to the very top, and looked out. The stars hung in the chilly sky, while the patterned lights of the city spread below him, street lights and car headlights and things in motion. He walked slowly down from the hill until he reached the graveyard's main gates, and he stopped there.

He could hear music.

Bod had listened to all kinds of music: the sweet chimes of the ice-cream van, the songs that played on workmen's radios, the tunes that Claretty Jake played the dead on his dusty fiddle, but he had never heard anything like this before: a series of deep swells, like the music at the beginning of something, a prelude, perhaps, or an overture.

He slipped through the locked gates, walked down the hill, and into the Old Town.

He passed the Lady Mayoress standing on a corner, and as he watched, she reached out and pinned a little white flower to the lapel of a passing businessman.

'I don't make personal charitable donations,' said the man. 'I leave that to the office.'

'It's not for charity,' said Mrs Caraway. 'It's a local tradition.'

'Ah,' he said, and he pushed his chest out, displaying the little white flower to the world, and walked off, proud as Punch.

A young woman pushing a baby buggy was the next to go past.

'Wossit for?' she asked suspiciously, as the Mayoress approached.

'One for you, one for the little one,' said the Mayoress.

She pinned the flower to the young woman's winter coat. She stuck the flower for the baby to its coat with tape.

'But wossit *for*?' asked the young woman.

'It's an Old Town thing,' said the Lady Mayoress, vaguely. 'Some sort of tradition.'

Bod walked on. Everywhere he went he saw people wearing the white flowers. On the other street corners, he passed the men who had been with the Lady Mayoress, each man with a basket, handing out the white flowers. Not everyone took a flower, but most people did.

The music was still playing: somewhere, at the edge of perception, solemn and strange. Bod cocked his head to one side, trying to locate where it was coming from, without success. It was in the air and all around. It was playing in the flapping of flags and awnings, in the rumble of distant traffic, the click of heels on the dry paving stones . . .

And there was an oddness, thought Bod, as he watched the people heading home. They were walking in time to the music.

The man with the beard and the turban was almost out of flowers. Bod walked over to him.

'Excuse me,' said Bod.

The man started. 'I did not see you,' he said, accusingly.

'Sorry,' said Bod. 'Can I have a flower as well?'

The man with the turban looked at Bod with suspicion. 'Do you live around here?' he asked.

'Oh yes,' said Bod.

The man passed Bod a white flower. Bod took it, then said, 'Ow,' as something stabbed into the base of his thumb.

'You pin it to your coat,' said the man. 'Watch out for the pin.'

A bead of crimson was coming up on Bod's thumb. He sucked at it while the man pinned the flower to Bod's sweater. 'I've never seen you around here,' he told Bod.

'I live here, all right,' said Bod. 'What are the flowers for?'

'It was a tradition in the Old Town,' said the man, 'before the city grew up around it. When the winter flowers bloom in the graveyard on the hill, they are cut and given out to everybody, man or woman, young or old, rich or poor.'

The music was louder now. Bod wondered if he could hear it better because he was wearing the flower – he could make out a beat, like distant drums, and a skirling, hesitant melody that made him want to pick up his heels and march in time to the sound.

Bod had never walked anywhere as a sightseer before. He had forgotten the prohibitions on leaving the grave-yard, forgotten that tonight in the graveyard on the hill the dead were no longer in their places; all that he thought of was the Old Town, and he trotted through it down to the municipal gardens in front of the old town hall, which was now a museum and tourist information centre, the town hall itself having moved into much more imposing, if newer and duller, offices halfway across the city.

There were already people around, wandering the municipal gardens – now in mid-winter, little more than a large grassy field with, here and there, some steps, a shrub, a statue.

Bod listened to the music, entranced. There were people trickling into the square, in ones and twos, in fami-lies or alone. He had never seen so many living people at one time. There must have been hundreds of them, all of them breathing, each of them as alive as he was, each with a white flower.

'Is this what living people do?' thought Bod, but he knew that it was not: that *this*, whatever it was, was special.

The young woman he had seen earlier pushing a baby buggy stood beside him, holding her baby, swaying her head to the music.

'How long does the music go on for?' Bod asked her, but she said nothing, just swayed and smiled. Bod did not think she smiled much normally. And only when he was certain that she had not heard him, that he had Faded, or was simply not someone she cared enough about to listen to, she said, 'Blimmen 'eck. It's like Christmases.' She said it like a woman in a dream, as if she were seeing herself from the outside. In the same not-really-there tone of voice, she said, 'Puts me in mind of me gran's sister, Aunt Clara. The night before Christmas we'd go to her, after me gran passed away, and she'd play music on her old piano, and she'd sing, sometimes, and we'd eat chocolates and nuts and I can't remember any of the songs she sung. But that music, it's like all of them songs playing at once.'

The baby seemed asleep with its head on her shoulder, but even it was swaying its hands gently in time to the music.

And then the music stopped and there was silence in the square, a muffled silence, like the silence of falling snow, all noise swallowed by the night and the bodies in the square, no one stamping or shuffling, scarcely even breathing.

A clock began to strike somewhere close at hand: the chimes of midnight, and they came.

They walked down the hill in a slow procession, all stepping gravely, all in time, filling the road, five abreast. Bod knew them or knew most of them. In the first row he recognised Mother Slaughter and Josiah Worthington, and the old earl who had been wounded in the Crusades and came home to die, and Doctor Trefusis, all of them looking solemn and important.

There were gasps from the people in the square. Someone began to cry, saying, 'Lord have mercy, it's a judgement on us, that's what it is!' Most of the people simply stared, as unsurprised as they would have been if this had happened in a dream.

The dead walked on, row on row, until they reached the square.

Josiah Worthington walked up the steps until he reached Mrs Caraway, the Lady Mayoress. He extended his arm and said, loud enough that the whole square could hear him, 'Gracious lady, this I pray: join me in the Macabray.'

Mrs Caraway hesitated. She glanced up at the man beside her for guidance: he wore a dressing gown and slippers, and he had a white flower pinned to his lapel. He smiled and nodded to her. 'Of course,' Mr Caraway said.

She reached out a hand. As her fingers touched Josiah Worthington's, the music began once more. If the music Bod had heard until then was a prelude, it was a prelude no longer. This was the music they had all come to hear, a melody that plucked at their feet and fingers.

They took hands, the living with the dead, and they began to dance. Bod saw Mother Slaughter dancing with the man in the turban, while the businessman was dancing with Louisa Bartleby. Mistress Owens smiled at Bod as she took the hand of the old newspaper seller, and Mr Owens reached out and took the hand of a small girl, without condescension, and she took his hand as if she had been waiting to dance with him her whole life. Then Bod stopped looking because someone's hand closed around his, and the dance began.

Liza Hempstock grinned at him. 'This is fine,' she said, as they began to tread the steps of the dance together.

Then she sang, to the tune of the dance:

> 'Step and turn, and walk and stay,
> Now we dance the Macabray.'

The music filled Bod's head and chest with a fierce joy, and his feet moved as if they knew the steps already, had known them forever.

He danced with Liza Hempstock, and then, when that measure ended, he found his hand taken by Fortinbras Bartleby, and he danced with Fortinbras, stepping past lines of dancers, lines that parted as they came through.

Bod saw Abanazer Bolger dancing with Miss Borrows, his former teacher. He saw the living dancing with the dead. And the one-on-one dances became long lines of people stepping together in unison, walking and kicking (*La-la-la-oomp! La-la-la-oomp!*) a line dance that had been ancient a thousand years before.

Now he was in the line beside Liza Hempstock. He said, 'Where does the music come from?'

She shrugged.

'Who's making all this happen?'

'It always happens,' she told him. 'The living may not remember, but we always do . . .' And she broke off, excited. '*Look!*'

Bod had never seen a real horse before, only in the

pages of picture books, but the white horse that clopped down the street towards them was nothing like the horses he had imagined. It was bigger, by far, with a long, serious face. There was a woman riding on the horse's bare back, wearing a long grey dress that hung and gleamed beneath the December moon like cobwebs in the dew.

She reached the square, and the horse stopped, and the woman in grey slipped off it easily and stood on the earth, facing them all, the living and the dead of them.

She curtseyed.

And, as one, they bowed or curtseyed in return, and the dance began anew.

'Now the Lady on the Grey leads us in the Macabray,' sang Liza Hempstock, before the whirl of the dance took her off and away from Bod. They stomped to the music, and stepped and spun and kicked, and the lady danced with them, stepping and spinning and kicking with enthusiasm. Even the white horse swayed its head and stepped and shifted to the music.

The dance sped up, and the dancers with it. Bod was breathless, but he could not imagine the dance ever stopping: the Macabray, the dance of the living and the dead, the dance with Death. Bod was smiling, and everyone was smiling.

He caught sight of the lady in the grey dress from time to time, as he spun and stomped his way across the municipal gardens.

Everyone, thought Bod, everyone is dancing! He thought it, and as soon as he thought it, he realised that he was mistaken. In the shadows by the old town hall, a man was standing, dressed all in black. He was not dancing. He was watching them.

Bod wondered if it was longing that he saw on Silas's face, or sorrow, or something else, but his guardian's face was unreadable.

He called out, 'Silas!' hoping to make his guardian come to them, to join the dance, to have the fun they were having, but when he heard his name, Silas stepped back into the shadows and was lost to sight.

'Last dance!' someone called, and the music skirled up into something stately and slow and final.

Each of the dancers took a partner, the living with the dead, each to each. Bod reached out his hand and found himself touching fingers with, and gazing into the grey eyes of, the lady in the cobweb dress.

She smiled at him.

'Hello, Bod,' she said.

'Hello,' he said, as he danced with her. 'I don't know your name.'

'Names aren't really important,' she said.

'I love your horse. He's so big! I never knew horses could be that big.'

'He is gentle enough to bear the mightiest of you away on his broad back, and strong enough for the smallest of you as well.'

'Can I ride him?' asked Bod.

'One day,' she told him, and her cobweb skirts shimmered. 'One day. Everybody does.'

'Promise?'

'I promise.'

And with that, the dance was over. Bod bowed low to

his dancing partner, and then, and only then, did he feel exhausted, feel as if he had been dancing for hour after hour. He could feel all his muscles aching and protesting. He was out of breath.

A clock somewhere began to strike the hour, and Bod counted along with it. Twelve chimes. He wondered if they had been dancing for twelve hours or twenty-four or for no time at all.

He straightened up and looked around him. The dead had gone, and the Lady on the Grey. Only the living remained, and they were beginning to make their way home – leaving the town square sleepily, stiffly, like people who had awakened from a deep sleep, walking without truly waking.

The town square was covered with tiny white flowers. It looked as if there had been a wedding.

Bod woke the next afternoon in the Owenses' tomb feeling like he knew a huge secret, that he had done something important, and was burning to talk about it.

When Mistress Owens got up, Bod said, 'That was amazing last night!'

Mistress Owens said, 'Oh yes?'

'We danced,' said Bod. 'All of us. Down in the Old Town.'

'Did we indeed?' said Mistress Owens, with a snort. 'Dancing is it? And you know you aren't allowed down into the town.'

Bod knew better than even to try to talk to his mother when she was in this kind of mood. He slipped out of the tomb into the gathering dusk.

He walked up the hill, to the black obelisk, and

Josiah Worthington's stone, where there was a natural amphitheatre, and he could look out at the Old Town and at the lights of the city around it.

Josiah Worthington was standing beside him.

Bod said, 'You began the dance. With the Mayoress. You danced with her.'

Josiah Worthington looked at him and said nothing.

'You *did*,' said Bod.

Josiah Worthington said, 'The dead and the living do not mingle, boy. We are no longer part of their world, they are no part of ours. If it happened that we danced the *danse macabre* with them, the dance of death, then we would not speak of it, and we certainly would not to speak of it to the living.'

'But I'*m* one of you.'

'Not yet, boy. Not for a lifetime.'

And Bod realised why he had danced as one of the living, and not as one of the crew that had walked down the hill, and he said only, 'I see . . . I think.'

He went down the hill at a run, a ten-year-old boy in a hurry, going so fast he almost tripped over Digby Poole (1785–1860, As I Am So Shall You Be), righting himself by effort of will, and charged down to the old chapel, scared he would miss Silas, that his guardian would already be gone by the time Bod got there.

Bod sat down on the bench.

There was a movement beside him, although he heard nothing move, and his guardian said, 'Good evening, Bod.'

'You were there last night,' said Bod. 'Don't try and say you weren't there or something because I know you were.'

'Yes,' said Silas.

'I danced with her. With the lady on the white horse.'

'Did you?'

'You saw it! You watched us! The living and the dead! We were dancing. Why won't anyone *talk* about it?'

'Because there are mysteries. Because there are things that people are forbidden to speak about. Because there are things they do not remember.'

'But you're speaking about it right now. We're talking about the Macabray.'

'I have not danced it,' said Silas.

'You saw it, though.'

Silas said only, 'I don't know what I saw.'

'I danced with the lady, Silas!' exclaimed Bod. His guardian looked almost heartbroken then, and Bod found himself scared, like a child who has woken a sleeping panther.

But all Silas said was, 'This conversation is at an end.'

Bod might have said something – there were a hundred things he wanted to say, unwise though it might have been to say them then – when something distracted his attention: a rustling noise, soft and gentle, and a cold feather-touch as something brushed his face.

All thoughts of dancing were forgotten then, and his fear was replaced with delight and with awe.

It was the third time in his life that he had seen it.

'Look, Silas, it's snowing!' he said, joy filling his chest and his head, leaving no room for anything else. 'It's really snow!'

INTERLUDE

The Convocation

A small sign in the hotel lobby announced that the Washington Room was taken that night by a private function, although there was no information as to what kind of function this might be. Truthfully, if you were to have looked at the inhabitants of the Washington Room that night, you would have had no clearer idea of what was happening, although a rapid glance would have told you that there were no women in there. They were all men, that much was clear, and they sat at round dinner tables, and they were finishing their dessert.

There were about a hundred of them, all in sober black suits, but the suits were all they had in common. They had white hair or dark hair or fair hair or red hair or no hair at all. They had friendly faces or unfriendly, helpful or sullen, open or secretive, brutish or sensitive. The majority of them were pink-skinned, but there were black-skinned men and brown-skinned. They were European, African, Indian, Chinese, South American, Filipino, American. They all spoke English when they talked to each other, or to the waiters, but the accents were as diverse as the gentlemen. They came from all across Europe and from all over the world.

The men in black suits sat around their tables while up on a platform one of their number, a wide, cheery man dressed in a morning suit, as if he had just come from a wedding, was announcing Good Deeds Done. Children from poor places had been taken on exotic holidays. A bus had been bought to take people who needed it on excursions.

The man Jack sat at the front centre table, beside a dapper man with silver-white hair. They were waiting for coffee.

'Time's a-ticking,' said the silver-haired man, 'and we're none of us getting any younger.'

The man Jack said, 'I've been thinking. That business in San Francisco a few years ago –'

'Was unfortunate, but like the flowers that bloom in the spring, tra-la, absolutely nothing to do with the case. You failed, Jack. You were meant to take care of them all. That included the baby. Especially the baby. *Nearly* only counts in horseshoes and hand grenades.'

A waiter in a white jacket poured coffee for each of the men at the table: a small man with a pencil-thin black moustache, a tall blond man good-looking enough to be a film star or a model, and a dark-skinned man with a huge head who glared out at the world like an angry bull. These men were making a point of not listening to Jack's conversation, and instead were paying attention to the speaker, even clapping from time to time. The silver-haired man added several heaped spoonfuls of sugar to his coffee, stirred it briskly.

'*Ten years*,' he said. 'Time and tide wait for no man. The babe will soon be grown. And then what?'

'I still have time, Mister Dandy,' the man Jack began, but the silver-haired man cut him off, stabbing a large pink finger in his direction.

'You *had* time. Now, you just have a deadline. Now, you've got to get smart. We can't cut you any slack, not any more. Sick of waiting, we are, every man Jack of us.'

The man Jack nodded, curtly. 'I have leads to follow,' he said.

The silver-haired man slurped his black coffee. 'Really?'

'Really. And I repeat, I think it's connected with the trouble we had in San Francisco.'

'You've discussed this with the secretary?' Mr Dandy indicated the man at the podium, who was, at that moment, telling them about hospital equipment bought in the previous year from their generosity. ('Not one, not two, but *three* kidney machines,' he was saying. The men in the room applauded themselves and their generosity politely.)

The man Jack nodded. 'I've mentioned it.'

'And?'

'He's not interested. He just wants results. He wants me to finish the business I started.'

'We all do, sunshine,' said the silver-haired man. 'The boy's still alive. And time is no longer our friend.'

The other men at the table, who had pretended not to be listening, grunted and nodded their agreement.

'Like I say,' Mr Dandy said, without emotion. 'Time's a-ticking.'

'I think,' said Silas, 'it is time to talk about
where you came from.'

CHAPTER 6

Nobody Owens' School Days

Rain in the graveyard, and the world puddled into blurred reflections. Bod sat, concealed from anyone, living or dead, who might come looking for him, under the arch that separated the Egyptian Walk and the north-western wilderness beyond it from the rest of the graveyard, and he read his book.

'Damm'ee!' came a shout from down the path. 'Damm'ee sir and blast your eyes! When I catch you – and find you I shall – I shall make you rue the day you were born!'

Bod sighed and he lowered the book, and leaned out enough to see Thackeray Porringer (1720–1734, *son of the above*) come stamping up the slippery path. Thackeray was a big boy – he had been fourteen when he died, following his initiation as an apprentice to a master house painter: he had been given eight copper pennies and told not to come back without a half-a-gallon of red and white striped paint for painting barber's poles. Thackeray had spent five hours being sent all over the town one slushy January morning, being laughed at in each establishment he visited and then sent on to the next; when he realised he had been made a fool of, he had taken an angry case of apoplexy, which carried him off within the week, and he died glaring furiously at the other apprentices and even at Mr Horrobin, the master painter, who had undergone so much worse back when *he* was a 'prentice that he could scarcely see what all the fuss was about.

So Thackeray Porringer had died in a fury, clutching his copy of *Robinson Crusoe*, which was, apart from a silver sixpence with the edges clipped and the clothes he had formerly been standing up in, all that he owned, and, at his mother's request, he was buried with his book. Death had not improved Thackeray Porringer's temper, and now he was shouting, 'I know you're here somewhere! Come out and take your punishment, you, you thief!'

Bod closed the book. 'I'm not a thief, Thackeray. I'm only borrowing it. I promise I'll give the book back when I've finished it.'

Thackeray looked up, saw Bod nestled behind the statue of Osiris. 'I told you not to!'

Bod sighed. 'But there are so few books here. It's just up to a good bit anyway. He's found a footprint. It's not his. That means someone else is on the island!'

'It's my book,' said Thackeray Porringer, obstinately. 'Give it back.'

Bod was ready to argue or simply to negotiate, but he saw the hurt look on Thackeray's face, and he relented. Bod clambered down the side of the arch, jumped the last few feet. He held out the book. 'Here.' Thackeray took it, gracelessly, and glared.

'I could read it to you,' offered Bod. 'I could do that.'

'You could go and boil your fat head,' said Thackeray, and he swung a punch at Bod's ear. It connected, and it stung, although judging from the look on Thackeray Porringer's face, Bod realised it must have hurt his fist as much as it hurt Bod.

The bigger boy stomped off down the path, and Bod watched him go, ear hurting, eyes stinging. Then he walked through the rain back down the treacherous ivy-covered path. At one point he slipped and scraped his knee, tearing his jeans.

There was a willow grove beside the wall, and Bod almost ran into Miss Euphemia Horsfall and Tom Sands, who had been stepping out together for many years. Tom had been buried so long ago that his stone was just a weath-ered rock, and he had lived and died during the Hundred Years' War with France, while Miss Euphemia (1861–1883, *She Sleeps, Aye, Yet She Sleeps with Angels*) had been buried in Victorian times, after the graveyard had been expanded and extended and became, for some fifty years, a successful commercial enterprise, and she had a whole tomb to herself behind a black door in the Willow Walk. But the couple seemed to have no troubles with the difference in their historical periods.

'You should slow down, young Bod,' said Tom. 'You'll do yourself an injury.'

'You already did,' said Miss Euphemia. 'Oh dear, Bod. I have no doubt that your mother will have words with you about that. It's not as if we can easily repair those pantaloons.'

'Um. Sorry,' said Bod.

'And your guardian was looking for you,' added Tom.

Bod looked up at the grey sky. 'But it's still daylight,' he said.

'He's up betimes,' said Tom, a word which, Bod knew, meant *early*, 'and said to tell you he wanted you. If we saw you.'

Bod nodded.

'There's ripe hazelnuts in the thicket just beyond the Littlejohns' monument,' said Tom with a smile, as if softening a blow.

'Thank you,' said Bod. He ran on, pell-mell, through the rain and down the winding path into the lower slopes of the graveyard, running until he reached the old chapel.

The chapel door was open and Silas, who had love for neither the rain or for the remnants of the daylight, was standing inside, in the shadows.

'I heard you were looking for me,' said Bod.

'Yes,' said Silas. Then, 'It appears you've torn your trousers.'

'I was running,' said Bod. 'Um. I got into a bit of a fight with Thackeray Porringer. I wanted to read *Robinson Crusoe*. It's a book about a man on a boat – that's a thing that goes in the sea, which is water like an enormous puddle, and how the ship is wrecked on an island, which is a place on the sea where you can stand, and – '

Silas said, 'It has been eleven years, Bod. Eleven years that you have been with us.'

'Right,' said Bod. 'If you say so.'

Silas looked down at his charge. The boy was lean, and his mouse-coloured hair had darkened slightly with age.

Inside the old chapel, it was all shadows.

'I think,' said Silas, 'it is time to talk about where you came from.'

Bod breathed in deeply. He said, 'It doesn't have to be now. Not if you don't want to.' He said it as easily as he could, but his heart was thudding in his chest.

Silence. Only the patter of the rain and the wash of the water from the drainpipes. A silence that stretched until Bod thought that he would break.

Silas said, 'You know you're different. That you are alive. That we took you in – *they* took you in here – and that I agreed to be your guardian.'

Bod said nothing.

Silas continued, in his voice like velvet, 'You had parents. An older sister. They were killed. I believe that you were to have been killed as well, and that you were not was due to chance, and the intervention of the Owenses.'

'And you,' said Bod, who had had that night described to him over the years by many people, some of whom had even been there. It had been a big night in the graveyard.

Silas said, 'Out there, the man who killed your family is, I believe, still looking for you, still intends to kill you.'

Bod shrugged. 'So?' he said. 'It's only death. I mean, all of my best friends are dead.'

'Yes.' Silas hesitated. 'They are. And they are for the most part, done with the world. You are not. You're *alive*, Bod. That means you have infinite potential. You can do anything, make anything, dream anything. If you change the world, the world will change. Potential. Once you're dead, it's gone. Over. You've made what you've made, dreamed your dream, written your name. You may be buried here, you may even walk. But that potential is finished.'

Bod thought about this. It seemed almost true, although he could think of exceptions – his parents adopting him, for example. But the dead and the living were different, he knew that, even if his sympathies were with the dead.

'What about you?' he asked Silas.

'What about me?'

'Well, you aren't alive. And you go around and do things.'

'I,' said Silas, 'am precisely what I am, and nothing more. I am, as you say, not alive. But if I am ended, I shall simply cease to be. My kind *are*, or we are *not*. If you see what I mean.'

'Not really.'

Silas sighed. The rain had stopped and the cloudy gloaming had become true twilight. 'Bod,' he said, 'there are many reasons why it is important that we keep you safe.'

Bod said, 'The person who hurt my family. The one who wants to kill me. You are certain that he's still out there?' It was something he had been thinking about for a while now, and he knew what he wanted.

'Yes. He's still out there.'

'Then,' said Bod, and said the unsayable, 'I want to go to school.'

Silas was imperturbable. The world could have ended, and he would not have turned a hair. But now his mouth opened and his brow furrowed, and he said only, 'What?'

'I've learned a lot in this graveyard,' said Bod. 'I can Fade and I can Haunt. I can open a ghoul-gate and I know the constellations. But there's a world out there, with the sea in it, and islands, and shipwrecks and pigs. I mean, it's filled with things I don't know. And the teachers here have taught me lots of things, but I need more. If I'm going to survive out there, one day.'

Silas seemed unimpressed. 'Out of the question. Here we can keep you safe. Outside, anything could happen. How could we keep you safe, out there?'

'Yes,' agreed Bod. 'That's the potential thing you were talking about.' He fell silent. Then, 'Someone killed my mother and my father and my sister.'

'Yes. Someone did.'

'A man?'

'A man.'

'Which means,' said Bod, 'you're asking the wrong question.'

Silas raised an eyebrow. 'How so?'

'Well,' said Bod. 'If I go outside in the world, the question isn't, "Who will keep me safe from him?"'

'No?'

'No. It's "Who will keep him safe from me?"'

Twigs scratched against the high windows, as if they needed to be let in. Silas flicked an imaginary speck of dust from his sleeve with a fingernail as sharp as a blade. He said, 'We will need to find you a school.'

No one noticed the boy, not at first. No one even noticed that they hadn't noticed him. He sat halfway back in class. He didn't answer much, not unless he was directly asked a question, and even then his answers were short and forgettable, colourless: he faded, in mind and in memory.

'Do you think they're religious, his family?' asked Mr Kirby, in the staffroom. He was marking essays.

'Whose family?' asked Mrs McKinnon.

'Owens in Eight B,' said Mr Kirby.

'The tall spotty lad?'

'I don't think so. Sort of medium height.'

Mrs McKinnon shrugged. 'What about him?'

'Handwrites everything,' said Mr Kirby. 'Lovely handwriting. What they used to call copperplate.'

'And that makes him religious because . . . ?'

'He says they don't have a computer.'

'And?'

'He doesn't have a phone.'

'I don't see why that makes him religious,' said Mrs McKinnon, who had taken up crocheting when they had banned smoking in the staffroom, and was sitting and crocheting a baby blanket for no one in particular.

Mr Kirby shrugged. 'He's a smart lad,' he said. 'There's just stuff he doesn't know. And in History he'll throw in little made-up details, stuff not in the books . . .'

'What kind of stuff?'

Mr Kirby finished marking Bod's essay and put it down on the pile. Without something immediately in front of him the whole matter seemed vague and unimportant.

'Stuff,' he said, and forgot about it. Just as he forgot to enter Bod's name on the roll. Just as Bod's name was not to be found on the school databases.

The boy was a model pupil, forgettable and easily forgotten, and he spent much of his spare time in the back of the English class where there were shelves of old paperbacks, and in the school library, a large room filled with books and old armchairs, where he read stories as enthusiastically as some children ate.

Even the other kids forgot about him. Not when he was sitting in front of them: they remembered him then. But when that Owens kid was out of sight he was out of mind. They didn't think about him. They didn't need to. If someone asked all the kids in Eight B to close their eyes and list the twenty-five boys and girls in the class, that Owens kid wouldn't have been on the list. His presence was almost ghostly.

It was different if he was there, of course.

Nick Farthing was twelve, but he could pass – and did sometimes – for sixteen: a large boy with a crooked smile, and little imagination. He was practical, in a basic sort of way, an efficient shoplifter, and occasional thug, who did not care about being liked as long as the other kids, all smaller, did what he said. Anyway, he had a friend. Her name was Maureen Quilling, but everyone called her Mo, and she was thin and had pale skin and pale yellow hair, watery blue eyes, and a sharp, inquisitive nose. Nick liked to shoplift, but Mo told him what to steal. Nick could hit and hurt and intimidate, but Mo pointed him at the people who needed to be intimidated. They were, as she told him sometimes, a perfect team.

They were sitting in the corner of the library splitting their take of the Year Sevens' pocket money. They had eight or nine of the eleven-year-olds trained to hand over their pocket money every week.

'The Singh kid hasn't coughed up yet,' said Mo. 'You'll have to find him.'

'Yeah,' said Nick. 'He'll pay.'

'What was it he nicked? A CD?'

Nick nodded.

'Just point out the error of his ways,' said Mo, who wanted to sound like the hard cases from the television.

'Easy,' said Nick. 'We're a good team.'

'Like Batman and Robin,' said Mo.

'More like Doctor Jekyll and Mister Hyde,' said somebody, who had been reading, unnoticed, in a window seat, and he got up and walked out of the room.

Paul Singh was sitting on a window sill by the changing rooms, his hands deep in his pockets, thinking dark thoughts. He took one hand out of his pocket, opened it, looked at the handful of pound coins, shook his head, closed his hand around the coins once more.

'Is that what Nick and Mo are waiting for?' somebody asked, and Paul jumped, scattering money all over the floor.

The other boy helped him pick the coins up, handed them over. He was an older boy, and Paul thought he had seen him around before, but he could not be certain. Paul said, 'Are you with them? Nick and Mo?'

The other boy shook his head. 'Nope. I think that they

are fairly repulsive.' He hesitated. Then he said, 'Actually, I came to give you a bit of advice.'

'Yeah?'

'Don't pay them.'

'Easy for you to say.'

'Because they aren't blackmailing me?'

The boy looked at Paul and Paul looked away, ashamed.

'They hit you or threatened you until you shoplifted a CD for them. Then they told you that unless you handed over your pocket money to them, they'd tell on you. What did they do, film you doing it?'

Paul nodded.

'Just say no,' said the boy. 'Don't do it.'

'They'll kill me. And they said . . .'

'Tell them that you think the police and school authorities could be a lot more interested in a couple of kids who are getting younger kids to steal for them and then forcing them to hand over their pocket money than they ever would be in one kid forced to steal a CD against his will. That if they touch you again, you'll make the call to the police. And that you've written it all up, and if anything happens to you, anything at all, if you get a black eye or anything, your friends will automatically send it to the school authorities and the police.'

Paul said, 'But. I can't.'

'Then you'll pay them your pocket money for the rest of your time in this school. And you'll stay scared of them.'

Paul thought. 'Why don't I just tell the police anyway?' he asked.

'Can if you like.'

'I'll try it your way first,' Paul said. He smiled. It wasn't a big smile, but it was a smile, right enough, his first in three weeks.

So Paul Singh explained to Nick Farthing just how and why he wouldn't be paying him any longer, and walked away while Nick Farthing just stood and didn't say anything, clenching and unclenching his fists. And the next day another five eleven-year-olds found Nick Farthing in the playground, and told him they wanted their money back, all the pocket money they'd handed over in the previous month, or *they'd* be going to the police, and now Nick Farthing was an extremely unhappy young man.

Mo said, 'It was *him*. He started it. If it wasn't for him . . . they'd never have thought of it on their own. He's the one we have to teach a lesson. Then they'll all behave.'

'Who?' said Nick.

'The one who's always reading. The one from the library. Bob Owens. Him.'

Nick nodded slowly. Then he said, 'Which one is he?'

'I'll point him out to you,' said Mo.

Bod was used to being ignored, to existing in the shadows. When glances naturally slip from you, you become very aware of eyes upon you, of glances in your direction, of attention. And if you barely exist in people's minds as another living person, then being pointed to, being followed around . . . these things draw attention to themselves.

They followed him out of the school and up the road,

past the corner newsagent, and across the railway bridge. He took his time, making certain that the two who were following him, a burly boy and a fair, sharp-faced girl, did not lose him, then he walked into the tiny churchyard at the end of the road, a miniature graveyard behind the local church and he waited beside the tomb of Roderick Persson and his wife Amabella, and also his second wife, Portunia, (*They Sleep To Wake Again*).

'You're that kid,' said a girl's voice. 'Bob Owens. Well, you're in really big trouble Bob Owens.'

'It's Bod, actually,' said Bod, and he looked at them. 'With a D. And you're Jekyll and Hyde.'

'It was you,' said the girl. 'You got to the Year Sevens.'

'So we're going to teach you a lesson,' said Nick Farthing, and he smiled without humour.

'I quite like lessons,' said Bod. 'If you paid more attention to yours, you wouldn't have to blackmail younger kids for pocket money.'

Nick's brow crinkled. Then he said, 'You're dead, Owens.'

Bod shook his head, and he gestured around him, 'I'm not actually,' he said. 'They are.'

'Who are?' said Mo.

'The people in this place,' said Bod. 'Look. I brought you here to give you a choice –'

'You didn't bring us here,' said Nick.

'You're here,' said Bod. 'I wanted you here. I came here. You followed me. Same thing.'

Mo looked around nervously. 'You've got friends here?' she asked.

173

Bod said, 'You're missing the point, I'm afraid. You two need to stop this. Stop behaving like other people don't matter. Stop hurting people.'

Mo grinned a sharp grin. 'For heaven's sake,' she said to Nick. 'Hit him.'

'I gave you a chance,' said Bod. Nick swung a vicious fist at Bod, who was no longer there, and Nick's fist slammed into the side of the gravestone.

'Where did he go?' said Mo. Nick was swearing and shaking his hand. She looked around the shadowy cemetery, puzzled. 'He was here. You know he was.'

Nick had little imagination, and he was not about to start thinking now. 'Maybe he ran away,' he said.

'He didn't run,' said Mo. 'He just wasn't there any more.' Mo had an imagination. The ideas were hers. It was twilight in a spooky churchyard, and the hairs on the back of her neck were prickling. 'Something is really, really wrong,' said Mo. Then she said, in a higher-pitched panicky voice, 'We have to get out of here.'

'I'm going to find that kid,' said Nick Farthing. 'I'm going to beat the stuffing out of him.' Mo felt something unsettled in the pit of her stomach. The shadows seemed to move around them.

'Nick,' said Mo, 'I'm scared.'

Fear is contagious. You can catch it. Sometimes all it takes is for someone to say that they're scared for the fear to become real. Mo was terrified, and now Nick was too.

Nick didn't say anything. He just ran, and Mo ran close on his heels. The street lights were coming on as they ran back towards the world, turning the twilight into night, making the shadows into dark places in which anything could be happening.

They ran until they reached Nick's house, and they went inside and turned on all the lights, and Mo called her mother and demanded, half crying, to be picked up and driven the short distance to her own house, because she wasn't walking home that night.

Bod had watched them run with satisfaction.

'That was good, dear,' said someone behind him, a tall women in white. 'A nice Fade, first. Then the Fear.'

'Thank you,' said Bod. 'I hadn't even tried the Fear out on living people. I mean, I knew the theory, but. Well.'

'It worked a treat,' she said, cheerfully. 'I'm Amabella Persson.'

'Bod. Nobody Owens.'

'The *live* boy? From the big graveyard on the hill? Really?'

'Um.' Bod hadn't realised that anyone knew who he was beyond his own graveyard. Amabella was knocking on the side of the tomb. 'Roddy? Portunia? Come and see who's here!'

There were three of them there, then, and Amabella was introducing Bod and he was shaking hands and saying, 'Charmed, I am sure,' because he could greet people politely in over nine hundred years of changing manners.

'Master Owens here was frightening some children who doubtless deserved it,' Amabella was explaining.

'Good show,' said Roderick Persson. 'Bounders guilty of reprehensible behaviour, eh?'

'They were bullies,' said Bod. 'Making kids hand over their pocket money. Stuff like that.'

'A Frightening is certainly a good beginning,' said Portunia Persson, who was a stout woman, much older than Amabella. 'And what have you planned if it does not work?'

'I hadn't really thought –' Bod began, but Amabella interrupted.

'I should suggest that Dreamwalking might be the most efficient remedy. You *can* Dreamwalk, can you not?'

'I'm not sure,' said Bod. 'Mister Pennyworth showed me how, but I haven't really – well, there's things I only really know in theory, and –'

Portunia Persson said, 'Dreamwalking is all very well, but might I suggest a good Visitation? That's the only language that these people understand.'

'Oh,' said Amabella. 'A Visitation? Portunia, my dear, I don't really think so –'

'No, you don't. Luckily, one of us thinks.'

'I have to be getting home,' said Bod, hastily. 'They'll be worrying about me.'

'Of course,' said the Persson family, and, 'Lovely to meet you,' and, 'A very good evening to you, young man.' Amabella Persson and Portunia Persson glared at each other. Roderick Persson said, 'If you'll forgive me asking, but your guardian. He is well?'

'Silas? Yes, he's fine.'

'Give him our regards. I'm afraid a small churchyard like this, well, we're never going to meet an actual member of the Honour Guard. Still. It's good to know that they're there.'

'Goodnight,' said Bod, who had no idea what the man was talking about, but filed it away for later. 'I'll tell him.'

He picked up his bag of school books, and he walked home, taking comfort in the shadows.

Going to school with the living did not excuse Bod from his lessons with the dead. The nights were long, and sometimes Bod would apologise and crawl to bed exhausted before midnight. Mostly, he just kept going.

Mr Pennyworth had little to complain of these days. Bod studied hard, and asked questions. Tonight Bod asked about Hauntings, getting more and more specific, which exasperated Mr Pennyworth, who had never gone in for that sort of thing himself.

'How exactly do I make a cold spot in the air?' he asked, and, 'I think I've got Fear down, but how do I take it up all the way to Terror?' and Mr Pennyworth sighed and hurrumphed and did his best to explain, and it was gone four in the morning before they were finished.

Bod was tired at school the next day. The first class was History – a subject Bod mostly enjoyed, although he often had to resist the urge to say that it hadn't happened like that, not according to people who had been there anyway – but this morning Bod was fighting to stay awake.

He was doing all he could do to concentrate on the lesson, so he was not paying attention to much else going on around him. He was thinking about King Charles the First, and about his parents, of Mr and Mrs Owens and of the other family, the one he could not remember, when there was a knock on the door. The class and Mr Kirby all looked to see who was there (it was a Year Seven, who had been sent to borrow a textbook). And as they turned, Bod felt something stab in the back of his hand. He did not cry out. He just looked up.

Nick Farthing grinned down at him, a sharpened pencil in his fist. 'I'm not afraid of you,' whispered Nick Farthing. Bod looked at the back of his hand. A small drop of blood welled up where the point of the pencil had punctured it.

Mo Quilling passed Bod in the corridor that afternoon, her eyes so wide he could see the whites all around them.

'You're weird,' she said. 'You don't have any friends.'

'I didn't come here for friends,' said Bod truthfully. 'I came here to learn.'

Mo's nose twitched. 'Do you know how weird *that* is?' she asked. 'Nobody comes to school to *learn*. I mean, you come because you have to.'

Bod shrugged.

'I'm not afraid of you,' she said. 'Whatever trick you did yesterday. You didn't scare me.'

'OK,' said Bod, and he walked on down the corridor.

He wondered if he had made a mistake, getting involved. He had made a mis-step in judgement, that was for certain. Mo and Nick had begun to talk about him, probably the Year Sevens had as well. Other kids were looking at him, pointing him out to each other. He was becoming a presence, rather than an absence, and that made him uncomfortable. Silas had warned him to keep a low profile, told him to go through school partly Faded, but everything was changing.

He talked to his guardian that evening, told him the whole story. He was not expecting Silas's reaction.

'I cannot believe,' said Silas, 'that you could have been so . . . so stupid. Everything I told you about remaining just this side of invisibility. And now you've become the talk of the school?'

'Well, what did you want me to do?'

'Not this,' said Silas. 'It's not like the olden times. They can keep track of you, Bod. They can find you.' Silas's unmoving exterior was like the hard crust of rock over molten lava. Bod knew how angry Silas was only because he knew Silas. He seemed to be fighting his anger, controlling it.

Bod swallowed.

'What should I do?' he said, simply.

'Don't go back,' said Silas. 'This school business was an experiment. Let us simply acknowledge that it was not a successful one.'

Bod said nothing. Then he said, 'It's not just the learning stuff. It's the other stuff. Do you know how nice it is to be in a room filled with people and for all of them to be breathing?'

'It's not something in which I've ever taken pleasure,' said Silas. 'So. You don't go back to school tomorrow.'

'I'm *not* running away. Not from Mo or Nick or school. I'd leave here first.'

'You will do as you are told, boy,' said Silas, a knot of

velvet anger in the darkness.

'Or what?' said Bod, his cheeks burning. 'What would you do to keep me here? Kill me?' And he turned on his heel and began to walk down the path that led to the gates and out of the graveyard.

Silas began to call the boy back, then he stopped, and stood there in the night alone.

At the best of times his face was unreadable. Now his face was a book written in a language long forgotten, in an alphabet unimagined. Silas wrapped the shadows around him like a blanket, and stared after the way the boy had gone, and did not move to follow.

Nick Farthing was in his bed, asleep and dreaming of pirates on the sunny blue sea, when it all went wrong. One moment he was the captain of his own pirate ship – a happy place, crewed by obedient eleven-year-olds, except for the girls, who were all a year or two older than Nick and who looked especially pretty in their pirate costumes – and the next he was alone on the deck, and a huge, dark ship the size of an oil tanker, with ragged black sails and a skull for a figurehead, was crashing through the storm towards him.

And then, in the way of dreams, he was standing on the black deck of the new ship, and someone was looking down at him.

'You're not afraid of me,' said the man standing over him.

Nick looked up. He *was* scared, in his dream, scared of this dead-faced man in pirate costume, his hand on the hilt of a cutlass.

'Do you think you're a pirate, Nick?' asked his captor, and suddenly something about him seemed familiar to Nick.

'You're that kid,' he said. 'Bob Owens.'

'I,' said his captor, 'am Nobody. And you need to change. Turn over a new leaf. Reform. All that. Or things will get very bad for you.'

'Bad how?'

'Bad in your head,' said the Pirate King, who was now only the boy from his class and they were in the School Hall, not the deck of the pirate ship, although the storm had not abated and the floor of the hall pitched and rolled like a ship at sea.

'This is a dream,' Nick said.

'Of course it's a dream,' said the other boy. 'I would have to be some kind of monster to do this in real life.'

'What can you do to me in a dream?' asked Nick. He smiled. 'I'm not afraid of you. You've still got my pencil in the back of your hand.' He pointed to the back of Bod's hand, at the black mark the graphite point had made.

'I was hoping it wouldn't have to be like this,' said the other boy. He tipped his head on one side as if he were listening to something. 'They're hungry,' he said.

'What are?' asked Nick.

'The things in the cellar. Or below decks. Depends whether this is a school or a ship, doesn't it?'

Nick felt himself beginning to panic. 'It isn't . . . spiders . . . is it?' he said.

'It might be,' said the other boy. 'You'll find out, won't you?'

Nick shook his head.

'No,' he said. '*Please* no.'

'Well,' said the other boy. 'It's all up to you, isn't it? Change your ways or visit the cellar.'

The noise got louder – a scuttling sort of a scuffling noise, and while Nick Farthing had no idea what it was, he was utterly, completely certain that whatever it would turn out to be would be the most scary terrible thing he had ever – would ever – encounter . . .

He woke up screaming.

Bod heard the scream, a shout of terror, and felt the satisfaction of a job well done.

He was standing on the pavement outside Nick Farthing's house, his face damp from the thick night mist. He was exhilarated and exhausted: he had felt barely in control of the Dreamwalk, had been all too aware that there was nothing else in the dream but Nick and himself, and that all Nick had been scared of was a noise.

But Bod was satisfied. The other boy would hesitate before tormenting smaller kids.

And now?

Bod put his hands in his pockets and began to walk, not certain where he was going. He would leave the school, he thought, just as he had left the graveyard. He would go somewhere no one knew him, and he would sit in a library all day and read books and listen to people breathing. He wondered if there were still deserted islands in the world, like the one on which Robinson Crusoe had been shipwrecked. He could go and live on one of those.

Bod did not look up. If he had, he would have seen a pair of watery blue eyes watching him intently from a bedroom window.

He stepped into an alley, feeling more comfortable out of the light.

'Are you running away, then?' said a girl's voice.

Bod said nothing.

'That's the difference between the living and the dead, ennit?' said the voice. It was Liza Hempstock talking, Bod knew, although the witch-girl was nowhere to be seen. 'The dead dun't disappoint you. They've had their life, done what they've done. We dun't change. The living, they always disappoint you, dun't they? You meet a boy who's all brave and noble, and he grows up to run away . . .'

'That's not fair!' said Bod.

'The Nobody Owens I knew wouldn't've run off from the graveyard without saying so much as a fare-thee-well to those who cared for him. You'll break Mistress Owens' heart.'

Bod had not thought of that. He said, 'I had a fight with Silas.'

'So?'

'He wants me to come back to the graveyard. To stop school. He thinks it's too dangerous.'

'Why? Between your talents and my bespellment, they'll barely notice you.'

'I was getting involved. There were these kids bullying other kids. I wanted them to stop. I drew attention to myself . . .'

Liza could be seen now, a misty shape in the alleyway

keeping pace with Bod.

'He's out here, somewhere, and he wants you dead,' she said. 'Him as killed your family. Us in the graveyard, we wants you to stay alive. We wants you to surprise us and disappoint us and impress us and amaze us. Come home, Bod.'

'I think . . . I said things to Silas. He'll be angry.'

'If he didn't care about you, you couldn't upset him,' was all she said.

The fallen autumn leaves were slick beneath Bod's feet, and the mists blurred the edges of the world. Nothing was as clean-cut as he had thought it, a few minutes before.

'I did a Dreamwalk,' he said.

'How did it go?'

'Good,' he said. 'Well, all right.'

'You should tell Mr Pennyworth. He'll be pleased.'

'You're right,' he said. 'I should.'

He reached the end of the alley, and instead of turning right, as he had planned and off into the world, he turned left, on to the high street, the road that would take him back to Dunstan Road and the graveyard on the hill.

'What?' said Liza Hempstock. 'What you doin'?'

'Going home,' said Bod. 'Like you said.'

There were shop lights now. Bod could smell the hot grease from the chip shop on the corner. The paving stones glistened.

'That's good,' said Liza Hempstock, now only a voice once more. Then the voice said, 'Run! Or Fade! Something's wrong!'

Bod was about to tell her that there was nothing

wrong, that she was being foolish, when a large car with a light flashing on the top came veering across the road and pulled up in front of him.

Two men got out from it. 'Excuse me, young man,' said one of the men. 'Police. Might I ask what you're doing out so late?'

'I didn't know there was a law against it,' said Bod.

The largest of the policemen opened the rear door of the car. 'Is this the young man you saw, miss?' he said.

Mo Quilling got out of the car, and looked at Bod, and smiled. 'That's him,' she said. 'He was in our back garden breaking things. And then he ran away.' She looked Bod in the eye. 'I saw you from my bedroom,' she said. 'I think he's the one who's been breaking windows.'

'What's your name?' asked the smaller policeman. He had a ginger moustache.

'Nobody,' said Bod. Then, 'Ow,' because the ginger policeman had taken Bod's ear between finger and thumb, and had given it a hard squeeze. 'Don't give me that,' said the policeman. 'Just answer the questions politely. Right?'

Bod said nothing.

'Where exactly do you live?' asked the policeman.

Bod said nothing. He tried to Fade, but Fading – even when boosted by a witch – relies on people's attention sliding away from you, and everybody's attention – not to mention a large pair of official hands – was on him then.

Bod said, 'You can't arrest me for not telling you my name or address.'

'No,' said the policeman. 'I can't. But I can take you down to the station until you give us the name of a parent,

185

guardian or responsible adult, into whose care we can release you.'

He put Bod into the back of the car, where Mo Quilling sat, with the smile on her face of a cat who has eaten all the canaries. 'I saw you from my front window,' she said, quietly. 'So I called the police.'

'I wasn't doing anything,' said Bod. 'I wasn't even in your garden. And why are they bringing you out to find me?'

'Quiet back there!' said the large policeman. Everyone was quiet until the car pulled up in front of a house that had to be Mo's. The large policeman opened the door for her, and she got out.

'We'll call you tomorrow, let your mum and dad know what we found,' said the large policeman.

'Thanks Uncle Tam,' said Mo, and she smiled. 'Just doing my duty.'

They drove back through the town in silence, Bod trying to Fade as best he could, with no success. He felt sick and miserable. In one evening, he had had his first real argument with Silas, had attempted to run away from home, had failed to run away, and now failed to return home. He could not tell the police where he lived, or his name. He would spend the rest of his life in a police cell, or in a prison for kids. *Do they have prison for kids?* He didn't know.

'Excuse me? Do they have prisons for kids?' he asked the men in the front seat.

'Getting worried, now, are you?' said Mo's Uncle Tam. 'I don't blame you. You kids. Running wild. Some of you need locking up, I'll tell you.'

Bod wasn't sure if that was a yes or a no. He glanced out of the car window. Something huge was flying through the air, above the car and to one side, something darker and bigger than the biggest bird. Something man-sized that flickered and fluttered as it moved, like the strobing flight of a bat.

The ginger policeman said, 'When we get to the station, best if you just give us your name, tell us who to call to come and get you, we can tell them we gave you a bollocking, they can take you home. See? You cooperate, we have an easy night, less paperwork for everyone. We're your friends.'

'You're too easy on him. A night in the cells isn't that hard,' said the large policeman to his friend. Then he looked back at Bod, and said, 'Unless it's a busy night, and we have to put you in with some of the drunks. They can be nasty.'

Bod thought, *He's lying!* and *They're doing this on purpose, the friendly one and the tough one . . .*

Then the police car turned a corner, and there was a *thump!* Something big rode up on to the bonnet of the car and was knocked off into the dark. A screech of brakes as the car stopped, and the ginger policeman began to swear under his breath.

'He just ran out into the road!' he said. 'You saw it!'

'I'm not sure what I saw,' said the larger policeman. 'You hit something, though.'

They got out of the car, shone lights around. The ginger policeman said, 'He was wearing black! You can't see it.'

'He's over here,' shouted the large policeman. The two

men hurried over to the body on the ground, holding torches.

Bod tried the door handles on the back seat. They did not work. And there was a metal grille between the back and the front. Even if he Faded, he was still stuck in the back seat of a police car.

He leaned over as far as he could, craning to try and see what had happened, what was on the road.

The ginger policeman was crouched down beside a body, looking at it. The other, the large one, was standing above it, shining a light down into its face.

Bod looked at the face of the fallen body – then he began to bang on the window, frantically, desperately.

The large policeman came over to the car.

'What?' he said, irritably.

'You hit my – my dad,' said Bod.

'You're kidding.'

'It looks like him,' said Bod. 'Can I look properly?'

The large policeman's shoulders slumped. 'Oi! Simon, the kid says it's his dad.'

'You've got to be bloody kidding me.'

'I think he's serious.' The large policeman opened the door, and Bod got out.

Silas was sprawled on his back, on the ground, where the car had knocked him. He was deathly still.

Bod's eyes prickled.

He said, 'Dad?' Then he said, 'You killed him.' He wasn't lying, he told himself – not really.

'I've called an ambulance,' said Simon, the ginger-moustached policeman.

'It was an accident,' said the other.

Bod crouched by Silas, and he squeezed Silas's cold hand in his. If they had already called an ambulance, there was not much time. He said, 'So that's your careers over, then.'

'It was an accident – you saw!'

'He just stepped out –'

'What I saw,' said Bod, 'is that you agreed to do a favour for your niece, and frighten a kid she's been fighting with at school. So you arrested me without a warrant for being out late, and then when my dad runs out into the road to try and stop you or to find out what was going on, you intentionally ran him over.'

'It was an accident!' repeated Simon.

'You've been fighting with Mo at school?' said Mo's Uncle Tam, but he didn't sound convincing.

'We're both in Eight B at the Old Town School,' said Bod. 'And you killed my dad.'

Far off, he could hear the sound of sirens.

'Simon,' said the large man, 'we have to talk about this.' They walked over to the other side of the car, leaving Bod alone in the shadows with the fallen Silas. Bod could hear the two policemen talking heatedly – 'Your bloody niece!' was used, and so was 'If *you'd* kept your eyes on the road!' Simon jabbed his finger into Tam's chest . . .

Bod whispered, 'They aren't looking. Now.' And he Faded.

There was a swirl of deeper darkness, and the body on the ground was now standing beside him.

Silas said, 'I'll take you home. Put your arms around my neck.'

Bod did, holding tightly to his guardian, and they plunged through the night, heading for the graveyard.

'I'm sorry,' said Bod.

'I'm sorry too,' said Silas.

'Did it hurt?' asked Bod. 'Letting the car hit you like that?'

'Yes,' said Silas. 'You should thank your little witch-friend. She came and found me, told me you were in trouble, and what kind of trouble you were in.'

They landed in the graveyard. Bod looked at his home as if it were the first time he had ever seen it. He said, 'What happened tonight was stupid, wasn't it? I mean, I put things at risk.'

'More things than you know, young Nobody Owens. Yes.'

'You were right,' said Bod. 'I won't go back. Not to that school, and not like that.'

Maureen Quilling had had the worst week of her life: Nick Farthing was no longer speaking to her; her Uncle Tam had shouted at her about the Owens kid thing, then told her not to mention anything about that evening ever to anyone, as he could lose his job, and he wouldn't want to be in her shoes if that happened; her parents were furious with her; she felt betrayed by the world; even the Year Sevens weren't scared of her any longer. It was rotten. She wanted to see that Owens kid, who she blamed for everything that had happened to her so far, writhing in miserable agony. If he thought being *arrested* was bad . . . and then she would concoct elaborate revenge schemes in her head, complex and vicious. They were the only thing that made her feel better, and even they didn't really help.

If there was one job that gave Mo the creeps, it was cleaning up the science labs – putting away the Bunsen burners, making sure that all test tubes, Petri dishes, unused filter papers and the like were returned to their places. She only had to do it, on a strict rotation system, once every two months, but it stood to reason that here, in the worst week of her life, she would be in the science lab, all on her own.

At least Mrs Hawkins, who taught General Sciences, was there, collecting papers, gathering things up at the end of the day. Having her there, having anybody there, was comforting.

'You're doing a good job, Maureen,' said Mrs Hawkins.

A white snake in a jar of preservative stared blindly down at them. Mo said, 'Thanks.'

'Aren't there meant to be two of you?' asked Mrs Hawkins.

'I was supposed to be doing it with the Owens kid,' said Mo. 'But he hasn't been to school in days now.'

The teacher frowned. 'Which one was he?' she asked, absently. 'I don't have him down on my list.'

'Bob Owens. Brownish hair, a bit too long. Didn't talk much. He was the one who named all the bones of the skeleton in the quiz. Remember?'

'Not really,' admitted Mrs Hawkins.

'You must remember! Nobody remembers him! Not even Mr Kirby!'

Mrs Hawkins pushed the rest of the sheets of paper into her bag and said, 'Well, I appreciate you doing it on your own, dear. Don't forget to wipe down the working surfaces, before you go.' And she went, closing the door behind her.

The science labs were old. There were long, dark wooden tables, with gas jets and taps and sinks built in to them, and there were dark wooden shelves upon which were displayed a selection of things in large bottles. The things that floated in the bottles were dead, had been dead for a long time. There was even a yellowed human skeleton in one corner of the room: Mo did not know if it was real or not, but right now it was creeping her out.

Every noise she made echoed, in that long room. She turned all of the overhead lights on, even the light on the whiteboard, just to make the place less scary. The room began to feel cold. She wished she could turn up the heat. She walked over to one of the large metal radiators and touched it. It was burning hot. But still, she was shivering.

The room was empty and unsettling in its emptiness, and Mo felt as if she were not alone, as if she were being watched.

Well, of course I'm being watched, she thought. *A hundred dead things in jars are all looking at me, not to mention the skeleton.* She glanced up at the shelves.

That was when the dead things in the jars began to move. A snake with unseeing milky eyes uncoiled in its alcohol-filled jar. A faceless, spiny sea-creature twisted and revolved in its liquid home. A kitten, dead for decades, showed its teeth and clawed the glass.

Mo closed her eyes. *This isn't happening*, she told herself. *I'm imagining it.* 'I'm not frightened,' she said, aloud.

'That's good,' said someone, standing in the shadows, by the rear door. 'It seriously sucks to be frightened.'

She said, 'None of the teachers even remember you.'

'But you remember me,' said the boy, the architect of all her misfortunes.

She picked up a glass beaker and threw it at him, but her aim went wide and it smashed against a wall.

'How's Nick?' asked Bod, as if nothing had happened.

'You know how he is,' she said. 'He won't even talk to me. Just shuts up in class, goes home and does his homework. Probably building model railways.'

'Good,' he said.

'And you,' she said. 'You haven't been at school for a week. You're in such trouble, Bob Owens. The police came in the other day. They were looking for you.'

'That reminds me ... How's your Uncle Tam?' said Bod.

Mo said nothing.

'In some ways,' said Bod, 'you've won. I'm leaving school. And in other ways, you haven't. Have you ever been haunted, Maureen Quilling? Ever looked in the mirror wondering if the eyes looking back at you were yours? Ever sat in an empty room, and realised you were not alone? It's not pleasant.'

'You're going to haunt me?' Her voice trembled.

Bod said nothing at all. He just stared at her. In the far corner of the room, something crashed: her bag had slipped off the chair on to the floor and when she looked back, she was alone in the room. Or, at least, there was nobody that she could see in there with her.

Her way home was going to be very long and very dark.

The boy and his guardian stood at the top of the hill, looking out at the lights of the town.

'Does it still hurt?' asked the boy.

'A little,' said his guardian. 'But I heal fast. I'll soon be as good as ever.'

'Could it have killed you? Stepping out in front of that car?'

His guardian shook his head. 'There are ways to kill people like me,' he said. 'But they don't involve cars. I am very old and very tough.'

Bod said, 'I *was* wrong, wasn't I? The whole idea was to do it without anybody noticing. And then I had to get involved with the kids in the school, and the next thing you know, there's police and all sorts of stuff. Because I was selfish.'

Silas raised an eyebrow. 'You weren't selfish. You need to be among your own kind. Quite understandable. It's just harder out there in the world of the living, and we cannot protect you out there as easily. I wanted to keep you perfectly safe,' said Silas. 'But there is only one perfectly safe place for your kind and you will not reach it until all your adventures are over and none of them matter any longer.'

Bod rubbed his hand over the stone of Thomas R. Stout (1817–1851, *Deeply regretted by all who knew him*), feeling the moss crumble beneath his fingers.

'He's still out there,' said Bod. 'The man who killed my first family. I still need to learn about people. Are you going to stop me leaving the graveyard?'

'No. That was a mistake and one that we have both learned from.'

'Then what?'

'We should do our best to satisfy your interest in stories and books and the world. There are libraries. There are other ways. And there are many situations in which there might be other, living people around you, like the theatre or the cinema.'

'What's that? Is it like football? I enjoyed watching them play football at school.'

'Football. Hmm. That's usually a little early in the day for me,' said Silas, 'but Miss Lupescu could take you to see a football match the next time she's here.'

'I'd like that,' said Bod.

They began to walk down the hill. Silas said, 'We have both left too many tracks and traces in the last few weeks. They are still looking for you, you know.'

'You said that before,' said Bod. 'How do you know? And who *are* they? And what do they want?'

But Silas only shook his head, and would be drawn no further, and with that, for the time being, Bod had to be satisfied.

The four men stood at the door to Number 33.

CHAPTER 7

Every Man Jack

Silas had been preoccupied for the previous several months. He had begun to leave the graveyard for days, sometimes weeks, at a time. Over Christmas, Miss Lupescu had come out for three weeks in his place, and Bod had shared her meals in her little flat in the Old Town. She had even taken him to a football match, as Silas had promised that she would, but she had gone back to the place she called 'The Old Country' after squeezing Bod's cheeks and calling him 'Nimini', which had become her pet name for him.

Now Silas was gone, and Miss Lupescu also. Mr and Mrs Owens were sitting in Josiah Worthington's tomb talking to Josiah Worthington. None of them was happy.

Josiah Worthington said, 'You mean to say that he did not tell either of you where he was going or how the child was to be cared for?'

When the Owenses shook their heads, Josiah Worthington said, 'Well, where *is* he?'

Neither Owens was able to answer. Master Owens said, 'He's never been gone for so long before. And he promised, when the child came to us, promised he would be here, or someone else would be here to help us care for him. He *promised*.'

Mrs Owens said, 'I worry that something must have happened to him.' She seemed close to tears, and then her tears turned to anger, and she said, 'This is too bad of him! Is there no way to find him, to call him back?'

'None that I know,' said Josiah Worthington. 'But I believe that he's left money in the crypt, for food for the boy.'

'Money!' said Mrs Owens. 'What use is *money*?'

'Bod will be needing money if he's to go out there to buy food,' began Mr Owens, but Mrs Owens turned on him.

'You're all as bad as each other!' she said.

She left the Worthington tomb, then, and she went looking for her son, whom she found, as she expected to, at the top of the hill, staring out over the town.

'Penny for your thoughts,' said Mrs Owens.

'You don't have a penny,' said Bod. He was fourteen, now, and taller than his mother.

'I've got two in the coffin,' said Mrs Owens. 'Probably a bit green by now, but I've still got them right enough.'

'I was thinking about the world,' said Bod. 'How do we even know that the person who killed my family is still alive? That he's out there?'

'Silas says he is,' said Mrs Owens.

'But Silas doesn't tell us anything else.'

Mrs Owens said, 'He means only the best for you. You know that.'

'Thanks,' said Bod, unimpressed. 'So where is he?'

Mrs Owens made no reply.

Bod said, 'You saw the man who killed my family, didn't you? On the day you adopted me.'

Mrs Owens nodded.

'What was he like?'

'Mostly, I had eyes for you. Let me see . . . he had dark hair, very dark. And I was frightened of him. He had a sharp face. Hungry and angry all at once, he was. Silas saw him off.'

'Why didn't Silas just kill him?' said Bod, fiercely. 'He should have just killed him then.'

Mrs Owens touched the back of Bod's hand with her cold fingers. She said, 'He's not a monster, Bod.'

'If Silas had killed him back then, I would be safe now. I could go anywhere.'

'Silas knows more than you do about all this, more than any of us do. And Silas knows about life and death,' said Mrs Owens. 'It's not that easy.'

Bod said, 'What was his name? The man who killed them.'

'He didn't say it. Not then.'

Bod put his head on one side, and stared at her with eyes as grey as thunderclouds. 'But you know it, don't you?'

Mrs Owens said, 'There's nothing you can do, Bod.'

'There is. I can learn. I can learn *everything* I need to know, all I can. I learned about ghoul-gates. I learned to Dreamwalk. Miss Lupescu taught me how to watch the stars. Silas taught me silence. I can Haunt. I can Fade. I know every inch of this graveyard.'

Mrs Owens reached out a hand, touched her son's shoulder. 'One day,' she said ... and then she hesitated. One day, she would not be able to touch him. One day, he would leave them. One day. And then she said, 'Silas told me the man who killed your family was called Jack.'

Bod said nothing. Then he nodded. 'Mother?'

'What is it, son?'

'When will Silas come back?'

The midnight wind was cold and it came from the north.

Mrs Owens was no longer angry. She feared for her son. She said only, 'I wish I knew, my darling boy, I wish I knew.'

Scarlett Amber Perkins was fifteen, and, at that moment, sitting on the upper deck of the elderly bus, she was a mass of angry hate. She hated her parents for splitting up. She hated her mother for moving away from Scotland, hated her father because he didn't seem to care that she had gone. She hated this town for being so different – nothing like Glasgow, where she had grown up – and she hated it because every now and again she would turn a corner and see something and the world would all become achingly, horribly familiar.

She had lost it with her mother that morning. 'At least in Glasgow I had friends!' Scarlett had said, and she wasn't quite shouting and she wasn't quite sobbing. 'I'll never see them again!' All her mother had said in reply was, 'At least you're somewhere you've been before. I mean, we lived here when you were little.'

'I don't remember,' said Scarlett. 'And it's not like I still know anyone. Do you want me to find my old friends from when I was five? Is *that* what you want?'

And her mother said, 'Well, I'm not stopping you.'

Scarlett had gone through the whole of the school day angry, and she was angry now. She hated her school and she hated the world, and right now she particularly hated the town bus service.

Every day, when school was over, the 97 bus to the city centre would take her from her school gates all the way to the end of the street where her mother had rented a small flat. She had waited at the bus stop on that gusty April day for almost half an hour and no 97 buses had appeared, so when she saw a 121 bus with *City Centre* as its destination she had climbed aboard. But where her bus always turned right, this one turned left, into the Old Town, past the municipal gardens in the old town square, past the statue of Josiah Worthington, Bart, and then crept up a winding hill lined with high houses, as Scarlett's heart sank and her anger was replaced with misery.

She walked downstairs, edged forward, eyed the sign telling her not to speak to the driver when the vehicle was in motion, and said, 'Excuse me. I wanted to go to Acacia Avenue.'

The driver, a large woman, her skin even darker than Scarlett's said, 'You should have got the 97, then.'

'But this goes to the city centre.'

'Eventually. But even when you get there, you'll still need to get back.' The woman sighed. 'Best thing you can do, get off here, walk back down the hill, there's a bus stop in front of the town hall. From there, you can catch the number 4 or a 58, both of them will take you most of the way to Acacia Avenue. You could get off by the sports centre and walk up from there. You got all that?'

'The 4 or the 58.'

'I'll let you off here.' It was a request stop on the side of the hill, just past a large pair of open iron gates, and it looked uninviting and dismal. Scarlett stood in the open doorway of the bus until the bus driver said, 'Go on. Hop it.' She stepped down on to the pavement and the bus belched black smoke and roared away.

The wind rattled the trees on the other side of the wall.

Scarlett began to walk back down the hill – *this* was why she needed a mobile phone, she thought. If she was so much as five minutes late, her mother would *freak* but she still wouldn't buy Scarlett a phone of her own. Oh well. She would have to endure another one of her mother's shouting matches. It wouldn't be the first and it wouldn't be the last.

By now she was level with the open gates. She glanced inside and ...

'That's odd,' she said, aloud.

There's an expression, *déjà vu*, that means that you feel like you've been somewhere before, that you've somehow already dreamed it or experienced it in your mind. Scarlett had experienced it – the knowledge that a teacher was just about to tell them that she'd been to Inverness on holiday, or that someone had dropped a spoon in just that way before. This was different. This wasn't a feeling that she had been here before. This was the real thing.

Scarlett walked through the open gates into the grave-yard.

A magpie flew up as she walked in, a flash of black and white and iridescent green, and settled in the branches of a yew tree, watching her. *Around that corner*, she thought, *is a church, with a bench in front of it*, and she turned a corner to see a church – much smaller than the one in her head, a sinister blocky little Gothic building of grey stone, with a jutting spire. In front of it was a weathered wooden bench. She walked over, sat down on the bench, and swung her legs as if she were still a little girl.

'Hullo. Um, hullo?' said a voice from behind her. 'Awful cheek of me, I know, but would you help me hold down this, er, just really need another pair of hands, if it's not too much trouble.'

Scarlett looked around, and saw a man in a fawn-coloured raincoat squatting in front of a gravestone. He was holding a large sheet of paper which was blowing about in the wind. She hurried over to him.

'You hold on to it here,' said the man. 'One hand here, one hand there, that's it. Frightful imposition, I know. Ridiculously grateful.'

He had a biscuit tin next to him, and from the tin he pulled what looked like a crayon the size of a small candle. He began rubbing it back and forth across the stone with easy, practised movements.

'There we go,' he said, cheerfully. 'And here she comes . . . oops. A wiggly bit, down at the bottom here, I think it's meant to be ivy – the Victorians loved putting ivy on things, deeply symbolic you know ... and there we are. You can let go now.'

He stood up, ran one hand through his grey hair. 'Ow. Needed to stand. Legs got a bit pins-and-needlesy,' he said. 'So. What do you reckon to that?'

The actual headstone was covered in green and yellow lichen, and so worn and faded as to almost be undecipherable, but the rubbing was clear. 'Majella Godspeed, Spinster of this Parish, 1791–1870, *Lost to All But Memory*,' Scarlett read aloud.

'And probably now lost even to that,' said the man. His hair was thinning, and he smiled hesitantly and blinked at her through small, round glasses which made him look a little like a friendly owl.

A large raindrop splashed down on the paper, and the man hurriedly rolled it up and grabbed his tin box of crayons. Another handful of raindrops, and Scarlett picked up the portfolio the man pointed to, propped up beside a nearby gravestone, and followed him into the tiny porch of the chapel, where the rain could not touch them.

'Thank you so much,' said the man. 'I don't think it's really going to rain much. Weather forecast for this afternoon said mostly sunny.'

As if in reply, the wind gusted coldly and the rain began to beat down in earnest.

'I know what you're thinking,' the gravestone-rubbing man said to Scarlett.

'You do?' she said. She had been thinking, *My mum will kill me.*

'You're thinking, is this a church or a chapel? And the answer is, as far as I can ascertain, that on this site there was indeed a small church, and the original graveyard would have been its churchyard. That's as long ago as eight, perhaps nine hundred AD. Rebuilt and extended several times in there. But there was a fire here in the 1820s and by that time it was already much too small for the area. People around here were using St Dunstan's in the village square as their parish church, so when they came to rebuild here, they made it a funeral chapel, keeping many of the original features – the stained glass windows in the far wall are said to be original . . .'

'Actually,' said Scarlett, 'I was thinking that my mum is going to kill me. I got the wrong bus and I am already so late home . . .'

'Good Lord, you poor thing,' said the man. 'Look, I only live just down the road. You wait here –' and with that he thrust his portfolio, his tin of crayons and his rolled-up sheet of paper into her hands and he set off at a trot down to the gates, his shoulders hunched against the driving rain. A couple of minutes later, Scarlett saw the lights of a car and heard the sound of a car horn.

Scarlett ran down to the gates, where she could see the car, an elderly green Mini. The man she had been talking to was sitting in the driver's seat. He wound down his window.

'Come on,' he said, 'where exactly am I taking you?'

Scarlett stood there, the rain running down her neck. 'I don't take lifts from strangers,' she said.

'Quite right too,' said the man. 'But one good turn

deserves, and, um, all that. Here, put the stuff in the back before it gets soaked.' He pulled open the passenger door, and Scarlett leaned inside and put his grave-rubbing equipment down on the back seat as best she could. 'Tell you what,' he said. 'Why don't you phone your mother – you can use my phone – and tell her my car's number plate? You can do it from inside the car. You're getting soaked out there.'

Scarlett hesitated. Rain was beginning to plaster her hair down. It was cold.

The man reached over and handed her his mobile phone. Scarlett looked at it. She realised she was more afraid of calling her mother than she was of getting into the car. Then she said, 'I could call the police too, couldn't I?'

'You certainly can, yes. Or you can walk home. Or you can just call your mother and ask her to come and pick you up.'

Scarlett got into the passenger seat and closed the door. She kept hold of the man's phone.

'Where do you live?' the man asked.

'You really don't have to. I mean, you could just take me to the bus stop . . .'

'I'll take you home. Address?'

'102a Acacia Avenue. It's off the main road, a wee bit past the big sports centre . . .'

'You *are* out of your way, aren't you? Right. Let's get you home.' He took off the handbrake, swung the car around and drove down the hill.

'Been living here long?' he said.

'Not really. We moved here just after Christmas. We

lived here when I was five, though.'

'Is that a brogue I detect in your accent?'

'We've been living in Scotland for ten years. There, I sounded like everyone else, and then I came down here, and now I stick out like a sore thumb.' She had wanted it to sound like a joke, but it was true, and she could hear it as she said it. Not funny, just bitter.

The man drove to Acacia Avenue, parked in front of the house, then insisted on coming up to the front door with her. When the door was opened, he said, 'Frightfully sorry. I took the liberty of bringing your daughter back to you. Obviously, you taught her well, shouldn't accept lifts from strangers. But, well, it was raining, she took the wrong bus, wound up on the other side of town. Bit of a mess all around really. Say you can find it in your heart to forgive. Forgive her. And, um, me.'

Scarlett expected her mother to shout at both of them, and was surprised and relieved when her mother only said, well, you couldn't be too careful these days, and was Mr Um a teacher, and would he like a cup of tea?

Mr Um said his name was Frost, but she should call him Jay, and Mrs Perkins smiled and said he should call her Noona, and she'd put the kettle on.

Over tea, Scarlett told her mother the story of her wrong bus adventure, and how she had found herself at the graveyard, and how she met Mr Frost by the little church . . .

Mrs Perkins dropped her teacup.

They were sitting around the table in the kitchen, so the cup didn't fall very far, and it didn't break, just spilled tea. Mrs Perkins apologised awkwardly, and went and got a cloth from the sink to mop it up.

Then she said, 'The graveyard on the hill, in the Old Town? That one?'

'I live over that way,' said Mr Frost. 'Been doing a lot of grave rubbings. And you know it's technically a nature reserve?'

Mrs Perkins said, 'I know,' thin-lipped. Then she said, 'Thank you so much for giving Scarlett a ride home, Mr Frost.' Each word might have been an ice cube. Then, 'I think you should leave now.'

'I say, that's a bit much,' said Frost, amiably. 'Didn't mean to hurt your feelings. Was it something I said? The rubbings, they're for a local history project, it's not as if I'm, you know, digging up bones or anything.'

For a heartbeat, Scarlett thought that her mother was going to strike Mr Frost, who just looked worried. But Mrs Perkins shook her head and said, 'Sorry, family history. Not your fault.' As if she were making a conscious effort, she said, brightly, 'You know, Scarlett actually used to play in that graveyard when she was little. This is, oh, ten years ago. She had an imaginary friend, too. A little boy called Nobody.'

A smile twitched at the corner of Mr Frost's lips. 'A ghostie?'

'No, I don't think so. He just lived there. She even pointed out the tomb he lived in. So I suppose he *was* a ghost. Do you remember, love?'

Scarlett shook her head. 'I must have been a funny kid,' she said.

'I'm sure that you were nothing of the, um,' said Mr Frost. 'You are raising a fine girl here, Noona. Well, lovely cup of tea. Always a joy to make new friends. I'll be toddling off now. Got to make myself a little dinner, then I've got a meeting of the Local History Society.'

'You're making your own dinner?' said Mrs Perkins.

'Yes, making it. Well, defrosting it really. I'm also a master of the boil-in-the-bag. Eating for one. Living on my own. Bit of a crusty old bachelor. Actually, in the papers, that always means gay, doesn't it? Not gay, just never met the right woman.' And for a moment, he looked rather sad.

Mrs Perkins, who hated to cook, announced that she always cooked too much food at the weekend, and as she ushered Mr Frost out into the hall, Scarlett heard him agree that he would love to come round for dinner on Saturday night.

When Mrs Perkins came back from the front hall, all she said to Scarlett was, 'I hope you've done your homework.'

Scarlett was thinking about the afternoon's events as she lay in bed that night listening to the sound of the cars grinding their way along the main road. She *had* been there, in that graveyard, when she was little. That was why everything had seemed so familiar.

In her mind she imagined and she remembered, and somewhere in there she fell asleep, but in sleep she still walked the paths of the graveyard. It was night, but she could see everything as clearly as if it were day. She was on the side of a hill. There was a boy of about her own age standing with his back to her, looking at the lights of the city.

Scarlett said, 'Boy? What're you doing?'

He looked around, seemed to have trouble focusing. 'Who said that?' and then, 'Oh, I can see you, sort of. Are you Dreamwalking?'

'I think I'm dreaming,' she agreed.

'Not quite what I meant,' said the boy. 'Hullo. I'm Bod.'

'I'm Scarlett,' she said.

He looked at her again, as if he were seeing her for the first time. 'Of course, you are! I knew you looked familiar. You were in the graveyard today with that man, the one with the paper.'

'Mr Frost,' she said. 'He's really nice. He gave me a lift home.' Then she said, 'Did you see us?'

'Yeah. I keep an eye on most things that happen in the graveyard.'

'What kind of a name is Bod?' she asked.

'It's short for Nobody.'

'Of course!' said Scarlett. 'That's what this dream is about. You're my imaginary friend, from when I was little, all grown up.'

He nodded.

He was taller than she was. He wore grey, although she could not have described his clothes. His hair was too long, and she thought it had been some time since he had received a haircut.

He said, 'You were really brave. We went deep into the hill and we saw the Indigo Man. And we met the Sleer.'

212

Something happened, then, in her head. A rushing and a tumbling, a whirl of darkness and a crash of images . . .

'I *remember*,' said Scarlett. But she said it to the empty darkness of her bedroom, and heard nothing in reply but the low trundle of a distant lorry, making its way through the night.

Bod had stores of food, the kind that lasted, cached in the crypt, and more in some of the chillier tombs and vaults and mausoleums. Silas had made sure of that. He had enough food to keep him going for a couple of months. Unless Silas or Miss Lupescu was there, he simply would not leave the graveyard.

He missed the world beyond the graveyard gates, but he knew it was not safe out there. Not yet. The graveyard, though, was his world and his domain, and he was proud of it and loved it as only a fourteen-year-old boy can love anything.

And yet . . .

In the graveyard, no one ever changed. The little children Bod had played with when he was small were still little children; Fortinbras Bartleby, who had once been his best friend, was now four or five years younger than Bod was, and they had less to talk about each time they saw each other; Thackeray Porringer was Bod's height and age, and seemed to be in much better temper with him; he would walk with Bod in the evenings, and tell stories of unfortunate things that had happened to his friends. Normally the stories would end in the friends being hanged until they were dead for no offence of theirs and by mistake, although sometimes they were simply transported to the American colonies and they didn't have to be hanged unless they came back.

Liza Hempstock, who had been Bod's friend for the last six years, was different in another way; she was less likely to be there for him when Bod went down to the nettle patch to see her, and on the rare occasions when she was, she would be short-tempered, argumentative and often downright rude.

Bod talked to Mr Owens about this, and, after a few moments' reflection, his father said, 'It's just women, I reckon. She liked you as a boy, probably isn't sure who you are now you're a young man. I used to play with one little girl down by the duck-pond every day until she turned about your age, and then she threw an apple at my head and did not say another word to me until I was seventeen.'

Mrs Owens sniffed. 'It was a pear I threw,' she said, tartly, 'and I was talking to you again soon enough, for we danced a measure at your cousin Ned's wedding, and that was but two days after your sixteenth birthday.'

Mr Owens said, 'Of course you are right, my dear.' He winked at Bod, to tell him that it was none of it serious. And then he mouthed 'Seventeen' to show that, really, it was.

Bod had allowed himself no friends among the living. That way, he had realised back during his short-lived schooldays, lay only trouble. Still, he had remembered Scarlett, had missed her for years after she went away, had long ago faced the fact he would never see her again. And now she had been here in his graveyard, and he had not known her ...

He was wandering deeper into the tangle of ivy and trees that made the graveyard's north-west quadrant so dangerous. Signs advised visitors to keep out, but the signs were not needed. It was uninviting and creepy once you were past the ivy-tangle that marked the end of the Egyptian Walk and the black doors in the mock-Egyptian walls that led to people's final resting places. In the north-west, nature had been reclaiming the graveyard for almost a hundred years, and the stones were tipped over, graves were forgotten or simply lost beneath the green ivy and the leaf-fall of fifty years. Paths were lost and impassible.

Bod walked with care. He knew the area well, and he knew how dangerous it could be.

When Bod was nine, he had been exploring in just this part of the world when the soil had given way beneath him, tumbling him into a hole almost twenty feet down. The grave had been dug deep, to accommodate many coffins, but there was no headstone and only one coffin, down at the bottom, containing a rather excitable medical gentleman named Carstairs who seemed thrilled by Bod's arrival and insisted on examining Bod's wrist (which Bod had twisted in the tumble, grabbing on to a root) before he could be persuaded to go and fetch help.

Bod was making his way through the north-west quadrant, a sludge of fallen leaves, a tangle of ivy, where the foxes made their homes and fallen angels stared up blindly, because he had an urge to talk to the Poet.

Nehemiah Trot was the Poet's name, and his grave-stone, beneath the greenery, read:

Here lie the mortal remains of
NEHEMIAH TROT
POET
1741–1774
SWANS SING BEFORE THEY DIE

Bod said, 'Master Trot? Might I ask you for advice?'

Nehemiah Trot beamed, wanly. 'Of course, brave boy. The advice of poets is the cordiality of kings! How may I smear unction on your, no, not unction, how may I give balm to your pain?'

'I'm not actually in pain. I just – well, there's a girl I used to know, and I wasn't sure if I should find her and talk to her or if I should just forget about it.'

Nehemiah Trot drew himself up to his full height, which was less than Bod's, raised both hands to his chest excitedly, and said, 'Oh! You must go to her and implore her. You must call her your Terpsichore, your Echo, your Clytemnestra. You must write poems for her, mighty odes – I shall help you write them – and thus – and only thus – shall you win your true love's heart.'

'I don't actually need to win her heart. She's not my true love,' said Bod. 'Just someone I'd like to talk to.'

'Of all the organs,' said Nehemiah Trot. 'The tongue is the most remarkable. For we use it both to taste our sweet wine and bitter poison, thus also do we utter words both sweet and sour with the same tongue. Go to her! Talk to her!'

'I shouldn't.'

'You should, sir! You must! I shall write about it, when the battle's lost and won.'

'But if I Unfade for one person, it makes it easier for other people to see me . . .'

Nehemiah Trot said, 'Ah, listen to me young Leander, young Hero, young Alexander. If you dare nothing, then when the day is over, nothing is all you will have gained.'

'Good point.' Bod was pleased with himself, and glad he had thought of asking the Poet for advice. *Really,* he thought, *if you couldn't trust a poet to offer sensible advice, who could you trust?* Which reminded him . . .

'Mister Trot?' said Bod. 'Tell me about revenge.'

'Dish best served cold,' said Nehemiah Trot. 'Do not take revenge in the heat of the moment. Instead, wait until the hour is propitious. There was a Grub Street hack named O'Leary – an Irishman, I should add – who had the nerve, the confounded cheek to write of my first slim volume of poems A *Nosegay of Beauty Assembled for Gentlemen of Quality*, that it was inferior doggerel of no worth whatsoever, and that the paper it was written on would have been better used as – no, I cannot say. Let us simply agree that it was a most vulgar statement.'

'But you got your revenge on him?' asked Bod, curious.

'On him and on his entire pestilent breed! Oh, I had my revenge, Master Owens, and it was a terrible one. I wrote, and had published, a letter, which I nailed to the doors of the public houses in London where such low scribbling folk were wont to frequent. And I explained that, given the fragility of the genius poetical, I would henceforth write not for them, but only for myself and posterity, and that I should, as long as I lived, publish no more poems – for them! Thus I left instructions that upon my death my poems were to be buried with me, unpublished, and that only when posterity realised my genius, realised that hundreds of my verses had been lost – lost!– only then was my coffin to be disinterred, only then could my poems be removed from my cold dead hand, to finally be published to the approbation and delight of all. It is a terrible thing to be ahead of your time.'

'And after you died, they dug you up, and they printed the poems?'

'Not yet, no. But there is still plenty of time. Posterity is vast.'

'So . . . that was your revenge?'

'Indeed. And a mightily powerful and cunning one at that!'

'Ye-es,' said Bod, unconvinced.

'Best. Served. Cold,' said Nehemiah Trot, proudly.

Bod left the north-west of the graveyard, returned through the Egyptian Walk to the more orderly paths and untangled ways, and, as dusk fell, he wandered back towards the old chapel – not because he hoped Silas had returned from his travels, but because he had spent his life visiting the chapel at dusk, and it felt good to have a rhythm. And anyway, he was hungry.

Bod slipped through the crypt door, down into the crypt. He moved a cardboard box filled with curled and damp parish papers and took out a carton of orange juice, an apple, a box of breadsticks and a block of cheese, and he ate while pondering how and whether he would seek out Scarlett – he would Dreamwalk, perhaps, since that was how she had come to him . . .

He headed outside, was on his way to sit on the grey wooden bench, when he saw something and he hesitated. There was someone already there, sitting on his bench. She was reading a magazine.

Bod Faded even more, became a part of the graveyard, no more important than a shadow or a twig.

But she looked up. She looked straight at him, and she said, 'Bod? Is that you?'

He said nothing. Then he said, 'Why can you see me?'

'I almost couldn't. At first I thought you were in shadow or something. But you look like you did in my dream. You sort of came into focus.'

He walked over to the bench. He said, 'Can you actually read that? Isn't it too dark for you?'

Scarlett closed the magazine. She said, 'It's odd. You'd think it would be too dark, but I could read it fine, no problem.'

'Are you . . .' He trailed off, uncertain of what he had wanted to ask her. 'Are you here on your own?'

She nodded. 'I helped Mr Frost do some grave-rubbings, after school. And then I told him I wanted to sit and think here, for a bit. When I'm finished here, I promised to go and have a cup of tea with him and he'll run me home. He didn't even ask why. Just said he loves sitting in graveyards too, and that he thinks they can be the most peaceful places in the world.' Then she said, 'Can I hug you?'

'Do you want to?' said Bod.

'Yes.'

'Well then.' He thought for a moment. 'I don't mind if you do.'

'My hands won't go through you or anything? You're really there?'

'You won't go through me,' he told her, and she threw her arms around him and squeezed him so tightly he could hardly breathe. He said, 'That hurts.'

Scarlett let go. 'Sorry.'

'No. It was nice. I mean. You just squeezed more than I was expecting.'

'I just wanted to know if you were real. All these years I thought you were just something in my head. And then I sort of forgot about you. But I *didn't* make you up, and you're back, you're in my head, and you're in the world too.'

Bod smiled. He said, 'You used to wear a sort of a coat, it was orange, and whenever I saw that particular colour orange, I'd think of you. I don't suppose you still have the coat.'

'No,' she said. 'Not for a long time. It would be a wee bit too small for me now.'

'Yes,' said Bod. 'Of course.'

'I should go home,' said Scarlett. 'I thought I could come up at the weekend, though.' And then, seeing the expression on Bod's face, she said, 'Today's Wednesday.'

'I'd like that.'

She turned to go. Then she said, 'How will I find you, next time?'

Bod said, 'I'll find you. Don't worry. Just be on your own and I'll find you.'

She nodded, and was gone.

Bod walked back into the graveyard and up the hill, until he reached the Frobisher mausoleum. He did not enter it. He climbed up the side of the building, using the thick ivy root as a foothold, and he pulled himself up on to the stone roof, where he sat and thought looking out at the world of moving things beyond the graveyard, and he remembered the way that Scarlett had held him and how safe he had felt, if only for a moment, and how fine it would be to walk safely in the lands beyond the graveyard, and how good it was to be master of his own small world.

Scarlett said that she didn't want a cup of tea, thank you. Or a chocolate biscuit. Mr Frost was concerned.

'Honestly,' he told her, 'you look like you've seen a ghost. Well, a graveyard, not a bad place to see one, if you were going to, um, I had an aunt once who claimed her parrot was haunted. She was a scarlet macaw. The parrot. The aunt was an architect. Never knew the details.'

'I'm fine,' said Scarlett. 'It was just a long day.'

'I'll give you a lift home then. Any idea what this says? Been puzzling over it for half an hour.' He indicated a grave-rubbing on the little table, held flat by a jam jar in each corner. 'Is that name Gladstone, do you think? Could be a relative of the prime minister. But I can't make out anything else.'

'Fraid not,' said Scarlett. 'But I'll take another look when I come out on Saturday.'

'Is your mother likely to put in an appearance?'

'She said she'd drop me off here in the morning. Then she has to go and do the shopping for our dinner. She's cooking roast chicken.'

'Do you think,' asked Mr Frost, hopefully, 'there are likely to be roast potatoes?'

'I expect so, yes.'

Mr Frost looked delighted. Then he said, 'I wouldn't want her to go out of her way, I mean.'

'She's loving it,' said Scarlett, truthfully. 'Thank you for giving me a lift home.'

'More than welcome,' said Mr Frost. They walked together down the steps in Mr Frost's high narrow house, to the little entrance hall at the bottom of the stairs.

In Krakow, on Wawel Hill, there are caves called the Dragon's Den, named after a long dead dragon. These are the caves that the tourists know about. There are caves beneath those caves that the tourists do not know and do not ever get to visit. They go down a long way, and they are inhabited.

Silas went first, followed by the grey hugeness of Miss Lupescu, padding quietly on four feet just behind him. Behind them was Kandar, a bandage-wrapped Assyrian mummy with powerful eagle-wings and eyes like rubies, who was carrying a small pig.

There had originally been four of them, but they had lost Haroun in a cave far above, when the Ifrit, as naturally overconfident as are all of its race, had stepped into a space bounded by three polished bronze mirrors and had been swallowed up in a blaze of light. In moments the Ifrit could only be seen in the mirrors, and no longer in reality. In the mirrors his fiery eyes were wide open, and his mouth was moving as if he were shouting at them to leave and beware, and then he faded and was lost to them.

Silas, who had no problems with mirrors, covered one of them with his coat, rendering the trap useless. 'So,' said Silas. 'Now there are only three of us.'

'And a pig,' said Kandar.

'Why?' asked Miss Lupescu, with a wolf-tongue, through wolf teeth. 'Why the pig?'

'It's lucky,' said Kandar.

Miss Lupescu growled, unconvinced.

'Did Haroun have a pig?' asked Kandar, simply.

'Hush,' said Silas. 'They are coming. From the sound of it, there are many of them.'

'Let them come,' whispered Kandar.

Miss Lupescu's hackles were rising. She said nothing, but she was ready for them, and it was only by an effort of will that she did not throw back her head and howl.

'It's beautiful up this way,' said Scarlett.

'Yes,' said Bod.

'So, your family were all killed?' said Scarlett. 'Does anyone know who did it?'

'No. Not that I know. My guardian only says that the man who did it is still alive, and that he'll tell me the rest of what he knows one day.'

'One day?'

'When I'm ready.'

'What's he scared of? That you'd strap on your gun and ride out to wreak vengeance on the man who killed your family?'

Bod looked at her seriously. 'Well, obviously,' he said. 'Not a gun, though. But yes. Something like that.'

'You're joking.'

Bod said nothing. His lips were tight-pressed together. He shook his head. Then he said, 'I'm not joking.'

It was a bright and sunny Saturday morning. They were just past the entrance to the Egyptian Walk, out of the direct sunlight, under the pines and the sprawling monkey puzzle tree.

'Your guardian. Is he a dead person too?'

Bod said, 'I don't talk about him.'

Scarlett looked hurt. 'Not even to me?'

'Not even to you.'

'Well,' she said. 'Be like that.'

Bod said, 'Look, I'm sorry, I didn't mean –' just as Scarlett said, 'I promised Mr Frost I wouldn't be too long. I'd better be getting back.'

'Right,' said Bod, worried he had offended her, unsure what he should say to make things better.

He watched Scarlett head off on the winding path back to the chapel. A familiar female voice said, with derision, 'Look at her! Miss High and Mighty!' but there was no one to be seen.

Bod, feeling awkward, walked back to the Egyptian Walk. Miss Lillibet and Miss Violet had let him store a cardboard box filled with old paperback books in their vault, and he wanted to find something to read.

Scarlett helped Mr Frost with his grave-rubbings until midday, when they stopped for lunch. He offered to buy her fish and chips as a thank you, and they walked down to the chip shop at the bottom of the road, and as they walked back up the hill they ate their steaming fish and chips, drenched in vinegar and glittering with salt, out of paper bags.

Scarlett said, 'If you wanted to find out about a murder, where would you look? I already tried the internet.'

'Um. Depends. What kind of murder are we talking about?'

'Something local, I think. About thirteen or fourteen years ago. A family was killed around here.'

'Crikey,' said Mr Frost. 'This really happened?'

'Oh yes. Are you all right?'

'Not really. Bit too . . . well, bit of a wimp, really. Things like that, I mean, local true crime, you don't like to think about it. Things like that, happening here. Not something I'd expect a girl of your age to be interested in.'

'It's not actually for me,' admitted Scarlett. 'It's for a friend.'

Mr Frost finished off the last of his fried cod. 'The library, I suppose. If it's not on the internet, it'll be in their newspaper files. What set you off after this?'

'Oh.' Scarlett wanted to lie as little as possible. She

said, 'A boy I know. He was asking about it.'

'Definitely the library,' said Mr Frost. 'Murder. Brrr. Gives me the shivers.'

'Me too,' said Scarlett. 'A bit.' Then, hopefully, 'Could you maybe, possibly, drop me off at the library, this afternoon?'

Mr Frost bit a large chip in half, chewed it, and looked at the rest of the chip, disappointed. 'They get cold so fast, don't they, chips. One minute, you're burning your mouth on them, the next you're wondering how they cool off so quickly.'

'I'm sorry,' said Scarlett. 'I shouldn't be asking for lifts everywhere –'

'Not at all,' said Mr Frost. 'Just wondering how best to organise this afternoon, and whether or not your mother likes chocolates. Bottle of wine or chocolates? Not really sure. Both maybe?'

'I can make my own way home from the library,' said Scarlett. 'And she loves chocolates. So do I.'

'Chocolates it is, then,' said Mr Frost, relieved. They had reached the middle of the row of high, terraced houses on the hill, and the little green Mini parked outside. 'Get in. I'll run you over to the library.'

The library was a square building, all brick and stone, dating back to the beginning of the last century. Scarlett looked around, and then went up to the desk.

The woman said, 'Yes?'

Scarlett said, 'I wanted to see some old newspaper clippings.'

'Is it for school?' said the woman.

'It's local history,' said Scarlett, nodding, proud that she hadn't actually lied.

'We've got the local paper on microfiche,' said the woman. She was large, and had silver hoops in her ears. Scarlett could feel her heart pounding in her chest; she was certain she looked guilty or suspicious, but the woman led her into a room with boxes that looked like computer screens, and showed her how to use them, to project a page of the newspaper at a time on to the screen. 'One day we'll have it all digitised,' said the woman. 'Now, what dates are you after?'

'About thirteen or fourteen years ago,' said Scarlett, 'I can't be more specific than that. I'll know it when I see it.'

The woman gave Scarlett a small box with five years' worth of newspapers on microfilm in it. 'Go wild,' she said.

Scarlett assumed that the murder of a family would have been front-page news but instead, when she eventually found it, it was almost buried on page five. It had happened in October, thirteen years earlier. There was no colour in the article, no description, just an understated list of events:

Architect Ronald Dorian, 36, his wife, Carlotta, 34, a publisher, and their daughter, Misty, 7, were found dead at 33 Dunstan Road. Foul play is suspected. A police spokesman said that it was too early to comment at this stage in their investigations, but that significant leads are being followed.

*

There was no mention of how the family died, and nothing said about a missing baby. In the weeks that followed, there was no follow-up, and the police did not ever comment, not that Scarlett could see.

But that was it. She was certain. Thirty-three Dunstan Road. She knew the house. She had been in there.

She returned the box of microfilm to the front desk, thanked the librarian, and walked home in the April sunshine. Her mother was in the kitchen cooking – not entirely successfully, judging from the smell of burnt-bottom-of-the-saucepan that filled most of the flat. Scarlett retreated to her bedroom and opened the windows wide to let the burnt smell out, then she sat on her bed and made a phone call.

'Hello? Mr Frost?'

'Scarlett. Everything still all right for this evening? How's your mother?'

'Oh, it's all under control,' said Scarlett, which was what her mother had said when she had asked. 'Um, Mr Frost, how long have you lived at your house?'

'How long? About, well, four months now.'

'How did you find it?'

'Estate agents' window. It was empty and I could afford it. Well, more or less. Well, I wanted something within walking distance of the graveyard, and this was perfect.'

'Mister Frost,' Scarlett wondered how to say it, and then just said it. 'About thirteen years ago, three people were murdered in your house. The Dorian family.'

There was a silence at the other end of the phone.

'Mister Frost? Are you there?'

'Um. Still here, Scarlett. Sorry. Not the sort of thing you expect to hear. It's an old house, I mean, you expect things to happen a long time ago. But not . . . well, what happened?'

Scarlett wondered how much she could tell him. She said, 'There was a little piece on it in an old newspaper, it only gave the address and nothing else. I don't know how they died or anything.'

'Well. Good Lord.' Mr Frost sounded more intrigued by the news than Scarlett could have expected. 'This, young Scarlett, is where we local historians come into our own. Leave it with me. I'll find out everything I can and report back.'

'Thank you,' said Scarlett, relieved.

'Um. I assume this phone call is because if Noona thought there were murders going on in my home, even thirteen-year-old-ones, you'd never be allowed to see me or the graveyard again. So, um, suppose I won't mention it unless you do.'

'Thank you, Mr Frost!'

'See you at seven. With chocolates.'

Dinner was remarkably pleasant. The burnt smell had gone from the kitchen. The chicken was good, the salad was better, the roast potatoes were too crispy, but a delighted Mr Frost had proclaimed that this was precisely the way he liked them, and had taken a second helping.

The flowers were popular, the chocolates, which they had for dessert, were perfect, and Mr Frost sat and talked then watched television with them until about 10 p.m., when he said that he needed to get home.

'Time, tide and historical research wait for no man,' he said. He shook Noona's hand with enthusiasm, winked at Scarlett conspiratorially, and was out the door.

Scarlett tried to find Bod in her dreams that night; she thought of him as she went to sleep, imagined herself walking the graveyard looking for him, but when she did dream it was of wandering around Glasgow city centre with her friends from her old school. They were hunting for a specific street, but all they found, one after another, was a succession of dead ends.

Deep beneath the hill in Krakow, in the deepest vault beneath the caves they call the Dragon's Den, Miss Lupescu stumbled and fell.

Silas crouched beside her and cradled Miss Lupescu's head in his hands. There was blood on her face, and some of it was hers.

'You must leave me,' she said. 'Save the boy.' She was halfway now, halfway between grey wolf and woman, but her face was a woman's face.

'No,' said Silas. 'I won't leave you.'

Behind him, Kandar cradled its piglet like a child might hold a doll. The mummy's left wing was shattered, and it would never fly again, but its bearded face was implacable.

'They will come back, Silas,' Miss Lupescu whispered. 'Too soon, the sun will rise.'

'Then,' said Silas, 'we must deal with them before they

are ready to attack. Can you stand?'

'Da. I am one of the Hounds of God,' said Miss Lupescu. 'I will stand.' She lowered her face into the shadows, flexed her fingers. When she raised her head again, it was a wolf's head. She put her front paws down on the rock, and, laboriously, pushed herself up into a standing position: a grey wolf bigger than a bear, her coat and muzzle flecked with blood.

She threw back her head and howled a howl of fury and of challenge. Her lips curled back from her teeth and she lowered her head once more. 'Now,' growled Miss Lupescu. 'We end this.'

Late on Sunday afternoon the telephone rang. Scarlett was sitting downstairs, copying faces from the manga she had been reading on to scrap paper. Her mother picked up the phone.

'Funny, we were just talking about you,' said her mother, although they hadn't been. 'It was wonderful,' her mother continued. 'I had the best time. Honestly, it was no trouble. The chocolates? They were perfect. Just perfect. I told Scarlett to tell you, any time you want a good dinner, you just let me know.' And then, 'Scarlett? Yes, she's here. I'll put her on. *Scarlett?*'

'I'm just here, Mum,' said Scarlett. 'You don't have to shout.' She took the phone. 'Mr Frost?'

'Scarlett?' He sounded excited. 'The. Um. The thing we were talking about. The thing that happened in my house. You can tell this friend of yours that I found out – um, listen, when you said "a friend of yours" did you mean it in the sense of "we're actually talking about you", or is there a real person, if it's not a personal question –'

'I've got a real friend who wants to know,' said Scarlett, amused.

Her mother shot her a puzzled look.

'Tell your friend that I did some digging – not literally, more like rummaging, well, a fair amount of actual looking around – and I think I might have unearthed some very real information. Stumbled over something hidden. Well, not something I think we should spread around . . . I, um. I found things out.'

'Like what?' asked Scarlett.

'Look . . . don't think I'm mad. But, well, as far as I can tell, three people were killed. One of them – the baby, I think – wasn't. It wasn't a family of three, it was a family of four. Only three of them died. Tell him to come and see me, your friend. I'll fill him in.'

'I'll tell him,' said Scarlett. She put down the phone, her heart beating like a snare.

Bod walked down the narrow stone stairs for the first time in six years. His footsteps echoed in the chamber inside the hill.

He reached the bottom of the steps and waited for the Sleer to manifest. And he waited, and waited, but nothing appeared, nothing whispered, nothing moved.

He looked around the chamber, untroubled by the deep darkness, seeing it as the dead see. He walked over to the altar stone set in the floor, where the cup and the brooch and the stone knife sat.

He reached down and touched the edge of the knife. It was sharper than he had expected, and it nicked the skin of his finger.

IT IS THE TREASURE OF THE SLEER, whispered a triple voice, but it sounded smaller than he remembered, more hesitant.

Bod said, 'You're the oldest thing here. I came to talk to you. I want advice.'

A pause. NOTHING COMES TO THE SLEER FOR ADVICE. THE SLEER GUARDS. THE SLEER WAITS.

'I know. But Silas isn't here. And I don't know who else to talk to.'

Nothing was said. Just a silence in reply, that echoed of dust and loneliness.

'I don't know what to do,' Bod said, honestly. 'I think I can find out about who killed my family. Who wanted to kill me. It means leaving the graveyard, though.'

The Sleer said nothing. Smoke-tendrils twined slowly around the inside of the chamber.

'I'm not frightened of dying,' said Bod. 'It's just, so many people I care for have spent so much time keeping me safe, teaching me, protecting me.'

Again, silence.

Then he said, 'I have to do this on my own.'

YES.

'That's all, then. Sorry I bothered you.'

It whispered into Bod's head, then, in a voice that was a sleek insinuating glide, THE SLEER WAS SET TO GUARD THE TREASURE UNTIL OUR MASTER RETURNED. ARE YOU OUR MASTER?

'No,' said Bod.

And then, with a hopeful whine, WILL YOU BE OUR MASTER?

'I'm afraid not.'

IF YOU WERE OUR MASTER, WE COULD HOLD YOU IN OUR COILS FOREVER. IF YOU WERE OUR MASTER, WE WOULD KEEP YOU SAFE AND PROTECT YOU UNTIL THE END OF TIME AND NEVER LET YOU ENDURE THE DANGERS OF THE WORLD.

'I am not your master.'

NO.

Bod felt the Sleer writhing through his mind. It said, THEN FIND YOUR NAME. And his mind was empty, and the room was empty, and Bod was alone.

Bod walked back up the stairs carefully yet quickly. He had come to a decision and needed to act fast, while the decision still burned in his mind.

Scarlett was waiting for him on the bench by the chapel. 'Well?' she said.

'I'll do it. Come on,' he said, and side by side they walked the path down to the graveyard gates.

Number 33 was a tall house, spindly-thin, in the middle of a terraced row. It was red-brick and unmemorable. Bod looked at it uncertainly, wondering why it did not seem familiar, or special. It was only a house, like any other. There was a small concreted space in front of it that wasn't a garden, a green Mini parked on the street. The front door had once been painted a bright blue, but had been dimmed by time and the sun.

'Well?' said Scarlett.

Bod knocked on the door. There was nothing, then a clatter of feet on the stairs from inside, and the door opened to reveal an entrance hall and stairs. Framed in the doorway was a bespectacled man with receding grey hair, who blinked at them, then stuck out his hand at Bod, and smiled nervously, and said, 'You must be Miss Perkins' mysterious friend. Good to meet you.'

'This is Bod,' said Scarlett.

'Bob?'

'Bod. With a D,' she said. 'Bod, this is Mr Frost.'

Bod and Frost shook hands. 'Kettle's on,' said Mr Frost. 'What say we swap information over a cuppa?'

They followed him up the steps to a kitchen, where he poured three mugs of tea, then led them into a small sitting room. 'The house just keeps going up,' he said. 'The toilet's on the next floor up, and my office, then bedrooms above that. Keeps you fit, all the stairs.'

They sat on a large, extremely purple sofa ('It was already here when I came') and they sipped their tea.

Scarlett had worried that Mr Frost would ask Bod lots of questions, but he didn't. He just seemed excited, as if he had identified the lost gravestone of someone famous and desperately wanted to tell the world. He kept moving impatiently in his chair, as if he had something enormous to impart to them and not immediately blurting it out was a physical strain.

Scarlett said, 'So what did you find out?'

Mr Frost said, 'Well, you were right. I mean, this was the house where those people were killed. And it . . . I think the crime was ... well, not exactly hushed up, but forgotten about, let go ... by the authorities.'

'I don't understand,' said Scarlett. 'Murders don't get swept under the carpet.'

'This one was,' said Frost. He drained his tea. 'There are people out there who have influence. It's the only explanation for that, and for what happened to the youngest child ...'

'And what was that?' asked Bod.

'He lived,' said Frost. 'I'm sure of it. But there wasn't a manhunt. A missing toddler normally would be national news. But they, um, they must have squashed it somehow.'

'Who *are* they?' asked Bod.

'The same people who had the family killed.'

'Do you know any more than that?'

'Yes. Well, a little ...' Frost trailed off. 'I'm sorry. I'm. Look. Given what I found. It's all too incredible.'

Scarlett was starting to feel frustrated. 'What was? What did you find?'

Frost looked shamefaced. 'You're right. I'm sorry. Getting into keeping secrets. Not a good idea. Historians don't bury things. We dig them up. Show people. Yes.' He stopped, hesitated, then he said, 'I found a letter. Upstairs. It was hidden under a loose floorboard.' He turned to Bod. 'Young man, would I be correct in assuming your, well, your interest in this business, this dreadful business, is personal?'

Bod nodded.

'I won't ask any more,' said Mr Frost, and he stood up.

236

'Come on,' he said to Bod. 'Not you, though,' to Scarlett, 'not yet. I'll show *him*. And if he says it's all right, I'll show you as well. Deal?'

'Deal,' said Scarlett.

'We won't be long,' said Mr Frost. 'Come on, lad.'

Bod stood up, darted a concerned look at Scarlett. 'It's OK,' she said, and smiled at him as reassuringly as she could. 'I'll wait here for you.'

She watched their shadows as they walked out of the room and up the stairs. She felt nervous, but expectant. She wondered what Bod would learn, and was happy that he would learn it first. It was his story, after all. It was his right.

Out on the stairs, Mr Frost led the way.

Bod looked around as he walked up towards the top of the house, but nothing seemed familiar. It all seemed strange.

'All the way to the very top,' said Mr Frost. They went up another flight of stairs. He said, 'I don't – well, you don't have to answer if you don't want to, but – um, you're the boy, aren't you?'

Bod said nothing.

'Here we are,' said Mr Frost. He turned the key in the door at the top of the house, pushed it open and they went inside.

The room was small, an attic room with a sloping ceiling. Thirteen years before, it had held a cot. It barely held the man and the boy.

'Stroke of luck, really,' said Mr Frost. 'Under my own nose, so to speak.' He crouched down, pulled back the threadbare carpet.

'So you know why my family were murdered?' asked Bod.

Mr Frost said, 'It's all in here.' He reached down to a short length of floorboard and pushed at it until he was able to lever it out. 'This would have been the baby's room,' said Mr Frost, 'I'll show you the … you know, the only thing we don't know is just who did it. Nothing at all. We don't have the tiniest clue.'

'We know he has dark hair,' said Bod, in the room that had once been his bedroom. 'And we know that his name is Jack.'

Mr Frost put his hand down into the empty space where the floorboard had been. 'It's been almost thirteen years,' he said. 'And hair gets thin and goes grey, in thirteen years. But yes, that's right. It's Jack.'

He straightened up. The hand that had been in the hole in the floor was holding a large, sharp knife.

'Now,' said the man Jack. 'Now, boy. Time to finish this.'

Bod stared at him. It was as if Mr Frost had been a coat or a hat the man had been wearing, that he had now discarded. The affable exterior had gone.

The light glinted on the man's spectacles, and on the blade of the knife.

A voice called up to them from further down the stairs – Scarlett's. 'Mr Frost? There's someone knocking at the front door. Should I get it?'

The man Jack only glanced away for a moment, but Bod knew that the moment was all he had, and he Faded, as completely, as utterly as he could. The man Jack looked back to where Bod had been, then stared around the room, puzzlement and rage competing on his face. He took a step further into the room, his head swinging from side to side like an old tiger scenting prey.

'You're here somewhere,' growled the man Jack. 'I can smell you!'

Behind him, the little door to the attic bedroom slammed closed, and as he swung around he heard the key turn in the lock.

The man Jack raised his voice. 'It buys you moments, but it won't stop me, boy,' he called through the locked door. Then added, simply, 'We have unfinished business, you and I.'

Bod threw himself down the stairs, bouncing into the walls, almost tumbling headlong in his rush to reach Scarlett.

'Scarlett!' he said, when he saw her. 'It's him! Come on!'

'It's who? What are you talking about?'

'Him! Frost. He's Jack. He tried to kill me!'

A *bang!* from above as the man Jack kicked at the door.

'But.' Scarlett tried to make sense of what she was hearing, 'But he's *nice.*'

'No,' said Bod, grabbing her hand and pulling her down the stairs, into the hallway. 'No, he's not.'

Scarlett pulled open the front door.

'Ah. Good evening, young lady,' said the man at the door, looking down at her. 'We are looking for Mr Frost. I believe this is his neck of the woods.' He had silver-white hair, and he smelled of cologne.

'Are you friends of his?' she asked.

'Oh yes,' said a smaller man, standing just behind. He had a small black moustache and was the only one of the men to wear a hat.

'Certainly are,' said a third, a younger man, huge and Nordic blond.

'Every man Jack of us,' said the last of the men, wide and bull-like, with a massive head. His skin was brown.

'He. Mr Frost. He had to go out,' she said.

'But his car's here,' said the white-haired man, as the blond one said, 'Who are you, anyway?'

'He's a friend of my mum's,' said Scarlett.

She could see Bod, now, on the other side of the group of men, gesturing frantically to her to leave the men and follow him.

She said, as breezily as she could. 'He just popped out. Popped out for a newspaper. From the corner shop down there.' And she closed the door behind her, stepped around the men and began to walk away.

'Where are you going?' asked the man with the moustache.

'I've got a bus to catch,' she said. Scarlett walked up the hill towards the bus stop and the graveyard, and did not, resolutely did not, look back.

Bod walked beside her. Even to Scarlett he seemed shadowy in the deepening dusk, like something that was almost not there, a shimmer of heat haze, a skittery leaf that for a moment had seemed to be a boy.

'Walk faster,' said Bod. 'They're all looking at you. But don't run.'

'Who are they?' asked Scarlett, quietly.

'I don't know,' said Bod. 'But they all felt weird. Like they weren't properly people. I want to go back and listen to them.'

'Of course they're people,' said Scarlett, and she walked up the hill as fast as she could without actually running, no longer certain that Bod was by her side.

The four men stood at the door to Number 33. 'I don't like this,' said the big man with the bull-neck.

'You don't like this, Mr Tar?' said the white-haired man. 'None of us like it. All wrong. Everything's going wrong.'

'Krakow's gone. They aren't answering. And after Melbourne and Vancouver . . .' said the man with the moustache. 'For all we know, we four are all that's left.'

'Quiet, please, Mr Ketch,' said the white-haired man. 'I'm thinking.'

'Sorry, sir,' said Mr Ketch, and he patted his moustache with one gloved finger, looked up the hill and down again, and whistled through his teeth.

'I think . . . we should go after her,' said the bull-necked man, Mr Tar.

'I think you people should listen to me,' said the white-haired man. 'I said quiet. And what I meant was, *quiet*.'

'Sorry, Mr Dandy,' said the blond man.

They were quiet.

In the silence, they could hear thumping sounds coming from high inside the house.

'I'm going in,' said Mr Dandy. 'Mr Tar, you're with me. Nimble and Ketch, get that girl. Bring her back.'

'Dead or alive?' asked Mr Ketch, with a smug smile.

'Alive, you moron,' said Mr Dandy. 'I want to know what she knows.'

'Maybe she's one of them,' said Mr Tar. 'The ones who done for us in Vancouver and, Melbourne and –'

'Get her,' said Mr Dandy. 'Get her *now*.' The blond man and the hat-and-moustache hurried up the hill.

Mr Dandy and Mr Tar stood outside the door to Number 33.

'Force it,' said Mr Dandy.

Mr Tar put his shoulder against the door and began to lean his weight on it. 'It's reinforced,' he said. 'Protected.'

Mr Dandy said, 'Nothing one Jack can do that another can't fix.' He pulled off his glove, put his hand against the door, muttered something in a language older then English. 'Now try it,' he said.

Tar leaned against the door, grunted and pushed. This time the lock gave and the door swung open.

'Nicely done,' said Mr Dandy.

There was a crashing noise from far above them, up at the top of the house.

The man Jack met them halfway down the stairs. Mr Dandy grinned at him, without any humour but with perfect teeth. 'Hello, Jack Frost,' he said. 'I thought you had the boy.'

'I did,' said the man Jack. 'He got away.'

'Again?' Jack Dandy's smile grew wider and chillier and even more perfect. 'Once is a mistake, Jack. Twice is a disaster.'

'We'll get him,' said the man Jack. 'This ends tonight.'

'It had better,' said Mr Dandy.

'He'll be in the graveyard,' said the man Jack. The three men hurried down the stairs.

The man Jack sniffed the air. He had the scent of the boy in his nostrils, a prickle at the nape of his neck. He felt like all this had happened, years before. He paused, pulled on his long black coat, which had hung in the front hall, incongruous beside Mr Frost's tweed jacket and fawn mackintosh.

The front door was open to the street, and the daylight had almost gone. This time the man Jack knew exactly which way to go. He did not pause, but simply walked out of the house, and hurried up the hill towards the graveyard.

The graveyard gates were closed when Scarlett reached them. Scarlett pulled at them desperately, but the gates were padlocked for the night. And then Bod was beside her. 'Do you know where the key is?' she asked.

'We don't have time,' said Bod. He pushed close to the metal bars. 'Put your arms around me.'

'You what?'

'Just put your arms around me and close your eyes.'

Scarlett stared at Bod, as if daring him to try something, then she held him tightly and screwed her eyes shut. 'OK.'

Bod leaned against the bars of the graveyard gates. They counted as part of the graveyard, and he hoped that his Freedom of the Graveyard might just, possibly, just this time, cover other people too. And then, like smoke, Bod slipped through the bars.

'You can open your eyes,' he said.

She did.

'How did you do that?'

'This is my home,' he said. 'I can do things here.'

The sound of shoes slapping against the pavement, and two men were on the other side of the gates, rattling them, pulling at them.

'Hul-lo,' said Jack Ketch, with a twitch of his moustache, and he smiled at Scarlett through the bars like a rabbit with a secret. He had a black silk cord tied around his left forearm, and now he was tugging at it with his gloved right hand. He pulled it off his arm and into his hand, testing it, running it from hand to hand as if he were about to make a cat's cradle. 'Come on out, girlie. It's all right. No one's going to hurt you.'

'We just need you to answer some questions,' said the big blond man, Mr Nimble. 'We're on official business.' (He lied. There was nothing official about the Jacks of All Trades, although there had been Jacks in governments and in police forces and in other places besides.)

'Run!' said Bod to Scarlett pulling at her hand. She ran.

'Did you see that?' said the Jack they called Ketch.

'What?'

'I saw somebody with her. A boy.'

'The boy?' asked the Jack called Nimble.

'How would I know? Here. Give me a hand up.' The bigger man put his hands out, linked them to make a step, and Jack Ketch's black-clad foot went into it. Lifted up, he scrambled on to the top of the gates and jumped down to the drive, landing on all fours like a frog. He stood up, said, 'Find another way in. I'm going after them.' And he sprinted off up the winding path that led into the graveyard.

Scarlett said, 'Just tell me what we're doing.' Bod was walking fast through the twilit graveyard, but he was not running, not yet.

'How do you mean?'

'I think that man wanted to kill me. Did you see how he was playing with that black cord?'

'I'm sure he does. That man Jack – your Mister Frost – *he* was going to kill me. He's got a knife.'

'He's not *my* Mister Frost. Well, I suppose he is, sort of. Sorry. Where are we going?'

'First we put you somewhere safe. Then I deal with them.'

All around Bod, the inhabitants of the graveyard were waking and gathering, worried and alarmed.

'Bod?' said Caius Pompeius. 'What is happening?'

'Bad people,' said Bod. 'Can our lot keep an eye on them? Let me know where they are at all times. We have to hide Scarlett. Any ideas?'

'The chapel crypt?' said Thackeray Porringer.

'First place they'll look.'

'Who are you talking to?' asked Scarlett, staring at Bod

as if he had gone mad.

Caius Pompeius said, 'Inside the hill?'

Bod thought. 'Yes. Good call. Scarlett, do you remember the place where we found the Indigo Man?'

'Kind of. A dark place. I remember there wasn't anything to be scared of.'

'I'm taking you up there.'

They hurried up the path. Scarlett could tell that Bod was talking to people as he went, but could only hear his side of the conversation. It was like hearing someone talk on a phone. Which reminded her . . .

'My mum's going to go spare,' she said. 'I'm dead.'

'No,' said Bod. 'You're not. Not yet. Not for a long time.' Then, to someone else, 'Two of them, now. Together? OK.'

They reached the Frobisher mausoleum. 'The entrance is behind the bottom coffin on the left,' Bod said. 'If you hear anyone coming and it's not me, go straight down to the very bottom . . . do you have anything to make light?'

'Yeah. A little LED thing on my key ring.'

'Good.'

He pulled open the door to the mausoleum. 'And be careful. Don't trip or anything.'

'Where are you going?' asked Scarlett.

'This is my home,' said Bod. 'I'm going to protect it.'

Scarlett squeezed the LED key ring, and went down on her hands and knees. The space behind the coffin was tight, but she went through the hole into the hill and pulled the coffin back as best she could. In the dim LED light she could see stone steps. She stood upright, and, hand on the wall, walked down three steps, then stopped and sat, hoping that Bod knew what he was doing, and she waited.

Bod said, 'Where are they now?'

His father said, 'One fellow's up by the Egyptian Walk, looking for you. His friend's waiting down by the alley wall. Three others are on their way over, climbing up the alley wall on all they big bins.'

'I wish Silas was here. He'd make short work of them. Or Miss Lupescu.'

'You don't need them,' said Mr Owens encouragingly.

'Where's Mum?'

'Down by the alley wall.'

'Tell her I've hidden Scarlett in the back of the Frobishers' place. Ask her to keep an eye on her if anything happens to me.'

Bod ran through the darkened graveyard. The only way into the north-west part of the graveyard was through the Egyptian Walk. And to get there he would have to go past the little man with the black silk rope. A man who was looking for him, and who wanted him dead . . .

He was Nobody Owens, he told himself. He was a part of the graveyard. He would be fine.

He nearly missed the little man – the Jack called Ketch – as he hurried into the Egyptian Walk. The man was almost part of the shadows.

Bod breathed in, Faded as deeply as he could, and moved past the man like dust blown on an evening breeze.

He walked down the green-hung length of the

Egyptian Walk, and then, with an effort of will, he became as obvious as he could, and kicked at a pebble.

He saw the shadow by the arch detach itself and come after him, almost as silent as the dead.

Bod pushed through the trailing ivy that blocked the end of the Walk and into the north-west corner of the graveyard. He would have to time this just right, he knew. Too fast and the man would lose him, yet if he moved too slowly a black silk rope would wrap itself around his neck, taking his breath with it and all his tomorrows.

He pushed noisily through the tangle of ivy, disturbing one of the graveyard's many foxes, which sprinted off into the undergrowth. It was a jungle here, of fallen headstones and headless statues, of trees and holly bushes, of slippery piles of half-rotted fallen leaves, but it was a jungle that Bod had explored since he had been old enough to walk and to wander.

Now he was hurrying carefully, stepping from root-tangle of ivy to stone to earth, confident that this was his graveyard. He could feel the graveyard itself trying to hide him, to protect him, to make him vanish, and he fought it, worked to be seen.

He saw Nehemiah Trot, and hesitated.

'Hola, young Bod!' called the poet. 'I hear that excitement is the master of the hour, that you fling yourself through these dominions like a comet across the firmament. What's the word, good Bod?'

'Stand there,' said Bod. 'Just where you are. Look back the way I came. Tell me when he comes close.'

Bod skirted the ivy-covered Carstairs' grave, and then

he stood, panting as if out of breath, with his back to his pursuer.

And he waited. It was only for a few seconds, but it felt like a small forever.

('He's here, lad,' said Nehemiah Trot. 'About twenty paces behind you.')

The Jack called Ketch saw the boy in front of him. He pulled his black silk cord tight between his hands. It had been stretched around many necks, over the years, and had been the end of every one of the people it had embraced. It was very soft and very strong and invisible to X-rays.

Ketch's moustache moved, but nothing else. He had his prey in his sight, and did not want to startle it. He began to advance, silent as a shadow.

The boy straightened up.

Jack Ketch darted forward, his polished black shoes almost soundless on the leaf-mould.

('He comes, lad!' called Nehemiah Trot.)

The boy turned around, and Jack Ketch made a leap towards him –

And Mr Ketch felt the world tumbling away beneath him. He grabbed at the world with one gloved hand, but tumbled down and down into the old grave, all of twenty feet, before crash-landing on Mr Carstairs' coffin, splintering the coffin-lid and his ankle at the same time.

'That's one,' said Bod, calmly, although he felt anything but calm.

'Elegantly accomplished,' said Nehemiah Trot. 'I shall compose an Ode. Would you like to stay and listen?'

'No time,' said Bod. 'Where are the other men?'

Euphemia Horsfall said, 'Three of them are on the south-western path, heading up the hill.'

Tom Sands said, 'And there's another. Right now he's just walking around the chapel. He's the one who's been all around the graveyard for the last month. But there's something different about him.'

Bod said, 'Keep an eye on the man in with Mr Carstairs – and please apologise to Mr Carstairs for me . . .'

He ducked under a pine branch and loped around the hill, on the paths when it suited him, off the paths, jumping from monument to stone, when that was quicker.

He passed the old apple tree. 'There's four of them, still,' said a tart female voice. 'Four of them, and all killers. And the rest of them won't all fall into open graves to oblige you.'

'Hullo, Liza. I thought you were angry at me.'

'I might be and I mightn't,' she said, nothing more than a voice. 'But I'm not going to let them cut you up, nohow.'

'Then trip them for me, trip them and confuse them and slow them down. Can you do that?'

'While you runs away again? Nobody Owens, why don't you just Fade, and hide in your mam's nice tomb, where they'll never find you, and soon enough Silas will be back to take care of them –'

'Maybe he will and maybe he won't,' said Bod. 'I'll meet you by the lightning tree.'

'I am still not talking to you,' said Liza Hempstock's voice, proud as a peacock and pert as a sparrow.

'Actually, you are. I mean, we're talking right now.'

'Only during this emergency. After that, not a word.'

Bod made for the lightning tree, an oak that had been burned by lightning twenty years ago and now was nothing more than a blackened limb clutching at the sky.

He had an idea. It was not fully formed. It depended on whether he could remember Miss Lupescu's lessons, remember everything he had seen and heard as a child.

It was harder to find the grave than he had expected, even looking for it, but he found it – an ugly grave tipped at an odd angle, its stone topped by a headless, water-stained angel that had the appearance of a gargantuan fungus. It was only when he touched it and felt the chill, that he knew it for certain.

He sat down on the grave, forced himself to become entirely visible.

'You've not Faded,' said Liza's voice. 'Anyone could find you.'

'Good,' said Bod. 'I want them to find me.'

'More know Jack Fool than Jack Fool knows,' said Liza.

The moon was rising. It was huge now and low in the sky. Bod wondered if it would be overdoing it if he began to whistle.

'I can see him!'

A man ran towards him, tripping and stumbling, two other men close behind.

Bod was aware of the dead clustered around them, watching the scene, but he forced himself to ignore them. He made himself more comfortable on the ugly grave. He felt like the bait in a trap, and it was not a good feeling.

The bull-like man was the first to reach the grave, followed closely by the man with the white hair who had done all the talking, and the tall blond man.

Bod stayed where he was.

The man with the white hair said, 'Ah. The elusive Dorian boy, I presume. Astonishing. There's our Jack Frost hunting the whole world over, and here you are, just where he left you, thirteen years ago.'

Bod said, 'That man killed my family.'

'Indeed he did.'

'Why?'

'Does it matter? You're never going to tell anyone.'

'Then it's no skin off your nose to tell me, is it?'

The white-haired man barked a laugh. 'Hah! Funny boy. What I want to know is, how have you lived in a graveyard for thirteen years without anyone catching wise?'

'I'll answer your question if you answer mine.'

The bull-necked man said, 'You don't talk to Mr Dandy like that, little snot! I split you, I will –'

The white-haired man took another step closer to the grave. 'Hush, Jack Tar. All right. An answer for an answer. We – my friends and I – are members of a fraternal organisation, known as the Jacks of All Trades, or the Knaves, or by other names. We go back an extremely long way. We know...we remember things that most people have forgotten. The Old Knowledge.'

Bod said, 'Magic. You know a little magic.'

The man nodded agreeably. 'If you want to call it that. But it's a very specific sort of magic. There's a magic you take from death. Something leaves the world, something else comes into it.'

'You killed my family for – for what? For magic powers? That's ridiculous.'

'No. We killed you for protection. Long time ago, one of our people – this was back in Egypt, in pyramid days – he foresaw that one day, there would be a child born who would walk the borderland between the living and the dead. That if this child grew to adulthood it would mean the end of our Order and all we stand for. We had people casting nativities before London was a village, we had your family in our sights before New Amsterdam became New York. And we sent what we thought was the best and the sharpest and the most dangerous of all the Jacks to deal with you. To do it properly, so we could take all the bad Juju and make it work for us instead, and keep everything tickety-boo for another five thousand years. Only he didn't.'

Bod looked at the three men.

'So where is he? Why isn't he here?'

The blond man said, 'We can take care of you. He's got a good nose on him, has our Jack Frost. He's on the trail of your little girlfriend. Can't leave any witnesses. Not to something like this.'

Bod leaned forward, dug his hands into the wild weed-grass that grew on the unkempt grave.

'Come and get me,' was all that he said.

The blond man grinned, the bull-necked man lunged,

and – yes – even Mr Dandy took several steps forward.

Bod pushed his fingers as deeply as he could into the grass, and he pulled his lips back from his teeth, and he said three words in a language that was already ancient before the Indigo Man was born.

'Skagh! Thegh! Khavagah!'

He opened the ghoul-gate.

The grave swung up like a trapdoor. In the deep hole below the door Bod could see stars, a darkness filled with glimmering lights.

The bullman, Mr Tar, at the edge of the hole, could not stop, and stumbled, surprised, into the darkness.

Mr Nimble jumped towards Bod, his arms extended, leaping over the hole. Bod watched as the man stopped in the air at the zenith of his spring, and hung there for a moment, before he was sucked through the ghoul-gate, down and down.

Mr Dandy stood at the edge of the ghoul-gate, on a lip of stone and looked into the darkness beneath him. Then he raised his eyes to Bod, and thin-lipped, he smiled.

'I don't know what you just did,' said Mr Dandy. 'But it didn't work.' He pulled his gloved hand out of his pocket, holding a gun, pointed directly at Bod. 'I should have just done this thirteen years ago,' said Mr Dandy. 'You can't trust other people. If it's important, you have to do it yourself.'

A desert wind came up from the open ghoul-gate, hot and dry, with grit in it. Bod said, 'There's a desert down there. If you look for water, you should find some. There's things to eat if you look hard, but don't antagonise the night-gaunts. Avoid Ghûlheim. The ghouls might wipe your memories and make you into one of them, or they might wait until you've rotted down, and then eat you. Either way, you can do better.'

The gun barrel did not waver. Mr Dandy said, 'Why are you telling me this?'

Bod pointed across the graveyard. 'Because of them,' he said, and as he said it, as Mr Dandy glanced away, only for a moment, Bod Faded. Mr Dandy's eyes flickered away and back, but Bod was no longer by the broken statue. From deep in the hole something called, like the lonely wail of a night bird.

Mr Dandy looked around, his forehead a slash, his body a mass of indecision and rage. 'Where are you?' he growled. 'The deuce take you! Where *are* you?'

He thought he heard a voice say, 'Ghoul-gates are made to be opened and then closed again. You can't leave them open. They want to close.'

The lip of the hole shuddered and shook. Mr Dandy had been in an earthquake once, years before, in Bangladesh. It felt like that: the earth juddered, and Mr Dandy fell, would have fallen into the darkness, but he caught hold of the fallen headstone, threw his arms about it and locked on. He did not know what was beneath him, only that he had no wish to find out.

The earth shook, and he felt the headstone begin to shift, beneath his weight.

He looked up. The boy was there, looking down at him curiously.

'I'm going to let the gate close now,' he said. 'I think if

255

you keep holding on to that thing, it might close on you, and crush you, or it might just absorb you and make you into part of the gate. Don't know. But I'm giving you a chance, more than you ever gave my family.'

A ragged judder. Mr Dandy looked up into the boy's grey eyes, and he swore. Then he said, 'You can't ever escape us. We're the Jacks of All Trades. We're everywhere. It's not over.'

'It is for you,' said Bod. 'The end of your people and all you stand for. Like your man in Egypt predicted. You didn't kill me. You were everywhere. Now it's all over.' Then Bod smiled. 'That's what Silas is doing, isn't it? That's where he is.'

Mr Dandy's face confirmed everything that Bod had suspected.

And what Mr Dandy might have said to that Bod would never know, because the man let go of the headstone and tumbled slowly down into the open ghoul-gate.

Bod said, '*Wegh Khârados*.'

The ghoul-gate was a grave once again, nothing more.

Something was tugging at his sleeve. Fortinbras Bartleby looked up at him. 'Bod! The man by the chapel. He's going up the hill.'

The man Jack followed his nose. He had left the others, not least because the stink of Jack Dandy's cologne made finding anything subtler impossible.

He could not find the boy by scent. Not here. The boy smelled like the graveyard. But the girl smelled like her mother's house, like the dab of perfume she had touched to

256

her neck before school that morning. She smelled like a victim too, like fear-sweat, thought Jack, like his quarry. And wherever she was, the boy would be too, sooner or later.

His hand closed around the handle of his knife and he walked up the hill. He was almost at the top of the hill when it occurred to him – a hunch he knew was a truth – that Jack Dandy and the rest of them were gone. *Good*, he thought. *There's always room at the top.* The man Jack's own rise through the Organisation had slowed and stopped after he had failed to kill all of the Dorian family. It was as if he had no longer been trusted.

Now, soon, everything would change.

At the top of the hill the man Jack lost the girl's scent. He knew she was near.

He retraced his steps, almost casually, caught her perfume again about fifty feet away, beside a small mausoleum with a closed metal gateway. He pulled on the gate and it swung wide.

Her scent was strong now. He could smell that she was afraid. He pulled down the coffins, one by one, from their shelves, and let them clatter on to the ground, shattering the old wood, spilling their contents on to the mausoleum floor. No, she was not hiding in any of those...

Then where?

He examined the wall. Solid. He went down on his hands and knees, pulled the last coffin out and reached back. His hand found an opening...

'Scarlett,' he called, trying to remember how he would

257

have called her name when he was Mr Frost, but he could not even find that part of himself any longer: he was the man Jack now, and that was all he was. On his hands and knees he crawled through the hole in the wall.

When Scarlett heard the crashing noise from above, she made her way, carefully, down the steps, her left hand touching the wall, her right hand holding the little LED key ring, which cast just enough light to allow her to see where she was placing her feet. She made it to the bottom of the stone steps and edged back in the open chamber, her heart thumping.

She was scared: scared of nice Mr Frost and his scarier friends; scared of this room and its memories; even, if she were honest, a little afraid of Bod. He was no longer a quiet boy with a mystery, a link to her childhood. He was something different, something not quite human.

She thought, I *wonder what Mum's thinking right now. She'll be phoning Mr Frost's house over and over to find out when I'm going to get back.* She thought, *If I get out of this alive, I'm going to force her to get me a phone. It's ridiculous. I'm the only person in my year who doesn't have her own phone, practically.*

She thought, *I miss my mum.*

She had not thought anyone human could move that silently through the dark, but a gloved hand closed upon her mouth, and a voice that was only barely recognisable as Mr Frost's said, without emotion, 'Do anything clever – do anything at all – and I will cut your throat. Nod if you understand me.'

Scarlett nodded.

*

Bod saw the chaos on the floor of the Frobisher mausoleum, the fallen coffins, with their contents scattered across over the aisle. There were many Frobishers and Frobyshers, and several Pettyfers, all in various states of upset and consternation.

'He is already down there,' said Ephraim.

'Thank you,' said Bod. He clambered through the hole into the inside of the hill, and he went down the stairs.

Bod saw as the dead see: he saw the steps, and he saw the chamber at the bottom. And when he got halfway down the steps, he saw the man Jack holding Scarlett. He had her arm twisted up behind her back, and a large, wicked, boning-knife at her neck.

The man Jack looked up in the darkness.

'Hello, boy,' he said.

Bod said nothing. He concentrated on his Fade, took another step.

'You think I can't see you,' said the man Jack. 'And you're right. I can't. Not really. But I can smell your fear. And I can hear you move and hear you breathe. And now that I know about your clever vanishing trick, I can *feel* you. Say something now. Say it so I can hear it, or I start to cut little pieces out of the young lady. Do you understand me?'

'Yes,' said Bod, his voice echoing in the chamber room. 'I understand.'

'Good,' said Jack. 'Now, come here. Let's have a little chat.'

Bod began to walk down the steps. He concentrated

on the Fear, on raising the level of panic in the room, of making the Terror something tangible . . .

'Stop that,' said the man Jack. 'Whatever it is you're doing. Don't do it.'

Bod let it go.

'You think,' said Jack, 'that you can do your little magics on me? Do you know what I am, boy?'

Bod said, 'You're a Jack. You killed my family. And you should have killed me.'

Jack raised an eyebrow. He said, 'I should have killed you?'

'Oh yes. The old man said that if you let me grow to adulthood your Order would be destroyed. I did. You failed and you lost.'

'My Order goes back before Babylon. Nothing can harm it.'

'They didn't tell you, did they?' Bod was standing five paces from the man Jack. 'Those four, they were the last of the Jacks. What was it . . . Krakow and Vancouver and Melbourne. All gone.'

Scarlett said, 'Please. Bod. Make him let go of me.'

'Don't worry,' said Bod, with a calm he did not feel. He said to Jack, 'There's no point in hurting her. There's no point in killing me. Don't you understand? There isn't even an Order of Jacks of All Trades. Not any more.'

Jack nodded thoughtfully. 'If this is true,' said Jack, 'and if I am now a Jack-all-alone, then I have an excellent reason for killing you both.'

Bod said nothing.

'Pride,' said the man Jack. 'Pride in my work. Pride in

finishing what I began.' And then he said, 'What are you doing?'

Bod's hair prickled. He could feel a smoke-tendril presence twining through the room. He said, 'It's not me. It's the Sleer. It guards the treasure that's buried here.'

'Don't lie.'

Scarlett said, 'He's not lying. It's true.'

Jack said, 'True? Buried treasure? Don't make me –'

THE SLEER GUARDS THE TREASURE FOR THE MASTER.

'Who said that?' asked the man Jack, looking around.

'You heard it?' asked Bod, puzzled.

'I heard it,' said Jack. 'Yes.'

Scarlett said, 'I didn't hear anything.'

The man Jack said, 'What is this place, boy? Where are we?'

Before Bod could speak, the Sleer's voice spoke, echoing through the chamber, THIS IS THE PLACE OF THE TREASURE. THIS IS THE PLACE OF POWER. THIS IS WHERE THE SLEER GUARDS AND WAITS FOR OUR MASTER TO RETURN.

Bod said, 'Jack?'

The man Jack tilted his head on one side. He said, 'It's good to hear my name in your mouth, boy. If you'd used it before, I could have found you sooner.'

'Jack. What was my real name? What did my family call me?'

'Why should that matter to you now?'

Bod said, 'The Sleer told me to find my name. What was it?'

Jack said, 'Let me see. Was it Peter? Or Paul? Or Roderick – you look like a Roderick. Maybe you were a

Stephen . . .' He was playing with the boy.

'You might as well tell me. You're going to kill me anyway,' said Bod. Jack shrugged and nodded in the darkness, as if to say *obviously*.

'I want you to let the girl go,' said Bod. 'Let Scarlett go.'

Jack peered into the darkness, then said, 'That's an altar stone, isn't it?'

'I suppose so.'

'And a knife? And a cup? And a brooch?'

He was smiling now, in the darkness. Bod could see it on his face: a strange, delighted smile that seemed out of place on that face, a smile of discovery and of understanding. Scarlett couldn't see anything but a blackness that sometimes erupted in flashes inside her eyeballs, but she could hear the delight in Jack's voice.

The man Jack said, 'So the Brotherhood is over and the Convocation is at an end. And yet, if there are no more Jacks of All Trades but me, what does it matter? There can be a new Brotherhood, more powerful than the last.'

POWER, echoed the Sleer.

'This is perfect,' said the man Jack. 'Look at us. We are in a place for which my people have hunted for thousands of years, with everything necessary for the ceremony waiting for us. It makes you believe in Providence, doesn't it? Or in the massed prayers of all the Jacks who have gone before us, that at our lowest ebb, we are given this.'

Bod could feel the Sleer listening to Jack's words, could feel a low susurrus of excitement building in the chamber.

The man Jack said, 'I am going to put out my hand,

boy. Scarlett, my knife is still at your throat – do not try to run when I let go of you. Boy, you will place the cup and the knife and the brooch in my hand.'

THE TREASURE OF THE SLEER, whispered the triple voice. IT ALWAYS COMES BACK. WE GUARD IT FOR THE MASTER.

Bod bent down, took the objects from the altar stone, put them in Jack's open, gloved hand. Jack grinned.

'Scarlett. I am going to release you. When I take the knife away, I want you to lie, face down, on the ground, with your hands behind your head. Move or try anything, and I will kill you painfully. Do you understand?'

She gulped. Her mouth was dry, but she took one shaky step forward. Her right arm, which had been twisted up to the small of her back, was now numb, and she felt only pins and needles in her shoulder. She lay down, her cheek resting on the packed earth.

We are dead, she thought, and it was not even tinged with emotion. It felt as if she were watching something happening to other people, a surreal drama that had turned into a game of Murder in the Dark. She heard the noise of Jack taking hold of Bod . . .

Bod's voice said, 'Let her go.'

The man Jack's voice: 'If you do everything I say, I won't kill her. I won't even hurt her.'

'I don't believe you. She can identify you.'

'No.' The adult voice seemed certain. 'She can't.' And then it said, 'Ten thousand years, and the knife is still sharp . . .' The admiration in the voice was palpable. 'Boy. Go and kneel on that altar stone. Hands behind your back. Now.'

IT HAS BEEN SO LONG, said the Sleer, but all Scarlett heard was a slithering noise, as if of enormous coils winding around the chamber.

But the man Jack heard. 'You want to know your name, boy, before I spill your blood on the stone?'

Bod felt the cold of the knife at his neck. And in that moment, Bod understood. Everything slowed. Everything came into focus. 'I know my name,' he said. 'I'm Nobody Owens. That's who I am.' And, kneeling on the cold altar stone, it all seemed very simple.

'Sleer,' he said, to the chamber. 'Do you still want a master?'

THE SLEER GUARDS THE TREASURE UNTIL THE MASTER RETURNS.

'Well,' said Bod, 'haven't you finally found the master you've been looking for?'

He could sense the Sleer writhing and expanding, hear a noise like the scratching of a thousand dead twigs, as if something huge and muscular were snaking its way around the inside of the chamber. And then, for the first time, Bod saw the Sleer. Afterwards, he was never able to describe what he had seen: something huge, yes; something with the body of an enormous snake, but with the head of a what . . .? There were three of them: three heads, three necks. The faces were dead, as if someone had constructed dolls from parts of the corpses of humans and of animals. The faces were covered in purple patterns, tattooed in swirls of indigo, turning the dead faces into strange, expressive monstrous things.

The faces of the Sleer nuzzled the air about Jack tentatively, as if they wanted to stroke or caress him.

'What's happening?' said Jack. 'What is it? What does it do?'

'It's called the Sleer. It guards the place. It needs a master to tell it what to do,' said Bod.

Jack hefted the flint knife in his hand. 'Beautiful,' he said to himself. And then, 'Of course. It's been waiting for me. And yes. Obviously, I *am* its new master.'

The Sleer encircled the interior of the chamber. MASTER? it said, like a dog who had waited patiently for too long. It said MASTER? again, as if testing the word to see how it tasted. And it tasted good, so it said one more time, with a sigh of delight and of longing: MASTER . . .

Jack looked down at Bod. 'Thirteen years ago I missed you, and now, now we are reunited. The end of one Order. The beginning of another. Goodbye, boy.' With one hand he lowered the knife to the boy's throat. The other hand held the goblet.

'Bod,' said Bod. 'Not Boy. Bod.' He raised his voice. 'Sleer,' he said. 'What will you do with your new Master?'

The Sleer sighed. WE WILL PROTECT HIM UNTIL THE END OF TIME. THE SLEER WILL HOLD HIM IN ITS COILS FOREVER AND NEVER LET HIM ENDURE THE DANGERS OF THE WORLD.

'Then protect him,' said Bod. 'Now.'

'I am your Master. You will obey me,' said the man Jack.

THE SLEER HAS WAITED SO LONG, said the triple voice of the Sleer, triumphantly. SO LONG A TIME. It began to loop its huge, lazy coils around the man Jack.

The man Jack dropped the goblet. Now he had a knife

in each hand – a flint knife, and a knife with a black bone handle – and he said, 'Get back! Keep away from me! Don't get any closer!' He slashed out with the knife, as the Sleer twined about him, and in a huge crushing movement, engulfed the man Jack in its coils.

Bod ran over to Scarlett, and helped her up. 'I want to see,' she said. 'I want to see what's happening.' She pulled out her LED light, and turned it on . . .

What Scarlett saw was not what Bod saw. She did not see the Sleer, and that was a mercy. She saw the man Jack, though. She saw the fear on his face, which made him look like Mr Frost had once looked. In his terror he was once again the nice man who had driven her home. He was floating in the air, five, then ten feet above the ground, slashing wildly at the air with two knives, trying to stab something she could not see, in a display that was obviously having no effect.

Mr Frost, the man Jack, whoever he was, was pulled away from them, forced back until he was spread-eagled, arms and legs wide and flailing, against the side of the chamber wall.

It seemed to Scarlett that Mr Frost was being pulled through the wall, pulled into the rock, was being swallowed up by it. Now there was nothing visible but a face. He was shouting wildly, desperately, shouting at Bod to call the thing off, to save him, please, please . . . and then the man's face was pulled through the wall, and the voice was silenced.

Bod walked back to the altar stone. He picked up the stone knife, and the goblet, and the brooch, from the ground and he replaced them where they belonged. He left the black metal knife where it fell.

Scarlett said, 'I thought you said the Sleer couldn't hurt people. I thought all it could do was frighten us.'

'Yes,' said Bod. 'But it wanted a master to protect. It told me so.'

Scarlett said, 'You mean you knew. You *knew* that would happen . . .'

'Yes. I hoped it would.'

He helped her up the steps and out into the chaos of the Frobisher mausoleum. 'I'll need to clean this all up,' said Bod, casually. Scarlett tried not to look at the things on the floor.

They stepped out into the graveyard. Scarlett said, dully, once more, 'You knew that would happen.'

This time Bod said nothing.

She looked at him as if unsure of what she was looking at. 'So you knew. That the Sleer would take him. Was *that* why you hid me down there? Was it? What was I, then, *bait*?'

Bod said, 'It wasn't like that.' Then he said, 'We're still alive, aren't we? And he won't trouble us any longer.'

Scarlett could feel the anger and the rage welling up inside her. The fear had gone, and now all she was left with was the need to lash out, to shout. She fought the urge. 'And what about those other men? Did you kill them too?'

'I didn't kill anyone.'

'Then where are they?'

'One of them's at the bottom of a deep grave, with a

267

broken ankle. The other three are, well, they're a long way away.'

'You didn't kill them?'

'Of course not.' Bod said, 'This is my home. Why would I want them hanging around here for the rest of time?' Then, 'Look, it's OK. I dealt with them.'

Scarlett took a step away from him. She said, 'You aren't a person. People don't behave like you. You're as bad as he was. You're a monster.'

Bod felt the blood drain from his face. After everything he had been through that night, after everything that had happened, this was somehow the hardest thing to take. 'No,' he said. 'It wasn't like that.'

Scarlett began to back away from Bod.

She took one step, two steps, and was about to flee, to turn and run madly, desperately away through the moonlit graveyard, when a tall man in black velvet put a hand on her arm, and said, 'I am afraid you do Bod an injustice. But you will undoubtedly be happier if you remember none of this. So let us walk together, you and I, and discuss what has happened to you over the last few days, and what it might be wise for you to remember, and what it might be better for you to forget.'

Bod said, 'Silas. You can't. You can't make her forget me.'

'It will be safest that way,' said Silas, simply. 'For her, if not for all of us.'

'Don't – don't I get a say in this?' asked Scarlett.

Silas said nothing. Bod took a step towards Scarlett, said, 'Look, it's over. I know it was hard. But. We did it. You and me. We beat them.'

Her head was shaking gently, as if she were denying everything she saw, everything she was experiencing.

She looked up at Silas, and said only, 'I want to go home. Please?'

Silas nodded. He walked, with the girl, down the path that would eventually lead them both out of the graveyard. Bod stared at Scarlett as she walked away, hoping that she would turn and look back, that she would smile or just look at him without fear in her eyes. But Scarlett did not turn. She simply walked away.

Bod went back into the mausoleum. He had to do something, so he began to pick up the fallen coffins, to remove the debris, and to replace the tangle of tumbled bones into the coffins, disappointed to discover that none of the many Frobishers and Frobyshers and Pettyfers gathered around to watch seemed to be quite certain whose bones belonged in which container.

A man brought Scarlett home. Later, Scarlett's mother could not remember quite what he had told her, although disappointingly, she had learned that that nice Jay Frost had unavoidably been forced to leave town.

The man talked with them, in the kitchen, about their lives and their dreams, and by the end of the conversation Scarlett's mother had somehow decided that they would be returning to Glasgow: Scarlett would be happy to be near her father, and to see her old friends again.

Silas left the girl and her mother talking in the kitchen, discussing the challenges of moving back to

Scotland, with Noona promising to buy Scarlett a phone of her own. They barely remembered that Silas had ever been there, which was the way he liked it.

Silas returned to the graveyard and found Bod sitting in the amphitheatre by the obelisk, his face set.

'How is she?'

'I took her memories,' said Silas. 'They will return to Glasgow. She has friends there.'

'How could you make her forget me?'

Silas said, 'People want to forget the impossible. It makes their world safer.'

Bod said, 'I liked her.'

'I'm sorry.'

Bod tried to smile, but he could not find a smile inside himself. 'The men . . . they spoke about trouble they were having in Krakow and . . . and Melbourne and Vancouver. That was you, wasn't it?'

'I was not alone,' said Silas.

'Miss Lupescu?' said Bod. Then, seeing the expression on his guardian's face. 'Is she all right?'

Silas shook his head, and for a moment his face was terrible for Bod to behold. 'She fought bravely. She fought for you, Bod.'

Bod said, 'The Sleer has the man Jack. Three of the others went through the ghoul-gate. There's one injured but still alive at the bottom of the Carstairs' grave.'

Silas said, 'He is the last of the Jacks. I will need to talk to him, then, before sunrise.'

The wind that blew across the graveyard was cold, but neither the man nor the boy seemed to feel it.

Bod said, 'She was scared of me.'

'Yes.'

'But why? I saved her life. I'm not a bad person. And I'm just like her. I'm alive too.' Then he said, 'How did Miss Lupescu fall?'

'Bravely,' said Silas. 'In battle. Protecting others.'

Bod's eyes were dark. 'You could have brought her back here. Buried her here. Then I could have talked to her.'

Silas said, 'That was not an option.'

Bod felt his eyes stinging. He said, 'She used to call me "Nimini". No one will ever call me that again.'

Silas said, 'Shall we go and get food for you?'

'We? You want me to come with you? Out of the grave-yard?'

Silas said, 'No one is trying to kill you. Not right now. There are a lot of things they are not going to be doing, not any longer. So, yes. What would you like to eat?'

Bod thought about saying that he wasn't hungry, but that simply was not true. He felt a little sick, and a little lightheaded, and he was starving. 'Pizza?' he suggested.

They walked through the graveyard, down to the gates. As Bod walked, he saw the inhabitants of the grave-yard, but they let the boy and his guardian pass among them without a word. They only watched.

Bod tried to thank them for their help, to call out his gratitude, but the dead said nothing.

The lights of the pizza restaurant were bright, brighter than Bod was comfortable with. He and Silas sat near the back, and Silas showed him how to use a menu, how to order food. (Silas ordered a glass of water and a small salad for himself, which he pushed around the bowl with his fork but never actually put to his lips.)

Bod ate his pizza with his fingers and enthusiasm. He did not ask questions. Silas would talk in his own time, or he would not.

Silas said, 'We had known of them ... of the Jacks ... for a long, long time, but we knew of them only from the results of their activities. We suspected there was an organisation behind it, but they hid too well. And then they came after you, and they killed your family. And, slowly, I was able to follow their trail.'

'Is *we* you and Miss Lupescu?' asked Bod.

'Us and others like us.'

'The Honour Guard,' said Bod.

'How did you hear about –' said Silas. Then, 'No matter. *Little pitchers have big ears*, as they say. Yes. The Honour Guard.' Silas picked up his glass of water. He put the water glass to his lips, moistened them, then put it down on the polished black table-top.

The surface of the table-top was almost mirrored, and, had anyone cared to look, they might have observed that the tall man had no reflection.

Bod said, 'So. Now you're done ... done with all this. Are you going to stay?'

'I gave my word,' said Silas. 'I am here until you are grown.'

'I'm grown,' said Bod.

'No,' said Silas. 'Almost. Not yet.'

He put a ten-pound note down on the table-top.

'That girl,' said Bod. 'Scarlett. Why was she so scared of me, Silas?'

But Silas said nothing, and the question hung in the air as the man and the youth walked out of the bright pizza restaurant into the waiting darkness; and soon enough they were swallowed by the night.

There was a passport in his bag, money in his pocket.

CHAPTER 8

Leavings and Partings

Sometimes he could no longer see the dead. It had begun a month or two previously, in April or in May. At first it had only happened occasionally, but now it seemed to be happening more and more.

The world was changing.

Bod wandered over to the north-western part of the graveyard, to the tangle of ivy that hung from a yew tree and half-blocked the far exit from the Egyptian Walk. He saw a red fox and a large black cat with a white collar and paws, who sat conversing together in the middle of the path. At Bod's approach they looked up, startled, then fled into the undergrowth, as if they had been caught conspiring.

'Odd,' he thought. He had known that fox since it had been a cub, and the cat had prowled through the graveyard for as long as Bod could remember. They knew him. If they were feeling friendly, they even let him pet them.

Bod started to slip through the ivy but he found his way blocked. He bent down, pushed the ivy out of the way and squeezed through. He walked down the path carefully, avoiding the ruts and holes until he reached the impressive stone that marked the final resting place of Alonso Tomás García Jones (1837–1905, *Traveller Lay Down Thy Staff*).

Bod had been coming down here every few days for several months: Alonso Jones had been all over the world, and he took great pleasure in telling Bod stories of his travels. He would begin by saying, 'Nothing interesting has ever happened to me,' then would add, gloomily, 'and I have told you all my tales.' And then his eyes would flash, and he would remark, 'Except . . . did I ever tell you about . . .' And whatever the next words were – 'the time I had to escape from Moscow?' or 'the time I lost an Alaskan gold mine, worth a fortune?' or 'the cattle stampede on the pampas?' – Bod would always shake his head and look expectant and soon enough his head would be swimming with tales of derring-do and high adventure, tales of beautiful maidens kissed, of evil-doers shot with pistols or fought with swords, of bags of gold, of diamonds as big as the tip of your thumb, of lost cities and of vast mountains, of steam trains and clipper ships, of oceans, deserts, tundra.

Bod walked over to the pointed stone – tall, carved with upside-down torches, and he waited, but saw no one. He called to Alonso Jones, even knocked on the side of the stone, but there was no response. Bod leaned down, to push his head into the grave and call his friend, but instead of his head slipping through the solid matter like a shadow passing through a deeper shadow, his head met the ground with a hard and painful thump. He called again, but saw nothing and no one, and, carefully, he made his way out of the tangle of greenery and of grey stones and back to the path. Three magpies perched in a hawthorn tree took wing as he passed them.

He did not see another soul until he reached the graveyard's south-western slope, where the familiar shape of Mother Slaughter, tiny in her high bonnet and her cloak, could be seen, walking between the gravestones, head bent, looking at wildflowers.

'Here, boy!' she called. 'There's nasturshalums growing wild over here. Why don't you pick some for me, and put them over by my stone.'

So Bod picked the red and yellow nasturtiums, and he carried them over to Mother Slaughter's headstone, so cracked and worn and weathered that all it said now was:

LAUGH

which had puzzled the local historians for over a hundred years. He put down the flowers in front of the stone, respectfully.

Mother Slaughter smiled at him. 'You're a good lad. I don't know what we'll do without you.'

'Thank you,' said Bod. Then, 'Where is everyone? You're the first person I've seen tonight.'

Mother Slaughter peered at him sharply. 'What did you do to your forehead?' she asked.

'I bumped it, on Mr Jones's grave. It was solid. I . . .'

But Mother Slaughter was pursing her lips and tilting her head. Bright old eyes scrutinised Bod from beneath her bonnet. 'I called you *boy*, didn't I? But time passes in the blink of an eye, and it's a young man you are now, isn't it? How old are you?'

'About fifteen, I think. Though I still feel the same as I always did,' Bod said, but Mother Slaughter interrupted, 'And I still feels like I done when I was a tiny slip of a thing, making daisy chains in the old pasture. You're always you, and that don't change, and you're always changing, and there's nothing you can do about it.'

She sat down on her broken stone, and said, 'I remember you the night you came here, boy. I says, "We can't let the little fellow leave," and your mother agrees, and all of them starts argufying and what-not until the Lady on the Grey rides up. "People of the Graveyard," she says, "Listen to Mother Slaughter. Have you not got any charity in your bones?" and then all of them agreed with me.' She trailed off, shook her little head. 'There's not much happens here to make one day unlike the next. The seasons change. The ivy grows. Stones fall over. But you coming here... well, I'm glad you did, that's all.'

She stood up and pulled a grubby piece of linen from her sleeve, spat on it, and reached up as high as she could and scrubbed the blood from Bod's forehead. 'There, that ought to make you look presentable,' she said, severely. 'Seeing as I don't know when next I'll see you, anyway. Keep safe.'

Feeling discomfited in a way he could not remember having felt before, Bod made his way back to the Owenses' tomb, and was pleased to see both of his parents waiting for him beside it. As he got closer, his pleasure turned into concern: why did Mr and Mrs Owens stand like that, arranged on each side of the tomb like characters from a stained-glass window? He could not read their faces.

His father took a step forward and said, 'Evening, Bod. I trust you are keeping well.'

'Tolerably well,' said Bod, which was what Mr Owens always said to his friends when they asked him the same question.

Mr Owens said, 'Mistress Owens and I spent our lives wishing that we had a child. I do not believe that we could have ever had a better young man than you, Bod.' He looked up at his son with pride.

Bod said, 'Well, yes, thank you, but . . .' He turned to his mother, certain he could get her to tell him what was happening, but she was no longer there. 'Where did she go?'

'Oh. Yes.' Mr Owens seemed ill at ease. 'Ah, you know Betsy. There's things, times. Well, you don't know what to say. You know?'

'No,' said Bod.

'I expect Silas is waiting for you,' said his father, and then he was gone.

It was past midnight. Bod began to walk towards the old chapel. The tree that grew out of the gutter on the spire had fallen in the last storm, taking a handful of the slate-black roof tiles with it.

Bod waited on the grey wooden bench, but there was no sign of Silas.

The wind gusted. It was late on a summer's night, when the twilight lasts forever, and it was warm, but still, Bod felt goose pimples rising on his arms.

A voice by his ear said, 'Say you'll miss me, you lumpkin.'

'Liza?' said Bod. He had not seen or heard from the witch-girl for over a year – not since the night of the Jacks of All Trades. 'Where have you been?'

'Watching,' she said. 'Does a lady have to tell everything she does?'

'Watching *me*?' asked Bod.

Liza's voice, close to his ear, said, 'Truly, life is wasted on the living, Nobody Owens. For one of us is too foolish to live, and it is not I. Say you will miss me.'

'Where are you going?' asked Bod. Then, 'Of course I will miss you, wherever you go . . .'

'Too stupid,' whispered Liza Hempstock's voice, and he could feel the touch of her hand on his hand. 'Too stupid to live.' The touch of her lips against his cheek, against the corner of his lips. She kissed him gently and he was too perplexed, too utterly wrong-footed, to know what to do.

Her voice said, 'I will miss you too. Always.' A breath of wind ruffled his hair, if it was not the touch of her hand, and then he was, he knew, alone on the bench.

He got up.

Bod walked over to the chapel door, lifted the stone beside the porch and pulled out the spare key, left there by a long-dead sexton. He unlocked the big wooden door without even testing to see if he could slip through it. It creaked open, protesting.

The inside of the chapel was dark, and Bod found himself squinting as he tried to see.

'Come in, Bod.' It was Silas's voice.

'I can't see anything,' said Bod. 'It's too dark.'

'Already?' said Silas. He sighed. Bod heard a velvet rustle, then a match was struck, and it flamed, and was used to light two huge candles that sat on great carved wooden candlesticks at the back of the room. In the candlelight, Bod could see his guardian standing beside a large leather chest, of the kind they call a steamer trunk – big enough that a tall man could have curled up and slept inside it. Beside it was Silas's black leather bag, which Bod had seen before, on a handful of occasions, but which he still found impressive.

The steamer trunk was lined with whiteness. Bod put a hand into the empty trunk, touched the silk lining, touched dried earth.

'Is this where you sleep?' he asked.

'When I am far from my house, yes,' said Silas.

Bod was taken aback: Silas had been here as long as he could remember and before. 'Isn't *this* your home?'

Silas shook his head. 'My house is a long, long way from here,' said Silas. 'That is, if it is still habitable. There have been problems in my native land, and I am far from certain what I will find on my return.'

'You're going back?' asked Bod. Things that had been immutable were changing. 'You're really leaving? But. You're my guardian.'

'I *was* your guardian. But you are old enough to guard yourself. I have other things to protect.'

Silas closed the lid of the brown leather trunk, and began to do up the straps and the buckles.

'Why can't I just stay here? In the graveyard?'

'You must not,' said Silas, more gently than Bod could remember him ever saying anything. 'All the people here have had their lives, Bod, even if they were short ones. Now it's your turn. You need to live.'

'Can I come with you?'

Silas shook his head.

'Will I see you again?'

'Perhaps.' There was kindness in Silas's voice, and something more. 'And whether you see me or not, I have no doubt that I will see you.' He put the leather trunk against the wall, walked over to the door in the far corner. 'Follow me.' Bod walked behind Silas, followed him down the small spiral staircase to the crypt. 'I took the liberty of packing a case for you,' Silas explained, as they reached the bottom.

On top of the box of mildewed hymn books was a small leather suitcase, a miniature twin to Silas's own. 'Your possessions are all in there,' said Silas.

Bod said, 'Tell me about the Honour Guard, Silas. You're in it. Miss Lupescu was. Who else? Are there a lot of you? What do you do?'

'We don't do enough,' said Silas. 'And mostly, we guard the borderlands. We protect the borders of things.'

'What kind of borders?'

Silas said nothing.

'You mean like stopping the man Jack and his people?'

Silas said, 'We do what we have to.' He sounded weary.

'But you did the right thing. I mean, stopping the Jacks. They were terrible. They were monsters.'

284

Silas took a step closer to Bod, which made the youth tilt back his head to look up at the tall man's pale face. Silas said, 'I have not always done the right thing. When I was younger . . . I did worse things than Jack. Worse than any of them. I was the monster, then, Bod, and worse than any monster.'

It did not even cross Bod's mind to wonder if his guardian was lying or joking. He knew that he was being told the truth. He said, 'But you aren't that any longer, are you?'

Silas said, 'People can change,' and then fell silent. Bod wondered if his guardian – if Silas – was remembering. Then, 'It was an honour to be your guardian, young man.' His hand vanished inside his cloak, reappeared holding a battered old wallet. 'This is for you. Take it.'

Bod took the wallet, but did not open it.

'It contains money. Enough to give you a start in the world, but nothing more.'

Bod said, 'I went to see Alonso Jones today but he wasn't there, or if he was I couldn't see him. I wanted him to tell me about distant places he'd visited. Islands and porpoises and glaciers and mountains. Places where people dress and eat in the strangest ways.' Bod hesitated. Then, 'Those places. They're still there. I mean, there's a whole world out there. Can I see it? Can I go there?'

Silas nodded. 'There is a whole world out there, yes. You have a passport in the inner pocket of your suitcase. It's made out in the name of Nobody Owens. And was not easy to obtain.'

Bod said, 'If I change my mind, can I come back here?'

285

And then he answered his own question. 'If I come back, it will be a place, but it won't be home any longer.'

Silas said, 'Would you like me to walk you to the front gate?'

Bod shook his head. 'Best if I do it on my own. Um. Silas. If you're ever in trouble, call me. I'll come and help.'

'I,' said Silas, 'do not get into trouble.'

'No. I don't suppose you do. But still.'

It was dark in the crypt, and it smelled of mildew and damp and old stones, and it seemed, for the first time, very small.

Bod said, 'I want to see life. I want to hold it in my hands. I want to leave a footprint on the sand of a desert island. I want to play football with people. I want,' he said, and then he paused and he thought. 'I want *everything*.'

'Good,' said Silas. Then he put up his hand as if he were brushing away the hair from his eyes – a most uncharacteristic gesture. He said, 'If ever it transpires that I am in trouble, I shall indeed send for you.'

'Even though you don't get into trouble?'

'As you say.'

There was something at the edge of Silas's lips that might have been a smile, and might have been regret, and might just have been a trick of the shadows.

'Goodbye, then, Silas.' Bod held out his hand, as he had when he was a small boy, and Silas took it, in a cold hand the colour of old ivory, and shook it gravely.

'Goodbye, Nobody Owens.'

Bod picked up the little suitcase. He opened the door

to let himself out of the crypt, walked back up the gentle slope to the path without looking back.

It was well after the gates were locked. He wondered as he reached them if the gates would still let him walk through them, or if he would have to go back into the chapel to get a key, but when he got to the entrance he found the small pedestrian gate was unlocked and wide open, as if it were waiting for him, as if the graveyard itself were bidding him goodbye.

One pale, plump figure waited in front of the open gate, and she smiled up at him as he came towards her, and there were tears in her eyes in the moonlight.

'Hullo, Mother,' said Bod.

Mistress Owens rubbed her eyes with a knuckle, then dabbed at them with her apron, and she shook her head. 'Do you know what you're going to do now?' she asked.

'See the world,' said Bod. 'Get into trouble. Get out of trouble again. Visit jungles and volcanoes and deserts and islands. And people. I want to meet an awful lot of people.'

Mistress Owens made no immediate reply. She stared up at him, and then she began to sing a song that Bod remembered, a song she used to sing him when he was a tiny thing, a song that she had used to lull him to sleep when he was small.

> 'Sleep my little babby-oh
> Sleep until you waken
> When you wake you'll see the world
> If I'm not mistaken . . .'

'You're not,' whispered Bod. 'And I shall.'

> 'Kiss a lover
> Dance a measure,
> Find your name
> And buried treasure . . .'

Then the last lines of the song came back to Mistress Owens, and she sang them to her son.

> 'Face your life
> Its pain, its pleasure,
> Leave no path untaken'

'Leave no path untaken,' repeated Bod. 'A difficult challenge, but I can try my best.'

He tried to put his arms around his mother then, as he had when he was a child, although he might as well have been trying to hold mist, for he was alone on the path.

He took a step forward, through the gate that took him out of the graveyard. He thought a voice said, 'I am so proud of you, my son,' but he might, perhaps, have imagined it.

The midsummer sky was already beginning to lighten in the east, and that was the way that Bod began to walk: down the hill, towards the living people, and the city, and the dawn.

There was a passport in his bag, money in his pocket. There was a smile dancing on his lips, although it was a wary smile, for the world is a bigger place than a little graveyard on a hill; and there would be dangers in it and mysteries, new friends to make, old friends to rediscover, mistakes to be made and many paths to be walked before he would, finally, return to the graveyard or ride with the Lady on the broad back of her great grey stallion.

But between now and then, there was Life; and Bod walked into it with his eyes and his heart wide open.

ACKNOWLEDGEMENTS

First, foremost and for ever: I owe an enormous debt, conscious and, I have no doubt, unconscious, to Rudyard Kipling and the two volumes of his remarkable work *The Jungle Book*. I read them as a child, excited and impressed, and I've read and reread them many times since. If you are only familiar with the Disney cartoon, you should read the stories.

My son Michael inspired this book. He was only two years old, riding his little tricycle between gravestones in the summer, and I had a book in my head. Then it just took me twenty-something years to write it.

When I started writing the book (I started with Chapter Four), only my daughter Maddy's request to know what happened next kept me writing beyond the first couple of pages. Holly did nothing specific, but made everything better.

Gardner Dozois and Jack Dann were the first people to publish 'The Witch's Headstone'. Professor Georgia Grilli talked about what this book was without having read it, and listening to her talk helped throw the themes into focus.

Kendra Stout was there when I saw the first ghoul-gate, and was kind enough to walk through several grave-yards with me. She was the audience for the first chapters, and her love for Silas was awesome.

Artist and author Audrey Niffenegger is also a grave-yard guide, and she showed me around the ivy-covered marvel that is Highgate Cemetery West. A lot of what she told me crept into Chapters Seven and Eight. Former Web Elf Olga Nunes and Scary God-daughter Hayley Campbell made it happen and walked with me.

Many friends read this book as it was being written, and all of them offered wise suggestions, Dan Johnson, Gary K. Wolfe, John Crowley, Moby, Farah Mendlesohn, and Joe Sanders, among others. They all spotted things I needed to fix. Still, I missed John M. Ford (1957–2006), who was my best critic of all.

Isabel Ford, Elise Howard, Sarah Odedina, and Clarissa Hutton were the book's editors on both sides of the Atlantic. They made me look good. Michael Conroy directed the audiobook version with aplomb. Mr McKean and Mr Riddell both drew wonderfully, and differently. Merrilee Heifetz is the best agent in the world, and Dorie Simmonds made it happen excellently in the UK. Jon Levin offered advice and took care of the film rights. The Fabulous Lorraine Garland, the Wonderful Cat Mihos and the Amazing Kelli Bickman all struggled with my handwriting, mostly successfully.

I wrote this book in many places: among other places, Jonathan and Jane's Florida house, a cottage in Cornwall, a hotel room in New Orleans; and I failed to write in Tori's house in Ireland because I had flu there instead. But she helped and inspired me, nonetheless.

And as I finish these thanks, the only thing I'm certain of is that I have forgotten not just one very important person but dozens of them. Sorry. But thank you all anyway.

Neil Gaiman

I said
She's gone
but I'm alive, I'm alive
I'm coming in the graveyard
to sing you to sleep now

Tori Amos, 'Graveyard'

'Will delight fans of both Stephen King and Mark Twain. Darkly romantic, chilling and rousing by turns, moody and memorable. A thundering success.' Roger Zelazny

'A haunting, moving tale . . . I loved it.' Ramsey Campbell

'The subtle atmosphere of menace grows and grows.'
Whitley Strieber

'The milieu is arresting, the pace hellbent, the characters vibrant. Martin's tale is splendid, and then some. *Fevre Dream* runs red with original, high adventure.' Harlan Ellison

ALSO BY GEORGE R. R. MARTIN

Novels
Dying of the Light (1977)
Windhaven *with Lisa Tuttle* (1981)
The Armageddon Rag (1983)
A Game of Thrones (1996)
A Clash of Kings (1998)
A Storm of Swords (2000)

Short Story collections
A Song for Lya and Other Stories (1974)
Songs of Stars and Shadows (1977)
Sandkings (1981)
Songs the Dead Men Sing (1983)
Nightflyers (1985)
Tuf Voyaging (1986)
Portraits of His Children (1987)

As Editor
New Voices in Science Fiction, Volumes 1-4
The Science Fiction Weight-Loss Book
with Isaac Asimov and Martin Harry Greenberg
The John W. Campbell Awards, Volume 5
Night Visions 3
Wild Cards I-XV

FEVRE DREAM

GEORGE R. R. MARTIN

The right of George R. R. Martin to be identified as the
author of this work has been asserted by him in accordance
with the Copyright, Designs and Patents Act 1988.

This edition published in Great Britain in 2001 by
Gollancz
An imprint of the Orion Publishing Group
Orion House, 5 Upper St Martin's Lane,
London WC2H 9EA

A CIP catalogue record for this book is available
from the British Library.

ISBN 1 85798 331 9

Printed in Great Britain by
The Guernsey Press Co. Ltd, Guernsey, C.I.

For Howard Waldrop,
a helluva writer, a helluva friend,
and a fevered dreamer if ever there was one.

St. Louis,
April 1857 ———————————————————

ABNER Marsh rapped the head of his hickory walking stick smartly on the hotel desk to get the clerk's attention. "I'm here to see a man named York," he said. "Josh York, I believe he calls hisself. You got such a man here?"

The clerk was an elderly man with spectacles. He jumped at the sound of the rap, then turned and spied Marsh and smiled. "Why, it's Cap'n Marsh," he said amiably. "Ain't seen you for half a year, Cap'n. Heard about your misfortune, though. Terrible, just terrible. I been here since '36 and I never seen no ice jam like that one."

"Never you mind about that," Abner Marsh said, annoyed. He had anticipated such comments. The Planters' House was a popular hostelry among steamboatmen. Marsh himself had dined there regularly before that cruel winter. But since the ice jam he'd been staying away, and not only because of the prices. Much as he liked Planters' House food, he was not eager for its brand of company: pilots and captains and mates, rivermen all, old friends and old rivals, and all of them knowing his misfortune. Abner Marsh wanted no man's pity. "You just say where York's room is," he told the clerk peremptorily.

The clerk bobbed his head nervously. "Mister York won't be in his room, Cap'n. You'll find him in the dining room, taking his meal."

"Now? At *this* hour?" Marsh glanced at the ornate hotel clock, then loosed the brass buttons of his coat and pulled out his own gold pocket watch. "Ten past midnight," he said, incredulous. "You say he's *eatin'?*"

"Yes sir, that he is. He chooses his own times, Mister York, and he's not the sort you say no to, Cap'n."

Abner Marsh made a rude noise deep in his throat, pocketed his watch, and turned away without a word, setting off across the richly appointed lobby with long, heavy strides. He was a big man, and not a patient one, and he was not accustomed to business meetings at midnight. He carried his walking stick with a flourish, as if he had never had a misfortune, and was still the man he had been.

The dining room was almost as grand and lavish as the main saloon on a big steamer, with cut-glass chandeliers and polished brass fixtures and tables covered with fine white linen and the best china and crystal. During normal hours, the tables would have been full of travelers and steamboatmen, but now the room was empty, most of the lights extinguished. Perhaps there was something to be said for midnight meetings after all, Marsh reflected; at least he would have to suffer no condolences. Near the kitchen door, two Negro waiters were talking softly. Marsh ignored them and walked to the far side of the room, where a well-dressed stranger was dining alone.

The man must have heard him approach, but he did not look up. He was busy spooning up mock turtle soup from a china bowl. The cut of his long black coat made it clear he was no riverman; an Easterner then, or maybe even a foreigner. He was big, Marsh saw, though not near so big as Marsh; seated, he gave the impression of height, but he had none of Marsh's girth. At first Marsh thought him an old man, for his hair was white. Then, when he came closer, he saw that it was not white at all, but a very pale blond, and suddenly the stranger took on an almost boyish aspect. York was clean-shaven, not a mustache nor side whiskers on his long, cool face, and his skin was as fair as his hair. He had hands like a woman, Marsh thought as he stood over the table.

He tapped on the table with his stick. The cloth muffled the sound, made it a gentle summons. "You Josh York?" he said.

York looked up, and their eyes met.

Till the rest of his days were done, Abner Marsh remembered that moment, that first look into the eyes of Joshua York. Whatever thoughts he had had, whatever plans he had made, were sucked up in the maelstrom of York's eyes. Boy and old man and dandy and foreigner, all those were gone in an instant, and there was only York, the man himself, the power of him, the dream, the intensity.

York's eyes were gray, startlingly dark in such a pale face. His pupils were pinpoints, burning black, and they reached right into

Marsh and weighed the soul inside him. The gray around them seemed alive, moving, like fog on the river on a dark night, when the banks vanish and the lights vanish and there is nothing in the world but your boat and the river and the fog. In those mists, Abner Marsh saw things; visions swift-glimpsed and then gone. There was a cool intelligence peering out of those mists. But there was a beast as well, dark and frightening, chained and angry, raging at the fog. Laughter and loneliness and cruel passion; York had all of that in his eyes.

But mostly there was force in those eyes, terrible force, a strength as relentless and merciless as the ice that had crushed Marsh's dreams. Somewhere in that fog, Marsh could sense the ice moving, slow, so slow, and he could hear the awful splintering of his boats and all his hopes.

Abner Marsh had stared down many a man in his day, and he held his gaze for the longest time, his hand closed so hard around his stick that he feared he would snap it in two. But at last he looked away.

The man at the table pushed away his soup, gestured, and said, "Captain Marsh. I have been expecting you. Please join me." His voice was mellow, educated, easy.

"Yes," Marsh said, too softly. He pulled out the chair across from York and eased himself into it. Marsh was a massive man, six foot tall and three hundred pounds heavy. He had a red face and a full black beard that he wore to cover up a flat, pushed-in nose and a faceful of warts, but even the whiskers didn't help much; they called him the ugliest man on the river, and he knew it. In his heavy blue captain's coat with its double row of brass buttons, he was a fierce and imposing figure. But York's eyes had drained him of his bluster. The man was a fanatic, Marsh decided. He had seen eyes like that before, in madmen and hell-raising preachers and once in the face of the man called John Brown, down in bleeding Kansas. Marsh wanted nothing to do with fanatics, with preachers, and abolitionists and temperance people.

But when York spoke, he did not sound like a fanatic. "My name is Joshua Anton York, Captain. J. A. York in business, Joshua to my friends. I hope that we shall be both business associates and friends, in time." His tone was cordial and reasonable.

"We'll see about that," Marsh said, uncertain. The gray eyes across from him seemed aloof and vaguely amused now; whatever he had seen in them was gone. He felt confused.

"I trust you received my letter?"

"I got it right here," Marsh said, pulling the folded envelope from the pocket of his coat. The offer had seemed an impossible stroke of fortune when it arrived, salvation for everything he feared lost. Now he was not so sure. "You want to go into the steamboat business, do you?" he said, leaning forward.

A waiter appeared. "Will you be dining with Mister York, Cap'n?"

"Please do," York urged.

"I believe I will," Marsh said. York might be able to outstare him, but there was no man on the river could outeat him. "I'll have some of that soup, and a dozen oysters, and a couple of roast chickens with taters and stuff. Crisp 'em up good, mind you. And something to wash it all down with. What are you drinking, York?"

"Burgundy."

"Fine, fetch me a bottle of the same."

York looked amused. "You have a formidable appetite, Captain."

"This is a for-mid-a-bul town," Marsh said carefully, "and a for-mid-a-bul river, Mister York. Man's got to keep his strength up. This ain't New York, nor London neither."

"I'm quite aware of that," York said.

"Well, I hope so, if you're going into steamboatin'. It's the for-mid-a-bullest thing of all."

"Shall we go directly to business, then? You own a packet line. I wish to buy a half-interest. Since you are here, I take it you are interested in my offer."

"I'm considerable interested," Marsh agreed, "and considerable puzzled, too. You look like a smart man. I reckon you checked me out before you wrote me this here letter." He tapped it with his finger. "You ought to know that this last winter just about ruined me."

York said nothing, but something in his face bid Marsh continue.

"The Fevre River Packet Company, that's me," Marsh went on. "Called it that on account of where I was born, up on the Fevre near Galena, not 'cause I only worked that river, since I didn't. I had six boats, working mostly the upper Mississippi trade, St. Louis to St. Paul, with some trips up the Fevre and the Illinois and the Missouri. I was doing just fine, adding a new boat or two most every year, thinking of moving into the Ohio trade, or maybe even New Orleans. But last July my *Mary Clarke* blew a boiler and burned, up near to Dubuque, burned right to the water line with a hundred dead. And this winter—this was a terrible winter. I had four of my boats wintering here at St. Louis. The *Nicholas Perrot*, the *Dunleith*, the *Sweet*

Fevre, and my *Elizabeth A.*, brand new, only four months in service and a sweet boat too, near 300 feet long with 12 big boilers, fast as any steamboat on the river. I was real proud of my lady Liz. She cost me $200,000, but she was worth every penny of it." The soup arrived. Marsh tasted a spoonful and scowled. "Too hot," he said. "Well, anyway, St. Louis is a good place to winter. Don't freeze too bad down here, nor too long. This winter was different, though. Yes, sir. Ice jam. Damn river froze *hard*." Marsh extended a huge red hand across the table, palm up, and slowly closed his fingers into a fist. "Put an egg in there and you get the idea, York. Ice can crush a steamboat easier than I can crush an egg. When it breaks up it's even worse, big gorges sliding down the river, smashing up wharfs, levees, boats, most everything. Winter's end, I'd lost my boats, all four of 'em. The ice took 'em away from me."

"Insurance?" York asked.

Marsh set to his soup, sucking it up noisily. In between spoons, he shook his head. "I'm not a gambling man, Mister York. I never took no stock in insurance. It's gambling, all it is, 'cept you're bettin' against yourself. What money I made, I put into my boats."

York nodded. "I believe you still own one steamboat."

"That I do," Marsh said. He finished his soup and signaled for the next course. "The *Eli Reynolds*, a little 150-ton stern-wheeler. I been using her on the Illinois, 'cause she don't draw much, and she wintered in Peoria, missed the worse of the ice. That's my asset, sir, that's what I got left. Trouble is, Mister York, the *Eli Reynolds* ain't worth much. She only cost me $25,000 new, and that was back in '50."

"Seven years," York said. "Not a very long time."

Marsh shook his head. "Seven years is a powerful long time for a steamboat," he said. "Most of 'em don't last but four or five. River just eats 'em up. The *Eli Reynolds* was better built than most, but still, she ain't got that long left." Marsh started in on his oysters, scooping them up on the half shell and swallowing them whole, washing each one down with a healthy gulp of wine. "So I'm puzzled, Mister York," he continued after a half-dozen oysters had disappeared. "You want to buy a half-share in my line, which ain't got but one small, old boat. Your letter named a price. Too high a price. Maybe when I had six boats, then Fevre River Packets was worth that much. But not now." He gulped down another oyster. "You won't earn back your investment in ten years, not with the *Reynolds*.

She can't take enough freight, nor passengers neither." Marsh wiped his lips on his napkin, and regarded the stranger across the table. The food had restored him, and now he felt like his own self again, in command of the situation. York's eyes were intense, to be sure, but there was nothing there to fear.

"You need my money, Captain," York said. "Why are you telling me this? Aren't you afraid I will find another partner?"

"I don't work that way," Marsh said. "Been on the river thirty years, York. Rafted down to New Orleans when I was just a boy, and worked flatboats and keelboats both before steamers. I been a pilot and a mate and a striker, even a mud clerk. Been everything there is to be in this business, but one thing I never been, and that's a sharper."

"An honest man," York said, with just enough of an edge in his voice so Marsh could not be sure if he was being mocked. "I am glad you saw fit to tell me the condition of your company, Captain. I knew it already, to be sure. My offer stands."

"Why?" Marsh demanded gruffly. "Only a fool throws away money. You don't look like no fool."

The food arrived before York could answer. Marsh's chickens were crisped up beautifully, just the way he liked them. He sawed off a leg and started in hungrily. York was served a thick cut of roasted beef, red and rare, swimming in blood and juice. Marsh watched him attack it, deftly, easily. His knife slid through the meat as if it were butter, never pausing to hack or saw, as Marsh so often did. He handled his fork like a gentleman, shifting hands when he set down his knife. Strength and grace; York had both in those long, pale hands of his, and Marsh admired that. He wondered that he had ever thought them a woman's hands. They were white but strong, hard like the white of the keys of the grand piano in the main cabin of the *Eclipse*.

"Well?" Marsh prompted. "You ain't answered my question."

Joshua York paused for a moment. Finally he said, "You have been honest with me, Captain Marsh. I will not repay your honesty with lies, as I had intended. But I will not burden you with the truth, either. There are things I cannot tell you, things you would not care to know. Let me put my terms to you, under these conditions, and see if we can come to an agreement. If not, we shall part amiably."

Marsh hacked the breast off his second chicken. "Go on," he said. "I ain't leaving."

York put down his knife and fork and made a steeple of his fingers.

"For my own reasons, I want to be master of a steamboat. I want to travel the length of this great river, in comfort and privacy, not as passenger but as captain. I have a dream, a purpose. I seek friends and allies, and I have enemies, many enemies. The details are none of your concern. If you press me about them, I will tell you lies. Do not press me." His eyes grew hard a moment, then softened as he smiled. "Your only interest need be my desire to own and command a steamboat, Captain. As you can tell, I am no riverman. I know nothing of steamboats, or the Mississippi, beyond what I have read in a few books and learned during the weeks I have spent in St. Louis. Obviously, I need an associate, someone who is familiar with the river and river people, someone who can manage the day-to-day operations of my boat, and leave me free to pursue my own purposes.

"This associate must have other qualities as well. He must be discreet, as I do not wish to have my behavior—which I admit to be sometimes peculiar—become the talk of the levee. He must be trustworthy, since I will give all management over into his hands. He must have courage. I do not want a weakling, or a superstitious man, or one who is overly religious. Are you a religious man, Captain?"

"No," said Marsh. "Never cared for bible-thumpers, nor them for me."

York smiled. "Pragmatic. I want a pragmatic man. I want a man who will concentrate on his own part of the business, and not ask too many questions of me. I value my privacy, and if sometimes my actions seem strange or arbitrary or capricious, I do not want them challenged. Do you understand my requirements?"

Marsh tugged thoughtfully on his beard. "And if I do?"

"We will become partners," York said. "Let your lawyers and your clerks run your line. You will travel with me on the river. I will serve as captain. You can call yourself pilot, mate, co-captain, whatever you choose. The actual running of the boat I will leave to you. My orders will be infrequent, but when I do command, you will see to it that I am obeyed without question. I have friends who will travel with us, cabin passage, at no cost. I may see fit to give them positions on the boat, with such duties as I may deem fitting. You will not question these decisions. I may acquire other friends along the river, and bring them aboard as well. You will welcome them. If you can abide by such terms, Captain Marsh, we shall grow rich together and travel your river in ease and luxury."

Abner Marsh laughed. "Well, maybe. But it ain't my river, Mister York, and if you think we're going to travel in luxury on the old *Eli*

Reynolds, you're going to be awful sore when you come on board. She's a rackety old tub with some pretty poor accommodations, and most times she's full of foreigners taking deck passage to one unlikely place or the other. I ain't been on her in two years—old Cap'n Yoerger runs her for me now—but last time I rode her, she smelled pretty bad. You want luxury, you ought to see about buying into the *Eclipse* or the *John Simonds*."

Joshua York sipped at his wine, and smiled. "I did not have the *Eli Reynolds* in mind, Captain Marsh."

"She's the only boat I got."

York set down his wine. "Come," he said, "let us settle up here. We can proceed up to my room, and discuss matters further."

Marsh made a weak protest—the Planters' House offered an excellent dessert menu, and he hated to pass it up. York insisted, however.

York's room was a large, well-appointed suite, the best the hotel had to offer, and usually reserved for rich planters up from New Orleans. "Sit," York said commandingly, gesturing Marsh to a large, comfortable chair in the sitting room. Marsh sat, while his host went into an inner chamber and returned a moment later, bearing a small iron-bound chest. He set it on a table and began to work the lock. "Come here," he said, but Marsh had already risen to stand behind him. York threw back the lid.

"Gold," Marsh said softly. He reached out and touched the coins, running them through his fingers, savoring the feel of the soft yellow metal, the gleam and the clatter of it. One coin he brought to his mouth and tasted. "Real enough," he said, spitting. He chunked the coin back in the chest.

"Ten thousand dollars in twenty-dollar gold coins," York said. "I have two other chests just like it, and letters of credit from banks in London, Philadelphia, and Rome for sums considerably larger. Accept my offer, Captain Marsh, and you shall have a second boat, one far grander than your *Eli Reynolds*. Or perhaps I should say that *we* shall have a second boat." He smiled.

Abner Marsh had meant to turn down York's offer. He needed the money bad enough, but he was a suspicious man with no use for mysteries, and York asked him to take too much on faith. The offer had sounded too good; Marsh was certain that danger lay hidden somewhere, and he would be the worse for it if he accepted. But now, staring at the color of York's wealth, he felt his resolve weakening. "A new boat, you say?" he said weakly.

"Yes," York replied, "and that is over and above the price I would pay you for a half-interest in your packet line."

"How much . . ." Marsh began. His lips were dry. He licked them nervously. "How much are you willin' to spend to build this new boat, Mister York?"

"How much is required?" York asked quietly.

Marsh took up a handful of gold coins, then let them rattle through his fingers back into the chest. The gleam of them, he thought, but all he said was, "You oughtn't carry this much about with you, York. There's scoundrels would kill you for *one* of them coins."

"I can protect myself, Captain," York said. Marsh saw the look in his eyes and felt cold. He pitied the robber who tried to take Joshua York's gold.

"Will you take a walk with me? On the levee?"

"You haven't given me my answer, Captain."

"You'll get your answer. Come first. Got something I want you to see."

"Very well," York said. He closed the lid of the chest, and the soft yellow gleam faded from the room, which suddenly seemed close and dim.

The night air was cool and moist. Their boots sent up echoes as they walked the dark, deserted streets, York with a limber grace and Marsh with heavy authority. York wore a loose pilot's coat cut like a cape, and a tall old beaver hat that cast long shadows in the light of the half-moon. Marsh glared at the dark alleys between the bleak brick warehouses, and tried to present an aspect of solid, scowling strength sufficient to scare off ruffians.

The levee was crowded with steamboats, at least forty of them tied up to landing posts and wharfboats. Even at this hour all was not quiet. Huge stacks of freight threw black shadows in the moonlight, and they passed roustabouts lounging against crates and bales of hay, passing a bottle from hand to hand or smoking their cob pipes. Lights still burned in the cabin windows of a dozen or more boats. The Missouri packet *Wyandotte* was lit and building steam. They spied a man standing high up on the texas deck of one big side-wheel packet, looking down at them curiously. Abner Marsh led York past him, past the procession of darkened, silent steamers, their tall chimneys etched against the stars like a row of blackened trees with strange flowers on their tops.

Finally he stopped before a great ornate side-wheeler, freight piled high on her main deck, her stage raised against unwanted intruders as she nuzzled against her weathered old wharfboat. Even in the dimness of the half-moon the splendor of her was clear. No steamer on the levee was quite so big and proud.

"Yes?" Joshua York said quietly, respectfully. That might have decided it right there, Marsh thought later—the respect in his voice.

"That's the *Eclipse*," Marsh said. "See, her name is on the wheel-house, there." He jabbed with his stick. "Can you read it?"

"Quite well. I have excellent night vision. This is a special boat, then?"

"Hell yes, she's special. She's the *Eclipse*. Every goddamned man and boy on this river knows her. Old now—she was built back in '52, five years ago. But she's still grand. Cost $375,000, so they say, and worth all of it. There ain't never been a bigger, fancier, more for-mid-a-bul boat than this one right here. I've studied her, taken passage on her. I know." Marsh pointed. "She measures 365 feet by 40, and her grand saloon is 330 feet long, and you never seen nothin' like it. Got a gold statue of Henry Clay at one end, and Andy Jackson at the other, the two of 'em glaring at each other the whole damn way. More crystal and silver and colored glass than the Planters' House ever dreamed of, oil paintings, food like you ain't never tasted, and mirrors—*such* mirrors. And all that's nothin' to her speed.

"Down below on the main deck she carries 15 boilers. Got an 11-foot stroke, I tell you, and there ain't a boat on any river can run with her when Cap'n Sturgeon gets up her steam. She's done eighteen miles an hour upstream, easy. Back in '53, she set the record from New Orleans to Louisville. I know her time by heart. Four days, nine hours, thirty minutes, and she beat the goddamned *A. L. Shotwell* by fifty minutes, fast as the *Shotwell* is." Marsh rounded to face York. "I hoped my Lady Liz would take the *Eclipse* some day, beat her time or race her head to head, but she never could of done it, I know that now. I was just foolin' myself. I didn't have the money it takes to build a boat that can take the *Eclipse*.

"You give me that money, Mister York, and you've got yourself a partner. There's your answer, sir. You want half of Fevre River Packets, and a partner who runs things quiet and don't ask you no questions 'bout your business? Fine. Then you give me the money to build a steamboat like that."

Joshua York stared at the big side-wheeler, serene and silent in the darkness, floating easily on the water, ready for all challengers. He turned to Abner Marsh with a smile on his lips and a dim flame in his dark eyes. "Done," was all he said. And he extended his hand.

Marsh broke into a crooked, snaggle-toothed grin, wrapped York's slim white hand within his own meaty paw, and squeezed. "Done, then," he said loudly, and he brought all his massive strength to bear, squeezing and crushing, as he always did in business, to test the will and the courage of the men he dealt with. He squeezed until he saw the pain in their eyes.

But York's eyes stayed clear, and his own hand clenched hard around Marsh's with a strength that was surprising. Tighter and tighter it squeezed, and the muscles beneath that pale flesh coiled and corded like springs of iron, and Marsh swallowed hard and tried not to cry out.

York released his hand. "Come," he said, clapping Marsh solidly across the shoulders and staggering him a bit. "We have plans to make."

SOUR Billy Tipton arrived at the French Exchange just after ten, and watched them auction four casks of wine, seven crates of dry goods, and a shipment of furniture before they brought in the slaves. He stood silently, elbows up against the long marble bar that extended halfway around the rotunda, sipping an absinthe while he observed the *encanteurs* hawk their wares in two languages. Sour Billy was a dark, cadaverous man, his long horseface scarred by the pox he'd had as a boy, his hair thin and brown and flaky. He seldom smiled, and he had frightening ice-colored eyes.

Those eyes, those cold and dangerous eyes, were Sour Billy's protection. The French Exchange was a grand place, altogether too grand for his tastes, and for a fact he did not like to come there. It was in the rotunda of the St. Louis Hotel, beneath a towering dome from which daylight cascaded down onto auction block and bidders. The dome was eighty feet across, easily. Tall pillars circled the room, galleries ran round the inside of the dome, the ceiling was elaborate and ornamental, the walls were covered with odd paintings, the bar was solid marble, the floor was marble, the desks of the *encanteurs* were marble. The patrons were as fine as the decor; rich planters from upriver, and young Creole dandies from the old city. Sour Billy loathed the Creoles, them with their rich clothes and haughty ways and dark, contemptuous eyes. He did not like to go among them. They were hot-blooded and quarrelsome, much given to dueling, and sometimes one of the young ones would take offense at Sour Billy, at the way he mangled their language and looked at their women, at the disreputable, scruffy, presumptuous *Americanness* of him. But then they would catch sight of his eyes, pale and staring and edged with malice—and, often as not, they would turn away.

Still, left to his own devices, he'd do his nigger-buying over at the American Exchange in the St. Charles, where manners were less refined, English was spoken in place of French, and he felt less out of place. The grandeur of the rotunda in the St. Louis did not impress him, except for the quality of the drinks they served.

He came there once a month, nonetheless, and had no choice about it. The American Exchange was a good place to buy a field hand or a cook, dark-skinned as you please, but for a fancy girl, one of the young dusky octaroon beauties that Julian preferred, you had to come to the French Exchange. Julian wanted beauty, insisted on beauty.

Sour Billy did as Damon Julian told him.

It was about eleven when the last of the wine was cleared away, and the traders began to bring in their merchandise from the slave pens on Moreau and Esplanade and Common Streets; men and women, old and young, and children too, a disproportionate number of them light of skin and fair of face. Intelligent as well, Sour Billy knew, probably French-speaking. They were lined up along one side of the room for inspection, and several of the young Creole men walked along the row jauntily, making light comments to one another and viewing today's stock at close hand. Sour Billy stayed by the bar and ordered another absinthe. He had visited most of the yards yesterday, looked over what there was to offer. He knew what he wanted.

One of the auctioneers brought down a mallet on his marble desk, and at once the patrons ceased their conversation and turned to give him their attention. He gestured, and a young woman of about twenty climbed unsteadily to the top of a nearby crate. She was a slight quadroon with wide eyes, pretty in her way. She wore a calico dress and had green ribbons in her hair, and the auctioneer began singing her praises effusively. Sour Billy watched with disinterest while two young Creoles bid her up. She was finally sold for some $1400.

Next an older woman, said to be a fine cook, was auctioned off, and then a young mother with two children, all sold together. Sour Billy waited through several other sales. It was a quarter past noon and the French Exchange was jammed with bidders and spectators when the item he had chosen came up.

Her name was Emily, the *encanteur* told them. "Look at her, sirs," he babbled in French, "just look at her. Such perfection! It has been years since such a lot has been sold here, years, and it will be years before we see another like her." Sour Billy was inclined to agree. Emily was sixteen or seventeen, he judged, but already very much a woman. She looked a little frightened up on the auction block, but the dark simplicity of her dress set off her figure to good advantage, and she had a beautiful face—big soft eyes and fine café-au-lait skin. Julian will like this one.

The bidding was spirited. The planters had no use for such a fancy girl, but six or seven of the Creoles were hot after her. No doubt the other slaves had given Emily some idea what might be in store for her. She was pretty enough to get her freedom, in time, and to be kept by one of those fine Creole dandies in a little house on Ramparts Street, at least until he married. She'd go to the Quadroon Balls in the Orleans Ballroom, wear silk gowns and ribbons, be the cause of more than one duel. Her daughters would have skin even lighter, and grow into the same fine life. Maybe when she got old she'd learn to dress hair or run a boarding house. Sour Billy sipped at his drink, cold-faced.

The bids rose. By $2,000 all but three of the bidders had fallen out. At that point one of them, a swarthy bald-headed man, demanded that she be stripped. The *encanteur* snapped a curt command, and Emily gingerly undid her dress and stepped out of it. Someone shouted up a lewd compliment that drew a round of laughter from the audience. The girl smiled weakly while the auctioneer grinned and added a comment of his own. Then the bidding resumed.

At $2,500 the bald-headed man dropped out, having gotten his look. That left two bidders, both Creoles. They topped one another three times in succession, forcing the price up to $3,200. Then came the hesitation. The auctioneer coaxed a final bid from the younger of the two men: $3,300.

"Thirty-four hundred," his opponent said quietly. Sour Billy recognized him. He was a lean young Creole named Montreuil, a notorious gambler and duelist.

The other man shook his head; the auction was over. Montreuil was smirking at Emily with anticipation. Sour Billy waited three heartbeats, until the mallet was about to fall. Then he set aside his absinthe glass and said, "Thirty-seven hundred," in a loud clear voice.

Encanteur and girl both looked up in surprise. Montreuil and several of his friends gave Billy dark, threatening looks. "Thirty-eight hundred," Montreuil said.

"Four thousand," said Sour Billy.

It was a high price, even for such a beauty. Montreuil said something to two men standing near him, and the three of them suddenly spun on their heels and strode from the rotunda without another word, their footsteps ringing angrily on the marble.

"It seems like I won the auction," Sour Billy said. "Get her dressed and ready to go." The others were all staring at him.

"But of course!" the *encanteur* said. Another auctioneer rose at his desk, and with his mallet summoned yet another fancy girl to the attention of the crowd, and the French Exchange began to buzz again.

Sour Billy Tipton led Emily down the long arcade from the rotunda to St. Louis Street, past all the fashionable shops where idlers and wealthy travelers gave them curious looks. As he stepped out into daylight, blinking at the glare, Montreuil came up beside him. "*Monsieur,*" he began.

"Talk English if you want to talk to me," Sour Billy said sharply. "It's Mister Tipton out here, Montreuil." His long fingers twitched, and he fixed the other with his cold ice eyes.

"Mister Tipton," Montreuil said in a flat, unaccented English. His face was vaguely flushed. Behind him, his two companions stood stiffly. "I have lost girls before," the Creole said. "She is striking, but it is nothing, losing her. But I take offense at the way you bid, Mister Tipton. You made a mockery of me in there, taunting me with victory and playing me for a fool."

"Well, well," Sour Billy said. "Well, well."

"You play a dangerous game," Montreuil warned. "Do you know who I am? If you were a gentleman, I would call you out, sir."

"Dueling's illegal, Montreuil," Sour Billy said. "Hadn't you heard? And I'm no gentleman." He turned back to the quadroon girl, who was standing up near the wall of the hotel, watching them. "Come," he said. He walked off down the sidewalk, and she followed.

"You shall be paid in kind for this, *monsieur,*" Montreuil called after him.

Sour Billy paid him no mind and turned a corner. He walked briskly, a swagger in his step that had been absent inside the French Exchange. The streets were where Sour Billy felt at home; there he had grown up, there he had learned to survive. The slave girl Emily scurried after him as best she could, her bare feet pounding on the brick sidewalks. The streets of the Vieux Carré were lined with brick and plaster houses, each with its graceful wrought-iron balcony overhanging the narrow walk, fancy as you please. But the roads themselves were unpaved, and the recent rains had turned them into a sea of mud. Along the walks were open gutters, deep ditches of cypress full of standing water, fragrant with filth and raw sewage.

They passed neat little shops and slave pens with heavily barred windows, passed elegant hotels and smoky grog shops full of surly free niggers, passed close, humid alleys and airy courtyards each with its well or fountain, passed haughty Creole ladies with their escorts and chaperones and a gang of runaway slaves in iron collars and chains cleaning the gutters under the careful watch of a hard-eyed white man with a whip. Shortly they passed out of the French Quarter entirely, into the rawer, newer American section of New Orleans. Sour Billy had left his horse tied up outside a grog shop. He mounted it, and told the girl to walk along beside him. They struck out south from the city, and soon left the main roads, stopping only once, briefly, so Sour Billy could rest his horse and eat some of the dry, hard bread and cheese in his saddlebag. He let Emily suck up some water from a stream.

"Are you my new massa, sir?" she asked him then, in remarkably good English.

"Overseer," said Sour Billy. "You'll meet Julian tonight, girl. After dark." He smiled. "He'll *like* you." Then he told her to shut up.

Since the girl was afoot their pace was laggardly, and it was near dusk when they reached the Julian plantation. The road ran along the bayou and wound through a thick stand of trees, limbs heavy with Spanish moss. They rounded a large, barren oak and came out into the fields, red-tinged in the somber light of the setting sun. They lay fallow and overgrown from the water's edge to the house. There was an old, rotting wharf and a woodyard along the bayou for passing steamers, and behind the great house a row of slave shanties. But there were no slaves, and the fields had not been worked in some years. The house was not large as plantation houses go, nor particularly grand; it was a stolid, square structure of graying wood, paint flaking from its sides, its only striking aspect a high tower with a widow's walk around it.

"Home," said Sour Billy.

The girl asked if the plantation had a name.

"Used to," Sour Billy said, "years ago, when Garoux owned it. But

22

he took sick and died, him and all his fine sons, and it don't got no name now. Now shut your mouth and hurry."

He led her around back, to his own entrance, and opened the padlock with a key he wore on a chain around his neck. He had three rooms of his own, in the servants' portion of the house. He pulled Emily into the bedroom. "Get out of them clothes," Sour Billy snapped.

The girl fumbled to obey, but looked at him with fear in her eyes.

"Don't look like that," he said. "You're Julian's, I ain't going to mess with you. I'll be heatin' some water. There's a tub in the kitchen. You'll wash the filth off you, and dress." He threw open a wardrobe of intricately carved wood, pulled out a dark brocade gown. "Here, this'll fit."

She gasped. "I can't wear nothin' like that. That's a white lady's dress."

"You shut your mouth and do like I tell you," Sour Billy said. "Julian wants you pretty, girl." Then he left her and went through into the main part of the house.

He found Julian in the library, sitting quietly in darkness in a great leather chair, a brandy snifter in his hand. All around him, covered with dust, were the books that had belonged to old René Garoux and his sons. None of them had been touched in years. Damon Julian was not a reader.

Sour Billy entered and stood a respectful distance away, silent until Julian spoke.

"Well?" the voice from the darkness asked at last.

"Four thousand," Sour Billy said, "but you'll like her. A young one, nice and tender, beautiful, real beautiful."

"The others will be here soon. Alain and Jean are here already, the fools. The thirst is on them. Bring her to the ballroom when she is ready."

"Yes," Sour Billy said quickly. "There was trouble at the auction, Mister Julian."

"Trouble?"

"A Creole sharper, name of Montreuil. He wanted her too, didn't like being outbid. Think he might get curious. He's a gambler, seen a lot around the gaming rooms. Want me to take care of him some night?"

"Tell me about him," Julian commanded. His voice was liquid, soft and deep and sensuous, rich as a fine cognac.

"Young, dark. Black eyes, black hair. Tall. A duelist, they say.

Hard man. Strong and lean, but he's got a pretty face, like so many of them do."

"I will see to him," Damon Julian said.

"Yes, sir," said Sour Billy Tipton. He turned and went back to his rooms.

Emily was transformed when she slipped into the brocade gown. Slave and child alike vanished; washed and dressed properly, she was a woman of dark, almost ethereal beauty. Sour Billy inspected her carefully. "You'll do," he said. "Come, you're goin' to a ball.'"

The ballroom was the largest and grandest chamber in the house, lit by three huge cut-glass chandeliers burning with a hundred tiny candles. Bayou landscapes done in rich oils hung on the walls, and the floors were beautifully polished wood. At one end of the room wide double doors opened out onto a foyer; at the other, a great staircase rose and branched off to either side, its banisters gleaming.

They were waiting when Sour Billy led her in.

Nine of them were on hand, including Julian himself; six men, three women, the men in dark suits of European cut, the women in pale silken gowns. Except for Julian, they waited on the staircase, still and silent, respectful. Sour Billy knew them all: the pale women who called themselves Adrienne and Cynthia and Valerie, dark handsome Raymond with the boy's face, Kurt whose eyes burned like hot coals, all the others. One of them, Jean, trembled slightly as he waited, his lips pulled back from long white teeth, his hand moving in small spasms. The thirst was on him badly, but he did not act. He waited for Damon Julian. All of them waited for Damon Julian.

Julian walked across the ballroom to the slave girl Emily. He moved with the stately grace of a cat. He moved like a lord, like a king. He moved like darkness flowing, liquid and inevitable. He was a dark man, somehow, though his skin was very pale; his hair was black and curling, his clothing somber, his eyes glittering flint.

He stopped before her and smiled. Julian had a charming, sophisticated smile. "Exquisite," he said simply.

Emily blushed and stammered. "Shut up," Sour Billy told her sharply. "Don't you talk unless Mister Julian tells you to."

Julian ran his finger along one soft, dark cheek, and the girl trembled and tried to stand still. He stroked her hair languidly, then raised her face toward his and let his eyes drink from her own. At that Emily shied and cried out with alarm, but Julian placed his hands on either side of her face, and would not let her look away. "Lovely," he

said. "You are beautiful, child. We appreciate beauty here, all of us."
He released her face, took one of her small hands in his own, raised
it, and turned it over and bowed to plant a soft kiss on the inside of
her wrist.

The slave girl was still shaking, but she did not resist. Julian turned
her slightly, and gave her arm to Sour Billy Tipton. "Will you do the
honors, Billy?"

Sour Billy reached behind him, and pulled the knife from the
sheath in the small of his back. Emily's dark eyes bulged wide and
frightened and she tried to pull away, but he had a firm grip on her
and he was fast, very fast. The blade had scarcely come into view
and suddenly it was wet; a single swift slash across the inside of her
wrist, where Julian had planted his lips. Blood welled from the wound
and began to drip onto the floor, the patters loud in the stillness of
the ballroom.

Briefly the girl whimpered, but before she quite knew what was
happening Sour Billy had sheathed his knife and stepped away and
Julian had taken her hand again. He raised her slim arm up once
more, and bent his lips to her wrist, and began to suck.

Sour Billy retreated to the door. The others left the stair and came
closer, the women's gowns whispering softly. They stood in a hungry
circle about Julian and his prey, their eyes dark and hot. When Emily
lost consciousness, Sour Billy sprang forward and caught her beneath the arms, supporting her. She weighed almost nothing at all.

"Such beauty," Julian muttered when he broke free of her, lips
moist, eyes heavy and sated. He smiled.

"*Please*, Damon," implored the one called Jean, shaking like a man
with the fever.

Blood ran slowly, darkly down Emily's arm as Julian gave Jean a
cold, malignant stare. "Valerie," he said, "you are next." The pale
young woman with the violet eyes and yellow gown came forward,
knelt daintily, and began to lick at the terrible flow. Not until she had
licked the arm clean did she press her mouth to the open wound.

Raymond went next, by Julian's leave, then Adrienne, then Jorge.
Finally, when the others were done, Julian turned to Jean with a
smile and a gesture. He fell on her with a stifled sob, wrenching her
from Sour Billy's embrace, and began to tear at the soft flesh of her
throat. Damon Julian grimaced with distaste. "When he is done," he
told Sour Billy, "clean it up."

CHAPTER THREE

New Albany, Indiana, June 1857

THE mists were thick on the river and the air damp and chilly. It was just after midnight when Joshua York, finally arrived from St. Louis, met Abner Marsh in the deserted boatyards of New Albany. Marsh had been waiting for almost half an hour when York appeared, striding out of the fog like some pale apparition. Behind him, silent as shadows, came four others.

Marsh grinned toothily. "Joshua," he said. He nodded curtly to the others. He had met them briefly back in April, in St. Louis, before he had taken passage to New Albany to supervise the building of his dream. They were York's friends and traveling companions, but an odder bunch Marsh had never met. Two of them were men of indeterminate age with foreign names that he could neither remember nor pronounce; he called 'em Smith and Brown, to York's amusement. They were always yapping at each other in some outlandish gibble-gabble. The third man, a hollow-cheeked Easterner who dressed like a mortician, was called Simon and never spoke at all. The woman, Katherine, was said to be a Britisher. She was tall and kind of stooped, with a sickly, decaying look to her. She reminded Marsh of a great white vulture. But she was York's friend, all of them were, and York had warned him that he might have peculiar friends, so Abner Marsh held his tongue.

"Good evening, Abner," York said. He stopped and glanced around the yards, where the half-built steamers lay like so many skeletons amid the gray flowing mists. "Cold night, isn't it? For June?"

"That it is. You come far?"

"I've taken a suite at the Galt House over in Louisville. We hired a boat to take us across the river." His cool gray eyes studied the nearest steamboat with interest. "Is this one ours?"

Marsh snorted. "This little thing? Hell no, that's just some cheap stern-wheeler they're building for the Cincinnati trade. You don't think I'd put no damned stern-wheel on *our* boat, do you?"

York smiled. "Forgive my ignorance. Where is our boat, then?"

"Come this way," Marsh said, gesturing broadly with his walking stick. He led them half across the boatyard. "There," he said, pointing.

The mists gave way for them, and there she stood, high and proud, dwarfing all the other boats around her. Her cabins and rails gleamed with fresh paint pale as snow, bright even in the gray shroud of fog. Way up on her texas roof, halfway to the stars, her pilot house seemed to glitter; a glass temple, its ornate cupola decorated all around with fancy woodwork as intricate as Irish lace. Her chimneys, twin pillars that stood just forward of the texas deck, rose up a hundred feet, black and straight and haughty. Their feathered tops bloomed like two dark metal flowers. Her hull was slender and seemed to go on forever, with her stern obscured by the fog. Like all the first-class boats, she was a side-wheeler. Set amidship, the huge curved wheelhouses loomed gigantic, hinting at the vast power of the paddle wheels concealed within them. They seemed all the larger for want of the name that would soon be emblazoned across them.

In the night and the fog, amid all those smaller, plainer boats, she seemed a vision, a white phantom from some riverman's dream. She took the breath away, Marsh thought as they stood there.

Smith was gibbling and Brown was gabbling back at him, but Joshua York just looked. For the longest time he looked, and then he nodded. "We have created something beautiful, Abner," he said.

Marsh smiled.

"I had not expected to find her so close to finished," York said.

"This is New Albany," said Marsh. "That's why I came here, instead of one of the boatyards in St. Louis. They been buildin' steamboats here since I was a boy, built twenty-two of 'em just last year, probably have almost that many this year. I knew they could do the job for us. You should have been here. I came in with one of those little chests of gold, and I dumped it all over the superintendent's desk, and I says to him, I says, 'I want a steamer built, and I want it built *quick*, and I want it to be the fastest and prettiest and best damn heller of a boat that you ever damn built, you hear? Now you get me some engineers, your best, I don't care if you got to drag 'em out of some cathouse over to Louisville, you get 'em to me tonight, so we can begin. And you get me the best damn carpenters and painters and boilermakers and all the damn rest, cause if I get anything *but* the best, you're goin' to be a mighty sorry man.' " Marsh laughed. "You should of seen him, didn't know whether to look at that gold or lissen to me, both scared him half to death. But he did us right, that he did." He nodded toward the boat. "Course, she's not finished. Trim needs to be painted, goin' do it up mostly in blue and silver, to go with all that silver you wanted in the saloon. And we're still waitin' on some of the fancy furniture and mirrors you ordered from Philadelphia, and such things. But mostly she's done, Joshua, mostly she's ready. Come, I'll show you."

Workmen had abandoned a lantern atop a pile of lumber near the stern of the boat. Marsh struck a match on his leg, lit the lantern, and thrust it imperiously at Brown. "Here, you, carry this," he said brusquely. He went clomping heavily up a long board onto the main deck, the others trailing behind. "Careful what you touch," he said, "some of the paint's still wet."

The lowest, or main, deck was full of machinery. The lantern burned with a clear, steady light, but Brown kept moving it around, so the shadows of the hulking machines seemed to shift and jump ominously, as if they were things alive. "Here, hold that still," Marsh commanded. He turned to York and began to point, his stick jabbing like a long hickory finger toward the boilers, great metal cylinders that ran along either side of the forepart of the deck. "Eighteen boilers," Marsh said proudly, "three more than the *Eclipse*. Thirty-eight-inch diameters, twenty-eight-foot long, each of 'em." His stick waggled. "Furnaces are all done up with firebrick and sheet iron, got 'em up on brackets clear of the deck, cuts down on the chance of fires." He traced the path of the steam lines overhead, running from the boilers back to the engines, and they all turned toward the stern. "We got thirty-six-inch cylinders, high pressure, and we got ourselves an eleven-foot stroke, same as the *Eclipse*. This boat is goin' chew up that old river something terrible, I tell you."

Brown gabbled, Smith gibbled, and Joshua York smiled.

"Come on up," Marsh said. "Your friends don't seem too interested in the engines, but they ought to like it just fine upstairs."

The staircase was wide and ornate, polished oak with graceful fluted banisters. It began up near the bow, its width hiding the boilers and engines from those boarding, then broke in two and curled gracefully to either side to open on the second, or boiler, deck. They walked along the starboard side, with Marsh and his stick and Brown and the lantern leading the way, their boots clacking on the hardwood deck of the promenade as they marveled at the fine gothic detail of the pillars and the guard rails, all the painstakingly shaped wood, carved with flowers and curlicues and acorns. Stateroom doors and windows ran fore and aft in a long, long row; the doors were dark walnut, the windows stained glass. "Staterooms aren't furnished yet," Marsh said, opening a door and leading them into one, "but we're getting nothing but the best, featherbeds and feather pillows, a mirror and an oil lamp for each room. Our cabins are larger than usual, too—won't be able to take quite as many passengers as some other boat our size, but they'll have more room." He smiled. "We can charge 'em more too."

Each cabin had two doors; one leading out onto the deck, the other inward, to the grand saloon, the main cabin of the steamer. "Main cabin isn't near finished," Marsh said, "but come look at it anyway."

They entered and stopped, while Brown raised the lantern to cast light all up and down the vast, echoing length of it. The grand saloon extended the length of the boiler deck, continuous and unobstructed except by a midship gangway. "Fore portion is the gents' cabin, aft for the ladies," Marsh explained. "Take a look. Ain't done yet, but she'll be something. That marble bar there is forty foot long, and we're going to put a mirror behind it just as big. Got it on order now. We'll have mirrors on every stateroom door too, with silver frames around 'em, and a twelve-foot-high mirror there, at the aft end of the ladies' cabin." He pointed upward with his stick. "Can't see nothing now, with it being dark and all, but the skylights are stained glass, run the whole length of the cabin. We're going to put down one of them Brussels carpets, and carpets in all the staterooms too. We got a silver water cooler with silver cups that's going to stand on a fancy wooden table, and we got a grand piano, and brand new velvet chairs, and real linen tablecloths. None of it is here yet, though."

Even empty of carpeting, mirrors, and furniture, the long cabin had a splendor to it. They walked down it slowly, in silence, and in the moving light of the lantern bits of its stately beauty suddenly took form from the darkness, only to vanish again behind them: The high arched ceiling with its curving beams, carved and painted with detail as fine as fairy lace. Long rows of slim columns flanking the stateroom doors, trimmed with delicate fluting. The black marble bar with its thick veins of color. The oily sheen of dark wood. The double row of chandeliers, each with four great crystal globes hanging from a spiderweb of wrought iron, wanting only oil and a flame and all those mirrors to wake the whole saloon to glorious, glittering light.

"I thought the cabins too small," Katherine said suddenly, "but this room will be grand."

Marsh frowned at her. "The cabins are big, ma'am. Eight foot square. Six is usual. This is a steamer, you know." He turned away from her, pointed with his walking stick. "Clerk's office will be all the way forward there, the kitchen and the washrooms are by the wheelhouses. I know just the cook I want to get, too. Used to work on my Lady Liz."

The roof of the boiler deck was the hurricane deck. They walked up a narrow stair and emerged forward of the great black iron smokestacks, then up a shorter stair to the texas deck, which ran back from the stacks to the wheelhouses. "Crew's cabins," Marsh said, not bothering with a tour. The pilot house stood atop the texas. He led them up and in.

From here, the whole yards were visible; all the lesser boats wrapped in mist, the black waters of the Ohio River beyond, and even the distant lights of Louisville, ghostly flickers in the fog. The interior of the pilot house was large and plush. The windows were of the best and clearest glass, with stained glass trim around them. Everywhere shone dark wood, and polished silver pale and cold in the lantern light.

And there was the wheel. Only the top half of it was visible, so huge was it, and even that stood as high as Marsh himself, while the bottom half was set in a slot in the floorboards. It was fashioned of soft black teak, cool and smooth to the touch, and the spokes wore ornamental silver bands like a dancehall girl wears garters. The wheel seemed to cry out for a pilot's hands.

Joshua York came up to the wheel and touched it, running a pale hand over the black wood and silver. Then he took hold of it, as if he were a pilot himself, and for a long moment he stood like that, the wheel in his hands and his gray eyes brooding as they stared out into the night and the unseasonable June fog. The others all fell silent, and for a brief moment Abner Marsh could almost feel the steamboat move, over some dark river of the mind, on a voyage strange and endless.

Joshua York turned then, and broke the spell. "Abner," he said, "I would like to learn to steer this boat. Can you teach me to pilot?"

"Pilot, eh?" Marsh said, surprised. He had no difficulty imagining York as a master and a captain, but piloting was something else—yet somehow the very asking made him warm to his partner, made him understandable after all. Abner Marsh knew what it was to want to pilot. "Well, Joshua," he said, "I've done my share of piloting, and it's the grandest feeling in the world. Being a captain, that ain't nothin' to piloting. But it ain't something you just pick up, if you know what I'm saying."

"The wheel looks simple enough to master," York said.

Marsh laughed. "Hell yes, but it's not the wheel you got to learn. It's the river, York, the river. The old Mississippi hisself. I was a pilot for eight years, before I got my own boats, licensed for the upper Mississippi and the Illinois. Never for the Ohio, though, or the lower Mississippi, and for all I knew about steamboatin' I couldn't have piloted no boat on those rivers to save my life—didn't know 'em. Those I did know, it took me years to learn 'em, and the learnin' never stopped. By now I been out of the pilot house for so long that I'd have to learn 'em all over again. The river changes, Joshua, that it does. Ain't never the same twice in a row, and you got to know every inch of it." Marsh strolled to the wheel and put one of his own hands on it, fondly. "Now, I plan to pilot this boat, at least once. I dreamed about her too long not to want to take her in my hands. When we go against the *Eclipse*, I mean to stand a spell in the pilot house, that I do. But she's too grand a boat for anything but the New Orleans trade, and that means the lower river, so I'm going to have to start learnin' myself, learn every damn foot. Takes time, takes work." He looked at York. "You still want to pilot, now that you know what it means?"

"We can learn together, Abner," York replied.

York's companions were growing restless. They wandered from window to window, Brown shifting the lantern from one hand to another, Simon as grim as a cadaver. Smith said something to York in their foreign tongue. York nodded. "We must be going back," he said.

Marsh glanced around one final time, reluctant to leave even now, and led them from the pilot house.

When they had trudged partway through the boatyards, York

turned and looked back toward their steamboat where she sat on her pilings, pale against the darkness. The others stopped as well, and waited silently.

"Do you know Byron?" York asked Marsh.

Marsh thought a minute. "Know a fellow named Blackjack Pete used to pilot on the *Grand Turk*. I think his last name was Brian."

York smiled. "Not Brian, Byron. Lord Byron, the English poet."

"Oh," said Marsh. "Him. I'm not much a one for poems. I think I heard of him, though. Gimp, wasn't he? And quite a one for the ladies."

"The very one, Abner. An astounding man. I had the good fortune to meet him once. Our steamboat put me in mind of a poem he once wrote." He began to recite.

> *She walks in Beauty, like the night*
> *Of cloudless climes and starry skies;*
> *And all that's best of dark and bright*
> *Meet in her aspect and her eyes:*
> *Thus mellowed to that tender light*
> *Which Heaven to gaudy day denies.*

"Byron wrote of a woman, of course, but the words seem to fit our boat as well, do they not? Look at her, Abner! What do you think?"

Abner Marsh didn't quite know what to think; your average steamboatman didn't go around spouting poetry, and he didn't know what to say to one that did. "Very interesting, Joshua," was all he managed.

"What shall we name her?" York asked, his eyes still fixed on the boat, and a slight smile on his face. "Does the poem suggest anything?"

Marsh frowned. "We're not going to name her after any gimp Britisher, if that's what you're thinking," he said gruffly.

"No," said York, "I wasn't suggesting that. I had in mind something like *Dark Lady*, or—"

"I had somethin' in mind myself," Marsh said. "We're Fevre River Packets, after all, and this boat is all I ever dreamed come true." He lifted his hickory stick and pointed at the wheelhouse. "We'll put it right there, big blue and silver letters, real fancy. *Fevre Dream*." He smiled. "*Fevre Dream* against the *Eclipse*, they'll talk about that race till all of us are dead."

For a moment, something strange and haunted moved in Joshua

32

York's gray eyes. Then it was gone as swiftly as it had come. *"Fevre Dream,"* he said. "Don't you think that choice a bit . . . oh, ominous? It suggests sickness to me, fever and death and twisted visions. Dreams that . . . dreams that should not be dreamed, Abner."

Marsh frowned. "I don't know about that. I like it."

"Will people ride in a boat with such a name? Steamboats have been known to carry typhoid and yellow fever. Do we wish to remind them of such things?"

"They rode my *Sweet Fevre,*" Marsh said. "They ride the *War Eagle,* and the *Ghost,* even boats named after Red Indians. They'd ride her."

The gaunt, pale one named Simon said something then, in a voice that rasped like a rusty saw and a language strange to Marsh, though it was not the one Smith and Brown babbled in. York heard him and his face took on a thoughtful cast, though it still seemed troubled. *"Fevre Dream,"* he said again. "I had hoped for a—a healthier name, but Simon has made a point to me. Have your way then, Abner. The *Fevre Dream* she is."

"Good," Marsh said.

York nodded absently. "Let us meet tomorrow for dinner at the Galt House. At eight. We can make plans for our voyage to St. Louis, discuss crew and provisioning, if that is agreeable to you."

Marsh voiced a gruff assent, and York and his companions went off toward their boat, vanishing into the mists. Long after they had gone Marsh stood in the boatyards, staring at the still, silent steamer. *"Fevre Dream,"* he said loudly, just to test the taste of the words on his tongue. But oddly, for the first time, the name seemed wrong in his ears, fraught with connotations he did not like. He shivered, unaccountably cold for a moment, then snorted and set off for bed.

CHAPTER FOUR

Aboard the Steamer FEVRE DREAM, Ohio River, July 1857

THE *Fevre Dream* left New Albany by dark, on a sultry night early in July. In all his years on the river, Abner Marsh had never felt so alive as he did that day. He spent the morning attending to last minute details in Louisville and New Albany; hiring a barber and lunching with the men from the boatyards and posting a handful of letters. In the heat of the afternoon, he settled into his cabin, made a last check round the steamer to make certain everything was right, and greeted some of the cabin passengers as they arrived. Supper was a rushed affair, and then he was off to the main deck to check the engineer and the strikers checking the boilers, and to supervise the mate as he supervised the loading of the last of the cargo. The sun beat down relentlessly and the air hung thick and still, so the roustabouts gleamed with sweat as they carried crates and bales and barrels up the narrow loading planks, the mate cussing at them all the while. Across the river to Louisville, Marsh knew, other steamers were departing or loading up as well: the big, low-pressure *Jacob Strader* of the Cincinnati Mail Line, the swift *Southerner* of the Cincinnati & Louisville Packet Company, a half-dozen smaller boats. He watched to see if any of 'em went down the river, feeling awful good despite the heat and the swarms of mosquitoes that had risen from the river when the sun went down.

The main deck was crammed with cargo fore and aft, filling most all the space not taken up by the boilers and furnaces and engines. She was carrying a hundred-fifty tons of bale leaf tobacco, thirty tons of bar iron, countless barrels of sugar and flour and brandy, crates of fancy furniture for some rich man in St. Louis, a couple blocks of salt, some bolts of silk and cotton, thirty barrels of nails, eighteen boxes of rifles, some books and papers and sundries. And lard. One dozen big barrels of the finest lard. But the lard wasn't cargo, properly; Marsh had bought it himself and ordered it stowed on board.

The main deck was crammed with passengers as well, men and women and children, thick as the river mosquitoes, swarming and milling amid the cargo. Near three hundred of 'em had crowded on, paying a dollar each for passage to St. Louis. Passage was all they got; they ate what food they brought on board with them, and the lucky ones found a place to sleep on the deck. They were mostly foreigners, Irish and Swedes and big Dutchmen all yelling at each other in languages Marsh didn't know, drinking and cussing and slapping their kids. A few trappers and common laborers were down there as well, too poor for anything but deck passage at Marsh's bargain rates.

The cabin passengers had paid a full ten dollars, at least those who were going all the way to St. Louis. Almost all the cabins were full, even at that rate; the clerk told Marsh they had one hundred seventy-seven cabin passengers aboard, which Marsh figured had to be a good number, with all those sevens in it. The roster included a dozen planters, the head of a big St. Louis fur company, two bankers, a rich Britisher and his three daughters, and four nuns going to Iowa. They also had a preacher on board, but that was all right since they weren't carrying no gray mare; it was well known among rivermen that having a preacher and a gray mare on board was an invitation to disaster.

As for the crew, Marsh was right pleased with it. The two pilots, now, were nothing special, but they were only hired on temporary to take the steamer to St. Louis, since they were Ohio River pilots and the *Fevre Dream* was going to work the New Orleans trade. He had already written letters to St. Louis and New Orleans, and he had a couple of lightning lower Mississippi pilots waiting for them at the Planters' House. The rest of the crew, though, were as good as any steamboatmen on any river anywhere, Marsh was sure. The engineer was Whitey Blake, a peppery little man whose fierce white whiskers always had grease stains in 'em from the engines. Whitey had been with Abner Marsh on the *Eli Reynolds*, and later on the *Elizabeth A.* and the *Sweet Fevre*, and there wasn't no one understood a steam engine better than he did. Jonathon Jeffers, the clerk, had gold spectacles and slicked-back brown hair and fancy button gaiters, but he was a terror at ciphering and dickering, never forgot anything, struck a mean bargain and played a meaner game of chess. Jeffers had been in the line's main office until Marsh had written him to come down to the *Fevre Dream*. He'd come right away; for all of his dandified appearance, Jeffers was a riverman through to his dark ciphering soul. He carried a gold-handled sword cane too. The cook was a free colored man named Toby Lanyard, who had been with Marsh fourteen years, ever since Marsh tasted his cooking down in Natchez, bought him, and gave him his freedom. And the mate—who was named Michael Theodore Dunne though nobody ever called him anything but Hairy Mike except for the roustabouts, who called him Mister Dunne Sir—was one of the biggest and meanest and stubbornest men on the river. He was well over six foot tall, with green eyes and black whiskers and thick black curly hair all over his arms and legs and chest. He had a foul mouth and a bad temper and never went noplace without his three-foot-long black iron billet. Abner Marsh had never seen Hairy Mike hit anyone with that billet, except once or twice, but it was always wrapped in his hand, and there was talk among the roustabouts that he'd once split open the head of a man who'd dropped a cask of brandy in the river. He was a hard, fair mate, and no one dropped anything when he was watching. Everyone on the river respected the hell out of Hairy Mike Dunne.

It was a damn fine crew, those men on the *Fevre Dream*. Right from the first day, they all did their jobs, so by the time the stars were all out over New Albany, the cargo and the passengers were on board and on the records, the steam was up and the furnaces were roaring with a terrible ruddy light and enough heat to make the main deck warmer than Natchez-under-the-hill on a good night, and a fine meal was a-cooking in the kitchen. Abner Marsh checked it all, and when he was satisfied he climbed on up to the pilot house, which stood resplendent and dignified above all the chaos and bellowing below. "Back her out," he said to his pilot. And the pilot called down for some steam, and set the two great side wheels to backing. Abner Marsh stood back of him respectfully, and the *Fevre Dream* slid smoothly out onto the black, starlit waters of the Ohio.

Once out in the river, the pilot reversed the wheels and turned her to downstream, and the big steamer vibrated a little and slipped into the main channel easy as you please, the wheels going *chunkachunka chunkachunka* as they churned and roiled the water, the boat moving along faster and faster, with the speed of the current and her own steam, sparklin' along swift as a steamboater's dream, swift as sin, swift as the *Eclipse* herself. Above their heads, the chimneys gave off two long streamers of black smoke, and clouds of sparks flew out and vanished behind them, settling to the river to die like so many red and orange fireflies. To Abner Marsh's eyes, the smoke and steam and sparks they trailed behind them were a finer, grander sight than all the fireworks they'd seen in Louisville on the Fourth. The pilot reached up and sounded their steam whistle then, and the long shrill scream of it deafened them; it was a wonderful whistle, with a wild keening edge to it and a blast that could be heard for miles.

Not until the lights of Louisville and New Albany disappeared behind them and the *Fevre Dream* was steaming between banks as black and empty as they'd been a century ago did Abner Marsh become aware that Joshua York had come up to the pilot house and was standing by his side.

He was done up all fine, in trousers and tailcoat of the purest white, with a deep blue vest, a white shirt full of ruffles and fancies, and a blue silk tie. The watch chain that stretched across his vest was silver, and on one pale hand York wore a big silver ring, with a bright blue stone set in it, gleaming. White and blue and silver; those were the boat's colors, and York looked a part of her. The pilot house was hung with showy blue and silver curtains, and the big stuffed couch to the back of it was blue, and the oilcloth, too. "Why, I like your getup, Joshua," Marsh said to him.

York smiled. "Thank you," he said. "It seemed appropriate. You look striking as well." Marsh had bought himself a new pilot's jacket with shiny brass buttons, and a cap with the steamer's name embroidered on it in silver thread.

"Yeah," Marsh replied. He was never at ease with compliments; cussing was easier and more comfortable to him. "Well," he said, "were you up when we left?" York had been sleeping in the captain's cabin on the texas deck most of the day, while Marsh sweated and worried and performed most of the captain's actual duties. Marsh had slowly grown accustomed to the way York and his companions lived up the nights and slept during the day. He'd known others who'd done the same, and the one time he'd asked York about it, Joshua had just smiled and spouted that poem about "gaudy day" at Marsh again.

"I was standing on the hurricane deck, forward of the chimneys, watching everything. It was cool up there, once we got underway."

"A fast steamer makes her own wind," Marsh said. "Don't matter how hot the day is or how fierce the wood's burning, it's always fine and cool up above. Sometimes I feel a mite sorry for those down on the main deck, but what the hell, they're only payin' a dollar."

"Of course," Joshua York agreed.

The boat gave a heavy *thunk* just then, and shook slightly.

"What was that?" York asked.

"We just run over a log, probably," Marsh replied. "That so?" he asked the pilot.

"Grazed it," the man replied. "Don't fret, Cap'n. No damage done."

Abner Marsh nodded and turned back to York. "Well, should we be going on down to the main cabin? The passengers will all be up and about, seeing as how this is the first night out, so we can meet a few of 'em, talk 'em up, see that everything is good and proper."

"I'd be glad to," York replied. "But first, Abner, will you join me in my cabin for a drink? We ought to celebrate our departure, don't you agree?"

Marsh shrugged. "A drink? Well, I don't see why not." He tipped his cap at the pilot. "Good night, Mister Daly. I'll have some coffee sent up for you, if you'd like."

They left the pilot house and repaired to the captain's cabin, pausing for a moment while York unlocked the door—he had insisted that his cabin, and indeed all the staterooms on the boat, have good locks. That was a bit peculiar, but Marsh had been willing to acquiesce. York wasn't used to life on a steamer, after all, and most of his other requests had been sensible enough, like all that silver and the mirrors that made the main saloon such a splendid place.

York's cabin was three times the length of the passenger staterooms and twice as wide, so by steamer standards it was immense. But this was the first time Abner Marsh had been inside it since York had taken possession, so he looked around curiously. A pair of oil lamps on opposite sides of the cabin gave the interior a warm, cozy light. The wide stained-glass windows were dark now, shuttered off and curtained with heavy black velvet that looked soft and rich in the lamplight. In one corner was a tall chest of drawers with a basin of water set atop it, and a silver-framed mirror on the wall. There was a narrow but comfortable-looking featherbed, and two big leather chairs, and a great wide rosewood desk with lots of drawers and nooks and crannies. It stood flush against one wall. Above it, a fine old map of the Mississippi river system had been tacked up. The top of the desk was covered with leather-bound ledgers and piles and piles of newspapers. That was another of Joshua York's peculiarities; he read an inordinate number of newspapers, from just about all over—papers from England, papers in foreign languages, Mr. Greeley's *Tribune* of course and the *Herald* from New York as well, just about all the St. Louis and New Orleans papers, and all kinds of little river-town weeklies. He got packets of newspapers delivered to him every day. Books too; there was a tall bookcase in the cabin, and it was crammed full, and more books were stacked up on the little table by the bed, with a half-melted reading candle on top of them.

Abner Marsh didn't waste time looking at books, though. Next to the bookcase was a wooden wine rack, with twenty or thirty bottles lying neatly on their sides. He went directly to it and pulled out a bottle. The bottle was unlabeled, and the liquid within was a somber red, so dark it was almost black. A cap of shiny black wax sealed the cork on. "You got a knife?" he asked York, turning with the bottle in his hand.

"I don't think you'd care much for that vintage, Abner," York said. He was holding a tray with two silver goblets and a crystal decanter. "I have some excellent sherry here. Why don't we have that instead?"

Marsh hesitated. York's sherry was usually just fine and he hated to pass it up, but knowing Joshua he figured that any wine he kept a private stock of had to be superlative. Besides, he was curious. He shifted the bottle from one hand to the other. The liquid within flowed slowly, creeping along languidly like some sweet liqueur. "What is this anyway?" Marsh asked, frowning.

"A home brew of sorts," York replied. "Part wine and part brandy and part liqueur, tasting like none of them. A rare drink, Abner. My companions and I have a fondness for it, but most people find it not to their liking. I'm sure you'd prefer the sherry."

"Well," Marsh said, hefting the bottle, "anything you drink is probably just fine for me, Joshua. You do serve up good sherry, though, that's true enough." He brightened. "Say, we're in no hurry, and I got myself a fierce thirst. Why don't we try both?"

Joshua York laughed, a laugh of pure spontaneous delight, deep and musical. "Abner," he said, "you are singular, and most formidable. I like you. You, however, will not like my little drink. Still, if you insist, we shall have both."

They settled themselves into the two leather chairs, York putting the tray on the low table between them. Marsh handed over the bottle of wine, or whatever it was. From somewhere within the pristine folds of his white suit, York produced a skinny little knife, with an ivory handle and a long silver blade. He sliced away the wax, and with one single deft twist flicked the knife point into the cork and brought it out with a pop. The liquor poured slowly, flowing like red-black honey into the silver goblets. It was opaque, and seemed full of tiny black specks. Strong, though; Marsh lifted his goblet and sniffed at it, and the alcohol in it brought tears to his eyes.

"We ought to have a toast," York said, lifting his own goblet.

"To all the money we're going to make," Marsh joked.

"No," York said seriously. Those demon gray eyes of his had a kind of grave melancholy in them, Marsh thought. He hoped that York wasn't going to start reciting poetry again. "Abner," York continued, "I know what the *Fevre Dream* means to you. I want you to know that she means much to me, as well. This day is the start of a grand new life for me. You and I, together, we made her what she is, and we shall go on to make her a legend. I have always admired beauty, Abner, but this is the first time in a long life that I have created it, or helped in its creation. It is a good feeling, to bring something new and fine into the world. Particularly for me. And I have you to thank for it." He lifted his goblet. "Let us drink for the *Fevre Dream* and all she represents, my friend—beauty, freedom, hope. To our boat and a better world!"

"To the fastest steamer on the river!" Marsh replied, and they drank. He almost gagged. York's private drink went down like fire, searing the back of his throat and spreading warm tendrils in his innards, but there was a kind of cloying sweetness to it as well, and a hint of an unpleasant smell that all its strength and sweetness could not quite conceal. Tasted like something had rotted in the bottle, he thought.

Joshua York drained his own goblet in a single long motion, his head thrown back. Then he set it aside and looked at Marsh and laughed again. "The look on your face, Abner, is wonderfully grotesque. Don't feel you have to be polite. I warned you. Why don't you have some sherry?"

"I believe I will," Marsh replied, "I do believe I will."

Later, when two glasses of sherry had wiped the aftertaste of York's drink from Marsh's mouth, they got to talking.

"What is our next step after St. Louis, Abner?" York asked.

"The New Orleans trade. Ain't no other run for a boat as grand as this one."

York gave an impatient shake of his head. "I know that, Abner. I was curious about how you intend to realize your dream of beating the *Eclipse*. Will you seek her out and issue a challenge? I'm willing, so long as it does not delay us unduly or take us out of our way."

"Wish it were that simple, but it ain't. Hell, Joshua, there's thousands of steamers on the river, and all of them would like to beat the *Eclipse*. She's got runs to make, just like we do, passengers and freight to move. Can't be just racing all the time. Anyhow, her cap'n be a fool to lissen to any challenge from us. Who're we anyway? Some new steamer fresh out of New Albany that nobody ever heard of. *Eclipse*'d have everything to lose and nothin' to gain by racing us." He emptied another glass of sherry and held it out to York for a refill. "No, first we got to work our trade, build ourselves a reputation. Get known up and down the river as a fast boat. Pretty soon folks will get to talkin' about how fast she is, and get to wonderin' how *Fevre Dream* and *Eclipse* would match up. Maybe we run into her on the river a couple times, say, and pass her up. We build up the talk, and folks start to betting. Maybe we make some of the runs the *Eclipse* makes, and we beat her time. A fast steamer gets the trade, y'know. The planters and shippers and such, they want to get their wares to market soon as they can, so they go with the fastest boat around. And passengers, why they all love to ride on a famous boat if they got the money. So what happens, you see, is that after a time people start thinking we're the fastest boat on the lower river, and the trade starts moving our way, and the *Eclipse* gets hurt a little where it counts, in the purse. Then you just watch how easy we get us a race, to prove once and for all who's faster."

"I see," said York. "Is this run to St. Louis going to start our reputation, then?"

"Well, I ain't trying for no record time. She's a new boat, and we got to break her in. Don't even have our regular pilots on board yet, no one is real familiar with how she handles, and we got to give Whitey time to work out all the little problems with the engines and get his strikers trained proper." He set down his empty glass. "Don't mean we can't start in some other ways, though," he said, smiling. "Got something or other in mind along those lines. You'll see."

"Good," said Joshua York. "More sherry?"

"No," Marsh said. "We ought to get on down to the saloon, I think. I'll buy you a drink at our bar. Guarantee you it'll taste better than that damned stuff of yours."

York smiled. "My pleasure," he said.

That night was not like other nights for Abner Marsh. It was a magic night, a dream. There seemed to be at least forty or fifty hours in it, he could have sworn, and each of them was priceless. He and York were up till dawn, drinking and talking up a storm, wandering all over the wonder of a boat they had built. The day after, Marsh woke with such a head that he could barely recall half of what he'd done the night before. But some moments were indelible in his memory.

He remembered entering the grand saloon, and it was better than entering the finest hotel in the world. The chandeliers were brilliant, lamps aglow and prisms glittering. The mirrors made the long narrow cabin seem twice as wide as it really was. A crowd was gathered around the bar, talking politics and such, and Marsh joined them for a while and listened to them complain about abolitionists and argue over whether Stephen A. Douglas ought to be president, while York said hello to Smith and Brown, who were at one of the tables playing cards with some planters and a notorious gambler. Someone was tinkling on the grand piano, stateroom doors opened and closed all the time, and the whole place was bright with light and laughter.

Later they went down to a different world on the main deck; cargo piled everywhere, roustabouts and deckers asleep on coils of rope and bags of sugar, a family gathered around a little fire they'd built cooking something or other, a drunk passed out behind the stairs. The engine room was awash in the hellish red glow of the furnaces, and Whitey was in the middle of it all, with his shirt soaked by sweat and grease in his beard, bellowing at his strikers to be heard above the hiss of the steam and the *chunkachunka* of the wheels churning water. The rods were awesome, moving back and forth in their long powerful strokes. They watched for a while, York and he, until the heat and smell of machine oil got to be too much for them.

Some time later they were up on the hurricane deck, passing a bottle between them, strolling and talking in their own cool wind. The stars were bright as a lady's diamonds overhead, the Fevre River banner was flapping on both fore and verge flagpoles, and the river around them was blacker than the blackest slave Marsh had ever seen.

They ran all night, Daly standing the long watch up in the pilot house, keeping them moving at a smart clip—though nothing to what they could do if pressed, Marsh knew—along the dark Ohio, with nothingness all around them. It was a charmed run, with no snags or sawyers or sandbars to bedevil them. Only twice did they have to send out a yawl ahead of them for soundings, and both times they found good water when they dropped lead, and the *Fevre Dream* steamed on. A few houses were glimpsed on the shore, most dark and shuttered for the night, but one with a light burning in a high window. Marsh wondered who was awake up there, and what they thought when the steamer went on by. She must have been a fine sight, with her decks all lit and the music and laughter drifting out over the water, the sparks and smoke from her chimneys, and her name big on the wheelhouse, *Fevre Dream* done all in thick fancy blue lettering with silver trim around it. He almost wished he was on shore just to see it.

The big excitement of the night came just before midnight, when they first sighted another steamer churning water ahead of them. When Marsh saw, he took York by the elbow and led him on up to the pilot house. It was crowded up there, Daly still at the wheel, sipping coffee, two other pilots and three passengers sitting on the couch behind him. The pilots weren't nobody hired by Marsh, but pilots rode free if they wanted to, that was a custom of the river, and they usually rode in the pilot house to chat with the man at the wheel and keep up on the river. Marsh ignored them. "Mister Daly," he said to his pilot, "there's a steamer up ahead."

"I see it, Cap'n Marsh," Daly replied with a laconic grin.

"Wonder what boat that is? You got any idea, Daly?" Whatever boat it was, it wasn't much; some squat stern-wheeler with a pilot house square as a cracker box.

"Sure don't," the pilot replied.

Abner Marsh turned to Joshua York. "Joshua," he said, "You're the real captain, now, and I don't want to be givin' you too many suggestions. But the truth is, I'm awful curious as to what steamer that is on up ahead of us. Why don't you tell Daly here to catch her for us, so I can relax a bit."

York smiled. "Certainly," he said. "Mister Daly, you heard Captain Marsh. Do you think the *Fevre Dream* can catch that boat on ahead?"

"She can catch *anything*," the pilot said. He called down to the engineer for more steam, and pulled the steam whistle again, and the wild banshee scream echoed over the river, as if to warn the steamer up ahead that the *Fevre Dream* was coming after her.

The blast was enough to bring all the passengers out of the main saloon onto the deck. It even got the deck passengers up off their bags of flour. A couple of pasengers came wandering up and tried to enter the pilot house, but Marsh chased 'em all down below again, along with the three who'd already been up there. As passengers will, all of them rushed to the front of the boat, and later to the larboard side, when it became clear that was the side they'd pass the other boat on. "Damn passengers," Marsh muttered to York. "Never will trim boat. One of these days they'll all rush to the same side and tip some poor steamer right on over, I swear it."

For all his complaining, Marsh was delighted. Whitey was chucking in more wood down below, the furances were roaring, and the big wheels moved faster and faster. It was over in hardly no time at all. The *Fevre Dream* seemed to eat up the miles between her and the other boat, and when she passed her a ragged cheer came up from the lower decks, sweet music to Marsh's ears.

As they surged past the small stern-wheeler, York read her name off the pilot house. "She seems to be the *Mary Kaye*," he said.

"Well, boil me for an egg!" Marsh said.

"Is she a well-known boat?" York asked.

"Hell no," said Marsh. "I never heard of her. Can you beat that?" Then he laughed uproariously and clapped York on the back, and before long everyone in the pilot house was laughing.

Before the night was over, the *Fevre Dream* had caught and passed a half-dozen steamers, including one side-wheeler near as big as she was, but it never got as exciting as that first time, catching the *Mary Kaye*. "You wanted to know how we'd begin it," Marsh said to York when they left the pilot house. "Well, Joshua, it's begun."

"Yes," said York, glancing back behind them, where the *Mary Kaye* was growing small in the distance. "Indeed it has."

CHAPTER FIVE

Aboard the Steamer FEVRE DREAM, Ohio River, July 1857————

HEADACHE or no, Abner Marsh was too good a riverman to sleep away the day, especially a day as important as this one. He sat up in bed around eleven, after a scant few hours sleep, splashed some tepid water on his face from the basin on the nightstand, and dressed. There was work to be done, and York wouldn't be up and around till dusk. Marsh set his cap on his head, scowled at himself in the mirror and fluffed out his beard a little, then gathered up his walking stick and lumbered on down from the texas to the boiler deck. He visited the washrooms first, then ducked back to the kitchen. "Missed breakfast, Toby," he said to the cook, who was already preparing dinner. "Have one of your boys fix me up a half-dozen eggs and a slab of ham, and sent it on up to the texas, will you? Coffee, too. Lots of coffee."

In the grand saloon, Marsh had a quick drink or two, which made him feel somewhat better. He mumbled a few polite words at passengers and waiters, then hastened back to the texas to wait for his food.

After he'd eaten, Abner Marsh felt like his old self again.

He climbed on up to the pilot house after breakfast. The watch had changed, and the other pilot was at the wheel, with only one of the freeloaders keeping him company. "Morning, Mister Kitch," Marsh said to his pilot. "How's she drawin'?"

"I ain't complainin'," the pilot replied. He glanced at Marsh. "This here boat of yours is a frisky one, Cap'n. You take her down to New Orleans, you better get yourself some good pilots. She takes a good hand at the wheel, she does."

Marsh nodded. That wasn't unexpected; frequently the faster boats were hard to handle. It didn't bother him. No pilot who didn't know what he was about was going to get anywhere near the *Fevre Dream*'s wheel.

"What kind of time we makin'?" Marsh asked.

"Smart enough," the pilot replied with a shrug. "She can do better, but Mister Daly said you weren't in no hurry, so we're just lazing along."

"Put in at Paducah when we get there," Marsh ordered. "Got a couple passengers to set off and some freight to discharge." He spent a few minutes chatting with the pilot and finally went on back down to the boiler deck.

The main cabin had been set up for dinner. Bright noon sunlight was pouring from the skylights in a cascade of colors, and beneath it a long row of tables ran the length of the cabin. The waiters were setting silverware and china; crystal glasses gleamed brilliantly in the light. From the kitchen, Marsh caught hints of the most marvelous, mouth-watering smells. He paused and found himself a menu, glanced over it and decided he was still hungry. Besides, York wasn't about yet, and it was only fitting that one of the captains join the cabin passengers and other officers for dinner.

The dinner, Marsh thought, was excellent. Marsh put away a big plate of roast lamb in parsley sauce, a small pigeon, lots of Irish potatoes and green corn and beets, and two pieces of Toby's famous pecan pie. By the time dinner was over, he was feeling quite amiable. He even gave the preacher permission to give a little lecture on bringing Christianity to the Indians, though he didn't normally hold with no bible-thumping on his boats. Had to keep the passengers amused somehow, Marsh figured, and even the prettiest scenery got boring after a while.

Early in the afternoon, the *Fevre Dream* put into Paducah, which lay on the Kentucky side of the river, where the Tennessee emptied into the Ohio. It was their third stop on the run, but the first lengthy one. They'd put in briefly at Rossborough during the night, to drop off three passengers, and they'd taken on wood and a small amount of freight at Evansville while Marsh had been asleep. But they had to discharge twelve tons of bar iron at Paducah, as well as some flour and sugar and books, and there was supposed to be some forty or fifty tons of lumber waiting there to be loaded. Paducah was a big lumbering town, with log rafts all the time coming down the Tennessee, clogging up the river and getting in the way of the steamboats. Like most steamboatmen, Marsh didn't have much use for rafters. Half the time they didn't show no lights at night, and they got run over by some unlucky steamer, and then they had the gumption to cuss and yell and throw things.

Fortunately, there were no rafts about when they put into Paducah and tied up. Marsh took one look at the cargo waiting on the riverfront—which included several towering stacks of crates and some bales of tobacco—and decided that it would be easy to get some more freight onto the main deck. It would be a shame, he decided, to steam away from Paducah and leave all this custom to some other boat.

Already the *Fevre Dream* was secure to the wharf, and swarms of roustabouts were laying down planks and starting to unload. Hairy Mike moved out among them, yelling "Quick now, you ain't no cabin passenger out for no stroll," and "You drop that, boy, and I'm gone drop this here iron right longside you head," and other such things. The stage came down with a *whunk*, and a few Paducah passengers began to disembark.

Marsh made up his mind. He went to the clerk's office, where he found Jonathon Jeffers working over some bills of lading. "You got to do those now, Mister Jeffers?" he asked.

"Hardly, Cap'n Marsh," Jeffers replied. He removed his spectacles and wiped them on a neckerchief. "These are for Cairo."

"Good," Marsh said. "Come on with me. Going to go ashore and find out who owns all that freight settin' out there in the sun, and where it's bound to. Figure it's got to be going St. Louis way, some of it, and maybe we can make ourself some money."

"Excellent," Jeffers replied. He got off his stool, straightened his neat black coat, checked to make sure the big iron safe was locked, and picked up his sword cane. "I know a fine grog shop in Paducah," he added as they left.

Marsh's venture proved well worthwhile. They found the tobacco shipper easily enough, and took him to the grog shop, where Marsh persuaded him to consign his goods to the *Fevre Dream* and Jeffers dickered out a good price. It took some three hours, but Marsh was feeling damned pleased with the bit of work when he and Jeffers came strolling back to the riverfront and the *Fevre Dream*. Hairy Mike was lounging on the wharf, smoking a black cigar and talking with the mate from some other boat, when they returned. "That's ours now," Marsh told him, pointing out the tobacco with his stick. "Get your boys to load it quick, so we can get underway."

Marsh leaned on the railing of the boiler deck, shaded and content, watching them scramble and tote the bales while Whitey got the steam up. He chanced to notice something else; a line of horse-drawn hotel omnibuses waiting on the road just off the steamboat landing. Marsh stared at them curiously for a moment, pulling at his whiskers, then went on up to the pilot house.

The pilot was having a slice of pie and a cup of coffee. "Mister Kitch," Marsh told him, "don't take her out until I tell you so."

"Why's that, Cap'n? She's almost loaded, and the steam's up."

"Look out there," Marsh said, lifting his stick. "Them omnibuses are bringing passengers to the landing, or waiting for 'em to arrive. Not our passengers, neither, and they don't meet every little stern-wheeler that puts in. I got myself a hunch."

A few moments later, his hunch was rewarded. Spewing steam and smoke and sparkling down the Ohio fast as the devil, a long classy side-wheeler came into sight. Marsh recognized her almost at once, even before he could read her name; the *Southerner*, of the Cincinnati & Louisville Packet Company. "I knew it!" he said. "She must have left Louisville a half-day after we did. She made better time, though." He moved to the side window, brushed aside the fancy curtains that were shutting out the hot afternoon sun, and watched the other steamer pull in, tie up, and begin to discharge passengers. "She won't take long," Marsh said to his pilot. "No freight to load or unload, just passengers. You let her pull out first, you understand? Let her get down the river a bit, then you back out and go after her."

The pilot finished his last forkful of pie and wiped a bit of meringue from the corner of his mouth with his napkin. "You want me to let the *Southerner* get ahead of us and then try to catch her? Cap'n, we'll be breathin' her steam all the way to Cairo. After that she'll be out of sight."

Abner Marsh clouded up like a thunderhead about to break. "What do you think you're sayin', Mister Kitch? I don't want to lissen to no talk like that. If you ain't pilot enough to do it, just say so, and I'll kick Mister Daly out of bed and get him on up here to take the wheel."

"That's the *Southerner*," Kitch insisted.

"And this is the *Fevre Dream*, and don't you forget it!" Marsh shouted. He turned and stormed from the cabin, scowling. Damn pilots all thought they were kings of the river. Of course they were, once the boat was on the river, but that didn't give them no cause to go bellyaching about a little race and doubting his steamer.

His fury faded when he saw that the *Southerner* was taking on passengers already. He had been hoping for something like this from the minute he spied the *Southerner* over across the river back in Louisville, but he hadn't dared hope too hard. If *Fevre Dream* could catch the *Southerner*, her reputation was halfway made, once folks along the river heard about it. The other steamer, and her sister boat the *Northerner*, were the pride of their line. They were special boats, built back in '53 especially for speed. Smaller than the *Fevre Dream*, they were the only steamers Marsh knew of that didn't carry freight, only passengers. He couldn't see for a minute how they turned a profit, but that wasn't important. What was important was how fast they were. The *Northerner* had set a new record for the Louisville–St. Louis run back in '54. The *Southerner* broke it the following year, and still had the fastest time; one day and nineteen hours even. High up on her pilot house, she wore the gilded antlers that marked her as the fleetest steamer on the Ohio.

The more he considered the prospect of taking her on, the more excited Abner Marsh grew. All of a sudden it occurred to him that this was not something Joshua would care to miss, beauty sleep or no. Marsh stomped forward to York's cabin, determined to roust him out. He rapped sharply on the door with the head of his walking stick.

No answer. Marsh rapped again, louder and more insistently. "Hallo in there!" he boomed. "Get yourself out of bed, Joshua, we're goin' to run us a race!"

Still no sound came from within York's cabin. Marsh tried the door and found it locked. He rattled it, pounded on the walls, knocked on the shuttered window, shouted; all to no avail. "Damn you, York," he said, "get yourself up or you're goin' to miss it." Then he had an idea. He walked back near the pilot house. "Mister Kitch, sir," he shouted up. Abner Marsh could shout with the best of them when he put his lungs into it good. Kitch popped his head out the door and looked down at him. "You blow that whistle," Marsh told him, "and keep blowing it till I wave at you, you hear?"

He returned to York's locked door and began pounding again, and suddenly the steam whistle began to shriek. Once. Twice. Three times. Long angry blasts. Marsh flailed away with his stick.

York's cabin door came open.

Marsh took one look at York's eyes and his mouth hung open in mid-shout. The steam whistle sounded again, and he waved hurriedly. It fell silent. "*Get in here,*" Joshua York said in a cold whisper.

Marsh entered, and York swung the door shut behind him. Marsh heard him throw the lock. He didn't see it. He didn't see anything. Once the door closed, York's cabin was black as the pit. Not even a crack of light snuck in through the door or the shuttered, curtained windows. Marsh felt like he'd gone blind. But in his mind's eye, a vision lingered, the last thing he'd seen before the darkness closed in: Joshua York, standing in the doorway naked as the day he was born, his skin deathly white as alabaster, his lips drawn back in animal rage, his eyes like two smoky gray slits opening onto hell.

"Joshua," Marsh said, "can you turn on a lamp? Or pull back a curtain, or something? I can't see."

"I can see just fine," York's voice replied from the darkness behind him. Marsh hadn't heard him move. He turned, and blundered into something. "*Hold still,*" York commanded, with such force and fury in his tone that Marsh had no choice but to obey. "Here, I'll give you a light, before you wreck my cabin."

A match flared across the room, and York touched it to his reading candle, then seated himself on the edge of his rumpled bed. He'd donned a pair of trousers, somehow, but his face was hard and terrible. "There," he said. "Now, *why are you here?* I warn you, you had better have a reason!"

Marsh began to grow angry. No one talked to him that way, no one. "The *Southerner* is next to us, York," he snapped. "The fastest damn boat on this river, got the horns and everything. I'm fixin' to run *Fevre Dream* after her, and I thought you'd want to see. If you don't think that's reason enough for getting you out of bed, then you ain't no steamboatman and you never will be! And you watch your manners with me, you hear?"

Something flared in Joshua York's eyes, and he started to rise, but even as he did he checked himself, and turned away. "Abner," he said. He paused, frowning. "I am sorry. I did not intend to treat you with disrespect, or to frighten you. Your intent was good." Marsh was startled to see his hand clench violently, before he steadied it. York crossed the dim cabin with three quick, purposeful strides. On his desk rested the bottle of his private drink, the one Marsh had caused him to open the night before. He poured out a full goblet of it, tossed back his head, and drained it straightaway. "Ah," he said softly. He swung about to face Marsh again. "Abner," he said, "I've given you your dream boat, but not as a gift. We struck a bargain. You are to obey such orders as I give, respect my eccentric behavior, and ask no questions. Do you mean to live up to your half of our bargain?"

"I'm a man of my word!" Marsh said stoutly.

"Good," said York. "Now listen. You meant well, but it was wrong of you to wake me as you did. Never do it again. Never. For any reason."

"If the boiler blows and we catch afire, I'm to let you crisp in here, is that it?"

York's eyes glittered in the half-light. "No," he admitted. "But it might be safer for you if you did. I am unruly when woken suddenly. I am not myself. I have been known, at such times, to do things I later regret. That was why I was so short with you. I apologize for it, but it would happen again. Or worse. Do you understand, Abner? Never come in here when my door is locked."

Marsh frowned, but he could think of nothing to say. He had struck the bargain, after all; if York wanted to get all upset about a little sleep, it was his business. "I understand," he said. "Your apology is accepted, and you got mine, if it matters. Now, do you want to come up and watch us take the *Southerner?* Seein' as how you're woke already and all?"

"No," said York, grim-faced. "It is not that I have no interest, Abner. I do. But—you must understand—I need my rest, vitally. And I do not care for daylight. The sun is harsh, burning. Have you ever had a bad burn? If so, you can understand. You've seen how fair I am. The sun and I do not agree. It is a medical condition, Abner. I do not care to discuss it further."

"All right," Marsh said. Beneath his feet, the deck began to vibrate slightly. The steam whistle sounded its ear-piercing wail. "We're backing out," Marsh said. "I got to go. Joshua, I'm sorry to have bothered you, truly I am."

York nodded, turned away, and began to pour himself more of his noxious drink. "I know." He sipped at it this time. "Go," he said. "I will see you this evening, at supper." Marsh moved toward the door, but York's voice stopped him before he could open it. "Abner."

"Yes?" Marsh said.

Joshua York favored him with a pale thin smile. "Beat her, Abner. Win."

Marsh grinned, and left the cabin.

When he reached the pilot house, the *Fevre Dream* had backed clear of the landing, and was reversing her paddles. The *Southerner* was already well down the river. The pilot house was crowded with a good half-dozen off-duty pilots, talking and chewing tobacco and making side wagers on whether or not they'd catch the other boat. Even Mister Daly had interrupted his leisure to come up and observe. The passengers all knew something was afoot; the lower decks were crowded as they sat along the railings and pushed onto the forecastle for a good view.

Kitch swung the great black-and-silver wheel, and the *Fevre Dream* angled out toward the main channel, sliding into the brisk current behind her rival. He called down for more steam. Whitey threw some pitch in the furnaces and they gave the folks on shore a show, puffing out great clouds of dense black smoke as they steamed away. Abner Marsh stood behind the pilot, leaning on his stick and squinting. The afternoon sun shone on the clear blue water ahead of them, leaving blinding reflections that danced and shimmered and hurt the eyes, except where the churning wake of the *Southerner's* paddle wheels had cut them all up into a thousand fiery pieces.

For a few moments it looked easy. The *Fevre Dream* surged forward, steam and smoke flying from her, American flags fore and aft flapping like the devil, her wheels slapping against the water in an ever-faster tempo, engines rumbling below. The gap between her and the other steamer began to diminish visibly. But the *Southerner* was no *Mary Kaye*, no two-bit stern-wheeler to be left behind at will. It wasn't long before her captain or her pilot realized what was going on, and her reply was a taunting lurch of speed. Her smoke thickened and came streaming back at them, and her wake grew even more violent and choppy, so Kitch had to swing the *Fevre Dream* wide a bit to avoid it, losing part of the current as he did. The distance between them widened again, then held steady.

"Keep after her," Marsh told his pilot after it was clear that the two steamers were holding their positions. He left the pilot house and went searching for Hairy Mike Dunne, who he finally located on the forecastle of the main deck, with his boots up on a crate and a big cigar in his mouth. "Round up the roustas and deckhands," Marsh said to the mate. "I want 'em to trim boat." Hairy Mike nodded, rose, ground out his smoke, and started bellowing.

In a few moments most of the crew could be found aft and larboard, to partially offset the weight of the passengers, the majority of whom were crowded up forward and starboard to watch the race. "Damn passengers," Marsh muttered. The *Fevre Dream*, now slightly better balanced, began to creep up on the *Southerner* once more. Marsh returned to the pilot house.

Both boats were going at it hard now, and they were pretty well matched. Abner Marsh figured the *Fevre Dream* was more powerful but it wasn't enough. She was heavily laden with freight and running low in the water and in the *Southerner's* wake to boot, so the waves kicked up over her head a bit and slowed her, while the *Southerner* skipped along easy as you please, with nothing aboard but passengers and nothing ahead but a clear river. Now, barring breakdowns or accidents, it was up to the pilots. Kitch was intent at the wheel, handling her easy, doing his damndest to pick up a few minutes at every chance. Behind him, Daly and the vagabond pilots were babbling away, full of advice on the river and its stage and how best to run it.

For more than an hour the *Fevre Dream* chased the *Southerner*, losing sight of her once or twice around bends, but edging closer each time as Kitch shaved it tight coming around. Once they got close enough so Marsh could make out the faces of the passengers leaning on the other boat's aft railings, but then the *Southerner* kicked forward again and restored the distance between them. "Bet you they just changed pilots," Kitch said, spitting a wad of tobacco juice into a nearby cuspidor. "See the way she perked up there?"

"I seen," Marsh growled. "Now I want to see us perk up a mite too."

Then they got their break. One moment the *Southerner* was holding steady in front of them, sweeping around a densely wooded bend. Then all of a sudden her whistle started to hooting, and she slowed, and trembled, and her side wheels started to back.

"Careful," Daly said to Kitch. Kitch spat again and moved the wheel, carefullike, and the *Fevre Dream* nosed across the turbulent wake of the *Southerner* to go wide and starboard of her. When they were halfway round the bend, they saw the cause of the trouble; another big steamer, main deck all but buried beneath bales of tobacco, had run aground on a sandbar. Her mate and crew were out with spars and winches, trying to grasshopper her over. The *Southerner* had almost run right into 'em.

For a long few minutes the river was chaotic. The men on the bar were all shouting and waving, the *Southerner* backed like the devil, the *Fevre Dream* steamed toward clear water. Then the *Southerner* reversed her wheels again, and her head turned and it looked as though she was trying to cross right in front of the *Fevre Dream*. "Damn egg-suckin' idyut," Kitch said, and he swung the wheel a little more and told Whitey to ease up on the larboard. But he didn't back, or try to stop her. The two big steamers edged toward each other, closer and closer. Marsh could hear passengers crying out in alarm down below, and there was a second or two when even *he* thought they were going to collide.

But then the *Southerner* eased off herself, and her pilot swung her bow downstream again, and the *Fevre Dream* nosed by her with feet to spare. Someone began to cheer below.

"Keep her goin'," Marsh muttered, so low that no one could have heard him. The *Southerner* had her wheels kicking up spray and was hot after them, behind now, but not by much, running a bare boat's length astern. All the damn passengers on the *Fevre Dream* rushed aft, of course, and all the crew had to rush forward, so the steamer shook to all the running footsteps.

The *Southerner* was gaining on them again. She was running to their larboard, parallel and just behind. Her bow came up to the *Fevre Dream*'s stern now, and she was creeping up inch by inch. The sides of the two steamers were close enough so that passengers could have jumped from one to the other, if they'd had a mind to, though the *Fevre Dream* stood taller. "Damn," said Marsh, when the other boat drew almost abreast of them. "Enough is enough. Kitch, call down and tell Whitey to use my lard."

The pilot glanced his way, grinning ear to ear. "Lard, cap'n? Oh, I knew you was a sly one!" He barked a command down the speaking tube to the engine room.

The two steamers were running head to head. Marsh's grip on his stick was all sweat. Down below, probably, the deckhands were arguing with some damn foreigners, who'd gone and perched on those lard barrels and had to be dislodged before the lard could be dragged off to the stokers. Marsh was burning with impatience, hot as his lard would be. Good lard was expensive, but it came in handy on a steamer. The cook could use it, and it burned damned *hot*, and that was what they needed now, a good hot head of high-pressure steam they couldn't get from wood alone.

When the lard got chucked in, there was no doubt in the pilot house. Long high columns of white steam came a-hissing up out of the 'scape-pipes, and smoke rolled from the high chimneys, and the *Fevre Dream* snorted fire and shook just a mite, and then she was sparkling, *chunkachunkachunka* fast as a train wheel, the stroke pounding the deck. She went flying right on out ahead of the *Southerner*, and when she was safely clear of her Kitch eased her right in front of the other steamer's bow, leaving them to ride her waves. All those worthless berthless pilots were chuckling and passing around smokes and yapping about what a heller of a boat this *Fevre Dream* was, while the *Southerner* receded behind them and Abner Marsh grinned like a fool.

They were a full ten minutes ahead of the *Southerner* when they put into Cairo, where the broad Ohio's clear waters merged with the muddy Mississippi. By then Abner Marsh had almost forgot about that little incident with Joshua York.

CHAPTER SIX

Julian Plantation, Louisiana, July 1857

SOUR Billy Tipton was out front, chucking his knife at the big dead tree that fronted the gravel path, when the riders approached. It was morning but already hot as hell, and Sour Billy was working himself up a good sweat and thinking of going down for a swim when he finished up his knife-throwing. Then he saw the riders emerge from the woods where the old road crooked around. He went over to the dead tree and pulled loose his knife and slid it back into its sheath behind his back, all thoughts of swimming forgotten.

The riders came on real slow, but bold as brass, riding straight up in broad daylight like they belonged here. They couldn't be from these parts, Sour Billy figured; what neighbors they had all knew that Damon Julian didn't like no one coming onto his land without his leave. When they were still too far away to make out good, he wondered if maybe they weren't some of Montreuil's Creole friends come to make trouble. If so, they were going to regret it.

Then he saw why they were riding so slow, and Sour Billy relaxed. Two niggers in chains were stumbling along behind the two men on horseback. He crossed his arms and leaned against the tree, waiting for them to reach him.

Sure enough, they reined up. One of the men on horseback looked at the house, with its peeling paint and half-rotted front steps, spat out a wad of tobacco juice, and turned to Sour Billy. "This the Julian plantation?" he said. He was a big red-faced man with a wart on his nose, dressed in smelly leathers and a slouchy felt hat.

"Sure is," Sour Billy replied. But he was looking past the horseman and his companion, a lean pink-cheeked youth who was probably the other's son. He went walking over to the two haggard-looking niggers, downcast and miserable in their chains, and Sour Billy smiled. "Why," he said, "if it ain't Lily and Sam. Never thought you two be dropping by again. Must be two years since you went and run off. Mister Julian will be real pleased to know that you come back."

Sam, a big powerful-looking buck, raised his head and stared at Sour Billy, but there was no defiance in his eyes. Only fear. "We come on 'em up to Arkansas, my boy and me," the red-faced man said. "Tried to claim they was free niggers, but they didn't fool me for a minute, no sir."

Sour Billy looked at the slave catchers and nodded. "Go on."

"They was awful stubborn, these two. Couldn't get 'em to tell us where they was from for the longest while. Whipped 'em right smart, used a few other tricks I know. Usually, with niggers, you just scares 'em a bit and it pops right out. Not with these." He spat. "Well, we finally got it out of 'em. Show him, Jim."

The boy dismounted, went over to the woman, and lifted her right arm. Three fingers were missing from her hand. One of the stumps was still crusted over with a scab.

"We started with the right cause we noticed she was left-handed," the man said. "Didn't want to cripple her up too bad, you unnerstand, but we couldn't find nothin' in the papers, no posters out neither, so . . ." He shrugged eloquently. "Got to the third finger, like you see, and the man finally told us. The woman cussed him out somethin' fierce." He guffawed. "Anyway, here they is. Two slaves like that, got to be worth somethin' to us for catchin' 'em. This Mister Julian at home?"

"No," said Sour Billy, looking up at the sun. It was still a couple of hours shy of noon.

"Well," said the red-faced man, "you must be the overseer, right? The one they call Sour Billy?"

"That's me," he said. "Sam and Lily talk about me?"

The slave catcher laughed again. "Oh, they did a powerful lot of talkin' once we knew where they come from. Talked all the way here. We shut 'em up a time or two, my boy and me, but then they'd just start to talkin' again. Some stories, too."

Sour Billy looked at the two runaways with his cold, malicious eyes, but neither one would meet his gaze.

"Maybe you can just take charge of these two, and give us our reward, and we'll be ridin' on our way," the man said.

"No," said Sour Billy Tipton. "You got to wait. Mister Julian will want to give you his thanks personal. Won't be too long. He'll be back by dark."

"By dark, huh?" the man said. He and his son exchanged glances. "Funny, Mister Sour Billy, but these here niggers said you'd say jest that very thing. They tell queer stories bout what goes on here after dark. My boy and I, we'd jest sooner take our money and leave, if it's all the same to you."

"It won't be all the same to Mister Julian," Sour Billy said. "And I can't give you no money neither. You going to believe some fool story told you by a couple niggers?"

The man frowned, working his tobacco all the while. "Nigger stories is one thing," he said finally, "but I knowed niggers to tell the truth once in a while too. Now, what we'll do, Mister Sour Billy, is wait, like you say, for this Mister Julian to come home. But don't you think we're gonna let ourself be cheated." He had a pistol by his side. He patted it. "I'm gonna wear my friend here whiles I wait, and my boy he's got one too, and we're both of us handy with our knives. You unnerstand? These niggers learned us all about that little knife you got hid behind your back, so don't you go a-reachin' back there, like to scratch on anything, or else our fingers might get a little bit itchy too. Let's jest all of us wait and be friends."

Sour Billy turned his eyes on the slave catcher and gave him a cold stare, but the big man was too stupid to even notice. "We'll wait inside," Sour Billy said, keeping his hands well clear of his back.

"Jest fine," the slave catcher said. He dismounted. "My name is Tom Johnston, by the way, and that's my boy Jim."

"Mister Julian will be pleased to meet you," Sour Billy said. "Tie up your horses and bring the niggers on inside. Careful on the steps. They's rotted through in places."

The woman started to whimper as they led her toward the house, but Jim Johnston gave her a smart crack across the mouth and she fell silent again.

Sour Billy led them to the library, and drew back the heavy curtains to admit some light into the dim, dusty room. The slaves sat on the floor, while the two catchers stretched out in the heavy leather chairs. "Now," said Tom Johnston, "this here is real nice."

"Everything is all rotten and dusty, daddy," the youth said. "Jest like them niggers said it'd be."

"Well, well," said Sour Billy, looking at the two niggers. "Well, well. Mister Julian ain't going to be pleased you been spreadin' tales about his house. You two earned yourself a whippin'."

The big black buck, Sam, found the courage to raise his head and glower. "I ain't scared o' no whippin'."

Sour Billy smiled just slightly. "Why then, there's worse things than whippin', Sam. Indeed there is."

That was too much for the woman, Lily. She looked at the youth. "He's tellin' the truth, massa Jim, he is. You got to lissen. Take us outta here 'fore dark. You and your daddy kin own us, work us, we work real hard for you, we will. Won't run away. We're good niggers. Never would have run away, but for . . . for . . . *don't* wait till dark, massa, don't. It'll be too late then."

The boy hit her, hard, with the butt of his pistol, leaving a welt across her cheek and knocking her backward to the carpet where she lay, shuddering and weeping. "Shut your lyin' black mouth," he said.

"You want a drink?" Sour Billy asked him.

The hours passed. They went through most of two bottles of Julian's best brandy, swilling it down like it was cheap whiskey. They ate. They talked. Sour Billy didn't do much talking himself, just asked questions to draw out Tom Johnston, who was drunk and vain and in love with his own voice. The slave catchers operated out of Napoleon, Arkansas, it seemed, but they weren't there much, traveling like they did. There was a Missus Johnston, but she stayed at home with her daughter. They didn't tell her much of their business. "Woman ain't got no reason to know about her man's comin's and goin's. You tell 'em somethin' or other, jest you don't see if they don't go and bother you about it if you're late. Then you got to slap 'em around." He spat. "Easier just to keep 'em guessing, so they's grateful when you shows up." Johnston left Sour Billy with the impression that he preferred topping nigger wenches anyway, so his wife was no loss to him.

Outside, the sun was sinking toward the west.

When the shadows lay thick across the room. Sour Billy rose and drew the curtains and lit some candles. "I'll go and get Mister Julian," he said.

The younger Johnston looked awful pale as he turned to his father, Sour Billy thought. "Daddy, I didn't hear no one ride up," he said.

"Wait," said Sour Billy Tipton. He left them, walked through the darkened, deserted ballroom, and climbed the grand staircase. Upstairs, he entered a large bedroom, the wide French windows boarded up, the ornate bed shrouded by a black velvet canopy. "Mister Julian," he called softly, from the door. The room was black and stifling.

Behind the canopy, something stirred. The velvet hangings were pushed back. Damon Julian emerged; pale, quiet, cold. His black eyes seemed to reach right out of the darkness and touch Sour Billy. "Yes, Billy?" came the soft voice.

Sour Billy told him everything.

Damon Julian smiled. "Bring them into the dining room. I'll join you in a few moments."

The dining room had a great old chandelier, but it had not been lit in Sour Billy's memory. After bringing in the slave catchers, he found some matches and touched off a small oil lamp, which he set on the middle of the long table, so it threw a small ring of light on the white linen tablecloth but left the rest of the narrow, high-ceilinged room in shadow. The Johnstons took seats, the younger one peering around uneasily, his hand never leaving his pistol. The niggers held each other miserably at one end of the table.

"Where's this Julian?" Tom Johnston growled.

"Soon, Tom," said Sour Billy. "Wait."

For nearly ten minutes no one spoke. Then Jim Johnston sucked in his breath. "Daddy," he said, "look. Somebody's standin' in that door!"

The door led to the kitchen. It was black back there. Full night had fallen, and the only illumination in this part of the house was the oil lamp on the table. Beyond the kitchen door nothing could be seen but vague, threatening shadows—and something that looked like the outline of a human form, standing very still.

Lily whimpered, and the nigger Sam held her more closely. Tom Johnston got to his feet, his chair scraping over the wooden floor, his face hard. He drew and cocked his pistol. "Who's that?" he demanded. "Come out!"

"No need to be alarmed," said Damon Julian.

They all turned, Johnston jumping like he'd been spooked. Julian stood beneath the archway to the foyer, framed against darkness, smiling charmingly, dressed in a long dark suit with a red silk tie shining at his neck. His eyes were dark and amused, the flame of the lamp reflected in them. "That's only Valerie," Julian said.

With a rustle of her skirts, she emerged and stood in the kitchen door, pale and quiet yet still strikingly beautiful. Johnston looked at her and laughed. "Ah," he said, "only a woman. Sorry, Mister Julian. Them nigger stories got me all jumpy."

"I understand perfectly," said Damon Julian.

"There's others behind him," Jim Johnston whispered. They all saw them now; dim figures, indistinct, lost in the darkness at Julian's back.

"Only my friends," said Damon Julian, smiling. A woman in a light blue gown emerged at his right. "Cynthia," he said. Another woman, in green, stood to his left. "Adrienne," Julian added. He raised his arm in a weary, languid gesture. "And that is Raymond, and Jean, and Kurt." They emerged together, moving silent as cats, from other doors ringing the long room. "And behind you are Alain and Jorge and Vincent."

Johnston whirled, and there they were, stepping out from the shadows. Still more came into view behind Julian himself. Except for the whisperings of cloth against cloth, none of them made any sound as they moved. And they all stared, and smiled invitingly.

Sour Billy wasn't smiling, though he was vastly amused at the way Tom Johnston clutched his gun and cast his eyes about like a frightened animal. "Mister Julian," he said, "I ought to tell you that Mister Johnston here don't intend to be cheated. He's got him a *gun*, Mister Julian, and his boy too, and they're both handy with their knives."

"Ah," said Damon Julian.

The niggers began to pray. Young Jim Johnston looked at Damon Julian and drew his own pistol. "We brung you your niggers," he said. "We won't bother you for no reward, neither. We'll jest be goin'."

"Going?" Julian said. "Now, would I let you leave without a reward? When you've come all the way from Arkansas just to bring us a few darkies? I wouldn't hear of it." He crossed the room. Jim Johnston, caught in those dark eyes of his, held his pistol up and did not move. Julian took it from his hand and laid it on the table. He touched the youth's cheek. "Beneath the dirt, you're a handsome boy," he said.

"What are you doin' to my boy?" Tom Johnston demanded. *"Get away from him!"* He flourished his pistol.

Damon Julian glanced around. "Your boy has a certain rude beauty," he said. "You, on the other hand, have a wart."

"He *is* a wart," Sour Billy Tipton suggested.

Tom Johnston glared and Damon Julian smiled. "Indeed," he said. "Amusing, Billy." Julian gestured to Valerie and Adrienne. They glided toward him, and each took young Jim Johnston by the arm.

"You want help?" Sour Billy offered.

"No," said Julian, "thank you." With a graceful, almost offhand gesture, he raised his hand and brought it lightly across the youth's long neck. Jim Johnston made a wet, choking sound. A thin line of red suddenly appeared across his throat, a little looping scarlet necklace, whose bright red beads swelled larger and larger as they watched, bursting one by one to send trickles down his neck. Jim Johnston began to thrash, but the iron embrace of the two pale women held him immobile. Damon Julian leaned forward, and pressed his open mouth to the flow, to catch the hot bright blood.

Tom Johnston made an incoherent animal noise deep in his chest, and took the longest time to react. Finally he cocked his pistol again and took aim. Alain stepped in his path, and suddenly Vincent and Jean were beside him, and Raymond and Cynthia touched him from behind with cold white hands. Johnston cursed at them and fired. There was a flash and a whiff of acrid smoke, and weed-thin Alain staggered back and fell, driven by the force of the bullet. A flow of dark blood seeped through the white ruffled shirtfront he wore. Half-sprawled, half-seated, Alain touched his chest, and his hand came away bloody.

Raymond and Cynthia had Johnston firmly by then, and Jean took the gun from his hand with a smooth, easy motion. The big red-faced man did not resist. He was staring at Alain. The flow of blood had stopped. Alain smiled, showing long white teeth, terrible and sharp. He rose and came on. "No," screamed Johnston, "no, I shot ya, you gotta be dead, I shot ya."

"Niggers sometimes tell the truth, Mister Johnston," said Sour Billy Tipton. "All the truth. You should of lissened."

Raymond reached under Johnston's slouchy hat and got a good grip on his hair, jerking his head back to expose his thick red neck. Alain laughed and tore Johnston's throat out with his teeth. Then the others closed in.

Sour Billy Tipton reached back and pulled his knife and sauntered over to the two niggers. "Come on," he said, "Mister Julian don't need you tonight, but you two ain't goin' to be running off no more. Down to the cellar. Come on, be quick about it, or I'll leave you here with *them*." That got them moving right proper, as Sour Billy knew it would.

The cellar was small and dank. You had to go through a trap door under a rug to get to it. The land around here was too wet for a proper cellar, but this cellar wasn't proper. Two inches of standing water covered the floor, the ceiling was so low a man couldn't stand upright, and the walls were green with mold. Sour Billy chained the niggers up good, close enough so that they could touch. He figured that was real nice of him. He brought them a hot dinner, too.

Afterward he made his own dinner and washed it down with what was left of the second bottle of brandy the Johnstons had opened. He was just finishing up when Alain came into the kitchen. The blood had dried on his shirt and there was a burnt black hole where the shot had gone through, but otherwise he looked none the worse for wear. "It's finished," Alain told him. "Julian wants you in the library."

Sour Billy pushed away his plate and went to answer the summons. The dining room badly wanted cleaning, he noted when he passed through. Adrienne and Kurt and Armand were enjoying some wine amid the dim silence there, the bodies—or what was left of them— just feet away. Some of the others were off in the drawing room, talking.

The library was pitch dark. Sour Billy had expected to find Damon Julian alone, but when he entered he saw three indistinct figures in the shadows, two seated, one standing. He couldn't make out who they were. He waited in the door until Julian finally spoke. "In the future, do not ever bring such people into my library," the voice said. "They were filthy. They left a smell."

Sour Billy felt a brief stab of fear. "Yes, sir," he said, facing the chair from which Julian had spoken. "I'm sorry, Mister Julian."

After a moment of silence, Julian said, "Close the door, Billy. Come in. You may use the lamp."

The lamp was made of showy red-stained glass; its flame gave the dusty room the red-brown cast of dried blood. Damon Julian sat in a high-backed chair, his fine long fingers steepled beneath his chin, a faint smile on his face. Valerie sat at his right hand. The sleeve of her gown had gotten torn in the struggles, but she didn't seem to have noticed. Sour Billy thought she was even paler than usual. A few feet away, Jean stood behind another chair, looking guarded and nervous, twisting a big gold ring on his finger.

"Must *he* be here?" Valerie asked Julian. She glanced at Billy briefly, contempt in her big purple eyes.

"Why, Valerie," Julian replied. He reached out and took her hand. She trembled and pressed her lips together tightly. "I brought Billy to reassure you," Julian continued.

Jean gathered up his courage and stared right at Sour Billy, frowning. "This Johnston had a wife."

So that was it, Sour Billy thought. "You scared?" he asked Jean mockingly. Jean was not one of Julian's favorites, so it was safe to taunt him. "He had a wife," Billy said, "but it ain't nothin' to worry over. He never talked to her much, never told her where he was goin' or when he'd be back. She ain't goin' to be comin' after you."

"I do not like it, Damon," Jean grumbled.

"What about the slaves?" Valerie demanded. "They've been gone two years. They said things to the Johnstons, dangerous things. They must have talked to others as well."

"Billy?" Julian said.

Sour Billy shrugged. "I expect they told stories to every damn nigger between here and Arkansas," he said. "It don't worry me none. Just a pack of nigger stories, ain't nobody goin' to believe it."

"I wonder," said Valerie. She turned to Damon Julian, pleading. "Damon, please. Jean is right. We have been here too long. It is not safe. Remember what they did to that Lalaurie woman in New Orleans, the one who tortured her slaves for pleasure? The talk finally caught up with her. And what she did was nothing to . . ." She hesitated, swallowed, and added, quietly, ". . . to the things we do. The things we must do." She turned her face away from Julian.

Slowly, gently, Julian reached out a pale hand, touched her cheek, drew a finger down the side of her face in a tender caress, then caught her under the chin and made her look at him. "Are you so timid now, Valerie? Must I remind of who you are? Have you been listening to Jean again? Is he the master now? Is he bloodmaster?"

"No," she said, her deep violet eyes wider than ever, her voice afraid. "No."

"Who is the bloodmaster, dear Valerie?" Julian asked. His eyes were lambent and heavy and bored right into her.

"You are, Damon," she whispered. "You."

"Look at me, Valerie. Do you think I need fear any tales told by a pack of slaves? What do I care what they say of me?"

Valerie opened her mouth. No words came out.

Satisfied, Damon Julian released his hold on her. There were deep red marks on her flesh where his fingers had pressed. He smiled at Sour Billy as Valerie drew back. "What do you think, Billy?"

Sour Billy Tipton looked down at his feet and shuffled nervously.

He knew what he ought to say, but he'd been doing some figuring lately, and there were things he had to tell Julian that Julian wouldn't take kindly to hearing. He'd been putting it off, but now he didn't see as how he had any more choice. "I don't know, Mister Julian," he said weakly.

"You don't know, Billy? What is it you don't know?" The tone was cold and vaguely threatening.

Sour Billy plunged on regardless. "I don't know how long we can go on, Mister Julian," he said boldly. "I been thinking on this some, and there's things I don't like. This here plantation brought in a lot of money when Garoux was runnin' it, but it's near worthless now. You know I can get work out of any slave, damned if I can't, but them what's dead or run off I can't work. When you and your friends started takin' kids from them shanties, or ordering the likely wenches up to the big house where they never come out, that was the start of our troubles. You ain't had no slaves for more'n a year now, excepting those fancy girls, and they sure don't stay around long." He laughed nervously. "We don't got no crops. We sold half the plantation, all the best parcels of land. And them fancy girls, Mister Julian, they're expensive. We got us bad money troubles.

"And that ain't all. Doing in niggers is one thing, but using white folks for the thirst, that's dangerous. In New Orleans, well, maybe that's safe enough, but you and I know it was Cara killed Henri Cassand's youngest boy. He's a neighbor, Mister Julian. They all know there's somethin' peculiar over here anyway; if their slaves and children start to dyin' we're goin' to have us real trouble."

"Trouble?" said Damon Julian. "We are almost twenty strong, with you. What can the cattle do to us?"

"Mister Julian," said Sour Billy, "what if they come by day?"

Julian waved a hand casually. "It will not happen. If it does, we will deal with them as they deserve."

Sour Billy grimaced. Julian might be unconcerned, but it was Sour Billy took the biggest risks. "I think maybe she's right, Mister Julian," he said unhappily. "I think we ought to go somewheres. We've drained this place. It's dangerous to stay on."

"I am comfortable here, Billy," Julian said. "I feed on the cattle. I do not run from them."

"Money, then. Where we goin' to get money?"

"Our guests left horses. Take them to New Orleans tomorrow, sell them. See that they aren't traced. You may sell off more of the land as well. Neville of Bayou Cross will want to buy again. Call on him, Billy." Julian smiled. "You might even invite him to dinner here, to discuss my proposition. Ask him to bring along his lovely wife and that lithe young son of theirs. Sam and Lily can serve. It will be just as it used to be, before the slaves ran off."

He was taunting, Sour Billy thought. But it was never safe to treat any of Julian's words lightly. "The house," Billy said. "They'll come to eat and they'll see how far it's gone. Isn't safe. They'll tell stories when they go home."

"If they go home, Billy."

"Damon," Jean said shakily, "you can't mean . . ."

The dim, red-drenched room was hot. Sour Billy had begun to sweat. "Neville is—please, Mister Julian, you can't take Neville. You can't go on takin' folks from around here and buyin' fancy girls."

"Your creature is right for once," Valerie said in a very small voice. "Listen to him." Jean was nodding too, emboldened by having others on his side.

"We could sell the whole place," Billy said. "It's all rotted out anyhow. Move to New Orleans, all of us. It'd be better down there. With all them Creoles and free niggers and river trash, a few more or less won't be missed, you know?"

"No," said Damon Julian. Icily. His voice told them he would stand no further argument. Sour Billy shut up real quick. Jean began to toy with his ring again, his mouth sullen and afraid.

But Valerie, astoundingly, spoke up. "Let *us* go, then."

Julian turned his head languidly. "Us?"

"Jean and I," she said. "Send us away. It will be . . . better that way. For you, too. It's safer when there are fewer of us. Your fancy girls will last longer."

"Send you away, dear Valerie? Why, I would miss you. And I would be concerned for you, too. Where would you go, I wonder?"

"Somewhere. Anywhere."

"Do you still hope to find your dark city in a cave?" Julian said mockingly. "You faith is touching, child. Have you mistaken poor weak Jean for your pale king?"

"No," said Valerie. "No. We only want a rest. Please, Damon. If we all stay, they will find us out, hunt us, kill us. Let us go away."

"You are so beautiful, Valerie. So exquisite."

"*Please*," she said, trembling. "Away. A rest."

"Poor small Valerie," Julian said. "There is no rest. Wherever you go, your thirst will travel with you. No, you shall stay."

"*Please,*" she repeated, numbly. "My bloodmaster."

Damon Julian's dark eyes narrowed just slightly, and the smile faded. "If you are that eager to be away, perhaps I should give you what you ask for."

Both Valerie and Jean looked at him hopefully.

"Perhaps I should send you away," Julian mused. "Both of you. But not together, no. You are so beautiful, Valerie. You deserve better than Jean. What do you think, Billy?"

Sour Billy smirked. "Send them all away, Mister Julian. You don't need them none. You got me. Send them off, and they'll see how much they like it."

"Interesting," said Damon Julian. "I will think on it. Now leave me, all of you. Billy, go sell the horses. See Neville about the land."

"No dinner?" Sour Billy asked with relief.

"No," said Julian.

Sour Billy was the last to reach the door. Behind him, Julian snuffed the light, and darkness filled the room. But Sour Billy hesitated at the threshold, and turned back again.

"Mister Julian," he said, "your promise—it's been years now. When?"

"When I do not need you, Billy. You are my eyes by day. You do the things I cannot. How could I spare you now? But have no fear. It will not be long. And time will seem as nothing to you when you join us. Years and days are alike to one who has the life eternal." The promise filled Sour Billy with reassurance. He left to do Julian's bidding.

That night he dreamt. In his dreams he was as dark and graceful as Julian himself, elegant and predatory. It was always night in his dreams, and he roamed the streets of New Orleans beneath a full, pale moon. They watched him pass from their windows and their little iron-lace balconies, and he could feel their eyes upon him, the men full of fear, the women drawn to his dark power. Through the dark he stalked them, gliding soundlessly over the brick sidewalks, hearing their frantic footsteps and their panting. Beneath the swaying fire of a hanging oil lamp, he caught a fine young dandy and tore his throat out, laughing. A sultry Creole beauty watched him from afar, and he came after her, hunting her down alleys and courtyards as she ran before him. Finally, in a court lit by a wrought-iron flambeau, she turned to face him. She looked a bit like Valerie. Her eyes were violet and full of fire. He came to her and pushed her back and took her. Creole blood was as hot and rich as Creole food. The night was his, and all the nights forever, and the red thirst was on him.

When he woke from the dream, he was hot and fevered, and his sheets were wet.

CHAPTER SEVEN

THE *Fevre Dream* lay up in St. Louis for twelve days.

It was a busy time for the entire crew, but for Joshúa York and his strange companions. Abner Marsh was up and about early every morning, and on the streets by ten, making calls on shippers and hotel proprietors, talking up his boat and trying to scare up business. He had a mess of handbills printed for Fevre River Packets—now that he had more than one packet again—and hired some boys to paste them up all over the city. Drinking and eating in all the best places, Marsh told and retold the story of how the *Fevre Dream* took the *Southerner,* to make sure the word got around. He even took out advertisements in three of the local papers.

The lightning pilots that Abner Marsh had hired for the lower river came aboard as soon as the *Fevre Dream* put in to St. Louis, and drew their wages for the time they'd idled away waiting. Pilots didn't come cheap, especially pilots like these two, but Marsh didn't begrudge the money too much, since he wanted the best for his steamer. Once paid, the new men resumed their idling; pilots drew full wages all the time, but didn't do a lick of work until the steamer was in the river. Anything besides piloting was beneath their dignity.

The two pilots Marsh had found had their own individual styles of idling, though. Dan Albright, prim and taciturn and fashionable, strolled aboard the day the *Fevre Dream* put in, surveyed the boat, the engines, and the pilot house, nodded with satisfaction, and immediately took up residence in his cabin. He spent his days reading in the steamer's well-stocked library, and played a few games of chess with Jonathon Jeffers in the main saloon, although Jeffers invariably beat him. Karl Framm, on the other hand, could usually be found in the billiard halls along the riverfront, grinning crookedly beneath his wide-brimmed felt hat and bragging about how him and his new boat were going to run everyone else off the river. Framm had a heller's reputation. He liked to joke about how he kept one wife in St. Louis, one in New Orleans, and a third in Natchez-under-the-hill.

Abner Marsh didn't have the time to worry over much about what his pilots were doing; he was too busy with this task or that one. Nor did he see much of Joshua York and his friends, although he understood that York frequently went on long nightly walks into the city, often with Simon, the silent one. Simon was also learning how to mix drinks, since Joshua had told Marsh he had a mind to use him as night bartender on the run down to New Orleans.

Marsh did frequently see his partner over supper, which Joshua York was in the habit of taking in the main cabin with the other officers, before he retired to his own cabin or the library to read newspapers, packets of which were delivered to him every day, fresh off incoming steamers. Once York announced that he was going in to the city to see a group of players perform. He invited Abner Marsh and the other officers to accompany him, but Marsh was having none of it, so York wound up going with Jonathon Jeffers. "Poems and plays," Marsh muttered to Hairy Mike Dunne as they sauntered off, "it makes you wonder what this damn river is comin' to." Afterward, Jeffers began to teach York to play chess.

"He has quite a mind, Abner," Jeffers told Marsh a few days later, on the morning of their eighth day in St. Louis.

"Who?"

"Why, Joshua of course. I taught him the moves two days ago. Last night I found him in the saloon playing over the score of one of Morphy's games, from one of those New York newspapers he takes. A strange man. How much do you know about him?"

Marsh frowned. He didn't want his people getting too curious about Joshua York; that was part of the bargain. "Joshua don't like to talk much about himself. I don't ask him. A man's past is none of my business, I figure. You ought to take the same attitude, Mister Jeffers. In fact, see that you do."

The clerk arched his thin, dark eyebrows. "If you say so, Cap'n," he replied. But there was a cool smile on his face that Abner Marsh found disquieting.

Jeffers was not the only one to ask questions. Hairy Mike came to Marsh, too, and said that the roustabouts and stokers were spreading some funny talk about York and his four guests, and did Marsh want him to do anything about it?

"What kind of talk?"

Hairy Mike shrugged eloquently. "Bout him only comin' out at night. Bout those queer friends o' his, too. You know Tom, who stokes the middle larboard? He been tellin' this story—says that night we left Louisville, well, you 'member how thick the skeeters were, well, Tom says he saw that old Simon down on the main deck, jest kind o' looking around, and a skeeter landed on his hand, and he went and swatted it with his other hand. Squashed it. But you know how full up skeeters git sometimes, so when you squash 'em they jest bust with the blood. Tom says that happen'd with the skeeter on the back of Simon's hand, so it smeared up all bloody when he got it. Only then, Tom tells it, that Simon jest kind of stared at his hand for the longest while, then lifted it up, and damned if he didn't lick it clean."

Abner Marsh scowled. "You tell your boy Tom that he better stop telling such stories, or he's goin' to be stokin' the middle larboard on somebody else's steamer." Hairy Mike nodded, brought his iron billet into his other hand with a meaty thwack, and turned to go. But Marsh stopped him. "No," he said. "Wait. You tell him not to go spreadin' no stories. But if he sees anything else funny, he should come to you, or to me. Tell him we'll give him a half-dollar."

"He'll lie for the half-dollar."

"Well, forget the half-dollar then, but you tell him the rest of it."

The more Abner thought about Tom's story, the more it bothered him. He was just as glad that Joshua York was going to install Simon as bartender, where he'd be out in public and a man could keep an eye on him. Marsh had never liked morticians, and Simon still reminded him of one something ungodly, when he didn't remind him of one of their patrons, that is. He only hoped that Simon didn't go licking up no mosquitoes while he was serving drinks to the cabin passengers. That kind of thing could ruin a boat's reputation awful fast.

Marsh soon put the incident out of his mind, and plunged back into business. On the night before their scheduled departure, however, something else bothered him. He had called on Joshua York in his cabin to go over a few details of their trip. York was sitting at his desk, with his slim ivory-handled knife in hand, slicing an article out of a newspaper. He and Marsh chatted briefly for a few minutes about the business at hand, and Marsh was about to take his leave when he noticed a copy of the *Democrat* on York's desk. "They were supposed to run one of our advertisements today," Marsh said, reaching for the paper. "You finished with this, Joshua?"

York dismissed the paper with a wave of his hand. "Take it if you'd like," he said.

Abner Marsh carried the paper under his arm to the main cabin, and paged through it while Simon made him a drink. He was annoyed. He couldn't locate their advertisement. Of course, it might not be an omission; York had sliced out a story on the page that backed up the shipping news, so there was a hole just in the prime place. Marsh drained his glass, folded up the paper, and went forward to the clerk's office.

"You got the latest number of the *Democrat?*" Marsh asked Jeffers. "I think that damn Blair left out my advertisement."

"It's there yonder," Jeffers replied, "but he didn't. Look on the shipping page."

And sure enough, there it was, a box smack in the middle of a column of similar boxes:

FEVRE RIVER PACKET COMPANY

The splendid fleet steamer *Fevre Dream* will leave for New Orleans, Louisiana, and all intermediate points and landings, on Thursday, making the best time and manned by all experienced officers and crew. For freight or passage, apply on board or at the company office at the foot of Pine St.

—Abner Marsh, presdn't

Marsh inspected the advertisement, nodded, and flipped back a page, to see what Joshua York had cut out. The item looked to be a reprint lifted from some downriver paper, about some old no-count woodyard man found dead in his cabin on the river north of New Madrid. The mate of a steamer that had put in for wood found him, when no one answered their calls. Some thought that Indians did it, some others said wolves, since the body had been all ripped up, and half eaten. That was just about all it said.

"Something wrong, Cap'n Marsh?" Jeffers asked. "You got a queer look on your face."

Marsh folded up Jeffers' *Democrat* and stuck it under his arm with York's. "No, nothin', damn paper just spelled a couple things wrong."

Jeffers smiled. "Are you certain? I know spelling isn't your strong suit, Cap'n."

"Don't you go joshing me about that again, or I'll chuck you over the side, Mister Jeffers," Marsh replied. "I'm going to be takin' your paper, if you don't mind."

"Go ahead," Jeffers said, "I'd finished."

Back at the bar Marsh reread the story about the woodyard man. Why should Joshua York be cutting out some item about some fool trash killed by wolves? Marsh couldn't figure an answer, but it bothered him. He looked up and noticed Simon's eyes on him in the big mirror over the bar. Marsh quickly folded up the *Democrat* again and stuffed it into a pocket. "Let me have a little glass of whiskey," he said.

Marsh drank the whiskey straight down, and made a long "Aaaaaaah" as the burning spread down through his chest. It cleared his head a mite. There were ways he could find out more about this, but then again it wasn't rightly his business what kind of newspaper stories Joshua York liked to read. Besides, he had given his word not to go prying into York's business, and Abner Marsh fancied himself a man of his word. Resolute, Marsh set down his glass and moved away from the bar. He clomped down the grand, curving stair to the main deck, and tossed both newspapers into one of the dark furnaces. The deckhands looked at him strangely, but Marsh felt better immediately. A man shouldn't go around entertaining suspicions about his partner, especially one as generous and well-mannered as Joshua York. "What are you lookin' at?" he barked at the deckhands. "Ain't you got no work to do? I'll find Hairy Mike and see he gets you some!" Immediately the men were busy. Abner Marsh went back up to the main cabin and had himself another drink.

The next morning Marsh went over to Pine Street, to his company's main office, and tended to business for several hours. He lunched at the Planters' House, surrounded by old friends and old rivals, feeling grand. Marsh bragged up a storm about his steamer, and had to endure Farrell and O'Brien flapping their jaws about their boats, but that was all right, he just smiled and said, "Well, boys, maybe we'll meet on the river. Wouldn't that be grand?" Not a soul mentioned his previous misfortune, and three different men came up to his table and asked Marsh if he needed a pilot for the lower Mississippi. It was a fine couple of hours.

Strolling back to the river, Marsh chanced to pass a tailor's shop. He hesitated, tugging at his beard thoughtfully while he mulled over an idea that had struck him real sudden. Then he went inside, grinning, and ordered up a new captain's coat for himself. A white one, with a double row of silver buttons, just like Joshua's. Marsh left two dollars on account, and arranged to pick up the coat when the *Fevre Dream* returned to St. Louis. He left feeling very satisfied with himself.

The riverfront was chaotic. A consignment of dry goods had arrived late, and the roustabouts were sweating to get it loaded up in time. Whitey had the steam up; tall white plumes were rising from the 'scape-pipes, and dark smoke rolled out of the chimney's flowered tops. The steamer to the left of the *Fevre Dream* was backing out, with great gouts of smoke and much whistle-blowing and shouting. And the big side-wheeler to the right was unloading freight onto its wharfboat, an old decrepit shell of a steamer tied permanently to the landing. All up and down the riverfront there were steamboats, as far as the eye could see in either direction, more boats than Marsh could count. Nine boats up was the luxurious, three-decked *John Simonds*, taking on passengers. Down from her was the side-wheeler *Northern Light*, with a picture of the Aurora painted gaudy on her paddle boxes; she was a brand new upper-Mississippi steamer, and the Northwestern Line said she was faster than any boat that had plied those waters yet. Coming downriver was the *Grey Eagle*, which the *Northern Light* was going to have to take to live up to her brag. There was the *Northerner*, and the crude, powerful stern-wheeler *St. Joe*, and the *Die Vernon II*, and the *Natchez*.

Marsh looked at each of them in turn, at the intricate devices suspended between their chimneys, at their fancy jigsaw carpentry and their bright paint, at their hissing, billowing steam, at the power in their wheels. And then he looked at his own boat, the *Fevre Dream*, all white and blue and silver, and it seemed to him that her steam rose higher than any of the others, and her whistle had a sweeter, clearer tone, and her paint was cleaner and her wheels more for-mid-a-bul, and she stood taller than all but three or four of the other boats, and she was longer than just about any of them. "We'll take 'em all," he said to himself, and he went on down to his lady.

CHAPTER EIGHT

Aboard the Steamer FEVRE DREAM, Mississippi River, July 1857 ——————

ABNER Marsh cut a wedge of cheddar from the wheel on the table, positioned it carefully atop what remained of his apple pie, and forked them both up with a quick motion of his big red hand. He belched, wiped his mouth with his napkin and shook a few crumbs from his beard, and sat back with a smile on his face.

"Good pie?" asked Joshua York, smiling at Marsh over a brandy snifter.

"Toby don't bake no other kind," Marsh replied. "You should of tried a piece." He pushed away from the table and stood up. "Well, drink up, Joshua. It's time."

"Time?"

"You wanted to learn the river, didn't you? You ain't goin' to learn it settin' to table, I'll tell you that much."

York finished his brandy, and they went up to the pilot house together. Karl Framm was on duty. He was lounging on the couch, smoke curling up from his pipe, while his cub—a tall youth with lank blonde hair hanging down to his collar—worked as steersman. "Cap'n Marsh," Framm said, nodding. "And you must be the mysterious Cap'n York. Pleased to meet you. Never been on a steamer with two captains before." He grinned, a wide lopsided grin that flashed a gold tooth. "This boat got almost as many captains as I got wives. Of course, it stands to reason. Why, this boat got more boilers and more mirrors and more silver than any boat I ever seen, so it ought to have more captains too, I figure." The lanky pilot leaned forward and knocked some ashes from his pipe into the belly of the big iron stove. It was cold and dark, the night being hot and thick. "What can I do for you gentlemen?" Framm asked.

"Learn us the river," said Marsh.

Framm's eyebrows rose. "Learn you the river? I got myself a cub here. Ain't that right, Jody?"

"Sure is, Mister Framm."

Framm smiled and shrugged. "Now, I'm learnin' Jody here, and it's all been arranged, I'm to get six hundred dollars from the first wages he gets after he's been licensed and taken into the association. I'm only doin' it so cheap cause I know his family. Can't say I know your families, though, can't say that *a-tall*."

Joshua York undid the buttons on his dark gray vest. He was wearing a money belt. He brought out a twenty-dollar gold piece, and placed it on top of the stove, the gold gleaming softly against the black iron. "Twenty," said York. He set another gold piece atop it. "Forty," he said. Then a third. "Sixty." When the count reached three hundred York buttoned up his vest. "I'm afraid that is all I have on me, Mister Framm, but I assure you I am not without funds. Let us agree to seven hundred dollars for yourself, and an equal amount for Mister Albright, if the two of you will instruct me in the rudiments of piloting, and refresh Captain Marsh here so he can steer his own boat. Payable immediately, not from future wages. What say you?"

Framm was real cool about it, Marsh thought. He sucked on his pipe thoughtfully for a moment, like he was considering the offer, and finally reached out and took the stack of gold coins. "Can't speak for Mister Albright, but for myself, I was always fond of the color of gold. I'll learn you. What say you come on up tomorrow during the day, at the start of my watch?"

"That may be fine for Captain Marsh," York said, "but I prefer to begin immediately."

Framm looked around. "Hell," he said. "Can't you see? It's *night*. Been learning Jody for near a year now, and it's only been a month I been lettin' him steer by night. Running at night ain't never easy. No." His tone was firm. "I'll learn you by day first, when a man can see where's he runnin' to."

"I will learn by night. I keep strange hours, Mister Framm. But you need not worry. I have excellent night vision, better than yours, I suspect."

The pilot unfolded his long legs, stood up, and stalked over and took the wheel. "Go below, Jody," he said to his cub. When the youth had gone, Framm said, "Ain't no man sees good enough to run a bad stretch of river in the dark." He stood with his back to them, intent on the black starlit waters ahead. Far up the river they could see the distant lights of another steamer. "Tonight is a good clear night, no clouds to speak of, a half decent moon, good stage on the river. Look at that water out there. Like black glass. Look at the banks. Real easy to see where they're at, ain't it?"

"Yes," said York. Marsh, smiling, said nothing.

"Well," said Framm, "it ain't always like that. Sometimes there ain't no moon, sometimes there's clouds covering everything. Gets awful black then. Gets so a man can't see much of nothin'. The banks pull back so you can't see where they are, and if you don't know what you're doin' you can steer right into 'em. Other times you get shadows that hulk up like they were solid land, and you got to know they ain't, otherwise you'll spend half the night steerin' away from things that ain't really there. How do you suppose a pilot knows such things, Cap'n York?" Framm gave him no chance to reply. He tapped his temple. "By memory is how. By seeing the dern river by day and rememberin' it, all of it, every bend and every house along the shore, every woodyard, where it runs deep and where it's shallow, where you got to cross. You pilot a steamer with what you know, Cap'n York, not with what you see. But you got to see before you can know, and you can't see good enough by night."

"That's the truth, Joshua," Abner Marsh affirmed, putting a hand up on York's shoulder.

York said quietly, "The boat up ahead of us is a side-wheeler, with what appears to be an ornate K between her chimneys, and a pilot house with a domed roof. Right now she's passing a woodyard. There's an old rotten wharf there, and a colored man is sitting on the end of it, looking out at the river."

Marsh let go of York's shoulder and moved to the window, squinting. The other boat was a long way ahead. He could make out that she was a side-wheeler right enough, but the device between her chimneys . . . the chimneys were black against a black sky, he could barely see them, and then only because of the sparks flying from them. "Damn," he said.

Framm glanced around at York with surprise in his eyes. "I can't make out half that stuff myself," he said, "but I do believe you're right." A few moments later the *Fevre Dream* steamed past the woodyard, and there was the old colored man, just like York had described. "He's smokin' a pipe," Framm said, grinning. "You left that out."

"Sorry," Joshua York said.

"Well," said Framm thoughtfully, "well." He chewed on his pipe, his eyes on the river ahead. "You surely do have good night eyes, I'll give you that. But I'm still not sure. It ain't hard to see a woodyard up ahead on a clear night. Seein' an old darkie is a mite harder, with the way they blend in and all, but still, that's one thing, and the river is another. There's lots of little things a pilot has got to see that your cabin passenger would never notice a-tall. The look of the water when a snag or a sawyer is hidin' underneath it. Old dead trees that'll tell you the stage of the river a hundred miles further on. The way to tell a bluff reef from a wind reef. You got to be able to read the river like it was a book, and the words is just little ripples and eddies, sometimes all faded so they can't be made out properly, and then you got to rely on what you remember about the last time you read that page. Now you wouldn't go try readin' a book in the dark, would you?"

York ignored that. "I can see a ripple on the water as easily as I can see a woodyard, if I know what to look for. Mister Framm, if you can't teach me the river, I'll find a pilot who can. I remind you that I am the owner and master of the *Fevre Dream*."

Framm glanced around again, frowning now. "More work by night," he said. "If you want to learn by night, it'll cost you eight hundred."

York's expression melted into a slow smile. "Done," he said. "Now, let us begin."

Karl Framm pushed back his slouchy hat until it sat on the back of his head, and gave a long sigh, like a man who was inordinately put upon. "All right," he said, "it's your money, and your boat too. Don't come botherin' me when you tear out her bottom. Now listen up. The river runs pretty straight from St. Louis down to Cairo, before the Ohio comes in. But you got to know it anyhow. This here stretch is called the graveyard from time to time, cause a lot of boats went down here. Some, you can still see the chimneys peeping up above the water, or the whole damn wreck lyin' in the mud if the river's low —the ones that are down under the waterline, though, you better know where they lie, or the next damn boat comin' down is goin' to have to know where *you* lie. You got to learn your marks, too, and how to handle the boat. Here, step on up and take the wheel, get the feel of her. You couldn't touch bottom with a church steeple right now, it's safe enough." York and Framm changed places. "Now, the first point below St. Louis . . ." Framm began. Abner Marsh sat himself down on the couch, listening, while the pilot went on and on, meandering from the marks to tricks of steering to long stories about the steamers that lay sunken in the graveyard they were running. He was a colorful storyteller, but after every tale he'd recollect the task at hand and meander back to the marks again. York drank it all in, quietlike. He seemed to pick up the knack of steering quickly, and whenever Framm stopped and asked him to repeat some bit of information, Joshua just reeled it back at him.

At length, after they'd caught and passed the side-wheeler that had been running ahead of them, Marsh found himself yawning. It was such a fine sharp night, though, that he hated to go to bed. He hoisted himself up and went down to the texas-tender, coming back with a pot of hot coffee and a plate of tarts. When he returned, Karl Framm was spinning the yarn about the wreck of the *Drennan Whyte*, lost above Natchez in '50 with a treasure aboard her. The *Evermonde* tried to raise her, caught fire and went to the bottom. The *Ellen Adams*, a salvage steamer, came looking for the treasure in '51, struck a bar and half sank. "The treasure's cursed, y'see," Framm was saying, "either that or that old devil river just don't want to give it up."

Marsh smiled and poured the coffee. "Joshua," he said, "that story's true enough, but don't you go believing everything he says. This man's the most notorious liar on the river."

"Why, Cap'n!" Framm said, grinning. He turned back to the river. "See that old cabin yonder, with the tumbly-down porch?" he said. "Good, cause you got to recollect it . . ." and he was off again. It was a solid twenty minutes before he got distracted by the story of *E. Jenkins*, the steamer that was thirty miles long, with hinges in the middle so it could make the turns in the river. Even Joshua York gave Framm an incredulous look for that one. But he was smiling.

Marsh retired about an hour after he'd eaten the last of the tarts. Framm was amusing enough, but he'd take his lessons by day, when he could damn well see the marks the pilot was talking about.

When he woke, it was morning and the *Fevre Dream* was at Cape Girardeau, taking on a load of grist. Framm had elected to put in there sometime during the night, he learned, when some fog closed in around them. Cape Girardeau was a haughty town perched up on its bluffs, some 150 miles below St. Louis, and Marsh did some figuring and was pleased with their time. It was no record, but it was good.

Within the hour the *Fevre Dream* was back on the river, heading downstream. The July sun was fierce overhead, the air thick with heat and humidity and insects, but up on the texas deck it was cool and serene. Stops were frequent. With eighteen big boilers to keep hot, the steamer ate wood like nobody's business, but fuel was never a problem; woodyards dotted both banks regularly. Whenever they got low the mate would signal up to the pilot, and they'd put in near some ramshackle little cabin surrounded by big stacks of split beech or oak or chestnut, and Marsh or Jonathan Jeffers would go ashore and dicker with the woodyard man. When they gave the signal, the deckhands would swarm ashore at those cords of wood, and in three blinks of your eye it would be gone, stowed aboard the steamer. Cabin passengers always liked to watch the wooding operations from the railings on the boiler deck. Deck passengers always liked to get in the way.

They stopped at all manner of towns as well, causing no end of excitement. They stopped at an unmarked landing to discharge one passenger, and a private dock to pick one up. Around noon they stopped for a woman and child who hailed them from a bank, and close to four they had to slow and back their wheels so three men in a rowboat could catch them and clamber aboard. The *Fevre Dream* didn't run far that day, or fast. By the time the westering sun was turning the broad waters a deep burnished red, they were in sight of Cairo, and Dan Albright chose to tie up there for the night.

South of Cairo the Ohio flowed into the Mississippi, and the two rivers made an odd sight. They wouldn't merge all at once, but kept each to itself, the clear blue flow of the Ohio a bright ribbon down the eastern bank, against the murkier brown waters of the Mississippi. Here too was where the lower river took on its own peculiar character; from Cairo to New Orleans and the Gulf, a distance of nearly 1100 miles, the Mississippi coiled and looped and bent round and about like a writhing snake, changing its course at the merest whim, eating through the soft soil unpredictably, sometimes leaving docks high and dry, or putting whole towns under water. The pilots claimed the river was never the same twice. The upper Mississippi, where Abner Marsh had been born and had learned his trade, was an entirely different place, confined between high, rocky bluffs and running straight as often as not. Marsh stood up on the hurricane deck for a long time, looking at the passing scenery and trying to feel the *difference* of it, and the difference it would make to his future. He had crossed from the upper river to the lower, he thought, and into a new part of his life.

Shortly after, Marsh was jawing with Jeffers in the clerk's office when he heard the bell sound three times, the signal for a landing. He frowned, and looked out Jeffers' window. Nothing was visible except densely wooded banks. "I wonder why we're landin'," Marsh said. "New Madrid's the next stop. I may not know this part of the river, but this sure ain't New Madrid."

Jeffers shrugged. "Perhaps we were hailed."

Marsh begged his pardon and went on up to the pilot house. Dan Albright was at the wheel. "Was there a hail?" Marsh asked.

"No, sir," answered Albright. He was a laconic sort. He answered what you asked him, barely.

"Where we stopping?"

"Woodyard, Cap'n."

Marsh saw there was indeed a woodyard up ahead, on the west bank. "Mister Albright, I do believe we wooded up not an hour ago. We can't have burned it all already. Did Hairy Mike ask you to land?" The mate was supposed to keep track of when a steamer needed wood.

"No, sir. This is Captain York's order. The word was passed along that I was to put in at this particular woodyard, whether we wanted wood or not." Albright glanced over. He was a trim little fellow, with a thin dark moustache, a red silk tie, and patent leather boots. "Are you telling me to pass by?"

"No," Abner Marsh said hastily. York might have warned him, he thought, but their bargain gave Joshua the right to give queer orders. "You know how long we're goin' to be here?"

"I hear York has business ashore. If he don't get up till dark, that's all day."

"Damn. Our schedule—the passengers will be askin' no end of bothersome questions." Marsh frowned. "Well, I suppose there's no help for it. We might as well take on some more wood long as we're here. I'll go see to it."

Marsh struck up a bargain with the boy running the woodyard, a slender Negro in a thin cotton shirt. The boy wasn't much for dickering; Marsh got beech from him at cottonwood prices, and made him throw in some pine knots too. As the roustabouts and deckhands meandered over to load up, Marsh looked the colored boy square in the eye, smiled, and said, "You're new at this, ain't you?"

The boy nodded. "Yassuh, Cap'n." Marsh nodded, and was starting to turn back to the steamer, but the boy continued, "I jest been here a week, Cap'n. Ol' white man useta be here got hisself et up by wolves."

Marsh looked at the boy hard. "We're only a couple miles north of New Madrid, ain't we, boy?"

"Thass right, Cap'n."

When Abner Marsh returned to the *Fevre Dream*, he was feeling very agitated. Damn Joshua York, he thought. What was the man up to, and why did they have to waste a whole day at this fool woodyard? Marsh had a good mind to go storming up to York's cabin and give him a good talking to. He considered the idea briefly, then thought better of it. It was none of his business, Marsh reminded himself forcibly. He settled down to wait.

The hours passed slowly as the *Fevre Dream* lay dead in the water off the woodyard. A dozen other steamers slid by downriver, much to Abner Marsh's annoyance. Almost as many came struggling upstream. A brief knife fight between two deck passengers in which no one was injured provided the afternoon's excitement. Mostly the passengers and crew of the *Fevre Dream* lazed about on her decks, chairs tilted back in the sun, smoking or chewing or arguing politics. Jeffers and Albright played chess in the pilot house. Framm told wild stories in the grand saloon. Some of the ladies started talk of getting up a dance. And Abner Marsh grew more and more impatient.

At dark, Marsh was sitting up on the texas porch, drinking coffee and swatting mosquitoes, when he happened to glance toward shore in time to see Joshua York leave the steamer. Simon was with him. They stopped by the cabin and talked briefly to the woodyard boy, then vanished down a rutted mud road into the woods. "Well, I'll be," Marsh said, rising. "With not even a by-your-leave or a hello." He frowned. "No supper neither." That reminded him, though, and he went on down to the main cabin to eat.

The night went by; passengers and crew alike grew restless. Drinking was heavy around the bar. Some planter started up a game of brag, and others began to sing, and one stiff-necked young man got himself hit with a cane for calling for abolition.

Near midnight, Simon returned alone. Abner Marsh was in the saloon when Hairy Mike tapped him on the shoulder; Marsh had left orders to be summoned as soon as York came back. "Get your roustas aboard and tell Whitey to get our steam up," he snapped at the mate, "we got us some time to make up." Then he went to see York. Only York wasn't there.

"Joshua wants you to go on," Simon reported. "He will travel by land, and meet you in New Madrid. Wait for him." Heated questioning drew nothing more out of him; Simon only fixed Marsh with his small, cold eyes and repeated the message, that the *Fevre Dream* was to wait for York at New Madrid.

Once steam was up, it was a short, pleasant voyage. New Madrid was a bare few miles downriver from the woodyard where they had been tied up all day. Marsh gladly bid the desolate place farewell as they steamed off into the night. "Damn that Joshua," he muttered.

They lost almost two full days in New Madrid.

"He's dead," Jonathon Jeffers opined when they had been tied up for a day and a half. New Madrid had hotels, billiard parlors, churches, and diverse other recreations not available in woodyards, so the time spent at the landing was not near as boring, but nonetheless everyone was anxious to be off. A half-dozen passengers, impatient with the delay when the weather was good—the boat seemed in fine fettle, and the stage was high—came up to Marsh and demanded a refund of their passage money. They were indignantly refused, but Marsh still seethed and wondered aloud where Joshua York had got himself to.

"York ain't dead," Marsh said. "I'm not sayin' he ain't goin' to wish he was dead when I get ahold of him, but he ain't dead yet."

Behind the gold spectacles, Jeffers' eyebrow arched. "No? How can you be so sure, Cap'n? He was alone, on foot, going through the woods by night. There are scoundrels out there, and animals, too. I do believe there have been a number of deaths around New Madrid the last few years."

Marsh stared at him. "What's that?" he demanded. "How do you know?"

"I read the papers," said Jeffers.

Marsh scowled. "Well, it don't make no difference. York ain't dead. I know that, Mister Jeffers, I know that for a fact."

"Lost, then?" suggested the clerk, with a cool smile. "Shall we get up a party and go look for him, Cap'n?"

"I'll think on that," said Abner Marsh.

But there was no need. That night, an hour after the sun had set, Joshua York came striding up to the landing. He did not look like a man who had spent two days off by himself in the woods. His boots and trouser legs were dusty, but other than that his clothing looked as elegant as on the night he had left. His gait was rushed but graceful. He bounded up the stage, and smiled when he saw Jack Ely, the second engineer. "Find Whitey and get the steam up," York said to Ely, "we're leaving." Then, before anyone could question him, he was halfway up the grand staircase.

Marsh, for all his anger and restlessness, found himself remarkably relieved at Joshua's return. "Go ring the goddamned bell so them that went ashore know we're leaving," he told Hairy Mike. "I want to get us out on the river again soon as we can."

York was in his cabin, washing his hands in the basin of water that sat atop his chest of drawers. "Abner," he said politely when Marsh came rushing in after a brief, thunderous knock. "Do you think I might trouble Toby for a late supper?"

"I'll trouble you to ask why we been wastin' all this time," Marsh said. "Damn it, Joshua, I know you said you'd act queer, but *two days!* Ain't no way to run a steam packet, I tell you that."

York dried his long, pale hands carefully, and turned. "It was important. I warn you that I may do it again. You will have to accustom yourself to my ways, Abner, and see that I am not questioned."

"We got freight to deliver, and passengers who paid for passage, not for loungin' around at woodyards. What do I tell them, Joshua?"

"Whatever you choose. You are ingenious, Abner. I provided the money in our partnership. I expect you to provide the excuses." His tone was cordial but firm. "If it is any solace, this first trip will be the worst. On future trips, I anticipate few if any mysterious excursions. You'll get your record run without any trouble from me." He smiled. "I hope you can be satisfied with that. Take hold of your impatience, friend. We'll reach New Orleans eventually, and then things will go easier. Can you accept that, Abner? Abner? Is anything wrong?"

Abner Marsh had been squinting hard, and scarcely listening to York at all. He must have had an odd look on his face, he realized. "No," he said quickly, "just two days, that's all that's wrong. But it's no matter. No matter at all. Whatever you say, Joshua."

York nodded, seemingly satisfied. "I am going to change, and bother Toby for a meal, and then go on up to the pilot house to learn more of your river. Who has the after-watch tonight?"

"Mister Framm," said Marsh.

"Good," York said. "Karl is very entertaining."

"That he is," replied Marsh. "Excuse me, Joshua. Got to get down below and see to things, if we're goin' to get underway tonight." He turned abruptly and left the cabin. But outside, in the heat of the night, Abner Marsh leaned heavily on his walking stick and stared off into the star-flecked darkness, trying to summon up the thing he thought he'd seen across the cabin.

If only his eyes were better. If only York had lit both oil lamps, instead of just one. If only he had dared to walk closer. It had been hard to make out, all the way over there on the chest of drawers. But Marsh couldn't get it out of his mind. The cloth on which York had been wiping his hands had stains on it. Dark stains. Reddish.

And they'd looked too damn much like blood.

CHAPTER NINE

Aboard the Steamer FEVRE DREAM, Mississippi River, August 1857——

DAY after tedious day slipped by as the *Fevre Dream* crept down the Mississippi.

A fleet steamer could run from St. Louis to New Orleans and back in twenty-eight days or so, even allowing for intermediate stops and landings, for a week or more at wharfside loading or unloading, and for a reasonable amount of bad weather. But at the pace the *Fevre Dream* was keeping, it was going to take them a month just to reach New Orleans. It seemed to Abner Marsh as if the weather, the river, and Joshua York were all conspiring to slow him down. Fog lay over the water for two days, thick and gray as soiled cotton; Dan Albright ran through it for some six hours, cautiously steering the steamer into solid, shifting walls of mist that faded and gave way before her, leaving Marsh a mass of nerves. Had it been up to him, they would have laid up the moment the fog closed in rather than risk the *Fevre Dream*, but out on the river it was the pilot who decided such things, not the captain, and Albright pressed on. Finally, though, the mists grew too thick even for him, and they lost a day and a half at a landing near Memphis, watching the brown water rush past and tug at them, and listening to distant splashes in the fog. Once a raft came by, a fire burning on its deck, and they heard the raftsmen calling out to them, vague faint cries that echoed over the river before the gray swallowed raft and sound both.

When the fog had finally lifted enough so that Karl Framm judged it safe to try the river again, they steamed for less than an hour before coming up hard on a bar as Framm tried to run an uncertain cutoff and save some time. Deckhands and firemen and roustabouts spilled ashore, with Hairy Mike supervising, and walked the steamer over, but it took more than three hours, and afterward they crept along slow, with Albright out ahead in the yawl, taking soundings. Finally they got clear of the cutoff and into good water again, but that was not the end of their troubles. There was a thunderstorm three days later, and more than once the *Fevre Dream* had to take the long way around a bend in the river because of snags or low water in the chutes or cutoffs, or move along slow, paddles barely turning, while the sounding yawl edged out ahead with the off-duty pilot and an officer and a picked crew to drop lead and call back the news: "Quarter twain," or "Quarter less three," or "Mark three." The nights were black and overcast when they weren't foggy; if the steamer ran at all, she ran carefully, at quarter speed or less, with no smoking allowed up in the pilot house and all the windows below carefully curtained and shuttered so the boat gave off no light and the steersman could more easily see the river. The banks were pitch and desolate those nights, and moved around like restless corpses, shifting here and there so a man couldn't easily make out where the deep water ran, or even where water ended and land began. The river ran dark as sin, with no moonlight or stars upon it. Some nights it was hard even to spy the nighthawk, the device partway up the flagpole by which pilots gauged their marks. But Framm and Albright, different as they were, were both lightning pilots, and they kept the *Fevre Dream* moving when it was possible to move at all. The times when they tied up were times when *nothing* moved on the river, except rafts and logs, and a handful of flatboats and small steamers that didn't hardly draw nothing at all.

Joshua York helped them along; each night he was up in the pilot house to stand his watch like a proper cub. "I told him right off that a night like that weren't no good," Framm said to Marsh once over dinner. "I couldn't learn him marks that I couldn't rightly see myself, could I? Well, that man's got the damndest eyes for the darkness I ever seen. There's times I swear he's seein' right into the water, and it ain't nothin' to him how black it gets. I keep him by me and tell him the marks, and nine times out of ten he sees 'em before I do. Last night I think I would have tied her up halfway through the dog watch, but for Joshua."

But York delayed the steamer as well. Six additional landings were made on his order, at Greenville and at two smaller towns and at a private wharf in Tennessee and twice at woodyards. Twice he was gone all night. At Memphis York had no business ashore, but elsewhere he dragged out their layovers intolerably. When they put in at Helena he was gone overnight, and at Napoleon he held them up three days, him and Simon, doing god knows what off by themselves. Vicksburg was even worse; there they idled four nights away before Joshua York finally returned to the *Fevre Dream*.

The day they steamed out of Memphis, the sunset was especially pretty. A few lingering wisps of mist took on an orange glow, and the clouds in the west turned a vivid, fiery red, until the sky itself seemed aflame. But Abner Marsh, standing alone up on the texas deck, had eyes only for the river. No other steamers were in sight. The water ahead of them was calm; here the wind sent up a series of ripples, and there the current flowed around the wicked black limbs of a fallen tree jutting out from the shore, but mostly the old devil was placid. And as the sun went down, the muddy water took on a reddish tinge, a tinge that grew and spread and darkened until it seemed as if the *Fevre Dream* moved upon a flowing river of blood. Then the sun vanished behind the trees and the clouds, and slowly the blood darkened, going brown as blood does when it dries, and finally black, dead black, black as the grave. Marsh watched the last crimson eddies vanish. No stars came out that night. He went down to supper with blood on his mind.

Days had passed since New Madrid, and Abner Marsh had done nothing, said nothing. But he had done a considerable amount of thinking about what he had seen, or what he hadn't seen, in Joshua's cabin. He couldn't be sure he had seen anything, of course. Besides, what if he had? Perhaps Joshua had cut himself in the woods . . . though Marsh had looked closely at York's hands the following night, and had seen no signs of a cut or scab. Perhaps he had butchered an animal, or defended himself against thieves; a dozen good reasons presented themselves, but all fell before the simple fact of Joshua's silence. If York had nothing to hide, why was he so damn secretive? The more Abner Marsh thought on that, the less he liked it.

Marsh had seen blood before, plenty of it; fistfights and canings, duels and shootings. The river ran down into slave country, and blood flowed easily there for those whose skin was black. The free states weren't much better. Marsh had been in bleeding Kansas for a time, had seen men burned and shot. He had served in the Illinois militia when he was younger, and had fought in the Black Hawk War. He still dreamt at times of the Battle of Bad Axe, when they'd cut down Black Hawk's people, women and children too, as they tried to cross the Mississippi to the safety of the western shore. That had been a bloody day, but needed; Black Hawk had come a-warring and a-raiding over to Illinois, after all.

The blood that might or might not have been on Joshua's hands was different, somehow. It left Marsh uneasy, disquieted.

Still, he reminded himself, he had made a bargain. A bargain was a bargain to Abner Marsh, and a man was bound to keep those he made, whether good or bad, whether with a preacher or a sharper or the devil hisself. Joshua York had mentioned having enemies, Marsh recalled, and a man's dealings with his enemies were his own business. York had been fair enough with Marsh.

So he reasoned, and tried to put the whole matter from his mind.

But the Mississippi turned to blood, and there was bleeding in his dreams as well. Aboard the *Fevre Dream*, the mood began to grow bored and somber. A striker got careless and was scalded by the steam, and had to be set ashore at Napoleon. A roustabout ran off at Vicksburg, which was crazy, it being slave country and him a free colored man. Fights broke out among the deck passengers. It was the boredom and the thick, suffocating wet heat of August, Jeffers told him. Trash gets crazy when it gets hot, Hairy Mike echoed. Abner Marsh wasn't so sure. It seemed almost like they were being punished.

Missouri and Tennessee vanished behind them, and Marsh fretted. Cities and towns and woodyards drifted by, days turned into tortuously slow weeks, and they lost passengers and cargo because of York's layovers. Marsh went ashore, into saloons and hotels popular with steamboatmen, and listened, and didn't like the gab he heard about his boat. For all her boilers, one story ran, the *Fevre Dream* was built too big and heavy, and wasn't very fast at all. Engine trouble, another rumor claimed; seams near to bursting on the boilers. That was bad talk; boiler explosions were greatly feared. A mate from some New Orleans boat told Marsh in Vicksburg that the *Fevre Dream* looked sweet enough, but her captain was just some no-count upper-river man who didn't have the courage to run her full out. Marsh nearly broke open his head. There was talk about York as well, him and his queer friends and their ways. The *Fevre Dream* was starting to get herself a reputation, sure enough, but it was not one that Abner Marsh was over-partial to.

By the time they came steaming into Natchez, Marsh had had quite enough.

It was an hour shy of dusk when they first sighted Natchez in the distance, a few lights burning already in the ruddy afternoon, shadows lengthening from the west. It had been a fine day, but for the heat; they'd made their best time since leaving Cairo. The river had a golden sheen to it, and the sun shimmered upon it like a burnished brass ornament, gaudy as all get-out, rippling and dancing when the wind breathed upon the water. Marsh had taken to bed that afternoon, feeling a bit under the weather, but he got himself out of the cabin when he heard the whistle shriek, in answer to the call of another steamer that came high and sweet over the water. They were talking to each other, Marsh knew, an ascending and a descending boat deciding which would pass to the right and which to the left when they met. It happened a dozen times each day. But there was something in the voice of the other boat that called to him, dragged him from his sweaty sheets, and he came out of the texas just in time to see her pass; the *Eclipse*, swift and haughty, the gilded device between her chimneys glittering in the sun, her passengers thick on her decks, smoke rolling and tumbling from her. Marsh watched her recede upriver until only her smoke could be seen, a strange tightness in his gut all the while.

When the *Eclipse* had faded like a dream fades in the morning, Marsh turned, and there was Natchez up ahead of them. He heard the bells sounding the signal for a landing, and their whistle called again.

A tangle of steamers crowded the landing, and beyond them two cities waited for the *Fevre Dream*. Up on its lofty, precipitous bluffs was Natchez-on-the-hill, the proper city, with its broad streets, its trees and flowers, and all its grand houses. Each one had a name. Monmouth. Linden. Auburn. Ravenna. Concord and Belfast and Windy Hill. The Burn. Marsh had been in Natchez a half-dozen times in his younger days, before he'd had steamers of his own, and he had made it a point to go walking up there and see all those storied houses. They were goddamned palaces, every one of them, and Marsh didn't feel quite comfortable there. The old families who lived inside them acted like kings, too; aloof and arrogant, drinking their mint juleps and their sherry cobblers, icing their damned wine, amusing themselves by racing their highbred horses and hunting bears, dueling with revolvers and bowie knives over the slightest trifling affront. The nabobs, Marsh had heard them called. They were a fine lot, and every goddamned one of them seemed to be a colonel. Sometimes they showed up on the landing, and then you had to invite them aboard your steamboat for cigars and drinks, no matter how they behaved.

But they were a curiously blind bunch. From their great houses on the bluffs, the nabobs looked out over the shining majesty of the river, but somehow they couldn't see the things that were right underneath them.

For beneath the mansions, between the river and the bluffs, was another city: Natchez-under-the-hill. No marble columns stood there, and there were precious few flowers either. The streets were mud and dust. Brothels clustered round the steamer landing and lined Silver Street, or what was left of it. Much of the street had caved into the river twenty years ago, and the walks that remained were half-sunken and lined with tawdry women and dangerous, cold-eyed, foppish young men. Main Street was all saloons and billiard rooms and gambling halls, and each night the city below the city steamed and seethed. Brawls and brags and blood, crooked poker and Spanish burials, whores who'd do most anything and men who'd grin at you and take your purse and slit your throat in the bargain, that was Natchez-under-the-hill. Whiskey and flesh and cards, red lights and raucous song and watered gin, that was the way of it by the river. Steamboatmen loved and hated Natchez-under-the-hill and its milling population of cheap women and cutthroats and gamblers and free blacks and mulattoes, even though the older men swore that the city under the bluffs today wasn't nothing near as wild as it had been forty years back, or even before the tornado that God had sent to clean it out in 1840. Marsh didn't know about that; it was wild enough for him and he'd spent several memorable nights there, years ago. But this time he had a bad feeling about it.

Briefly Marsh entertained a notion to pass it by, to climb on up to the pilot house and tell Albright to keep on going. But they had passengers to land, freight to unload, and the crew would be looking forward to a night in fabled Natchez, so Marsh did nothing for all his misgivings. The *Fevre Dream* steamed in, and was made fast for the night. They quieted her down, damped her steam and let the fires die in her guts, and then her crew spilled from her like blood from an open wound. A few of them paused on the landing to buy frozen creams or fruit from the black peddlers with their carts, but most streamed right down Silver Street toward the hot bright lights.

Abner Marsh lingered on the texas porch until the stars began to peer out. Song came drifting over the water from the windows of the brothels, but it did not lighten his mood. At last Joshua York opened his cabin door and stepped out into the night. "You goin' ashore, Joshua?" Marsh asked him.

York smiled coolly. "Yes, Abner."

"How long will you be gone this time?"

Joshua York gave an elegant shrug. "I cannot say. I will return as soon as I can. Wait for me."

"I'd sooner go with you, Joshua," Marsh said. "That's Natchez out there. Natchez-under-the-hill. It's a rough place. We might be waitin' here a month, while you lay in some gutter with your throat cut. Let me come with you, show you around. I'm a riverman. You ain't."

"No," York said. "I have business ashore, Abner."

"We're partners, ain't we? Your business is my business, where the *Fevre Dream* is concerned."

"I have concerns beyond our steamboat, friend. Some things you cannot help me with. Some things I must do alone."

"Simon goes with you, don't he?"

"At times. That is different, Abner. Simon and I share . . . certain interests that you and I do not."

"You mentioned enemies once, Joshua. If that's what you're about, takin' care of those who wronged you, then tell me. I'll help."

Joshua York shook his head. "No, Abner. My enemies might not be your enemies."

"Let me decide that, Joshua. You been fair with me so far. Trust me to be fair with you."

"I cannot," York replied, sorrowfully. "Abner, we have a bargain. Ask me no questions. Please. Now, if you would, let me pass."

Abner Marsh nodded and moved aside, and Joshua York swept by him and started down the stairs. "Joshua," Marsh called out when York was almost to the bottom. The other turned. "Be careful, Joshua," Marsh said. "Natchez can be . . . bloody."

York stared up at him for a long time, his eyes as gray and unreadable as smoke. "Yes," he said finally, "I will take care." Then he turned and was gone.

Abner Marsh watched him go ashore and vanish into Natchez-under-the-hill, his lean figure throwing long shadows beneath the smoking lamps. When Joshua York was quite gone, Marsh turned and proceeded forward to the captain's cabin. The door was locked, as he had known it would be. Marsh reached in his ample pocket, and came out with the key.

He hesitated before putting it in the lock. Having duplicate keys made and stored in the steamer's safe, that was no betrayal, just plain sense. People died in locked cabins, after all, and it was better to have a spare key than to have to break the door in. But using the key, that was something else. He had made a bargain, after all. But partners had to trust each other, and if Joshua York would not trust him, how could he expect trust in return? Resolute, Marsh opened the lock, and entered York's cabin.

Inside, he lit an oil lamp, and locked the door behind him. He stood there uncertainly for a moment, looking around, wondering what he hoped to find. York's cabin was just a big stateroom, looking like it had all the other times Marsh had visited it. Still, there must be something here that would tell him something about York, give him some clue as to the nature of his partner's peculiarities.

Marsh moved to the desk, which seemed the most likely place to begin, carefully eased himself into York's chair, and began to sift through the newspapers. He touched them gingerly, noting the position of each paper as he slid it out for examination, so that he could leave all as he found it when he left. The newspapers were . . . well, newspapers. There must have been fifty of them on the desk, numbers old and new, the *Herald* and the *Tribune* from New York, several Chicago papers, all the St. Louis and New Orleans journals, papers from Napoleon and Baton Rouge and Memphis and Greenville and Vicksburg and Bayou Sara, weeklies from a dozen little river towns. Most of them were intact. A few had stories cut from them.

Beneath the litter of newspapers, Marsh found two leather-bound ledger books. He eased them out slowly, trying to ignore a nervous clenching in his stomach. Perhaps here he had a journal or a diary, Marsh thought, something to tell him where York had come from and where he aimed to go. He opened the first ledger, and frowned in disappointment. No diary. Only stories, carefully cut from newspapers and mounted with paste, each one labeled as to date and place in Joshua's flowing hand.

Marsh read the story before him, from a Vicksburg paper, about a body that had been found washed up on the riverfront. The date placed it six months back. On the opposite page were two items, both from Vicksburg as well; a family found dead in a shanty twenty miles from the city, a Negro wench—probably a runaway—discovered stiff in the woods, dead of unknown causes.

Marsh turned the pages, read, turned again. After a time he closed the book and opened the other. It was the same. Page after page of bodies, mysterious deaths, corpses discovered here and there, all arranged by city. Marsh closed the books and returned them to their place, and tried to consider. The newspapers had lots of accounts of deaths and killings that York hadn't bothered to cut out. Why? He searched through a few newspapers and read over them until he was sure. Then Marsh frowned. It appeared that Joshua had no interest in shootings or knifings, in rivermen drowned or blown up by boiler explosions or burned, in gamblers and thieves hanged by the law. The stories he collected were different. Deaths no one could account for. Folks with throats tore out. Bodies all mutilated and ripped up, or else too far rotted for anyone to know just how they'd died. Bodies unmarked as well, found dead for no reason anyone could find, found with wounds too small to notice at first, found whole but bloodless. Between the two ledgers, there must of been fifty or sixty stories, nine months' worth of death drawn from the whole length of the lower Mississippi.

Briefly Abner Marsh was afraid, sick at heart at the thought that perhaps Joshua was saving accounts of his own vile deeds. But a moment's thought proved that could not be. Some, perhaps, but in other cases the dates were wrong; Joshua had been with him in St. Louis or New Albany or aboard the *Fevre Dream* when these people met their ghastly ends. He could not be responsible.

Still, Marsh saw, there was a pattern to the stops York had ordered, to his secretive trips ashore. He was visiting the sites of these stories, one by one. What was York looking for? What . . . or who? An enemy? An enemy who had done all this, somehow, moving up and down the river? If so, then Joshua was on the side of right. But why the silence, if his purpose was just?

It had to be more than one enemy, Marsh realized. No single person could be responsible for all the killing in those ledgers, and Joshua had said "enemies," after all. Besides, he had come back from New Madrid with blood on his hands, but that did not end his quest.

He could not make sense of it.

Marsh began to go through the drawers and storage nooks in York's desk. Paper, fancy stationery impressed with a picture of the *Fevre Dream* and the name of the line, envelopes, ink, a half-dozen pens, a blotter, a map of the river system with marks on it, boot polish, sealing wax: in short, nothing useful. In one drawer he found letters, and turned to them hopefully. But they told him nothing. Two were letters of credit, the rest simple business correspondence with agents in London, New York, St. Louis, and other cities. Marsh did come on one letter from a banker in St. Louis bringing Fevre River Packets to York's attention. "I think it best suited to your purposes as you describe them," the man had written. "Its owner is an experienced riverman with a reputation for honesty, said to be exceedingly ugly but fair, and he has recently had reverses which should make him receptive to your offer." The letter went on, but told Marsh nothing he had not already known.

Replacing the letters as he had found them, Abner Marsh rose and moved about the cabin, looking for something else, something to enlighten him. He found nothing; clothing in the drawers, York's vile-tasting drink in the wine rack, suits hung in the closet, books everywhere. Marsh checked the titles of the volumes by York's bedside; one was a book of poetry by Shelley, the other some sort of medical book he could scarcely understand a line of. The tall bookcase offered more of the same; much fiction and poetry, a fair amount of history, books on medicine and philosophy and natural science, a dusty old tome on alchemy, an entire shelf of books in foreign languages. A few untitled books, hand-bound in finely tooled leather with gold-leaf pages, presented themselves, and Marsh pulled one out, hoping this might be the diary or log to answer his questions. But if it was, he could not read it; the words were in some grotesque, spindly code, and the hand was clearly not Joshua's airy script but rather crabbed and tiny.

Marsh went through the cabin one final time, to make sure he had overlooked nothing, and finally determined to leave, not much wiser than he had come. He inserted the key in the lock, turned it carefully, snuffed the lamp, stepped outside, and relocked the door behind him. It had gotten a trifle cooler outside. Marsh realized that he was drenched in sweat. He slipped the key back into his coat pocket and turned to go.

And stopped.

A few yards away, the ghastly old woman Katherine was standing and staring at him, cold malevolence in her eyes. Marsh decided to brazen it out. He tipped his cap. "Good evening, ma'am," he said to her.

Katherine smiled slowly, a creeping rictus of a smile that twisted her vulpine face into a mask of terrible glee. "Good evening, Captain," she said. Her teeth, Marsh noted, were yellow, and very long.

CHAPTER TEN

*New Orleans,
August 1857*

AFTER Adrienne and Alain had departed on the steamer *Cotton Queen*, bound for Baton Rouge and Bayou Sara, Damon Julian decided to take a stroll along the levee to a French coffee stall he knew. Sour Billy Tipton walked uneasily beside him, casting suspicious glances at everyone they passed. The rest of Julian's party followed; Kurt and Cynthia walked together, while Armand brought up the rear, furtive and ill-at-ease, already touched by the thirst. Michelle was back at the house.

The rest were gone, dispersed, sent up or down the river on one steamer or another by Julian's command, searching for money, safety, a new place to gather. Damon Julian had finally stirred.

The moonlight was soft and bright as butter upon the river. The stars were out. Along the levee, dozens of steamers crowded in next to the sailing ships with their high, proud masts and furled canvas sails. Niggers moved cotton and sugar and flour from one sort of boat to the other. The air was humid and fragrant, the streets crowded.

They found a table that gave them a good view of the bustle, and ordered café au lait and the fried sugar pastries the stall was famous for. Sour Billy bit into one and got sugar powder all over his vest and sleeves. He cussed loudly.

Damon Julian laughed, his laughter as sweet as the moonlight. "Ah, Billy. How amusing you are."

Sour Billy hated being laughed at worse than he hated anything, but he looked up at Julian's dark eyes and forced a grin. "Yes, sir," he said with a rueful shake of his head.

Julian ate his own pastry neatly, so no sugar whitened the rich dark gray of his suit, or the sheen of his scarlet tie. When he was done, he sipped at his café au lait while his gaze swept over the levee and wandered among the passersby on the street. "There," he said shortly, "the woman beneath the cypress." The others looked. "Is she not striking?"

She was a Creole lady, escorted by two dangerous-looking gentlemen. Damon Julian stared at her like a love-struck youth, his pale face unlined and serene, his hair a mass of fine dark curls, his eyes large and melancholy. But even across the table, Sour Billy could feel the heat in those eyes, and he was afraid.

"She is exquisite," Cynthia said.

"She has Valerie's hair," Armand added.

Kurt smiled. "Will you take her, Damon?"

The woman and her companions were going away from them, walking in front of an ornate wrought-iron fence. Damon Julian watched them thoughtfully. "No," he said at last, turning back to the table and sipping his café au lait. "The night is too young, the streets are too crowded, and I am weary. Let us sit."

Armand looked downcast and anxious. Julian smiled at him briefly, then leaned forward and laid a hand on Armand's sleeve. "We will drink before the dawn comes," he said. "You have my word."

"I know a place," Sour Billy added conspiratorially, "a real fancy house, with a bar, red velvet chairs, good drinks. The girls are all beautiful, you'll see. You can get one all night for a twenty-dollar gold piece. In the morning, well, well." He chuckled. "But we'll be gone when they find what they find, and it's cheaper than buyin' fancy girls. Yes, sir."

Damon Julian's black eyes were amused. "Billy makes me niggardly," he said to the others, "but whatever would we do without him?" He looked about again, bored. "I should come into the city more often. When one is sated, one loses sight of all the other pleasures." He sighed. "Can you feel it? The air is rank with it, Billy!"

"What?" said Sour Billy.

"Life, Billy." Julian's smile mocked him, but Billy made himself smile back. "Life and love and lust, rich food and rich wine, rich dreams and hope, Billy. All of it here around us. Possibilities." His eyes glittered. "Why should I pursue that beauty who went by us, when there are so many others, so many possibilities? Can you answer?"

"I—Mister Julian, I don't—"

"No, Billy, you don't, do you?" Julian laughed. "My whims are life and death to these cattle, Billy. If you are ever to be one of us, you must understand that. I am pleasure, Billy. I am power. And the essence of what I am, of pleasure and power, lies in possibility. My own possibilities are vast, and have no limit, as our years have no limit. But I am the limit to these cattle, I am the end of all their hopes, of all their possibilities. Do you begin to understand? To slake the red thirst, that is nothing, any old darkie on his deathbed will do for that. Yet how much finer to drink of the young, the rich, the beautiful, those whose lives stretch out ahead of them, whose days and nights glitter and shine with promise! Blood is but blood, any animal can sip at it, any of *them*." He gestured languidly, at the steamboatmen on the levee, the niggers toting their hogsheads, and all the richly dressed folk of the Vieux Carré. "It is not the blood that ennobles, that makes one a master. It is the *life*, Billy. Drink of their lives and yours becomes longer. Eat of their flesh and yours grows stronger. Feast on beauty and wax more beautiful."

Sour Billy Tipton listened eagerly; he had seldom seen Julian in so expansive a mood. Sitting in the darkness of the library, Julian tended to be brusque and frightening. Beyond it, out in the world again, he glittered, reminding Sour Billy of the way he had been when he first arrived with Charles Garoux at the plantation where Billy was overseer. He said as much.

Julian nodded. "Yes," he said, "the plantation is safe, but in safety and satiety is danger." His teeth were white when he smiled. "Charles Garoux," he mused. "Ah, the possibilities of that youth! He was beautiful in his way, strong, healthy. A firebrand, beloved by all the ladies, admired by other men. Even the darkies loved Master Charles. He would have had a grand life! His nature was so open as well, it was easy to befriend him, to win his undying trust by saving him from poor Kurt here." Julian interrupted himself with a laugh. "Then, once I had been welcomed into his house, easier still to come to him every night, and drain him, little by little, so he seemed to sicken and die. Once he woke when I was in his room, and thought I had come to comfort him. I leaned over his bed, and he reached up and clasped me to him, and I drank. Ah, the sweetness of Charles, all the strength and beauty of him!"

"The old man was damn upset when he up and died," Sour Billy put in. Personally, he'd been delighted. Charles Garoux had always been telling his father that Billy was too hard on the niggers, and trying to get him dismissed. As if you could get any work from a nigger by being soft.

"Yes, Garoux was distraught," said Julian. "How fortunate that I was there to comfort him in his grief. His son's best friend. How often he told me, afterward, that I had become like a fourth son to him as we mourned."

Sour Billy remembered it well. Julian had handled it real good. The younger sons had let down the old man; Jean-Pierre was a drunken lout, and Philip a weakling who wept like a woman at his brother's funeral, but Damon Julian had been a tower of manly strength. They had buried Charles out back of the plantation, in the family cemetery. The ground being so damp in these parts, he'd been laid to rest in a big marble mausoleum with a winged victory on top of it. It stayed nice and cool in there, even in the heat of August. Sour Billy had gone into the tomb many a time in the years since, to drink and piss on Charles's coffin. Once he'd dragged a nigger wench in there with him, slapped her around a little and had her three-four times, just so old Charles's ghost could see the proper way to handle niggers.

Charles had only been the beginning, Sour Billy recalled. Six months later Jean-Pierre rode off to do some whoring and gambling in the city, and he never did ride back, and it wasn't long after that when poor timid Philip got himself all ripped up by some kind of animal in the woods. Old Garoux was real sick at heart by then, but Damon Julian was by his side through all of it, helping. Finally Garoux adopted him, and wrote a new will leaving him just about everything.

There was a night not too long after that Sour Billy would never forget, when Damon Julian had demonstrated how thoroughly old René Garoux was in his power. It was up in the old man's bedroom. Valerie was there, and Adrienne and Alain as well, they'd all been living in the big house, since any friend of Julian's was welcome in the Garoux home. They watched with Sour Billy while Damon Julian stood at the side of the great canopied bed and pierced the old man through with his black eyes and his easy smile and told him the truth, all the truth about what had happened to Charles and Jean-Pierre and Philip. Julian was wearing Charles's signet ring, and Valerie had its twin on a chain about her neck. Hers had once belonged to the missing Jean-Pierre. She had not wanted to wear it. The thirst was on her, but she wanted to finish old Garoux quickly, without talk. But Damon Julian stilled her protests with soft words and cold eyes, so she wore the ring and stood meekly and listened.

When Julian had finished his story, Garoux had been shaking, his rheumy eyes full of tears and pain and hate. And then, astoundingly, Damon Julian had told Sour Billy to hand the old man his knife. "He ain't dead yet, Mister Julian," Billy had protested. "He'll cut your guts out."

But Julian only glanced at him and smiled, so Sour Billy reached back and produced the knife and put it into Garoux's wrinkled, liver-spotted grasp. The old man's hands shook so bad that Billy had been afraid he was going to drop the damn thing, but somehow he hung on to it. Damon Julian sat on the edge of the bed. "René," he said, "my friends are thirsty." His voice was so quiet, so liquid.

That was all he had to say. Alain produced a glass, a fine crystal etched with the family crest, and old René Garoux carefully cut open the vein in his wrist and filled the glass with his own steaming red blood, crying and trembling all the while. Valerie and Alain and Adrienne passed the glass from hand to hand, but it was left to Damon Julian to finish it off, while Garoux bled to death in his bed.

"Garoux gave us some good years," Kurt was saying. His words drew Sour Billy out of his memories. "Rich and safe, off by ourselves, the city here whenever we wanted it. Food and drink and niggers to wait on us, a fancy girl every month."

"Yet it ended," Julian said, a trifle wistfully. "All things must end, Kurt. Do you mourn it?"

"Things aren't the same," Kurt admitted. "Dust everywhere, the house rotting, rats. I'm not anxious to move again, Damon. Out in the world, we are never secure. After a hunt, there is always the fear, the hiding, the running. I do not want that again."

Julian smiled sardonically. "Inconvenient, true, but not without spice. You are young, Kurt. Remember, however they may hound you, you are the master. You will see them dead, and their children, and their children's children. The Garoux home falls into ruin. It is nothing. All these things the cattle make fall into ruin. I have seen Rome itself turn to dust. Only we go on." He shrugged. "And we may yet find another like René Garoux."

"So long as we are with you," Cynthia said anxiously. She was a slight, pretty woman with brown eyes, and she had become Julian's favorite since he had dismissed Valerie, but even Sour Billy could tell that she was insecure about her position. "It is worse when we are alone."

"So you do not wish to leave me?" Damon Julian asked her, smiling.

"No," she said. "Please." Kurt and Armand were looking at him as well. Julian had begun sending away his companions a month ago, very suddenly. Valerie was exiled first, as she had begged, though he sent her upriver not with the troublesome Jean, but with dark handsome Raymond, who was cruel and strong and—some said—Julian's own son. Raymond would be sure to keep her safe, Julian said mockingly as Valerie knelt before him that night. Jean was given his leave the next night, and went off alone, and Sour Billy thought that would be the end of it. He was wrong. Damon Julian had some new thought in his head, and so Jorge was sent away a week later, and then Cara and Vincent, and then the others, alone or in pairs. Now those who remained knew that none of them were safe.

"Ah," Julian said to Cynthia, amused. "Well, there are only five of us now. If we are careful, and we make each fancy girl last for, oh, a month or two, sipping slowly as it were—why then, I believe we can last until winter. By then one of the others will have sent word, perhaps. We shall see. Until then, you may stay, darling. And Michelle as well, and you, Kurt."

Armand looked stricken. "And me?" he blurted. "Damon, please."

"Is it the thirst, Armand? Is that why you tremble? Control yourself. Will you rip and tear when we reach these friends of Billy's? You know how I frown on that." His eyes narrowed. "I am still thinking about you, Armand."

Armand looked down at his empty cup.

"I'll stay," Sour Billy announced.

"Ah," said Damon Julian. "Of course. Why, Billy, what would we do without you?" Sour Billy Tipton didn't much like the smile Julian wore then, but there wasn't nothing to be done about it.

A short time later, they set off to the place Billy had promised to show them. The house was outside the Vieux Carré, in the American section of New Orleans, but within walking distance. Damon Julian went in front, walking through the narrow gaslit streets arm in arm with Cynthia, wearing a private ghost of a smile as he regarded the iron balconies, the gates opening on courtyards with their flambeaux and their fountains, the gas lamps atop iron poles. Sour Billy directed them. Soon they were in a darker, rawer part of town, where the buildings were wood or crumbling tabby-brick, made of ground oyster shells and sand. Even the gas lines had not extended this far, though the city had had its gas works for more than twenty years. At the corners, oil lamps swung from heavy iron chains hung diagonally across the streets and supported by great hooks driven into the sides of buildings. They burned with a sensual smoky light. Julian and Cynthia passed from pools of light into shadow, back into light, then again into shadow. Sour Billy and the others followed.

A party of three men stepped out from an alley and crossed their path. Julian ignored them, but one of the men glimpsed Sour Billy as he passed beneath a light. "*You!*" he said.

Sour Billy turned his stare on them, saying nothing. They were young Creoles, half-drunk and therefore dangerous.

"I know you, *monsieur*," the man said. He stepped up to Sour Billy, his dark face flush with drink and anger. "Have you forgotten me? I was with Georges Montreuil the day you affronted him in the French Exchange."

Sour Billy recognized him. "Well, well," he said.

"Monsieur Montreuil vanished one June night, after an evening of gaming at the St. Louis," the man said stiffly.

"I'm real grieved," Sour Billy said. "I guess he must of won too much, and got robbed for his trouble."

"He lost, *monsieur*. He had been losing steadily for some weeks. He had nothing worth stealing. No, I do not think it was robbery. I think it was you, Mister Tipton. He had been asking about you. He meant to deal with you like the trash you are. You are no gentleman, *monsieur*, or I would call you out. If you dare show your face in the Vieux Carré again, however, you have my word that I shall whip you through the streets like a nigger. Do you hear me?"

"I hear," said Sour Billy. He spat on the man's boot.

The Creole swore and his face paled with rage. He took a step forward and reached out for Sour Billy, but Damon Julian stepped between them, and stopped the man with a hand against his chest. "*Monsieur*," Julian said, in a voice like wine and honey. The man halted, confused. "I can assure you that Mister Tipton did no harm to your friend, sir."

"Who are you?" Even half-drunk, the Creole clearly recognized that Julian was a different sort of person than Sour Billy; his fine clothes, cool features, cultured voice, all marked him a gentleman. Julian's eyes glittered dangerously in the lamplight.

"I am Mister Tipton's employer," Julian said. "May we discuss this affair somewhere other than the public street? I know a place further on where we can sit beneath the moon and sip drinks while we talk. Will you let me buy your friends and you a refreshment?"

One of the other Creoles stepped up beside his friend. "Let us hear him out, Richard."

Grudgingly, the man consented. "Billy," Damon Julian said, "do show us the way." Sour Billy Tipton suppressed a smile, nodded, and led them off. A block away they turned into an alley, and followed it back into a dark court. Sour Billy sat down on the edge of a scum-covered pool. The water soaked through the seat of his pants, but he didn't care.

"What is this place?" demanded Montreuil's friend. "This is no tavern!"

"Well," said Sour Billy Tipton. "Well. I must have turned wrong." The other Creoles had entered the court, followed by the rest of Julian's party. Kurt and Cynthia stood by the mouth of the alley. Armand moved closer to the fountain.

"I do not like this," one of the men said.

"What is the meaning of this?"

"Meaning?" asked Damon Julian. "Ah. A dark court, the moonlight, a pool. Your friend Montreuil died in just such a place, *monsieur*. Not in this place, but one very much like it. No, do not look at Billy. He bears no blame. If you have a quarrel, take it up with me."

"You?" said Montreuil's friend. "As you will. Permit me to retire a moment. My companions will act as my seconds."

"Certainly," said Julian. The man moved away, conferred briefly with his two companions. One of them stepped forward. Sour Billy rose from the pool's edge and met him.

"I'm Mister Julian's second," Sour Billy said. "You want to talk terms?"

"You are no proper second," the man began. He had a long, pretty face and dark brown hair.

"Terms," Sour Billy repeated. His hand went behind his back. "Me, I'd favor knives."

The man gave a small grunt and staggered backward. He looked down in terror. Sour Billy's knife was buried hilt-deep in his gut, and a slow red stain was spreading across his vest. "God," the man whimpered.

"That's only me, though," Sour Billy continued. "And I'm not a gentleman, no sir, not a proper second. Knives ain't no proper weapon neither." The man dropped to his knees, and his friends suddenly noticed and started forward in alarm. "Mister Julian now, he's got different ideas. His weapon," Billy smiled, "is teeth."

Julian took Montreuil's friend, the one called Richard. The other turned to run. Cynthia embraced him by the alley, and gave him a lingering wet kiss. He thrashed and struggled but could not break free of her embrace. Her pale hands brushed the back of his neck, and long nails sharp and thin as razors slid across his veins. Her mouth and tongue swallowed his scream.

Sour Billy pulled free his knife while Armand bent to attend to his whimpering victim. In the moonlight, the blood running down the blade looked almost black. Billy started to clean it in the pool, then hesitated. He raised the knife to his lips and licked at the flat of it tentatively. Then he made a face. Tasted awful, not like in his dreams at all. Still, that would change when Julian made him over, he knew.

Sour Billy washed his knife and sheathed it. Damon Julian had given Richard over to Kurt, and was standing solitary, gazing up at the moon. Sour Billy approached him. "Saved us some money," he said.

Julian smiled.

CHAPTER ELEVEN

Aboard the Steamer FEVRE DREAM, Natchez, August 1857——

FOR Abner Marsh, that night went on and on. He had a small snack, to settle his stomach and calm his fears, and soon thereafter retired to his cabin, but sleep would not take him easily. For hours he lay staring at the shadows, his mind racing, his thoughts a jumble of suspicion and anger and guilt. Beneath the thin, starchy sheet, Marsh sweated like a hog. When he did sleep, he tossed and turned and woke often, and dreamed flushed, furtive, incoherent dreams of blood and burning steamboats and yellow teeth and Joshua Anton York, standing pale and cold beneath a scarlet light with fever and death behind his angry eyes.

The next day was the longest day Abner Marsh had ever known. All his thoughts led him round and round and back to the same place. By noon he knew what he must do. He'd been caught, no help for it. He had to fess up and have it out with Joshua. If that meant the end of their partnership, so be it, although the thought of losing his *Fevre Dream* made Marsh feel sick and weary, as full of despair as he had been the day he'd seen the splinters the ice had made of his steamers. It would be the end of him, Marsh thought, and perhaps it was all he deserved for betraying Joshua's trust. But things could not go on as they were. Joshua ought to hear the tale from his own mouth too, Marsh decided, which meant that he had to get to him before that woman Katherine did.

He spread the word. "I want to be told, the moment he gets back," he said, "no matter when it is, or what I'm about, come fetch me. You hear?" Then Abner Marsh waited, and took what solace he could in a lovely dinner of roast pork and green beans and onions, with half a blueberry pie afterward.

Two hours shy of midnight, one of the crew came to him. "Cap'n York's come back, Cap'n. Got some folks with him. Mister Jeffers is settlin' them into cabins."

"Has Joshua gone up to his cabin?" Marsh asked. The man nodded. Marsh snatched up his walking stick and made for the stairs.

Outside York's cabin, he hesitated briefly, threw back his ample shoulders, and brought the head of his stick sharply against the door. York opened on the third knock. "Come in, Abner," he said, smiling. Marsh stepped inside, shut the door behind him, and leaned against it, while York crossed the room and resumed what he'd been doing. He'd set out a silver tray and three glasses. Now he reached for a fourth. "I'm glad you came up. I've brought some people aboard I want you to meet. They'll be coming up for a drink as soon as they've settled into their staterooms." York pulled a bottle of his private drink from the wine rack, produced his knife, and sliced off the wax seal.

"Never mind about that," Marsh said brusquely. "Joshua, we got to talk."

York set the bottle down on the tray and turned to face Marsh. "Oh? What of? You sound upset, Abner."

"I got spare keys to every lock on this boat. Mister Jeffers keeps 'em for me in the safe. When you went into Natchez, I got myself a key and searched your cabin."

Joshua York scarcely moved, but when he heard Marsh's words his lips pressed together slightly. Abner Marsh looked him straight in the eye, as a man ought at a time like this, and felt coldness there, and the fury of betrayal. He would almost rather Joshua had screamed at him, or even drawn a weapon, than look at him with such eyes. "Did you find anything of interest?" York asked finally, in a voice gone flat.

Abner Marsh wrenched himself away from Joshua's gray eyes, and jabbed his stick at the desk. "Your ledgers," he said. "Full of dead men."

York said nothing. He glanced briefly at the desk, frowned, and sat himself down in one of his armchairs and poured out a measure of his thick, vile drink. He sipped it, and only then gestured to Marsh. "Sit down," he commanded. When Marsh was seated across from him, York added one final word: "Why?"

"Why?" Marsh said, a bit angrily. "Maybe cause I'm tired of havin' myself a partner who don't tell me nothin', who don't trust me."

"We had a bargain."

"I know that, Joshua. And I'm sorry, if that matters. Sorry I did it, and a damn sight sorrier I got caught." He grinned ruefully. "That Katherine saw me leave. She'll be talkin' to you. Look, I should have come direct to you, told you what was eatin' at me. I'm doin' that now. Maybe it's too late, but here I am. Joshua, I love this boat of ours much as I ever loved anything, and the day we take the horns off the *Eclipse* is goin' to be the grandest day of my life. But I been thinkin', and I know I got to give up that day, and this steamer, rather than go on like we are. This river is full of scoundrels and sharpers and Bible-thumpers and abolitionists and Republicans and all manner of queer folk, but you're the queerest of the lot, I swear. The night hours I don't mind, they don't fret me none. Books full of dead people, that's somethin' else, but it ain't nobody's business what a man cares to read. Why, I knew a pilot on the *Grand Turk* kept books that'd make even Karl Framm turn red with shame. But these stops of yours, these trips off by yourself, it's those I can't suffer no more. You're *slowing my steamer*, damn you, you're ruinin' our name before we even made it. And Joshua, that ain't all. I seen you the night you come back from New Madrid. You had blood on your hands. Deny it if you will. Cuss me if you want. But I know. You had blood on your hands, damned if you didn't."

Joshua York took a long drink, and frowned as he refilled his glass. When he looked at Marsh, the ice had melted in his eyes. He looked thoughtful. "Are you proposing we dissolve our partnership?" he asked.

Marsh felt like a mule had kicked him in the stomach. "If you want, you got that right. I ain't got the money to buy you out, of course. But you'd have the *Fevre Dream*, and I could keep my *Eli Reynolds* and maybe show a profit with her, send you a little as it come in."

"Is that the way you'd prefer it?"

Marsh glared at him. "Damn you, Joshua, you know it ain't."

"Abner," York said, "I need you. I cannot run the *Fevre Dream* by myself. I am learning a little of piloting, and I've become somewhat more familiar with the river and its ways, but we both know I am no steamboatman. If you left, half of the crew would go with you. Mister Jeffers and Mister Blake and Hairy Mike for certain, and no doubt others. They are loyal to you."

"I can order 'em to stay on with you," Marsh offered.

"I would rather you stayed on. If I agree to overlook your trespass, can we continue as before?"

The lump in Abner Marsh's throat was so thick he thought he would choke on it. He swallowed, and said the hardest thing that he had ever said, in all his born days: "No."

"I see," said Joshua.

"I got to trust my partner," Marsh said. "He's got to trust me. You talk to me, Joshua, you tell me what all this is about, and you got yourself a partner."

Joshua York grimaced, and sipped slowly at his drink, considering. "You will not believe me," he said at last. "It is a more outlandish story than any of Mister Framm's."

"Try it out on me. Can't do no harm."

"Oh, but it can, Abner, it *can*." York's voice was serious. He put down his glass and went over to the bookcase. "When you searched," he said, "did you look at my books?"

"Yes," Marsh admitted.

York pulled out one of the untitled volumes in the leather bindings, returned to his chair, and opened it to a page full of crabbed characters. "Had you been able to read it," he said, "this book and its companion volumes might have enlightened you."

"I looked at it. Didn't make no sense."

"Of course not," York said. "Abner, what I am about to tell you will be difficult for you to accept. Whether you accept it or not, however, it must not be repeated outside the confines of this cabin. Is that understood?"

"Yes."

York's eyes wondered. "I want no mistake this time, Abner. Is *that* understood?"

"I said yes, Joshua," Marsh grumbled, offended.

"Very well," Joshua said. He put his finger on the page. "This code is a relatively simple cipher, Abner, but to break it you must first realize that the language involved is a primitive dialect of Russian, one that has not been spoken in some hundreds of years. The original papers transcribed in this volume were very, very old. They told the story of some people who lived and died in the area north of the Caspian Sea many centuries ago." He paused. "Pardon. Not people. Russian is not among my best languages, but I believe the proper word is *odoroten*."

"What?" said Marsh.

"That is only one term, of course. Other languages have other names. *Krŭvnik, védomec, wieszczy. Vilkakis* and *vrkolák* as well, although those two have somewhat different meanings from the others."

"You're talkin' gibberish," Marsh said, although some of the words Joshua was reciting did kind of ring familiar, and sounded vaguely like the gibble-gabble Smith and Brown were always spouting.

"I won't give you the African names for them, then," said Joshua, "or the Asian, or any of the others. Does *nosferatu* have meaning for you?"

Marsh regarded him blankly.

Joshua York sighed. "How about *vampire?*"

Abner Marsh knew that one. "What kind of story you tryin' to tell me?" he said gruffly.

"A vampire story," said York with a sly smile. "Surely you've heard them before. The living dead, immortal, prowlers of the night, creatures without souls, damned to eternal wandering. They sleep in coffins filled with their native earth, shun daylight and the cross, and each night they rise and drink the blood of the living. They are shape-changers as well, able to take the forms of a bat or a wolf. Some, who utilize the wolf form frequently, are called werewolves and thought to be a different species entirely, but that is an error. They are two sides of a single dark coin, Abner. Vampires can also become mist, and their victims become vampires themselves. It is a wonder, multiplying so, that vampires have not displaced living men entirely. Fortunately, they have weaknesses as well as vast power. Though their strength is frightening, they cannot enter a house where they have not been invited, neither as human nor animal nor mist. They wield great animal magnetism, however, the force Mesmer wrote about, and can often compel their victims to ask them in. But a cross will send them fleeing, garlic can bar them, and they cannot cross running water. Though they look much like you and I, they have no souls, and therefore are not reflected in mirrors. Holy water will burn them, silver is anathema to them, daylight can destroy them if dawn catches them away from their coffins. And by severing their heads from their bodies and driving a wooden stake through their hearts, one can rid the world of them permanently." Joshua sat back and took up his drink, sipped, smiled. "*Those* vampires, Abner," he said. He tapped the book with a long finger. "This is the story of a few of

109

them. They are real. Old, eternal, and real. A sixteenth-century *odoroten* wrote this book, about those who had gone before him. A vampire."

Abner Marsh said nothing.

"You do not believe me," said Joshua York.

"It ain't easy," Marsh admitted. He tugged at the coarse hairs of his beard. There were other things he didn't say. Joshua's talk of vampires didn't bother him half so much as his own disquiet about where Joshua himself fit in. "Let's not worry if I believe or not," Marsh said. "If I can take Mister Framm's stories, I can at least lissen to yours. Go on."

Joshua smiled. "You're a clever man, Abner. You should be able to figure things out by yourself."

"I don't feel so damn clever," Marsh said. "Tell me."

York sipped, shrugged. "They are my enemies. They are real, Abner, and they are here, all along your river. Through books like these, through research in newspapers, through much painstaking work, I have tracked them from the mountains of Eastern Europe, the forests of the Germans and Poles, the steppes of Russia. Here. To your Mississippi Valley, to the new world. I know them, I bring an end to them and all the things they have ever been." He smiled. "Now do you comprehend my books, Abner? And the blood on my hands?"

Abner Marsh thought on that for a spell before he replied. He finally said, "I recollect how you wanted mirrors all up and down the grand saloon instead of oil paintings and such. For . . . protection?"

"Exactly. And silver. Did you ever know a steamer to wear so much silver?"

"No."

"And, of course, we have the river. The old devil river. The Mississippi. Running water such as the world has never seen! The *Fevre Dream* is a sanctuary. I can hunt them, you see, but they cannot come near us."

"I'm surprised you didn't tell Toby to season everything with garlic," Marsh said.

"I thought of it," Joshua said. "But I dislike garlic."

Marsh mulled it all over. "Just say I believe this," he said. "I ain't sayin' that's so, but just for the sake of argument I'll go along. Still got some things that bother me. How come you didn't tell me before?"

"If I'd told you at the Planters' House, you'd never have let me buy into your company. I need the power to go where I must."

"And how come you only go out by night?"

"*They* prowl by night. It is easier to find them when they go abroad than when they are safe in their sanctuaries, hidden. I know the ways of those I hunt. I keep their hours."

"And those friends of yours? Simon and the rest?"

"Simon has been my associate for a long time. The others have joined me more recently. They know the truth, they assist me in my mission. As I hope you shall, henceforth." Joshua chuckled. "Don't worry, Abner, all of us are as mortal as you are."

Marsh fingered his beard. "Let me have a drink," he said. When York leaned forward, he added quickly, "No, not that stuff, Joshua. Something else. Got any whiskey?"

York rose and poured him a glass. Marsh drained it straightaway. "I can't say I like any of this. Dead folks, blood drinkin', all that stuff, I never believed in none of it."

"Abner, this is a dangerous game I play. I never meant to involve you or your crew in any of it. I would never have told you as much as I have, but you insisted. If you wish to deal yourself out, I have no objections. Do as I tell you, run the *Fevre Dream* for me, that is all I ask. I will deal with *them*. Do you doubt my capacity to do so?"

Marsh looked at the easy way Joshua sat, remembered the force behind those gray eyes, the strength of his handshake. "No."

"I have been honest in many of things I've said to you," Joshua continued. "My purpose is not my only obsession. I love this steamer as you do, Abner, and share many of your dreams for her. I want to pilot her, to know the river. I want to be on hand the day we outrun the *Eclipse*. Believe me when I say—"

There was a knock on the door.

Marsh was startled. Joshua York smiled and shrugged. "My friends from Natchez come up for their drink," he explained. "A *moment!*" he called loudly. He said to Marsh in a low, urgent voice, "Think about all I have said, Abner. We can talk again, if you'd like. But keep my faith, and talk to no one about this. I have no wish to involve others."

"You got my word," Marsh said. "Hell, who'd believe it?"

Joshua smiled. "If you would be so kind as to let in my guests while I pour us some drinks," he said.

Marsh got up and opened the door. Outside a man and a woman stood talking in soft whispers. Beyond them, Marsh saw the moon standing between the chimneys like a glowing decoration. He heard snatches of a bawdy song from Natchez-under-the-hill, faint in the distance. "Come on in," he said.

The strangers were a fine-looking couple, Marsh saw as they entered. The man was young, almost boyish, very lean and handsome, with black hair and fair skin and heavy, sensual lips. He had a fierce cold look in his black eyes when he glanced briefly at Marsh. And the woman . . . Abner Marsh looked at her, and found it hard to look away. She was a real beauty. Long hair black as midnight, skin as fine as milk-white silk, high cheekbones. Her waist was so small Marsh wanted to reach out and see if his big hands would go all the way around. He looked up at her face instead, and found her staring at him. Her eyes were incredible. Marsh had never seen eyes that color before; a deep, velvety purple, full of promise. He felt like he could drown in those eyes. They reminded him of a color he'd seen on the river, once or twice, at twilight, a strange violet stillness glimpsed only briefly, before darkness came in for good and all. Marsh stared into those eyes helplessly for what seemed like ages, until the woman finally gave him an enigmatic smile and turned briskly away.

Joshua had filled four glasses; for Marsh, a tumbler of whiskey, for himself and the others, his private stock. "I am pleased to have you here," he said as he served the drinks. "I trust your accommodations are satisfactory?"

"Quite," the man said, taking up his glass and looking at it dubiously. Remembering his own taste of the stuff, Marsh didn't blame him one bit.

"You have a lovely steamboat, Captain York," the woman said in a warm voice. "I shall enjoy taking passage on it."

"I hope we shall be traveling together for some time," Joshua replied graciously. "As for the *Fevre Dream*, I am very proud of her, but your compliments should really be directed to my partner." He gestured. "If you will permit me to make introductions, this formidable gentleman here is Captain Abner Marsh, my associate in Fevre River Packets and the real master of the *Fevre Dream*, if truth be told."

The woman smiled at Abner again, while the man nodded stiffly.

"Abner," York continued, "may I present Mister Raymond Ortega, of New Orleans, and his fiancée, Miss Valerie Mersault?"

"Real glad to have you with us," Marsh said awkwardly.

Joshua raised his glass. "A toast," he said. "To new beginnings!"

They echoed his words, and drank.

CHAPTER TWELVE

Aboard the Steamer FEVRE DREAM, Mississippi River, August 1857————

ABNER Marsh had a mind that was not unlike his body. It was big all around, ample in size and capacity, and he crammed all sorts of things into it. It was strong as well; when Abner Marsh took something in his hand it did not easily slip away, and when he took something in his head it was not easily forgotten. He was a powerful man with a powerful brain, but body and mind shared one other trait as well: they were deliberate. Some might even say slow. Marsh did not run, he did not dance, he did not scamper or slide along; he walked with a straightforward dignified gait that nonetheless got him where he wanted to go. So it was with his mind. Abner Marsh was not quick in word or thought, but he was far from stupid; he chewed over things thoroughly, but at his own pace.

As the *Fevre Dream* steamed out of Natchez, Marsh was only beginning to mull over the story he had gotten from Joshua York. The more he mulled, the more he fretted. If you could credit it, Joshua's outlandish story about hunting for vampires did explain a respectable amount of the strange goings-on that had plagued the *Fevre Dream*. But it didn't explain everything. Abner Marsh's slow, but tenacious, memory kept throwing up questions and recollections that floated around in his head like dead wood floats on the river, good for nothing, but bothersome.

Simon, f'rinstance, licking up mosquitoes.

Joshua's extraordinary night vision.

And most of all, the way he'd raged the day Marsh had come barging into his cabin. He hadn't come outside neither, to see them run against the *Southerner*. That worried Marsh considerably. It was fine for Joshua to say he kept night hours on account of these vampires of his, but that still didn't explain the way he'd acted that afternoon. Most folks Abner Marsh knew kept normal daylight hours, but that didn't mean they wouldn't hoist themselves out of bed at three in the morning if there was something interesting to gawk at.

Marsh badly felt the need to talk it over with someone. Jonathan Jeffers was a demon for book learning, and Karl Framm probably knew every damn fool story that had ever been told along the damn fool river; either of 'em would likely know everything there was to know about these vampires. Only he couldn't talk to them. He'd promised Joshua, and he was beholden to the man, and wasn't about to go and betray him a second time. Not without cause, anyway, and all he had were half-formed suspicions.

The suspicions got more formed every day, though, as the *Fevre Dream* loafed down the Mississippi. Generally they ran by day now, and tied up at twilight, then set out again the next morning. They made better time than they had before Natchez, which heartened Marsh. Other changes pleased him less.

Marsh did not cotton to Joshua's new friends; he decided in short order that they were every bit as queer as Joshua's old friends, keeping the same night hours and all. Raymond Ortega struck Marsh as a restless, untrustworthy sort. The man wouldn't keep to passenger territory, and kept turning up in places he didn't belong. He was polite enough in a haughty, indolent fashion, but Marsh got a chill off him.

Valerie was warmer but almost as disturbing, with her soft words and provocative smiles and those eyes of hers. She didn't act like Raymond Ortega's fiancée at all. Right from the first, she was real friendly with Joshua. Too damned friendly, if you asked Marsh. It was bound to cause trouble. A proper lady would have stayed to the ladies' cabin, but Valerie spent her nights with Joshua in the grand saloon, and sometimes took walks on the deck with him. Marsh even heard one man say that they'd gone up to Joshua's cabin together. He tried to warn York about the kind of scandalous talk that was starting up, but Joshua just shrugged it off. "Let them have their scandal, Abner, if it pleases them," he said. "Valerie is interested in our boat, and it is my pleasure to show it to her. There is nothing between us but friendship, you have my word." He looked almost sad when he said that. "I might wish that it were otherwise, but that is the truth."

"You better be goddamned careful what you're wishin'," Marsh said bluntly. "That Ortega might have his own opinions on the matter. He's from New Orleans, probably one of those Creoles. They'll fight a duel over just about any damn thing, Joshua."

Joshua York smiled. "I have no fear of Raymond, but I thank you for your warning, Abner. Now, please, let Valerie and me conduct our own affairs."

Marsh did just that, but not comfortably. He was certain that Ortega would make trouble sooner or later, especially when Valerie Mersault went on to become Joshua's constant companion during the nights that followed. The goddamned woman was blinding him to the dangers all about him, but there wasn't a thing Marsh could do about it.

And that was only the start of it. At each landing, more strangers came aboard, and Joshua always gave them cabins. At Bayou Sara, he and Valerie left the *Fevre Dream* one night and returned with a pale, heavy man named Jean Ardant. A few minutes downriver, they'd put in at a woodyard, and Ardant had gone and fetched this sallow-faced dandy named Vincent. At Baton Rouge, four more strangers had taken passage; at Donaldsonville another three.

And then there were those dinners. As his strange company began to grow, Joshua York ordered a table set up in the texas parlor, and there he would dine at midnight with his companions, new and old. Supper they took with everyone else in the main cabin, but these dinners were private. The custom started in Bayou Sara. Abner Marsh allowed once to Joshua how the idea of a regular meal at midnight took his fancy, but that didn't get him invited. Joshua only smiled, and the meals went on, the number of diners growing each night. Finally Marsh's curiosity got the better of him, and he managed to walk by the parlor a couple of times to glance in the window. There wasn't much to see. Just some folks eating and talking. The oil lamps were dim and subdued, the curtains half-drawn. Joshua sat at the head of the table, Simon on his right-hand side and Valerie to his left. Everybody was sipping from glasses of Joshua's vile elixir, several bottles of which had been uncorked. The first time Marsh wandered by, Joshua was talking animatedly and the rest were listening. Valerie stared at him almost worshipfully. The second time Marsh peeked in, Joshua was listening to Jean Ardant, one hand resting casually on the tablecloth. As Marsh watched, Valerie placed her own hand on top of it. Joshua glanced at her and smiled fondly.

Valerie smiled back. Abner Marsh looked quickly for Raymond Ortega, muttered "Goddamn fool woman" under his breath, and hurried away, scowling.

Marsh tried to make sense of it, of all these queer strangers, these odd goings-on, of all Joshua York had told him about vampires. It wasn't easy, and the more he thought on it the more confused he got. The library on the *Fevre Dream* had no books about vampires or anything like that and he wasn't about to go stealing into Joshua's cabin again. At Baton Rouge, he took himself into town and bought a few rounds at some likely grog shops, hoping to find out something that way. When he could, he'd introduce the subject of vampires into the talk, usually by turning to his drinking companions and saying, "Say, you ever heard anything 'bout vampires along the river?" He figured that was safer than raising the subject on the steamer, where the very word might start some bad talk.

A few folks laughed at him or gave him odd looks. One free man of color, a burly soot-black fellow with a broken nose whom Marsh accosted in a particularly smoky tavern, ran off as soon as Marsh asked his question. Marsh tried to run after him, but was soon left behind wheezing. Others seemed to know considerable about vampires, though none of the stories had a damn thing to do with the Mississippi. All the stuff he'd heard from Joshua's lips, about crosses and garlic and coffins full of dirt, he heard repeated, and more besides.

Marsh took to watching York and his companions closely at supper, and afterward in the grand saloon. Vampires didn't eat nor drink, he'd been told, but Joshua and the others drank copious amounts of wine and whiskey and brandy when they weren't sipping York's private stock, and all of them were only too glad to do justice to a nice chicken or pork chop.

Joshua was always wearing his silver ring, with its sapphire big as a pigeon's eye, and none of them seemed bothered by all the silver about the cabin. They used the silverware proper enough when they ate, better than most of the *Fevre Dream*'s crew.

And when the chandeliers were lit by night, the mirrors all up and down the main cabin gleamed brilliantly and crowds of finely dressed reflections came to life on either side of them, and danced and drank and played cards just like the real folks in the real saloon. Abner Marsh, night after night, found himself looking into those mirrors. Joshua was always there where he was supposed to be, smiling, laughing, gliding from mirror to mirror arm in arm with Valerie, talking politics with a passenger, listening to Framm's river yarns, sharing private talks with Simon or Jean Ardant; each night a thousand Joshua Yorks walked the *Fevre Dream*'s carpeted deck, each as alive and grand as all the others. His friends cast reflections too.

That ought to have been enough, but Marsh's slow, suspicious mind was still disquieted. It wasn't until Donaldsonville that he hit on a plan to stop his fretting. He went into town with a canteen, and filled it up with holy water from a Papist church near to the river. Then he took aside the boy who waited their end of the table, and gave him fifty cents. "You fill Cap'n York's water glass from this tonight, you hear?" Marsh told him. "I'm playin' him a joke."

During supper the waiter kept looking at York expectantly, waiting for the joke to get funny. He was disappointed. Joshua drank down the holy water easy as you please. "Well, damn," Marsh muttered to himself afterwards. "That sure ought to settle it."

But it didn't, and that night Abner Marsh excused himself from the grand saloon to do some thinking. He'd been sitting up on the texas porch for a couple of hours, alone, his chair leaned back and his feet up on the railing, when he heard the rustle of skirts on the stairway.

Valerie drifted over and stood close beside him, smiling down. "Good evening, Captain Marsh," she said.

Abner Marsh's chair thumped back to the deck as he pulled his boots off the rail, scowling. "Passengers ain't supposed to be up on the texas," he said, trying to hide his annoyance.

"It was so warm down below. I thought it might be cooler up here."

"Well, that's true," Marsh replied uncertainly. He didn't know quite what to say next. The truth was, women had always made him feel uncomfortable. They had no place in a steamboatman's world, and Marsh had never quite known how to deal with them. Beautiful women made him even more ill at ease, and Valerie was as disconcerting as any fancy New Orleans matron.

She stood with one slender hand curled lightly around a carved post, looking off over the water toward Donaldsonville. "We'll reach New Orleans tomorrow, won't we?" she asked.

Marsh stood up, figuring it probably wasn't polite to be sitting down with Valerie standing. "Yes, ma'am," he said. "We ain't but a few hours upriver, and I mean to steam in sparklin', so it won't take hardly no time at all."

"I see." She turned suddenly, and her pale, shapely face was very serious as she fixed him with her huge purple eyes. "Joshua says you are the true master of the *Fevre Dream*. In some curious way, he has much respect for you. He will listen to you."

"We're partners," Marsh said.

"If your partner were in danger, would you come to his aid?"

Abner Marsh scowled, thinking of the vampire stories Joshua had told him, conscious of how pale and beautiful Valerie looked in the starlight, how deep her eyes were. "Joshua knows he can come to me if he's got trouble," Marsh said. "A man who wouldn't help his partner ain't no kind of a man at all."

"Words," Valerie said scornfully, tossing back her thick black hair. The wind was in it, and it moved about her face as she spoke. "Joshua York is a great man, a strong man. A king. He deserves a better partner than you, Captain Marsh."

Abner Marsh felt the blood rushing to his face. "What the hell you talkin' about?" he demanded.

She smiled slyly. "You broke into his cabin," she said.

Marsh was suddenly furious. "He told you that?" he said. "Goddamn him anyhow, we had it out over that. It ain't none of your never mind, neither."

"It is," she said. "Joshua is in great danger. He is bold, reckless. He must have help. I want to help him, but you, Captain Marsh, you only give him words."

"I don't have one goddamned idea what you're talkin' about, woman," Marsh said. "What kind of help does Joshua need? I offered to help him with these damned vam—with some troubles he got, but he didn't want to hear none of it."

Valerie's face softened suddenly. "Would you really help him?" she asked.

"He's my goddamned partner."

"Then turn your steamer, Captain Marsh. Take us away from here, take us to Natchez, to St. Louis, I don't care. But not to New Orleans. We must not go to New Orleans tomorrow."

Abner Marsh snorted. "Why the hell not?" he demanded. When Valerie looked away instead of answering, he went on. "This here is a steamboat, not some goddamned horse I can ride anyplace I got a notion. We got a schedule to keep, folks who've taken passage with us, freight to discharge. We got to go to New Orleans." He scowled. "And what about Joshua?"

"He'll be asleep in his cabin come dawn," Valerie said. "When he wakes, we'll be safely upriver."

"Joshua's my partner," Marsh said. "Man's got to trust his partner. Maybe I spied on him once, but I ain't goin' to do anything like that again, not for you and not for nobody. And I ain't goin' to turn the *Fevre Dream* around without tellin' him. Now if Joshua comes to me and says he don't want to go on to New Orleans, hell, maybe we can talk it over. But not otherwise. You want me to go ask Joshua about this?"

"*No!*" Valerie said quickly, alarmed.

"I got a good mind to tell him anyway," Marsh said. "He ought to know that you're plottin' when his back is turned."

Valerie reached out and took him by the arm. "Please, no," she implored. Her grip was strong. "Look at me, Captain Marsh."

Abner Marsh had been about to stomp away, but something in her voice compelled him to do as she bid. He looked into those purple eyes, and kept looking.

"I'm not so hard to look at," she said, smiling. "I've seen you look before, Captain. You can't keep your eyes away from me, can you?"

Marsh's throat was very dry. "I . . ."

Valerie tossed her hair back again in a wild, flamboyant gesture. "Steamboats can't be the only thing you dream of, Captain Marsh. This boat is a cold lady, a poor lover. Warm flesh is better than wood and iron." Marsh had never heard a woman talk like that before. He stood there thunderstruck. "Come closer," Valerie said, and she pulled him to her, until he stood only inches from her upturned face. "Look at me," she said. He could sense the trembling warmth of her, so near at hand, and her eyes were vast purple pools, cool and silky and inviting. "You want me, Captain," she whispered.

"No," Marsh said.

"Oh, you want me. I can see the desire in your eyes."

"No," Marsh protested. "You're . . . Joshua . . ."

Valerie laughed; light, airy laughter, sensuous, musical. "Don't concern yourself with Joshua. Take what you want. You're afraid, that's why you fight it so. Don't be afraid."

Abner Marsh shook violently, and in the back of his mind he realized with a start that he was trembling with lust. He had never wanted a woman so badly in his life. Yet somehow he was resisting, fighting it, though Valerie's eyes were drawing him closer, and the world was full of the scent of her.

"Take me to your cabin now," she whispered. "I'm yours tonight."

"You are?" Marsh said, weakly. He felt sweat dripping off his brow, clouding his eyes. "No," he muttered. "No, this ain't . . ."

"It can be," she said. "All you need do is promise."

"Promise?" Marsh repeated hoarsely.

The violet eyes beckoned, blazed. "Take us away, away from New Orleans. Promise me that and you can have me. You want it so much. I can feel it."

Abner Marsh brought his hands up, took her by the shoulders. He shook. His lips were dry. He wanted to crush her to him in a bearlike embrace, tumble her into his bed. But instead, somehow, he called up all the strength that was in him, and shoved her away roughly. She cried out, stumbled, went down to one knee. And Marsh, freed of those eyes, was roaring. "Get out of here!" he bellowed. "Get the hell off my texas, what the hell kind of woman are you, get the hell out of here, you're nothing but . . . get *out* of here!"

Valerie's face turned up again toward his, and her lips were drawn back. "I can make you . . ." she started angrily.

"*No,*" Joshua York said, firmly, quietly, from behind her.

Joshua had appeared from the shadows as suddenly as if the darkness itself had taken on human form. Valerie stared at him, made a small noise deep in her throat, and fled down the stairs.

Marsh felt so drained he could hardly stand up. "Goddamn," he muttered. He pulled a handkerchief from a pocket and wiped the sweat off his brow. When he finished, Joshua was looking at him patiently. "I don't know what you saw, Joshua, but it wasn't what you might think."

"I know exactly what it was, Abner," Joshua replied. He did not sound especially angry. "I have been here nearly the whole time. When I noticed that Valerie had left the saloon, I went in search of her, and I heard your voices as I came up the stairs."

"I never heard you," Marsh said.

Joshua smiled. "I can be very quiet when it suits my purposes, Abner."

"That woman," Marsh said. "She's . . . she offered to . . . hell, she's just a goddamned . . ." The words would not come. "She ain't no lady," he finished weakly. "Put her off, Joshua, her and Ortega both."

"No."

"Why the hell not?" Marsh roared. "You heard her!"

"It makes no difference," Joshua said calmly. "If anything, what I heard makes me cherish her all the more. It was for me, Abner. She cares for me more than I had hoped, more than I dared expect."

Abner Marsh cussed furiously. "You ain't makin' one goddamned bit of sense."

Joshua smiled softly. "Perhaps not. This is not your concern, Abner. Leave Valerie to me. She will not cause trouble again. She was only afraid."

"Afraid of New Orleans," Marsh said. "Of vampires. She knows."

"Yes."

"You sure you can handle whatever we're steamin' into?" Marsh said. "If you want to skip New Orleans, say so, damn it! Valerie thinks . . ."

"What do you think, Abner?" York asked.

Marsh looked at him for a long, long time. Then he said, "I think we're going to New Orleans," and both of them smiled.

And so it was that the *Fevre Dream* steamed into New Orleans the next morning, with dapper Dan Albright at her wheel and Abner Marsh standing proudly out on her bridge in his captain's coat and his new cap. The sun burned hot in a blue, blue sky and every little snag and bluff reef was marked by golden ripples on the water, so the piloting came easy and the steamer made crack time. The New Orleans levee was jammed with steamers and all manner of sailing ships; the river was alive to the music of their whistles and bells. Marsh leaned on his walking stick and watched the city loom large ahead, listening to the *Fevre Dream* call out to the other boats with her landing bell and her loud, wild whistle. He had been to New Orleans many a time in his days on the river, but never like this, standing on the bridge of his own steamer, the biggest and fanciest and fleetest boat in sight. He felt like the lord of creation.

Once they had tied up on the levee, though, there was work to do; freight to unload, consignments to hunt up for the return trip to St. Louis, advertisements to take in the local papers. Marsh decided that the company ought to see about opening a regular office down here, so he busied himself looking at likely sites and making arrangements for starting a bank account and hiring an agent. That night he dined at the St. Charles Hotel with Jonathon Jeffers and Karl Framm, but his mind kept wandering away from the food to the dangers that Valerie had seemed so afraid of, and he wondered what Joshua York was up to. When Marsh returned to the steamer, Joshua was talking with his companions in the texas parlor, and nothing seemed amiss, though Valerie—seated by his side—looked somewhat sullen and abashed. Marsh went to sleep and put the whole thing from his mind, and in the days that followed he hardly thought on it at all. The *Fevre Dream* kept him too busy by day, and by night he dined well in the city, bragged up his boat over drinks in taverns near the levee, strolled through the Vieux Carré admiring the lovely Creole ladies and all the courtyards and fountains and balconies. New Orleans was as fine as he remembered, Marsh thought at first.

But then, gradually, a disquiet began to grow in him, a vague sense of wrongness that made him look at familiar things from new eyes. The weather was beastly; by day the heat was oppressive, the air thick and wet once you shut yourself off from the cool river breezes. Day and night, fumes rose up stinking from the open sewers, rich rotten odors that wafted off the standing water like some vile perfume. No wonder New Orleans was so often taken by yellow fever, Marsh thought. The city was full of free men of color and lovely young quadroons and octoroons and *griffes* who dressed as fine as white women. But it was full of slaves as well. You saw them everywhere, running errands for their masters, sitting or milling forlornly in the slave pens on Moreau and Common streets, going in long chained lines to and from the great exchanges, cleaning out the gutters. Even down by the steamer landing, you couldn't escape the signs of slavery; the grand side-wheelers that plied the New Orleans trade were always taking black folks up and down the river, and Abner Marsh saw them come and go whenever he went down to the *Fevre Dream*. The slaves rode in chains as often as not, sitting together miserably amidst the cargo, sweating in the heat of the furnaces.

"I don't like it none," Marsh complained to Jonathon Jeffers. "It ain't *clean*. And I tell you, I won't have none of it on the *Fevre Dream*. Nobody is goin' to stink up my boat with that kind of stuff, you hear?"

Jeffers gave him a wry look of appraisal. "Why, Cap'n, if we don't traffic in slaves, we stand to lose a pile of money. You're sounding like an abolitionist."

"I ain't no damned abolitionist," Marsh said hotly, "but I mean what I said. If a gentleman wants to bring a slave or two along, servants and such, that's fine. I'll take 'em cabin passage or deck passage, don't matter none to me. But we ain't goin' to take 'em as freight, all chained up by some goddamned trader."

By their seventh night in New Orleans, Abner Marsh felt strangely sick of the city, and anxious to be off. That night Joshua York came down to supper with some river charts in his hand. Marsh had seen very little of his partner since their arrival. "How do you fancy New Orleans?" Marsh asked York as the other seated himself.

"The city is lovely," York replied in an oddly troubled voice that made Marsh look up from the roll he was buttering. "I have nothing but admiration for the Vieux Carré. It is utterly unlike the other river towns we've seen, almost European, and some of the houses in the American section are grand as well. Nonetheless, I do not like it here."

Marsh frowned. "Why's that?"

"I have a bad feeling, Abner. This city—the heat, the bright colors, the smells, the slaves—it is very alive, this New Orleans, but inside I think it is rotten with sickness. Everything is so rich and beautiful here, the cuisine, the manners, the architecture, but beneath that . . ." He shook his head. "You see all those lovely courtyards, each boasting an exquisite well. And then you see the teamsters selling river water from barrels, and you realize that the well water is unfit to drink. You savor the rich sauces and the spices of the food, and then you learn that the spices are intended to disguise the fact that the meat is going bad. You wander through the St. Louis and cast your eyes upon all that marble and that delightful dome with the light pouring through it down onto the rotunda, and then you learn it is a famous slave mart where humans are sold like cattle. Even the graveyards are places of beauty here. No simple tombstones or wooden crosses, but great marble mausoleums, each prouder than the last, with statuary atop them and fine poetic sentiments inscribed in stone. But inside every one is a rotting corpse, full of maggots and worms. They must be imprisoned in stone because the ground is no good even for burying, and graves fill up with water. And pestilence hangs over this beautiful city like a pall.

"No, Abner," Joshua said with an odd, distant look in his gray eyes, "I love beauty, but sometimes a thing lovely to behold conceals vileness and evil within. The sooner we are quit of this city, the better I shall like it."

"Hell," said Abner Marsh. "Damned if I can say why, but I feel just the same way. Don't fret, we can get out of here real quick."

Joshua York grimaced. "Good," he said. "But first, I have one final task." He moved aside his plate and opened the chart he had brought to the table with him. "Tomorrow at dusk, I want to take the *Fevre Dream* downriver."

"*Downriver?*" Marsh said in astonishment. "Hell, ain't nothin' downstream of here for us. Some plantations, lots of Cajuns, swamps and bayous and then the Gulf."

"Look," said York. His finger traced a path down the Mississippi. "We follow the river down around through here, turn off onto this bayou and proceed about a half-dozen miles to here. It won't take us long, and we can return the next night to pick up our passengers for St. Louis. I want to make a brief landing *here.*" He jabbed.

Abner Marsh's ham steak was set in front of him, but he ignored it, leaning over to see where Joshua was pointing.

"Cypress Landing," he read from the chart. "Well, I don't know." He looked around the main cabin, three-quarters empty now with no passengers aboard. Karl Framm, Whitey Blake, and Jack Ely were eating down to the far end of the table. "Mister Framm," Marsh called out, "come on down here a minute." When Framm arrived, Marsh pointed out the route York had traced. "Can you pilot us downriver, and up this here bayou? Or do we draw too much?"

Framm shrugged. "Some of them bayoux is pretty wide and deep, others you'd have trouble gettin' up with a yawl, let alone a steamer. But probably I can do it. There's landings and plantations down there, and other steamers get to 'em. Most of 'em ain't so big as this lady, though. It'll be slow goin', I know that. We'll have to sound all the way, and be real careful of snags and sandbars, and likely as not we'll have to saw off a mess of tree limbs if we don't want 'em knockin' off our chimneys." He leaned over to look at the chart. "Where we goin'? I been down that way once or twice."

"Place called Cypress Landing," said Marsh.

Framm pursed his lips thoughtfully. "Shouldn't be too bad. That's the old Garoux plantation. Steamers used to put in there regular, takin' sweet potaters and sugar cane to N'Orleans. Garoux died, though, him and his whole family, and Cypress Landing ain't been heard of much since. Although, now that I recollect, there's some funny stories about them parts. Why we goin' there?"

"A personal matter," said Joshua York. "Just see that we get there, Mister Framm. We'll leave tomorrow at dusk."

"You're the cap'n," Framm said. He went on back to his meal.

"Where the hell is my milk?" Abner Marsh complained. He looked around. The waiter, a slender Negro youth, lingered at the kitchen door. "Come on with my supper," Marsh bellowed at him, and the boy started visibly. Marsh turned back to York. "This trip," he said. "Is it—part of that thing you told me about?"

"Yes," York said curtly.

"Dangerous?" Marsh asked.

Joshua York shrugged.

"I don't like this none," Marsh said, "this vampire stuff." He dropped his voice to a whisper when he said *vampire*.

"It will soon be over, Abner. I will make a call at this plantation, attend to some business, bring some friends back with me, and that will be the end of it."

"Let me go with you," Marsh said. "On this business of yours. I ain't sayin' I don't believe you, but it'd all be easier to credit if I could see one of these—you know—with my own eyes."

Joshua looked at him. Marsh glanced into his eyes briefly, but something in there seemed to reach out and touch him, and suddenly without meaning to he had looked away. Joshua folded up the river chart. "I do not think it would be wise," he said, "but I will think about it. Excuse me. I have things to attend to." He rose and left the table.

Marsh watched him go, unsure of what had just passed between them. Finally he muttered, "Damn him anyhow," and turned his attention to his ham steak.

Hours later, Abner Marsh had visitors.

He was in his cabin, trying to sleep. The soft knock on his door woke him as if it had been a thunderclap, and Marsh could feel the pounding of his heart. For some reason he was scared. The cabin was pitch dark. "Who is it?" he called out. "Damn you!"

"Jest Toby, Cap'n," came the soft whispered reply.

Marsh's fear suddenly melted away and seemed silly. Toby Lanyard was the gentlest old soul ever set foot on a steamboat, and one of the meekest as well. Marsh called out, "Comin'," and lit a lamp by his bedside before going to open the door.

Two men stood outside. Toby was about sixty, bald but for a fringe of iron gray hair around his black skull, his face worn and wrinkled and black as a pair of old comfortable boots. With him was a younger Negro, a short stout brown man in an expensive suit. In the dim light, it was a moment before Marsh recognized him as Jebediah Freeman, the barber he had hired up in Louisville. "Cap'n," said Toby, "we wants to talk to you, private, if we kin."

Marsh waved them in. "What's this about, Toby?" he asked, closing the door.

"We's kind of spokesmen," said the cook. "You knowed me a long time, Cap'n, you knows I wouldn't lie to you."

"Course I do," said Marsh.

"I wouldn't run off neither. You done give me my freedom and all, jest fer cookin' fer you. But some of them other niggers, the stokers and sech, they won't lissen to Jeb and me here 'bout what a fine man you is. They's scared, and likely to run off. The boy at supper tonight, he heard you and Cap'n York a-talkin' about goin' down to this Cypress place, and now all the niggers is talkin'."

"What?" Marsh said. "You never been down here before, neither of you. What's Cypress Landing to you?"

"Nuthin' a-tall," Jeb said. "But some of these other niggers heard of it. There's stories 'bout this place, Cap'n. Bad stories. All the niggers run off from that place, cause of things went on there. Terrible things, Cap'n, jest terrible."

"We come to ask you not to go on down there, Cap'n," Toby said. "You know I never ast you for nuthin' before."

"No cook and no barber are goin' to tell me where to take my steamboat," Abner Marsh said sternly. But then he looked at Toby's face, and softened. "Ain't nothin' goin' to happen," he promised, "but if you two want to wait here in New Orleans, you go ahead. Won't need no cookin' or no barberin' on a short run like this."

Toby looked grateful, but said, "The stokers, though . . ."

"Them I need."

"They ain't goin' to stay, Cap'n, I tell you."

"I reckon Hairy Mike will have a thing or two to say about that."

Jeb shook his head. "Them niggers is scared o' Hairy Mike sure 'nough, but they's more scared of this place you're fixin' to take us. They'll run off, sure as anythin'."

Marsh swore. "Damn fools," he said. "Well, we can't get up steam without no stokers. But it was Joshua wanted to make this trip, not me. Give me a few moments to dress, boys, and we'll hunt up Cap'n York and speak to him about this."

The two black men exchanged looks, but said nothing.

Joshua York was not alone. When Marsh strode up to the door of the captain's cabin, he heard his partner's voice, loud and rhythmic, from within. Marsh hesitated, then groaned when he realized that Joshua was reading poetry. Aloud, even. He hammered at the door with his stick, and York broke off his reading and told them to come in.

Joshua sat calmly with a book in his lap, a long pale finger marking his place, a glass of wine on the table beside him. Valerie was in the other chair. She looked up at Marsh and quickly away; she had been avoiding him since that night on the texas, and Marsh found it easy to ignore her. "Tell him, Toby." he said.

Toby seemed to have far more difficulty finding words than he had with Marsh, but he finally got it all out. When he was done he stood with his eyes downcast, twisting his old battered hat in his hands.

Joshua York wore a grim look. "What do the men fear?" he asked in a polite, cold tone.

"Gettin' et, suh."

"Give them my word that I will protect them."

Toby shook his head. "Cap'n York, no disrespeck, but them niggers is 'fraid of you, too, 'specially now that you want us to go down *there*."

"They think you's one of *them*," Jeb put in. "You and you friends, lurin' us down there to the others, like it were. Them stories say those folks there don't come out by day, and you's the same, Cap'n, jest the same. Course, me and Toby knows better, but not them others."

"Tell 'em we'll double their wages for the time on the bayou," Marsh said.

Toby didn't look up, but shook his head. "They don't care 'bout no money. They's goin' to run off."

Abner Marsh swore. "Joshua, if neither money nor Hairy Mike can get 'em to do it, they ain't a-goin' to do it. We'll have to discharge 'em all and get us some new stokers and roustas and such, but that'll take us some time."

Valerie leaned forward and laid her hand on Joshua York's arm. "Please, Joshua," she said quietly. "Listen to them. This is a sign. We were not meant to go. Take us back to St. Louis. You've promised to show me St. Louis."

"I shall," Joshua said, "but not until my business is concluded." He frowned at Toby and Jeb. "I can reach Cypress Landing overland easily enough," he said. "No doubt that would be the quickest and simplest way to accomplish my goals. But that does not satisfy me, gentlemen. Either this is my steamer or it is not. Either I am captain here or I am not. I will not have my crew distrusting me. I will not have my men afraid of me." He set the book of poems on the table with an audible thump, clearly frustrated. "Have I done anything to harm you, Toby?" Joshua demanded. "Have I mistreated any of your people? Have I done anything at all to earn this suspicion?"

"No, suh," Toby said softly.

"No, you say. Yet they will desert me despite that?"

"Yessuh, Cap'n, 'fraid so," Toby said.

Joshua York took on a hard, determined look. "What if I proved I was not what they think me?" His eyes went from Toby to Jeb and back again. "If they saw me in daylight, would they trust me?"

"No," Valerie said. She looked aghast. "Joshua, you can't . . ."

"I can," he said, "and will. Well, Toby?"

The cook raised his head, saw York's eyes, and nodded slowly. "Well, maybe . . . if they seed you wasn't . . ."

Joshua studied the two black men for a long time. "Very well," he said at last. "I will dine with you tomorrow afternoon, then. Have a place set for me."

"Well I'll be damned," said Abner Marsh.

CHAPTER THIRTEEN

Aboard the Steamer FEVRE DREAM, New Orleans, August 1857———

JOSHUA wore his white suit down to dinner, and Toby outdid himself. Word had gotten around, of course, and virtually the entire crew of the *Fevre Dream* was on hand. The waiters, neat as pins in their smart white jackets, glided to and fro, bearing Toby's feast out from the kitchen on big steaming platters and fine china bowls. There was turtle soup and lobster salad, stuffed crabs and larded sweetbreads, oyster pie and mutton chops, terrapin, pan-fried chicken, turnips and stuffed peppers, roast beef and breaded veal cutlets, Irish potatoes and green corn and carrots and artichokes and snap beans, a profusion of rolls and breads, wine and spirits from the bar and fresh milk in from the city, plates of new-churned butter, and for dessert plum pudding and lemon pie and floating islands and sponge cake with chocolate sauce.

Abner Marsh had never had a better meal in his life. "Damn," he said to York, "I wish you came to dinner more often, so we'd eat like this most every day."

Joshua barely touched his food, however. In the bright light of day, he seemed a different person; shrunken somehow, less imposing. His fair skin took on an unhealthy pallor beneath the skylights, and Marsh thought there was a chalky grayish tinge to it. York's movements seemed lethargic, and occasionally jerky, with none of that grace and power that was normally so much a part of him. But the biggest difference was in his eyes. Beneath the shade of the wide-brimmed white hat he wore, his eyes appeared tired, infinitely tired. The pupils were shrunken down to tiny black pinpricks, and the gray around them was pale and faded, without the intensity Marsh had seen in them so often.

But he was there, and that seemed to make all the difference in the world. He had come out of his cabin in broad daylight, and walked across the open decks and down the stairs, and set himself down to dine before God, the crew, and everyone. Whatever stories and fears his night hours had given birth to seemed damned silly now, as the good light of day washed down on Joshua York and his fine white suit.

York was quiet through most of the meal, though he gave diffident answers whenever someone asked a question of him, and infrequently tossed a comment of his own into the table talk. When the desserts were served, he pushed his plate aside and put down his knife wearily. "Ask Toby to come out," he said.

The cook came forward from the kitchen, spotted with flour and cooking oil. "Din' you like the food, Cap'n York?" he asked. "You hardly et none of it."

"It was fine, Toby. I'm afraid I don't have much appetite at this time of day. I am here, however. I trust I've proved something."

"Yessuh," said Toby. "Won't be no trouble now."

"Excellent," York said. When Toby had returned to his kitchen, York turned to Marsh. "I've decided to lay over another day," he said. "We'll steam out of here tomorrow at nightfall, not tonight."

"Well, sure, Joshua," Marsh said. "Pass me down another piece of that pie, will you?"

York smiled and passed it to him.

"Cap'n, tonight'd be better'n tomorrow," said Dan Albright, who was cleaning his teeth with a bone toothpick. "I smell a storm comin' up."

"Tomorrow," York said.

Albright shrugged.

"Toby and Jeb can stay behind. In fact," York continued, "I want to take only the bare complement necessary to man the boat. Any passengers who boarded early are to be put ashore for a few days, until our return. We won't be taking on any freight, so the roustabouts can be given a few days off as well. We'll take only one watch with us. Can that be done?"

"I reckon," Marsh said. He glanced down the long table. The officers were all looking at Joshua curiously.

"Tomorrow at nightfall, then," York said. "Excuse me. I must rest." He stood up, and for a brief instant seemed unsteady on his feet. Marsh got up from the table hurriedly, but York waved him away. "I'm fine," he said. "I'll be retiring to my cabin now. See that I am not disturbed until we are ready to leave New Orleans."

"Won't you be down for supper tonight?" Marsh asked.

"No," said York. His eyes moved up and down the cabin. "I do think I prefer it by night," he said. "Lord Byron was right. Day is far too gaudy."

"Eh?" Marsh said.

"Don't you remember?" York said. "The poem I recited to you at the boatyards in New Albany. It fits the *Fevre Dream* so well. *She walks in beauty . . .*"

". . . *like the night*," said Jeffers, adjusting his spectacles. Abner Marsh looked at him, flabbergasted. Jeffers was a demon for chess and ciphering and even went to plays, but Marsh had never heard him recite no poetry before.

"You know Byron!" Joshua said, delighted. For an instant, he looked almost like his own self.

"I do," Jeffers admitted. One eyebrow arched as he regarded York. "Cap'n, are you suggesting that our days are spent in goodness here on the *Fevre Dream?*" He smiled. "Why, that'll sure come as news to Hairy Mike and Mister Framm here."

Hairy Mike guffawed, while Framm protested, "Hey, now, three wives don't mean I ain't good, why most every one of 'em 'ud vouch for me!"

"What the hell you talkin' about?" Abner Marsh put in. Most of the officers and crew looked as confused as he was.

Joshua played with an elusive smile. "Mister Jeffers is reminding me of the final stanza of Byron's poem," he said. He recited:

> And on that cheek, and o'er that brow,
>   So soft, so calm, yet eloquent,
> The smiles that win, the tints that glow,
>   But tell of days in goodness spent,
> A mind at peace with all below,
>   A heart whose love is innocent!

"Are we innocent, Cap'n?" Jeffers asked.

"No one is entirely innocent," Joshua York replied, "but the poem speaks to me nonetheless, Mister Jeffers. The night *is* beautiful, and we can hope to find peace and nobility in its dark splendor as well. Too many men fear the dark unreasoningly."

"Perhaps," said Jeffers. "Sometimes it ought to be feared, though."

"No," said Joshua York, and with that he left them, breaking off the verbal fencing match with Jeffers abruptly. As soon as he was gone, others began to leave the table to attend to their duties, but Jonathon Jeffers remained in his place, lost in thought, staring off across the cabin. Marsh sat down to finish his pie. "Mister Jeffers," he said, "I don't know what's goin' on along this river. Damn poems. What good did all that fancy talk ever do anyhow? If this Byron had somethin' to say, why didn't he just out and say it in plain, simple language? Answer me that."

Jeffers looked over at him, blinking. "Sorry, Cap'n," he said. "I was trying to remember something. What was it you said?"

Marsh swallowed a forkful of pie, washed it down with some coffee, and repeated his question.

"Well, Cap'n," Jeffers said, with a wry smile, "the main thing is that poetry is pretty. The way the words fit together, the rhythms, the pictures they paint. Poems are pleasant when said aloud. The rhymes, the inner music, just the way they *sound*." He sipped some coffee. "It's hard to explain if you don't feel it. But it's sort of like a steamer, Cap'n."

"Ain't never seen no poem pretty as a steamer," said Marsh gruffly.

Jeffers grinned. "Cap'n, why does the *Northern Light* have that big picture of the Aurora on her wheelhouse? She don't need it. The paddles would turn just as smartly without it. Why is our pilot house, and so many others, all fancied up with curlicues and carvings and trim, why is every steamer worth her name full of fine wood and carpets and oil paintings and jigsaw carpentry? Why do our chimneys have flowered tops? The smoke would come out just as easy if they were plain."

Marsh burped, and frowned.

"You could make steamers plain and simple," Jeffers concluded, "but the way they are, that makes them finer to look at, to ride on. It's the same with poetry, Cap'n. A poet could maybe say something straight out, sure enough, but when he puts it in rhyme and meter it becomes grander."

"Well, maybe," Marsh said dubiously.

"I bet I could find a poem even you would like," Jeffers said. "Byron wrote one, in fact. 'The Destruction of Sennacherib,' it's called."

"Where's that?"

"It's a who, not a where," Jeffers corrected. "A poem about a war,

Cap'n. There's a marvelous rhythm to it. It gallops along as lively as 'Buffalo Gals.' " He stood up and straightened his coat. "Come with me, I'll show you."

Marsh finished the dregs of his coffee, pushed off from the table, and followed Jonathon Jeffers aft to the *Fevre Dream*'s library. He collapsed gratefully in a big overstuffed armchair while the head clerk searched up and down the bookcases that filled the room and rose clear to the high ceiling. "Here it is," Jeffers said at last, pulling down a fair-sized volume. "I knew we had to have a book of Byron's poems somewhere." He leafed through the pages—a few had never been cut, and he sliced them apart with his fingernail—until he found what he was looking for. Then he struck a pose and read "The Destruction of Sennacherib."

The poem did have quite a rhythm to it, Marsh had to admit, especially with Jeffers reciting it. It wasn't no "Buffalo Gals," though. Still, he kind of liked it. "Not bad," he admitted when Jeffers had finished. "Didn't care for the end, though. Damn Bible-thumpers got to drag the Lord in most everywhere."

Jeffers laughed. "Lord Byron was no Bible-thumper, I can assure you," he said. "He was immoral, in fact, or so it was said." He took on a thoughtful look and began turning pages again.

"What are you lookin' for now?"

"The poem I was trying to recollect at the table," Jeffers said. "Byron wrote another poem about night, quite at odds with—ah, here it is." He glanced up and down the page, nodded. "Listen to this, Cap'n. The title is 'Darkness.' " He commenced to recite:

> *I had a dream, which was not all a dream,*
> *The bright sun was extinguish'd, and the stars*
> *Did wander darkling in the eternal space,*
> *Rayless, and pathless, and the icy Earth*
> *Swung blind and blackening in the moonless air;*
> *Morn came and went—and came, and brought no day,*
> *And men forgot their passions in the dread*
> *Of this their desolation; and all hearts*
> *Were chill'd into a selfish prayer for light. . . .*

The clerk's voice had taken on a hollow, sinister tone as he read; the poem went on and on, longer than any of the others. Marsh soon lost track of the words, but they touched him nonetheless, and cast a chill that was somehow frightening over the room. Phrases and bits of lines lingered in his mind; the poem was full of terror, of vain prayer and despair, of madness and great funeral pyres, of war and famine and men like beasts.

> . . . —*a meal was brought*
> *With blood, and each sate sullenly apart*
> *Gorging himself in gloom; no Love was left;*
> *All earth was but one thought—and that was Death*
> *Immediate and inglorious; and the pang*
> *Of famine fed upon all entrails—men*
> *Died and their bones were tombless as their flesh;*
> *The meagre by the meagre were devour'd, . . .*

and Jeffers read on, evil dancing after evil, until at last he concluded:

> *They slept on the abyss without a surge—*
> *The waves were dead; the tides were in their grave,*
> *The Moon, their mistress, had expired before;*
> *The winds were wither'd in the stagnant air,*
> *And the clouds perish'd; Darkness had no need*
> *Of aid from them—She was the Universe.*

He closed the book.

"Ravings," Marsh said. "He sounds like a man taken with fever."

Jonathon Jeffers smiled wanly. "The Lord didn't even put in an appearance." He sighed. "Byron was of two minds about darkness, it seems to me. There's precious little innocence in *that* poem. I wonder if Cap'n York is familiar with it?"

"Of course he is," Marsh said, hoisting himself out of his chair. "Give that here." He extended his hand.

Jeffers handed him the book. "Taking an interest in poetry, Cap'n?"

"Never you mind about that," Marsh replied, slipping the book into his pocket. "Ain't there any business to attend to in your office?"

"Certainly," said Jeffers. He took his leave.

Abner Marsh stood in the library for three or four minutes, feeling mighty odd; the poem had had a very unsettling effect on him. Maybe there was something to this poetry business after all, he thought. He resolved to look into the book at his leisure and figure it out for himself.

Marsh had his own errands to run, however, and they kept him busy through most of the afternoon and early evening. Afterward he forgot all about the book in his pocket. Karl Framm was going into New Orleans to sup at the St. Charles, and Marsh decided to join him. It was almost midnight when they returned to the *Fevre Dream*. Undressing up in his cabin, Marsh came upon the book again. He put it carefully on his bedside table, donned his nightshirt, and settled down to read a bit by candlelight.

"Darkness" seemed even more sinister by night, in the dim loneliness of his little steamer cabin, although the words on the page didn't have quite the cold menace that Jeffers had given them. Still, they disquieted him. He turned pages and read "Sennacherib" and "She Walks in Beauty" and some other poems, but his thoughts kept wandering into "Darkness." Despite the heat of the night, Abner Marsh had gooseflesh creeping up his arms.

In the front of the book, there was a picture of Byron. Marsh studied it. He looked pretty enough, dark and sensual like a Creole; it was easy to see why the women went for him so, even if he was supposed to be a gimp. Of course, he was a nobleman too. It said so right beneath his picture:

GEORGE GORDON, LORD BYRON
1788–1824

Abner Marsh studied Byron's face for a time, and found himself envying the poet's features. Beauty was never something he had experienced from within; if he dreamed of grand gorgeous steamers, perhaps it was because he so conspicuously lacked beauty himself. With his bulk, his warts, his flat squashed nose, Marsh had never had to worry over much about women neither. When he'd been younger, rafting and flatboating down the river, and even after he'd worked a spell on steamers, Marsh had frequented places in Natchez-under-the-hill and New Orleans where a riverman could find a night's fun for a reasonable price. And later, when Fevre River Packets was going strong, there were some women in Galena and Dubuque and St. Paul who would have married him for the asking; good, stout, hard-faced widow women who knew the worth of a sound strong man like him, with all those steamboats. But they had lost interest quick enough after his misfortune, and anyway they had never been what he'd wanted. When Abner Marsh let himself think of such things, which wasn't often, he dreamed of women like the dark-eyed Creole ladies and dusky free quadroons of New Orleans, lithe and graceful and proud as his steamers.

Marsh snorted and blew out his candle. He tried to sleep. But his dreams were flushed and haunted; words echoed dimly and frighteningly in the darkened alleys of his mind.

> *. . . Morn came and went—and came, and brought no day.*
>
> *. . . Gorging himself in gloom: no Love was left.*
>
> *. . . men forgot their passions in the dread*
> *Of this their desolation.*
>
> *. . . a meal was brought,*
> *With blood.*
>
> *. . . an astounding man.*

Abner Marsh sat bolt upright in his bed, wide awake, listening to the thumping of his heart. "Damn," he muttered. He found a match, lit his bedside candle, and opened the book of poems to the page with Byron's picture. "Damn," he repeated.

Marsh dressed quickly. He yearned for company something fierce, for Hairy Mike's muscles and black iron billet, or Jonathon Jeffers and his sword cane. But this was between him and Joshua alone, and he had given his word not to talk to no one.

He splashed some water on his face, took up his hickory stick, and went out onto the deck, wishing he had a preacher on board, or even a cross. The book of poems was in his pocket. Far down the landing, another steamer was building steam and loading; Marsh could hear her roustabouts singing a slow, melancholy chant as they toted cargo across the planks.

At the door to Joshua's cabin, Abner Marsh raised his stick to knock, then hesitated, suddenly full of doubts. Joshua had given orders not to be disturbed. Joshua was going to be almighty displeased by what Marsh had to say. The whole thing was tomfoolery, that poem had just plagued him with bad dreams, or maybe it was something he ate. Still, still . . .

He was still standing there, frowning in thought, his stick upraised, when the cabin door swung silently open.

Inside was as dark as the belly of a cow. Moon and stars cast some small light across the door frame, but beyond was hot velvet blackness. Several paces back from the door, a shadowy figure stood. The moon touched bare feet, and the vague shape of the man was dimly felt. "Come in, Abner," came the voice from the darkness. Joshua spoke in a raspy whisper.

Abner Marsh stepped forward across the threshold.

The shadow moved, and suddenly the door was closed. Marsh heard it lock. It was utterly dark. He couldn't see a thing. A powerful hand gripped him tightly by the arm and drew him forward. Then he was pushed backward, and he was afraid for an instant until he felt the chair beneath him.

A rustle of motion in the darkness. Marsh looked around, blindly, trying to make sense out of the black. "I didn't knock," he heard himself say.

"No," came Joshua's reply. "I heard you approach. And I have been expecting you, Abner."

"He said you would come," came another voice, from a different part of the darkness. A woman's voice, soft, bitter. Valerie.

"You," Marsh said in astonishment. He had not expected that. He was confused, angry, uncertain, and Valerie's presence made it even more difficult. "What are *you* doin' here?" Marsh demanded.

"I might ask the same of you," her soft voice answered. "I am here because Joshua needs me, Captain Marsh. To help him. And that is more than you have done, for all your words. You and your kind, with all your suspicion, all your pious—"

"Enough, Valerie," Joshua said curtly. "Abner, I do not know why you have come tonight, but I knew you would come sooner or later. I might have done better to take a dullard as a partner, a man who would take orders without questions. You are too shrewd perhaps for your own good, and mine. I knew it was only a matter of time until you saw through the tale I spun for you at Natchez. I've seen you watching us. I know about your little tests." He gave a rough, forced chuckle. "Holy water, indeed!"

"How . . . you knew, then?" Marsh said

"Yes."

"Damn that boy."

"Don't be too hard on him. He had little to do with it, Abner, though I did notice him staring at me all during supper." Joshua's laugh was a strained, terrible sound. "No, it was the water itself that told me. A glass of clear clean water shows up in front of me a few days after our talk, and what am I to think? All the time we've been on the river, we've been getting water full of mud and sediment. I could have started a garden with the river mud I've left at the bottom of my glass." He made a dry, clacking sound of amusement. "Or even filled my coffin."

Abner Marsh ignored the last. "Stir it up and drink it down with the water," he said. "Make a riverman of you." He paused. "Or maybe just a man," he added.

"Ah," said Joshua, "so we come to the point." He said nothing more for a long time, and the cabin seemed suffocating, thick with darkness and silence. When Joshua finally spoke, his tone was chilled and serious. "Did you bring a cross with you, Abner? Or a stake?"

"I brung this," Marsh said. He pulled out the book of poems and tossed it through the air, to where he judged Joshua was sitting.

He heard a motion, a snap as the spinning book was snatched from the air. Pages rustled. "Byron," Joshua said, bemused.

Abner Marsh couldn't have seen his fingers wriggling an inch in front of his face, so thoroughly was the cabin shuttered and curtained. But Joshua could not only see well enough to catch the book, but to read it as well. Marsh felt goosebumps rise on him again, despite the heat.

"Why Byron?" asked Joshua. "You puzzle me. Another test, a cross, questions, those I might have anticipated. Not Byron."

"Joshua," said Marsh, "how old are you?"

Silence.

"I'm a fair judge of age," Marsh said. "You're a hard one, with your white hair and all. Still, from the looks of you—your face, your hands—I'd say thirty, thirty-five at the most. That book there, it says he died thirty-three years ago. And you say you knew him."

Joshua sighed. "Yes." He sounded rueful. "A stupid mistake. I was so taken by the sight of this steamer that I forgot myself. Afterward I thought it would not matter. You knew nothing of Byron. I was sure you would forget."

"I ain't always quick. But I don't forget." Marsh took a hard, reassuring grip on his stick, and leaned forward. "Joshua, I want us to talk. Get the woman out of here."

Valerie laughed icily in the darkness. She seemed closer now, though Marsh had not heard her move. "He is a bold fool," she said.

"Valerie will stay, Abner," Joshua said bluntly. "She can be trusted to hear anything you might care to say to me. She is as I am."

Marsh felt cold and very alone. "Like you are," he echoed heavily. "Well then. *What are you?*"

"Judge for yourself," Joshua replied. A match flared suddenly, startlingly, in the black cabin.

"Oh, my God," Marsh croaked.

The brief small flame threw harsh light on Joshua's features. His lips were swollen and cracked. Burned, blackened skin pulled tight across his forehead and cheeks. Blisters, swollen with water and pus, bulged beneath his chin and clustered on the raw red hand that cupped the match. His gray eyes gaped whitened and rheumy from hollow pits. Joshua York smiled grimly, and Marsh heard the seared flesh crackle and tear. Pale white fluid ran slowly down one cheek from a fissure freshly torn open. A piece of skin fell away, revealing raw pink flesh beneath.

Then the match went out, and darkness was a blessing.

"His partner, you said," Valerie said accusingly. "You would help him, you said. This is the help you gave him, you and your crew with your suspicions and your threats. He might have died for your sake. He is the pale king, and you are nothing, but he did *this* to himself to win your worthless loyalty. Are you satisfied, Captain Marsh? It seems not, since you are here."

"What the hell *happened* to you?" Marsh asked, ignoring Valerie.

"I was in the light of your gaudy day for less than two hours," Joshua replied, and now Marsh understood his pained whispering. "I was aware of the risk. I have done it before, when it was necessary. Four hours might have killed me. Six hours, most certainly. But two hours or less, most of it spent out of direct sunlight—I knew my limits. The burns look worse than they are. The pain is bearable. And this shall pass quickly. By tomorrow at this time, no one will ever know anything had touched me. Already my flesh heals itself. The blisters burst, the dead skin sloughs off. You saw for yourself."

Abner Marsh shut his eyes, opened them. It made no difference. The darkness was as full either way, and he could still see the pale blue after-image of the match hanging before him, and the awful specter of Joshua's ravaged face. "Then it don't matter about the holy water, and the mirrors," he said. "It don't matter. You can't go out by day, not really. What you said—those goddamned vampires of yours. They're real. Only you lied to me. You *lied* to me, Joshua! You ain't no vampire hunter, you're one of them. You and her and all the rest of them. *You're vampires your-goddamned-selves!*" Marsh held his walking stick out in front of him, an ineffective hickory sword warding off things he could not see. His throat felt raw and dry. He heard Valerie laugh lightly, and move closer.

"Lower your voice, Abner," Joshua said calmly, "and spare me your indignation. Yes, I lied to you. At our very first meeting, I warned you that if you pressed me for answers you would get lies. You forced the lies from me. I only regret that they were not better lies."

"My partner," Abner Marsh said angrily. "Hell, I can't believe it even now. A killer, or worse'n a killer. What have you been doin' all these nights? Goin' out and findin' somebody alone, drinkin' blood, rippin' them apart? And then moving on, yessir, now I see. A different town most every night, you're safe that way, by the time the folks ashore find what you've done you're gone off somewheres else. And not runnin' neither, just loafin' along in grand style in a fancy steamer with your own cabin and everything. No wonder you wanted yourself a steamboat so much, Mister Cap'n York. God damn you to hell."

"*Be silent*," York snapped, with such force in his voice that Marsh abruptly closed his mouth. "Lower that stick before you break something waving it around. *Lower* it, I say." Marsh dropped the walking stick to the carpet. "Good," said Joshua.

"He is like all the rest, Joshua," Valerie said. "He does not understand. He has nothing for you but fear and hate. We can't let him leave here alive."

"Perhaps," Joshua said reluctantly. "I think there is more to him than that, but perhaps I'm wrong. What of it, Abner? Be careful what you say. Speak as if your life hung on every word."

But Abner Marsh was too angry for thought. The fear that had filled him had given way to a fever of rage; he had been lied to, made a part of this, played for a big ugly fool. No man treated Abner Marsh like that, no matter if he wasn't a man at all. York had turned his *Fevre Dream*, his lady, into some kind of floating nightmare. "I been on this river a long time," Marsh said. "Don't you try to scare me none. When I was on my first steamer, I seen a friend o' mine get his guts cut out in a St. Joe saloon. I grabbed the scoundrel that did it, took the knife off him, and broke his damn back for him. I was at Bad Axe too, and down in bleeding Kansas, so no goddamned bloodsucker is goin' to bluff me. You want to come for me, you come right on. I'm twice your weight, and you're burned up all to hell. I'll twist your damned head off. Maybe I ought to do that anyhow, for what you done."

Silence. Then, astonishingly, Joshua York laughed, long and loud. "Ah, Abner," he said when he had quieted again, "you *are* a steamboatman. Half-dreamer and half-braggart and all fool. You sit there blind, when you know I can see perfectly well by the light leaking in through the shutters and drapes, and beneath the door. You sit there fat and slow, knowing my strength, my quickness. You ought to know how silently I can move." There was a pause, a creak, and suddenly York's voice came from across the cabin. "Like this." Another silence. "And this." Behind him. "And this." He was back where he had started; Marsh, who had turned his head every which way to follow the voice, felt dizzy. "I could bleed you to death with a hundred soft touches you'd hardly feel. I could creep up on you in the darkness and rip out your throat before you realized I'd stopped talking. And still, despite everything, you sit there looking in the wrong direction, with your beard stuck out, blustering and threatening." Joshua sighed. "You have spirit, Abner Marsh. Poor judgment, but lots of spirit."

"If you're fixin' to try to kill me, come on and get it done," Marsh said. "I'm ready. Maybe I never outrun the *Eclipse*, but I done most everything else I had a mind to. I'd rather be rottin' in one of those fancy N'Orleans tombs than runnin' a steamer for a pack of vampires."

"Once I asked you if you were a superstitious man, or a religious one," Joshua said. "You denied it. Yet now I hear you talking about vampires like some ignorant immigrant."

"What're you sayin'? You're the one *told* me . . ."

"Yes, yes. Coffins full of dirt, soulless creatures that don't show up in mirrors, things that can't cross running water, creatures who can turn into wolves and bats and mists yet cringe before a clove of garlic. You're too intelligent a man to believe such rubbish, Abner. Shrug off your fears and your angers for a moment, and *think!*"

That brought Abner Marsh up short. The mocking bite of Joshua's tone made it all sound mighty silly, in fact. Maybe York did get all burned up by a little daylight, but that didn't change the fact that he drank holy water and wore silver and showed up in mirrors. "You tellin' me you *ain't* no vampire now, or what?" Marsh said, lost.

"There are no such things as vampires," Joshua said patiently. "They are like those river stories Karl Framm tells so well. The treasure of the *Drennan Whyte*. The phantom steamer of Raccourci. The pilot who was so conscientious he got up to stand his watch even after he'd died. Stories, Abner. Idle amusements, not to be taken seriously by a grown man."

"Some of them stories is part true," Marsh protested feebly. "I mean, I know lots of pilots who claim they seen the lights of the phantom when they went down the Raccourci cutoff, and even heard her leadsmen cussin' and swearin'. And the *Drennan Whyte*, well, I don't believe in no curses, but she went down just like Mister Framm tells it, and them other boats that came to raise her went down too. As for that dead pilot, hell, I knew him. He was a sleep-walker, is what it was, and he piloted the steamer while he was dead asleep. Only the story got exaggerated a mite goin' up and down the river."

"You've made my point for me, Abner. If you insist on the word, then yes, vampires are real. But the stories about us have gotten exaggerated a mite as well. Your sleepwalker became a corpse in a few years of telling stories about him. Think of what he'll be in a century or two."

"What are you then, if you ain't no vampire?"

"I have no easy word for what I am," Joshua said. "In English, your kind might call me vampire, werewolf, witch, warlock, sorcerer, demon, ghoul. Other languages offer other names: *nosferatu, odoroten, upir, loup garou*. All names given by your people to such poor things as I. I do not like those names. I am none of them. Yet I have nothing to offer in their stead. We have no name for ourselves."

"Your own language . . ." Marsh said.

"We have no language. We use human languages, human names. Such has always been our way. We are not human, yet neither are we vampires. We are . . . another race. When we call ourselves anything, it is usually one of your words, in one of your languages, to which we have given a secret meaning. We are the people of the night, the people of the blood. Or simply the people."

"And us?" Marsh demanded. "If you're the people, what are we?"

Joshua York hesitated briefly, and Valerie spoke up. "The people of the day," she said quickly.

"No," Joshua said. "That is my term. It is not one my people use frequently. Valerie, the time for lies is past. Tell Abner the truth."

"He will not like it," she said. "Joshua, the risk . . ."

"Nonetheless," Joshua said. "Valerie, tell him."

Leaden silence for a moment. And then, softly, Valerie said, "The cattle. That's what we call you, Captain. The cattle."

Abner Marsh frowned and clenched a big, rough fist.

"Abner," Joshua said, "you wanted the truth. I have been giving you a great deal of thought of late. After Natchez, I feared I might have to arrange an accident for you. We dare not risk exposure, and you are a threat to us. Simon and Katherine both urged me to have you killed. Those of my newer companions whom I have taken into my confidence, like Valerie and Jean Ardant, tended to concur. Yet, though my people and I would undoubtedly be safer with you dead, I held back. I am sick of death, sick of fear, endlessly weary of the mistrust between our races. I wondered if perhaps we might try working together instead, but I was never certain that you could be trusted. Until that night in Donaldsonville, that is, that night when Valerie tried to get you to turn the *Fevre Dream*. You proved stronger than I had any right to expect when you resisted her, and more loyal as well. Then and there, I decided. You would live, and if you came to me again, I would tell you the truth, all of it, the good and the bad. Will you listen?"

"Do I got much choice?" Marsh asked.

"No," admitted Joshua York.

Valerie sighed. "Joshua, I plead with you to reconsider. He's one of *them*, however much you like him. He will not understand. They'll come up here with sharpened stakes, you know they will."

"I hope not," Joshua said. Then, to Marsh, he said, "She is afraid, Abner. This is a new thing I propose to do, and new things are always dangerous. Hear me out and do not judge me, and perhaps we can have a true partnership between us. I have never told the truth to one of you before . . ."

"To one of the cattle," Marsh grumbled. "Well, I never lissened to no vampire before neither, so we're even. Go on. This here bull is lissenin'."

CHAPTER FOURTEEN

Of Days Dark and Distant

LISTEN then, Abner, but first hear my conditions. I want no interruptions. I want no outraged outbursts, no questions, no judgments from you. Not until I am finished. Much of what I have to say you will find grim and terrible, I warn you, but if you let me take you from the beginning to the end, then perhaps you will understand. You have called me a killer, a vampire, and in a sense I am. But you have killed as well, by your own admission. You believe your acts justified by the circumstances. So do I. If not justified, then at least mitigated. Hear *all* I have to say before you condemn me and my kind.

Let me begin with myself, my own life, and tell you the rest as I learned it.

You asked my age. I am young, Abner, in the first flush of adult life by the standards of my race. I was born in provincial France in the year 1785. I never knew my mother, for reasons I shall reveal later. My father was a minor noble. That is, he granted himself a title as he moved through French society. He had been in France several generations, so he enjoyed a certain status, though he claimed to be of Eastern European origin. He had wealth, a small amount of land. He accounted for his longevity by a ruse in the 1760s, whereby he posed as his own son and eventually succeeded himself.

So, you see, I am some 72 years old, and I did indeed enjoy the good fortune of meeting Lord Byron. That was some time later, however.

My father was as I am. So were two of our servants, two who were not truly servants but companions. The three adults of my race taught me languages, manners, much of the world . . . and cautions. I slept by day, went out only by night, learned to fear the dawn as children of your race, having been burned, learn to fear fire. I was different from others, I was told, superior and apart, a lord. I must not talk of those differences, though, lest the cattle fear me and kill me. I must pretend that my hours were simply a matter of preference. I must learn and observe the forms of Catholicism, even take communion at special midnight masses in our private chapel. I must —well, I will not go on. You must realize, Abner, I was only a child. I might have learned more in time, might have begun to comprehend the why and the wherefore of those around me and the life we led, had things continued. I would then have been another person.

In 1789, however, the fires of the Revolution changed my life irrevocably. When the Terror came, we were taken. For all his cautions, his chapels and his mirrors, my father had aroused suspicion by his nocturnal habits, his solitude, his mysterious wealth. Our servants—our human servants—denounced him as a warlock, a satanist, a disciple of the Marquis de Sade. And he called himself an aristocrat as well, the blackest sin of all. His two companions, being seen only as servants themselves, managed to slip away, but my father and I were taken.

Young as I was, I have vivid memories of the cell in which we were imprisoned. It was cold and damp, all rough stone, with a great door of iron so thick and heavily barred that even my father's great strength was no use against it. The cell stank of urine, and we slept without blankets, in filthy straw scattered over the floor. There was one window, but it was far above us, slanting through a solid stone wall at least ten feet thick. It was very small, and the outside was heavily barred. We were actually below the ground, I think, in a sort of cellar. Very little light filtered down to us, but of course that was a blessing in disguise.

When we were alone, my father told me what I must do. He could not even get to the window, the gap in the stone being so narrow, but I could; I was still small. And I had the strength to deal with the bars. He ordered me to leave him. He gave me other advice as well. To wear rags and draw no attention to myself. To hide by day, and pilfer food by night. Never to tell anyone how I was different. To find myself a cross, and wear it. I did not understand half of what he said, and soon forgot much of it, but I promised to obey. He told me to leave France, and to seek out the servants who had fled. I was not to try to avenge him, he said. I would have vengeance enough in time, for all these people would die and I would live. Then he said something I have never forgotten. "They cannot help themselves. The red thirst is on this nation, and only blood will sate it. It is the bane of us all." I asked him what the red thirst was. "You will know it soon enough," he told me. "It cannot be mistaken." Then he bid me go. I squeezed up the narrow aperture to the window. The bars were old and rusted through. Since it was impossible to get to them, no one had given thought to their replacement. They broke away in my hands.

I never saw my father again, but later, after the Restoration that followed Napoleon, I made inquiries after him. My disappearance had sealed his fate. He was clearly a sorcerer as well as an aristocrat. He was tried, convicted. He lost his head to a provincial guillotine. Afterward they burnt his body, because of the charge of sorcery.

But I knew none of this then. I fled the prison and the province and wandered to Paris, where survival was easy in those days, so chaotic was the situation. By day I took refuge in cellars, the darker the better. By night I came forth and stole food. Meat, chiefly. I had little taste for vegetables or fruits. I became a proficient thief. I was fast, silent, and terribly strong. My nails seemed sharper and harder each day. I could claw through wood when I had a mind to. No one noticed me or questioned me. I spoke good, cultured French, fair English, and a smattering of low German. In Paris I picked up the gutter tongue as well. I searched for our vanished servants, the only others of my race I had ever known, but I had no clue how to find them, and my efforts came to nothing.

So I grew up among your people. The cattle. The people of the day. I was clever and observant. Much as I looked like those around me, I soon realized how truly different I was. And better, as I had been told. Stronger, quicker, and—I believed—longer-lived as well. Daylight was my only weakness. I kept my secret well.

The life I led in Paris, however, was mean and degraded and boring. I wanted more. I began to steal money as well as food. I found someone to teach me how to read, and thereafter I stole books whenever I could. Once or twice I was almost caught, but I always got away. I could melt into shadows, scale walls in the winking of an eye, move as quietly as a cat. Perhaps those who pursued me thought I changed into a mist. It must have seemed that way at times.

When the Napoleonic Wars began, I was careful to avoid the army, since I knew they would require me to expose myself to daylight. But I followed behind them in their campaigns. I traveled through Europe in that fashion, saw much burning and killing. And where the Emperor went, there was loot for me.

In Austria in 1805, I saw my great chance. On the road by night, I chanced upon a wealthy Viennese merchant fleeing before the French armies. He had all his money with him, converted to gold and silver, a fabulous sum. I stalked him to the inn where he spent the night, and when I was sure he was asleep, broke in to make my fortune. He was not asleep, however. The war had made him afraid. He was waiting for me, and he was armed. He pulled a pistol from beneath his blankets, and shot me.

Shock and pain overwhelmed me. The blow drove me to the floor. It had caught me in the stomach, square, and I bled profusely. But then, suddenly, the flow began to ebb, and the pain lessened. I got up. I must have been a terrible sight, pale-faced and covered with blood. And a strange feeling came over me, one I had never felt before. The moon was coming in through the window, and the merchant was screaming, and before I knew quite what I was doing I was on him. I wanted to silence him, to clamp my hand over his mouth, but . . . something took hold of me. My hands went to him, my nails —they are very sharp, very hard. I tore open his throat. He choked on his own blood.

I stood there, trembling, watching the black blood spurt out from him, his body thrashing on the bed in the pale moonlight. He was dying. I had seen people die before, in Paris, in the war. This was different. *I* had killed him. A great passion seemed to fill me, and I felt . . . *desire*. I had read often of desire in the books I stole, of lust and the carnal urges to which man is heir. I had never felt any of it. I had looked on naked women, on men, on couples locked in sexual congress, and none of it had touched me. I could not comprehend all this nonsense I read of uncontrollable passions, lusts like fire. But now I knew them. The blood flowing, this fat rich man dying in my hands, the noises he made, his feet beating on the bed. It all excited some animal deep within me. The blood drenched my hands. It was so dark and hot. It steamed as it came from his throat. So I leaned forward and tasted it. The taste made me mad, feverish. Suddenly I had plunged my face into his neck, ripping with my teeth, sucking up the blood, tearing, swallowing. He stopped thrashing. I fed. And

148

then the door opened, and there were men with knives and rifles. I looked up, startled. How I must have terrified them. Before they could act, I was through the window and gone into the night. I had the presence of mind to grab the money belt as I went. It had only a fraction of the man's fortune in it, but it was enough.

I ran long and far that night, and passed the next day in the root cellar of a farmhouse that had been burned and abandoned.

I was twenty years old. Among the people of the night, a child still, but now coming into adulthood. When I woke that night in the root cellar, covered with dried blood and clutching the money belt to me, I remembered my father's words. I knew what the red thirst was at last. And only blood will sate it, he had said. I was sated. I felt stronger and healthier than ever in my life. Yet I was sick and horrified as well. I had grown up among your people, you see, and I thought as you did. I was no animal, no monster. There and then, I resolved to change the way I lived, so such a thing might never happen again. I washed, stole clothes, the finest I could find. I moved west, away from the fighting. Then north. I took rooms in inns by day, hired coaches to travel from town to town each night. Finally, with difficulty due to the war, I made my way to England. I took a new name, determined to make myself a gentleman. I had the money. I could learn the rest.

My journeys had taken me about a month. My third night in London, I felt strange, sick. I had never been ill in my life. The next night was worse. The night after, finally, I knew the feeling for what it was. The red thirst was on me. I screamed and raged. I ordered up a fine meal, a great rich red slab of meat I thought would slake the yearning. I ate it, and willed myself to calm. It was no use. Within the hour I was out on the streets. I found an alley, waited. A young woman was the first to pass. Part of me admired her beauty; it burned in me like a flame. Another part simply hungered. I almost tore her head off, but at least it was over quickly. Afterward I wept.

For months I despaired. From my readings, I knew what I must be. I had learned those words. For twenty years I had thought myself superior. Now I found I was something unnatural, a beast, a soulless monster. I could not decide whether I was a vampire or a werewolf, which puzzled me. Neither I nor my father had the power to turn into anything, but my red thirst came on me monthly, in what seemed a lunar cycle—although it did not always coincide with the full moon. That was a characteristic of the werewolf, I read. I read a great deal on those subjects at that time, trying to understand myself. Like the werewolf of legend, I often tore out the throat, and I did eat some small amount of flesh, especially if the thirst was on me badly. And when the thirst was not on me, I seemed a decent enough person, which also fit the werewolf legends. On the other hand, silver had no power over me, nor wolfbane, I did not change my shape or grow hair. Like the vampire, I could only walk by night. And it seemed to me that it was the blood I truly craved, not flesh. But I slept in beds, not coffins, and had crossed running water hundreds of times, easily. I was certainly not dead, and religious objects bothered me not at all. Once, to be sure, I spirited away the body of a victim, wondering if it would rise as a wolf or a vampire. It stayed a corpse. After a while it began to smell, and I buried it.

You can imagine my terror. I was not human, but neither was I one of these legendary creatures. I decided my books were useless to me. I was on my own.

Month after month the red thirst came upon me. Those nights were filled with an awful exultation, Abner. In taking life I *lived* as never before. But there was always an afterward, and then I was filled with loathing for the thing I had become. I slayed the young, the innocent, the beautiful, they above all. They seemed to have an inner light that inflamed the thirst as old and sick people could not. And yet at other times I loved the selfsame qualities I was drawn to kill.

Desperately I tried to change myself. My will, so strong normally, was nothing when the red thirst was on me. I turned to religion with hope. When I felt the first tendrils of the fever in me, I sought a church, and confessed everything to the priest who answered my knock. He did not believe me, but he agreed to sit and pray with me. I wore a cross, knelt at the altar, prayed fervently, with the candles and statues all around me, safe in the house of God, one of his ministers by my side. Within three hours, I turned on him, and killed him right there, in the church. It caused a small sensation when the body was found the next day.

I tried reason next. If religion had no answers, then what drove me could not be supernatural. I slaughtered animals instead of humans. I stole human blood from a doctor's office. I broke into a mortician's office where I knew a fresh corpse had been taken. Each of these helped, they quieted the thirst somewhat, but they did not end it. The best of the half-measures lay in killing a living animal, and drinking its blood still warm from its body. It was the life, you see, the life as well as the blood itself.

Through all of this, I protected myself. I moved about England several times, so the deaths and disappearances of my victims would not be concentrated in one locale. I buried as many bodies as I could. And I finally began to apply my intellect to my hunting. I needed money, so I sought out wealthy prey. I became rich, and then richer. Money breeds more money, and once I had some, more came to me honestly, cleanly. I had become quite fluent in English by then. I changed my name again, styled myself a gentleman, bought myself an isolated house on the moors in Scotland where my behavior would draw little attention, hired some discreet servants. Each month I went away on business, always overnight. None of my prey lived anywhere near me. The servants suspected nothing.

Finally I hit upon what I thought might be the answer. One of my servants, a pretty young maid, had been growing more and more familiar with me. She seemed to like me, and not simply as an employer. I returned her affection. She was honest, cheerful, and quite intelligent, if uneducated. I began to think of her as my friend, and I saw in her a way out. Often I had considered the alternative of chaining myself up, or otherwise confining myself until the red thirst had passed, but I had never hit on a scheme to make it work. If I put the key in reach, I would use it when the thirst was on me. If I tossed it away, how would I get unchained? No, I needed the help of another, but I had always heeded my father's warning to trust none of *you* with my secret.

Now I decided to take a risk. I dismissed my other servants and sent them away, hired no one to replace them. I had a room built in my house. A small windowless room with thick stone walls and an iron door as thick as I remembered from the cell I'd shared with my father. It could be secured from the outside with three great metal bolts. I would have no way out. When it was complete, I called my pretty little maid in, and gave her instructions. I did not trust her sufficiently to tell her the full truth. I was afraid, Abner, that if she knew what I truly was, she would denounce me, or flee at once, and the solution that seemed so close at hand would be gone, along with my house and property and the life I had built. So I told her only that a brief madness came on me each month, a fit such as epilepsy brings on. During my fits, I said, I would enter my special room, and she must bolt me in and keep me there for three full days. I would take food and water in with me, including some live chickens, to take some of the edge off the thirst.

She was shocked, concerned, and quite puzzled, but at last she agreed to do as I bid her. She loved me in her way, I think, and was willing to do almost anything for my sake. So I entered the room, and she locked the door behind me.

And the thirst came. It was frightening. Despite the lack of windows, I could feel when day had come and gone. I slept by day, as always—but the nights were a blur of horror. I killed all the chickens the first night, gorged on them. I demanded to be set free, and my loyal maid refused. I screamed abuse at her. Then I simply screamed, incoherent sounds like an animal. I threw myself at the walls, pounded against the door until my fists were bloody, then squatted to suck at my own blood eagerly. I tried to claw through the soft stone. But I could not get out.

On the third day I grew clever. It was as if my fever had broken. I was on the downhill side now, becoming myself again. I could feel the thirst waning. I called my maid to the door, and told her it was over, that she could let me out. She refused, and said I told her to keep me confined for three full nights, as indeed I had. I laughed and admitted that was true, but said the fit had come and gone, that I knew it would not come again for another month. Still she would not unbar the door. I did not rave at her. I said I understood, praised her for following orders so well. I asked her to stay and talk, since I was lonely in my prison. She agreed, and we talked for almost an hour. I was calm and articulate, charming even, very reconciled to another night inside. We spoke so reasonably that soon she admitted that I sounded quite like myself. I told her what a good girl she was to be so conscientious. I enlarged on her merits and my affection for her. Finally, I asked her to marry me when I was free again.

She opened the door. She looked so happy, Abner. So very happy and alive. She was full of life. She came to kiss me, and I put my arms around her and pulled her to me. We kissed several times. Then my lips trailed down to her neck, and I found the artery, and opened it. I . . . fed . . . for a long time. I was so thirsty, and her life was so sweet. But when I let her go and she staggered back from me, she was still alive, just barely, bled white and dying but still conscious. The look in her eyes, Abner. The look in her eyes.

Of all the things I have ever done, that was most terrible. She will be with me always. The look in her eyes.

Afterward my despair was boundless. I tried to kill myself. I bought a silver knife with a handle fashioned in the shape of a cross—the superstitions still had a grip on me, you see. And I cut my wrists open, and lay down in a warm bath to die. I healed. I fell on my sword in the manner of the ancient Romans. I healed. I was learning more of my abilities every day. I mended so quickly, with only a brief time of pain. My blood clotted virtually instantaneously, no matter how gaping the wound I inflicted. Whatever I might be, I was clearly a wonder.

Finally I hit on the way. Outside my house, I attached two great iron chains to the wall. By night I donned the manacles, and threw the key as far as I was able. A very long way. I waited for the dawn. The sun was worse than I remembered. It burned and blinded me. Everything blurred. My skin was on fire. I think I began to scream. I know I closed my eyes. I was out there for hours, closer and closer to death. There was nothing in me except guilt.

And then, somehow, in the fever of my death, I decided to live. How, why, I cannot tell you. But it seemed to me that I had always loved life, in myself and in others. That was why health and beauty and youth drew me so. I loathed myself because I gave death to the world, and yet here I was, killing once more, though this time the victim was myself. I could not wash out my sins with more blood, more death, I thought. To atone, I must live, bring life and beauty and hope back into the world to take the place of all that I had taken. I remembered my father's vanished servants then. There were others of my race in the world. Vampires, werewolves, warlocks, whatever they might be, they were out there in the night. How did they deal with the red thirst, I wondered. If only I could find them. I could trust my own kind where I could not trust humans. We could help each other conquer the evil that consumed us. I could learn from them.

I decided I would not die.

The chains were very strong. I had seen to that, fearful that I would seek escape from pain and death. But now I found a strength in my resolve greater than anything I had ever known, even when the thirst was driving me on. I determined to break the chains, to pull them from the stone walls where I had fastened them. I pulled and strained and yanked. They would not give. They were strong chains. I had been in the sun for hours and hours. What kept me conscious I cannot say. My skin was black and burned. The pain had grown so terrible I scarcely felt it any more. Still I worked at those chains.

Finally one of them broke free. The left. The ring set into the wall came out in a crumble of masonry. I was half free. But I was sick unto death, having strange visions. I knew I would faint soon, and once I slipped to the ground there would be no getting up again, ever. And the right chain seemed as strong and secure as when I had begun my struggle, an endless time before.

The chain never gave, Abner. Yet I won free, and sought the safety of my cool black cellars, where I lay for more than a week, dreaming and burning and writhing in pain, but healing all the while. I turned on myself, you see. I gnawed through my own wrist and left my right hand lying there while I slipped the stump through the manacle.

When I regained consciousness, a week later, I had a hand again. It was soft and small, half-formed, and it hurt. It hurt terribly. But in time the skin hardened. Then the hand swelled up, and the skin cracked and split, oozing a thick pale fluid. When it dried and peeled away, the flesh beneath was healthier. Three times that happened. The process took more than three weeks, but when it was over you would never have known that anything had happened to my hand at all. I was astounded.

That was in the year 1812, which marked a turning point in my life.

When I had recovered my strength, I found I had emerged from the ordeal with a great resolve; to change my way of life and that of my people, to free us from what my father had called the bane of the red thirst, to enable us to restore the life and beauty we drank from the world. To do this, I had first to seek out others of my kind, and the only others I knew of were my father's vanished servants. Yet a search for them was not possible just then. England warred on the Empire of the French, and there was no commerce between the two. The enforced delay did not trouble me. I knew I had all the years I might require.

As I waited, I took up the study of medicine. Nothing was known of my people, of course. Our very existence was legend. But there was much to learn of your race, so like and yet unlike my own. I befriended a number of doctors, a leading surgeon of the time, several faculty members of a well-known medical school. I read medical texts, old and new. I delved into chemistry, biology, anatomy, even alchemy, searching for insights. I built my own laboratory for experimentation, in the very room I had once used as my ill-fated prison. Now, when I took a life—as I did each month—I would carry the body back with me whenever I could, study it, dissect it. How I yearned for a cadaver of my own species, Abner, so I might see the differences!

In my second year of study, I cut a finger from my left hand. I knew it would regenerate. I wanted flesh of my flesh for analysis and dissection.

A severed finger was not sufficient to answer a hundredth of my questions, but the pain was nonetheless worthwhile, for what I learned. Bone, flesh, and blood all showed significant differences from the human. The blood was paler, like the flesh, and lacking several elements found in human blood. The bones, on the other hand, contained more of these elements. They were at once stronger and more flexible than human bone. Oxygen, that miracle gas of Priestley and Lavoisier, was present in blood and muscle tissue to a much greater degree than in comparable samples taken from your race.

I did not know what to make of any of this, but it made me feverish with theories. It seemed to me that perhaps the lacks in my blood had some relation to my drive to drink the blood of others. That month, when the thirst had come and gone and I had taken my victim, I bled myself and studied the sample. The composition of my blood had changed! Somehow I had converted the blood of my victim into my own, thickening and enriching it, at least for a time. Thereafter I bled myself daily. Study showed that my blood thinned each day. Perahps it was when the balance reached a certain critical point that the red thirst came on, I thought.

My supposition left many questions unanswered. Why was animal blood insufficient to quell the thirst? Or even human blood taken from a corpse? Did it lose some property in death? Why had the thirst not come upon me until I was twenty? What of all the years before? I did not know any of the answers, nor how to find them, but now at least I had a hope, a starting point. I began to make potions.

What can I tell you of that? It took years, endless experiments, study. I used human blood, animal blood, metals and chemicals of all sorts. I cooked blood, dried it, drank it raw, mixed it with wormwood, brandy, with foul-smelling medicinal preservatives, with herbs, salts, irons. I drank a thousand potions to no avail. Twice I made myself sick, so my stomach churned and heaved until I vomited forth the concoction I had downed. Always it was fruitless. Potions and jars of blood and drugs I could consume by the hundreds, but still the red thirst drove me forth to hunt by night. I killed without guilt now, knowing that I was striving for an answer, that I would conquer my bestial nature yet. I did not despair, Abner.

And finally, in the year 1815, I found my answer.

Some of my mixtures had worked better than others, you see, and those I had cont.nued to work with, improving them, making this change or addition, then that one, patiently, trying one after the other and all the time searching out new approaches as well. The compound I finally produced had as its base sheep's blood in large measure, mixed with a strong portion of alcohol which acted to preserve its properties, I believe. Yet that description oversimplifies vastly. There is a good part of laudanum in it as well, for calm and sweet visions, plus potassium salts and iron and wormwood, and various herbs and alchemical preparations long disused. For three years I had searched for it, and one night in the summer of 1815 I drank it down, as I had so many other potions before. That night the red thirst did not come upon me.

The night following I felt the beginnings of the hot restlessness which marks the onset of the thirst, and I poured a glass of my drink and sipped at it, half-afraid my triumph would be a dream, illusory. But the feeling faded. I did not thirst that night either, nor go abroad to hunt and kill.

At once I set to work, making the fluid in large quantities. It is not always easy to get it exactly right, and if the mixture is not exact, it has no effect. My labor was painstaking, however. You have seen the result, Abner. My special drink. It is never far from me. Abner, I accomplished what none of my race had ever done before, though I did not know it then, in that hot flush of triumph. I had begun a new epoch for my people, and yours as well. Darkness without fear, an end to hunter and prey, to hiding and despair. No more nights of blood and degradation. Abner, *I conquered the red thirst!*

I know now that I was extraordinarily fortunate. My understanding was superficial and limited. I thought the differences between our peoples lay solely in the blood. Later I learned how wrong that was. I felt that excess of oxygen was somehow responsible for the way the fevers of the red thirst coursed through my veins. Today I think it more likely that oxygen gives my race its strength, and helps it heal. Much of what I thought I knew in 1815 I know now for nonsense. But it does not matter, for my solution was no nonsense.

I have killed since, Abner, I will not deny that. But in the fashion humans kill, for human reasons. And since that night in Scotland in 1815, I have not tasted blood, or felt the ravages of the red thirst.

I did not stop learning, not then or ever. Knowledge has a beauty to me, and I rejoice in all beauty, and there was still much to know of myself and my people. But with my great discovery the emphasis of the quest changed, and I began to search for others of my race. At first I employed agents and letters. Later, when peace had come, I traveled on the continent myself. Thus I discovered how my father had ended. More importantly, in old provincial records I found where he had come from—or at least where he claimed to have come from. I followed the trail through the Rhineland, through Prussia and Poland. To the Poles he was a dimly remembered, much-feared recluse their great-grandfathers had whispered about. Some said he had been a Teutonic Knight. Others pointed me further east, to the Urals. It made no difference; the Teutonic Knights were centuries dead, and the Urals were a great range of mountains, too vast for me to search blindly.

At a dead end, I decided to take a risk. Wearing a great silver ring and a cross, which I hoped would be sufficient to dispel any talk or superstition, I began to inquire openly about vampires, werewolves, and other such legends. Some laughed at me or mocked me, a few crossed themselves and slunk away, but most gladly told the simple-minded Englishman the folk tales he wanted to hear, in exchange for a drink or a meal. From their stories I took directions. It was never easy. Years passed while I searched. I learned Polish, Bulgar, some Russian. I read papers in a dozen languages, looking for accounts of death that sounded like the red thirst. Twice I was forced to return to England, to brew more of my drink and give some attention to my affairs.

And finally, *they* found me.

I was in the Carpathians, in a rude country inn. I had been asking questions, and word of my inquiries had passed from mouth to mouth. Tired and despondent, and beginning to feel the first twinges of the thirst, I had returned to my room early, well before dawn. I was sitting before a crackling fire, sipping my drink, when I heard a clatter that at first I thought was the storm rattling the frost-rimed windows. I turned to look—the room was dark but for the blaze in the hearth—and the window was opened from outside, and there outlined against the blackness and the snow and the stars was a man, standing on the sill. He came inside easy as a cat, making no noise as he landed, a cold wind whipping around him from the winter that howled outside. He was dark, but his eyes burned, Abner, they *burned*. "You are curious about vampires, Englishman," he whispered in passable English as he shut the windows softly behind him.

It was a frightening moment, Abner. Perhaps it was the chill from outside that filled the room and made me tremble, but I think not. I saw this stranger as so many of your people had seen me, before I took them and feasted on their life's blood; dark and hot-eyed and terrible, a shadow with teeth that moved with a sure grace and spoke in a sinister whisper. As I started to rise from my chair, he moved forward into the light. I saw his nails. They were claws, grown five inches long, the ends black and sharp. Then I looked up and saw his face. And it was a face I had known in childhood, and as I looked on it again the name came to me as well. "Simon," I said.

He stopped. Our eyes met.

You have looked into my eyes, Abner. You have seen the power in them, I think, and perhaps other things as well, darker things. So it is with all of our race. Mesmer wrote of animal magnetism, of a strange force that resides in all living things, in some more strongly than others. I have seen this force in humans. In war, two officers may order their men to the same foolhardy course. One will be killed for his troubles by his own troops. The second, using the same words in the same situation, will compel his men to follow him willingly into certain death. Bonaparte had the power in great measure, I think. But our race, we have it most of all. It resides in our voices, and especially in our eyes. We are hunters, and with our eyes we can captivate and quiet our natural prey, bend them to our will, sometimes even compel them to assist in their own slaughter.

I knew none of this then. All I knew was Simon's eyes, the heat of them, the rage and suspicion there. I could feel the thirst burning within him, and the sight of it woke my own long-buried bloodlust dimly, like calling to like until I was afraid. I could not look away. Nor could he. We faced each other silently, moving but slightly in a wary circle, eyes locked. My glass fell and shattered on the floor.

How much time passed I cannot say. But finally Simon looked down, and it was over. Then he did something startling and strange. He knelt before me, and bit open a vein in his own wrist so the blood flowed out, and held it up to me in submission. "Bloodmaster," he said in French.

The flowing blood, so close at hand, woke a dryness in my throat.

I reached out and grabbed his arm, trembling, and began to bend toward it. And then I remembered. I slapped him and spun away, and the bottle was on the table by the hearth. I poured two glasses, drained one and thrust the other at him while he looked on, uncomprehending. "Drink," I commanded him, and he did as he was told. I was bloodmaster, and my word was law.

That was the beginning, there in the Carpathians in 1826.

Simon had been one of my father's two followers, as I had known. My father had been bloodmaster. With his death, Simon led, being stronger than the other. He brought me to the place he lived the following night, a snug chamber buried in the ruins of an old mountain fortress. There I met the others; a woman whom I recognized as the other servant of my childhood, and two more of my people, whom you call Smith and Brown. Simon had been their master. Now I was. More, I brought with me freedom from the red thirst.

So we drank, and passed many nights, while from their lips I began to learn the history and ways of the people of the night.

We are an *old* people, Abner. Long before your race raised its cities in the hot south, my ancestors swept through the dark winters of northern Europe, hunting. Our tales say we came from the Urals, or perhaps the steppes, spreading west and south through the centuries. We lived in Poland long before the Poles, prowled German forests before the coming of the Germanic barbarians, held sway over Russia before the Tartars, before Novgorod-the-Great. When I saw *old*, I do not speak of hundreds of years, but of thousands. Millennia passed in the cold and the darkness. We were savage, the stories say, cunning naked animals, one with the night, swift and deadly and free. Long-lived beyond all other beasts, impossible to kill, the masters and lords of creation. So our stories go. All that walked on two legs or four, ran in fear of us. All that lived was but food for us. By day we slept in caves, packs of us, families. By night we ruled the earth.

Then, up from the south, your race came into our world. The day people, so like us and yet so unlike. You were weak. We killed you easily, and took joy in it, for we found beauty in you, and always my people had been drawn to beauty. Perhaps it was your likeness to us we found so captivating. For centuries you were simply our prey.

But changes came with time. My race was very long-lived, but few in number. The mating urge is curiously absent in us, while in you humans it rules as surely as the red thirst rules us. Simon told me, when I asked him of my mother, that the males of my race feel desire only when the female enters heat, and that happens but rarely—most frequently when male and female have shared a kill together. Even then, the women are seldom fertile, and for that they are thankful, for conception usually means death for our females. I killed my mother, Simon told me, ripping my way out of her womb, doing such damage inside that even our recuperative powers were of no avail. So it is most often when my people enter this world. We begin our lives in blood and death, even as we live them.

There is a certain balance in that. God, if you believe in him, or Nature, if not, gives and takes away. We may live for a thousand years or more. Were we as fertile as you, we would soon fill this world. Your race breeds and breeds and breeds, swarming in numbers like flies, but you die like flies as well, of little wounds and illnesses my kind shrugs off.

It is no wonder we thought little of you at first. But you bred, and you built cities, and you learned. You had minds, even as we did, but we had never had cause to use ours, so strong were we. Your kind brought fire into the world, armies, bows and spears and clothing, art and writing and language. Civilization, Abner. And, civilized, you were no longer prey. You hunted us down, killed us with flame and stake, came upon our caves by day. Our numbers, never great, diminished steadily. We fought you and died, or fled you, but where we went your kind soon followed. Finally we did as we were forced to do. We learned from you.

Clothing and fire, weapons and language, all of it. We never had our own, you see. We borrowed yours. We organized as well, began to think and plan, and finally melted into you entirely, living in the shadows of the world your race built, pretending we were your kind, stealing out by night to slake our thirst on your blood, hiding by day in fear of you and your vengeance. Such has been the story of my race, the people of the night, through most of history.

I heard it from Simon's lips, as he had heard it years before from those now slain and gone. Simon was the oldest of the group I had found, claiming almost six hundred years.

I heard other things as well, legends that went beyond our oral history back to our ultimate origins in the dim dawn of time itself. Even there I saw the hand of your people, for our myths were taken from your Christian Bible. Brown, who had once posed as a preacher, read me passages from Genesis, about Adam and Eve and their children, Cain and Abel, the first men, the only men. But when Cain slew Abel, he went forth in exile and took a wife from the land of Nod. Where *she* came from, if the others were the only people in the world, Genesis did not explain. Brown did, however; Nod was the land of night and darkness, he said, and that woman was the mother of our race. From her and Cain are we descended, and thus it is we who are the children of Cain, not the black peoples as some of your kind believes. Cain slew his brother and hid, and so it is that we must kill our distant cousins and hide ourselves when the sun rises, since the sun is the face of God. We remain long-lived, as all men were in the first days described by your Bible, but our lives are accursed and must be spent in fear and darkness. So many of my people have believed, I was told. Others held to different myths, some even accepting the vampire tales they had heard, and believing themselves to be undying avatars of evil.

I listened to the stories of ancestors long vanished, of struggles and persecutions, of our migrations. Smith told me of a great battle on the desolate shores of the Baltic a thousand years before, when a few hundred of my race descended by night on a horde of thousands, so the sun came up on a field of blood and corpses. I was reminded of Byron's "Sennacherib." Simon spoke of splendid ancient Byzantium, where many of our race had lived and prospered for centuries, invisible in that great teeming city until the crusaders came through, plundering and destroying, putting many of us to the torch. They bore the cross, those invaders, and I wondered if perhaps *that* was the truth behind the legend that my race fears and abhors that Christian symbol. From all lips I heard a legend of a city we had built, a great city of the night, wrought in iron and black marble in some dark caverns in the heart of Asia, by the shores of an underground river and a sea never touched by the sun. Long before Rome or even Ur, our city had been great, they avowed, in flagrant contradiction to the history they had told me earlier, of running naked through moonlit winter forests. According to the myth, we had been expelled from our city for some crime, had wandered forgetful and lost for thousands of years. But the city was still there, and some day a king would be born to our people, a bloodmaster greater than any who had ever come before, one who would gather our scattered race together and lead us back to the city of the night beside its sunless sea.

Abner, of all that I heard and learned, that tale affected me most greatly. I doubt that any such vast underground city exists, doubt that it ever existed, but the very telling of such a story proved to me that my people were not the evil, empty vampires of legend. We had no art, no literature, not even a language of our own—but the story showed we had the capacity to dream, to imagine. We had never built, never created, only stolen your garments and lived in your cities and fed ourselves on your life, your vitality, your very blood—but we *could* create, given a chance, we had it within us to whisper stories of cities of our own. The red thirst has been a curse, has made my race and yours enemies, has robbed my people of all noble aspirations. The mark of Cain, indeed.

We have had our great leaders, Abner, bloodmasters real and imagined in ages past. We have had our Caesars, our Solomons, our Prester Johns. But we are waiting for our deliverer, you see, waiting for our Christ.

Huddled in the ruins of that grim castle, listening to the wind howl outside, Simon and the others drank my liquor and told me stories and studied me from potent, feverish eyes, and I realized what they must think. Each of them was hundreds of years older than I, but I was the stronger, I was bloodmaster. I brought them an elixir that banished the red thirst. I seemed almost half-human. Abner, they saw *me* as the deliverer of legend, the promised king of the vampires. And I could not deny it. It was my destiny, I knew then, to lead my race from darkness.

There are so many things I want to do, Abner, so many things. Your own people are fearful and superstitious and full of hate, so my kind must stay hidden for now. I have seen the way you war on each other, read of Vlad Tepes—who was *not* one of us, by the way—of him and Gaius Caligula and other kings, I have seen your race burn old women because they were suspected of being one of us, and here in New Orleans I have witnessed the way you enslave your own kind, whip them and sell them like animals simply because of the darkness of their skin. The black people are closer to you, more kin, than ever my kind can be. You can even get children on their women, while no such interbreeding is possible between night and day. No, we must remain hidden from your people, for our safety. But, free from the red thirst, I hope in time we can reveal ourselves to the enlightened among you, men of science and learning, your leaders. We can help each other so much, Abner! We can teach you your own histories, and from us you may learn how to heal yourselves, how to live longer. For our part, we have only just begun. I have defeated the red thirst, and with help I dream some day of conquering the very sun, so we can go abroad by day. Your surgeons and men of medicine could help our females in childbirth, so procreation need not mean death.

There is no limit to what my race can create and accomplish. I realized then, listening to Simon, that I could make us one of the great peoples of the earth. But first I had to *find* my race, before any of it could begin.

The task was not easy. Simon said that in his youth there had been almost a thousand of us, scattered over Europe from the Urals to Britain. Legend said some of us had migrated south to Africa or east to Mongolia and Cathay, but no one had any proof of such treks. Of the thousand who had dwelled in Europe, most had died in wars or witch trials, or had been hunted down when they grew careless. Perhaps a hundred of us were left, Simon guessed, perhaps fewer. Births had been few. And those who did survive were scattered and hidden.

So we began a search that took a decade. I will not bore you with all the details. In a church in Russia, we found those books you saw in my cabin, the only literature known to have come from the hand of one of my race. I deciphered them in time, and read the melancholy story of a community of fifty of the people of the blood, their woes and migrations and battles, their deaths. They were all gone, the last three crucified and burned centuries before my birth. In Transylvania we found the burnt-out shell of a mountain fastness, and in caves beneath, the skeletal remains of two of my race, rotten wooden stakes protruding from their ribs, skulls mounted on poles. I learned a good deal from study of those bones, but we had no living survivors. In Trieste we found a family that never went out by day, and were whispered to be strangely pale. Indeed they were. Albinos. In Buda-Pest we came upon a rich woman, a dreadful sick woman who whipped her maids and bled them with leeches and knives, and rubbed the blood into her skin to preserve her beauty. She was one of you, however. I confess, I killed her with my own hands, so sick at heart did she make me. She was under no compulsion from the thirst; only an evil nature made her do as she did, and that made me furious. Finally, finding nothing, we returned to my home in Scotland.

Years passed. The woman in our group, Simon's companion and

the servant of my childhood, died in 1840, of causes I was never able to determine. She was less than five hundred years old. I dissected her, and learned how very different, how very inhuman, we are. She had at least three organs I have never seen in human cadavers. I have only a vague idea of their function. Her heart was half again the size of a human heart, but her intestines were a mere fraction of the length, and she had a secondary stomach—I think solely for the digestion of blood. And more, but that is of no matter.

I read widely, learned other languages, wrote some poetry, dabbled in politics. We attended all the best society gatherings, Simon and I at least. Smith and Brown, as you call them, never did show much interest in English, and kept to themselves. Twice Simon and I went to the continent together on new searches. Once I sent him to India for three years, alone.

Finally, barely two years ago, we found Katherine, living in London, right under our noses. She was of our race, of course. But more important was the story she told.

She said that around 1750, a sizeable group of our people had been scattered over France and Bavaria and Austria and even Italy. She mentioned some names; Simon recognized them. We had searched for these people unsuccessfully for years. Katherine told us that one of their number had been tracked and killed by police in Munich in 1753 or so, that the others had grown very frightened. Their bloodmaster decided that Europe had become too populated, too organized for safety. We lived in the cracks and shadows, and those were fewer and fewer, it seemed. So he had chartered a ship, and all of them had departed from Lisbon, bound for the New World, where the savagery and endless forests and rude colonial conditions promised easy prey and safety. Why my father and his group had not been included in the migration she could not say. She was to go with them, but rains and storms and a broken carriage wheel plagued her trip to Lisbon, and when she arrived they had departed.

Of course I went at once to Lisbon, and pored through whatever old shipping records the Portugese had preserved. In time, I found it. The ship had never returned from its charter, as I had suspected. At sea for all that time, they would have had no choice but to feed on the crew, one by one. The question was, had the ship ever arrived safely in the New World? I could find no record of it. But I did find the intended destination; the port of New Orleans. From there, via the Mississippi, the whole continent would be open to them.

164

The rest should be obvious. We came. I felt certain I would find them. It seemed to me that by having a steamboat I would enjoy the luxury I have grown accustomed to, and the mobility and freedom I needed for my search. The river was full of eccentrics. A few more would not be noticed. And if tales of our fabulous boat and the strange captain who only came out by night spread up and down the river, so much the better. The tales might come to the right ears, and they would come to me as Simon did so many years ago. So I made inquiries, and we met one night in St. Louis.

You know the rest, I think, or can guess it. Let me say one other thing, however. In New Albany, when you showed our steamer to me, I did not feign my satisfaction. The *Fevre Dream* is beautiful, Abner, and that was as it should be. For the first time, a thing of beauty is come into the world because of us. It is a new beginning. The name frightened me a bit—fever has been another word for the red thirst among my people. But Simon pointed out that such a name would likely intrigue any of our race who might hear it.

There is my story, almost all of it. The truth, which you insisted on. You have been honest with me, in your way, and I believe you when you say you are not superstitious. If my dreams are to come true, there must come a time when day and night clasp hands across the twilight of fear that lies between us. There must come a time for risk. Let it be now, with you. My dream and yours, our steamer, the future of my people and your own, vampires and cattle—I give them all over to your judgment, Abner. What will it be? Trust or fear? Blood or good wine? Friends or enemies?

CHAPTER FIFTEEN

Aboard the Steamer FEVRE DREAM, New Orleans, August 1857——

IN the heavy silence that followed Joshua's story, Abner Marsh could hear his own steady breathing and the thump of his heart laboring in his chest. Joshua had been talking for hours, it seemed, but in the black stillness of the cabin there was no way to be sure. Outside it might be getting light. Toby would be cooking breakfast, the cabin passengers would be taking their morning strolls along the promenade on the boiler deck, the levee would be bustling with activity. But inside Joshua York's cabin, night went on and on, forever.

The words of that damned poem came back to him, and Abner Marsh heard himself say, "Morn came and went—and came, and brought no day."

"*Darkness,*" said Joshua, softly.

"And you've lived in it your whole damn life," Marsh said. "No morning, not ever. God, Joshua, how d'you stand it?"

York made no reply.

"It ain't sensible," Marsh said. "It's the goddamndest story I ever sat still for. But damned if I don't believe you."

"I'd hoped you would," said York. "And now, Abner?"

That was the hard part, Abner Marsh thought. "I don't know," he said honestly. "All them people you say you killed, and still I kind of feel sorry for you. Don't know if I ought to. Maybe I ought to try to kill you, maybe that's the only damn Christian thing to do. Maybe I ought to try to help you." He snorted, annoyed at the dilemma. "I guess what I ought to do is hear you out a little more, and wait before I make up my mind. Cause you left somethin' out, Joshua. That you did."

"Yes?" York prompted.

"New Madrid," said Abner Marsh firmly.

"The blood on my hands," Joshua said. "What can I tell you, Abner? I took a life in New Madrid. But it was not as you might suspect."

"Tell me how it was, then. Go on."

"Simon told me many things of the history of our people; our secrets, our customs, our ways. One thing he said I found greatly disturbing, Abner. This world that your people have built is a daylight world, not easy for us to live in. Sometimes, to make it easier, one of us will turn to one of you. We can use the power that dwells within our eyes and our voice. We can use our strength, our vitality, the promise of life unending. We can use the very legends your people have erected around us, for our own purposes. With lies and fear and promises, we can fashion for ourselves a human thrall. Such a creature can be very useful. He can protect us by day, go where we cannot go, move among men without suspicion.

"In New Madrid there had been a killing. At the very woodyard where we stopped. From what I read in the newspapers, I had great hopes of finding one of my own race. Instead I found—call him what you will. A slave, a pet, an associate. A thrall. He was an old, *old* man. A mulatto, bald and wrinkled and hideous, with a milk-glass eye and a face terribly scarred by some ancient fire. He was not pleasing to look at, and inside—inside he was foul. Corrupt. When I came upon him, he leapt up, brandishing an axe. And then he looked at my eyes. He recognized me, Abner. He knew what I was at once. And he fell to his knees, crying and blubbering, *worshipping* me, groveling as a dog to a man, begging me to fulfill the promise. 'The promise,' he kept saying, 'the promise, the *promise.*'

"Finally I bid him stop, and he did. At once. Cringing away in fear. He had been taught to heed a bloodmaster's words, you see. I asked him to tell me the story of his life, hoping he might lead me to my own people.

"His story was grim as my own. He was born a free man of color in a place called the Swamp, which I gather is a notorious district of New Orleans. He lived as a pimp, a cutpurse, finally a cutthroat, preying on the flatboatmen who came down to the city. He'd killed two men before he was ten. Later he served under Vincent Gambi, the bloodiest of the pirates of Barataria. He was overseer to the slaves Gambi stole from Spanish slavers and resold in New Orleans. He was a voodoo man as well. And he had served us.

"He told me of his bloodmaster, the man who took him in thrall, who laughed at his voodoo and promised to teach him greater, darker magic. Serve me, the bloodmaster had promised, and I will make you one of us. Your scars will heal, your eye will see again, you will drink blood and live forever, never aging. So the mulatto had served. For almost thirty years he did everything he was bid. He lived for the promise. He killed for the promise, was taught to eat warm flesh, to drink blood.

"Until finally his master saw a better opportunity. The mulatto, old and sickly now, became a hindrance. His usefulness passed, so he was discarded. It might have been merciful to kill him, but instead he was sent away, upriver, to fend for himself. A thrall does not go against his bloodmaster, even if he knows the promise made him to be a lie. So the old mulatto had wandered on foot, living by robbery and murder, moving up the river slowly. Sometimes he earned honest money as a slave catcher or laborer, but mostly he kept to himself in the woods, a recluse who lived by night. When he dared, he ate the flesh and drank the blood of his victims, still believing it would help restore his youth and health. He had been living around New Madrid for a year, he told me. He used to chop some wood for the woodyard man, who was too old and feeble to do it himself. He knew how seldom anyone visited that woodyard. So . . . well, you know the rest.

"Abner, your people can learn much from mine. But not the things that he had learned. Not *that*. I felt pity for him. He was old and hideous and without hope. Yet I was angry as well, as angry as I had been in Buda-Pest with the rich woman who liked to wash in blood. In the legends of your race, my people have been made the very essence of evil. The vampire has no soul, no nobility, no hope of redemption, it is said. I will not accept that, Abner. I have killed countless times, have done many terrible things, but I am not evil. I did not *choose* to be the way I was. Without choice, there can be no good nor evil. My people have never had that choice. The red thirst has ruled us, condemned us, robbed us of all we might have been. But *your* people, Abner—they have no such compulsion. That thing I encountered in the forest beyond New Madrid, he had never felt the red thirst, he could have been anything, done anything. Instead he had chosen to become what he was. Oh, to be sure, one of my own race shares the guilt—the man who lied to him, promised him things that could never be. Yet I can understand the reason for that, much as I might loathe it. An ally among your people can make all the difference. All of us know fear, Abner, my race and yours alike.

"What I cannot understand is why one of you would lust so after a life in darkness, would desire the red thirst. Yet he did desire it, with a great passion. He begged me not to leave him, as the other bloodmaster had done. I could not give him what he wanted. I would not, even if it had been possible. I gave him what I could."

"You tore his damn throat out for him, didn't you?" Abner Marsh said to the darkness.

"I told you," Valerie said. Marsh had almost forgotten she was there, quiet as she'd been. "He doesn't understand. Listen to him."

"I killed him," Joshua admitted, "with my bare hands. Yes. His blood ran off my fingers, soaked into the earth. But it did not touch my lips, Abner. And I buried him intact."

Another great silence filled the cabin while Abner Marsh pulled at his beard, and thought. "Choice, you said," he volunteered finally. "That's the difference between good and evil, you said. Now it looks like I'm the one got to make a choice."

"We all make our choices, Abner. Every day."

"Maybe that's so," said Marsh. "I don't much care for this one, though. You say you want my help, Joshua. Let's say I give it. How's that goin' to make me any different from that damned old mulatto you killed, answer me that!"

"I would never make you into—something like that," Joshua said. "I have never tried. Abner, I will live for centuries after you are dead and gone. Have I ever tried to tempt you with that?"

"You tempted me with a goddamn steamboat instead," Marsh replied. "And you sure as hell told me a pack of lies."

"Even my lies have held a kind of truth, Abner. I told you I sought out vampires to put an end to their evil. Can't you see the truth in that? I need your help, Abner, but as a partner, not as a bloodmaster needs a human thrall."

Abner Marsh considered that. "All right," he said. "Maybe I believe you. Maybe I should trust you. But if you want me for a partner, you're goin' to have to trust me, too."

"I've taken you into my confidence. Isn't that enough?"

"Hell, no," said Abner Marsh. "Yeah, you told me the truth, and now you're waitin' for an answer. Only if I give the wrong answer, I don't get to leave this cabin alive, do I? Your lady friend there will see to that even if you don't."

"Very perceptive, Captain Marsh," Valerie said from the darkness. "I bear you no malice, but Joshua must not be harmed."

Marsh snorted. "See what I mean? That ain't trust. We ain't partners on this steamer no more. Things are too goddamned uneven. You can kill me any damn time you want. I got to behave myself or else I'm dead. The way I see it, that makes me a slave, not no partner. I'm alone, too. You got all your damn blood-drinkin' friends aboard to help you out if there's trouble. God knows what you're plannin', you sure don't tell me. But I can't talk to nobody, you say. Hell, Joshua, maybe you ought to kill me right now. I don't think I like this here kind of partnership."

Joshua York considered that in silence for a time. Then he said, "Very well. I see your point. What would you have me do to demonstrate my trust?"

"For a start," said Marsh, "supposin' I wanted to kill you. How would I go about it?"

"*No!*" Valerie cried in alarm. Marsh heard her footsteps as she moved toward Joshua. "You *can't* tell him that. You don't know what he's planning, Joshua. Why would he ask that if he didn't intend to—"

"To make us even," Joshua said softly. "I understand him, Valerie, and it is a risk we must take." She started to plead again, but Joshua hushed her and said to Marsh, "Fire will do it. Drowning. With a gun, aim for the head. Our brains are vulnerable. A shot through the skull would kill me, while a shot to the heart would only knock me down until I healed. The legends are accurate in one respect. If you cut off our heads and hammer a stake through our hearts, we die." He gave a raspy chuckle. "One of your kind would do the same, I think. The sun can be deadly as well, as you have seen. The rest, the silver and garlic, that is all nonsense."

Abner Marsh let out his breath noisily, scarcely aware he'd been holding it. "Boil me for an egg," he said.

"Satisfied?" York asked.

"Almost," Marsh said. "One more thing."

A match scratched against leather, and suddenly a little dancing flame burned in York's cupped palm. He touched it to an oil lamp so the flame crept across to the wick, and a dusky yellow illumination filled the cabin. "There," Joshua said, extinguishing the match with a wave of his hand. "Better, Abner? More even? Partnership demands a little light, don't you think? So we can look each other in the eye."

Abner Marsh found he was blinking back tears; after so long in darkness, even a little light seemed terribly bright. But the room looked larger now, the terror and the suffocating closeness of it melted away. Joshua York was regarding Marsh calmly. His face was covered with husks of dry, dead skin. When he smiled, one crackled and flaked away. His lips were still puffy and he looked as though he had two black eyes, but the burns and blisters were all but gone. The change was astonishing. "What is this other thing, then, Abner?"

Marsh took York at his word and looked him straight in the eye. "I ain't goin' to go this alone," he said. "I'm goin' to tell . . ."

"No," Valerie said, from where she stood by Joshua's side. "One is bad enough, we can't let him spread this. They'll kill us."

"Hell, woman, I wasn't figurin' on putting' no advertisement in the *True Delta*, you know."

Joshua steepled his fingers and regarded Marsh thoughtfully. "Just what were you figuring then, Abner?"

"One or two people," Marsh said. "I ain't the only one who's been suspicious, you know. And it could be you'll need more help than I can give you. I'll only talk to them I know I can trust. Hairy Mike, for one. And Mister Jeffers, he's damn smart and he's already been wonderin' over you. The rest don't need to know. Mister Albright is a mite too prim and godly to hear all this, and if you told Mister Framm it'd be all over the river inside of a week. The whole damn texas could burn off without Whitey Blake noticin', so long as his engines weren't bothered none. But Jeffers and Hairy Mike, they ought to know. They're good men, and you may need 'em."

"Need them?" Joshua said. "How is that, Abner?"

"What if one of your folks don't fancy that drink of yours?"

Joshua York's genial smile vanished abruptly. He stood up, walked across the cabin, and poured himself a drink: whiskey, neat. When he turned back he was still frowning. "Perhaps," he said. "I need to think on this. If they can truly be trusted . . . I have certain misgivings about the trip down the bayou."

For once, Valerie did not utter the expected protest. Marsh glanced at her, and saw that her lips were pressed tightly together, and in her eyes was something that might just have been the beginnings of fear. "What's wrong?" Marsh said. "Both of you look . . . queer."

Valerie's head snapped up. "*Him*," she said. "I asked you to turn back upriver. I would ask it again, if I thought either of you might listen. *He* is down there at Cypress Landing."

"Who?" Marsh asked, baffled.

"A bloodmaster," Joshua said. "Abner, understand that all my kind do not think as I do. Even among my own followers, well, Simon is loyal, Smith and Brown are passive, but Katherine—from the very beginning, I have felt the resentment in her. I think there is a darkness at the center of her, something that prefers the old ways, that grieves for the ship she missed and chafes under my domination. She obeys because she must. I am bloodmaster. But she does not like it. And the others, those we have taken aboard on the river—I am not sure of them. Except for Valerie and Jean Ardant, I trust none of them fully. Remember your warnings to me about Raymond Ortega? I share your misgivings about him. Valerie means nothing to him, so you were wrong in thinking jealousy a motive, yet otherwise right. To bring Raymond aboard at Natchez, I had to conquer him, as I conquered Simon so long ago in the Carpathians. With Cara de Gruy and Vincent Thibaut, there were other struggles. Now they follow me, because they must. It is the way of my people. Yet I wonder if some of them, at least, are not waiting. Waiting to see what will happen when the *Fevre Dream* steams down the bayou, and I come face to face with he who was master of them all.

"Valerie has told me much of him. He is old, Abner. Older than Simon or Katherine, older than any of us. His age itself disturbs me. Now he calls himself Damon Julian, but before that name he was Giles Lamont, the same Giles Lamont whom that wretched mulatto served for thirty futile years. I am told he has another human thrall now—"

"Sour Billy Tipton," Valerie said with loathing.

"Valerie is afraid of this Julian," Joshua York said. "The others also speak of him with fear, but sometimes with a certain loyalty as well. As bloodmaster, he took care of them. He gave them sanctuary, wealth, and feasts. They feasted on slaves. No wonder he chose to settle where he did."

Valerie shook her head. "Leave him, Joshua. Please. For me, if for no other reason. Damon will not welcome your coming, will not cherish the freedom you bring."

Joshua scowled in annoyance. "He still has others of our people with him. Would you have me abandon them as well? No. And you may be wrong about Julian. He has been in the grip of the red thirst for uncounted centuries, and I can soothe that fever."

Valerie crossed her arms, her violet eyes furious. "And if he will not be soothed? You do not know him, Joshua."

"He is educated, intelligent, cultured, a lover of beauty," York said stubbornly. "You said as much."

"He is *strong* as well."

"As with Simon, and Raymond, and Cara. They follow me now."

"Damon is different," Valerie insisted. "It is not the same!"

Joshua York made an impatient gesture. "It makes no difference. I will control him."

Abner Marsh had watched them argue in thoughtful silence, but now he spoke up. "Joshua's right," he said to Valerie. "Hell, I looked in his eyes once or twice myself, and he nearly busted every bone in my hand the first time we shook. Besides, what was it you called him? A king?"

"Yes," Valerie admitted. "The pale king."

"Well, if he's this pale king of yours, it stands to reason that he's got to win, don't it?"

Valerie glanced from Marsh to York and back again. Then she trembled. "You haven't seen him, either of you." She hesitated a moment, tossed her dark hair back with a pale slender hand, and faced Abner Marsh squarely. "Perhaps I was wrong about you, Captain Marsh. I do not have Joshua's strength, nor his trust. I have been ruled by the red thirst for half a century. Your people were my prey. You cannot befriend your prey. You *cannot*. You cannot trust them either. That was why I urged Joshua to kill you. You cannot just cast aside the cautions of a lifetime. Do you understand?"

Abner Marsh nodded warily.

"I am still uncertain," Valerie continued, "but Joshua has been showing us many new things, and I am willing to admit that perhaps you can be trusted. Perhaps." She scowled fiercely. "But whether or not I was wrong about you, I am *right* about Damon Julian!"

Abner Marsh frowned, not knowing what to say. Joshua reached out and took Valerie's hand in his own. "I think you are wrong to be so fearful," he said. "But for your sake, I will move with all caution. Abner, do as you wish, tell Mister Jeffers and Mister Dunne. It will be good to have their help if Valerie is right. Choose the men for a special watch, and let the rest ashore. When the *Fevre Dream* steams up the bayou, I want her manned only by our best and most reliable, the bare minimum needed to run her. No religious fanatics, no one who is easily frightened, no one prone to rashness."

"Hairy Mike and I will do the pickin'," Marsh said.

"I will meet Julian on my own steamer, in my own time, with you and the best of your men behind me. Be careful how you tell Jeffers and Dunne. It must be done correctly." He looked at Valerie. "Satisfied?"

"No," she said.

Joshua smiled. "I can do no more." He looked back at Abner Marsh. "Abner, I am glad you are not my enemy. I am close now, my dreams at hand. In beating the red thirst, I had my first great triumph. I would like to think that here, tonight, you and I have fashioned a second, the beginning of friendship and trust between -our races. The *Fevre Dream* will steam on the razor edge between night and day, banishing the specter of old fear wherever she goes. We will achieve great things together, friend."

Marsh didn't care over much for flowery talk, but Joshua's passion reached him nonetheless and he gave a grudging smile. "Got a lot of work to do before we achieve any goddamned thing at all," Marsh said, gathering up his walking stick and getting to his feet. "I'll be goin', then."

"Fine," Joshua said, smiling. "I will take my rest, and see you once again at twilight. Make certain the boat is ready to depart. We'll get this done with as quickly as we can."

"I'll have our steam up," Marsh said as he took his leave.

Outside, day had come.

It looked to be about nine, Abner Marsh thought as he stood blinking outside the captain's cabin, after Joshua had locked the door behind him. The morning was dismal; hot and muggy, with a heavy gray overcast that hid the sun. Soot and smoke from steamers on the river hung in the air. There's going to be a storm, Abner Marsh thought, and the prospect was one he found disheartening. He was suddenly aware of how little sleep he'd gotten, and felt inutterably tired, but there was so much to do that he dared not even consider a nap.

He descended to the main saloon, figuring that breakfast would give him some spirit. He drank a gallon of hot black coffee while Toby cooked him up some boiled beefcakes and waffles, with blueberries on the side. As he was eating, Jonathon Jeffers entered the saloon, saw him, and came striding over to the table.

"Sit down and eat somethin'," Marsh said. "Want to have a long talk with you, Mister Jeffers. Not here, though. Better wait till I'm through and then go to my cabin."

"Fine," Jeffers replied, in a distracted sort of way. "Cap'n, where have you been? I've been looking for you for hours. You weren't in your cabin."

"Joshua and I were chattin'," Marsh said. "What . . . ?"

"There's a man here to see you," Jeffers said. "He came aboard in the middle of the night. He's very insistent."

"Don't like to be kept around waitin', like I'm some no-count trash," the stranger said. Marsh hadn't even seen the man enter. Without so much as a by-your-leave, the man pulled out a chair and sat down. He was an ugly, haggard-looking cuss, his long face cratered by the pox. Thin, limp brown hair hung down in strands across his forehead. His complexion was unhealthy, and patches of hair and skin were covered by scaly white flakes, like he'd been in his own private snowfall. Yet he wore an expensive black broadcloth suit, and a ruffled white shirtfront, and a cameo ring.

Abner Marsh didn't care for his looks, his tone, the flat press of his lips, his ice-colored eyes. "Who the hell are you?" he said gruffly. "You better have a damn good reason for botherin' me at breakfast, or I'll have you chucked over the damn side." Just saying so made Marsh feel somewhat better. He'd always figured there was no use being a steamboat captain if you couldn't tell somebody to go to hell once in a while.

The stranger's sour expression changed not a flicker, but he fixed his icy eyes on Marsh with a kind of smirking malice. "I'm goin' to be takin' passage on this fancy raft of yours."

"The hell you are," Marsh said.

"Shall I call Hairy Mike to deal with this ruffian?" Jeffers offered coolly.

The man looked at the clerk with brief contempt. His eyes moved back to Marsh. "Cap'n Marsh, I come last night to bring you an invite, for you and your partner. Figured one o' you, at least, be out and about by night. Well, it's day now, so it'll have to be tonight instead. Dinner at the St. Louis, along about an hour past sunset, you and Cap'n York."

"I don't know you and I don't care for you," Marsh said. "I sure ain't goin' to have dinner with you. Besides, the *Fevre Dream* is steamin' out tonight."

"I know. Know where, too."

Marsh frowned. "What are you sayin'?"

"You don't know niggers, I can tell. Nigger hears somethin', before long ever' nigger in the city knows it. And me, I lissen good. You don't want to take this big ol' steamer of yours up the bayou to where you're fixin' to go. You'll ground yourself for sure, maybe rip out your bottom. I can save you all the trouble. Y'see, the man you lookin' for is right here waitin' for you. So, when dark comes, you go tell that to your master, you hear? You tell him that Damon Julian is waiting for him at the St. Louis Hotel. Mister Julian is right eager to make his acquaintance."

CHAPTER SIXTEEN

New Orleans,
August 1857

SOUR Billy Tipton returned to the St. Louis Hotel that evening more than a little fearful. Julian would not like the message he carried from the *Fevre Dream*, and Julian was dangerous and unpredictable when displeased.

In the darkened parlor of their lavish suite, only a single small candle had been lighted. Its flame was reflected in Julian's black eyes as he sat in the deep velvet chair near the window, sipping a sazerac. The room was full of silence. Sour Billy felt the weight of the stares upon him. The latch made a small, deadly *snick* when the door shut behind him. "Yes, Billy?" said Damon Julian, softly.

"They won't come, Mister Julian," Sour Billy said, a little too quickly, a little too breathlessly. In the dim light he could not see Julian's reaction. "He says you got to come to him."

"He says," repeated Julian. "Who is *he*, Billy?"

"Him," said Sour Billy. "The . . . the other bloodmaster. Joshua York, he calls hisself. The one that Raymond wrote you about. The other cap'n, Marsh, the fat one with the warts and the whiskers, he wouldn't come neither. Damned rude, too. But I waited for dark, waited for the bloodmaster to get up. Finally they took me to 'im." Sour Billy still felt cold, remembering the way that York's gray, gray eyes had touched his own, and found him wanting. There had been such bitter contempt there that Billy had wrenched his gaze away at once.

"Tell us, Billy," said Damon Julian, "what is he like, this other? This Joshua York. This *bloodmaster*."

"He's . . . " Billy began, fumbling for words, "he's . . . *white*, I mean, his skin and all is real pale, and his hair ain't got no color in it. He even wore a white suit, like some kind of ha'nt. And silver, he wore lots of silver. The way he moves . . . like one of them damn Creoles, Mister Julian, high and lordly. He's . . . he's like you, Mister Julian. His *eyes* . . ."

"Pale and strong," murmured Cynthia from the far corner of the room. "And with a wine that conquers the red thirst. Is he the one, Damon? He must be. It must be true. Valerie always believed the stories, and I mocked her for it, but it must be so. He will bring us all together, lead us back to the lost city, the dark city. Our kingdom, our own. It *is* true, isn't it? He is bloodmaster of bloodmasters, the king we have waited for." She looked at Damon Julian for an answer.

Damon Julian tasted his sazerac and smiled a sly, feline smile. "A king," he mused. "And what did this king say to you, Billy? Tell us."

"He said to come to the steamer, all of you. Tomorrow, after dark. For dinner, he said. Him and Marsh, they won't come here, not like you wanted, alone. Marsh, he said that if they come to you it's goin' to be with others."

"The king is strangely timid," Julian commented.

"Kill him!" Sour Billy blurted suddenly. "Go to that damn boat and kill him, kill 'em all. He's *wrong*, Mister Julian. His eyes, like some damn Creole, the way he looked at me. Like I was a bug, a no-count, even though I come from *you*. He thinks he's better'n you, and them others, that warty cap'n and this damn clerk, all dandied up, let me cut him, bleed him some all over them fine clothes of his, you got to go kill him, you *got* to."

The room was silent after Sour Billy's outburst. Julian stared out the window, off into the night. The windows had been thrown wide, so the curtains stirred lazily in the night air and street noises drifted up from below. Julian's eyes were dark, hooded, fixed on distant lights.

When at last he turned his head, his pupils caught the gleam of the single candle flame again, and held it within, red and flickering. His face took on a lean, feral cast. "The drink, Billy," he prompted.

"He makes 'em all drink it," Sour Billy said. He leaned back against the door and pulled out his knife. It made him feel better to have it in hand. He began scraping crud out from under his nails as he spoke. "It ain't just blood, Cara said. Something else in it. It kills the thirst, they all say that. I went all over that boat, talked to Raymond

and Jean and Jorge, a couple others. They told me. Jean kept ravin'
about this drink, about what a relief it was, if you can believe that."

"Jean," said Julian with disdain.

"It *is* true, then," Cynthia said. "He is greater than the thirst."

"There's more," Sour Billy added. "Raymond says York has taken
up with Valerie."

The stillness in the parlor was full of tension. Kurt frowned. Michelle averted her eyes. Cynthia sipped at her drink. All of them
knew that Valerie, beautiful Valerie, had been Julian's special pet; all
of them watched him carefully. Julian seemed pensive. "Valerie?" he
said. "I see." Long, pale fingers tapped on the arm of his chair.

Sour Billy Tipton picked at his teeth with the point of his knife,
pleased. He'd figured that bit about Valerie would settle it. Damon
Julian had had plans for Valerie, and Julian did not like his plans
disturbed. He'd told Billy all about it, with an air of sly amusement,
when Billy had asked him why he'd gone and sent her away. "Raymond is young and strong, and he can hold her," Julian had said.
"They will be alone, the two of them, alone with each other and the
thirst. Such a romantic vision, don't you think? And in a year, or
two, or five, Valerie will be with child. I would almost bet on it,
Billy." And then he had laughed that deep musical laugh of his. But
he was not laughing now.

"What will we do, Damon?" Kurt asked. "Are we going?"

"Why, of course," Julian said. "We could hardly refuse such a kind
invitation, and from a king at that. Don't you want to taste this wine
of his?" He looked at each of them in turn, and none of them dared
speak. "Ah," said Julian, "where is your enthusiasm? Jean recom-
mends this vintage to us, and Valerie as well, no doubt. A wine
sweeter than blood, thick with the stuff of life. Think of the peace it
will bring us." He smiled. No one spoke, He waited. When the quiet
had gone on a long while, Julian shrugged and said, "Well, then, I
hope the king will not think less of us if we prefer other drinks."

"He makes the rest of 'em drink it," Sour Billy said. "Whether they
want to or not."

"Damon," Cynthia said, "will you . . . refuse him? You can't. We
must go to him. We must do as he bids us. We *must*."

Julian turned his head slowly to look at her. "Do you really think
so?" he asked, smiling thinly.

"Yes," Cynthia whispered. "We must. He is bloodmaster." She
averted her eyes.

"Cynthia," said Damon Julian, "look at me."

Slowly, with infinite reluctance, she raised her head again, until her gaze met Julian's. "No," she whimpered. "Please. Oh, please."

Damon Julian said nothing. Cynthia did not look away. She slipped from her chair, knelt on the carpet, trembling. A bracelet of spun gold and amethysts shone on her small wrist. She pushed it aside, and her lips parted slowly, as if she were about to speak, and then she raised her hand and touched mouth to wrist. The blood began to flow.

Julian waited until she had crawled across the carpet, her arm extended in offering. With grave courtesy he took her hand in his, and drank long and deeply. When he was done Cynthia got to her feet unsteadily, slipped back to one knee, and rose again, shaking. "Bloodmaster," she said, head bowed. "Bloodmaster."

Damon Julian's lips were red and wet, and a tiny bead of blood had trickled down one corner of his mouth. Julian took a handkerchief from his pocket, carefully blotted the thin line of moisture from his chin, and tucked it neatly away. "Is it a large steamer, Billy?" he asked.

Sour Billy sheathed his knife behind him with a practiced, easy motion, smiling. The wound on Cynthia's wrist, the blood on Julian's chin, it all left him hot, excited. Julian would show those damn steamboat people, he thought. "Big as any steamboat I ever seen," he answered, "and fancy too. Silver and mirrors and marble, lots of stained glass and carpet. You'll like her, Mister Julian."

"A steamboat," mused Damon Julian. "Why did I never think of the river, I wonder? The advantages are so obvious."

"Then we are going?" said Kurt.

"Yes," said Julian. "Oh yes. Why, the bloodmaster has summoned us. The king." He laughed, throwing back his head, roaring. "The king!" he cried between gusts of laughter. "The *king!*" One by one the others began to laugh with him.

Julian rose abruptly, like a jackknife unfolding, his face gone solemn again, and the uproar quieted as suddenly as it had begun. He stared out into the darkness beyond the hotel. "We must bring a gift," he said. "One does not call upon royalty without a gift." He turned to Sour Billy. "Tomorrow you will go down to Moreau Street, Billy. There is something I wish you to get for me. A little gift, for our pale king."

CHAPTER SEVENTEEN

Aboard the Steamer FEVRE DREAM, New Orleans, August 1857————

IT seemed as though half the steamers in New Orleans had decided to leave that afternoon, Abner Marsh thought as he stood upon the hurricane deck and watched them all depart.

The custom was for boats going upriver to make their departure from the levee about five o'clock. At three the engineers would fire the furnaces and start to get the steam up. Rosin and pitch-pine would get chucked into the steamers' hungry maws, along with wood and coal, and from one boat after another the black smoke would start to rise, ascending from the lofty flowered chimneys in tall hot columns, dark pennants of farewell. Four miles of steamboats packed solid along the levee can generate a lot of smoke. The sooty columns would start to blend together into one massive black cloud a couple hundred feet above the river; a cloud shot through with ash, full of hot bright cinders, adrift on the wind. Larger and larger the cloud would swell as still more steamers fired up and poured out smoke, until the pall blotted out the sun and began to creep across the face of the city.

From Abner Marsh's vantage point on the hurricane deck, it looked as though the whole city of New Orleans was going up in flames, and all the steamers were about to flee. It made him feel uneasy, as if somehow the other captains knew something he did not, as if the *Fevre Dream*, too, ought to be getting up her steam and making ready to back out. Marsh was anxious to be off. For all the wealth and glamour of the New Orleans trade, he yearned for the rivers he knew: for the upper Mississippi with its bluffs and dense woods, for the wild muddy Missouri that ate steamers like nobody's business, for the narrow Illinois and the silty, bustling Fevre. The *Fevre Dream*'s maiden voyage down the Ohio seemed almost idyllic to him now, a remembrance of simpler, better days. Not even two months gone, it seemed an eternity ago. Ever since they'd left St. Louis and come downriver, things had been going wrong, and the further south they'd come the worse they'd gotten. "Joshua is right," Marsh muttered to himself as he looked out over New Orleans. "There's something rotten here." It was too damn hot, too damn wet, with too damn many bugs, enough to make a man think there was a curse on the whole damn place. And maybe there was, on account of the slavery, though Marsh wasn't sure about that. All he was sure of was that he wanted to tell Whitey to fire up the boilers, and roust Framm or Albright up to the pilot house, so he could back the *Fevre Dream* clear of the landing and get her upriver. Now. Before sunset. Before *they* arrived.

Abner Marsh wanted to shout those orders so bad he could taste the words, lying bitter and unspoken on his tongue. He felt a kind of superstitious dread about this evening, though he told himself over and over that he was not a superstitious man. Still, he wasn't blind either—the sky was hot and suffocating, and west of them a storm was building, a big one, a ripper, the storm that Dan Albright had smelled a couple days back. And the steamers were leaving, one after another, dozens of them, and as Marsh watched them recede upriver and vanish in the shimmering waves of heat, he felt more and more alone, as if each steamboat that faded into the distance carried a small bit of him aboard her, a piece of courage, a hunk of his certainty, a dream or a small, sooty hope. Lots of steamers left New Orleans every day, Marsh thought to himself, and today is no different, it's just a day like any other day on the river in August: hot and smoky and lazy, everyone moving slow, waiting, maybe for a breath of cool air or for the clean, fresh rain that would wash the smoke from the sky.

But another part of him, an older and deeper part, knew that what they waited for was neither cool nor clean, and it would bring no relief from the heat, the dampness, the bugs, the fear.

Down below, Hairy Mike was roaring at his roustabouts, and making threatening gestures with his black iron billet, but the noises from the landing and the bells and whistles of the other steamers drowned out his words. A mountain of cargo waited on the levee, almost a thousand tons, the *Fevre Dream*'s top capacity. Hardly a quarter of it had been carried across the narrow planks to the main deck. It would take hours to get the rest aboard. Even if he wanted to, Marsh could not take them out, not with all that freight a-waiting on the landing. Hairy Mike and Jeffers and the rest would think he'd gone mad.

He wished he'd been able to tell them, like he'd intended to, to make plans with them. But there wasn't time. Everything had begun to move so quickly, and tonight after dark this Damon Julian would come aboard the *Fevre Dream* to dine. There was no time to talk to Hairy Mike or Jonathon Jeffers, no time to explain or persuade or deal with the doubts and questions they'd surely have. So tonight Abner Marsh would be alone, or almost alone, just him and Joshua in a room full of *them*, the night folks. Marsh did not count Joshua York with the others. He was different, somehow. And Joshua said that everything would go well, Joshua had his drink, Joshua was full of fine sounding words and dreams. But Abner Marsh had his misgivings.

The *Fevre Dream* was quiet, almost deserted. Joshua had sent almost everyone ashore; the dinner tonight would be as private as he could make it. That wasn't the way Abner Marsh would have liked it, but there was no arguing with Joshua when he got a notion in his head. In the main cabin, the table was already set. The lamps had not been lighted yet, and the smoke and steam and building storm outside had all conspired to make the illumination that poured through the skylights dim and somber and tired. It seemed to Marsh as if twilight had already come to the saloon, and to his steamer. The carpets looked almost black, the mirrors were full of shadows. Behind the long black marble bar, a man was cleaning glasses, but even he was indistinct somehow, faded. Marsh nodded to him nonetheless, and made his way to the kitchen, aft of the wheelhouse. Behind the kitchen doors he found activity; a couple of Toby's kitchen boys were stirring big copper pots or pan-frying chicken, while the waiters lounged around and joked with each other. Marsh could smell pies baking in the huge ovens. It made his mouth water, but he pushed past, resolute. He found Toby in the starboard galley, surrounded on all sides by stacks of cages full of chickens and pigeons and here and there some robins and ducks and such. The birds were making a terrible racket. Toby looked up when Marsh entered. The cook had been killing chickens. Three headless birds were piled up by his elbows, and a fourth was on the block in front of him, struggling fitfully. Toby had the cleaver in hand. "Why, Cap'n Marsh," he said, smiling. He brought the cleaver down smartly, with a solid *thunk*.

Blood spurted, and the headless chicken thrashed crazily when Toby released it. His hard black hands were drenched with blood. He wiped them on his apron. "What kin I do fer you?" he asked.

"I just wanted to tell you, tonight, when dinner's done, I want you off the boat," Marsh said. "You serve us up good and proper, and then you get. And take your kitchen boys and them waiters with you. You understand, do you? You hear what I'm sayin'?"

"I surely do, Cap'n," Toby said with a grin. "I surely do. Goin' to have a lil' party, is you?"

"Never you mind about that," Marsh said. "Just see that you get ashore when you're done workin'." He turned to go, stern-faced. But something made him turn back. "Toby," he said.

"Yessuh?"

"You know I never held much with slavery, even if I never done much against it neither. I would of, but those damned abolitionists were such Bible-thumpers. Only I been thinkin', and it seems to me maybe they was right after all. You can't just go . . . usin' another kind of people, like they wasn't people at all. Know what I mean? Got to end, sooner or later. Better if it ends peaceful, but it's got to end even if it has to be with fire and blood, you see? Maybe that's what them abolitionists been sayin' all along. You try to be reasonable, that's only right, but if it don't work, you got to be ready. Some things is just wrong. They got to be ended."

Toby was looking at him queerly, still absent-mindedly wiping his hands across the front of his apron, back and forth, back and forth. "Cap'n," he said softly, "you is talkin' abolition. This here is slave country, Cap'n. You could git kilt fo' sech talk."

"Maybe I could, Toby, but right is right, that's what I say."

"You done good by ol' Toby, Cap'n Marsh, givin' me my freedom and all so's I could cook fo' you. That you did."

Abner Marsh nodded. "Toby," he said, "why don't you go fetch me a knife from the kitchen. Don't say nothing about it, you hear? Just go fetch me a good sharp knife. It ought to be able to slide down into my boot, I think. Can you get me a knife?"

"Yessuh, Cap'n Marsh," said Toby. His eyes narrowed just a little in his worn black face. "Yessuh." Then he ran to obey.

Abner Marsh walked a little strangely for the next couple hours, with the long kitchen knife snugly tucked into his high leather boot. By the time dark had fallen, however, the blade had begun to feel damned comfortable, and he almost forgot that it was there.

The storm came just before sunset. Most of the steamers headed upriver were long gone by then, although others had come to take their places along the New Orleans levee. The storm broke, with a terrible roaring sound like a steamer's boilers going up, and the lightning flashed overhead, and the rain came a-screaming down, torrential as a spring flood. Marsh stood beneath the cover of the boiler deck promenade, listening to the water pound against his steamer and watching folks on the landing scramble for cover. He had been standing there for the longest time, leaning on the rail and thinking, when suddenly Joshua York was there beside him. "It's rainin', Joshua," Marsh said, pointing his stick out into the storm. "Maybe this Julian won't be coming tonight. Maybe he don't want to get wet."

Joshua York wore a strange solemn look. "He will come," he said. That was all. Just, "He will come."

And—finally—he did.

The storm had subsided by then. The rain still came down and down, but it was gentler, softer, hardly more than a mist. Abner Marsh was still on the boiler deck, and he saw them coming, striding across the deserted, rain-slick levee. Even at a distance, he knew it was them. There was something about the way they walked, something graceful and predatory, full of a terrible beauty. One of them walked different, swaggering and sliding like he was trying to be one of them but couldn't and when they came closer Marsh saw that it was Sour Billy Tipton. He was carrying something awkwardly.

Abner Marsh went on into the grand saloon. The others were all at table: Simon and Katherine, Smith and Brown, Raymond and Jean and Valerie and all the others that Joshua had gathered along the river. They were talking softly, but they fell silent when Marsh entered. "They're coming," Marsh said. Joshua York rose from his seat at the head of the table and went to meet them. Abner Marsh went to the bar and poured himself a whiskey. He drained it in a gulp, had another quickly, then went to the table. Joshua had insisted Marsh sit right up by the head, on his left-hand side. The chair to his right was saved for this Damon Julian. Marsh plopped down heavily and scowled at the empty place across from him.

And then they entered.

Only the four night folks came into the saloon, Marsh noted. Sour Billy had been left behind somewhere, which suited him just fine. There were two women, and a huge white-faced man who frowned darkly and shook the moisture from his coat. And the other, *him*, Marsh knew him instantly. He had a smooth ageless face framed by black curls, and he looked like some kind of lord in his dark burgundy suit, with a loose-collared silk shirt all ruffled down the front. On one finger he wore a gold ring with a sapphire the size of a sugar cube, and fastened to his black vest was a headlight, a polished chunk of black diamond in a soft web of yellow gold. He moved across the room and then—rounding the table—he paused, and stood by Joshua's place, behind the chair at the head of the table. He put his smooth white hands up on the chair back, and he *looked* at them, one by one, all along the table.

And they rose.

The three who had come with him first, and then Raymond Ortega, and then Cara, and then the rest, in ones and twos, Valerie last of all. Everyone in the room was standing, everyone but Abner Marsh. Damon Julian smiled a charming, warm smile. "It is good to be together with all of you once again," he said. He looked especially at Katherine. "My dear, how many years has it been? How very many years?"

The grin that lit her vulture-face was terrible to behold, Marsh thought. He decided to take matters into his own hands. "Sit down," he barked up at Damon Julian. He tugged him by the sleeve. "I'm hungry, and we've waited supper just about long enough."

"Yes," said Joshua, and that broke the spell, and everyone took seats again. But Julian took Joshua's seat, the seat at the head of the table.

Joshua came and stood over Julian. "You are in my seat," he said. His voice seemed flat and tense. "This one is yours, sir. If you will be so kind." York gestured. His eyes were fixed on Damon Julian, and Marsh glanced up at Joshua's face and saw the power there, the cold intensity, the determination.

Damon Julian smiled. "Ah," he said softly. He shrugged slightly. "Pardon." Then, never looking up at Joshua York for even an instant, he rose and moved to the other seat.

Joshua seated himself stiffly, and made an impatient motion with his fingers. A waiter came hurrying from the shadows and deposited a bottle on the table in front of York. "Kindly leave the room," Joshua told the youth.

The bottle was unlabeled. Beneath the chandeliers, surrounded by gleaming crystal and silver, it seemed dark and threatening. It had been opened. "You know what this is," Joshua York said flatly to Damon Julian.

"Yes."

York reached out, took up Julian's wine glass, and poured. He filled the glass to the brim, and put it down again squarely in front of the other. "Drink," he ordered.

York's eyes were on Julian. Julian stared at the glass, a faint smile playing around the corners of his mouth, as if he were involved in some secret amusement. The grand saloon was utterly silent. Far off in the distance, Marsh heard the faint wail of a steamer struggling through the rain. The moment seemed to last forever.

Damon Julian reached out, took up the glass, and drank. In a single long draught, he emptied the glass, and it was as if he drank all the tension from the room. Joshua smiled, Abner Marsh grunted, and down at the far end of the table, others traded wary, puzzled glances. York poured three more glasses, and had them passed down to Julian's three companions. All of them drank. Conversations began in low whispers.

Damon Julian smiled at Abner Marsh. "Your steamer is most impressive, Captain Marsh," he said cordially. "I hope the food is as excellent."

"The food," said Marsh, "is better." He bellowed, feeling almost like his own self again, and the waiters began bringing out the feast that Toby had cooked up. For more than an hour, they ate. The night folks had fine manners, but their appetites were healthy as any riverman's. They went at the food like a bunch of roustabouts who'd just heard the mate shout, "Grub-pile!" All except Damon Julian, that was. Julian ate slowly, almost delicately, pausing often to sip at his wine, smiling frequently for no apparent reason. Marsh had cleaned off his third platter, and Julian's plate was still half-full. Conversation was relaxed and inconsequential. Those far away talked low and heatedly, so Marsh couldn't make out what they were saying. Up close, Joshua York and Damon Julian mouthed a lot of words about the storm, the heat, the river, and the *Fevre Dream*. Except for when they were talking about his steamer, Abner Marsh took little interest, preferring to concentrate on his plate.

Finally coffee and brandy were served, and then the waiters faded away, and the main cabin of the steamer was empty but for Abner Marsh and the night folks. Marsh sipped at his brandy and heard the noise he made sucking it up before he quite realized that all conversations had ceased. "We are together at last," Joshua said, in a quiet voice, "and this is a new beginning for us, for the people of the night.

Those who live by day might call it a new dawning." He smiled. "For us, a new sunset might be a more appropriate metaphor. Listen, all of you. Let me tell you of my plans." Then Joshua rose, and began to speak in earnest.

How long he spoke Abner Marsh was not sure. Marsh had heard it all before; freedom from the red thirst, an end of fear, trust between day and night, the things that would be achieved by partnership, the grand new epoch. On and on Joshua went, eloquent, impassioned, his speech full of little snatches of poems and five-dollar words. Marsh paid more attention to the others, to the rows of pale faces all up and down the table. All of them had their eyes on Joshua, all of them were listening, silent. But they weren't all the same. Simon seemed a little jumpy, and kept glancing from York to Julian and back again. Jean Ardant looked rapt and worshipful, but some of the other faces were blank and cold and hard to read. Raymond Ortega was smiling slyly, and the big one called Kurt was frowning, and Valerie looked nervous, and Katherine—she had on her thin, hard face such a look of utter loathing that Marsh flinched to see it.

Then Marsh looked directly across the table to where Damon Julian was seated, and found Julian staring back at him. His eyes were black, hard and shiny as a lump of the best coal. Marsh saw pits there, endless bottomless pits, a chasm waiting to swallow them all up. He wrenched his eyes away, unwilling to even try to stare down Julian, as he had foolishly tried to stare down York so long ago at the Planters' House. Julian smiled, glanced up again at Joshua, sipped at his cold coffee, and listened. Abner Marsh did not like that smile, nor the depth of those eyes. All at once he was afraid again.

And finally Joshua finished, and sat down.

"The steamboat is a fine idea," Julian said pleasantly. His soft voice carried the length of the saloon. "Your drink may even have its uses. From time to time. The rest, dear Joshua, you must forget." His tone was charming, his smile relaxed and brilliant.

Someone drew in his breath sharply, but no one dared to speak. Abner Marsh sat up very straight. Joshua frowned. "Excuse me," he said.

Julian made a languid gesture of dismissal. "Your story makes me sad, dear Joshua," he said. "Raised among the cattle, now you think as they do. It is not your fault, of course. In time you will learn, you will celebrate your true nature. They have corrupted you, these little animals you have lived among, they have filled you with their small moralities, their feeble religions, their tedious dreams."

"What are you saying?" Joshua's voice was angry.

Julian did not answer him directly. Instead he turned to Marsh. "Captain Marsh," he asked, "that roast you so enjoyed was once part of a living animal. Do you suppose that, if that beast could talk, he would consent to being eaten?" His eyes, those fierce black eyes, were locked on Marsh, demanding an answer.

"I . . . hell, no . . . but . . ."

"But you eat him anyway, do you not?" Julian laughed lightly. "Of *course* you do, Captain, don't be ashamed of it."

"I ain't ashamed," Marsh said stoutly. "It's only a cow."

"Of course it is," said Julian, "and cattle are cattle." He looked back at Joshua York. "But the cattle may see it differently. However, that ought not trouble the captain here. He is a higher order of being than his cow. It is his nature to kill and eat, and the cow's to be killed and eaten. You see, Joshua, life is really very simple.

"Your errors rise from being raised among cows, who have taught you not to consume them. *Evil*, you talk about. Where did you learn that concept? From them, of course, from the cattle. Good and evil, those are cattle words, empty, intended only to preserve their worthless lives. They live and die in mortal dread of us, their natural superiors. We haunt even their dreams, so they seek solace in lies, and invent gods who have power over *us*, wanting to believe that somehow crosses and holy water can master us.

"You must understand, dear Joshua, that there is no good or evil, only strength and weakness, masters and slaves. You are feverish with their morality, with guilt and shame. How foolish that is. These are *their* words, not ours. You preach of new beginnings, but what shall we begin? To be as cattle? To burn beneath their sun, work when we might take, bow to cattle gods? No. They are animals, our natural inferiors, our great and beautiful prey. That is the way of things."

"*No*," said Joshua York. He pushed back his chair and rose, so he stood over the table like a pale, slender goliath. "They *think*, they dream, and they have built a world, Julian. You are wrong. We are cousins, both sides of the same coin. They are not prey. Look at all they have done! They bring beauty into the world. What have *we* created? Nothing. The red thirst has been our bane."

Damon Julian sighed. "Ah, poor Joshua," he said. He sipped his brandy. "Let the cattle create—life, beauty, what you will. And we shall take their creations, use them, destroy them if we choose. That is the way of it. We are the masters. Masters do not labor. Let them make the suits. We shall wear them. Let them build the steamboats. We shall ride upon them. Let them dream of life eternal. We shall live it, and drink of their lives, and savor the blood. We are the lords of this earth, and that is our heritage. Our destiny, if you will, dear Joshua. Exult in your nature, Joshua, do not seek to change it. Those cattle who truly know us envy us. Any of them would be as we are, given the choice." Julian smiled maliciously. "Have you ever wondered why this Jesus Christ of theirs bid his followers to drink his blood, if they would live forever?" He chuckled. "They burn to be like us, just as the darkies dream of being white. You see how far they go. To play at being masters, they even enslave their own kind."

"As you do, Julian," said Joshua York, dangerously. "What else do you call the dominion you have held over our people? Even those you call masters you make slaves to your own twisted will."

"Even we have strong and weak among us, dear Joshua," said Damon Julian. "It is fitting that the strong should lead." Julian set down his glass and looked far down the table. "Kurt," he said, "summon Billy."

"Yes, Damon," said the big man, rising.

"Where are you going?" Joshua demanded, as Kurt strode from the room, his image moving purposefully across a dozen mirrors.

"You have played at being cattle long enough, Joshua," said Julian. "I am going to teach you what it means to be a master."

Abner Marsh felt cold and frightened. All the eyes in the room were glassy, transfixed, watching the drama at the head of the table. Standing, Joshua York seemed to tower over the seated Damon Julian, but somehow he did not dominate. Joshua's gray eyes looked as strong and passionate as a man's could be. But Julian wasn't a man at all, Marsh thought.

Kurt was back in less than a moment. Sour Billy must have been just outside somewhere, like a slave waiting for his master's summons. Kurt took his place again. Sour Billy Tipton sauntered right up to the head of the table, carrying something, with a strange sort of excitement in his icy eyes.

Damon Julian swept the plates aside with an arm, clearing a space on the table. Sour Billy shifted his burden and set a small brown infant down on the tablecloth in front of Joshua York.

"What the *hell!*" Marsh roared. He pushed back from the table, glaring, and started to rise.

"Sit down and keep real quiet, boy," Sour Billy said in a flat, quiet voice. Marsh started to turn toward him, and felt something cold and very sharp press gently against the side of his neck. "You open your mouth and I'm goin' to have to bleed you," Sour Billy said. "Can you just imagine what *they'll* do when they see all that nice hot blood?"

Trembling, caught between rage and terror, Abner Marsh sat very still. The point of Billy's knife pressed a little harder, and Marsh felt something warm and wet trickle down into his collar. "Good," whispered Billy, "real nice."

Joshua York glanced briefly at Marsh and Sour Billy, then turned his attention back to Julian. "I find this obscene," he said coldly. "Julian, I do not know why you had this child brought here, but I do not like it. This game will end right now. Tell your man to take his knife away from the captain's throat."

"Ah," said Julian. "And if I do not choose to?"

"You *will* choose to," said Joshua. "I am bloodmaster."

"Are you?" asked Julian lightly.

"Yes. I do not like to use your methods of compulsion, Julian, but if I must, I shall."

"Ah," said Julian. He smiled. He stood up, stretched lazily, like some great dark cat waking from a nap, then extended a hand across the table toward Sour Billy. "Billy, give your knife to me," he said.

"But—what about *him?*" Sour Billy said.

"Captain Marsh will behave himself now," said Julian. "The knife."

Billy handed it over, hilt first.

"Good," said Joshua.

He got no further. The baby—undersized, scrawny, very brown and very naked—made a sort of gurgling noise just then, and stirred feebly. And Damon Julian did the most horrible thing that Abner Marsh had ever seen in all his born days. Swiftly and very delicately, he leaned over the table and brought down Sour Billy's knife and cut the infant's small right hand clean off with a single smooth stroke.

The baby began to howl. Blood spurted onto the table, over the crystal glasses and the silverware and the fine white linen. The baby's limbs thrashed feebly, and the blood began to pool. And Julian impaled the severed hand—it was so impossibly tiny, hardly the size of Marsh's big toe—on the blade of Billy's knife. He held it up, dripping, in front of Joshua York. "*Drink,*" he said, and all the lightness was gone from his voice.

York slapped the knife aside. It spun from Julian's hand, the hand still impaled upon it, and landed six feet away on the carpet. Joshua looked like death. He reached down, put two strong fingers on either side of the infant's thrashing wrist, and *pressed*. The bleeding stopped. "Get me a cord," he commanded.

No one moved. The infant was still screaming.

"There is an easier way to quiet him," Julian said. He took his own hard pale hand and clamped it down across the child's mouth. The hand enveloped the small brown head completely, and stifled all sound. Julian began to squeeze.

"*Release him!*" shouted York.

"Look at me," said Julian. "Look at me, *bloodmaster*."

And their eyes met as they stood there above the table, each with a hand on the small brown piece of humanity before them.

Abner Marsh just sat there, thunderstruck, sick and furious and wanting to do something, but somehow unable to move. Like all the rest of them, he stared at York and Julian, at the strange, silent battle of wills.

Joshua York was trembling. His mouth was tight with anger, and cords stood up in his neck, and his gray eyes were as cold and forceful as an ice jam. He stood there like a man possessed, a pale wrathful god in white and blue and silver. It was impossible for anything to withstand that outpouring of will, of strength, Marsh thought. Impossible.

And then he looked at Damon Julian.

The eyes dominated the face: cold, black, malevolent, implacable. Abner Marsh looked into those eyes a moment too long, and suddenly he felt dizzy. He heard men screaming somewhere, distantly, and his mouth was warm with the taste of blood. He saw all the masks that were called Damon Julian and Giles Lamont and Gilbert d'Aquin and Philip Caine and Sergei Alexov and a thousand other men fall away, and behind each one was another, older and more horrible, layer on layer of them each more bestial than the last, and at the bottom the thing had no charm, no smile, no fine words, no rich clothing or jewels, the thing had nothing of humanity, *was* nothing of humanity, had only the thirst, the fever, red, *red*, ancient and insatiable. It was primal and inhuman and it was *strong*. It lived and breathed and drank the stuff of fear, and it was old, oh so old, older than man and all his works, older than the forests and rivers, older than dreams.

Abner Marsh blinked, and there across the table from him was an animal, a tall handsome animal in burgundy, and there was nothing the least bit human about it, and the lines of its face were the lines of terror, and its eyes—its eyes were red, not black at all, *red*, and lit from within, and *red*, burning, thirsting, *red*.

Joshua York released the infant's stump. A sudden pent-up wash of blood spurted feebly out across the table. An instant later a sound like a terrible wet *crunch* filled the saloon.

And Abner Marsh, still half-dazed, slid the long kitchen knife out of his boot and came out of his seat screaming, raving, slashing. Sour Billy tried to grab him from behind, but Marsh was too strong, too wild. He brushed Billy aside, and flung himself across the dinner table at Damon Julian. Julian broke away from Joshua York's eyes just in time, and pulled back slightly. The knife missed his eye by a fraction of an inch, and left a long open gash down the right side of his face. Blood welled out of the wound, and Julian made a snarling sound deep in his throat.

Then someone seized Marsh from behind and dragged him off the table and *flung* him backward across the grand saloon, lifted him and flung him, all three hundred pounds of him, like he was a small child. It hurt something fierce when he landed, but somehow Marsh managed to roll over and get back to his feet.

It was Joshua had thrown him, he saw, and Joshua who was standing closest to him now, Joshua with pale hands trembling and gray eyes full of fear. "Run, Abner," he said. "Get off the steamer. *Run.*" Behind him the others had all risen from the table. White faces, eyes intent and staring, hands pale and hard and grasping. Katherine was smiling, smiling at him the way she'd smiled when she'd caught him coming from Joshua's cabin. Old Simon was shaking. Even Smith and Brown were drifting toward him, slowly, ringing him in, and their eyes were not friendly, and their lips were wet. They were all moving, all of them, and Damon Julian came gliding around the table, almost soundless, the blood drying on his cheek, the gash closing almost as Marsh watched. Abner Marsh looked down at his hands, and discovered that he had lost the knife. He backed up, step by step, until his back was up against a mirrored stateroom door.

"*Run*, Abner," Joshua York repeated.

Marsh fumbled and opened the door and backed into the cabin behind him, and he saw Joshua turn his back and stand between the cabin and the others, Julian and Katherine and all the rest, the night folks, the vampires. And that was the last thing he saw, before he broke and ran.

CHAPTER EIGHTEEN

Aboard the Steamer FEVRE DREAM, Mississippi River, August 1857————

WHEN the sun rose over New Orleans the next morning, a swollen yellow eye that turned the river mists to crimson and promised a scorching day, Abner Marsh was waiting on the levee.

He had run a long way the night before, plunging through the gaslit streets of the Vieux Carré like a madman, smashing into strollers, stumbling and panting, running as he had never run in all his years, until finally he realized, belatedly, that no one was pursuing him. Then Marsh had found a dim, smoky grog shop, and put down three quick whiskeys to stop his shaking hands. And finally, close to dawn, he had started back toward the *Fevre Dream*. Never in his life had Abner Marsh been angrier or more ashamed. They had run him off his own damn steamboat, stuck a knife to his neck, slaughtered a goddamn *baby* right in front of him, on his own table. No one got away with treating Abner Marsh like that, he thought; not white men nor coloreds nor Red Indians nor any goddamn vampires. Damon Julian was going to be mighty regretful, he swore to himself. Day had come now, and the hunters would become the prey.

The landing was already humming with activity when Marsh approached. Another big side-wheeler had put in beside the *Fevre Dream* and was unloading, peddlers were selling fruits and frozen creams from wheeled carts, one or two hotel omnibuses had put in an appearance. And the *Fevre Dream* had her steam up, Marsh saw with surprise and alarm. Dark smoke was curling upward from her chimneys, and down below a ragtag group of roustabouts was loading up the last of the freight. He quickened his pace, and accosted one of them. He shouted, "You there! Hold on!"

The rouster was a huge, thickly-built black man with a shiny bald head and one missing ear. He turned at Marsh's shout, a barrel on his right shoulder. "Yessuh, Cap'n."

"What's goin' on here?" Marsh demanded. "Why's the steam up? I didn't give no orders."

The rouster frowned. "I just loads 'em up, Cap'n. Don't know nuthin', suh."

Marsh swore and moved past him. Hairy Mike Dunne came swaggering across the stage, his iron billet in hand. "Mike," called Marsh.

Hairy Mike frowned, a fierce look of concentration on his dark face. "Mornin', Cap'n. You really sell this here boat?"

"*What?*"

"Cap'n York, he says you sold you half to him, says you ain't a-comin' with us. I got back a couple hours past midnight, me an' some of them boys, an' York he says you'n' him figgered two cap'n were one too many, an' he bought you out. An' he tole Whitey to get the steam up, he did, and here we is. That the truth o' it, Cap'n?"

Marsh scowled. The roustabouts were gathering round curiously, so he grabbed Hairy Mike by the arm and drew him across the stage onto the main deck. "I ain't got no time for no long stories," he said when the two of them were reasonably apart from everybody else. "So don't pester me with no questions, you hear? Just do like I tell you."

Hairy Mike nodded. "Trouble, Cap'n?" he said, whacking his iron club into a big, meaty palm.

"How many is back?" Marsh asked.

"Most all the crew, some passengers. Ain't but a few."

"We ain't goin' to wait for no others," Marsh said. "The fewer folks on board, the better. You go hunt up Framm or Albright, I don't care which one, and get them on up to the pilot house, and take us out. Right *now*, you hear? I'm goin' to find Mister Jeffers. After you get a pilot up there, you meet me in the clerk's office. Don't tell anybody what's goin' on."

Between his thick black whiskers, a small grin could be seen. "What we gone do, buy this steamboat back cheap, maybe?"

"No," said Abner Marsh. "No, we're goin' to kill a man. And not Joshua neither. Now get on! Meet me in the clerk's office."

Jonathon Jeffers wasn't in his office, however, so Marsh had to go round to the head clerk's cabin, and pound until a sleepy-looking Jeffers opened the door, still in his nightshirt. "Cap'n Marsh," he said, stifling a yawn. "Cap'n York said you'd sold out. I didn't think it made much sense, but you weren't around so I didn't know what to think. Come in."

"Tell me what happened last night," Marsh said when he was safely inside the clerk's cabin.

Jeffers yawned again. "Pardon, Cap'n," he said. "I haven't had much sleep." He went to the basin perched atop his chest of drawers and splashed some water on his face, fumbled for his spectacles, and came back over to Marsh, looking more like himself. "Well, let me think a minute. We were at the St. Charles, where I said we'd be. We figured to stay there all night so Cap'n York and you could have your private dinner." His eyebrow arched sardonically. "Jack Ely was with me, and Karl Framm, and Whitey and a few of his strikers, and . . . well, there was a whole bunch of us. Mister Framm's cub had come along too. Mister Albright dined with us, but went up to bed after dinner, while the rest of us stayed up drinking and talking. We had rooms and everything, but no sooner had we gone to bed . . . must have been two or three in the morning . . . when Raymond Ortega and Simon and that Sour Billy Tipton character came to bring us back to the steamer. They said York wanted us straightaway." Jeffers shrugged. "So we came, and Cap'n York met everyone in the grand saloon and said he'd bought you out, and we were leaving some time in the morning. Some of us were sent out to find those still in New Orleans, and notify the passengers. Most of the crew is here now, I believe. I got the freight all signed in, and decided to get some sleep. Now, what's *really* happening?"

Marsh snorted. "I ain't got time, and you wouldn't believe it anyhow. You see anything strange in that saloon last night?"

"No," Jeffers said. One eyebrow went up. "Should I have?"

"Maybe," said Marsh.

"Everything was all cleared away from dinner," Jeffers said. "That was odd, come to think on it, with the waiters all gone ashore."

"Sour Billy cleaned it up, I reckon," Marsh said, "but it don't matter. Was Julian there?"

"Yes, him and a few others I'd never met before. Cap'n York had me assign them cabins. That Damon Julian is a strange one. He stayed real close to Cap'n York. Polite enough, though, and nice-looking except for that scar."

"You gave 'em cabins, you say?"

"Yes," said Jeffers. "Cap'n York said Julian was to have your cabin, but I wouldn't go along with that, not with all your property in there.

I insisted he take one of the passenger staterooms along the saloon, until I'd had a chance to talk to you. Julian said that would be fine, so there wasn't really any trouble."

Abner Marsh grinned. "Good," he said. "And Sour Billy, where's he?"

"He got the cabin right next to Julian," said Jeffers, "but I doubt that he's in it. Last I saw he was wandering around the main cabin, acting like he owned the boat and playing with that little knife of his. We had a bit of a run-in. You wouldn't believe what he was doing—he was chucking his knife into one of your fancy colonnades as if it were an old dead tree. I told him to stop or I'd have Hairy Mike chuck him over the side, and he did, but he stared at me belligerently. He's trouble, that one."

"He's still in the main cabin, you think?"

"Well, I've been asleep, but he was there last I saw, sort of dozing in a chair."

"Get dressed," Abner Marsh told him. "Quicklike. And meet me down by your office."

"Certainly, Cap'n," Jeffers said, puzzled.

"And bring your sword cane," Marsh told him as he went out the door.

Less than ten minutes later, he and Jeffers and Hairy Mike Dunne were together in the clerk's office. "Sit down and keep quiet and lissen," Marsh said. "This is goin' to sound crazy, but you two have known me for years and you damn well know I ain't no half-wit and I don't go around telling stories like Mister Framm. This is the goddamn truth, I swear it, may the goddamn boiler blow up underneath me if I'm lyin'."

Abner Marsh took a deep breath and plunged into the story. He told them everything, in one long rush of a speech, stopping only once, when the wild scream of the steamer's whistle interrupted him and the deck began to vibrate.

"Pullin' out," said Hairy Mike, "Goin' upstream, like you ast."

"Good," said Marsh, and he went on with the story while the *Fevre Dream* backed clear of the New Orleans levee, reversed her great paddles, and started back up the Mississippi beneath a hot clean sun.

When Marsh was finished, Jonathon Jeffers looked thoughtful. "Well," he said, "fascinating. Perhaps we should have called in the police."

Hairy Mike Dunne snorted. "You know bettuh. On the river, you handle you own trouble." He hefted his billet.

Abner Marsh agreed with him. "This here is my steamboat, and I ain't callin' in no outsiders, Mister Jeffers." That was the way of the river; it was less bother to club a troublemaker and toss him over the side, or leave the paddles to chew him up. The old devil river kept its secrets. "Specially ain't callin' in no New Orleans police. They ain't goin' to care about no colored slave baby, and we ain't even got a body. They're a bunch of scoundrels anyway, and they wouldn't believe us. And if they did, then what? They'd come in with pistols and clubs, worse than useless against Julian and his bunch."

"So we're to handle it ourselves," Jeffers said. "How?"

"I round up the boys an' we kills 'em all," said Hairy Mike amiably.

"No," said Abner Marsh. "Joshua can control the others, I figure. He done it before. He tried to do right, to stop what went on last night, only Julian was too much for him. We just got to get rid of Julian before dark."

"Ain't gone be hard," offered Hairy Mike.

Abner Marsh scowled. "I ain't so sure of that," he said. "This ain't like the stories. They ain't helpless by day. They're only sleepin'. And if you wake 'em up, they're awful strong and awful fast and they ain't never easy to hurt. This has to be done right. I reckon the three of us can handle it, no sense gettin' others involved. If anything goes wrong, we'll get everybody off this steamer well before dark, and put in someplace upriver where nobody can interfere, where none of the night folks can get away if it comes to havin' to kill more'n just Julian. Don't think it will, though." Marsh looked at Jeffers. "You got the duplicate key to that cabin you put Julian in?"

"In my safe," the clerk said, pointing towards the black iron strongbox with his sword cane.

"Good," said Marsh. "Mike, how hard can you hit with that thing of yours?"

Hairy Mike smiled and thwacked the iron billet into his palm. It made a satisfactorily loud sound. "How hard you want me to hit, Cap'n?"

"I want you to crush his goddamn head in," Marsh said. "And you got to do it right off, with one swing. Ain't goin' to be time for no second try. You just break his nose for him and a second later he's goin' to be up tearin' out your throat."

"One hit," said Hairy Mike. "Jest one."

Abner Marsh nodded, confident that the huge mate was true to his word. "Only one more problem, then. Sour Billy. He's Julian's little watchdog. Maybe he's dozing in some chair, but I wager he'll wake up quick enough if he sees us goin' for Julian's door. So he ain't goin' to see us. Those boiler deck cabins got two doors. If Billy is in the saloon, we go in from the promenade. If he's outside, we go in from the saloon. Before we do anything, we make sure we know where Billy is. That's your job, Mister Jeffers. You're goin' to find Mister Sour Billy Tipton for us, and tell us where he is, and then you're to make sure he don't go wanderin'. If he hears a ruckus or heads for Julian's cabin, I want you to take that sword cane of yours and stick it clean through his sour little belly, you hear?"

"Understood," the clerk said grimly. He adjusted his spectacles.

Abner Marsh paused a moment and looked hard at his two allies: the slim dandy of a clerk in his gold specs and button gaiters, his mouth tight, his hair as neatly slicked back as ever, and beside him the huge mate with his rough clothing and his rough face and his rough ways, his green eyes hard and spoiling for a fight. They were a strange pair but a most formidable one, Abner Marsh thought. He snorted, satisfied. "Well, what are we waitin' for?" he asked. "Mister Jeffers, you go find where Sour Billy is at."

The clerk rose and brushed himself off. "Certainly," he said.

He was back in under five minutes. "He's in the main cabin, sitting to breakfast. The whistle must have wakened him. He's eating eggs and boiled beefcakes and drinking plenty of coffee, and he's sitting where he can see the door to Julian's cabin."

"Good," Marsh said. "Mister Jeffers, why don't you go break fast yourself?"

Jeffers smiled. "I do believe I have a sudden appetite."

"The keys first, though."

Jeffers nodded and bent to his safe. Keys in hand, Marsh gave the clerk a good ten minutes to find his way back to the grand saloon before he stood and took a deep breath. His heart was thumping. "C'mon," he said to Hairy Mike Dunne, opening the door to the world outside.

The day was bright and hot, which Marsh took for a good omen. The *Fevre Dream* was surging up the river easy as you please, her wake a churning double line of white-flecked foam. She must be doing eighteen miles an hour, Marsh thought, riding smooth as a Creole's manners. He found himself wondering what her time to

Natchez would be, and all of a sudden he wanted to be up in her pilot house more than anything, looking out on the river he loved so well. Abner Marsh swallowed and blinked back tears, feeling sick and unmanly.

"Cap'n?" Hairy Mike said uncertainly.

Abner Marsh cussed. "It's nothin'," he said. "It's just . . . god-damn it all . . . c'mon." He stomped off, the key to Damon Julian's cabin clenched tightly in a huge red hand. His knuckles were turning white.

Outside the cabin, Marsh paused to look around. The promenade was mostly empty. A lady was standing by the railing a good ways aft of them, and about a dozen doors forward there was a fellow in a white shirt and a slouchy hat sitting with his chair tilted back against a stateroom door, but neither of them seemed much interested in Marsh and Hairy Mike. Marsh slid the key carefully into the hole. "You 'member what I told you," he whispered to the mate. "Quick and quiet. One hit."

Hairy Mike nodded, and Marsh turned the key. The door clicked open, and Marsh pushed.

It was close and dark inside, everything curtained and shuttered the way the night folks liked their rooms, but they saw a pale form sprawled beneath the sheet by the light that spilled in from the door. They slid through, moving as quietly as two big, noisy men could move, and then Marsh was closing the door behind them and Hairy Mike Dunne was moving forward, raising his three-foot-long black iron billet high over his head, and dimly Marsh saw the thing in the bed stir, rolling over toward the noise, toward the light, and Hairy Mike was there in two long quick strides, all so fast, and the iron fell in a terrible arc at the end of his huge arm, fell and fell toward that dim pale head and it seemed to take *forever*.

Then the cabin door shut completely, the last thread of light snapped, and in the blind pitch darkness Abner Marsh heard a sound like a piece of meat being slapped down on a butcher's counter, and under that was another sound, like an eggshell breaking, and Marsh held his breath.

The cabin was very still, and Marsh could not see a thing. From the darkness came a low, throaty chuckle. A cold sweat covered Marsh's body. "Mike," he whispered. He fumbled for a match.

"Yessuh, Cap'n," came the mate's voice. "One hit, thass all." He chuckled again.

Abner Marsh scratched the match on the wall, and blinked. Hairy Mike was standing over the bed, his iron in hand. The business end was smeared and wet. The thing beneath the sheet had a staved-in red ruin for a face. Half the top of its skull had been taken away, and a slow trickle of blood was soaking into the sheet. Bits of hair and other dark stuff were spattered on the pillow and the wall and Hairy Mike's clothes. "Is he dead?" Marsh asked, suddenly and wildly suspicious that the smashed-in head would begin to knit itself together, and the pale corpse would rise and smile at them.

"I ain't never seen nuthin' deader," said Hairy Mike.

"Make sure," Abner Marsh ordered. "Make damn sure."

Hairy Mike Dunne shrugged a big, slow shrug, and raised his bloody iron and brought it down again onto skull and pillow. A second time. A third. A fourth. When it was over, the thing hardly could be said to have a head at all. Hairy Mike Dunne was an awful strong man.

The match burned Marsh's fingers. He blew it out. "Let's go," he said harshly.

"What'll we do with *him?*" Hairy Mike asked.

Marsh pulled open the cabin door. The sun and the river were before him, a blessed relief. "Leave him there," he said. "In the dark. Come nightfall, we'll chuck him in the river." The mate followed Marsh outside, and he locked the door behind him. He felt sick. He leaned his ample bulk up against the boiler deck railing, and struggled to keep from heaving over the side. Blood-sucker or not, what they'd gone and done to Damon Julian was terrible to behold.

"Need help, Cap'n?"

"No," said Marsh. He straightened himself with an effort. The morning was already hot, the yellow sun above beating down on the river with an almighty vengeance. Marsh was drenched with sweat. "I ain't had much sleep," he said. He forced a laugh. "I ain't had none, in fact. It takes a bit out of a man, too, what we just done."

Hairy Mike shrugged. It hadn't taken much out of him, it seemed. "Go sleep," he said.

"No," said Marsh. "Can't. Got to go see Joshua, tell him what we done. He's got to know, so he'll be ready to deal with them others." All of a sudden Abner Marsh found himself wondering just how Joshua York would react to the brutal murder of one of his people. After last night, he couldn't think Joshua would be too bothered, but he wasn't sure—he didn't really know the night folks and how they thought, and if Julian had been a baby-killer and a blood-sucker, well, the rest of them had done things near as bad, even Joshua. And Damon Julian had been Joshua's bloodmaster too, the king of the vampires. If you kill a man's king—even a king he hates—ain't he obliged to do something about it? Abner Marsh remembered the cold force of Joshua's anger, and with that memory found himself none too eager to go rushing on up to the captain's cabin on the texas, especially now, when Joshua would be at his worst once roused. "Maybe I can wait," Marsh found himself saying. "Sleep a little."

Hairy Mike nodded.

"I got to get to Joshua first, though," Marsh said. He really was feeling sick, he thought: nauseated, feverish, weary. He had to go lie down for a couple hours. "Can't let him get up." He licked his lips, which were dry as sandpaper. "You go talk to Jeffers, tell him how it come out, and one of you come and fetch me before sunset. *Well* before, you hear? Give me at least an hour to go on up and speak to Joshua. I'll wake him up and tell him, and then when it gets dark he'll know how to handle the other night folks. And you . . . you have one of your boys keep a sharp eye on Sour Billy . . . we're goin' to have to deal with him, too."

Hairy Mike smiled. "Let the river deal with *him*."

"Maybe we will," said Marsh. "Maybe. I'm going to go rest now, but make sure I'm up before dark. Don't you go let it get dark on me, you understand?"

"Yep."

So Abner Marsh climbed wearily up to the texas, feeling sicker and more tired with every step. Standing at the door of his own cabin, he felt a sudden stab of fear—what if one of *them* should be inside after all, despite what Mister Jeffers had said? But when he threw the door open and let the light come pouring into the room, it was empty. Marsh staggered in, drew the curtains back and opened the window to let in as much light and air as possible, locked the door, and sat heavily on the bed to remove his sweat-soaked clothing. He didn't even bother with a nightshirt. The cabin was stifling, but Marsh was too exhausted to notice. Sleep took him almost at once.

CHAPTER NINETEEN

Aboard the Steamer FEVRE DREAM, Mississippi River, August 1857——————

THE sharp, insistent rapping on his cabin door finally summoned Abner Marsh back from his deep, dreamless sleep. He stirred groggily and sat up in bed. "A minute!" he shouted. He lumbered over to his basin like a big naked bear just out of hibernation, and none too happy about it. It wasn't until Marsh had splashed some water on his face that he remembered. "Goddamn it all to hell!" he swore angrily, staring at the gray shadows gathering in every corner of the small dim cabin. Beyond the window, the sky was dark and purple. "Goddamn," he repeated, pulling on a pair of clean trousers. He stomped over and yanked open the door. "What the *hell* is the meaning of lettin' me sleep so long?" Marsh shouted at Jonathon Jeffers. "I told Hairy Mike to wake me a whole goddamn hour before sunset, damnit."

"It *is* an hour before sunset," Jeffers said. "It clouded up, that's why it looks so dark. Mister Albright says we're going to get another thunderstorm." The clerk stepped into Marsh's cabin and shut the door behind him. "I brought you this," he said, handing over a hickory walking stick. "I found it in the main cabin, Cap'n."

Marsh took the stick, mollified. "I lost it last night," he said. "Had other things on my mind." He leaned the stick up against the wall and glanced out the window again, frowning. Beyond the river, the whole western horizon was a mass of threatening clouds moving their way, like a vast wall of darkness about to collapse on them. The setting sun was nowhere to be seen. He didn't like it one bit. "I better get on up to Joshua," he said, pulling out a shirt and commencing the business of getting dressed.

Jeffers leaned on his sword cane. "Shall I accompany you?" he asked.

"I ought to talk to Joshua by myself," Marsh said, tying his tie with an eye on the mirror. "I don't relish it though. Why don't you come on up and wait outside. Maybe Joshua will want to call you in and talk about what we're goin' to do." Left unspoken was the other reason that Marsh wanted the clerk close at hand—maybe *he'd* want to call him in, if Joshua York didn't take kindly to the news of Damon Julian's demise.

"Fine," said Jeffers.

Marsh shrugged into his captain's coat and snatched up his stick. "Let's go then, Mister Jeffers. It's too damn dark already."

The *Fevre Dream* was steaming along briskly, her flags snapping and swirling in a strong wind, dark smoke pouring from her chimneys. Under the scant light of the strange purple sky, the waters of the Mississippi looked almost black. Marsh grimaced and strode forward briskly to Joshua York's cabin, Jeffers at his side. This time he did not hesitate at the door; he raised his stick and knocked. On the third knock he called out, "Joshua, let me in. We got to talk." On the fifth knock the door opened, moving slowly inward to reveal a soft still blackness. "Wait for me," Marsh said to Jeffers. He stepped into the cabin and closed the door. "Don't get mad now, Joshua," he said to the dark, with a tight feeling in his gut. "I wouldn't bother you, but this is important and it's almost night anyhow." There was no reply, though Marsh heard the sound of breathing. "Goddamnit," he said, "why do we always have to talk in the dark, Joshua? It makes me damn uncomfortable." He frowned. "Light a candle, will you?"

"No." The voice was curt, low, liquid. And it was not Joshua's.

Abner Marsh took a step backward. "Oh Jesus God, *no*," he said, and there was a rustling sound even as his shaking hand found the door behind him and threw it open. He opened it wide and by now his eyes had accustomed themselves to the darkness, and even the purplish glow of the storm-laden sky was enough to give brief form to the shadows within the captain's cabin. He saw Joshua York sprawled on his bed, pale and naked, his eyes closed, one arm hanging down to the floor, and on his wrist was something that looked like a terrible dark bruise, or a crust of dried blood. And he saw Damon Julian moving toward him, swift as death, smiling. "We *killed* you," Marsh roared, disbelieving, and he stumbled backward out of the cabin, tripped, and fell practically at Jonathon Jeffers' feet.

Julian stopped in the doorway. A thin dark line—hardly more than a cat scratch—ran down his cheek where Marsh had opened a yawning gash the night before. Otherwise he was unmarked. He had taken off his jacket and vest, and his ruffled silk shirt was without stain or blemish. "Come in, Captain," Julian said quietly. "Don't run away. Come in and talk."

"You're *dead*. Mike bashed your goddamn head to pieces," Marsh said, choking on his own words. He did not look at Julian's eyes. It was still day, he thought, he was safe outside, beyond Julian's reach until the sun went down, so long as he did not look in those eyes, so long as he did not go back into that cabin.

"Dead?" Julian smiled. "Ah. The other cabin. Poor Jean. He wanted so to believe Joshua, and see what you have done to him. Smashed his head in, did you say?"

Abner Marsh climbed to his feet. "You changed cabins," he said hoarsely. "You damn devil. You made him sleep in your bed."

"Joshua and I had so much to discuss," Julian replied. He made a beckoning gesture. "Now come, Captain, I am tired of waiting. Come and let us drink together."

"Burn in hell!" Marsh said. "Maybe we missed you this morning, but you ain't got away yet. Mister Jeffers, run on down and get Hairy Mike and his boys. A dozen of them ought to do, I reckon."

"No," said Damon Julian, "you won't do that."

Marsh waved his stick threateningly. "Oh yes, I will. You goin' to stop me?"

Julian glanced up at the sky; a deep violet now, shot through with black, a vast bruised and overcast twilight. "Yes," he said, and he stepped out into the light.

Abner Marsh felt the cold, clammy hand of terror close around his heart. He raised his walking stick and said, "*Stay away!*" in a voice gone suddenly shrill. He stepped backward. Damon Julian smiled and came on. It wasn't light enough, Marsh thought with sick despair.

And then there was a whisper of metal on wood, and Jonathon Jeffers stepped smoothly in front of him, his sword cane unsheathed, the sharp steel circling dangerously. "Go for help, Cap'n," Jeffers said quietly. He pushed up his spectacles with his free hand. "I'll keep Mister Julian occupied." Lightly, with a fencer's practiced speed, Jeffers darted forward at Julian, slashing. His blade was a rapier, double-edged and wickedly pointed. Damon Julian reeled back barely in time, his smile fading from his lips as the clerk's slash passed inches in front of his face.

"Step aside," Julian said darkly.

Jonathon Jeffers said nothing. He was in a fencer's stance, advancing slowly on the balls of his feet, crowding Julian back toward the door of the captain's cabin. He thrust suddenly, but Julian was too fast, sliding backward out of the reach of the sword. Jeffers made an impatient *tsk*. Damon Julian set one foot back inside the cabin, and answered with a laugh that was almost a snarl. His white hands rose and opened. Jeffers thrust again.

And Julian lunged, hands extended.

Abner Marsh saw it all. Jeffers' thrust was true, and Julian made no effort to avoid it. The rapier entered him just above the groin. Julian's pale face twisted, and a grunt of pain escaped him, but he came on. Jeffers ran him clean through even as Julian ran up the blade, and before the startled clerk had time to pull back, Julian had wrapped his hands around Jeffers' throat. Jeffers made a horrible choking sound, and his eyes bulged, and as he tried to wrench free his gold-rimmed spectacles spun off and fell to the deck.

Marsh leaped forward and smashed Julian with his stick, raining blows around his head and shoulders. Transfixed by the sword, Julian hardly seemed to feel it. He twisted savagely, and there was a noise like wood snapping. Jeffers went limp.

Abner Marsh whipped his stick around in one final blow, with all his strength in it, and caught Damon Julian square in the center of his forehead, staggering him briefly. When Julian opened his hands, Jeffers fell like a rag doll, his head twisted around grotesquely so it almost seemed it was on backwards.

Abner Marsh retreated hurriedly.

Julian touched his brow, as if gauging the effects of Marsh's blow. There was no blood, Marsh saw dismally. Strong as he was, he was no Hairy Mike Dunne, and hickory was not iron. Damon Julian kicked loose Jeffers' death-grip from the handle of the sword cane. Wincing, he drew the blood-slick blade awkwardly out of his own body. His shirt and trousers were damp and red, and stuck to him when he moved. He spun the blade off to one side, almost casually, and it whipped round and round like a top as it sailed off over the river, before vanishing into the dark moving water.

Julian staggered forward again, leaving bloody footsteps behind him on the deck. But he came.

Marsh retreated before him. There was no killing him, he thought in a blind sick panic; there is nothing to be done. Joshua and his dreams, Hairy Mike and his iron billet, Mister Jeffers and his sword, none of them could take the measure of this Damon Julian. Marsh scrambled down the short stairway to the hurricane deck, and began to run. Panting, he hurried aft, to the companionway leading down from the hurricane deck to the promenade, where he'd find people and safety. It was nearly dark, he saw. He took three thunderous steps downstairs, then gripped the handrail tightly and reeled, trying to check himself.

Sour Billy Tipton and four of *them* were climbing toward him.

Abner Marsh turned and ascended. Rush forward and ring the bell, he thought wildly, ring the bell for help . . . but Julian had come down from the texas deck now, and cut him off. For a moment Marsh stood, dead with despair. He had no escape, he was trapped between Julian and the others, unarmed except for his useless goddamned stick, and it didn't matter, nothing hurt them anyway, fighting was useless, he might as well give in. Julian wore a thin, cruel smile as he advanced. In his mind Marsh saw that pale face descending on his own, teeth bared, those eyes bright with fever and thirst, red and ancient and invincible. If he'd had tears Marsh might have wept. He found he could not move his legs from where they were rooted, and even his stick seemed far too heavy.

Then, far up the river, another side-wheeler came round a bend, and Abner Marsh would never have noticed, but the pilot did, and the steam whistle of the *Fevre Dream* called out to tell the other steamer that she'd take the larboard when they passed. The shrill wail of the great whistle stirred Marsh from his paralysis, and he looked up and saw the far-off lights of the descending boat and the fires belching from the tops of her tall chimneys, and the near-black sky that loomed above it, and the lightning dim in the distance lighting up the clouds from within, and the river, the river black and endless, the river that was his home and his trade and his friend and his worst enemy and fickle, brutal, loving consort to his ladies. It flowed on like it always flowed, and it didn't know nothing nor care nothing about Damon Julian and all his kind, they were nothing to it, they would be gone and forgotten and the old devil river would still be rolling and cutting new channels and drowning towns and crops and raising up others and crushing steamboats in its teeth so it could spit out splinters.

Abner Marsh moved to where the tops of the great paddleboxes loomed above the deck. Julian came following him. "Captain," he called, his voice twisted but still seductive. Marsh ignored it. He pulled himself up on top of the paddlebox with a strength born of urgency, a strength he didn't know he had. Beneath his feet the great side-wheel turned. He could feel it shaking through the wood, could hear the *chunka-chunka*. He moved aft, carefully, not wanting to fall in the wrong place, where the wheels would suck him under and smash him up. He looked down. The light was almost gone, and the water seemed black, but where the *Fevre Dream* had gone it was boiling and churning. The glow from the steamer's furnaces touched it with red, so it looked like boiling blood. Abner Marsh stared down at it and froze. More blood, he thought, more goddamn blood, can't get away from it, can't get away nohow. The pounding of the steamer's stroke was thunder in his ears.

Sour Billy Tipton vaulted up on top of the paddlebox and moved warily toward him. "Mister Julian wants you, fat man," he said. "Come along now, you gone as far as you can go." He took out his little knife and smiled. Sour Billy Tipton had a truly frightening smile.

"It ain't blood," Marsh said loudly, "it's just the goddamn river." Still clutching his stick, he took a deep breath, and threw himself off the steamer. Sour Billy's curses were ringing in his ears when he hit the water.

Aboard the Steamer FEVRE DREAM, Mississippi River, August 1857———

RAYMOND and Armand were supporting Damon Julian between them when Sour Billy leaped down from the paddlebox. Julian looked like he'd slaughtered a pig; his clothing was soaked through with blood. "You allowed him to escape, Billy," he said coldly. His tone made Sour Billy nervous.

"He's finished," Billy insisted. "Them paddles will suck him under and smash him, or he'll drown. You ought to of seen the splash he made when he hit the water, that big belly of his first. Ain't goin' to have to look at his warts no more." As he spoke, Sour Billy was looking around, and he didn't like what he saw, not one bit; Julian all bloody, a red smeary trail leading down the texas stairs and half-way down the hurricane deck, and that dandy of a clerk hanging off the end of the texas porch, more blood coming out of his mouth.

"If you fail me, Billy, you will never be as we are," Julian said. "I hope he is dead, for your sake. Do you understand?"

"Yes," said Billy. "Mister Julian, what happened?"

"They attacked me, Billy. They attacked *us*. According to the good captain, they killed Jean. Bashed his goddamn head to pieces, I believe that was the phrase." He smiled. "Marsh and his wretch of a clerk and someone named Mike were responsible."

"Hairy Mike Dunne," said Raymond Ortega. "He is the mate of the *Fevre Dream*, Damon. Large, stupid, and uncouth. It is his job to shout at the darkies and beat them."

"Ah," Julian said. "Let me go," he said to Raymond and Armand. "I feel stronger now. I can stand."

The twilight had deepened. They stood in shadow. "Damon," warned Vincent, "the watch will change at supper. Crewmen will be coming up to their cabins. We must do something. We must get off this steamer, or they will find us out." He looked at the blood, the body.

"No," said Julian. "Billy will clean it up. Won't you, Billy?"

"Yes," said Sour Billy. "I'll just toss the clerk in after his Cap'n."

"Do it then, Billy, instead of telling me about it." Julian's smile was cold. "And then come to York's cabin. We will retire there now. I need a change of clothes."

It took Sour Billy Tipton nearly twenty minutes to remove the evidence of the death on the texas. He worked in haste, all too aware of how easy it would be for someone to come out of his cabin, or up the stairs. The darkness was almost complete by then, however, which helped. He dragged Jeffers' body down the deck, hauled it up on the paddlebox with some difficulty—the clerk was heavier than Billy ever would have guessed—and shoved it over. The night and the river swallowed it, and the splash wasn't nearly as big as the one Marsh had made. It was almost lost in the sound of the paddlewheels. Sour Billy had just stripped off his shirt and started cleaning up the blood when he had a stroke of luck—the storm that had been coming all afternoon finally broke. Thunder boomed in his ears, lightning came stabbing down at the river, and the rains began. Clean, cold, pounding rains, smashing down onto the deck, soaking Billy through to his bones, and washing away the blood.

Sour Billy was dripping when he finally entered Joshua York's cabin, his once-fine shirt a damp ball in his hand. "It's done," he said.

Damon Julian was sitting in a deep leather chair. He had changed into some fresh clothing, had a drink in hand, and looked as strong and healthy as ever. Raymond was standing at his side, Armand was in the other chair, Vincent was seated on the desk, Kurt in the desk chair. And Joshua York sat on his bed, staring down at his feet, head sunk, his skin white as chalk dust. He looked like a whipped cur, thought Sour Billy.

"Ah, Billy," said Julian. "What ever would we do without you?"

Sour Billy nodded. "I been thinking while I was out there, Mister Julian," he said. "The way I figger, we got two choices. This here steamer has a yawl, for doin' soundings and such. We could take her and light out. Or now that the storm's broke, we could just wait till the pilot ties her up, and then get ashore. We ain't far from Bayou Sara, maybe we'll put in there."

"I have no interest in Bayou Sara, Billy. I have no interest in leaving this excellent steamboat. The *Fevre Dream* is ours now. Isn't that right, Joshua?"

Joshua York raised his head. "Yes," he said. His voice was so weak it was hardly audible.

"It's too dangerous," Sour Billy insisted. "The cap'n and the head clerk both gone, what are people goin' to think? They're goin' to be missed, questions are goin' to get asked. Real soon now too."

"He is right, Damon," Raymond put in. "I have been aboard this steamer since Natchez. The passengers may come and go, but the crew—we are in danger here. We are the strange ones, suspected, unknown. When Marsh and Jeffers are missed, they will look to us first."

"And then there's this mate," added Billy. "If he helped Marsh, he knows everything, Mister Julian."

"Kill him, Billy."

Sour Billy Tipton swallowed uneasily. "Suppose I do kill him, Mister Julian? Won't do no good. He'll be missed too, and there's others under him, a whole damn army of niggers and dumb Germans and big Swedes. We got less than twenty, and during the day there's only me. We got to get off this steamboat, and real quick, too. We can't fight the crew, and even if we could, I sure can't fight 'em alone all by myself. We got to go."

"We are staying. It is for them to fear us, Billy. How can you ever be one of the masters if you still think as a slave? We are staying."

"What will we do when Marsh and Jeffers are found gone?" asked Vincent.

"And what about the mate? He is a threat," said Kurt.

Damon Julian stared at Sour Billy and smiled. "Ah," he said. He sipped his drink. "Why, we will let Billy take care of these little problems for us. Billy will show us how clever he is, won't you, Billy?"

"Me?" Sour Billy Tipton stood open-mouthed. "I don't know . . ."

"*Won't you, Billy?*"

"Yes," Billy said quickly. "Yes."

"I can solve this without further bloodshed," Joshua York said, with a hint of his old resolve in his voice. "I am still captain aboard this steamer. Let me discharge Mister Dunne and any of the others that you may fear. We can get them off the *Fevre Dream* cleanly. There has been enough death."

"Has there?" asked Julian.

"Firing 'em won't work," Sour Billy said to York. "They'll only wonder why and demand to see Cap'n Marsh."

"Yes," agreed Raymond. "They don't follow York," he added, to Julian. "They don't trust him. He had to come out in broad daylight before any of them would agree to go down the bayou with him. With Marsh gone, and Jeffers too, he will never be able to control them."

Sour Billy Tipton looked at Joshua York with surprise and new respect. "You did that?" he blurted. "Went out by day?" The others sometimes dared the dusk, or lingered a short time after sunrise, but he had never seen any of them come out when the sun was high. Not even Julian.

Joshua York looked at him coldly, and did not answer.

"Dear Joshua likes to play at being cattle," Julian said, amused. "Perhaps he hoped his skin would turn brown and leathery."

The others laughed politely.

While they were laughing, Sour Billy got himself an idea. He scratched his head and let himself smile. "We won't fire them," he said suddenly to Julian. "I know. We'll make 'em run off. I know just how to do it."

"Good, Billy. What ever would we do without you?"

"Can you make *him* do like I tell him?" Billy asked, jerking a thumb in York's direction.

"I will do what I must to protect my people," Joshua York said, "and to protect my crew as well. There is no need for compulsion."

"Well, well," said Sour Billy. "Real nice." This was going to be even easier than he'd figured. Julian would be real impressed. "I got to go get me a new shirt. You get dressed, Mister Cap'n York, and then we'll do us some *protectin*'."

"Yes," Julian added softly. "And Kurt will go with you as well." He raised his glass to York. "Just in case."

A half hour later, Sour Billy led Joshua York and Kurt down to the boiler deck. The rain had let up a little, and the *Fevre Dream* had put in at Bayou Sara and was tied up next to a dozen smaller steamers. In the main saloon, supper had been served. Julian and his people were in there with the rest, eating inconspicuously. The captain's chair was empty, though, and someone was bound to comment sooner or later. Fortunately, Hairy Mike Dunne was down below on the main deck, bellowing at the rousters as they loaded up some freight and a dozen cords of wood. Sour Billy had watched him carefully from above before starting in on his plan; Dunne was the dangerous one.

"The body first," Sour Billy said, leading them straight to the outer door of the cabin where Jean Ardant had met his end. Kurt broke the lock with a single swing of his hand. Inside, Billy lit the lamp, and they took in the thing on the bed. Sour Billy Tipton whistled. "Well, well," he said. "Those friends of yours sure did a job on ol' Jean," he said to York. "Half his brains is on the sheets and half is on the wall."

York's gray eyes were full of disgust. "Get on with it," he said. "I suppose you want us to throw the body in the river."

"Hell, no," said Sour Billy. "Why, we're goin' to *burn* this body. Right down in one of your furnaces, Cap'n. And we're not sneakin' it down neither. We'll just go right on out into the saloon with it, and down the main staircase."

"Why, Billy?" York said coldly.

"Just do it!" Sour Billy snapped. "And I'm Mister Tipton to you, *Captain!*"

They wrapped Jean's corpse in a sheet, so nothing could be seen of it. York went to help Kurt lift it, but Sour Billy chased him off and took up the other end himself. "Wouldn't look right for a half-owner and cap'n to be a-totin' a dead man. You just walk along with us and look worried."

York didn't have trouble with the looking worried part. They opened the door to the grand saloon and went out, Jean's sheeted body between Billy and Kurt. The supper table was half-full. Someone gasped, and all conversation stopped.

"Can I help, Cap'n York?" asked a small man with white whiskers and oil stains on his vest. "What is it? Somebody die?"

"Stay away!" Sour Billy shouted when the man took a step toward them.

"Do as he says, Whitey," York said.

The man stopped. "Why, sure, but . . ."

"It's just a dead man," Sour Billy said. "Died in his cabin. Mister Jeffers found him. He got on at New Orleans, must of been sick. He was burnin' up when Jeffers heard him moanin'."

Everyone at the table looked concerned. One man turned very pale and fled toward his own stateroom. Sour Billy made certain not to smile.

"Where's Mister Jeffers?" asked Albright, the trim little pilot.

"Went to his cabin," Billy said quickly. "He wasn't feelin' good. Marsh is with him. Mister Jeffers was lookin' kind of yaller, I reckon seeing a man die didn't agree with him."

His words had the effect he'd figured on, especially when Armand leaned across the table to Vincent and said—in a loud whisper, like Billy had told him to—"*Bronze John.*" Then the two of them got up and left, their suppers half-eaten.

"It ain't Bronze John!" Billy said loudly. He had to say it loudly, because all of a sudden everybody at this table was trying to talk, and half of them were getting to their feet. "We got to go burn this body, come on now," he added, and he and Kurt started shuffling toward the grand staircase again. Joshua York lingered behind, hands upraised, trying to fend off a hundred frightened questions. Passengers and crew alike avoided Kurt and Billy and their burden.

A couple of scroungy-looking foreigners taking deck passage were the only ones down on the main deck, except for the rousters coming in and out with crates and firewood. The furnaces had been shut down, but they were still hot, and Sour Billy burned his fingers when he and Kurt stuffed the sheeted body into the nearest one. He was still swearing and shaking his hand in the air when Joshua York came down and found him again. "They're leaving," York said, his pale features puzzled. "Nearly all the passengers are already packing their bags, and half the crew must have come up to me to ask for their wages. Strikers, chambermaids, waiters, even Jack Ely, the second engineer. I don't understand."

"Bronze John is taking a ride up the river on your steamer," Sour Billy Tipton said. "Leastwise, that's what *they* think."

Joshua York frowned. "Bronze John?"

Sour Billy smiled. "Yaller fever, Cap'n. I can tell you never been in New Orleans when Bronze John made a call. Ain't nobody goin' to stay on this boat longer than he has to, nor look close at this body, nor go to talk with Jeffers or Marsh. I let 'em think they got the fever, you see. The fever is real catching. Fast, too. You turn yaller and heave up black stuff and burn like the devil, and then you die. Only now we better burn up ol' Jean here, so they think we're takin' this serious."

It took them ten minutes to get the furnace going again, and they finally had to call over a big Swedish fireman to help them, but that was all right. Sour Billy saw his eyes when he spied the body crammed in with the wood, and smiled at how fast he run off. Pretty soon Jean was going good. Sour Billy watched him smoke, then turned away, bored. He noticed the barrels of lard standing near to hand. "Use that for racing, do you?" he asked Joshua York.

York nodded.

Sour Billy spat. "Down here, when a cap'n gets into the race and needs some more steam, he just has 'em chuck in a nice fat nigger. Lard's too expensive. You see, I know something about steamers, too. Too bad we couldn't save Jean for a race."

Kurt smiled at that, but Joshua York only stared, glowering. Sour Billy didn't like that look, not one bit, but before he could say anything he heard the voice he'd been waiting for.

"YOU!"

Hairy Mike Dunne came swaggering in from the forecastle, all six foot of him. Rain was dripping off the wide brim of his black felt hat, and moisture beaded his black whiskers, and his clothes were stuck to his body. His eyes were hard little green marbles, and he had his iron club in hand, smacking it up against his palm threateningly. Behind him stood a dozen deckhands, stokers, and roustabouts. The big Swede was there, and an even bigger nigger with one ear, and a wiry mulatto with a two-by-four, and a couple guys with knives. The mate came closer, and the others followed him. "Who you burnin' there, boy?" he roared. "What's all this 'bout yaller fever? Ain't no yaller fever on this boat."

"Do like I told you," Sour Billy said to York in a low urgent voice. He backed away from the furnace as the mate advanced.

Joshua York stepped between them and raised his hands. "Stop," he said. "Mister Dunne, I'm discharging you, here and now. You are no longer mate of the *Fevre Dream*."

Dunne eyed him suspiciously. "I ain't?" he said. Then he grimaced. "Hell, you ain't firin' *me*!"

"I am the master and captain here."

"Is you? Well, I takes orders from Cap'n Marsh. He tells me to git, I git. Till then, I stay. An' don't tell me no lies 'bout buyin' him out. Heard them lies this mornin'." He took another step forward. "Now you git out of the way, Cap'n. I'm gone git me some answers from Mister Sour Billy here."

"Mister Dunne, there is sickness aboard this steamer. I am discharging you for your own safety." Joshua York lied with real nice sincerity, Sour Billy thought. "Mister Tipton will be the new mate. He's already been exposed."

"*Him?*" The iron billet smacked against the mate's palm. "He ain't no steamboater."

"Been an overseer," Billy said. "I can handle niggers." He moved forward again.

Hairy Mike Dunne laughed.

Sour Billy felt cold all over. If there was one thing in the world that he could not stand, it was being laughed at. Right then and there he decided not to scare Dunne off after all. Killing him would be much nicer. "You got all them niggers and white trash behind you," he said to the mate. "Looks to me like you're scared to face me by yourself."

Dunne's green eyes narrowed dangerously, and he smacked his club into his palm even harder than before. He came forward two quick steps, into the full glare of the furnace, and stood there, awash in the hellish glow, peering in at the burning corpse. Finally he turned to face Sour Billy again. "Only him in there," he said. "Thass good fo' you. If it'd been the Cap'n or Jeffers, I was gone break ever' bone in you body befo' I kilt you. Now I'm jest gone kill you right off."

"No," Joshua York said. He stepped in front of the mate again. "Get off my steamer," he said. "You're discharged."

Hairy Mike Dunne shoved him out of the way. "Stay out o' this, Cap'n. Fair fight, jest me an' him. If he whips me, he's mate. Only I'm gone bash his head in, an' then you an' me'll go find Cap'n Marsh and see who leaves this here steamboat."

Sour Billy reached behind him and pulled out his knife.

Joshua York looked from one to the other in despair. The other men had all drawn back now, and were calling out encouragement to Hairy Mike. Kurt moved forward smoothly and pulled York out of the way, to keep him from interfering.

Bathed in the furnace light, Hairy Mike Dunne looked like something straight out of hell, smoke curling up around him, his skin flushed and reddish, the water drying on his hair, his club smacking against his palm as he advanced. He smiled. "I fought boys with knifes befo'," he said, punctuating his words with smacks. "Lots o' dirty lil' boys." Smack. "I been cut befo' too." Smack. "Cuts heal up, Sour Billy." Smack. "Bust heads, thass another thing." Smack. Smack. Smack.

Billy had been steadily retreating, until his back came up hard against a stack of crates. The knife was loose in his hand. Hairy Mike

216

saw him cornered, and grinned, raising the iron billet high over head. He came forward roaring.

And Sour Billy Tipton tossed the knife in his hand, and sent it slicing through the air. It caught Hairy Mike right under his chin, driving up through his whiskers and into his head. He went to his knees and blood came pouring out of his mouth and then he pitched forward onto the deck.

"Well, well," Sour Billy said, sauntering over to the body. He kicked it in the head, and smiled, for the niggers and the foreigners and for Kurt, but mostly for Joshua York. "Well, well," he repeated. "Guess that makes me mate."

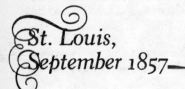

CHAPTER TWENTY-ONE

St. Louis, September 1857

ABNER Marsh slammed the door behind him when he came stomping into the Pine Street office of the Fevre River Packet Company. "Where is she?" Marsh demanded, striding across the room and leaning on the desk to stare down at the startled agent. A fly buzzed around his head, and Marsh brushed it away impatiently. "I said *where is she?*"

The agent was a gaunt, dark young man in a striped shirt and a green eyeshade. He was very flustered. "Why," he said, "why, Cap'n Marsh, why it's a pleasure, I never thought, that is, we didn't expect you, no sir, Cap'n, not a bit. Is the *Fevre Dream* come in, Cap'n?"

Abner Marsh snorted, straightened, and stamped his walking stick on the bare wooden floor in disgust. "Mister Green," he said, "quit your goddamn babblin' and pay attention now. I asked you, *where is she?* Now, what do you think I was asking about, Mister Green?"

The agent swallowed. "I reckon I don't know, Cap'n."

"*The Fevre Dream!*" Marsh bellowed, red in the face. "I want to know where she is! She ain't down by the landing, I know that much, I got eyes. And I didn't see her anywhere along the goddamn river. Did she come in and leave again? Did she steam up to St. Paul, or the Missouri? The Ohio? Don't look so damn thunderstruck, just tell me. *Where's my goddamn steamer?*"

"I don't know, Cap'n," said Green. "I mean, if *you* didn't bring her in, I got no idea. She's never been in St. Louis, not since you took her down the river back in July. But we heard . . . we . . ."

"Yes? What?"

"The fever, sir. We heard yellow fever broke out on the *Fevre Dream* down to Bayou Sara. Folks were dyin' like flies, we heard, just like flies. Mister Jeffers and you, we heard you had it, too. That's why I never expected . . . with everyone dyin' and all, we thought they'd burn her, Cap'n. The steamer." He slipped off his eyeshade and scratched his head. "I guess you got over the fever, Cap'n. Glad to hear it. Only . . . if the *Fevre Dream* ain't with you, where is she? Are you sure you didn't come in on her, and maybe forget? I hear the fever can make a man awful absentminded."

Abner Marsh scowled. "I ain't had the fever, and I sure as hell can tell one steamboat from another, Mister Green. I came in on the *Princess*. I was sick for a week or so, all right, but it wasn't no fever. I had the chills, on account of fallin' in the goddamn river and almost drownin'. That's how I lost the *Fevre Dream*, and now I aim to find her again, you hear me?" He snorted. "Where'd you hear all this stuff about yellow fever?"

"The crew, Cap'n, the ones who left her down in Bayou Sara. Some of 'em came in when they arrived in St. Louis, oh, 'bout a week ago it was. Some of 'em asked about jobs on the *Eli Reynolds*, Cap'n, but of course she's all full up, so I had to let 'em go. I hope I done right. You weren't here, of course, nor Mister Jeffers, and I thought maybe you was both dead, so I couldn't get no instructions."

"Never mind about that," Marsh said. The news heartened him somewhat. If Julian and his pack had taken over Marsh's steamer, at least some of his crew had gotten clear. "Who was here?"

"Why, I saw Jack Ely, the second engineer, and some waiters, and a couple of your strikers—Sam Kline and Sam Thompson, it was. There was a few others."

"Any of them still around?"

Green shrugged. "When I didn't hire 'em, they went looking around to other boats, Cap'n. I don't know."

"Damn," Marsh said.

"Wait!" the agent said, raising a finger. "I know! Mister Albright, the pilot, he was one of 'em told me about the fever. He was here about four days ago, and he didn't want no job—he's a lower river pilot, you know, so the *Eli Reynolds* wasn't for him. He said he was taking a room at the Planters' House until he could find a position on one of the classier boats, a big side-wheeler like."

"Albright, eh," Marsh said. "What about Karl Framm? You see him?" If Framm and Albright had both left the *Fevre Dream*, the steamer shouldn't be hard to find. Without qualified pilots, she couldn't move.

But Green shook his head. "No. Ain't seen Mister Framm."

Marsh's hopes sank. If Karl Framm was still aboard her, the *Fevre Dream* could be anywhere along the river. She might have gone off any one of a number of tributaries, or maybe the *Fevre Dream* had even steamed back down to New Orleans while he was laid up in that woodyard south of Bayou Sara. "I'm goin' to pay a call on Dan Albright," he told the agent. "While I'm gone, I want you to write some letters. To agents, pilots, anybody you know along the river, from here to New Orleans. Ask about the *Fevre Dream*. Somebody has got to have seen her. Steamer like that don't just vanish. You write those letters up this afternoon, you hear, and get down to the landing and post them on the fastest boats you see. I aim to find my steamer."

"Yes, sir," the agent said. He got out a stack of paper and a pen, dipped it in the inkwell, and began to write.

The clerk at the Planters' House desk bobbed his head in greeting. "Why, it's Cap'n Marsh," he said. "Heard about your misfortune, just awful, Bronze John's a wicked one, that he is. I'm glad you're better, Cap'n, I truly am."

"Never mind about that," Marsh said, annoyed. "What room is Dan Albright in?"

Albright had been polishing his boots. He let Marsh in with a cool, polite nod of greeting, took his seat again, stuck an arm into one boot, and resumed shining as if he'd never been called to the door.

Abner Marsh sat down heavily and wasted no time with pleasantries. "Why'd you leave the *Fevre Dream*?" he asked bluntly.

"Fever, Cap'n," Albright said. He studied Marsh briefly, then went back to work on his boot without another word.

"Tell me about it, Mister Albright. I wasn't there."

Dan Albright frowned. "You weren't? I understood you and Mister Jeffers found the first sick man."

"You understood wrong. Now tell me."

Albright polished his boots and told him; the storm, the supper, the body that Joshua York and Sour Billy Tipton and the other man had carried through the saloon, the flight of passengers and crew. He told it all in as few words as possible. When he was finished, his boots were gleaming. He slid them on.

"Everyone left?" Marsh said.

"No," said Albright. "Some stayed. Some don't know the fever as well as I do."

"Who?"

Albright shrugged. "Cap'n York. His friends. Hairy Mike. The stokers and roustabouts, too. Reckon they were too scared of Mike to run off. Specially down in slave country. Whitey Blake might have stayed. You and Jeffers, I thought."

"Mister Jeffers is dead," said Marsh.

Albright said nothing.

"What about Karl Framm?" Marsh asked.

"Can't say."

"You were partners."

"We were different. I didn't see him. I don't know, Cap'n."

Marsh frowned. "What happened after you took your wages?"

"I spent a day in Bayou Sara, then took a ride with Cap'n Leathers on the *Natchez*. I rode up to Natchez, looking over the river, spent about a week there, then came on up to St. Louis on the *Robert Folk*."

"What happened to the *Fevre Dream?*"

"She left."

"Left?"

"Steamed off, I figure. When I woke up, morning after the fever broke out, she was gone from Bayou Sara."

"Without a crew?"

"Must have been enough left to run her," Albright said.

"Where'd she go?"

Albright shrugged. "Didn't see her from the *Natchez*. I could have missed her, though. Wasn't looking. Maybe she went downstream."

"You're really quite a goddamn help, Mister Albright," Marsh said.

Albright said, "Can't tell you what I don't know. Maybe they burned her. The fever. Never should have given her that name, I figure. Unlucky."

Abner Marsh was losing patience. "She ain't been burned," he said. "She's on the river somewhere, and I'm goin' to find her. She ain't unlucky neither."

"I was the pilot, Cap'n. I saw it. Storms, fog, delays, and then the fever. She was cursed, that boat. If I was you, I'd give up on her. She's no good for you. Godless." He stood up. "That reminds me, I got something belongs to you." He fetched out two books, and handed them to Marsh. "From the *Fevre Dream* library," he explained. "I played a game of chess with Cap'n York back in New Orleans, and mentioned that I liked poetry, and he gave me these a day later. When I left, I took them along by mistake."

Abner Marsh turned the books over in his hands. Poetry. A volume of poems by Byron and one by Shelley. Just what he needed, he thought. His steamboat was gone, vanished off the river, and all he had left to show of her were two goddamn books of poems. "Keep them," he said to Dan Albright.

Albright shook his head. "Don't want them. Not the kind of poems I like, Cap'n. Immoral, both of them. No wonder your boat got struck down, carrying books like those."

Abner Marsh slid the books into his pocket and stood up, scowling. "I had about enough of that, Mister Albright. I won't hear that kind of talk about my boat. She's as fine a boat as any on the river, and she ain't cursed. Ain't no such thing as curses. The *Fevre Dream*'s a real heller of . . ."

"That she is," Dan Albright interrupted. He stood, too. "I got to see about a berth," he said, ushering Marsh toward the door. Marsh let himself be ushered. But as Albright was showing him out, the dapper little pilot said, "Cap'n Marsh, leave it be."

"What?"

"That steamer," Albright said. "She's no good for you. You know the way I can smell a storm coming?"

"Yes," Marsh said. Albright could smell storms better than anyone Marsh had ever known.

"Sometimes I can smell other things too," the pilot said. "Don't go looking for her, Cap'n. Forget about her. I figured you was dead. You're not. You ought to be thankful. Finding the *Fevre Dream* won't bring you no joy, Cap'n."

Abner Marsh stared at him. "You can say that. You stood at her wheel, and took her down the river, and you can say that."

Albright said nothing.

"Well, I ain't lissening," Marsh said. "That's *my* steamboat, Mister Albright, and someday I'm goin' to pilot her myself, I'm goin' to run her against the *Eclipse*, you hear, and . . . and . . ." Red-faced and angry, Marsh found himself choking on his own tongue. He could not go on.

"Pride can be sinful, Cap'n," Dan Albright said. "Leave it be." He closed the door, leaving Marsh out in the hallway.

Abner Marsh took his lunch in the Planters' House dining room, eating off by himself in the corner. Albright had shaken him, and he found himself thinking the same thoughts he had run through his head going upriver aboard the *Princess*. He ate a leg of lamb in mint sauce, a mess of turnips and snap beans, and three helpings of tapioca, but even that didn't calm him. As he drank his coffee, Marsh wondered if maybe Albright wasn't right. Here he was back in St. Louis, just like he'd been before he met Joshua York in this very same room. He still had his company, the *Eli Reynolds*, and some money in the bank, too. He was an upper river man; it had been a terrible mistake ever to go down to New Orleans. His dream had turned into a nightmare down there in slave country, in the hot fevered south. But now it was over, his steamer had gone and vanished, and if he wanted to he could just pretend that it had never happened at all, that there had never been a steamboat called the *Fevre Dream*, nor people named Joshua York and Damon Julian and Sour Billy Tipton. Joshua had come out of nowhere and now he was gone again. The *Fevre Dream* hadn't existed in April, and it didn't seem to exist now, as far as Marsh could see. A sane man couldn't believe that stuff anyhow, blood-drinking and skulking about by night and bottles of some foul liquor. It had *all* been a fever dream, Abner Marsh thought, but now the fever was gone from him, now he could get on with his life here in St. Louis.

Marsh ordered up some more coffee. They will go on killing, he thought to himself as he drank it, they will go on with the blood-drinking and the murder with no one to stop them. "Can't stop 'em anyway," he muttered. He'd done his best, him and Joshua and Hairy Mike and poor old Mister Jeffers, who'd never raise an eyebrow or move a chessman again. It hadn't gotten them anywhere. And it wouldn't do no good to go to the authorities, not with a story about a bunch of vampires who stole his steamboat. They'd just believe that yellow fever yarn, and figure he'd gone soft in the head, and maybe lock him up someplace.

Abner Marsh paid his bill and walked back to the office of Fevre River Packets. The landing was crowded and bustling. Above was a clear blue sky, and below was the river bright and clean in the sunlight, and the air had a tang to it, a scent of smoke and steam, and he heard the whistles of the boats passing each other on the river, and the big brass bell of a side-wheeler pulling in. The mates were bellowing and the roustabouts were singing as they loaded freight, and Abner Marsh stood and looked and listened. *This* was his life, the other had been a fever dream indeed. The vampires had been killing for thousands of years, Joshua had told him, so how could Marsh hope to change it? Maybe Julian had been right, anyway. It was their nature to kill. And it was Abner Marsh's nature to be a steamboatman, nothing more, he wasn't no fighter, York and Jeffers had tried to fight and they'd paid for it.

When he entered the office, Marsh had just about decided that Dan Albright was dead right. He would forget about the *Fevre Dream*, forget everything that had happened, that was the sensible thing to do. He'd just run his company and maybe make some money, and in a year or two he might have enough to build another boat, a bigger one.

Green was scurrying around the office. "I got twenty letters out, Cap'n," he said to Marsh. "Already posted, just like you said."

"Fine," said Marsh, sinking into a chair. He almost sat on the books of poems, jammed uncomfortably into his pocket. He pulled them out, leafed through them quickly, glancing at a few titles, then set them aside. They were poems all right. Marsh sighed. "Fetch out the books, Mister Green," he said. "I want to take a look at 'em."

"Yes, Cap'n," Green said. He went over and pulled them out. Then he saw something else, picked it up, and brought it over to Marsh with the ledgers. "Oh," he said, "I almost forgot about this." He handed Marsh a large package, wrapped with brown paper and cord. "Some little man brought this by about three weeks back, said you was supposed to pick it up but never showed. I told him you were still off with the *Fevre Dream* and paid him. I hope that was all right."

Abner Marsh frowned down at the package, snapped the cord with a twist of his bare hand, and ripped away the paper to open the box. Inside was a brand new captain's coat, white as the snow that covered the upper river in winter, pure and clean, with a double row of flashing silver buttons, and *Fevre Dream* written in raised letters on every damn one. He took it out and the box fell to the floor and suddenly, finally, the tears came.

"*Get out!*" roared Marsh. The agent took one look at his face and was gone. Abner Marsh rose and put on the white jacket, and buttoned up the silver buttons. It was a beautiful fit. It was cool, much cooler than the heavy blue captain's coat he'd been wearing. There was no mirror in the office, so Marsh couldn't see what he looked like, but he could imagine. In his mind he looked like Joshua York, he looked fine and regal and sophisticated. The cloth was so brilliantly *white*, he thought.

"I look like the cap'n of the *Fevre Dream*," Marsh said loudly, to himself. He stamped his stick hard on the floor, and felt the blood run to his face, and he stood there remembering. Remembering the way she'd looked in the mists of New Albany. Remembering the way her mirrors gleamed, remembering her silver, remembering the wild call of her steam whistle and stroke of her engine, loud as a thunderstorm. Remembering how she'd left the *Southerner* far behind her, how she'd gulped down the *Mary Kaye*. He remembered her people as well; Framm and his wild stories, Whitey Blake spotted with grease, Toby killing chickens, Hairy Mike roaring and cussing at the roustabouts and deckhands, Jeffers playing chess, defeating Dan Albright for the hundredth time. If Albright was so smart, Marsh thought, how come he could never beat Jeffers at chess?

And Marsh recalled Joshua most of all, Joshua all in white, Joshua sipping his liquor, Joshua sitting in the darkness and spinning out his dreams. Gray eyes and strong hands and poetry. "We all make our choices," whispered the memory. *Morn came and went, and came, and brought no day.*

"GREEN!" Abner Marsh roared at the top of his lungs.

The door opened and the agent poked his head in nervously.

"I want my steamboat," Marsh said. "Where the hell is she?"

Green swallowed. "Cap'n, like I said, the *Fevre Dream*—"

"Not *her!*" Marsh said, stamping his stick down hard. "My *other* steamboat. Where the hell is my *other* steamboat, now that I need her?"

CHAPTER TWENTY-TWO

Aboard the Steamer ELI REYNOLDS, Mississippi River, October 1857————

ON a cool evening in early autumn, Abner Marsh and the *Eli Reynolds* finally left St. Louis and headed downstream in search of the *Fevre Dream*. Marsh would just as soon have left several weeks earlier, but there had been too much to do. He'd had to wait for the *Eli Reynolds* to get back from her latest trip up the Illinois, and check her over to make sure she was fit for the lower river, and hire himself a couple of Mississippi pilots. Marsh had claims to settle as well, from planters and shippers who'd entrusted St. Louis-bound freight to the *Fevre Dream* down in New Orleans, and were irate at the steamer's disappearance. Marsh might have insisted they share his loss, but he'd always prided himself on being fair, so he paid them off fifty cents on the dollar. There was also the unpleasant task of talking to Mister Jeffers' relations—Marsh figured he could hardly tell them what had *really* happened, so he finally settled for the yellow fever yarn. Other folks had brothers or sons or husbands still unaccounted for and they pestered Marsh with questions he couldn't answer, and he had to deal with a government inspector and a man from the pilots' association, and he had accounts to square and books to go over and preparations to make, and it all toted up into a month of delay, frustration, and bother.

But all the while, Marsh kept on looking. When the letters that Green had sent out on his behalf got no response, he sent out more. He met incoming steamers as often as he could find the time, and asked after the *Fevre Dream*, after Joshua York, after Karl Framm and Whitey Blake and Hairy Mike Dunne and Toby Lanyard. He hired a couple of detectives and sent them downriver, with instructions to find out what they could. He even borrowed a trick from Joshua, and started buying newspapers from all up and down the river system; he spent his nights poring over the shipping columns, the advertisements, the lists of steamboat arrivals and departures from cities as distant as Cincinnati and New Orleans and St. Paul. He frequented the Planters' House and other river haunts even more than was his custom, and asked a thousand questions.

And learned nothing. The *Fevre Dream* was gone, it seemed, just plain gone from the river. No one had seen her. No one had talked to Whitey Blake or Mister Framm or Hairy Mike, or heard anything about them. The newspapers didn't list her coming or going.

"It ain't sensible," Marsh complained loudly to the officers of the *Eli Reynolds*, a week before their departure. "She's three hundred sixty-foot long, brand new, fast enough to make any steamboatman blink. A boat like that has got to get noticed."

"Unless she went down," suggested Cat Grove, the *Eli Reynolds'* short, wiry mate. "There's places on the river deep enough to drown whole towns. Could be she sunk, with all aboard."

"No," said Marsh stubbornly. He hadn't told them the whole story. He didn't see how he could. None of them had been aboard the *Fevre Dream*; they'd never believe him. "No, she ain't sunk. She's down there somewhere, hidin' from me. But I'm goin' to find her."

"How?" asked Yoerger, the captain of the *Eli Reynolds*.

"It's a long river," Marsh admitted, "and it's got lots of creeks and smaller rivers and bayous leadin' off it, cutoffs, and chutes, and bends, and all kinds of places a steamer can hide where she won't be seen easy. But it ain't so long that it can't be searched. We can start at one end and go to the other, and ask questions along the way, and if we reach New Orleans and we still ain't found her, then we can do the same on the Ohio and the Missouri and the Illinois and the Yazoo and the Red River and wherever the hell we got to go to find that goddamned boat."

"Could take a while," said Yoerger.

"And if it does?"

Yoerger shrugged, and the officers of the *Eli Reynolds* traded uncertain glances. Abner Marsh scowled. "Don't you worry your head about how long it's goin' to take," he snapped. "You just get my steamboat ready, you hear?"

"Yes sir, Cap'n," Yoerger said. He was a tall, stooped, gaunt old man with a quiet voice, and he'd been working steamboats since there had *been* steamboats, so nothing much surprised him anymore, and his tone said as much.

When the day came, Abner Marsh wore his white captain's coat with the double row of silver buttons. It seemed fitting somehow. He ate himself a huge supper at the Planters' House—the provisions on the *Eli Reynolds* weren't too good, and the cook was barely fit to scrub out Toby's fry pans—and walked down to the landing.

The *Eli Reynolds* had her steam up, Marsh saw with approval. Still, she didn't look like much. She was an upper river boat, built small and narrow and low for the shallow tight streams where she had to ply her trade. She was less than a fourth as long as the vanished *Fevre Dream*, and about half as wide, and full-loaded she could carry maybe 150 tons of cargo, against the thousand tons of the larger steamer. The *Reynolds* had only two decks; there was no texas, and the crew occupied the forward portion of the cabins on the boiler deck. She seldom had any cabin passengers anyway. A single big high-pressure boiler drove her stern wheel, and she was as plain as all get out. She was near empty of cargo now, so Marsh could see the boiler, sitting well forward. Rows of plain whitewashed wooden pillars supported the upper decks, looking like rickety stilts, and the columns that held up the weathered promenade roof were square and simple, plain as a picket fence. The aft wheelhouse was a big square wooden box, the stern wheel a sorry-looking afterthought, its red paint faded and streaked from long use. Elsewhere paint was flaking. The pilot house was a damn wood-and-glass outhouse set atop the steamboat, and the stubby chimneys were unadorned black iron. The *Eli Reynolds* showed her age sitting there in the water; she looked terribly weary and a bit lopsided, as if she was about to keel over and sink.

She was a damn unlikely match for the huge, powerful *Fevre Dream*. But she was all he had now, Abner Marsh reflected, and she would have to do. He walked on down to the steamer and climbed aboard, across a stage that had been badly worn by the tread of countless boots. Cat Grove met him on the forecastle. "All ready, Cap'n."

"Tell the pilot to take her out," Marsh said. Grove shouted up the order, and the *Eli Reynolds* sounded its whistle. The blast was thin and plaintive, and hopelessly brave, Marsh thought. He clomped up the steep, narrow stair to the main cabin, which was dim and cramped-feeling, barely forty foot long. The carpet was bare in spots, and the landscapes painted on the stateroom doors had long since faded into dullness. The whole interior of the steamer had an odor about it of stale food and sour wine and oil and smoke and sweat. It was unpleasantly hot, too, and the single plain skylight was too grimed-over to admit much light. Yoerger and the off-duty pilot were drinking cups of black coffee at a round table when Marsh entered. "My lard aboard?" Marsh asked.

Yoerger nodded.

"Not much else aboard, that I saw," Marsh commented.

Yoerger frowned. "I figured you'd like it that way, Cap'n. Loaded up, we'd be slower, and there'd be more stops to make, too."

Abner Marsh pondered that, and nodded in approval. "Good," he said. "Makes sense. My other package get delivered?"

"In your cabin," Yoerger said.

Marsh took his leave and retired to his stateroom. The bunk creaked beneath him when he sat down on its edge, opened the package, and took out the rifle and shells. He examined it carefully, hefting it in his hand, sighting down the barrel. It felt good. Maybe your ordinary pistol or rifle shot was nothing to the night folks, but this was something else again, custom made to his order by the best gunsmith in St. Louis. It was a buffalo gun, with a short, wide, octagonal barrel, designed to be fired from horseback and stop a charging buffalo in its tracks. The fifty custom shells were bigger than any the gunsmith had ever made before. "Hell," the man had complained, "these'll blow your game to pieces, won't be nothing left to et." Abner Marsh had only nodded. The rifle wouldn't be worth much for accuracy, especially in Marsh's hands, but it didn't need to be. At close range it would wipe Damon Julian's smile clean off his face, and blow his goddamn head off his shoulders for good measure. Marsh carefully loaded it up, and mounted it on the wall above his bed, where he could sit up and snatch it down in one easy motion. Only then did he let himself lie back.

And so it began. Day after day the *Eli Reynolds* steamed downriver, through rain and fog, through sunshine and overcast, stopping at every town and steamboat landing and woodyard to ask a question or two. Abner Marsh sat up on the hurricane deck, in a wooden chair beside the steamer's old cracked bell, and watched the river for hour after hour. Sometimes he even took his meals up there. When he had to sleep, Captain Yoerger or Cat Grove or the mud-clerk took his place, and the vigil went on. When rafts and flatboats and other steamers went sliding by, Marsh called out, "You there! You seen a steamer named the *Fevre Dream?*" But the answer, when he got an answer, always came back, "No, Cap'n, we sure ain't," and the folks on the landings and in the woodyards told them nothing, and the river was full of steamboats, steamboats day and night, steamboats big and little, going up the river or down it or lying half-sunk by the banks, but none of them were the *Fevre Dream.*

She was a slow small boat on a big river, the *Eli Reynolds,* and she crept along at a pace that would make most steamboatmen ashamed, and her stops and her questions delayed her even more. But still the towns passed, the woodyards passed, the forests and the houses and other steamboats drifted on by in a blur of days and nights, islands and sandbars were left behind them, their pilot steered them deftly past the snags and sawyers, and they moved south, ever south. Sainte Genevieve came and went, Cape Girardeau and Crosno went by, they put in for a bit at Hickman and longer at New Madrid. Caruthersville was lost in fog, but they found it. Osceola was still and Memphis was loud. Helena. Rosedale. Arkansas City. Napoleon. Greenville. Lake Providence.

When the *Eli Reynolds* came steaming into Vicksburg one blustery October morning, two men were waiting on the landing.

Abner Marsh sent most of the crew ashore. He and Captain Yoerger and Cat Grove met with the visitors in the main cabin of the steamer. One of the men was a big, hard sort with red muttonchop whiskers and a head bald as a pigeon's egg, dressed in a black broadcloth suit. The other was a slender, well-dressed black man with piercing dark eyes. Marsh sat them down and served them coffee. "Well?" he demanded. "Where is she?"

The bald man blew on his coffee and scowled. "Don't know."

"I paid you to find my steamer," Marsh said.

"She ain't to be found, Cap'n Marsh," the black man said. "Hank and me looked, I tell you that."

"Ain't sayin' we found nothin'," the bald man said. "Only that we ain't got the steamer pinned down yet."

"All right," Abner Marsh said. "Tell me what you found."

The black man pulled a sheet of paper from inside his jacket and unfolded it. "Most of your steamer's crew and near all her passengers left at Bayou Sara, after that yaller fever scare. Next morning, your

Fevre Dream steamed out. Went upriver, from all accounts. We found some woodyard niggers who swear she wooded up with 'em. Maybe they was lyin', but I can't see why. So we know the direction your steamer went in. We got enough folks to swear they seen her go by. Or they think they did, anyway."

"Only she never reached Natchez," his partner put in. "That's . . . what . . . eight, ten hours upriver."

"Less," said Abner Marsh. "The *Fevre Dream* was a damn fast boat."

"Fast or not, she got herself lost 'tween Bayou Sara and Natchez."

"The Red River branches off in there," Marsh said.

The black man nodded. "But your boat ain't been in Shreveport nor Alexandria neither, and none of the woodyards we checked can recall any *Fevre Dream*."

"Damn," said Marsh.

"Maybe she *did* sink," Cat Grove suggested.

"We got more," said the bald detective. He took a swallow of coffee. "Your steamer was never seen in Natchez, you understand. But some of the folks you were lookin' for were."

"Go on." Marsh said.

"We spent a lot of time on Silver Street," he said. "Askin' around. Man called Raymond Ortega, he was known there, and he was on your list, too. He came back one night, early in September, paid a social call to one of the nabobs on top of the hill, and a lot of calls down under the hill. Had four other men with him. One of 'em fits your description of this Sour Billy Tipton. They stayed about a week. Did some interesting things. Hired a lot of men, whites, colored, didn't matter. You know the kind of men you can hire from Natchez-under-the-hill."

Abner Marsh knew all right. Sour Billy Tipton had scared off Marsh's crew and replaced them with a gang of cutthroats like himself. "Steamboatmen?" he asked.

The bald man nodded. "There's more. This Tipton visited Fork-in-the-Road."

"It's a big slave mart," the black partner said.

"He bought a mess of slaves. Paid with *gold*." The bald man pulled a twenty-dollar gold piece from his pocket and set it on the table. "Like this. Bought some other stuff back in Natchez, too. Paid the same way."

"What kind of stuff?" Marsh asked.

"Slaver's stuff," the black man said. "Manacles. Chains. Hammers."

"Some paint, too," said the other.

And suddenly the truth of it burst on Abner Marsh like a shower of fireworks. "Jesus *God*," he swore. "*Paint!* No wonder no one has seen her. *Goddamn*. They're smarter than I thought, and I'm an egg-suckin' fool not to have seen it straight off!" He slammed his big fist down on the table hard enough to make the coffee cups jump.

"We figure just what you're thinkin'," the bald man said. "They painted her. Changed her name."

"A little paint ain't enough to change a famous steamer," objected Yoerger.

"No," said Abner Marsh, "but she wasn't famous yet. Hell, we made one damn trip down the river, never did make it back up. How many folks goin' to recognize her? How many even *heard* of her? There's new boats comin' out most every day. Slap a new name on her wheelhouse, maybe some new colors here and there, you got a new boat."

"But the *Fevre Dream* was *big*," said Yoerger. "And fast, you said."

"Lots of big steamers on the damn river," Marsh said. "Oh, she was bigger than nearly all of them except the *Eclipse*, but how many folks can tell that at a look, without another boat to measure her by? As for *fast*, hell, it's easy enough to keep her times down. That way she don't get talked about." Marsh was furious. That was just what they'd do, he knew; run her slow, at well under her capability, and thereby keep her inconspicuous. Somehow that seemed obscene to him.

"Problem is," the bald man said, "there ain't no way for us to know what name they painted on her. So findin' her ain't goin' to be easy. We can board ever' boat on the river, lookin' for these people you want, but . . ." He shrugged.

"No," Abner Marsh said. "I'll find her easier than that. No amount of paint is goin' to change the *Fevre Dream* so I can't tell her when I see her. We got this far, now we keep goin', all the way down to New Orleans." Marsh tugged at his beard. "Mister Grove," he said, turning to the mate, "fetch me those pilots of ours. They're lower river men, they ought to know the steamers down here pretty well. Ask 'em if they'll go over those piles of newspapers I been savin', and check off any boat that's strange to 'em."

"Sure thing, Cap'n," Grove said.

Abner Marsh turned back to the detectives. "I won't be needin' you gentlemen any more, I don't believe," he said. "But if you should happen to run into that steamer, you know how to reach me. I'll see that you get well paid." He stood up. "Now if you'll come back to the clerk's office, I'll give you the rest of what I owe you."

They spent the rest of the day tied up at Vicksburg. Marsh had just finished supper—a plate of fried chicken, sadly underdone, and some tired potatoes—when Cat Grove pulled up a chair next to him, a piece of paper in hand. "It took them most of the day, Cap'n, but they done it," Grove said. "There's too damn many boats, though. Must have been thirty neither of 'em knew. I went over the papers myself, checkin' the advertisements and such to see what they said about the size of the boats, who the masters were, that kind of thing. Some names I recognized, and I was able to cross off a lot of stern-wheelers and undersized boats."

"How many left?"

"Just four," said Grove. "Four big side-wheelers that nobody's ever heard of." He handed the list to Abner Marsh. The names were printed out carefully in block capitals, one beneath the other.

B. SCHROEDER

QUEEN CITY

OZYMANDIAS

F. D. HECKINGER

Marsh stared at the paper for a long time, frowning. Something there ought to mean something to him, he knew, but he couldn't figure out what or why for the life of him.

"Make any sense, Cap'n?"

"It ain't the *B. Schroeder,*" Marsh said suddenly. "They were puttin' her together up to New Albany the same time they were workin' on the *Fevre Dream.*" He scratched his head.

"That last boat," Grove said, pointing, "look at those initials, Cap'n. F. D. Like for *Fevre Dream,* maybe."

"Maybe," Marsh said. He said the names aloud. "F. D. Heckinger. Queen City. Ozy—" That one was hard. He was glad he didn't have to spell it. "Ozy-man-dee-us."

Then Abner Marsh's mind, his slow deliberate mind that never forgot anything, chucked the answer up in front of him, like a piece of driftwood thrown up by the river. He'd puzzled over that damn word before, very briefly and not so long ago, when flipping through a book. "Wait," he said to Grove. He rose and strode off to his cabin. The books were in the bottom drawer of his chest of drawers.

"What's that?" Grove asked when Marsh returned.

"Goddamn *poems*," Marsh said. He flipped through Byron, found nothing, turned to Shelley. And it was there in front of him. He read it over quickly, leaned back, frowned, read it over again.

"Cap'n Marsh?" Grove said.

"Listen to this," Marsh said. He read aloud:

> *"My name is Ozymandias, king of kings:*
> *Look on my works, ye Mighty, and despair!"*
> *Nothing beside remains. Round the decay*
> *Of that colossal wreck, boundless and bare*
> *The lone and level sands stretch far away.*

"What is it?"

"A poem," said Abner Marsh. "It's a goddamn poem."

"But what does it mean?"

"It means," said Marsh, closing the book, "that Joshua is feelin' sorry and beaten. You wouldn't understand why, though, Mister Grove. The important thing that it means is that we're lookin' for a steamboat name of *Ozymandias*."

Grove brought out another slip of paper. "I wrote down some stuff from the papers," he explained, squinting at his own writing. "Let's see, that Ozy . . . Ozy . . . whatever it is, it's workin' the Natchez trade. Master named J. Anthony."

"Anthony," said Marsh. "Hell. Joshua's middle name was Anton. Natchez, you say?"

"Natchez to New Orleans, Cap'n."

"We'll stay here for the night. Tomorrow, come dawn, we make for Natchez. You hear that, Mister Grove? I don't want to waste a minute of light. When that damn sun comes up, I want our steam up too, so we're ready to move." Maybe poor Joshua had nothing left but despair, but Abner Marsh had a lot more than that. There were accounts that wanted settling, and when he was through, there wasn't going to be any more left of Damon Julian than was left of that damned statue in the poem.

CHAPTER TWENTY-THREE

Aboard the Steamer ELI REYNOLDS, Mississippi River, October 1857———

ABNER Marsh did not sleep that night. He spent the long hours of darkness in his chair on the hurricane deck, his back to the smoky lights of Vicksburg, looking out over the river. The night was cool and quiet, the water like black glass. Once in a while some steamer would heave into view, wreathed in flame and smoke and cinders, and the tranquility would shatter while she passed. But then the boat would tie up or steam on, the sound of her whistle would die away, and the darkness would mend itself, grow smooth once again. The moon was a silver dollar floating on the water, and Marsh heard wet creaking sounds from the tired *Eli Reynolds*, and occasionally a voice or a footfall or maybe a snatch of song from Vicksburg, and always beneath it all the sound of the river, the rush of the endless waters surging past, pushing at his boat, trying to take her with them, south, south, to where the night folks and the *Fevre Dream* were waiting.

Marsh felt strangely filled with the night's beauty, with the dark loveliness that Joshua's gimp Britisher had been so moved by. He tilted his chair back against the old steamer's bell and gazed out over the moon and stars and river, thinking that maybe this would be the last moment of peace he would ever know. For tomorrow, or the day after for sure, they would find the *Fevre Dream*, and the summer's nightmare would begin again.

His head was full of forebodings, full of memories and visions. He kept seeing Jonathon Jeffers, him with his sword cane, so damned cocksure and so damned helpless when Julian ran right up the blade. He heard the sound the clerk's neck made when Julian snapped it,

235

and remembered the way Jeffers' spectacles had fallen off, the wink of gold as they tumbled to the deck, the terrible small sound that they had made. His big hands clenched tight around his walking stick. Against the dark river, he saw other things as well. That tiny hand impaled on a knife, dripping blood. Julian drinking Joshua's dark potion. The wet smears on Hairy Mike's iron billet when it had done its grisly work in the stateroom. Abner Marsh was afraid, afraid as he'd never been. To banish the specters that drifted across the night, he called up his own dream, a vision of him standing with the buffalo gun in hand at the door of the captain's cabin. He heard the gun roar and felt its awful kick, and saw Damon Julian's pale smile and dark curls burst apart, like a melon thrown from a height, a melon filled with blood.

But somehow, even when the face was gone and the smoke of the gun had blown away, the eyes were still there, staring, beckoning, waking things in him, anger and hatred and darker deeper feelings. The eyes were black as hell itself and filled with red, chasms endless and eternal as his river, calling to him, stirring his own lusts, his own red thirst. They floated before him, and Abner Marsh stared into them, into the warm black, and saw his answer there, saw the way to end them, better and surer than sword canes or stakes or buffalo guns.

Fire. Out on the river, the *Fevre Dream* was burning. Abner Marsh felt it all. The terrible sudden roar that ripped at the ears, worse than any thunder. The billows of flame and smoke, the burning chunks of wood and coal spilling everywhere, scalding-hot steam bursting free, clouds of white death enveloping the boat, the walls blowing out and burning, bodies flying through the air afire or half-cooked, the chimneys cracking, collapsing, the screams, the steamer listing and sinking into the river, sizzling and hissing and smoking, charred corpses floating face down amid the debris, the great side-wheeler coming apart until nothing was left but burnt wood and a chimney sticking up crookedly from the water. In the dream, when her boilers went, the name painted on her was still *Fevre Dream.*

It would be easy, Abner Marsh knew. A consignment of freight for New Orleans; they'd never suspect. Barrels of explosives, stowed down on the main deck carelessly near the red-hot furnaces and all those huge, unruly high-pressure boilers. He could arrange it, and that would be the end for Julian and all the night folks. A fuse, a timer, it could be done.

Abner Marsh closed his eyes. When he opened them again, the

burning steamer was gone, the sounds of the screams and the boiler explosion had faded, and the night was quiet once again. "Can't," he said aloud to himself, "Joshua is still aboard her. Joshua." And others as well, he hoped: Whitey Blake, Karl Framm, Hairy Mike Dunne and his rousters. And there was his lady herself to consider, his *Fevre Dream*. Marsh had a glimpse of a quiet bend of river on a night like tonight, and two great steamers running side by side, plumes of smoke behind them flattened by their speed, fires crowning their stacks, their wheels turning furiously. As they came on and on, one began to move ahead, a little now, then more and more, until she had opened up a boat's length lead. She was still pulling away when they passed out of sight, and Marsh saw the names written on them, and the leader was *Fevre Dream*, her flags flying as she moved upriver swift and serene, and behind came the *Eclipse*, glittering even in defeat. I will make it happen, Abner Marsh told himself.

The crew of the *Eli Reynolds* had largely returned by midnight. Marsh watched them straggle in from Vicksburg, and heard Cat Grove direct the wooding-up operation in the moonlight, with a series of short, snapped commands. Hours later, the first wisps of smoke began to curl upward from the steamer's chimneys, as the engineer fired her up. Dawn was still an hour off. It was about then that Yoerger and Grove appeared on the hurricane deck, with chairs of their own and a pot of coffee. They took seats next to Marsh in silence, and poured him a cup. It was hot and black. He sipped it gratefully.

"Well, Cap'n Marsh," Yoerger said after a time. His long face was gray and tired. "Don't you think it's time you told us what this is all about?"

"Since we got back to St. Louis," added Cat Grove, "you been talkin' nothin' but gettin' back your boat. Tomorrow, maybe, we'll have her. What then? You ain't told us much, Cap'n, 'cept that you don't intend to bring in no police. Why is that, if your boat was stole?"

"Same reason I ain't told you, Mister Grove. They wouldn't believe my story for a minute."

"Crew's curious," said Grove. "Me, too."

"It ain't none of their business," said Marsh. "I own this steamboat, don't I? You work for me, and them too. Just do like I tell you."

"Cap'n Marsh," said Yoerger, "this old gal and I been on the river some years now. You gave her over to me soon as you got your

237

second steamer, the old *Nick Perrot* I believe it was, back in '52. I took care of this lady ever since then, and you haven't relieved me, no sir. If I'm fired, why, tell me so. If I'm still your captain, then tell me what I'm taking my steamer into. I deserve that much."

"I told Jonathon Jeffers," said Marsh, seeing the little glint of gold once again, "and he died on account of it. Maybe Hairy Mike too, I don't know."

Cat Grove leaned forward gracefully and refilled Marsh's cup with lukewarm coffee from the pot. "Cap'n," he said, "from the little you told us, you ain't sure whether Mike is alive or not, but that ain't the point. You ain't sure 'bout some others as well. Whitey Blake, that pilot of yours, all them that stayed on the *Fevre Dream*. You tell all them, too?"

"No," Marsh admitted.

"Then it don't make no mind," said Grove.

"If there is danger downriver, we have a right to know," said Yoerger.

Abner Marsh thought on that, and saw the justice in it. "You're right," he said, "but you ain't goin' to believe it. And I can't have you leavin'. I need this steamer."

"We ain't goin' nowhere," said Grove. "Tell us the story."

So Abner Marsh sighed and told the story once again. When he was finished he stared at their faces. Both wore guarded expressions, careful, noncommittal.

"It is hard to credit," said Yoerger.

"I believe it," said Grove. "Ain't no harder to believe than ghosts. I seen ghosts myself, hell, dozens of times."

"Cap'n Marsh," said Yoerger, "you've talked a lot about finding the *Fevre Dream*, and seldom about your intentions after you find her. Do you have a plan?"

Marsh thought of the fire, the boilers roaring and blowing, the screams of his enemies. He pushed the thought away. "I'm takin' back my boat," he said. "You seen my gun. Once I blow Julian's head off, I figure Joshua can take care of the rest."

"You say you tried that, with Jeffers and Dunne, back when you still controlled the steamer and its crew. Now, if your detectives were right, the boat's full of slaves and cutthroats. You can't get aboard without being recognized. How will you get to Julian?"

Abner Marsh had not really given the matter much thought. But now that Yoerger had raised the point, it was plain to see that he couldn't hardly just stomp across the stage, buffalo gun in hand, alone, which is what he'd more or less intended. He thought on it a moment. If he could get aboard somehow as a passenger . . . but Yoerger was right, that was impossible. Even if he shaved, there was no one on the river looked even approximately like Abner Marsh. "We'll go in force," Marsh said after a brief hesitation. "I'll take the whole damn crew of the *Reynolds*. Julian and Sour Billy probably figure I'm dead; we'll surprise them. By day, of course. I ain't takin' no more chances with the light. None of the night folks ever seen the *Eli Reynolds*, and I reckon only Joshua ever heard the name. We'll steam right up next to her, wherever we find her landed, and we'll wait for a good bright sunny morning, and then me and all those who'll come with me will march over. Scum is scum, and whatever dregs Sour Billy found in Natchez ain't goin' to risk their skins against guns and knives. Maybe we'll have to take care of Billy hisself, but then the way's clear. This time I'll make goddamn sure it's Julian before I blow his head off." He spread his hands. "Satisfactory?"

"Sounds good," said Grove. Yoerger looked more dubious. But neither of them had any other suggestions worth a damn, so after a brief discussion, they agreed to his plan. By then dawn had brushed the bluffs and hills of Vicksburg, and the *Eli Reynolds* had her steam up. Abner Marsh rose and stretched, feeling remarkably fit for a man who hadn't slept a wink all night. "Take 'er out," he said loudly to the pilot, who had passed them on his way to the plain little pilot house. "Natchez!"

Deckhands cast loose the ropes that tied her to the landing, and the stern-wheeler backed out, reversed her paddle, and pushed out into the channel while red and gray shadows began to chase each other across the eastern shore, and the clouds in the west turned rose.

For the first two hours, they made good time, past Warrenton and Hard Times and Grand Gulf. Three or four larger steamers passed them up, but that was to be expected; the *Eli Reynolds* wasn't built for racing. Abner Marsh was satisfied enough with her progress so that he took himself below for thirty minutes, long enough to check and clean his gun and make sure it was loaded, and eat a quick breakfast of hotcakes and blueberries and fried eggs. Between St. Joseph and Rodney, the sky began to overcast, which Marsh didn't like one bit. A short time later, a small storm broke over the river, not enough thunder nor lightning nor rain to hurt a fly, Marsh thought, but the pilot respected it enough to keep them tied up for a hour at a woodyard, while Marsh prowled the boat restlessly. Framm or Albright would have just pushed on through the weather, but you couldn't expect to get a lightnin' pilot on a boat like this. The rain was cold and gray. When it finally ended, however, there was a nice rainbow in the sky, which Marsh liked quite a lot, and still more than enough time to reach Natchez before dark.

Fifteen minutes after casting off again, the *Eli Reynolds* fetched up hard against a sandbar.

It was a stupid, frustrating mistake. The young pilot, barely past being a cub, had tried to make up some lost time by running an uncertain cutoff instead of staying with the main channel, which made a wide bend to the east. A month or two back it might have been a slick bit of piloting, but now the river stage was too low, even for a steamer drawing as little as the *Eli Reynolds*.

Abner Marsh swore and fumed and stomped about angrily, especially when it became clear that they couldn't back her clear of the bar. Cat Grove and his men fetched out the winches and grasshopper poles and set to. It rained on them a couple times, just to make things more difficult, but four-and-a-half wet, weary hours later, the pilot started the stern wheel up again and the *Eli Reynolds* wrenched herself forward with a spray of mud and sand, shaking like she was about to fall to pieces. And then she was afloat. Her whistle blew in triumph.

They crept along the cutoff cautiously for another half-hour, but once they regained the river, the current took hold of them and the *Reynolds* picked up speed. She shot downriver smoking and rattling like the very devil, but there was no way to make up the time she'd lost.

Abner Marsh was sitting on the faded yellow couch in the pilot house when they first glimpsed the city, up ahead on its bluffs. He set down his coffee cup on top of the big pot-bellied stove and stood behind the pilot, who was busy making a crossing. Marsh paid him no mind; his eyes were on the distant landing, where twenty or more steamers were nuzzling up against Natchez-under-the-hill.

She was there, as he had known she'd be.

Marsh knew her right off. She was the biggest boat on the landing, and stuck out a good fifty feet beyond her nearest rival, and her stacks were tallest, too. As the *Eli Reynolds* drew nearer, Marsh saw that they hadn't changed her much. She was still mostly blue and white and silver, though they'd painted her wheelhouses a tawdry bright red, like the lips of a Natchez whore. Her name was spelled out in yellow lettering curved around the side of the paddlebox, crudely; OZYMANDIAS, it said. Marsh scowled. "See the big one there?" he said to the pilot, pointing. "You put us close to her as you can, you hear?"

"Yessuh, Cap'n."

Marsh looked at the town ahead with distaste. Already the shadows were growing in the streets, and the river waters wore the scarlet and gold tinge of sunset. It was cloudy too, too damn cloudy. They had lost too much time at the woodyard and the cutoff, he thought, and sunset came a lot earlier in October than in summer.

Captain Yoerger had entered the pilot house and moved to his side, and now he put words to Marsh's thoughts. "You can't go tonight, Cap'n Marsh. It's too late. It will be dark in less than an hour. Wait till tomorrow."

"What kind of damned fool you take me for?" Marsh said. "Course I'll wait. I made that damn mistake once, I ain't makin' it again." He stamped his walking stick hard against the deck in frustration. Yoerger started to say something else, but Marsh wasn't listening. He was still studying the big side-wheeler by the landing. "Hell," he said suddenly.

"What's wrong?"

Marsh pointed with his hickory stick. "Smoke," he said. "Damn them, they got her steam up! She must be leavin'."

"Don't be rash," Yoerger cautioned. "If she leaves, she leaves, but we'll catch up to her somewhere else downriver."

"They must run her by night," Marsh said, "tie up during the day. I should have figured that." He turned to the pilot. "Mister Norman," he said, "don't you land after all. Keep goin' downstream and put in at the first woodyard you see, wait till that boat there passes you by. Then follow her, well as you can. She's a hell of a lot faster'n the *Reynolds*, so don't you worry if she loses you, just keep on down-river as close behind her as you can."

"Whatever you say, Cap'n," the pilot replied. He swung the worn wooden wheel hand over hand, and the *Eli Reynolds* turned her head abruptly and began to angle back out into the channel.

They had been at the woodyard for ninety minutes, and it had been full night for at least twenty, when the *Fevre Dream* came steaming past. Marsh shivered when he saw her approach. The huge side-wheeler moved downriver with a terrible liquid grace, a quiet smoothness that reminded him somehow of Damon Julian and the way he walked. She was half-dark. The main deck glowed a faint reddish-pink from the fires of her furnaces, but only a few of the cabin windows on the boiler deck were lit up, and the texas was entirely black, as was the pilot house. Marsh thought he could see a solitary figure up there, standing at the wheel, but she was too far off to be sure. The moon and stars shone pale on her white paint and silver trim, and the red wheelhouses looked obscene. As she passed by, another steamer's lights appeared way downstream, ascending toward her, and they called out to one another in the night. Marsh would have known her whistle anywhere, he thought, but now it seemed to him that it had a cold and mournful sound to it that he had never heard before, a melancholy wail that spoke of pain and despair.

"Keep your distance," he said to his pilot, "but follow her." A deckhand cast off the rope holding them to the woodyard's snubbing post, and the *Eli Reynolds* swallowed a mess of tar and pine-knots and snorted out into the river after her larger, wayward cousin. A minute or two later, the stranger steamer ascending toward Natchez crossed the *Fevre Dream* and steamed toward them, sounding a deep three-toned blast on her whistle. The *Reynolds* answered, but her call sounded so thin and weak compared to the *Fevre Dream*'s wild shrill that it filled Marsh with unease.

He had expected that the *Fevre Dream* would outdistance them within minutes, but it did not turn out that way. The *Eli Reynolds* steamed downstream in her wake for two solid hours. She lost the bigger boat a half-dozen times around river bends, but always caught sight of her again within minutes. The distance between the two steamboats widened, but so gradually that it was hardly worth mentioning. "We're runnin' full out, or near it," Marsh said to Captain Yoerger, "but they're just loafin'. Unless they turn up the Red River, I reckon they'll stop at Bayou Sara. That's where we'll catch 'em." He smiled. "Fittin', ain't it?"

With eighteen big boilers to heat and a lot of boat to move, the *Fevre Dream* ate up a lot more wood than her small shadow. She stopped to wood up several times, and each time the *Eli Reynolds* crept up on her a bit, although Marsh was careful to have his pilot slow to quarter-speed so as not to catch the side-wheeler while she was taking on wood. The *Reynolds* herself stopped once to load up her neary-empty main deck with twenty cords of fresh-cut beech, and when she pushed back out into the river the lights of the *Fevre Dream* had receded to a vague reddish blur on the black waters ahead. But Marsh ordered a barrel of lard chucked into the furnace, and the burst of heat and steam soon made up most of the lost distance.

Near where the mouth of the Red River emptied into the wider Mississippi, a comfortable mile separated the two steamers. Marsh had just brought a fresh pot of coffee up to the pilot house, and was helping the pilot drink it, when the man squinted over the wheel and said, "Take a look here, Cap'n, appears the current's pushin' her sideways. Ain't no crossing to be made there."

Marsh put down his cup and looked. The *Fevre Dream* looked a lot closer all of a sudden, he thought, and the pilot was right, he could see a good portion of her larboard side. If she wasn't making a crossing, maybe the waters rushing in from the lesser river *were* responsible for her sheer, but he didn't see how a decent pilot would allow that. "She's just anglin' round a snag or a bar," Marsh said, but there was no certainty in his tone. As he watched, the side-wheeler seemed to turn even more, so she was practically at cross angles to them. He could read the lettering on her wheelhouse in the moonlight. She almost looked like she was drifting, but the smoke and sparks still steamed from her stacks, and now her bow was swinging into view.

"Goddamn," Marsh said loudly. He felt as cold as if he'd just taken another fall into the river. "She's turnin'. Damn it all to hell! She's *turnin'*!"

"What should I do, Cap'n?" asked the pilot.

Abner Marsh did not answer. He was watching the *Fevre Dream* with fear in his heart. A stern-wheeler like the *Eli Reynolds* had two ways to reverse directions, both of them clumsy. If the channel was wide enough, she could round to in a big U, but that took a lot of room and a lot of push. Otherwise she had to stop and reverse her paddle, back and turn, stop again and start forward to complete the turnabout. Either way took time, and Marsh didn't even know if they could round to right here. A side-wheeler was a damn sight more maneuverable. A side-wheeler could just reverse one wheel and keep the other going forward, so she'd spin about neat as you please like a dancer twirling on a toe. Now Abner Marsh could see the forecastle of the *Fevre Dream*. Her stages, drawn up, looked like two long white teeth in the moonlight, and pale-faced figures in dark clothing were clustered together on the forward portions of the main and boiler decks. The *Fevre Dream* loomed ahead of them bigger and more formidable than ever. She had almost completed her spin now, and the *Eli Reynolds* was still paddling toward her, *whapwhapwhap*, paddling toward those white maggot-faces and darkness and hot red eyes.

"You damn fool!" Marsh bellowed. "Stop her! Back her, dammit, *turn* her! Ain't you got eyes? *They're comin' after us!*"

The pilot gave him an uncertain glance, and moved to stop the paddle wheel and commence to turn, but even as he did Abner Marsh saw that it was too damn late. They'd never come around in time, and even if they did, the *Fevre Dream* would be on them in minutes anyway. Her power would be much more telling when both boats were struggling against the current. Marsh grabbed the pilot's arm. "No!" he said, "keep on! Faster! Go wide around them. Get some more lard in there quick, dammit, we got to shoot past 'em before they're on us, you hear?"

The *Fevre Dream* was creeping toward them now, her decks acrawl with the night folks. Smoke poured from her chimneys, and Marsh could almost count the waiting figures. The pilot reached for the steam whistle, but Marsh grabbed him again and said, "No!"

"We'll *collide!*" the pilot said. "Cap'n, we gotta let 'em know which side we're takin'."

"Keep 'em guessin'," Marsh said. "Damn you, it's our only chance! *And get that lard in there!*"

Across the dark moonlit waters, the *Fevre Dream* shrieked in triumph. It sounded like some demon wolf, thought Abner Marsh, howling after prey.

CHAPTER TWENTY-FOUR

Aboard the Steamer OZYMANDIAS, Mississippi River, October 1857————

"WELL, well," said Sour Billy Tipton, "he's comin' right to us. Ain't that nice of him?"

"You are certain it is Marsh, Billy?" asked Damon Julian.

"Take a look-see for yourself," Sour Billy said, handing Julian the telescope. "Right up there in the pilot house of that rattletrap. Ain't no one else so fat or so warty. Good thing I got to wonderin' why they was stayin' behind us like that."

Julian lowered the glass. "Yes," he said. He smiled. "What ever would we do without you, Billy?" Then the smile faded. "But Billy, you assured me that the captain was dead. When he fell into the river. I'm sure you recall. Don't you, Billy?"

Sour Billy looked at him warily. "We'll make sure this time, Mister Julian."

"Ah," said Julian. "Yes. Pilot, when we pass I want us within feet of their side. Do you understand, pilot?"

Joshua York looked away from the river briefly, without releasing his sure grip on the big black and silver wheel. His cold gray eyes met Julian's across the darkness of the pilot house, then dropped abruptly. "We will pass close to them," York said in a hollow voice.

On the couch behind the stove, Karl Framm stirred weakly, sat up, and came over to stand behind York, staring out over the river with filmy, half-dead eyes. He moved slowly, unsteady as a drunk or a weak old man. Looking at him, it was hard to recall how troublesome the pilot had been at first, Billy thought. Damon Julian had tended to Framm proper enough, though; that day he'd come lolly-gagging back to the boat, not realizing how things had changed, the lanky pilot had made some damn fool brag about his three wives within Julian's hearing. Damon Julian had been amused. "Since you won't be seeing the others anymore," Julian had said to Framm later, "you'll have three new wives aboard our steamer. A pilot has his privileges, after all." And now Cynthia, Valerie, and Cara took turns with him, careful not to drink too much all at once, but drinking regular enough. As the only licensed pilot, Framm couldn't be permitted to die, even though York did most of the steering now. Framm wasn't high and mighty anymore, nor troublesome. He hardly talked at all, and he sort of shuffled when he walked, and he had tooth marks and wounds and such all up and down his skinny arms, and a feverish look in his eyes.

Blinking at the approach of Marsh's squatty stern-wheeler, Framm almost seemed to perk up a mite. He even smiled. "Close," he muttered, "you bet she'll come close."

Julian looked at him. "What do you mean, Mister Framm?"

"Nothing a-tall," said Framm, "exceptin' that she's goin' to ram right into you." He grinned. "I bet ol' Cap'n Marsh has that dern boat stacked up to the boiler deck with explosives. It's an old river trick."

Julian flicked his gaze back to the river. The stern-wheeler was bearing straight down on the *Fevre Dream*, belching fire and smoke like nobody's business.

"He's lyin'," said Sour Billy, "he always lies."

"Look how fast she's coming," Framm said, and it was true. With the current behind her and her paddle churning furiously, the stern-wheeler was coming on like the very devil.

"Mister Framm is right," said Joshua York, and he was turning the huge wheel as he spoke, hand over hand, with smooth swift grace. The *Fevre Dream* swung her head sharply to the larboard. An instant later, the oncoming stern-wheeler sheered in the other direction, racing away from them. They could read the faded square lettering on her side: ELI REYNOLDS.

"It's a damn trick!" Sour Billy shouted. "He's lettin' them get past us!"

Julian said coldly, "There are no explosives. Put us close to them," and York began turning the wheel back at once, but it was too late; Marsh's boat had seen her chance and lurched forward with surprising speed, steam hissing from her 'scape-pipes in tall white plumes. The *Fevre Dream* responded quickly, her head moving back in line, but already the *Eli Reynolds* was thirty yards to the starboard and surging past them, away safely, heading downriver. A shot rang out from her as she receded, the report clear even above the thunderous stroke of the *Fevre Dream*'s engines and the noise of her paddles, but no damage was sustained.

Damon Julian turned to Joshua York, ignoring Framm's grin. "You will catch them for me, Joshua. Or I shall have Billy cast your bottles into the river, and you will thirst with the rest of us. Do you understand me?"

"Yes," said York. He called down for a full stop on both wheels, then set the larboard paddle slow forward, the starboard in reverse. The *Fevre Dream* began to come about again, assisted by the current. The *Eli Reynolds* was rushing away from her, stern-mounted paddle kicking wildly while sparks and flame poured from her stacks.

"Good," said Damon Julian. He turned to Sour Billy. "Billy, I am going to my cabin." Julian spent a lot of time in his cabin, sitting all alone in the dark without so much as a candle, sipping brandy and staring off at nothing. More and more he was leaving the running of the boat to Billy, just like he had let Billy run the plantation while he sat in his dark dusty library. "Stay here," Julian continued, "and see that our pilot does as I've told him. When we catch that steamer, bring Captain Marsh to me."

"What about the others?" Billy asked uncertainly.

Julian smiled. "I'm sure you'll think of something," he said.

When Julian had gone, Sour Billy turned to watch the river. The *Eli Reynolds* had sped downriver a good stretch while the *Fevre Dream* made her turn, and was several hundred yards ahead, but it was plain to see that it wouldn't last long. The *Fevre Dream* was surging forward like she hadn't done in months, both wheels turning full speed, the furnaces roaring, the decks pounding to the long massive stroke of the engines below. Even as Billy watched, the distance between the two boats seemed to diminish; the *Fevre Dream* was just eating up the river. Marsh would be paying a call on Damon Julian in no time at all. Sour Billy Tipton was looking forward to that, looking forward to it real keen.

Then Joshua York had them ease up on the starboard paddle, and began to turn the wheel.

"*Hey!*" Billy protested. "You're lettin' them get away! What are y' doin'?" He reached behind him and flicked out his knife, brandishing it at York's back. "What are y' doin'?"

"Crossing the river, Mister Tipton," answered York flatly.

"You turn that wheel right back. Marsh ain't doin' no crossin', not so I can see, and he's gettin' further ahead." York ignored the command, and Billy got angrier. "Turn back, I said."

"A moment ago we passed a creek," said York, "with a dead cottonwood by its mouth. That is the mark. At that mark, I must cross. If I kept straight on, I'd lose the deep water and sink us. There's a bluff reef on ahead there, too deep to show much of a sign on the water, but not so deep that it couldn't tear out our bottom. Isn't that right, Mister Framm?"

"Couldn't have said it better myself."

Sour Billy glared around suspiciously. "I don't believe you," he said. "Marsh didn't cross, and he didn't get his bottom tore out neither, not so I could notice." He flourished the knife. "You ain't goin' to let him get away," he said. The *Eli Reynolds* had already put another hundred feet between herself and the *Fevre Dream*. Only now was the smaller steamer starting to angle a bit to starboard.

"Some mate," Karl Framm said with contempt. "Hell, that little stern-wheeler we're chasin' don't draw nothin'. After a good rain, she could steam halfway across the city of N'Orleans without ever noticin' that she'd left the river."

"Abner is no fool," said Joshua York, "and neither is his pilot. They knew that reef was too deep to bother them, even with this stage on the river. They steamed right across it, hoping we would follow them and wreck ourselves. At best we'd have been grounded until dawn. Now do you understand, Mister Tipton?"

Sour Billy scowled, suddenly feeling like a fool. He put away his knife, and as he did Karl Framm laughed. It was a chuckle, kind of, but that was enough for Billy to hear. He snapped, "Shut up, or I'll call your missus." Then it was his turn to snicker.

The *Eli Reynolds* had gone around a point, but her smoke was still hanging in the air, and you could see her lights burning on the far side of the trees. Sour Billy stared off at the lights in silence.

"Why do you care so much if Abner escapes?" York asked quietly. "What has the captain ever done to cause you harm, Mister Tipton?"

"I don't care for warts," said Billy coldly, "and Julian wants him. I do like Julian wants."

"Whatever would he do without you," said Joshua York. Sour Billy didn't care for the way he said it, but before he could protest York was going on. "He is using you, Billy. Without you, he would be nothing. You think for him, act for him, you protect him by day. You make him what he is."

"Yeah," said Billy, proudly. He knew how important he was. He liked it just fine. It was even better on the steamer. He liked being a mate. The niggers he'd bought and the white trash he'd hired were all terrified of him, they called him "Mister Tipton" and rushed to do like he said, without him ever having to raise his voice or even stare at them. Some of the white rivermen had been unruly early on, till Sour Billy slit one open and stuffed him in a furnace with his belly hanging out. After that they got real respectful. The niggers were no trouble at all, except at landings, when Billy chained them up to the manacles he'd rigged on the main deck, so they couldn't run off. It was better than being a plantation overseer. An overseer was white trash, everybody looked down on him. But on the river, a steamer's mate was a man of substance, an officer, somebody you had to be polite to.

"The promise Julian has made you is a lie," York was saying. "You will never be one of us, Billy. We are different races. Our anatomy is different, our flesh, our very blood. He cannot make you over, no matter what he says."

"You must think I'm pretty damn stupid," Billy said. "I don't got to lissen to Julian. I heard the stories. I know how vampires can make other vampires. You were like me once, York, no matter what you say. Only you're weak, and I ain't. Are you afraid?" That was it, Billy thought. York wanted him to betray Julian so Julian wouldn't make him over, because once he was one of them, he'd be stronger than York, maybe as strong as Julian. "I scare you, Josh, don't I? You think you're so damn fine, but you wait till Julian makes me over, and I make you come crawlin' to me. Wonder what it tastes like, that blood of yours? Julian knows, don't he?"

York said nothing, but Sour Billy knew he'd struck a sore spot. Damon Julian had tasted York's blood a dozen times since that first night aboard the *Fevre Dream*. In fact, he had drunk of no one else. "Because you are so beautiful, dear Joshua," he would say with a pale smile, as he handed York a glass to be filled. It seemed to amuse him to make York submit.

"He is laughing at you all the time," York said after a time. "Every day and every night. He mocks you, he despises you. He thinks you are ugly and ludicrous, no matter how useful you may be. You are nothing but an animal to him, and he will cast you aside like so much trash if he finds a stronger beast to serve him. He will make sport of it, but by then you will be so corrupt and so rotten through that you will still believe, still grovel for him."

"I ain't no groveler," Billy said. "Shut up! Julian ain't lyin'!"

"Then ask him when he intends to make you over. Ask him how he will perform this miracle, how he will lighten your skin and make over your body and teach your eyes to see in darkness. Ask Julian if you think he is not lying. And listen, Mister Tipton. Listen to the mockery in his voice when he talks to you."

Sour Billy Tipton was seething. It was all he could do to stop from pulling out the knife and sticking it in Joshua York's broad back, but he knew that York would just turn on him, and Julian wouldn't be pleased either. "All right," he said. "Maybe I will ask him. He's older'n you, York, and he knows things you don't. Maybe I'll just ask him right now."

Karl Framm chuckled again, and even York glanced away from the wheel to smile tauntingly. "Why are you waiting, then?" he said. "Ask him." Sour Billy went below to the texas to ask.

Damon Julian had taken over the captain's cabin that had been Joshua York's. Billy knocked politely. "Yes, Billy," came the soft reply. He opened the door and entered. The room was black, but he could sense Julian sitting a few feet away, in the darkness. "Have we caught Captain Marsh yet?" Julian asked.

"He's still runnin'," Billy said, "but we're goin' to have him soon, Mister Julian."

"Ah. Then why are you here, Billy? I told you to stay with Joshua."

"I got to ask you something," Sour Billy said. He repeated all that Joshua York had told him. When he was done, the room was very quiet.

"Poor Billy," Julian said finally. "Do you have doubts, Billy, after all this time? If you doubt, you will never complete the change, Billy. That is why dear Joshua is so tormented. His doubts have left him in between, half-master and half-cattle. Do you understand? You must have patience."

"I want to start," Sour Billy insisted. "It's been years, Mister Julian. Now we got this steamer, things is better than they was. I want to be one of you. You promised me."

"So I did." Damon Julian chuckled. "Well then, Billy, we will have to start, won't we? You have served me well, and if you are so insistent, I can hardly refuse you, can I? You're so clever, I wouldn't want to lose you."

Sour Billy could hardly believe his ears. "You mean you'll do it?" Joshua York would be awful sorry for his tone, Billy thought wildly.

"Of course, Billy. I have given you a promise."

"When?"

"The change cannot be done in a single night. It will take time to transform you, Billy. Years."

"Years?" Sour Billy said, dismayed. He didn't care to wait no years. In the stories, it didn't take no *years*.

"I'm afraid so. As you grew from a boy into a man, slowly, you now must grow from a slave into a master. We will nourish you well, Billy, and from the blood you will gain power, beauty, speed. You will drink life and it will flow through your veins, until you are reborn into the night. It cannot be done quickly, but it can be done. It shall be as I have promised. You will have the life eternal, and the mastery, and the red thirst will fill you. We will begin soon."

"How soon?"

"To begin, you must drink, Billy. For that we need a victim." He laughed. "Captain Marsh," he said suddenly. "He will suffice for you, Billy. When we catch his steamer, bring him here to me, as I have told you. Unharmed. I shall not touch him. He will be yours, Billy. We will bind him up in his grand saloon, and you shall drink of him, night after night. A man his size must have a lot of blood in him. He will last a long time, Billy, and take you a long way into the change. Yes. You will begin with Captain Marsh, as soon as he is ours. Catch them, Billy. For me, and for yourself."

CHAPTER TWENTY-FIVE

Aboard the Steamer ELI REYNOLDS, Mississippi River, October 1857———

ABNER Marsh was watching from the pilot house of the *Eli Reynolds* when the *Fevre Dream* slid into her crossing. He stamped his stick down hard and cussed, but down under he wasn't sure whether he was disappointed or relieved. It would have cut the heart right out of him to see his lady rip herself asunder on that damned bluff reef, Marsh knew. On the other hand, now the *Fevre Dream* was still after them, and if she caught the *Reynolds*, no doubt Damon Julian would rip the heart right out of him. It seemed a losing game either way. Marsh stood there frowning while the pilot of the *Eli Reynolds* turned her rudder and began his own crossing. Steaming after them through the darkness, the *Fevre Dream* was a fearful sight. Marsh had built her to take the *Eclipse*, to be the fastest boat that ever got up a head of steam, and now he had to outrun her in one of the oldest, sorriest boats on the river. "No help for it," he said aloud, turning to his pilot. "We're in a race," he said. "See that we ain't caught."

The man looked at him like he was crazy, and maybe he was.

Abner Marsh took himself down to the main deck, to see what he could do. Cat Grove and the head engineer, Doc Turney, had already taken charge. The deck was awash with heat. The furnace was roaring and crackling, and gouts of flame were licking up and sometimes out every time the firemen tossed in fresh wood. Grove had all his stokers down there, sweating and feeding that red-orange maw, and coating the beech and pine knots with lard before they tossed them in. Grove was carrying a pail of whiskey with a big copper ladle, and he went around to each man in turn, so they could drink with only the briefest of pauses. Sweat ran down his bare chest in a steady stream, and like his stokers, his face was red from the terrible heat. It was hard to see how they could stand it, but the furnace was fed steadily.

Doc Turney was watching the pressure gauges on the boiler. Marsh went over and looked, too. Pressure was creeping higher and higher. The engineer looked at him. "Ain't had pressure up this high in the four years I been on her," he shouted. You had to shout to be heard above the sizzle and cough of the furnace, the hiss of the steam, the pounding of the engine. Marsh put out a hand tentatively, pulled it back quickly. The boiler was too hot to touch. "What'll I do about the safety cock, Cap'n?" asked Turney.

"Knock it back," Marsh shouted. "We need steam, Mister."

Turney frowned and did like he was told. Marsh watched the gauge; the needle rose steadily. The steam was practically shrieking through the pipes, but it was having its effect: the engine was shuddering and thumping like it was going to shake itself to pieces, and the wheel was turning, spinning faster than it had done in years, *whapwhapwhapwhapwhap*, spinning so the spray fanned out behind it and the whole boat vibrated, pushing like it had never pushed before.

The second engineer and the strikers were dancing around the engines, oiling and greasing, keeping the stroke smooth. They looked like little black monkeys drenched in tar. They moved as quick as monkeys too. They had to. It wasn't easy to grease up moving parts while they were moving, especially at the rate the *Reynolds'* old ratchedy engine was moving now.

"FASTER!" Grove roared. "Faster with that lard!" A big red-haired fireman staggered away from the mouth of the furnace, dizzy with the heat. He dropped to his knees, but another stoker took his place at once, and Grove moved to the fallen man and poured a ladle of whiskey over his head. The man looked up, wet and blinking, and opened his mouth, and the mate ladled some more alcohol down his gut. In a minute he was up again, smearing lard on pine knots.

The engineer grimaced and opened the 'scape-pipes, sending scalding-hot steam whistling up into the night and dropping the boiler pressure a mite. Then it began to build again. Solder was running and melting on some of the pipes, but men were standing ready to patch up any that split open. Marsh was soaked with sweat from the damp heat of the steam and the dry wash of the furnace's fury. Everywhere around him folks were running, shouting, passing wood and lard, feeding the furnace, tending the boiler and the engines. The stroke and the wheel made a terrible noise, the furnace flames drenched them all in shifting red light. It was a sweltering inferno, a hell of noise and activity and smoke and steam and danger. The steamer was shaking and coughing and trembling like a man about to collapse and die. But she *moved*, and down here there was nothing Abner Marsh could say or do to make her move faster.

He went out onto the forecastle gratefully, away from the awful heat, his jacket and shirt and pants as damp as if he'd just crawled out of the river. The wind moved around him, and Marsh felt wonderfully cold for a moment. Away ahead he saw an island dividing the river, and a light beyond that, on the western bank. They were moving toward it fast. "Damn," Marsh said. "Must be doing twenty miles an hour. Hell, maybe we're doing *thirty*." He said it loudly, almost shouting it, as if the thunder of his voice would make it true. The *Eli Reynolds* was an eight-mile-an-hour boat on a good day. Of course, now she had the current behind her.

Marsh thundered up the staircase, through the main cabin, and up onto the hurricane deck to get a look behind them. The tops of the short, stubby chimneys were throwing sparks everywhere and trailing fire, and as he watched steam came boiling up from the 'scape-pipes again as Doc Turney vented just enough to keep the damned boiler from blowing all of them to hell. The deck was unsteady underneath Marsh's feet, like the skin of something alive. The stern wheel was turning so fast that it was throwing up a goddamn wall of water, like a waterfall upside down.

And behind them came the *Fevre Dream*, half-dark, smoke and fire from her tall dark stacks rising halfway to the moon. She looked about twenty yards closer than when Marsh had gone downstairs.

Captain Yoerger stepped up beside Marsh. "We can't outrace her," he said in his weary gray tones.

"We need more steam! More heat!"

"The paddle can't turn any faster, Cap'n Marsh. If Doc sneezes at the wrong time, that boiler is goin' to blow and kill us all. Engine is seven years old, it's goin' to shake itself to pieces. The lard is running low, too. When it's gone we'll be firing her with just wood. This is an old lady, Cap'n. You got her dancing like it was her wedding night, but she can't take much more of it."

"*Damn*," Marsh said. He looked back past their paddle. The *Fevre Dream* came on and on. "Damn," he repeated. Yoerger was right, he knew. Marsh glanced ahead. They were steaming up on the island. The river, and the main channel, curved away to the east. The western fork was a cutoff, but a minor one. Even at this distance Marsh could see how it narrowed, how the trees leaned over the banks extending their black gnarled figures. He walked back to the pilot house and entered. "Take the cutoff," he told the pilot.

The pilot glanced back half in shock. On the river, the pilot decided such things. The captain maybe made casual suggestions, but he didn't give orders. "No, sir," the pilot replied, less furiously than an older man might have. "Look at the banks, Cap'n Marsh. The river is falling. I know that cutoff, and it ain't passable this time of year, if I take her in there we'll be setting on this boat till the spring floods."

"Maybe that's so," Marsh said, "but if we can't get through, there ain't no way in hell the *Fevre Dream* can. She'll have to go around. We'll lose her. Right now, losing her is more important than any damn snags or bars we might run into, you hear?"

The pilot frowned. "You got no call to be telling me how to run this river, Cap'n. I got my reputation. I never wrecked no boat yet and I don't aim to start tonight. We'll stay on the river."

Abner Marsh felt himself turning red. He looked back. The *Fevre Dream* was maybe three hundred feet behind them, and coming up quick. "You damn fool," Marsh said. "This is the most important race ever been run on this river, and I got a fool for a pilot. They'd have us already if Mister Framm was at her wheel, or if they had a mate who knew how to run her. They're probably firing her with *cottonwood*." He jabbed his stick back at the *Fevre Dream*. "But look, even slow as she's goin', she'll have us damn soon now, unless we out-pilot her. You hear me? *Take that damn cutoff!*"

"I could report you to the association," the pilot said stiffly.

"I could chuck you over the side," Abner Marsh replied. He moved forward threateningly.

"Send out a yawl, Cap'n," the pilot suggested. "We'll take soundings and see how she's running in there."

Abner Marsh snorted in disgust. "Out of the goddamn way," he said, shoving the pilot aside roughly. The man stumbled and fell. Marsh seized the wheel and turned it hard to the starboard, and the *Eli Reynolds* swung her head in answer. The pilot cussed and fumed.

Marsh ignored him and concentrated on steering until the steamer had crossed the island's high, muddy point, pounding down the crooked western bank. He glanced back over his shoulder just long enough to see the *Fevre Dream*—a bare two hundred feet behind now—slow and stop and begin to back furiously. When he looked again, a moment later, she was starting to veer off toward the eastern river bend. Then there was no more time for looking, as the *Eli Reynolds* hit something, hard, a big log by the sound of it. The impact jarred Marsh's teeth together so hard he almost bit off his tongue, and he had to hang on the wheel grimly to keep his feet. The pilot, who'd just gotten up, went down again and groaned. The steamboat's speed sent her climbing over the obstacle, and Marsh saw it briefly; a huge, black, half-submerged tree. A horrible racket ensued, a deafening clattering and thumping, and the boat trembled like some mad giant had gotten hold of her and started to shake, and then there was a violent wrench and the awful sound of wood smashing to splinters as the stern wheel came hammering down on the log.

"Damnation!" the pilot swore, climbing to his feet again. "Give me the wheel!"

"Gladly," Abner Marsh said, stepping out of the way. The *Eli Reynolds* had left the dead tree behind and was steaming madly down the shallow cutoff, shuddering as she ploughed through one sand bar after another. Each one slowed her, and the pilot slowed her even more, ringing the engine room bells like a wild man. "Full stop!" he called. "Full stop on the paddle!" The wheel turned a couple last leisurely licks and groaned to a halt, and two long tall plumes of white steam hissed as they came venting up from the 'scape-pipes. The *Eli Reynolds* lost her head and began to wobble a bit, and the steering wheel spun freely in the pilot's grip. "We've lost the rudder," he said, as the steamer bit into still another bar.

This one stopped her.

This time Abner Marsh *did* bite his tongue, as he stumbled forward into the wheel. Someone down below was screaming, he heard as he got back up and spit out a mouthful of blood. It hurt like hell. Fortunately he hadn't bitten it clean off.

"Damnation!" the pilot said. "Look. Just look."

Not only had the *Eli Reynolds* lost her rudder, but half of her paddle wheel as well. It was still attached to the steamer, but it hung crookedly, and half of the wooden buckets were shattered or missing. The boat vented steam once again, groaned, and settled into the mud, listing a bit to starboard.

"I *told* you we couldn't run this cutoff," the pilot said. "I *told* you. This time of year it's nothin' but sand and snags. This ain't *my* doing and I won't have nobody sayin' it was!"

"Shut your fool mouth," said Abner Marsh. He was looking back aft, where the river itself was still barely visible through the trees. The river looked empty. Maybe the *Fevre Dream* had gone on. Maybe. "How long to round that bend?" Marsh asked the pilot.

"Damnation, why the hell do you care? We ain't goin' nowhere till spring. You're goin' to need a new rudder and a new wheel both, and a good rise to get her off this bar."

"The bend," Marsh insisted. "How long around the bend?"

The pilot sputtered. "Thirty minutes, maybe twenty if she's sparklin' like she was, but why's it matter? I tell you—"

Abner Marsh threw open the door of the pilot house and roared for Captain Yoerger. He had to roar three times, and it took a good five minutes before Yoerger put in an appearance. "Sorry, Cap'n," the old man said, "I was down on the main deck. Irish Tommy and Big Johanssen got scalded pretty bad." He saw the ruins of the paddle and stopped. "My poor ol' gal," he murmured in a crestfallen tone.

"Some pipe bust?" Marsh asked.

"A lot of pipes," Yoerger admitted, tearing his gaze away from the battered paddle wheel. "Steam all over the place, might have been worse if Doc hadn't opened the 'scape-pipes quick and kept 'em open. That hit we took tore everything loose."

Marsh sagged. That was the final blow. Now even if they could winch themselves off the bar, rig up a new rudder, and somehow back clear of the cutoff on half a paddle, moving that damned tree somehow to get past it—none of which would be easy—they also had busted-up steampipes and maybe boiler damage to contend with. He cussed loud and long.

"Cap'n," said Yoerger, "we won't be able to hunt 'em down now, like you planned, but least we're safe. The *Fevre Dream* will steam round that bend and figure we're long gone and they'll go down river after us."

"No," said Marsh. "Cap'n, I want you to rig up stretchers for them that's burned, and start off through the woods." He pointed with his stick. The riverbank was ten feet away through shallow water. "Get to a town. Got to be one near."

"Two miles past the foot of this island," the pilot put in.

Marsh nodded at him. "Good. You take 'em there, then. I want all of you to go, and go quick." He remembered that glint of gold as

Jeffers's spectacles tumbled off him, that terrible little flash. Not again, Abner Marsh thought, not again on account of him. "Find a doctor to patch them up. You'll be safe, I reckon. They want me, not you."

"You aren't comin'?" asked Yoerger.

"I got my gun," said Abner Marsh. "And I got myself a feeling. I'm waitin'."

"Come with us."

"If I run, they'll follow. If they get me, you're safe. That's how I figure it, anyway."

"If they don't come—"

"Then I come trudging after you at first light," Marsh said. He stamped his walking stick impatiently. "I'm still cap'n here, ain't I? Quit jawin' with me, and do like I say. I want all of you off my steamer, you hear?"

"Cap'n Marsh," Yoerger said, "at least let Cat and me he'p you."

"No. Git."

"Cap'n—"

"GO!" shouted Marsh, red-faced. "GO!"

Yoerger blanched and took the startled pilot by the arm and drew him out of the pilot house. When they had hurried down, Abner Marsh glanced back at the river once more—still nothing—and then went downstairs to his cabin. He took the rifle from the wall, checked it and loaded it, and slid the box of custom shells into the pocket of his white coat. Armed, Marsh returned to the hurricane deck, and fixed up his chair where he could keep an eye on the river. If they were smart, Abner Marsh figured, they'd know how low the river stage was. They'd know that maybe the *Eli Reynolds* could run this cutoff and maybe she couldn't, but even at best she'd have to steam through slowly, sounding all the way. They'd know, once they came round the bend, that they'd beaten her. And if they knew that, they wouldn't steam downriver at all. They'd hold the *Fevre Dream* near the foot of the cutoff, waiting for the *Reynolds*. And meanwhile, the men—or night folks—that they'd let off near the head of the island would be crawling through the cutoff in a yawl, just in case the *Reynolds* stopped or got hung up. That was what Abner Marsh would have done, anyway.

The little stretch of river he could see was still empty. He felt a bit chilly, waiting. Any moment now he expected to see the yawl come round that stand of trees, full of silent dark figures with faces pale and smirking in the moonlight. He checked his gun again, and wished Yoerger would hurry.

Yoerger and Grove and the rest of the crew of the *Eli Reynolds* had been gone fifteen minutes, with still nothing moving on the river.

There were lots of noises in the night. The water gurgling around the wreck of his steamer, the wind rattling the trees together, animals off in the woods. Marsh rose, finger on the trigger of his rifle, and scanned upstream warily. There was nothing to see, nothing but silty river water washing across sandbars, gnarled roots, the fallen black corpse of the tree that had smashed up his steamer's paddle. He saw driftwood moving, and nothing else. "Maybe they ain't so smart," he muttered under his breath.

From the corner of his eye, Marsh glimpsed something pale on the island across the stream. He spun toward it, raising his gun to his shoulder, but there was nothing there, just black dense woods and thick river mud. Twenty yards of shallow water lay between him and the dark, silent island. Abner Marsh was breathing hard. What if they don't bring the yawl down the cutoff, he thought. What if they land it and come on foot?

The *Eli Reynolds* creaked beneath him, and Marsh grew more uneasy. Just settling, he told himself, she's aground and settling into the sand. But another part of him was whispering, whispering that maybe that creak was a footstep, that maybe they'd stole up on him while he was watching the river. Maybe they were on the boat already. Maybe Damon Julian was coming up the staircase even now, gliding through the main cabin—he knew how quiet Julian could walk—and searching the cabins, moving toward the stair that would lead him up here, up to the hurricane deck.

Marsh turned his chair so he faced the top of the stair, just in case a pale white face should suddenly heave into view. His hands were sweating where they held the rifle, making the stock all slippery. He wiped them on his pants leg.

The sound of soft whispering came drifting up the stairwell.

They were down there, Marsh thought, down there plotting how to get at him. He was trapped up here, alone. Not that being alone mattered. He'd had help before and it hadn't made no difference to them. Marsh rose and moved to the top of the stair, looking down into darkness streaked by wan moonlight. He gripped the gun hard, blinked, waited for something to show itself. He waited for the longest time, listening to those vague whispers, his heart thumping away like the *Reynolds'* old tired engine. They wanted him to hear them, Abner Marsh thought. They wanted him to be afraid. They'd come sneaking up on his steamer like haunts, so fleet and silent he hadn't seen them, and now they were trying to put the fear on him. "I know you're down there," he shouted. "Come on up. I got something for you, Julian." He hefted the gun.

Silence.

"Damn you," Marsh yelled.

Something moved at the foot of the stairs, a darting figure, pale and quick. Marsh jerked the gun up to fire, but it was gone before he could even begin to take aim. He swore and took two steps down the stairs, then stopped. This was what they wanted him to do, he thought. They were trying to lure him down there, to the promenade and the darkened cabins and the dim dusty saloon with the moonlight washing through its dirty skylight. Up here on the hurricane deck, he could hold them off. They couldn't get to him easy up here; he could see them sliding up the stairs, climbing the sides, whatever. But down *there*, he'd be at their mercy.

"*Captain*," a soft voice called up to him. "*Captain Marsh.*"

Marsh raised his gun, squinting.

"*Don't shoot, Captain. It's me. It's only me.*" She stepped into view at the bottom of the stairs.

Valerie.

Marsh hesitated. She was smiling up at him, dark hair catching the moonbeams, waiting. She wore trousers and a man's ruffled shirt, unbuttoned down the front. Her skin was soft and pale, and her eyes caught his and held them, shining violet beacons, deep, beautiful, endless. He could swim in those eyes forever. "*Come to me, Captain*," Valerie called. "I'm alone. Joshua sent me. Come down, so we can talk." Marsh took two steps downward, trapped by those brilliant eyes. Valerie held her arms out.

The *Eli Reynolds* moaned and settled, shifting suddenly to starboard. Marsh stumbled and hit his shin hard against the stair, and the pain brought tears to his eyes. He heard faint laughter drifting up from below, saw Valerie's smile waver and fade. Cussing, Marsh swung the rifle back up to his shoulder and fired. The kick near tore off his shoulder, and slammed him back against the steps. Valerie was gone, vanished like a ghost. Marsh swore and got to his feet and fumbled in his pocket for another cartridge, retreating backward up the stairway. "Joshua, *hell!*" he roared down at the darkness. "Julian sent you, damn him!"

When he stepped backward onto the hurricane deck, listing at a thirty-degree angle now, Marsh felt something very hard press between his shoulder blades. "Well, well," said the voice from behind him, "if it ain't Cap'n Marsh."

The others appeared, one by one, when Marsh had dropped the gun to clatter on the deck. Valerie came last of all, and would not look at him. Abner Marsh cussed her up and down and round about as a treacherous whore. Finally she gave him one terrible, accusing glance. "Do you think I have a choice?" she said bitterly, and Marsh ceased his tirade. It was not her words that quieted him; not her words, but the look in her eyes. For in those vast violet depths, glimpsed so briefly, Marsh saw shame and terror . . . and thirst.

"*Move,*" said Sour Billy Tipton.

"Damn you," said Abner Marsh.

CHAPTER TWENTY-SIX

Aboard the Steamer OZYMANDIAS, Mississippi River, October 1857

ABNER Marsh had expected darkness, but when Sour Billy shoved him through the door to the captain's cabin, the room gleamed in the soft light of its oil lamps. It was dustier than Marsh remembered, but otherwise just as Joshua had kept it. Sour Billy closed the door, and Marsh was alone with Damon Julian. He gripped his hickory stick hard—Billy had thrown the gun in the river, but allowed Marsh to retrieve the stick—and scowled. "If you're goin' to kill me, come on and try," he said. "I ain't in the mood for no games."

Damon Julian smiled. "Kill you? Why, Captain! I'd planned to feed you dinner." A silver serving tray had been set on the small table between the two big leather chairs. Julian lifted its cover to reveal a plate of pan-fried chicken and greens, turnips and onions on the side, and a slice of apple pie topped with cheese. "There is wine, too. Please have a seat, Captain."

Marsh looked at the food and smelled it. "Toby's still alive," he said, with a sudden certainty.

"Of course he is," Julian said. "Will you sit?"

Marsh moved forward warily. He couldn't figure what Julian was up to, but he considered it for a moment and decided he didn't care. Maybe the food was poisoned, but that didn't make no sense, they had easier ways of killing him. He sat down and picked up a chicken breast. It was still hot. He bit into it ravenously, and recalled how long it had been since he'd had a *decent* meal. Maybe he was going to die presently, but at least he'd die on a full stomach.

Damon Julian, resplendent in a brown suit and golden vest,

watched Marsh eat with an amused smile on his pale face. "Wine, Captain?" was all he said. He filled two glasses and sipped delicately from his own.

When Abner Marsh had polished off the pie, he sat back in his chair and belched, then screwed up his face in a scowl. "A good meal," he said grudgingly. "Now, why am I here, Julian?"

"The night you made your hasty departure, Captain, I tried to tell you I simply wanted to talk to you. You chose not to believe me."

"Damn right I didn't believe you," said Marsh. "Still don't. But now I ain't got much say on the matter, so talk."

"You are bold, Captain Marsh. And strong. I admire you."

"Can't say I got much use for you."

Julian laughed. His laughter was pure music. His dark eyes shone. "Amusing," he said. "Such bluster."

"I don't know why you're tryin' to butter me up, but it ain't goin' to do you no good. All the fried chicken in the world ain't goin' to make me forget what you did to that damned baby, and to Mister Jeffers."

"You seem to forget that Jeffers had just run me through with a sword," Julian said. "That is not something one takes lightly."

"That baby didn't have no sword."

"A slave," Julian said lightly. "Property, by the laws of your own nation. Inferior, according to your own people. I spared it a life of bondage, Captain."

"Go to hell," said Marsh. "It was just a damned baby, and you cut off its hand like you was cutting the head off a chicken, and then you crushed its head in. It didn't do nothin' to you."

"No," said Julian. "Nor did Jean Ardant harm you or your people. Yet you and your mate crushed his skull in while he slept."

"We thought he was you."

"Ah," said Julian. He smiled. "A mistake, then. But whether you acted in error or not, you slaughtered an innocent man. You do not seem unduly consumed by guilt."

"He wasn't no man. He was one of you. A vampire."

Julian frowned. "Please. I share Joshua's distaste for that term." Marsh shrugged.

"You contradict yourself, Captain Marsh," Julian said. "You judge me evil, for doing what you do without compunction—taking the lives of those unlike yourself. No matter. You defend your own kind. You even include the dark races. I admire that, you see. You know what you are, you understand your place, your nature. That is as it should be. You and I, we are alike in that."

"I ain't nothin' like you," Marsh said.

"Ah, but you are! We accept our natures, you and I, we do not seek to become things we are not, things we were never meant to be. I despise the weak, the changelings who so hate themselves that they must pretend to be something else. You feel the same way."

"I do not."

"No? Why do you hate Sour Billy so?"

"He's contemptible."

"Of course he is!" Julian looked highly amused. "Poor Billy is weak, and thirsts to be strong. He will do anything to be one of my people. Anything. I have known others like him, so many others. They are useful, often entertaining, but never admirable. You despise Billy because he apes our race and preys on your own, Captain Marsh. Dear Joshua feels the same way, little realizing that in Billy he sees his own reflection."

"Joshua and Billy Tipton ain't nothin' alike," Marsh said stoutly. "Billy is a goddamned weasel. Joshua's maybe done some vile things, but he's tryin' to make up for them. He would have helped you all."

"He would have made us as you are. Captain Marsh, your own nation is terribly divided on this issue of slavery, a slavery based on race. Suppose you could end it. Suppose you had a way to turn every white man in this land soot-black overnight. Would you do it?"

Abner Marsh scowled. He didn't much like the idea of turning soot-black, but he saw where Julian was heading and he didn't much want to go there either. So he said nothing.

Damon Julian sipped his wine and smiled. "Ah," he said. "You see. Even your abolitionists admit the dark races are inferior. They would have no patience with a slave trying to pretend at being white, and they would be disgusted if a white man should drink a potion in order to turn black. I did not hurt that slave child from malice, Captain Marsh. There is no malice in me. I did it to reach Joshua, dear Joshua. He is beautiful, but he sickens me.

"You are another case. Did you truly fear that I would harm you that night in August? Oh, perhaps I would have, in my pain and rage. But not before. Beauty draws me, Captain Marsh, and you have none of that." He laughed. "I don't think I've ever seen an uglier man. You are gross, rolling with fat, covered with coarse hair and warts, you stink of sweat, you have a flat nose and a pig's eyes, your teeth are crooked and stained. You could no more wake the thirst in me than Billy could. Yet you are strong, and you have a gross courage, and you know your place. All these I admire. You can run a steamboat, too. Captain, we should not be enemies. Join me. Run the *Fevre Dream* for me." He smiled. "Or whatever it's called now. Billy decided it had to be renamed, and Joshua found a name somewhere. You can change it back, if you'd prefer."

"She," Marsh said.

Julian frowned.

"Boat's a *she*, not an *it*," Marsh said.

"Ah," said Damon Julian.

"Billy Tipton is running this boat, ain't he?"

Julian shrugged. "Billy is an overseer, not a riverman. I can dispose of Billy. Would you like that, Captain? That can be your first reward, if you join me. Billy's death. I will kill him for you, or let you do it yourself. He killed your mate, you know."

"Hairy Mike?" Marsh said, feeling chilled.

"Yes," said Julian. "And your engineer too, after a few weeks. He caught him trying to weaken the boilers, so they'd explode. Would you like to revenge your people? It is within your power." Julian leaned forward intently, his dark eyes gleaming, excited. "You can have other things as well. Wealth. I care nothing for that. You can handle all my money."

"All you stole from Joshua."

Julian smiled. "A bloodmaster receives many gifts," he said. "I can offer you women as well. I have lived among your people for many years, I know your lusts, your thirsts. How long has it been since you've had a woman, Captain? Would you like Valerie? She can be yours. She is lovelier than any woman of your race, and she will not grow old and hideous, not in your lifetime. You can have her. The others as well. They will not harm you. What else would you like? Food? Toby is still alive. You can have his cooking six, seven times a day if you desire.

"You are a practical man, Captain. You do not share the religious delusions of your race. Consider what you are being offered. You will have the power to punish your enemies and protect your friends, a full stomach, money, women. And all for doing what you want to do desperately, for running this steamboat. Your *Fevre Dream*."

Abner Marsh snorted. "She ain't mine no more. You've fouled her."

"Look around you. Are things so bad? We have run between Natchez and New Orleans regularly, the steamer is in good repair, hundreds of passengers have come and gone without ever noticing anything amiss. A few vanish, most of them ashore, in the towns and cities we visit. Billy says it is safer that way. Only a handful have died aboard your steamer, those whose beauty and youth were too exceptional. More slaves die every day in New Orleans, yet you do not work against slavery. The world is full of evils, Abner. I do not ask you to condone or participate. Just run your steamer, and mind your own business. We need your expertise. Billy drives away passengers, we lose money on every run. Even Joshua's funds are not inexhaustible. Come, Abner, give me your hand. Agree. You want to. I can feel it in your eyes. You want this steamer back again. It is a thirst in you, a passion. Take it, then. Good and evil are silly lies, nonsense put forth to plague honest sensible men. I know you, Abner, and I can give you what you want. Join me, serve me. Take my hand, and together we will outrun the *Eclipse*." His dark eyes swirled and burned, endless depths, reaching deep inside Marsh, touching him, feeling him intimately, unclean and yet seductive, calling, *calling*. His hand was extended. Abner Marsh started to reach out for it. Julian smiled so nicely, and his words made so much sense. He wasn't asking Marsh to do nothing terrible, just run a steamboat, help protect him, protect his friends. Hell, he'd protected Joshua, and Joshua was a vampire too, wasn't he? And maybe there'd be some killing on the boat, but a man had been strangled on the *Sweet Fevre* back in '54, and two gamblers had been shot dead on the *Nick Perrot* when Marsh was running her; none of that had been his blame, he was just tending his own affairs, running his steamers, it wasn't like he'd kill anybody himself. Man had to protect his friends but not the whole world, he'd see to it that Sour Billy got what he deserved. It all sounded good, a damn good deal. Julian's eyes were black and hungry and his skin felt cool, hard like Joshua's, like Joshua's that night on the levee . . .

. . . and Abner Marsh snatched his hand away. "Joshua," he said loudly. "That's it. You ain't beaten him yet, have you? You got him whipped, but he's still alive, and you ain't got him to drink blood, you ain't got him to change. That's why." Marsh felt his blood rising to his face. "You don't care how much damn money this steamboat makes. If she sunk tomorrow, you wouldn't care a good goddamn, you'd just go somewheres else. And Sour Billy, maybe you want to get rid of him, use me instead, but that ain't it. It's Joshua. If I join you it will break whatever he's got left, prove you right. Joshua trusted me, and you want me 'cause you know what that'd do to him." Julian's hand was still extended, rings shining softly on his long pale fingers. "Damn you!" Marsh roared, and he picked up his walking stick and swung it hard, smashing the hand to the side. "*DAMN YOU!*"

The smile died on Damon Julian's lips and his face became something inhuman. There was nothing in his eyes but darkness and age and flickering dim fires that burned with ancient evil. He stood up, so he towered over Abner Marsh, and he snatched the stick away as Marsh swung it at his face. He broke it with his bare hands, as easily as Marsh might break a dead match, and tossed it to the side. The pieces clattered off the wall and dropped to the carpet. "You might have been remembered as the man who outran the *Eclipse*," Julian said with a malicious coldness. "Instead, you will die. It is going to last a long time, Captain Marsh. You are much too ugly for me. I am giving you to Billy, to teach him the taste of blood. Maybe dear Joshua should have a glass as well. It would do him good." He smiled. "As for your steamboat, Captain Marsh, don't worry. I will take good care of *her* after you are gone No one on the river will ever forget your *Fevre Dream*."

CHAPTER TWENTY-SEVEN

Aboard the Steamer OZYMANDIAS, Mississippi River, October 1857———

DAWN was breaking when Abner Marsh was led from the captain's cabin. Morning mists lay heavily on the river, gray wisps that drifted and curled smokily across the water and threaded themselves through the steamer's rails and colonnades, writhing like living things soon to burn and perish in the light of the morning sun. Damon Julian saw the red blush in the east, and remained in the dimness of his cabin. He pushed Marsh through the door. "Take the captain to his cabin, Billy," he said. "Keep him safe until dark. You will be so kind as to join us for supper, Captain Marsh?" He smiled. "I knew you would."

They were waiting just outside. Sour Billy, in a black suit and a checkered vest, was sitting with his chair tilted back against the wall of the texas, cleaning his fingernails with his knife. He stood up when the door opened, and tossed the knife easily in his hand. "Yes, sir, Mister Julian," he said, his ice-colored eyes fixed on Marsh.

He had two others with him. The night folks who'd helped Billy take Marsh from the *Eli Reynolds* had retreated back to their state-rooms to escape the touch of morning, so Billy had called up some of his river scum, it appeared. As Julian shut the cabin door, they moved in. One of them was a portly youth with ragged brown whiskers, a live oak cudgel stuck through his cord belt. The other one was a giant, and the ugliest damn thing Abner Marsh had ever seen. He must have stood near seven foot tall, but he had a tiny little head, squinty eyes, wooden teeth, and no nose at all. Abner Marsh stared.

"Don't you go looking at Noseless," Sour Billy said. "It ain't polite, Cap'n." Noseless, as if to agree, grabbed Marsh's arm roughly and twisted it up behind him so hard it hurt. "A gator bit off his nose," Sour Billy said. "Ain't his fault. You hold Cap'n Marsh tight now, Noseless. Cap'n Marsh is fond of jumpin' into the river, and we don't want none of that." Billy swaggered over and poked his knife into Marsh's stomach, just enough so Marsh felt the prick. "You swim better'n I figgered, Cap'n. Must be all this fat, makes it easier to float." He twisted the knife suddenly and sliced a silver button from Marsh's jacket. It fell clattering to the deck, and rolled around and around in a circle until Sour Billy stepped on it. "No swimming today, Cap'n. We're goin' to bed you down proper. You even get your own cabin. Don't think you're goin' to sneak out neither. Maybe the night folks is all asleep, but Noseless or me will be right outside all day. Come on, now." Billy flipped his knife in the air lazily, sheathed it, and turned. He led them aft, Noseless propelling Marsh along behind him, the third man bringing up the rear.

They rounded a corner of the texas, and nearly bowled right into Toby Lanyard.

"*Toby!*" Marsh exclaimed. He tried to step forward, but Noseless twisted his arm and Marsh grunted in pain and stopped.

Sour Billy Tipton stopped too, staring. "What the hell you doing up here, nigger?" he snapped.

Toby didn't look at him. He stood there in a frayed brown suit, his hands clasped behind his back, head bowed, scuffing one boot nervously against the deck.

"I said, *what the hell you doing here, nigger?*" Sour Billy said dangerously. "Why ain't you chained up in the kitchen? You gimme an answer now, or you're goin' to be one sorry nigger."

"*Chained!*" Marsh roared.

At that Toby Lanyard finally raised his head, and nodded. "Mister Billy says I is a slave agin, never mind I got no freedom papers. He chains us all up when we ain't workin'."

Sour Billy Tipton reached behind him and pulled out his knife. "How'd you get loose?" he demanded.

"I broke his chains, Mister Tipton," said a voice from above them. They all looked up. On top of the texas, Joshua York stood staring down at them. His white suit shone against the morning sun, and a gray cloak was rippling in the wind. "Now," said York, "kindly let go of Captain Marsh."

"It's daylight out," the stout young hand said, pointing at the sun with his oak cudgel. He sounded scared.

"You get yourself out of here," Sour Billy Tipton said to York, his neck craned back awkwardly so he could see the interloper. "You try anything and I'm calling Mister Julian."

Joshua York smiled. "Really?" he said, glancing at the sun. It was clearly visible now, a burning yellow eye amidst a blaze of red and orange clouds. "Do you imagine he'd come?"

Sour Billy's tongue flicked nervously across his thin lips. "You don't scare me none." He hefted his knife. "It's day and you're all alone."

"No he ain't,"said Toby Lanyard. Toby's hands had come out from behind his back. There was a meat cleaver in one of them and a big ragged-edged carving knife in the other. Sour Billy Tipton stared and took a step backward.

Abner Marsh glanced over his shoulder. Noseless was still squinting up at Joshua. His grip had loosened just a little. Marsh saw his chance. With all his strength he threw himself back into the giant, and Noseless stumbled and went down. Abner Marsh landed on top of him, all three hundred pounds, and the giant grunted like a cannonball had just caught him in the gut, and all the breath went out of him, and Marsh wrenched free his arm and rolled. He checked his roll barely in time—a knife sprung up quivering in the deck an inch in front of his face. Marsh swallowed hard, and then smiled. He yanked the blade free and got to his feet.

The man with the cudgel had taken two quick steps forward and thought better of it. Now he stepped back, and Joshua jumped quicker than Marsh could blink, landed behind the man, warded off a wild blow of the live oak club, and all of a sudden the heavy youth was on the deck, out cold. Marsh hadn't even seen the blow that did it.

"Leave me alone!" Sour Billy said. He was retreating before Toby. He retreated right into Marsh, who grabbed him and spun him around and slammed him up against a door. "Don't kill me!" Billy squealed. Marsh pressed an arm against his windpipe and leaned into him, pushing the knife up against Billy's skinny ribs, over the heart. Those ice-colored eyes had gone wide and scared. "Don't!" he choked.

"Why the hell not?"

"Abner!" warned Joshua, and Marsh glanced back just in time to see Noseless come surging to his feet. He made an animal noise and lunged forward, and then Toby moved faster than Marsh ever would have imagined, and the giant stumbled to his knees, choking on his own blood. Toby had made a single slash with that carving knife, and opened his throat for him. Blood came pouring out, and Noseless blinked his squinty little eyes and raised his hands up against his neck, as if to catch it as it fell. Finally he collapsed.

"That was not necessary, Toby," Joshua York said quietly. "I could have stopped him."

Gentle Toby Lanyard just frowned, holding his cleaver and the bloody knife. "I ain't so good as you is, Cap'n York," he said. He turned to Marsh and Sour Billy. "Cut him open, Cap'n Marsh," he urged. "I bet you Mister Billy ain't got no heart in dere."

"Don't, Abner. One killing is enough."

Abner Marsh heard both of them. He shoved the knife forward just enough to prick through Billy's shirt and start a little trickle of bleeding. "You like that?" Marsh asked. Sweat plastered Billy's lank hair to his brow. "You like it good enough when you're holdin' the knife, don't you?"

Billy choked on his reply, and Marsh let up the pressure on his skinny neck enough to let him talk. "*Don't kill me!*" Billy said, his voice gone thin and shrill. "It ain't my doing, it's Julian, he makes me do them things. He'll kill me if I don't do like he tells me!"

"He kilt ol' Hairy Mike, an' Whitey, too," Toby said, "an' a mess o' other folks. One man he burn up in the furnace, you could hear dat poor man screamin' all over. Tole me I was a slave agin, Cap'n Marsh, and when I shows him my freedom papers he done rip 'em up an' burn 'em. Cut him up, Cap'n."

"*He's lyin'! Them are damn nigger lies!*"

"Abner," said Joshua, "let him go. You have his weapon, he's harmless now. If you kill him like this, you're no better than he is. He can help us, if anyone challenges us as we're leaving. We still have to reach the yawl and get away."

"*Yawl,*" said Abner Marsh. "To hell with the yawl. I'm takin' my steamboat back." He smiled at Sour Billy. "Billy here can get us in to Julian's cabin, I reckon."

Sour Billy swallowed hard. Marsh felt the lump of his Adam's apple against his skin.

"If you attack Julian, you go alone," Joshua said. "I will not help you."

Marsh craned his head around and stared at York in astonishment. "After all he done?"

All of a sudden Joshua looked awful weak and tired. "I cannot," he whispered. "He is too strong, Abner. He is bloodmaster, he rules me. Even to dare this much goes against all the history of my people. He has bonded me to him a dozen times, forcing me to feed him with my blood. Each submission leaves me . . . weaker. More in his thrall. Abner, please understand. I could not do it. He would look at me with those eyes, and before I could take two steps I would be his. As likely as not it would be you I killed, not Julian."

"Toby and me will do it then," Marsh said.

"Abner, you would not have a chance. Listen to me. We can escape now. I've taken a great risk to save you. Do not throw it away."

Marsh looked back at helpless Billy and thought on it. Maybe Joshua was right. Besides, his gun was gone now, they didn't have nothing to hurt Julian with. Knives and meat cleavers sure wouldn't do it, and Marsh wasn't anxious to face Julian hand to hand. "We'll go," he said at last, "but after I kill this one."

Sour Billy whimpered. "No," he said. "Let me go, I'll help you." His pox-scarred face was moist. "It's easy for you, with your damn fancy steamboat and all, I never had no choice, ain't never had nothing, no family, no money, got to do like I'm told."

"You ain't the only one ever growed up poor," Marsh said. "It ain't no excuse. You made up your own goddamned mind to be like you are." His hand was shaking. He wanted to shove the knife in so bad it hurt, but somehow he couldn't, not like this. "Damn you," Marsh said grudgingly. He let go of Billy's throat and stepped backward, and Billy pitched forward to his knees. "Come on, you're gettin' us safe to that damn yawl."

Toby made a sound of disgust, and Sour Billy eyed him warily. "Keep that damn nigger cook away from me! Him and that cleaver, you keep 'em away."

"On your goddamn feet," Marsh said. He looked over to Joshua, who was holding a hand against his forehead. "You all right?"

"The sun," York said wearily. "We have to hurry."

"Others," said Marsh. "What about Karl Framm? He still alive?"

Joshua nodded. "Yes, and others, but we can't free them all. We don't have the time. This has taken too long as it is."

Abner Marsh frowned. "Maybe so," he said, "but I ain't leaving without Mister Framm. Him and you are the only ones can pilot this steamer. If we take both of you, she'll be stuck here, until we can come back."

Joshua nodded. "He's guarded. Billy, who is with Framm now?"

Sour Billy had struggled to his feet. "Valerie," he said, and Marsh remembered that pale form and beckoning violet eyes, drawing him down into the darkness.

"Good," said Joshua. "Hurry." And then they were moving, Marsh keeping a wary eye on Sour Billy, Toby concealing his weapons within the folds and pockets of his coat. Framm's cabin was up on the texas, but around on the far side of the boat. The window was curtained and shuttered, the door locked. Joshua shattered the lock with a single short blow of his hard white hand, and pushed it open. Marsh crowded in after him, pushing Sour Billy before him.

Framm was fully clothed, lying face down on the bed, dead to the world. But next to him a pale form sat up and stared at them from wide angry eyes. "*Who* . . . Joshua?" She rose from the bed swiftly. Her nightdress fell in white folds around her. "It's day. What do you want?"

"Him," said Joshua.

"It's *day*," Valerie insisted. Her eyes lingered on Marsh and Sour Billy. "What are you doing?"

"Leaving," said Joshua York, "and Mister Framm is going with us."

Marsh told Toby to keep an eye on Billy, and went over to the bed. Karl Framm didn't move. Marsh rolled him over. There were wounds on his neck, and dried blood on his shirt and his chin. He moved limply, heavily, and showed no signs of waking. But he was still his breathing.

"The thirst was on me," Valerie said, her voice small, looking from Marsh to York. "After the hunt . . . I had no choice . . . Damon gave him to me."

"Is he still alive?" Joshua asked.

"Yes," said Marsh. "We'll have to carry him, though." He stood up and gestured. "Toby, Billy, you take him down to the yawl."

"Joshua, *please*," Valerie pleaded. Standing there in her nightdress, she looked helpless and afraid. It was hard to see her the way she'd been on the *Eli Reynolds*, or imagine her drinking Framm's blood. "When Damon finds him gone, he will punish me. Please, don't."

Joshua hesitated. "We must take him, Valerie."

"Take me too, then!" she said. "Please."

"It is day."

"If you can risk it, I can. I'm strong. I'm not afraid."

"It's too dangerous," Joshua insisted.

"If you leave me here, Damon will be certain I helped you," Valerie said. "He'll punish me. Haven't I been punished enough? He hates me, Joshua . . . he hates me because I loved *you.* Help me. don't want it . . . the thirst. I *don't!* Please, Joshua, let me come with you!"

Abner Marsh could see her fear, and all of a sudden she no longer seemed like one of *them,* only like a woman, a human woman begging for help. "Let her come, Joshua."

"Dress, then," Joshua York said. "*Hurry.* Wear some of Mister Framm's clothing. It's heavier than your own, and will cover more of your skin."

"Yes," she said. She slipped off the nightdress to reveal a slender white body, high full breasts, strong legs. From a drawer she got one of Framm's shirts and buttoned it on. In barely a minute she was dressed; trousers, boots, vest and coat, a slouch hat. All of it was too big for her, but it didn't seem to hinder her movement.

"C'mon," Marsh snapped.

Billy and Toby carried Framm between them. The pilot was still unconscious, and his boots scraped along the deck as they hurried to the stair. Marsh came just behind them, his hand on the knife, which he kept shoved through his belt, concealed by the hang of his jacket. Valerie and Joshua brought up the rear.

The grand saloon was full of passengers, a few of whom eyed them curiously, but no one said anything. Down on the main deck, they had to step over sleeping deckhands, none of them men Marsh recognized. As they approached the sounding yawl, a couple of men moved toward them. "Where you goin'?" one demanded.

"None of your concern," Sour Billy said. "We're taking Framm here for some doctoring. Seems he ain't feeling good. Both of you, now, help us get him into the yawl."

One of the men hesitated, staring at Valerie and Joshua. Clearly it was the first time he'd seen either by day. "Does Julian know about this?" he said. Others were watching from all around the main deck, Marsh saw. He held the knife tightly, ready to slit Sour Billy's goddamn throat if he said one wrong word.

"You giving me lip, Tim?" Billy asked coldly. "You better think of what happened to Alligator George, maybe. Now move your damn ass and do like I told you!"

Tim flinched and jumped to obey. Three others rushed to help him, and in no time at all the yawl was in the water alongside the steamer, and Karl Framm had been lowered into it. Joshua helped Valerie step across, and Toby hopped down after them. The deck was lined with curious hands now. Abner Marsh moved real close to Sour Billy Tipton and whispered, "You done real good so far. Now get into the yawl."

Sour Billy looked at him. "You said you'd let me go," he said.

"I lied," Marsh said. "You're stayin' with us till we're out of here."

Sour Billy backed away. "No," he said. "You're just goin' to kill me." He raised his voice. "*Stop them!*" he shouted. "They had me prisoner, they're running off, *stop them!*" He wrenched backward, out of Marsh's reach. Marsh cussed and pulled loose the knife but it was too late, all the deckhands and rousters were moving toward him. A couple had knives of their own, he saw. "Kill him!" Sour Billy was yelling. "Get Julian, get help, kill them!"

Marsh grabbed the rope holding the yawl to the steamer, parted it with one swift stroke of the knife, and threw the blade at Billy's yapping mouth. But it was a bad throw, and anyhow Sour Billy ducked. Someone grabbed Marsh's jacket. He hit him hard across the face, and shoved him into the men behind him. The yawl was drifting with the current now. Marsh moved to step across before it went out of reach. Joshua was yelling for him to hurry, but somebody caught him around the throat and yanked him back. Abner Marsh kicked back furiously, but the man held on, and the yawl was getting further away, downstream, Joshua was yelling, and Marsh thought he was done for. Then Toby Lanyard's goddamn cleaver went whizzing by his ear, taking off a piece of it as it went, and the arm around his throat fell away as Marsh felt blood spatter his shoulder. He threw himself forward, towards the yawl, and made about half the distance, hitting the water heavily, belly first. It took all the breath out of him, and the cold was a shock. Abner Marsh flailed and thrashed and took in a mouthful of water and river mud before he surfaced. He saw the yawl drifting rapidly away, downstream, and paddled toward it. A rock or a knife or something splashed right alongside his head, and another fell a yard in front of him, but Toby had unshipped the oars and was slowing the boat a little, and Marsh reached it and threw an arm over the side. He nearly tipped the boat over trying to climb in, but Joshua had him, and he pulled, and before he knew it Marsh was lying on the bottom of the yawl, blowing out water. When he pulled himself up, they were twenty yards from the *Fevre Dream*, and moving off swiftly as the current got them firmly in its grasp. Sour Billy Tipton had gotten himself a pistol from somewhere, and was standing on the forecastle popping away at them, but he wasn't hitting anything.

"Damn him," Marsh said. "I should have killed him, Joshua."

"If you had, we would never had gotten away."

Marsh frowned. "Hell. Maybe. Maybe it would have been worth it anyway." He looked around the yawl. Toby was rowing, looking like he badly needed help. Marsh took another oar. Karl Framm was still unconscious. Marsh wondered how much blood Valerie had taken. Valerie herself didn't look so good. Huddled up in Framm's clothing, his hat pulled low over her face, she looked like she was shrivelling in the light. Her pale skin already looked vaguely pinkish, and those big violet eyes seemed small and dim and pained. He wondered if they'd got away after all, as he slipped the oar into the water and put his back into it. His arm hurt, his ear was bleeding, and the sun was bright and rising.

CHAPTER TWENTY-EIGHT

On the Mississippi River, October 1857

ABNER Marsh hadn't rowed a sounding yawl in more than twenty years. With only him and Toby pulling, it was damned hard work, even going with the current. His arms and back were complaining fiercely within the half-hour. Marsh grunted and kept on rowing. The *Fevre Dream* was out of sight now, vanished behind them. The sun was creeping up the sky, and the river had grown very wide. It looked to be almost a mile across.

"It hurts," Valerie said.

Joshua York said, "Cover yourself."

"I'm *burning*," she said. "I never thought it would be like this." She looked up at the sun and shied away as if struck. Marsh was startled by the vivid redness of her face.

Joshua York started to move toward her, and stopped suddenly, looking unsteady. He put a hand up against his brow and took a slow deliberate breath. Then, carefully, he edged closer. "Sit in my shadow," he said. "Pull down your hat."

Valerie curled up in the bottom of the yawl, practically in Joshua's lap. He reached down and straightened the collar of her jacket in an oddly tender manner, then rested his hand on the back of her head.

Down here, Marsh noted, the riverbanks were shorn of all timber but for an occasional row of ornamental saplings. Instead they saw carefully cultivated fields to either side, flat and endless, here and there interrupted by the splendor of a big Greek-Revival plantation house, its cupola overlooking the wide, tranquil river. Ahead on the western shore, a pile of smouldering bagasse, the refuse of sugarcane stalks, was sending up a column of acrid gray smoke. The pile was big as a house; the smoke spread in a shroud across the river. Marsh couldn't see no flames. "Maybe we ought to put in," he said to Joshua. "There's plantations all around us."

Joshua had closed his eyes. He opened them when Marsh spoke. "No," he said. "We are too close. We must put more distance between us and them. Billy may be coming after us on foot along the shore, and when night falls . . . " He left the rest unsaid.

Abner Marsh grunted and rowed. Joshua closed his eyes again, and pulled his wide-brimmed white hat lower.

For more than an hour they moved down the river in silence, the only sound the slap of the oars against water and the song of an occasional bird. Toby Lanyard and Abner Marsh rowed, while Joshua and Valerie lay huddled together as if they were asleep, and Karl Framm sprawled beneath a blanket. The sun rose in the sky. It was a chill, windy day, but a bright one. Marsh was thankful for the planters and the great piles of smoking bagasse that lined the shores since the drifting gray pall from their fires gave the only shade there was for the night folks.

Once Valerie cried out, as if in terrible pain. Joshua opened his eyes and bent over her, stroking her long black hair and whispering to her. Valerie whimpered. "I thought you were the one, Joshua," she said. "The pale king. I thought you'd come to change it all, to take us back." Her whole body trembled when she tried to talk. "The city, my father told me of the city. Is it there, Joshua? The dark city?"

"Quiet," said Joshua York. "Quiet. You weaken yourself."

"But is it there? I thought you would take us home, dear Joshua. I dreamt of it, I did. I was so tired of it all. I thought you had come to save us."

"*Quiet,*" Joshua said. He was trying to be forceful, but his voice was sad and weary.

"The pale king," she whispered. "Come to save us. I thought you had come to save us."

Joshua York kissed her lightly on her swollen, blistered lips. "So did I," he said bitterly. Then he pressed his fingers against her mouth to quiet her, and closed his eyes again.

Abner Marsh rowed, while the river flowed around them and the sun beat down overhead and the wind swept smoke and ash across the water. A cinder got in his eye somehow, and Marsh cussed and rubbed at it until the eye was red and swollen and the tearing had stopped. By then his whole body was one huge ache.

Two hours downstream Joshua began to talk, never opening his eyes, in a voice thick with pain. "He is mad, you know," he said. "It is true. He took me, night after night. The pale king, yes, I thought that, thought I was . . . but Julian vanquished me, time after time, and I submitted. His eyes, Abner, you have seen his eyes. Darkness, such darkness. And *old*. I thought he was evil, and strong, and clever. But I learned it was not so. Julian is not . . . Abner, he is mad, truly. Once, he must have been all that I thought him, but now . . . it is as though he sleeps. At times, he wakes, briefly, and one senses what he must have been. You saw it, Abner, that night at supper, you saw Julian stirred, awakened. But most of the time . . . Abner, he takes no interest in the boat, the river, the people and events around him. Sour Billy runs the *Fevre Dream*, devises the schemes that keep my people safe. Julian seldom gives orders, and when he does they are arbitrary, even stupid. He does not read, or talk, he does not play chess. He eats indifferently. I do not think he even tastes it. Since taking the *Fevre Dream*, Julian has descended into some dark dream. He spends most of his time in his cabin, in the darkness, alone. It was Billy who spied the steamer following us, not Julian.

"I thought him evil at first, a dark king leading his people into ruin, but watching him . . . he is ruined already, hollow, empty. He feasts on the lives of your people because he has no life of his own, not even a name that is truly his. Once I wondered what he thought of, alone, all those days and nights in darkness. I know now that he does not think at all. Perhaps he dreams. If so, I think he dreams of death, of an ending. He dwells in that black empty cabin as if it were a tomb, stirring from it only at the scent of blood. And the things he does . . . it is more than rashness. He courts destruction, discovery. He must want an end, a rest, I believe. He is so old. How tired he must be."

"He offered me a deal," Abner Marsh said. Without breaking his labored stroke, Marsh recounted his conversation with Damon Julian.

"You had half the truth, Abner," Julian said when he'd finished. "Yes, he would have liked to corrupt you, as a taunt to me. But that was not all. You might have agreed and never meant it. You might have lied to him, waited for a chance, and tried to kill him. I think Julian knew that. By bringing you aboard, he toyed with his own death."

Marsh snorted. "If he wants to die, he could cooperate more."

Joshua opened his eyes. They were small and faded. "When the danger is real and close to hand, it wakes him. The beast in him . . . the beast is old and mindless and weary, but when it wakes it struggles desperately to live . . . it is strong, Abner. And old." Joshua laughed feebly, a bitter laugh without humor. "After that night . . . after it all went wrong . . . I asked myself, over and over, *how* it could have happened. Julian had drained a full glass of my . . . my potion . . . it should have been enough, it should have killed the red thirst, it should have . . . I did not understand . . . it had always worked before, always, but not with Julian, not . . . not with *him*. At first I thought it was his strength, the power of him, the evil. Then . . . then one night he saw the question in my eyes, and he laughed and told me. Abner, you remember . . . when I told you my story . . . when I was very young, the thirst did not touch me. Do you remember?"

"Yeah."

Joshua nodded weakly. The skin was stretched tightly over his face, red and chafed-looking. "Julian is old, Abner, *old*. The thirst . . . he has not felt the thirst in years . . . hundreds, thousands of . . . years . . . that was why the drink . . . had no effect. I never knew, none of us did. You can outlive the thirst, and he . . . he did not thirst . . . but he fed, because he *chose* to, because of those things he said that night, you remember, strength and weakness, masters and slaves, all the things he said. Sometimes I think . . . the humanity of him is all hollow, a mask . . . he is only an old animal, so ancient it has lost even the taste for food, but it hunts on nonetheless, because that is all it remembers, that is all it *is*, the beast. The legends of your race, Abner, your vampire tales . . . the living dead, the undead, we bear those names in your stories. Julian . . . I think with Julian it is the truth. Even the thirst is gone. Undead. Cold and hollow and undead."

Abner Marsh was trying to frame a comment to the effect that he intended to erase the "un-" part from Joshua's description of Damon Julian, when Valerie suddenly sat bolt upright in the yawl. Marsh flinched and froze in mid-stroke. Beneath the slouchy felt hat, Valerie's skin was raw as an open wound, blistered and tight, with a color that had gone beyond red to the dark mottled purple of a bloody bruise. Her lips were cracked, and she drew them back in an insane giggle to reveal long white teeth. The whites of her eyes had swallowed up all the rest, so she looked blind and insane. "It *hurts!*" she screamed, lifting hands red as lobster claws above her head in an attempt to block out the sun. Then her eyes darted round the boat, and lighted on Karl Framm's softly breathing form, and she scrambled toward him, her mouth open.

"No!" Joshua York cried. He threw himself on top of her, and wrenched her aside before her teeth could close on Framm's throat. Valerie struggled crazily, and screamed. Joshua held her immobile. Valerie's teeth snapped together, again and again, until she had gnashed open her own lip. Her mouth dripped a froth of blood and spit. Struggle as she might, however, Joshua York was too much for her. Finally all the fight seemed to go out of her. She slumped back heavily, staring up at the sun out of blind white eyes.

Joshua cradled her in his arms, despairing. "Abner," he said, "the lead line. Under it. I hid it there last night, when they went out for you. Please, Abner."

Marsh stopped rowing and went to the lead line, the thirty-three-foot-long rope used for soundings, a pipe filled with lead at its end. Beneath its coils, Marsh found what Joshua wanted; an unlabeled wine bottle, more than three-quarters full. He passed it up to York, who pulled the cork and forced it to Valerie's swollen, cracked lips. The liquor dribbled down her chin and most of it wound up soaking her shirt, but Joshua got a little into her mouth. It seemed to help. All of a sudden she began to suck at the bottle greedily, like a baby sucking on a teat. "Easy," said Joshua York.

Abner Marsh moved the lead line around and frowned. "Is that the only bottle?" he asked.

Joshua York nodded. His own face looked scalded now, like the face of a second mate Marsh had once seen who'd stood too near to a steam pipe that burst. Blisters and cracks were appearing. "Julian kept my supply in his cabin, and doled it out a bottle at a time. I dared not protest. Often enough he toyed with the idea of destroying it all." He pulled the bottle away from Valerie. It was between a quarter and half-full now. "I thought . . . thought it would be enough, until I could make some more. I did not think Valerie would be with us." His hand shook. He sighed and put the bottle to his own lips, taking a long, deep draught.

"*Hurts*," Valerie whimpered. She curled up peacefully, her body trembling, but the fit clearly past her now.

Joshua York handed the bottle back to Marsh. "Keep it, Abner," he said. "It must last. We must ration it."

Toby Lanyard had stopped rowing and was staring back at them. Karl Framm stirred weakly in the bottom of the yawl. The boat drifted with the current, and up ahead Marsh saw the smoke of an ascending steamer. He picked up an oar. "Get us to shore, Toby," he said. "C'mon. I'm goin' to hail that goddamn boat down there. We got to get us into a cabin."

"Yessuh, Cap'n," said Toby.

Joshua touched his brow and flinched. "No," he said softly. "No, Abner, you shouldn't. Questions." He tried to stand up, and reeled dizzily, dropping back to his knees. "Burning," he said. "No. Listen to me. Not the boat, Abner. Keep on. A town, we'll reach a town. By dark . . . Abner?"

"Hell," said Abner Marsh, "you been out here maybe four hours now, and look at you. Look at her. It ain't even noon yet. Both of you will be burned to a crisp if we don't get you inside."

"No," said York. "They'll ask questions, Abner. You can't . . . "

"Shut your damn fool mouth," Marsh said, putting his aching back into the oar. The yawl moved across the river. The steamer was coming up at them, pennants waving in the wind, a handful of passengers strolling out on her promenade. It was a New Orleans packet boat, Marsh saw as they got near, a medium-sized side-wheeler named the *H. E. Edwards*. He waved an oar at her and called across the water, while Toby rowed and the yawl rocked. On the decks of the steamboat, passengers waved back and pointed. She gave a short, impatient blast on her whistle, and Abner Marsh craned his head around and saw another boat, way down the river, a white dot in the distance. His heart sunk. They were racing, he knew, and there was no steamer in the world going to stop for a hail in the middle of a race.

The *H. E. Edwards* surged past them at full speed, paddles kicking so hard the wake bobbed them up and down like they was shooting a rapids. Abner Marsh cussed and called after her and waved his oar threateningly. The second boat approached and passed even faster, her stacks trailing sparks. They were left drifting in midriver, with empty fields all around them, the sun above, and a pile of smouldering bagasse downstream sending up a gray pillar of smoke. "Land," Marsh said to Toby, and they made for the western bank. When they ran aground, he jumped out and pulled the yawl further in, standing knee-deep in mud. Even on the goddamn shore, he thought when he looked around, there was no shade, no trees to shelter them from the merciless sun. "Get on out of there," Marsh bellowed at Toby Lanyard. "We got to get them up on the bank," he said. "Then we'll drag out this goddamn boat and turn it over, get 'em under it." Toby nodded. They got Framm ashore first, then Valerie. When Marsh took her under the arms and lifted her, she shuddered wildly. Her face looked so bad he was scared to touch it, lest it come off in his hand.

When they returned for Joshua, he was already out of the boat. "I'll help," he said. "It's heavy." He was leaning against the side of the yawl.

Marsh nodded to Toby, and the three of them pushed the boat clear out of the river. It was hard. Abner Marsh put all his strength into it. The mud along the bank fought against him with wet, clutching fingers. Without Joshua, they might never have done it. But finally they got it over the embankment into the field, and flipping it over was easy. Marsh grabbed Valerie under the arms again and dragged her under the boat. "You get under here too, Joshua," he said, turning. Toby had Karl Framm and was ministering to him, forcing a handful of river water between the pilot's pale lips. Joshua was nowhere to be seen. Marsh scowled and went around the yawl. His pants, soaked and heavy with mud, clung to his legs. "Joshua," he roared, "where the hell you got yourself . . . "

Joshua York had collapsed on the river bank, his red, burned hand clawing at the mud. "God*damn*," Marsh roared. "*Toby!*"

Toby came running, and together they pulled York into the shade. His eyes were closed. Marsh fetched out the bottle and forced some down his throat. "Drink it, Joshua, drink it. Goddamn you anyway." Finally York began to swallow. He didn't stop swallowing until the bottle was empty. Abner Marsh held it in his hand, frowning. He turned it upside down. A last drop of Joshua York's private liquor ran out and fell on Marsh's mud-caked boot. "Hell," said Marsh. He flung the empty bottle into the river. "Stay with 'em, Toby," he said. "I'm goin' to fetch some help. Must be somebody round here."

"Yessuh, Cap'n Marsh," Toby replied.

Marsh started off across the field. The sugar cane had all been harvested. The fields were wide and empty, but off over a rise Marsh saw a thin trail of smoke. He walked toward it, hoping it was a house and not another goddamned pile of burning bagasse. He hoped in vain, but a few minutes past the fire he saw a bunch of slaves working in the fields, and called out to them, breaking into a run. They took him to the plantation house, where he told the overseer his sad story about the boiler explosion that had sunk their steamboat and killed everyone aboard, except for a few who'd gotten away in the sounding yawl. The man nodded and brought down the planter. "Got a couple folks burned bad," Marsh told him. "We got to be quick about it." A couple of minutes later, they'd hitched a pair of horses to a wagon and were off across the fields.

When they arrived at the overturned yawl, Karl Framm was standing up, looking dazed and weak. Abner Marsh jumped down from the wagon and gestured. "Get movin'," he said to the men who'd come with him, "we got them what was burned under there. Got to get 'em inside." He turned to Framm. "Are you all right, Mister Framm?"

Framm grinned weakly. "I been better, Cap'n," he said, "but I been a hell of a lot worse, too."

Two men were carrying Joshua York to the wagon. His white suit was stained with mud and wine, and he did not move. The third man, the planter's youngest son, came crawling out from under the yawl and wiped his hands on his pants, frowning. He looked a little sick. "Cap'n Marsh," he said, "That woman you got under there is burned to death."

CHAPTER TWENTY-NINE

Gray Plantation, Louisiana, October 1857

TWO of the houseboys lifted Joshua York from the back of the wagon, and carried him inside and up the wide, curving staircase to a bedroom. "A dark one!" Abner Marsh yelled up at them. "And pull the goddamned curtains, you hear me? I don't want no goddamned sunlight in there." He turned to his companions briefly, while the planter and his sons and a couple more slaves went back outside to see to Valerie's corpse. Framm had thrown an arm around Toby's shoulders to keep himself erect. "You get some damn food into you, Mister Framm," Marsh said.

The pilot nodded.

"And remember what happened. We was on the *Eli Reynolds*, and her boiler blew. Killed everybody, it did, except us. She sunk clean out of sight, a long ways upriver, where there's no bottom. That's all you know, you hear? Let me tell the rest."

"That's more'n I know," Framm said. "How the hell did I get here?"

"Never you mind about that. Just listen to what I told you." Marsh turned and stomped up the stairs while Toby helped Framm to a chair.

They had laid Joshua York on a wide canopied bed, and were undressing him when Marsh came in. Joshua's face and hands were the worst, seared horribly, but even beneath his clothing his pale white skin had reddened a bit. He moved feebly as they pulled off his boots, and moaned. "Lawd, this man burned up *bad*," one of the slaves said, shaking his head.

Marsh scowled and went to the windows, which were thrown wide. He pulled them shut and closed the shutters. "Fetch me a blanket or something," he ordered, "to hang across here. Too damn much light. And close them drapes round the bed, too." His tone was the bellow of a steamer captain, and brooked no argument.

Only when the room was black as Marsh could make it, and a gaunt haggard black woman had come up to tend to York's burns with herbs and healing salves and cold towels, did Abner Marsh leave. Downstairs, the planter—a bluff, stone-faced, lantern-jawed man who introduced himself as Aaron Gray—and two of his sons were sitting to table with Karl Framm. The scent of food made Marsh realize how long it had been since he'd eaten. He felt ravenous. "Do join us, Cap'n," Gray said, and Marsh gladly pulled out a chair and let them pile up fried chicken and cornbread and sweet peas and taters on his plate.

Joshua had been right about the questions, Marsh reflected as he wolfed down his food. The Grays asked a hundred of them, and Marsh answered as best he could, when his mouth wasn't full of food. Framm excused himself just as Marsh was taking seconds—the pilot was still looking poorly—and let himself be led to a bed. The more questions Marsh answered, the less comfortable he got. He wasn't a natural-born liar like some rivermen he knew, and that became more obvious with every damned word he uttered. Somehow, though, he made it through the meal, although Marsh fancied that Gray and his eldest boy were both looking at him kind of queer by the time he had done with dessert.

"Your nigger is fine," the second son said as they left the table, "and Robert has gone off to bring back Doctor Moore to attend to the other two. Sally will take care of 'em in the meanwhile. No sense you frettin', Cap'n. Maybe you'd like to rest up, too. You've been through a lot, losin' your steamboat and all those friends of yours."

"Yeah," said Abner Marsh. No sooner had the suggestion been made than Marsh felt incredibly weary. He hadn't slept in something like thirty hours now. "I'd appreciate that," he said.

"Show him to a room, Jim," the planter said. "And Cap'n, Robert will pay a call on the undertaker, too. For that unfortunate woman. Most tragic, most. What did you say her name was?"

"Valerie," Marsh said. For the life of him, he couldn't recall what last name she'd been using. "Valerie York," he improvised.

"She'll get a good Christian burial," Gray said, "unless you want to take her to her family, perhaps?"

"No," said Marsh, "no."

"Fine. Jim, take Cap'n Marsh upstairs. Put him near that poor burned-up friend of his."

"Yessuh, Daddy."

Marsh hardly bothered glancing at the room they gave him. He slept like a log.

When he woke, it was dark.

Marsh sat up in bed stiffly. The rowing had taken its toll. His joints creaked when he moved, he had a terrible cramp in his shoulders, and his arms felt like somebody had beaten on them with a big oak club. He groaned and edged slowly to the side of the mattress, lowering his bare feet to the floor. Every step sent pains through him as he went to the window and opened it wide to let some cool night air into the room. Outside was a small stone balcony, and beyond it a fringe of China trees and the fields, desolate and empty in the moonlight. In the distance Marsh could make out the dim glow of the bagasse, still sending up its veil of smoke. Beyond it, only a faint glimmering from here, was the river.

Marsh shivered, closed the window and went back to bed. It was chilly in the room now, so he pulled the blankets over himself and rolled onto his side. The moonlight etched darks and shadows everywhere, and the furniture, all strange to him, became stranger still in the faint light. He could not sleep. He found himself thinking of Damon Julian and the *Fevre Dream*, and worrying about whether the steamer was still where he'd left her. He thought of Valerie as well. He had gotten a good look at her when they'd pulled her out from under the yawl, and she hadn't been a pretty sight. You'd never have thought that she'd been beautiful, pale and graceful and sensual, with those great violet eyes. Abner Marsh felt sorry for her, and thought that was strange of him, seeing as how it was only last night around this time that he'd tried to kill her with that buffalo gun of his. The world was an awful queer place, he thought, when so goddamned much could change in a day.

Finally he slept again.

"*Abner*," came the whisper, disturbing his dreams. "*Abner*," came the voice, calling, "*let me in.*"

Abner Marsh sat up suddenly. Joshua York was standing on his balcony, rapping on the glass of his window with a pale, scarred hand.

"Hold on," Marsh said. It was still black outside and the house was quiet. Joshua smiled as Marsh climbed out of bed and padded toward him. His face was lined with cracks and fissures, husks of dying skin. Marsh opened the doors to the balcony, and Joshua stepped through, wearing his sad white suit, all stained and rumpled now. It wasn't until he was in the room that Abner Marsh remembered the empty bottle he'd tossed into the river. He stepped back suddenly. "Joshua, you ain't . . . you ain't *thirstin'*, are you?"

"No," said Joshua York. His gray cloak moved and curled in the wind that rustled through the open balcony doors. "I did not want to break the lock, or the glass. Do not be afraid, Abner."

"You're better," Marsh said, looking at him. York's lips were still cracked, his eyes were sunk in deep purple-black pits, but he was much improved. At noon he'd looked like death.

"Yes," Joshua said. "Abner, I've come to take my leave."

"What?" Marsh was flabbergasted. "You can't leave."

"I must, Abner. They saw me, whoever owns this plantation. I have a vague memory of being treated by a doctor. Tomorrow I will be healed. What will they think then?"

"What will they think when they go to bring you breakfast and you ain't there?" Marsh said.

"No doubt they will be puzzled, but it will be easier to account for nonetheless. You can be as shocked as they are, Abner. Tell them that I must have wandered off in a fever. I will never be found."

"Valerie is dead," Marsh said.

"Yes," said Joshua. "There is a wagon outside with a coffin in it. I guessed it was for her." He sighed and shook his head. "I failed her. I have failed all my people. We should never have taken her."

"She made her choice," Marsh said. "At least she got free of *him*."

"Free," Joshua York said bitterly. "Is this the freedom I bring my people? A poor gift. For a time, before Damon Julian came into my life, I dared to dream that Valerie and I might be lovers someday. Not in the fashion of my own people, inflamed by blood, but with a passion born of tenderness, and affection, and mutual desire. We talked of that." His mouth twisted in self-reproach. "She believed in me. I killed her."

"Like hell," Marsh said. "At the end, she said she loved you. She didn't have to come with us. She wanted to. We all got to choose, you said. I think she picked right. She was an awful pretty lady."

Joshua York shuddered. "She walks in beauty, like the night," he said very quietly, staring down at his clenched fist. "Sometimes I question whether there is an hour for my race, Abner. The nights are full of blood and terror, but the days are merciless."

"Where are you goin'?" Marsh asked.

Joshua looked grim. "Back."

Marsh scowled. "You *can't*."

"I have no other choice."

"You just *escaped* from there," Marsh said hotly. "After all we went through to get loose, you can't just up and go back. Wait. Hide in the woods or something, go to some town. I'll get loose of here and we'll join up, make some plans for getting that steamboat back."

"Again?" Joshua shook his head. "There is a story I never told you, Abner. It happened a long time ago, during my first months in England, when the red thirst still came upon me regularly, driving me out in search of blood. One night I had fought it, and lost, and I hunted through the midnight streets. I came upon a couple, a man and a woman hurrying somewhere. My habit was to shun such prey, to take only those who walked alone, for safety's sake. But the thirst was on me badly, and even from a distance I could see that the woman was very beautiful. She drew me like a flame draws the moth, and I came. I attacked from darkness, and got my hands around the man's neck, and ripped away half his throat, I thought. Then I shoved him aside and he fell. He was a huge man. I took the woman in my arms, and bent my teeth to her neck, ever so gently. My eyes held her still, entranced her. I had just tasted the first hot, sweet flow of blood when I was seized from behind and torn from her embrace. It was the man, her companion. I had not killed him after all. His neck was thick with muscle and fat, and while I had ripped it open so it dripped blood, he was still on his feet. He never said a word. He only put up his fists as a prizefighter might, and hit me square in the face. He was quite strong. The blow stunned me, and opened a gash above my eye. I was already distracted. Being pulled from your victim like that is a sickening feeling, dizzy, disorienting. The man hit me again, and I lashed out backhanded at him. He went down heavily, long gashes across his cheek, one of his eyes half-torn from his skull. I turned back to the woman, pressed my mouth to the open wound. And then he was on me again. I tore his arm loose of me and all but ripped it from its socket, and I broke one of his legs for good measure, with a kick. He went down. This time I watched. Painstakingly, he got up again, raised his fists, moved toward me. Twice more I knocked him down, and twice more he rose. Finally I broke his neck, and he died, and then I killed his woman.

"Afterward, I could not put him from my mind. He must have known that I was not entirely human. He must have realized, strong as he was, that he was no match for my strength, my speed, my thirst. I was distracted by my own fever, and the beauty of his companion, and I missed my kill. He might have been spared. He could have run. He could have called out for help. He could have taken a moment and found a weapon. But he did not. He saw his lady in my arms, saw me bleeding her, and all he could think of was to get up and come at me with those big, foolish fists of his. When I had time to reflect, I found myself admiring his strength, his mad courage, the love he must have had for that woman.

"But Abner, for all that, he was *stupid.* He saved neither his lady nor himself.

"You remind me of that man, Abner. Julian has taken your *Fevre Dream* from you, and all you can think of is getting her back, so you get up and cock your fists and come straight on, and Julian knocks you down again. One day you will not get up, if you continue these attacks. Abner, give it up!"

"What the hell you sayin'?" Marsh demanded in an angry voice. "It's Julian and his vampires got to worry now. That goddamn steamer ain't goin' no place without a pilot."

"I can pilot her," said Joshua York.

"Will you?"

"Yes."

Marsh felt sick with anger and betrayal. *"Why?"* he demanded. "Joshua, you ain't like them!"

"I will be, unless I return," York said gravely. "Unless I have my potion, the thirst will come on me, all the fiercer for the years I have held it at bay. And then I will kill, and drink, and be as Julian is. The next time I entered a bedroom by night, it would not be to talk."

"Go back then! Fetch your damned drink! But don't move that damned steamer, not until I can get there."

"With armed men. With sharpened stakes and hate in your hearts. To kill. I will not permit that."

"Whose side are you on?"

"The side of my people."

"Julian's side," spat Marsh.

"No," said Joshua York. He sighed. "Listen, Abner, and try to understand. Julian is the bloodmaster. He controls them, all of them. Some of them are like him, corrupt, evil. Katherine, Raymond, others, they follow him willingly. But not all of them. You saw Valerie, you heard her in the yawl today. I am not alone. Our races are not so very different. All of us have good and evil in us, and all of us dream. Yet if you attack the steamer, if you move against Julian, they will defend him, no matter what their private hopes may be. Centuries of enmity and fear will drive them. A river of blood flows between day and night, and it cannot be crossed easily. Those who hesitate, if any, will be compelled.

"If you come, Abner, you and your people, there will be death. And not Julian's alone. The others will guard him, and they will perish, and your people as well."

"Sometimes you got to take that risk," Marsh said. "And those who help Julian deserve to die."

"Do they?" Joshua looked sad. "Perhaps they do. Perhaps we all should die. We are out of place in this world your race has built. Your kind has killed all but a handful of us. Perhaps it is time to slaughter the last survivors as well." He smiled grimly. "If that is what you intend, Abner, then remember who I am. You are my friend, but they are blood of my blood, my people. I belong with them. I thought I was their king."

His tone was so bitter and despairing that Abner Marsh felt his anger fading. In its place was pity. "You tried," he said.

"I failed. I failed Valerie, and Simon, failed all those who believed in me. I failed you and Mister Jeffers, and that infant as well. I think I may even have failed Julian, in some strange way."

"It ain't your fault," Marsh insisted.

Joshua York shrugged, but there was a cold grim look in his gray eyes. "Past is past. My concern is with tonight and tomorrow night and the night after. I must go back. They need me, though they may not realize it. I must go back and do what I can, however little it may be."

Abner Marsh snorted. "And you tell *me* to give it up? You think *I'm* like that damned fool kept comin' at you? Hell, Joshua, what about *you?* How many times has Julian bled you now? It appears to me you're just as damned stubborn and stupid as you say I am."

Joshua smiled. "Perhaps," he admitted.

"Hell," Marsh swore. "All right. You're goin' back to Julian, like some egg-suckin' idyut. What the hell do you want me to do?"

"You had better leave here as quickly as you can," Joshua said, "before our hosts get more suspicious than they are already."

"I'd figured out that much."

"It's over, Abner. Don't come looking for us again."

Abner Marsh scowled. "Hell."

Joshua smiled. "You damned fool," he said. "Well, look if you must. You won't find us."

"I'll see about that."

"Maybe there's hope for us yet. I'll return and tame Julian and build my bridge between night and day, and together you and I will outrun the *Eclipse*."

Abner Marsh snorted derisively, but down inside he wanted to believe. "You take care of my goddamned steamboat," he said. "Ain't never been a faster one, and she better be in good repair when I get her back."

When Joshua smiled it made the dry, dead skin around his mouth crackle and tear. He lifted a hand to his face and tore it away. It peeled off whole, like it was only a mask he'd been wearing, an ugly mask full of scars and wrinkles. Beneath it his skin was milky white, serene and unlined, ready to begin anew, ready for the world to write upon it. York crumbled his old face in his hand; wisps of old pain and flakes of skin sifted through his fingers and fell to the floor. He wiped his hand on his coat and held it out to Abner Marsh. They shook.

"We all got to make choices," Marsh said. "You told me that, Joshua, and you was right. Them choices ain't always easy. Someday you're goin' to have to choose, I think. Between your night folks and . . . well, call it good. Doing right. You know what I mean. Make the right choice, Joshua."

"And you, Abner. Make your own choices wisely."

Joshua York turned, his cloak swirling behind him, and went outside. He vaulted over the balustrade with easy grace and dropped the twenty feet to the ground like it was something he did every day, landing on his feet. Then he was gone, vanished, moving so quick he seemed to fade into the night. Maybe he turned himself into a goddamned mist, Abner Marsh thought.

Away off on the distant shine that was the river, a steamer sounded her whistle, a faint melancholy call, kind of lost and kind of lonely. It was a bad night on the river. Abner Marsh shivered and wondered if there'd be a frost. He shut the balcony doors and walked on back to bed.

CHAPTER THIRTY

Fever Years: November 1857– April 1870

BOTH of them were true to their word: Abner Marsh kept on looking, but he did not find her.

They left Aaron Gray's plantation as soon as Karl Framm was strong enough to travel, several days after Joshua York had vanished. Marsh was glad to be gone. Gray and his kin were getting mighty curious by then about why there was nothing in the papers about a steamboat explosion, and why none of their neighbors had heard of it, and why Joshua had taken off. And Marsh was getting tangled up in his own lies. By the time he and Toby and Karl Framm got themselves upriver, the *Fevre Dream* was gone, as he'd known she would be. Marsh returned to St. Louis.

Through the long dreary winter, Marsh kept up his search. He wrote more letters, he loitered around the riverfront bars and billiard halls, he hired some more detectives, he read too damn many newspapers, he found Yoerger and Grove and the rest of the crew of the *Eli Reynolds* and sent them up and down the river, cabin passage, looking. All of it turned up nothing. No one had seen the *Fevre Dream*. No one had seen the *Ozymandias* either. Abner Marsh figured they'd changed her name again. He read every goddamned poem Byron and Shelley ever wrote, but this time it was no use. It got so bad he had the damn poems memorized, and he even went on to other poets, but the only thing he found that way was a sorry-looking Missouri stern-wheeler named the *Hiawatha*.

Marsh did get one report from his detectives, but it told him nothing he hadn't figured out already. The side-wheel steamer *Ozyman-*

dias had left Natchez that October night with about four hundred tons of freight, forty cabin passengers, and maybe twice as many deckers. The freight had never been delivered. Neither the steamer nor the passengers had ever been seen again, except at a few wood-yards just downstream of Natchez. Abner Marsh read over that letter a half dozen times, frowning. The numbers were way too low, which meant that Sour Billy was doing one damn poor job—unless he'd kept them down deliberate, so Julian and his night folks could have an easy time of it. A hundred and twenty people were gone, vanished. It gave Marsh a cold sweat. He stared at that letter and remembered what Damon Julian had said to him: *No one on the river will ever forget your Fevre Dream.*

For months Abner Marsh was plagued by terrible nightmares of a boat moving down the river, all black, every lamp and candle extinguished, the big black tarpaulins hung all around the main deck so even the ruddy light of the furnaces could not escape, a boat dark as death and black as sin, a shadow moving through moonlight and fog, hardly seen, quiet and fast. In his dreams she made no sound as she moved, and white shapes flitted about her decks silently and haunted her grand saloon, and inside their staterooms the passengers huddled in fear, until the doors opened one midnight, and then they began to scream. Once or twice Marsh woke up screaming as well, and even in his waking hours he could not forget her, his dream boat cloaked in shadows and screams, with smoke as black as Julian's eyes and steam the color of blood.

By the time the ice was breaking up on the upper river, Abner Marsh was faced with a hard choice. He had not found the *Fevre Dream*, and the search had brought him to the brink of ruin. His ledger books told a grim story; his coffers were almost empty. He owned a steamboat company without any steamboats, and he lacked even the funds to have a modest one built. So, reluctantly, Marsh wrote his agents and detectives and called off the hunt.

With the little money he had left he went downriver, to where the *Eli Reynolds* still sat in the cutoff that had wrecked her. They fitted a new rudder to her, and patched up her stern wheel a little, and waited for the spring floods. The floods came, the cutoff became passable once more, and Yoerger and his crew nursed the *Reynolds* back up to St. Louis, where she was fitted with a brand new paddle, a new engine with twice the push, and a second boiler. She even got a new paint job, and a bright yellow carpet for her main cabin. Then

Marsh launched her into the New Orleans trade, for which she was too small and too shabby and altogether poorly fitted, so he could continue his hunt personally.

Abner Marsh knew even before he started that it was near hopeless. Between Cairo and New Orleans alone, there was some eleven hundred miles of river. Then there was the upper Mississippi above Cairo all the way to the Falls of St. Anthony, there was the Missouri, there was the Ohio and the Yazoo and the Red River and about fifty other secondary rivers and tributaries navigable by steamer, most of which had tributaries of their own, not to mention all the little creeks and streams and cutoffs that were navigable part of the year, if you had a good pilot. She could be hiding up any one of them, and if the *Eli Reynolds* steamed past and missed her, it would mean starting all over again. Thousands of steamboats plied the Mississippi river system, with newcomers entering the trade every month, which meant lots of damned names to sort through in the papers. But Marsh was nothing if not stubborn. He searched, and the *Eli Reynolds* became his home.

She did not get much trade. The biggest, fastest, most luxurious steamboats on the river competed in the St. Louis-to-New Orleans run, and the *Reynolds*, old and slow as she was, attracted little custom away from the great side-wheelers. "It's not just that she's fast as a snail and twice as ugly," Marsh's New Orleans agent told him in the fall of 1858, while giving notice to take another job. "It's *you*, too, damned if I ain't telling the truth."

"Me?" Marsh roared. "What the hell you mean?"

"Folks on the river talk, y'know. They say you're the unluckiest man ever to own a steamboat. They say you got some kind of curse on you, worse'n the curse on the *Drennan Whyte*. One of your steamers blew her boilers, they say, and killed everybody. Four got crushed up in an ice jam. One got burned after everybody on her died of yaller fever. And the last one, they say you wrecked her yourself, after you went crazy and beat your pilot with a club."

"Damn that man," Marsh swore.

"Now, I ask you, who the hell is goin' to ride with a cursed man like that? Or work for him either. Not me, I tell you that for sure. Not me."

The man he'd hired to replace Jonathon Jeffers begged Marsh more than once to take the *Reynolds* out of the New Orleans trade, and have her work the upper Mississippi or the Illinois, where she'd be better suited, or even the Missouri, which was rough and dangerous but enormously profitable if your steamboat didn't get smashed to splinters. Abner Marsh refused, and fired the man when he persisted. He figured there was no chance that he'd find the *Fevre Dream* on the northern rivers. Besides, during the last few months he'd been making secret stops by night at certain Louisiana woodyards and deserted islands in Mississippi and Arkansas, taking on runaway slaves and bringing them up north to the free states. Toby had put him in touch with a bunch called the underground railroad, who made all the arrangements. Abner Marsh had no use for the goddamned railroads and insisted on calling it the underground river, but it made him feel good to help, kind of like he was hurting Damon Julian somehow. At times he'd hunker down with the runaways on the main deck, and ask them about night folks and the *Fevre Dream* and such, figuring that maybe the blacks knew things that white folks didn't, but none of them ever told him anything useful.

For nearly three years, Abner Marsh continued his hunt. They were hard years. By 1860 Marsh was heavily in debt due to the losses incurred in running the *Reynolds*. He had been forced to close the offices he had maintained in St. Louis, New Orleans, and other river towns. Nightmares no longer troubled him as they had, but he grew more and more isolated with the passage of years. At times it seemed to Marsh as if the time he had spent with Joshua York on the *Fevre Dream* was the last real life he had known, that the months and years since were drifting past as if in a dream. At other times, he felt just the opposite, felt that *this* was real, the red ink in his ledger books, the deck of the *Eli Reynolds* under him, the smell of her steam, the stains on her new yellow carpet. The memories of Joshua, the splendor of the great steamboat they had built together, the cold terror that Julian had stirred in him, *these* things were the dream, Marsh thought, and no wonder they had vanished, no wonder that folks along the river thought him mad.

The events of the summer of 1857 became even more dreamlike as, one by one, those who had shared some of Marsh's experiences began to drift out of his life. Old Toby Lanyard had gone east a month after they had returned to St. Louis. Being returned to slavery once had been enough for him, now he wanted to get as far from the slave states as possible. Marsh got a brief letter from him early in 1858, saying that he'd gotten a job cooking in a Boston hotel. After that he never heard from Toby again. Dan Albright had found himself a berth on a spanking new New Orleans side-wheeler. In the summer of 1858, however, Albright and his boat had the misfortune to be in New Orleans during a virulent outbreak of yellow fever. It killed thousands, including Albright, and eventually led to the city improving its sanitation so it wasn't quite so much like an open sewer in summer. Captain Yoerger ran the *Eli Reynolds* for Marsh until after the season of 1859, when he retired to his farm in Wisconsin, where he died peacefully a year later. When Yoerger had gone, Marsh took over captaining the stern-wheeler himself, to save money. By then only a handful of familiar faces remained among the crew. Doc Turney had been killed and robbed in Natchez-under-the-hill the previous summer, and Cat Grove had left the river entirely to go west, first to Denver, then to San Francisco, and eventually all the way to China or Japan or some such godforsaken place. Marsh hired Jack Ely, the old second engineer from the *Fevre Dream*, to replace Turney, and took on a few of the other crewmen who'd served on the vanished side-wheeler as well, but they died or drifted on or took other jobs. By 1860, only Marsh himself and Karl Framm were left of all those who had lived through the triumph and terror of 1857. Framm piloted the *Reynolds*, for all that his skills entitled him to a much bigger and more prestigious boat. Framm remembered a whole lot of things he wouldn't talk about, even to Marsh. The pilot was still good-natured, but he didn't tell near so many stories as he used to, and Marsh could see a grimness in his eyes that hadn't been there before. Framm wore a pistol now. "In case we find them," he said.

Marsh snorted. "That little thing ain't goin' to hurt Julian none."

Karl Framm's grin was still crooked, and his gold tooth caught the light, but there was nothing funny in his eyes when he answered. "Ain't for Julian, Cap'n. It's for me. They ain't getting me alive again." He looked at Marsh. "I could do the same for you, if it comes to that."

Marsh scowled. "It ain't comin' to that," he said, and he left the pilot house. He remembered that conversation for the rest of his days. He also remembered a Christmas party in St. Louis in 1859, given by the captain of one of the big Ohio boats. Marsh and Framm both attended, along with every other steamboatman in the town, and after everybody had been drinking some they got to telling river stories. He knew all the stories, but it was kind of peaceful and reassuring somehow to hear folks telling them all over again to the traders and bankers and pretty women who hadn't ever heard none of them. They talked about Old Al the alligator king, about the phantom steamer of Raccourci, about Mike Fink and Jim Bowie and Roarin' Jack Russell, about the great race between the *Eclipse* and the *A.L. Shotwell*, about the pilot who'd run a nasty stretch of river in the fog even though he'd gone and died, about the goddamn steamboat that had brought smallpox up the river twenty years before and killed something like twenty thousand Indians. "Ruined the hell out of the fur trade," the storyteller concluded, and everybody laughed, except Marsh and a couple of others. Then someone went through the brags about the impossibly big steamers, the *Hurricano* and the *E. Jenkins* and such, that grew their own wood with forests on their hurricane decks, and had wheels so big they took a whole year to make a full turn. Abner Marsh smiled.

Karl Framm pushed through the crowd, a brandy in his hand. "I know a story," he said, sounding a little drunk. " 'S true. There's this steamboat named the *Ozymandias*, y'see . . ."

"Never heard of it," somebody said.

Framm smiled thinly. "Y'better hope you never *see* it," he said, "cause them what does is done for. She only runs by night, this boat. And she's dark, all dark. Painted black as her stacks, every inch of her, except that inside she's got a main cabin with a carpet the color of blood, and silver mirrors everywhere that don't reflect nothing. Them mirrors is always empty, even though she's got lots of folks aboard her, pale-looking folks in fine clothes. They smile a lot. Only they don't show in the mirrors."

Someone shivered. They had all gone silent. "Why not?" asked an engineer Marsh knew slightly.

"Cause they're *dead*," Framm said. "Ever' damn one of 'em, dead. Only they won't lie down. They're sinners, and they got to ride that boat forever, that black boat with the red carpets and the empty mirrors, all up and down the river, never touching port, no sir."

"Phantoms," somebody said.

"Ha'nts," added a woman, "like that Raccourci boat."

"Hell no," said Karl Framm. "You can pass right through a ha'nt, but not the *Ozymandias*. She's real enough, and you'll learn it quick and to your sorrow if you come on her at night. Them dead folks is *hungry*. They drink blood, y'know. Hot red blood. They hide in the dark and when they see the lights of another steamer, they set out after her, and if they catch 'er they come swarming aboard, all those dead white faces, smiling, dressed so fine. And they sink the boat afterward, or burn her, and the next mornin' there's nothing to see but a couple stacks stickin' up out of the river, or maybe a wrecked boat full of corpses. Except for the sinners. The sinners go aboard that *Ozymandias*, and ride on her forever." He sipped his brandy and smiled. "So if you're out on the river some night, and you see a shadow on the water behind you, look close. It might be a steamer, painted black all over, with a crew white as ha'nts. She don't show no lights, that *Ozymandias*, so sometimes you can't see her till she's right behind you, her black wheels kicking up the water. If you see her, you better hope you got a lightnin' pilot, and maybe some coal oil on board, or a little lard. Cause she's big and she's fast, and when she catches you by night you're finished. Listen for her whistle. She only sounds her whistle when she knows she's got you, so if you hear it, start countin' up your sins."

"What does the whistle sound like?"

"Zactly like a man screaming," said Karl Framm.

"What's her name agin?" a young pilot asked.

"*Ozymandias*," said Framm. He knew how to say it right.

"What does *that* mean?"

Abner Marsh stood up. "It's from a poem," he said. "*Look on my works, ye Mighty, and despair.*"

The party crowd looked at him blankly, and one fat lady laughed a nervous, tittering sort of laugh. "There are curses and worse things on that old devil river," a short clerk started in. While he was talking, Marsh took Karl Framm by the arm and drew him outside.

"Why the hell did you tell that story?" Marsh demanded.

"To make them afraid," said Framm. "So if they see her, some damned night, they'll have the sense to run."

Abner Marsh considered that, and finally gave a reluctant nod. "I suppose it's alright. You called her by Sour Billy's name. If you'd said *Fevre Dream*, Mister Framm, I would have twisted your goddamned head off right then and there. You hear me?"

Framm heard, but it didn't matter. The story was out, for good or for ill. Marsh heard a garbled version of it from another man's lips a month later, while he was dining in the Planters' House, and twice more that winter. The story got changed some in the telling, of course, even to the name of the black steamboat. *Ozymandias* was too strange and too hard for most of the tellers, it seemed. But no matter what they named the boat, it was the same damned story.

A little over half a year later, Marsh heard another story, one that changed his life.

He had just sat down to dinner in a small St. Louis hotel, cheaper than the Planters' House and the Southern, but with good food. It was less popular with rivermen as well, which suited Marsh fine. His old friends and rivals looked at him queer in recent years, or avoided him as unlucky, or just wanted to sit down and talk about his misfortunes, and Marsh had no patience with any of that. He preferred to be left alone. That day in 1860 he was sitting there peacefully, drinking a glass of wine and waiting for the waiter to fetch out the roasted duck and yams and snap beans and hot bread he'd ordered, when he got interrupted. "Ain't seen you in a year," the man said. Marsh recognized him vaguely. The man had been a striker on the *A.L. Shotwell* a few years back. Grudgingly, he invited him to sit. "Don't mind if I do," the ex-striker said, and immediately pulled out a chair and commenced to gabbing. He was a second engineer on some New Orleans boat Marsh had never heard of, and full of gossip and river news. Marsh listened politely, wondering when his food would show up. He hadn't eaten all day.

The duck had just arrived, and Marsh was spreading butter over a chunk of good hot bread, when the engineer said, "Say, you heard 'bout that windstorm down to N'Orleans?"

Marsh chewed on his bread, swallowed, took another bite. "No," he said, not very interested. Isolated as he'd been, he didn't hear much talk of floods and windstorms and other like calamities.

The man whistled through a gap in his yellow teeth. "Hell, it was a bad'un. A bunch of boats tore loose and got busted up good. *Eclipse* was one of 'em. Smashed her up pretty bad, I hear."

Marsh swallowed his bread and put down the knife and fork he'd lifted to attack the duck. "The *Eclipse*," he said.

"Yessuh."

"How bad?" Marsh asked. "Cap'n Sturgeon'll fix her up, won't he?"

"Hell, she's too busted up for that," the engineer said. "I heard they'll use what's left as a wharfboat, up to Memphis."

"A wharfboat," Marsh repeated numbly, thinking of those tired old gray hulls that lined the landings in St. Louis and New Orleans and the other big river towns, boats gutted of engines and boilers, empty shells used only for stowing and transferring freight. "She ain't . . . she's . . ."

"Me, I figger that's bout what she deserves," the man said. "Hell, we would of beaten her with the *Shotwell*, only . . ."

Marsh made a strangled growling sound deep in his throat. "*Get the hell out of here*," he roared. "If you weren't a *Shotwell* man I'd kick your goddamned ass out in the street for what you just said. Now get out of here!"

The engineer got up real quickly. "You're crazy as they say," he blurted before he left.

Abner Marsh sat at that table for the longest time, his food untouched in front of him, staring off at nothing, a grim cold look settling over his face. Finally a waiter approached timidly. "Is somethin' wrong with yo' duck, Cap'n?"

Marsh looked down. The duck had gotten a little cold. Grease was starting to congeal around it. "I ain't hungry no more," he said. He pushed away the plate, paid his bill, and left.

He spent the following week going over his ledger books, adding up his debts. Then he called in Karl Framm. "It ain't no goddamn use," Marsh said to him. "She'll never run against the *Eclipse* now, even if we find her, which we won't. I'm tired of lookin'. I'm taking the *Reynolds* into the Missouri trade, Karl. I got to make some money."

Framm stared at him accusingly. "I'm not licensed for the Missouri."

"I know. I'm lettin' you go. You deserve a better boat than the *Reynolds* anyway."

Karl Framm sucked on his pipe and said nothing. Marsh could not look him in the eye. He shuffled some papers. "I'll pay you all the wages due you," he said.

Framm nodded and turned to go. At the door he stopped. "If I get a berth," he said, "I'll keep lookin'. If I find her, you'll hear."

"You won't find her," Marsh said bluntly. Then Framm closed the door and walked off his steamer and out of his life, and Abner Marsh was as alone as he had ever been. Now there was nobody left but him, nobody who remembered the *Fevre Dream* or Joshua's white suit or the hell that beckoned behind Damon Julian's eyes. Now it only lived because Marsh remembered, and Marsh was aiming to forget.

The years passed.

The *Eli Reynolds* made money in the Missouri trade. For almost a year she ran there, and Marsh captained her and sweated with her and tended to his freight and his passengers and his ledger books. He made enough in his first two trips to pay off three-quarters of his considerable debts. He might have grown rich, had not events in the larger world conspired against him: Lincoln's election (Marsh voted for him, despite the fact that he was a Republican), the secession, the firing on Ft. Sumter. Marsh thought of Joshua York's words as the carnage approached: *the red thirst is on this nation, and only blood will sate it.*

It took a great deal of blood, Marsh reflected afterward, bitterly. He seldom spoke about the war, or his experiences in it, and had little patience with those who fought the battles over and over again. "There was a war," he would say loudly. "We won. Now it's done with, and I don't see why we got to yammer about it endlessly, like it was something to be proud of. Only good thing come out of it was endin' slavery. The rest I got no use for. Shooting a man ain't nothin' to build a brag on, goddammit." Marsh and the *Eli Reynolds* returned to the upper Mississippi during the early years of the fighting, bringing troops down from St. Paul and Wisconsin and Iowa. Later on, he served on a Union gunboat, and saw action in a couple of river battles.

Karl Framm fought on the river, too. Marsh heard that he died in the fighting at Vicksburg, but he never knew for sure.

When peace came, Marsh returned to St. Louis, and took the *Eli Reynolds* into the upper Mississippi trade. He formed a brief association with the owner/captains of four rival boats, setting up a packet line with regular schedules to compete more effectively with the larger companies that ruled the upper river. But they were all strong-willed, stubborn men, and after a half year of quarrels and bluster the company was dissolved. By that time Abner Marsh found he had no appetite for the steamboat business anymore. The river had changed, somehow. After the war, there didn't seem to be a third as many steamers as there had been before it, yet the competition was fiercer, since the railroads were taking up more and more of the trade. Now when you steamed into St. Louis, you found maybe a dozen steamers along the levee, where once they had been crammed in for more than a mile. There were other changes as well, in those years following the war. Coal began to crowd out wood just about everywhere except on the wilder reaches of the Missouri. Federal regulators moved in with rules and laws that had to be followed, safety checks and registers and all manner of stuff, and even tried to prohibit racing. The steamboatmen changed too. Most of the men Marsh had known were dead or retired now, and those who took their places were strangers with strange ways. The old boisterous, cussing, free-spending, wild riverman who slapped you on the back, bought you drinks all night, and told you outrageous lies was a dying breed now. Even Natchez-under-the-hill was only a ghost of its former self, Marsh heard, nearly as sedate as the city on top of the hill with all its proper mansions with their fancy names.

One night in May of 1868, more than ten years after he had last seen Joshua York and the *Fevre Dream*, Abner Marsh took a walk along the levee. He thought back on the night when he and Joshua had first met, and walked along this same landing—the steamers had been crowded in then, great proud big side-wheelers and tough little stern-wheelers, old boats and new ones, and the *Eclipse* had been there among them, tied up to her wharfboat. Now the *Eclipse* had become a wharfboat herself, and there were boys on this river who called themselves strikers and mud-clerks and cub pilots who had never laid eyes on her. And the landing was nearly empty. Marsh stood and counted. Five boats. Six, if you counted the *Eli Reynolds*. The *Reynolds* was so old now that Marsh was half-afraid to take her out on the river. She must be the oldest damn steamboat in the world, he thought, with the oldest captain, and him and her were both just as tired.

The *Great Republic* was taking on freight. She was a huge new side-wheeler that had come out of some Pittsburgh boatyard the year before. They said she was 335 feet long, which made her the biggest steamer on the river now that the *Eclipse* and the *Fevre Dream* were both gone and forgotten. She was grand, too. Marsh had looked her over a dozen times, and gone aboard her once. Her pilot house was surrounded with all kinds of fancy trim and had an ornate cupola on top of it, and the paintings and glass and polished wood and carpets inside her were enough to break your heart. She was supposed to be the finest, prettiest steamboat ever built, luxurious enough to put all the older boats to shame. But she wasn't especially fast, Marsh had heard, and she was said to be losing money at a frightening rate. He stood with his arms folded against his chest, looking gruff and stern in his severe black coat, and he watched the roustabouts load her up. The rousters were black, every man among them. That was another change. All the roustabouts on the river were blacks now. The immigrants who'd worked as rousters and stokers and deckers before the war were gone, Marsh didn't know where, and the freedmen had taken their places.

As they worked, the rousters sung. Their song was a low, melancholy chant. *The night is dark, the day is long,* it went. *And we are far from home. Weep, my brothers, weep.* Marsh knew the chant. There was another verse, one that went, *The night is past, the long day done, And we are going home. Shout, my brothers, shout.* But they were not singing that verse. Not tonight, here on the empty steamer landing, loading up a boat that was spanking new and plush as any but still couldn't get enough trade. Watching them, listening, it seemed to Abner Marsh as if the whole river was dying, and him with it. He had seen enough dark nights and long days for the rest of his time on earth, and he was no longer certain he even had a home.

Abner Marsh walked slowly away from the landing back to his hotel. The next day he discharged his officers and crew, dissolved Fevre River Packets, and put the *Eli Reynolds* up for sale.

Marsh took what money he had, left St. Louis entirely, and bought a small house in his old hometown, Galena, within sight of the river. Only it wasn't the Fevre River any more. They'd gone and changed it to the Galena River, years ago, and now everyone was calling it that. The new name had better associations, folks said. Abner Marsh went on calling it the Fevre, like it was called when he was a boy.

He didn't do much in Galena. He read a lot of newspapers. That had gotten to be a habit with him, during the years he was searching for Joshua, and he liked to keep up with the fast boats and their times. There were still a few of them. The *Robert E. Lee* had come out of New Albany in 1866, and was a real heller. The *Wild Bob Lee,* some rivermen called her, or just the *Bad Bob.* And Cap'n Tom Leathers, as tough and mean and cussed a riverman as ever captained a steamer, had launched a new *Natchez* in 1869, the sixth of that name. Leathers named all his steamboats *Natchez.* The new *Natchez* was faster than any of the earlier ones, according to the papers. She cut through the water like a knife, and Leathers was bragging all up and down the river how he was going to show up Cap'n John Cannon and his *Wild Bob Lee.* The newspapers were full of it. He could smell a race coming on even clear up in Illinois, and it sounded like one they'd talk about for years. "I'd like to see that goddamned race," he said to the woman he'd hired to clean house for him one day. "Neither of 'em would have a chance against the *Eclipse,* though, you got my word on that."

"Both of 'em got better times than your ol' *Eclipse,*" she said. She liked to sass him, that woman.

Marsh snorted. "Don't mean nothin'. River's shorter now. River gets shorter every year. Pretty soon you'll be able to walk from St. Louis to New Orleans."

Marsh read more than just newspapers. Thanks to Joshua, he'd worked up a taste for poetry, of all the damn things, and he looked at an occasional novel, too. He also took up wood carving, and made himself detailed models of his steamboats, as he remembered them. He painted them and everything, and did them all to the same scale, so you could put them alongside each other and see how big they'd been. "That was my *Elizabeth A.*," he told his housekeeper proudly the day he finished the sixth and biggest model. "As sweet a boat as ever moved down the river. She would have set records, except for that damned ice jam. You can see how big she was, near three hundred feet. Look at how she dwarfs my ol' *Nick Perrot* there." He pointed. "And that's the *Sweet Fevre*, and the *Dunleith*—had a lot of trouble with the larboard engine on her, a lot of trouble—and next to her that's my *Mary Clarke*. She blew her boilers." Marsh shook his head. "Killed a lot of people, too. Maybe it was my fault. I don't know. I think about it sometimes. The little one on the end is the *Eli Reynolds*. Not much to look at, but she was a tough ol' gal. She took everything I could give her, and a lot more, and kept her steam up and her wheel turning. You know how long she lasted, that little ugly stern-wheeler?"

"No," the housekeeper said. "Didn't you have some other boat, too? A real fancy one? I heard—"

"Never mind what you heard, goddamn it. Yes, I had another boat. The *Fevre Dream*. Named her after the river."

The housekeeper made a rude noise at him. "No wonder this ain't never become the town it might have, with folks like you goin' on about the Fevre River. They must think we're all sick up here. Why didn't you call it right? It's named the *Galena* River now."

Abner Marsh snorted. "Changing the goddamn name of the goddamn river, I never heard of such goddamned foolishness. Far as I'm concerned it's the Fevre River and it's goin' to stay the Fevre River no matter what the hell the goddamned mayor says." He scowled. "Or you neither. Hell, the way they're lettin' it silt up pretty soon it's goin' to be the goddamned Galena *Creek!*"

"Such language. I'd think a man who reads poetry would be able to keep a civil tongue in his head."

"Never mind about my goddamned tongue," Marsh said. "And don't go yapping that poetry around town neither, you hear? I knew a man who liked those poems, that's the only reason I got them books. You just stop buttin' your nose in and keep my steamboats clean of dust."

"Certainly. Will you be making a model of that other boat, do you think? The *Fevre Dream?*"

Marsh settled into a big overstuffed chair and frowned. "No," he said. "No, I ain't. That's one boat I just want to forget about. So you just get to dusting and stop pesterin' me with your damned fool questions." He picked up a newspaper and began to read about the *Natchez* and Leathers's latest boast. His housekeeper made a clucking noise and finally commenced to dusting.

His house had a high round turret facing south. At evening, Marsh would often go up there, with a glass of wine or a cup of coffee, sometimes a piece of pie. He didn't eat like he used to, not since the war. Food just didn't seem to taste the same. He was still a big man, but he had lost at least a hundred pounds since his days with Joshua and the *Fevre Dream.* His flesh hung loose on him everywhere, like he'd bought it a couple sizes too large, expecting it to shrink. He had big droopy jowls, too. "Makes me even uglier than I used to be," he would growl when he glanced in a mirror.

Sitting by his turret window, Marsh could see the river. He spent a lot of nights there, reading, drinking, and looking out on the water. The river was pretty in the moonlight, flowing past him, on and on, like it had flowed before he was born, like it would flow after he was dead and buried. Seeing it made Marsh feel peaceful, and he treasured that feeling. Most of the time he just felt weary or melancholy. He had read one poem by Keats that said there wasn't nothing as sad as a beautiful thing dying, and it seemed to Marsh sometimes that every goddamned beatiful thing in the world was withering away. Marsh was lonely, too. He had been on the river so many years that he had no real friends left in Galena. He never had visitors, never talked to anyone but his damned annoying housekeeper. She vexed him considerably, but Marsh didn't really mind; it was about all he had left to keep his blood hot. Sometimes he thought his life was over, and that made him so angry he turned red. He still had so many goddamned things he'd never done, so much unfinished business . . . but there was no denying that he was getting old. He used to carry that old hickory walking stick to gesture with, and be fashionable. Now he had an expensive gold-handled cane to help him walk better. And he had wrinkles around his eyes and even between his warts, and a funny kind of brown spot on the back of his left hand. He'd look at it sometimes and wonder how it had got there. He'd never noticed. Then he would cuss and pick up a newspaper or a book.

Marsh was sitting in his parlor, reading a book by Mister Dickens about his travels on the river and through America, when his housekeeper brought in the letter to him. He grunted with surprise, and slammed down the Dickens book, muttering under his breath, "Goddamn fool of a Britisher, like to chuck him in the goddamn river." He took the letter and ripped it open, letting the envelope flutter to the floor. Getting a letter was pretty rare by itself, but this one was queerer still; it had been addressed to Fevre River Packets in St. Louis, and forwarded on up to Galena. Abner Marsh unfolded the crisp, yellowing paper, and suddenly sucked in his breath.

It was old stationery, and he remembered it well. He'd had it printed up some thirteen years before, to put in the desk drawer of every stateroom on his steamer. Across the top was a fancy pen-and-ink drawing of a great side-wheel steamer, and FEVRE DREAM in curved, ornate letters. He knew the hand too, that graceful, flowing hand. The message was short:

Dear Abner,

I have made my choice.
If you are well and willing, meet me in New Orleans as soon as possible. You will find me at the Green Tree on Gallatin Street.

—Joshua

"Goddamn it to hell!" Marsh swore. "After all this time, does that damned fool think he can just send me some goddamned letter and make me come all the goddamned way down to New Orleans? And with never a word of explanation, neither! Who the hell does he think he is?"

"I'm sure I don't know!" his housekeeper said.

Abner Marsh pulled himself to his feet. "Woman, where the hell did you go and put my white coat?" he roared.

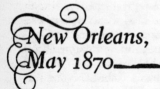

CHAPTER THIRTY-ONE

New Orleans, May 1870

GALLATIN Street by night looked like the main road through hell, Abner Marsh thought as he hurried along it. It was lined with dance halls, saloons, and whorehouses, all of them crowded, filthy, and raucous, and the sidewalks seethed with drunks and whores and cutpurses. The whores called after him as he walked, mocking invitations that turned to jeers when he ignored them. Rough, cold-eyed men with knives and brass knuckles appraised him with open contempt, and made Marsh wish he didn't look quite so prosperous and quite so goddamned old. He crossed the street to avoid one throng of men standing in front of a dance hall and hefting live oak cudgels, and found himself in front of the Green Tree.

It was a dance hall like all the others, a hellhole surrounded by other hellholes. Marsh pushed his way inside. The interior was crowded, smoky, and dim. Couples moved through the bluish haze, shuffling vaguely in time to the loud, cheap music. One of the men, a thickly-built unshaven lout in a red flannel shirt, staggered around the dance floor with a partner who looked to be unconscious. The man was squeezing her breast through her thin calico dress as he supported her and dragged her about. The other dancers all ignored them. The women were all typical dance hall girls, in faded calico shifts and tattered slippers. As Marsh looked on, the man in the red shirt stumbled and dropped his partner and collapsed on top of her, and a hoot of laughter went up. He cussed and got unsteadily to his feet while the woman lay sprawled out. Then, as the laughing subsided, he leaned over her and grabbed her by the front of her dress, and pulled. The cloth ripped, and he yanked the garment off and tossed it aside, grinning. She had nothing on underneath except for a red garter around one white, meaty thigh, with a little dagger stuck through it. The pommel was pink and heart-shaped. The man in the red shirt had started unbuttoning his pants when two bouncers moved in on either side of him. They were massive red-faced men with brass knuckles and thick wooden clubs. "Take 'er upstairs," one of them growled. The man in the red shirt started cussing a streak, but finally he lifted the woman onto a shoulder and staggered off through the smoke, accompanied by more laughter.

"Want to dance, Mister?" a slurred female voice whispered in Marsh's ear. He turned and scowled. The woman must have weighed as much as he did. She was pasty white and naked as the day she was born, except for a little leather belt with two knives hanging from it. She smiled and stroked Marsh's cheek before he turned away from her abruptly and pushed through the crowd. He made a circuit of the room, trying to find Joshua. In one particularly noisy corner a dozen men were crowded around a wooden box, belching and swearing as they watched a rat fight. Around the bar men stood two deep, near every one of them armed and glowering. Marsh muttered apologies and pushed past a weedy looking fellow with a garrote looped through his belt, who was talking intently to a short man wearing a brace of pistols. The man with the garrote stopped and eyed Marsh unpleasantly, until the other shouted something at him and drew him back into conversation. "Whiskey," Marsh demanded, leaning against the bar.

"This whiskey will rot a hole in your stomach, Abner," the barkeeper said softly, his quiet voice penetrating right through the din. Abner Marsh let his mouth fall open. The man behind the bar smiling at him wore rough-woven baggy trousers held up by a cord belt, a white shirt so dirty it was almost gray, and a black vest. But the face was the same as it had been thirteen years before, pale and unlined, framed by that straight white hair, a bit messy now. Joshua York's gray eyes seemed to shine with their own light in the dimness of the dance hall. He extended his hand across the bar, and clasped Marsh on the arm. "Come upstairs," he said urgently, "where we can talk."

As he came around the bar, the other barkeep stared at him, and a wiry weasel-faced man in a dark suit charged up to him and said, "Where the hell you goin'? Git back there an' pour them whiskeys!"

"I quit," Joshua told him.

"Quit? I'll hev yer damned throat slit!"

"Will you?" said Joshua. He waited, looking around the suddenly hushed room and challenging them all with his eyes. No one moved. "I'll be upstairs with my friend if any of you care to try," he said to the half-dozen bouncers who lined the bar. Then he took Marsh by the elbow and led him through the dancers to a narrow back stair. Upstairs was a short hall lit by a single flickering gas jet, and a half-dozen rooms. Noises were coming from behind one closed door, grunting and moaning. Another door was open, and a man was sprawled in front of it, face down, half-in and half-out of the room. As he stepped over him, Marsh saw that it was the red-shirted man from downstairs. "What the hell happened to him?" Marsh said loudly.

Joshua York shrugged. "Bridget probably woke up, clubbed him, and took his money. She is a real darling. I believe she's killed at least four men with that little knife of hers. She carves notches on that heart." He grimaced. "When it comes to bloodshed, Abner, my people have very little to teach your own."

Joshua opened the door to an empty room. "In here, if you will." He shut it behind them, after turning on one of the lamps.

Marsh sat heavily on the bed. "Goddamn," he said, "this is a hell of a place you got me to, Joshua. This is as bad as Natchez-under-the-hill was twenty, thirty years ago. Damned if I ever expected to find *you* in a place like this."

Joshua York smiled and sat down in a frayed old armchair. "Neither will Julian or Sour Billy. That is the point. They are searching for me, I know. But even if they think to search Gallatin Street, it will be difficult. Julian would be attacked for his obvious wealth, and Sour Billy is known here by sight. He has taken off too many women who have never returned. Tonight there were at least two men in the Green Tree who would have killed him on sight. The streets outside belong to the Live Oak Boys, who might beat Billy to death just for the fun of it, unless they decided to help him." He shrugged. "Even the police won't come to Gallatin Street. I am as safe here as I would be anywhere, and on this street my nocturnal habits draw no notice. They are commonplace."

"Never mind about that," Marsh said impatiently. "You sent me a letter. Said you'd made your choice. You know why I come, but I ain't sure why you sent for me. Maybe you better tell me."

"I scarcely know where to begin. It has been a long time, Abner."

"For both of us," Marsh said gruffly. Then his tone softened. "I looked for you, Joshua. For more goddamned years than I care to think about, I tried to find you and that steamboat of mine. But there was just too goddamned much river and not enough time nor money."

"Abner," said York, "you might have had all the time and money in the world, and you would never have found us on the river. For the past thirteen years, the *Fevre Dream* has been on dry land. She is hidden near the old indigo vats on the plantation that Julian owns, some five hundred yards from the bayou, but quite thoroughly concealed."

Marsh said, "How the *hell* . . ."

"It was my doing. Let me start from the beginning, and tell you all of it." He sighed. "I must go back thirteen years, to the night I took my leave from you."

"I remember."

"I went upriver as quickly as I could," Joshua began, "anxious to get back, worried that the thirst would come upon me. Travel was difficult, but I reached the *Fevre Dream* on the second night after my departure. She had moved only slightly. She now stood well away from the shore, the dark water rushing around her on both sides. It was a cold, foggy night when I approached her, and she was absolutely dead and dark. No smoke, no steam, not a flame showing anywhere, so silent that I almost missed her for the fog. I did not want to return, but I knew I must. I swam out to her." He hesitated briefly. "Abner, you know the sort of life I have led. I have seen and done many terrible things. But nothing prepared me for that steamer the way I found her, nothing."

Marsh's face grew hard. "Go on."

"I told you once that I thought Damon Julian was mad."

"I recollect it."

"Mad and heedless and dreaming of death," Joshua said. "And he had proven it. Oh, yes. He had proven it. When I pulled myself up onto deck, the steamer was deathly quiet. No sound, no movement, just the river rushing past. I wandered through the boat unmolested." His eyes were fixed on Abner Marsh, but they had a far-off glazed look, as if they were seeing something else, something they would always see. York stopped.

"Tell me, Joshua," Marsh said.

York's mouth grew tight. "It was a slaughterhouse, Abner." He let that simple statement hang in the air for a moment, before he went on. "Bodies were everywhere. Everywhere. And not intact, either. I walked through the main deck, and found corpses . . . among the freight and back with the engines. There were . . . arms, legs, other body parts. Ripped loose. Torn off. The slaves, the stokers Billy had bought, most of them were still in the manacles, dead, their throats torn out. The engineer had been hung upside down above the cylinder, and cut so . . . he must have bled down onto . . . as if blood could take the place of oil." Joshua gave a small grim shake of his head. "The number of dead, Abner. You can't imagine. And the way they were torn, the grotesque mutilations. The fog had seeped onto the boat, so I could not see the whole at once. I walked, I wandered, and these things would suddenly appear before me where, an instant before, there had been nothing but vague shadows and a drifting veil of fog. And I would look at whatever new terror the mist had yielded up to me, and move away, and take only two or three steps before the vapors dissolved yet again to reveal something even more vile.

"Finally, sick at heart and filled with a wrath that burned in me like a fever, I went up the grand staircase to the boiler deck. The saloon . . . it was more of the same. Bodies and pieces of bodies. So much blood had been spilled that the carpet was still wet with it, even then. Everywhere I found signs of struggle. Dozens of mirrors were shattered, three or four stateroom doors had been smashed in, tables were overturned. On one table that still stood there was a human head upon a silver platter. I have never known more horror than I did as I walked the length of that saloon, those terrible three hundred feet. Nothing moved in the darkness, in the fog. Nothing living. I moved back and forth listlessly, not knowing what to do. I stopped before the water cooler, that great silver ornamental water cooler you had placed at the forward end of the cabin. My throat was very dry. I picked up one of the silver cups and turned the handle. The water . . . the water came slowly, Abner. Very slowly. Even in the darkness of that saloon, I could see that it was black and viscous. Half . . . clotted.

"I stood with the cup in hand, looking about blindly, my nose filled with the smell . . . the *smell*, I have hardly mentioned that, the smell was terrible, it . . . you can imagine, I'm sure. I stood in the midst of it all watching that agonizing slow trickle from the water cooler. I felt as though I was choking. My horror, my outrage, I . . . felt them rise within me. I tossed the cup across the cabin, and I screamed.

"Then the noises began. Whispers, thumpings, begging sounds, weeping, threats. Voices, Abner, living human voices. I looked about me, and grew even sicker, even more angry. At least a dozen stateroom doors had been nailed shut, their occupants imprisoned within them. Waiting, I knew, for tonight or the night after. Julian's living larder. I began to tremble. I moved to the nearest door and started to pull loose the boards that held it shut. They pulled out with a loud creaking sound, almost a cry of agony. I was still working on that door when he said, 'Dear Joshua, you must stop that. Dear lost Joshua, come back to us.'

"When I turned, they were there. Julian smiling at me, Sour Billy at his side, and the others, all the others, even my own people, Simon, Smith and Brown, all of them that were left . . . watching me. I screamed at them all, wild and incoherent. They were my people, and yet they had done *this*. Abner, I was filled with such loathing . . .

"Later, days later, I heard the whole story, learned the full depth of Julian's madness. Perhaps it was my fault, in a sense. In saving you and Toby and Mister Framm, I brought on the death of more than a hundred innocent passengers."

Abner Marsh snorted. "Don't," he said. "Whatever happened, it was Julian that had done it, and him that has to answer for it. You weren't even there, so don't go blamin' yourself, you hear?"

Joshua's gray eyes were troubled. "So I have told myself many times," he said. "Let me finish the story. What had happened— Julian had woken that night to find us gone. He was furious. Wild. More—those words sound too feeble to convey what must have been his rage. Perhaps it was the red thirst in him that woke, after all those centuries. Moreover, it must have looked to him as if destruction were near to hand. His pilots were all gone. The steamer could not move without a pilot. And he must have known that you intended to return, to attack by day and destroy him. He could not have guessed that I would come back instead, to save them. No doubt my treachery and Valerie's desertion filled him with fear, with uncertainty about what would come next. He had lost control. He had been bloodmaster, and yet we had acted against him. In all the history of the people of the night, it had never happened before. I think, during that terrible night, that Damon Julian thought he saw the death he both hungered for and feared.

"Sour Billy, I learned later, urged that they go ashore, split up, travel overland separately and meet again in Natchez or New Orleans or somewhere. That would have been sensible. But Julian was past sense. He had just entered the main cabin, his madness seething in his eyes, when a passenger approached him and began to complain that the steamer was far behind schedule, that she had not moved all day. 'Ah,' Julian said, 'then we must move it immediately.' He had her taken a bit further out, so no one could get to shore. When it was done, he returned to the main cabin, where the passengers were dining, and approached the man who had complained, and killed him, in full view of all.

"Then the slaughter began. Of course, people screamed, ran, hid, locked themselves in their staterooms. But there was no place to go. And Julian used his power, used his voice and his eyes, and sent his people forth to kill. I understand the *Fevre Dream* had about a hundred thirty passengers aboard that night, against about twenty of my people, some driven by the thirst, some by Julian. But the thirst can be terrible at a time like that. Like a fever it can leap from one to the next, until all of them burn. And Sour Billy had the men he hired at Natchez-under-the-hill assist in the fighting, too. He told them it was all part of a plan to rob and kill the passengers, and that they would share in the loot. By the time my people turned against their human helpers, it was far too late.

"It was happening even as you and I stood talking that last night, Abner. The screams, the carnage, Julian's wild death spasm. He did not have everything his own way. The passengers fought back. I am told that virtually all my people sustained injuries, though of course they healed. Vincent Thibaut was shot through the eye, and died. Katherine was seized by two firemen and thrust into one of the furnaces. They burned her to death before Kurt and Alain intervened. So two of my people met their ends. Two of us, and well over a hundred of your kind. The survivors were penned within their own cabins.

"When it was over, Julian settled down to wait. The others were full of fear, and wanted to flee, but Julian would not permit it. He wanted to be discovered, I believe. They say he spoke of you, Abner."

"*Me?*" Marsh was thunderstruck.

"He said he had promised you that the river would never forget your *Fevre Dream*. He laughed and said he made good on that promise."

Abner Marsh's anger welled up in him and came out in a furious snort. "Damn him to hell!" he said, in a strangely quiet tone.

"That," said Joshua York, "was how it happened. But I knew none of that the night I returned to the *Fevre Dream*. I only knew what I saw with my eyes, what I smelled, what I could guess and imagine. And I was wild, Abner, wild. I was tearing free those boards, as I said, and then Julian was there, and suddenly I was screaming at him, screaming incoherently. I wanted vengeance. I wanted to kill him as badly as I have ever wanted to kill anyone, wanted to rip open that pale throat of his, and taste his damnable blood! My anger . . . ah, the words are so *useless!*

"Julian waited until I had finished screaming, and then he said quietly, 'There are two boards left, Joshua. Pull them off and let him out. You must be very thirsty.' Sour Billy sniggered. I said nothing. 'Go on, dear Joshua,' Julian said. 'Tonight you will *truly* join us, so you may never run again. Go on, dear Joshua. Free him. Kill him.' And his eyes held mine. I felt their force, pulling, pulling me inside him, trying to take hold of me and make me do his bidding. Once I had tasted blood again, I would be his, body and soul, forever. He had beaten me a dozen times, forced me to kneel to him, compelled me to let him drink of my own blood. But he had never been able to make me kill. It was my last protection of what I was and what I believed in and what I tried to do, and now his eyes were tearing it down, and behind it was only death and blood and terror, and the endless empty nights that soon would be my life."

Joshua York stopped then, and looked away. There had been something clouded and unreadable in his eyes. Abner Marsh saw to his astonishment that Joshua's hand was shaking. "Joshua," he said, "whatever happened, it was thirteen years ago. It's past, it's gone like all those folks you killed in England and such. And you didn't have no choice, no choice a-tall. It was you that told me you can't have good or evil without a choice. You ain't what Julian is, no matter if you did kill that man."

York looked at him straight on and gave a strange little smile. "Abner, I did *not* kill that man."

"No? Then what . . ."

"I fought back," said Joshua. "I was wild, Abner. I looked him in the eyes, and I defied him. I fought him. And this time I won. We stood there for a good ten minutes, and finally Julian broke away, snarling, and retreated up the stairs to his cabin, Sour Billy scurrying after him. The rest of my people stood staring at me astonished. Raymond Ortega stepped forward and challenged me. In less than a minute, he was kneeling. 'Bloodmaster,' he said, bowing his head. Then, one by one, the others began to kneel. Armand and Cara, Cynthia, Jorge and Michel LeCouer, even Kurt, all of them. Simon had such victory on his face. So did others. Julian's had been a bitter reign for several of them. Now they were free. I had vanquished Damon Julian, for all his strength, for all his age. I was the leader of my people once again. I realized then that I faced a choice. Unless I acted, and quickly, the *Fevre Dream* would be discovered, and I and Julian and all our race would die."

"What did you do?"

"I found Sour Billy. He had been mate, after all. He was outside Julian's cabin, confused, cowering. I put him in charge of the main deck, and told the others to do as he told them. They worked. As stokers, as strikers, as engineers. With Billy half-scared to death and giving orders, they got our steam up. We fueled her with wood and lard and corpses. Ghastly, I know, but we had to get rid of the bodies, and we could not stop to wood up without great risk. I went up to the pilot house and took the wheel. Up there, at least, no one had died. She ran with all her lights out, so no one could see us even if they had eyes to penetrate that fog. At times we had to take soundings and creep along, and other times—when the fog pulled back from us—we slid downriver fast enough to make you proud, Abner! We passed a few other steamboats in the dark, and I whistled to them and they whistled back, but no one got close enough to read our name. The river was empty that night, most of the traffic tied up because of the fog. I was being a reckless pilot, but the alternative was discovery and certain death. When dawn came, we were still on the river. I would not let them retire. Billy had the tarpaulins rigged around the main deck, as protection from the sun. I remained in the pilot house. We passed New Orleans near sunbreak, went downstream, and turned off into the bayou. It was narrow and shallow, the most difficult part of the trip. We had to sound every inch of it. But finally we reached Julian's old plantation. Only then did I let myself seek the shelter of my cabin. I was badly burned. Again." He smiled ruefully. "I seem to have made a habit of that," he said. "The next night I surveyed Julian's land. We had tied up the steamer at a half-rotted old wharf on the bayou, but she was too conspicuous. If you thought to come to Cypress Landing, you would find her easily. I was loath to destroy her, since we might need the mobility she gave us, yet I knew she had to be better hidden.

"I found my answer. The plantation had once been given over to indigo. The owners had begun growing the more lucrative sugarcane more than fifty years before, and of course Julian had grown nothing at all—but well south of the main house, I found the old, abandoned indigo vats on a waterway leading from the bayou. It was a still, stagnant backwater, overgrown and foul-smelling. Indigo is not wholesome. The channel was barely wide enough for the *Fevre Dream*, and clearly not deep enough.

"So I contrived to deepen it. We unloaded the steamer, and worked at clearing the undergrowth and cutting back the trees and dredging the backwater. A month of labor, Abner, nearly every night. And then I took the steamer down the bayou, angled her into the backwater with much difficulty, and squeezed her through. When I stopped her, we were scraping bottom, but she was essentially invisible, screened on all sides by foliage. In the weeks that followed we dammed up the mouth of the backwater where it met the bayou, replaced the mud and sand we had so laboriously dredged out, and endeavored to drain the waterway. Within a month or so, the *Fevre Dream* rested on damp, muddy ground, veiled by live oak and cypress, and one would never guess there had been water there."

Abner Marsh frowned unhappily. "That's no goddamned end for a steamboat," he said bitterly. "Not her, especially. She deserved better'n that."

"I know," said Joshua, "but I had the safety of my people to think about. I made my choice, Abner, and when it was done I was pleased and triumphant. We would never be found now. Most of the bodies had been burnt or buried. Julian had hardly been seen since the night I had defied and conquered him. He left his cabin infrequently, and then only for food. Sour Billy was the only one who spoke to him. Billy was afraid and obedient, and the others all followed me, drank with me. I had ordered Billy to remove my liquor from Julian's cabin and keep it behind the bar in the main saloon. We drank it every night with supper. There was only one major problem remaining before I went on to consider the future of my race—our prisoners, those passengers who had survived that night of terror. We had kept them confined all during our flight and labors, though none of them had suffered harm. I had seen that they were fed and well-treated. I had even tried to talk to them, to reason with them, but it was useless—when I entered their staterooms, they would become hysterical with fear. I had no appetite for keeping them caged up indefinitely, but they had seen everything, and I did not see how I could safely let them go.

"Then the problem was solved for me. One black night, Damon Julian left his cabin. He still lived on the steamer, as did a few others, those who had been closest to him. I was ashore that night, with a dozen others, working in the main house, which Julian had allowed to deteriorate shamefully. When I returned to the *Fevre Dream*, I found that two of our prisoners had been taken from their staterooms and killed. Raymond and Kurt and Adrienne were sitting in the grand saloon over the bodies, feeding, and Julian was presiding over it all."

Abner Marsh snorted. "Damn it, Joshua, you ought to have killed him when you had the chance."

"Yes," Joshua York agreed, much to Marsh's surprise. "I thought I could control him. A grievous error. Of course, that night he re-emerged, I tried to rectify that error. I was furious and sick. We exchanged bitter words, and I was determined that this would be the last crime of his long and monstrous life. I commanded him to face me. I intended to make him kneel and offer up his own blood, again and again if need be, until he was mine, until he was drained and broken and harmless. He rose and faced me and . . ." York gave a hard, hopeless laugh.

"He beat you?" Marsh said.

Joshua nodded. "Easily. As he had always done before, except that one night. I summoned up all the strength and will and anger that was in me, but I was no match for him. Even Julian did not expect it, I think." He shook his head. "Joshua York, king of the vampires. I failed them again. My reign lasted for just over two months. For the past thirteen years, Julian has been our master."

"Your prisoners?" Marsh asked, knowing the answer but hoping he was wrong.

"Dead. They took them one by one, over the months that followed."

Marsh grimaced. "Thirteen years, that's a long time, Joshua. Why didn't you run off? You must have had a chance."

"Many," Joshua York admitted. "I think Julian would have preferred that I vanish. He had been bloodmaster for a thousand years or more, the strongest and most terrible predator ever to walk the earth, and I had made him a slave for two months. Neither he nor I could account for my brief, bitter triumph, but neither could we forget it. We struggled again and again over the years, and each time, before Julian brought all his power to bear, I saw the flicker of doubt, the fear that maybe this time he would be overcome again. But it never happened. And I stayed. Where would I go, Abner? And what good could I do? My place was with my people. All that time, I continued to hope that someday I could take them back from him. Even in defeat, I believe my presence was a check on Julian. It was always I who initiated our contests for mastery, never him. He never attempted to make me kill. When supplies of my drink ran low, I set up my equipment and made more, and Julian did not interfere. He even allowed some of the others to join me. Simon, Cynthia, Michel, a few others. We drank, and stilled the thirst.

"For his part, Julian kept to his cabin. You might even say he was dormant. At times no one but Sour Billy would see him for weeks. Years passed that way, with Julian lost in his own dreams, though his presence hung over us. He had his blood, of course. At least once a month, Sour Billy would ride into New Orleans, and return with a victim. Slaves before the war. Afterward, dance-hall girls, prostitutes, drunks, scoundrels—whomever he could entice out to us. The war was difficult. Julian stirred during the war, and led parties into the city several times. Later he sent out the others. Wars often yield up easy prey for my people, but they can also be dangerous, and this war took its toll. Cara was attacked by a Union soldier one night in New Orleans. She killed him, of course, but he had companions . . . she was the first to die. Philip and Alain were arrested on suspicion, and imprisoned. They were shut up in an outdoor stockade, to wait for questioning. The sun came up, and both of them died. And troops fired the plantation house one night. It was half-ruined anyway, but not empty. Armand died in the blaze, and Jorge and Michel were horribly burned, though they recovered. The rest of us dispersed, and returned to the *Fevre Dream* when the marauders had gone. It has been our home ever since.

"The years have passed with a sort of uneasy truce between Julian and myself. There are fewer of us, barely a dozen, and we are divided. My followers have my liquor, and Julian's have their blood. Simon, Cynthia, and Michel are mine, the others his, some because they think as he does, others because he is bloodmaster. Kurt and Raymond are his strongest allies. And Billy." His expression was grim. "Billy is a cannibal, Abner. For thirteen years, Julian has been making him one of us, or so he says. After all that time, the blood still makes Billy sick. I have seen him retch on it a dozen times. But he eats human flesh eagerly now, though he cooks it first. Julian finds that amusing."

"You should have let me kill him."

"Perhaps. Though without Billy we would have died on the steamer that day. He has a quick mind, but Julian has twisted him terribly, as he twists all those who listen to him. Without Billy, this way of life Julian has constructed would collapse. It is Billy who rides into the city, and brings back Julian's sorry prey. It is Billy who sells off the silver from the boat, or parcels of land, or whatever else is needed to keep some money on hand. And, in a sense, it is because of Billy that you and I have met again."

"I figured you'd get to that sooner or later," Marsh said. "You been with Julian a long time, without runnin' off or doin' nothin'. Only now you're here, with Julian and Sour Billy hunting for you, and now you write me this goddamned letter. Why now? What's changed?"

Joshua's hands were tight on the ends of his armchair. "The truce I spoke of is over," he said. "Julian is awake again."

"How?"

"Billy," said Joshua. "Billy is our link with the world outside. When he goes into New Orleans, he often brings back newspapers and books, for me, along with food and wine and victims. Billy also hears all the stories, all the talk in the city and along the river."

"So?" said Abner Marsh.

"Of late much of that talk has been about one topic. The papers have been full of it, too. It is a topic dear to your heart, Abner. Steamboats. Two steamboats, in particular."

Abner Marsh frowned. "The *Natchez* and the *Wild Bob Lee*," he said. He couldn't see what Joshua was getting at.

"Precisely," said York. "From the papers I have read and the things Billy has said, it seems that a race is inevitable."

"Hell, yes," said Marsh. "Soon, too. Leathers has been braggin' all up and down the river, and he's starting to cut into the *Lee*'s trade bad, from what I hear. Cap'n Cannon ain't goin' to stand that long. It ought to be a hell of a race, too." He tugged at his beard. "Only I don't see what that's got to do with Julian and Billy and your damned night folks."

Joshua York smiled grimly. "Billy talked too much. Julian grew interested. And he remembers, Abner, he remembers that promise he made to you. I stopped him once. But now, damn him, he intends to do it again."

"Do it again?"

"He will recreate the slaughter I found on the *Fevre Dream*," said Joshua. "Abner, this business between the *Natchez* and the *Robert E. Lee* has caught the interest of the whole nation. Even in Europe large wagers are being placed, according to the papers. If they race from New Orleans to St. Louis, it will take them three or four days. And three or four nights, Abner. And three or four *nights*."

And all of a sudden Abner Marsh saw where Joshua was going, and a coldness settled on him such as he had never known. "The *Fevre Dream*," he said.

"They are floating her again," said York, "clearing out that waterway we had filled in. Sour Billy is raising money. Later this month he will come to the city and hire a crew, to help make her ready and man her when the time comes. Julian thinks it will all be very amusing. He intends to take her to New Orleans and land her until the day of the race. He will let the *Natchez* and the *Robert E. Lee* depart first, and then he will take the *Fevre Dream* upriver after them. When darkness falls, he will close in on whichever boat is leading, pull alongside her, and . . . well, you know what he intends. Both steamers will be lightly manned, without any passengers, to keep their weight down. Julian will have an easy time of it. And he will compel all of us to take part. I am his pilot." He laughed bitterly. "Or I was. When I first heard his madness, I fought him, and lost yet again. The next dawn I stole Billy's horse and fled. I thought that I could frustrate him by running. Without a pilot, he could not bring it off. But by the time I had recovered from my burns, I saw the fallacy in that. Billy will simply hire a pilot."

Abner Marsh had a heavy churning in the pit of his stomach. Part of him was sick and furious at Julian's plan to make the *Fevre Dream* some kind of demon steamer. But another part of him was entranced by the boldness of it, by the vision of his *Fevre Dream* showing up both of them, Cannon and Leathers and the whole damn world to boot. "Pilot, hell," Marsh said. "Them two steamers are the fastest things on the goddamned river, Joshua. If he lets them get off first, he ain't never goin' to catch them, nor kill nobody." But even as he said it, Marsh knew he did not really believe it.

"Julian thinks that makes it all the more amusing," Joshua York replied. "If they can stay ahead of him, they live. If not . . ." He shook his head. "And he says he has the greatest faith in your steamboat, Abner. He intends to make her famous. Afterward, both boats are to be wrecked, and Julian says we will all escape to the shore and make our way to the east, to Philadelphia or perhaps New York. He is weary of the river, he claims. I believe that is so much empty talk. Julian is weary of life. If he carries through this plan, it will mean the end of my race."

Abner Marsh got up off the bed and stamped his cane on the floor in fury. "*Goddamn it to hell!*" he roared. "She'll catch 'em, I know she will, she could have caught the goddamned *Eclipse* if she'd been given the chance, I swear it. She ain't goin' to have no goddamned trouble outrunnin' the likes of the *Natchez* and the *Bad Bob*. Hell, neither one of *them* could ever beat the *Eclipse*. Goddammit, Joshua, he ain't goin' to do this with my steamboat, I swear he ain't!"

Joshua York smiled a thin, dangerous smile, and when Abner Marsh looked into his eyes he saw the determination he had once seen in the Planters' House, and the cold anger he had once seen when he barged in on York by day. "No," York said. "He isn't. That's why I wrote you, Abner, and prayed that you were still alive. I have thought a long time about this. I am decided. We will kill him. There is no other way."

"Hell," said Marsh. "Took you long enough to see that. I could have told you that thirteen goddamned years ago. Well, I'm with you. Only—" He pointed his cane at York's chest. "—we don't hurt the steamer, you hear? The only thing wrong with that goddamned plan of Julian's is the part where everybody gets killed. The rest of it I like just fine." He smiled. "Cannon and Leathers is goin' to get such a goddamned surprise they ain't goin' to believe it."

Joshua rose smiling. "Abner, we will do our best, I promise you, to see that the *Fevre Dream* remains intact. Be sure to caution your men."

Marsh frowned. "What men?"

The smile faded from Joshua's face. "Your crew," he said. "I assumed that you came down here on one of your steamboats, with a party of men."

Marsh suddenly recollected that Joshua had mailed his letter to Fevre River Packets, in St. Louis. "Hell," he said, "Joshua, I ain't got no steamers anymore, nor any men neither. I came down by steamboat, all right. Cabin passage."

"Karl Framm," Joshua said. "Toby. The others, those men you had with you on the *Eli Reynolds* . . ."

"Dead or gone, all of 'em. I was near dead myself."

Joshua frowned. "I had thought we would attack in force, by day. This changes things, Abner."

Abner Marsh clouded up like a thunderhead about to break. "The hell it does," he said. "It don't change one goddamned thing, far as I can see. Maybe you figured we was goin' in there with an army, but *I* sure as hell knew better. I'm a goddamned old man, Joshua, and I'm probably goin' to die soon, and Damon Julian don't scare me no more. He's had my steamboat for too goddamned long and I ain't happy with what he's done with her and I'm goin' to get her back or die trying. You wrote that you made a choice, dammit. Now what is it? Are you comin' with me or not?"

Joshua York listened quietly to Marsh's furious outburst, and slowly a reluctant smile crept over his pale white features. "All right," he said at last. "We'll do it alone."

CHAPTER THIRTY-TWO

Julian Plantation, Louisiana, May 1870

THEY left New Orleans in the middle of the night, rolling and clattering over dark, rutted roads in a wagon that Joshua York had purchased. Dressed in dark brown, a hooded cloak billowing behind him, Joshua looked as fine as in the old days as he snapped the reins and urged the horses onward. Abner Marsh sat grimly beside him, bouncing and jouncing as they rattled over rocks and holes, holding tight to the double-barreled shotgun across his knees. The pockets of his coat bulged with shells.

Joshua pulled off the main road almost as soon as they were out of the city, and left the secondary road quickly as well, so they moved swiftly down pathways little traveled, and deserted now in the dead of night. The roads became narrow, twisting lanes, through thick stands of yellow pine and heart pine, magnolia and cypress, sour gum and live oak. At times the trees twined together overhead, so it seemed as though they were plunging through a long black tunnel. Marsh found he was nearly blind at times, when the trees pressed close and shut out the moon, but Joshua never let the pace slacken. He had eyes for the dark.

At length the bayou appeared on their left, and the road ran along it for a long time. The moon shone pale and still on the black, quiet water. Fireflies were drifting through the lazy night, and Marsh listened to the deep croaking of bullfrogs and smelled the heavy, rich odors that drifted off the backwaters, where the water lilies grew thickly and the banks were dense with snow-white dogwoods and daddy graybeard beneath the old, towering trees. It might be the last night of his life, Abner Marsh thought. So he breathed it deeply, snorted up all the smells it had to offer, the sweet ones and the sour ones alike.

Joshua York looked straight ahead, and kept them thundering through the dark, oblivious and hard-faced, lost in his own thoughts.

Near dawn—a vague light had just appeared in the east, and some of the stars seemed to be fading—they passed around an ancient Spanish oak, dead now, trailers of gray moss dripping feebly from its withered limbs, and into a wide, overgrown field. Marsh saw a row of shanties off in the distance, black as rotten teeth, and close at hand stood the charred and roofless walls of an old plantation house, its empty windows gaping at them. Joshua York brought them to a halt. "We will leave the wagon here and proceed on foot," he said. "It is not so far now." He looked up toward the horizon, where the brightness was spreading and eating up the stars. "At full light, we will strike."

Abner Marsh grunted assent and climbed down off the wagon, clutching the shotgun tightly. "Goin' to be a nice day," he said to Joshua. "Maybe just a trifle gaudy."

York smiled and pulled his hat down over his eyes. "This way," he said. "Remember the plan. I will smash the door in and confront Julian. When all his attention is fixed on me, step in and shoot for the face."

"Hell," said Marsh. "I ain't goin' to forget. I been shootin' at that face for years, in my dreams."

Joshua walked quickly, with long strides, and Abner Marsh moved heavily beside him, struggling to match his pace. Marsh had left his cane back in New Orleans. This morning, of all mornings, he felt young again. The air was sweet and cool and full of fragrance, and he was going to get his lady back, his sweet steamer, his *Fevre Dream*.

Past the plantation house. Past the slave shanties. Through another field, where indigo was growing wild in a profusion of pink and purple flowers. Around a tall old willow tree whose trailing tendrils brushed Marsh's face as gently as a woman's hand. Then into a denser stand of woods, cypress mostly, and some palmetto, with flowering reeds and dogwood and fleurs-de-lis of every color growing all about. The ground was damp, and grew damper as they walked. Abner Marsh felt the wetness soaking through the soles of his old boots.

Joshua ducked under a thick gray drape of Spanish moss that hung from a low, twisted limb, and Marsh did likewise one step behind him, and there she was.

Abner Marsh gripped the shotgun very tightly. "Hell," was all he said.

The water had returned to the old back channel, and it stood all about the *Fevre Dream*, but it was not deep enough, and the steamer was not afloat. She rested on a shoal of mud and sand, her head thrust up into the air, listing about ten degrees to larboard, her paddles high and mostly dry. Once she had been white and blue and silver. Now she was mostly gray, the gray of old rotting wood that has seen too much sun and too much dampness and not enough paint. It looked as if Julian and his goddamned vampires had sucked all the life out of it. On her wheelhouse, Marsh could see traces of the whore's scarlet that Sour Billy had slapped upon her, and the letters OZ real faint, like old memories. But the rest was gone, and the old true name could be seen again, where the newer paint had crumbled and peeled. The whitewash on her railings and colonnades had fared the worst, and that was where she was grayest, and here and there Marsh saw patches of green clinging to her wood, and spreading. He began to tremble as he looked at her. The damp and the heat and the rot, he thought, and there was something in his eye. He rubbed at it angrily. Her chimneys looked crooked because of the way she was listing. Spanish moss festooned one side of her pilot house, and drooped off her verge flagpole. The ropes that held up her larboard stage had snapped long ago, and the stage had come crashing to the forecastle. Her grand staircase, that great curving expanse of polished wood, was slimy with fungus. Here and there Marsh could see wildflowers that had taken root in cracks between the deck boards. "Goddamnit," he said. "*Goddamnit*, Joshua, how the hell could you let her get like this? How the hell could you . . ." But then his voice cracked and betrayed him, and Abner Marsh found he had no words.

Joshua York put a gentle hand on his shoulder and said, "I'm sorry, Abner. I did try."

"Oh, I know," Marsh swore. "It was him that did it to her, that turned her rotten like everything else he touches. Oh, I know who it was, I sure as hell know that. What I don't know is why the hell you lied to me, Mister York. All that business about the *Natchez* and the *Robert E. Lee*. Hell. She ain't goin' to outrun nobody, she ain't never goin' to move again." His face was beet red, he knew, and his voice was starting to get loud. "Goddamnit it all to hell, she's just goin' to sit and *rot*, goddamnit it, and *you knew it!*" He stopped suddenly, before he started to shout and woke up all the damned vampires.

"I knew it," Joshua York admitted, with sorrow in his eyes. The morning sun shone behind him, and made him look pale and weak. "But I needed you, Abner. It was not all lie. Julian did put forth the plan I told you, but Billy told him what bad shape the *Fevre Dream* was in, and he gave it up at once. The rest was all true."

"How the hell can I believe you?" Marsh said flatly. "After all we been through, you *lied* to me. Goddamn you to hell, Joshua York, you're my own goddamned partner, and you *lied* to me!"

"Abner, listen to me. Please. Let me explain." He put a hand up against his brow, and blinked.

"Go on," said Marsh. "Go on and tell me. I'm listening, damn you."

"I needed you. I knew there was no way I could conquer Julian alone. The others . . . even those who are with me, they cannot stand before him, before those eyes . . . he can make them do anything. You were my only hope, Abner. You and the men I thought you would bring with you. It has a painful irony. We of the night have preyed upon the people of the day for uncounted thousands of years, and now I must turn to you to save our race. Julian will destroy us. Abner, your dream may have rotted through, but mine can still live! I helped you once. You could not have built her without me. Help me now."

"You should have just asked me," Marsh said. "You could have told me the goddamned truth."

"I did not know if you would come to save my people. I knew you would come for her."

"I would have come for *you*, damn it. We're partners, ain't we? Well, ain't we?"

Joshua York regarded him with quiet gravity. "Yes," he said.

Marsh glared up at the gray rotten ruin that had been his proud lady, and saw that a goddamned bird had built a nest in one of her stacks. Other birds were stirring and fluttering from tree to tree, making little birdy sounds that vexed Abner Marsh no end. The morning sunlight fell upon the steamer in bright yellow shafts, slanting through the trees and swimming with dust motes. The last shadows were stealing away from the dawn, into the underbrush. "Why the hell now?" Marsh asked, frowning at York again. "If it wasn't the

Natchez and the *Robert E. Lee*, what was it? What makes today different from the last thirteen years, that all of a sudden you're runnin' off and writing me letters?"

"Cynthia is with child," said Joshua. "My child."

Abner Marsh remembered the things York had told him so long ago. "You killed somebody together?"

"No. For the first time in our history, conception was free of the taint of the red thirst. Cynthia has been using my drink for years. She became . . . sexually receptive . . . even without the blood, the fever. I responded. It was powerful, Abner. As strong as the thirst, but different, cleaner. A thirst for life instead of death. She will die when her time comes, unless your people can help. Julian would never permit that. And there is the child to think of. I do not want it corrupted, enslaved by Damon Julian. I want this birth to be a new beginning for my race. I had to take action."

A goddamned vampire baby, Abner Marsh thought. He was going to go in and face Damon Julian for a child that might grow up to be just like Julian was. But maybe not. Maybe it'd grow into Joshua instead. "If you want to do somethin'," Marsh said, "then why the hell ain't we in there, instead of yapping out here?" He jerked his shotgun in the direction of the huge ruined steamer.

Joshua York smiled. "I am sorry for the lie," he said. "Abner, there is no one like you. You have my thanks."

"Never mind about that now," Marsh said gruffly, embarrassed by Joshua's gratitude. He walked out from under the shadows of the trees, toward the *Fevre Dream* and the rotted, purple-stained indigo tanks that loomed behind her. When he got down near the water, the mud grabbed at his boots and made obscene sucking sounds as he pulled them free. Marsh checked again to make sure the gun was loaded. Then he found an old weathered plank lying in the shallow, still water, leaned it up against the side of her hull, and hefted himself up onto the main deck of the steamboat. Joshua York, moving quickly and silently, came behind him.

The grand staircase confronted them, leading up to the darkness of the boiler deck, to the curtained staterooms where their enemies slept, to the long echoing dimness of the saloon. Marsh did not move immediately. "I want to see my steamer," he said at last, and he walked around the stair into the engine room.

Seams had burst on a couple of the boilers. Rust had eaten through the steam pipes. The great engines were brown and flaking in spots. Marsh had to step warily to make sure his foot didn't crash through a rotten floorboard. He went to a furnace. Inside was old cold ash, and something else, something brown and yellow and blackened here and there. He reached in, and came out with a bone. "Bones in her furnace," he said. "Her deck rotted through. God-damned slave manacles still on the floor. Rust. Hell. *Hell.*" He turned. "I seen enough."

"I told you," said Joshua York.

"I wanted to see her." They walked back out into the sunlight of the forecastle. Marsh glanced back over his shoulder at the shadows, the rotten rusted shadows of all that she had been and all that he had dreamed. "Eighteen big boilers," he said hoarsely. "Whitey loved them engines."

"Abner, come. We must do what we came to do."

They ascended the grand staircase, climbing with care. The slime on the steps was foul-smelling and slippery. Marsh leaned too hard on a carved wooden acorn and it came off in his hand. The prome-nade was gray and deserted and looked unsafe. They entered the main cabin, and Marsh frowned at three hundred feet of decay and despair and beauty gone to rot. The carpet was stained and torn and eaten away by fungus and mold. Green splotches spread across it like cancer eating away at the soul of the steamer. Someone had painted over the skylight, had covered all that fine stained glass with black paint. It was dark. The long marble bar was covered with dust. State-room doors hung broken and shattered. One chandelier had fallen. They walked around the pile of broken glass. A third of the mirrors were cracked or missing. The rest had gone blind, their silver flaking away or turning black.

When they walked up to the hurricane deck, Marsh was glad to see the sun. He checked the gun again. The texas loomed above them, its cabin doors closed and waiting. "He still in the captain's cabin?" Marsh asked. Joshua nodded. They climbed the short flight of steps to the texas deck, and moved toward it.

In the shadows of the texas porch, Sour Billy Tipton was waiting.

But for the eyes, Abner Marsh might never have recognized him. Sour Billy was as ruined as the boat. He had always been skinny. Now he was an animated skeleton, sharp bones thrusting against sickly yellow flesh. His skin had the look of a man's who has been bedridden for years. His face was a damned skull, a yellowish pock-marked skull. Nearly all his hair had fallen out, and the top of his head was covered with scabs and raw red blotches. He was dressed in black rags, and his fingernails had grown four inches long. Only his eyes were the same: ice-colored and somehow feverish eyes, staring, trying to scare, trying to be little vampire eyes, just like Julian's. Sour Billy had known they were coming. He must have heard them. When they turned the corner he was there, his knife in his hand, his deadly practiced hand. He said, "Well—"

Abner Marsh snapped up the shotgun and fired both barrels, point-blank, at his chest. Marsh didn't much care to hear that second, "Well." Not this time.

The gun roared and kicked back hard, slamming into Marsh and bruising his arm. Sour Billy's chest turned red in a hundred places, and the blast threw him backward. The rotten railing of the texas porch gave way behind him, and he went crashing down to the hurricane deck. Still holding his knife, he tried to get to his feet. He reeled and staggered forward dizzily, like a drunk. Marsh jumped down to the hurricane deck after him, and reloaded the gun. Sour Billy grabbed for a pistol stuck through his belt. Marsh gave him two more barrels, and blew him clear off the hurricane deck. The pistol spun from his grip, and Abner Marsh heard Billy scream and smash into something on the way down. He peered down at the forecastle. Billy was lying face-down, twisted at an unnatural angle, a smear of red beneath him. He still had a hold of his goddamned knife, but it didn't look like he'd be doing any damage with it. Abner Marsh grunted, pulled a couple of fresh shells from his pocket, and turned back toward the texas.

The door to the captain's cabin stood wide open, and Damon Julian was out on the texas porch facing Joshua, a pale malevolence with black and beckoning eyes. Joshua York stood immobile, like a man entranced.

Marsh wrenched his eyes down to his shotgun and the shells he held in his hand. Pretend he ain't there, he told himself. You're in the sun, he can't come for you, don't look at him, just load, just load the gun and give him both goddamned barrels right in the face while Joshua holds him still. His hand shook. He steadied it and slid in one shell.

And Damon Julian laughed. At the sound of that laughter Marsh looked up in spite of himself, the second shell still between his fingers. Julian had such music in his laugh, such warmth and good humor, that it was hard to be afraid, hard to remember what he was and the things he could do.

Joshua had fallen to his knees.

Marsh cussed and took three impetuous strides forward, and Julian whirled, still smiling, and came at him. Or tried to. Julian vaulted down to the hurricane deck over the ruined porch, but Joshua saw him, rose, and came leaping after, catching Julian from behind. For a moment they grappled on the deck. Then Marsh heard Joshua cry out in pain, and he looked away and slid the second shell home and closed the gun and looked up again and saw Julian coming, that white face looming up before him and the teeth gleaming, the terrible teeth. His finger tightened convulsively on the trigger before he had the damned gun aimed, and the shot went wild. The recoil sent Marsh sprawling, and that was what probably saved his life. Julian missed him, spun . . . and hesitated when he saw Joshua rising, four long bleeding tracks down his right cheek. "Look at me, Julian," Joshua called softly. "Look at me."

Marsh had one shot left. Sprawled on the deck, he raised the shotgun, but he was too slow. Damon Julian tore his eyes away from Joshua and saw the barrel swinging toward him. He whirled, and the shot boomed through empty air. By the time Joshua York had helped Abner Marsh to his feet, Julian had vanished down the stairs. "Go after him!" Joshua said urgently. "And stay alert! He might be waiting for you."

"What about you?"

"I'll see he doesn't leave the boat," Joshua said. Then he spun and leaped from the edge of the hurricane deck, out over the forecastle, quick and nimble as a cat. He landed a yard from where Sour Billy lay, landed hard and rolled. An instant later he was back up, and darting up the grand staircase.

Marsh took out two more shells and reloaded. Then he went to the stair, peered down it warily, and began to descend step by careful step, the shotgun held at the ready. The wood creaked beneath his tread, but there was no other sound. Marsh knew that meant nothing. They moved so silently, all of them.

He had a hunch he knew where Julian would hide. In the grand saloon, or one of the staterooms off it. Marsh kept his trigger finger tensed, and went on in, pausing to let his eyes adjust to the darkness.

Way at the far end of the cabin, something moved. Marsh aimed and froze, then eased off. It was Joshua.

"He hasn't come out," Joshua called, his head moving as his eyes—so much better than Marsh's—raked the cabin.

"I figured he hadn't," Marsh said. All of a sudden it felt cold in the cabin. Cold and still, like the breath from a long-closed tomb. It was too dark. Marsh couldn't see anything but vaguely menacing shadows. "I need some goddamned light," he said. He jerked the shotgun upward and fired one barrel up at the skylight. The report echoed deafeningly in the enclosed cabin, and the glass disintegrated. Shards and sunlight came raining down. Marsh took out a shell to reload. "I don't see nothing," he said, stepping forward with the gun under his arm. The long cabin was utterly still and empty as far as he could see. Maybe Julian was crouched behind the bar, Marsh thought. Cautiously he moved toward it.

A vague tinkling sound touched his ears, the clatter of crystals clinking together in the wind. Abner Marsh frowned.

And Joshua cried, "*Abner! Above you!*"

Marsh looked up just as Damon Julian released his hold on the great swaying chandelier and came plunging down at him.

Marsh tried to raise and aim his shotgun, but it was too late and he was too damned slow. Julian landed right on top of him, and sent the gun spinning from Marsh's grasp, and both of them went down. Marsh tried to roll free. Something grabbed him, pulled. He smashed out blindly with a huge rough fist. The answering blow came out of nowhere and nearly tore his head off. For a moment he lay stunned. His arm was seized and wrenched roughly behind him. Marsh screamed. The pressure did not let up. He tried to push himself to his feet, and his arm was bent upward with awful force. He heard it snap, and he screamed again, louder, as the pain hammered through him. He was pushed roughly to the deck, his face hard against the moldy carpeting. "Struggle, my dear Captain, and I'll break your other arm," Julian's mellow voice told him. "Remain still."

"Get away from him!" Joshua said. Marsh lifted his eyes and saw him standing twenty feet away.

"I hardly think so," Julian replied. "Do not move, dear Joshua. If you come at me, I will tear out Captain Marsh's throat before you are within five feet. Stay where you are and I will spare him. Do you understand?"

Marsh tried to move, and bit his lip in anguish. Joshua stood his ground, hands poised like claws in front of him. "Yes," he said, "I understand." His gray eyes looked deadly, but uncertain. Marsh looked around for the shotgun. It lay five feet away, well beyond his reach.

"Good," said Damon Julian. "Now, why don't we make ourselves comfortable?" Marsh heard Julian pull over a chair. He seated himself just behind Marsh. "I'll sit here, in the shadows. You can take a seat beneath that shaft of sunlight the captain so obligingly let into the saloon. Go on, Joshua. Do as I say, unless you want to see him die."

"If you kill him, there will be nothing between us," Joshua said.

"Perhaps I am willing to take that risk," Julian replied. "Are you?"

Joshua York looked around slowly, frowned, took up a chair and moved it beneath the shattered skylight. He seated himself in the sun, a good fifteen feet away from them.

"Take off your hat, Joshua. I want to see your face."

York grimaced, removed his wide-brimmed hat, and sent it sailing off into the shadows.

"Fine," said Damon Julian. "Now we can wait together. For a while, Joshua." He laughed lightly. "Until dark."

CHAPTER THIRTY-THREE

Aboard the Steamer FEVRE DREAM, May 1870

SOUR Billy Tipton opened his eyes and tried to scream. Nothing passed his lips but a soft whimper. He sucked in his breath, and swallowed blood. Sour Billy had drunk enough blood to recognize the taste. Only this time it was his own blood. He coughed and fought for air. He didn't feel so good. His chest was on fire all over, and it was wet where he was lying. Blood, more blood. "Help me," he called out, weakly. No one could have heard him more than three feet away. He shuddered, and closed his eyes again, like he could maybe sleep and make the hurt go away.

But the hurt stayed. Sour Billy lay there for the longest time, his eyes closed, breathing ragged breaths that made his chest shake and scream. He couldn't think of nothing but the blood that was seeping out of him, the deck hard against his face, and the smell. There was some awful smell, all around him. Finally Sour Billy recognized it. He had gone and shit in his pants. He couldn't feel nothing, but he could smell it. He began to cry.

Finally Sour Billy Tipton could not cry anymore. His tears had dried up, and it hurt too much. It hurt awful bad. He tried to think about something else, about something besides the pain, so it would maybe leave him alone. Slowly it came back to him. Marsh and Joshua York, the shotgun going off in his face. They had come to hurt Julian, he remembered, and he had tried to stop them. Only this time he wasn't fast enough. He tried to call out again. "Julian!" he called, a little louder than he had before, but still not very loud.

No answer. Sour Billy Tipton whimpered, and opened his eyes

again. He had fallen, fallen all the way from the hurricane deck. He was on the forecastle, he saw. And it was daylight. Damon Julian couldn't hear him. And even if he did, it was so bright, it was the morning, Julian wouldn't come to him, Julian couldn't come until dark. By dark he would be dead. "I'll be dead by dark," he said aloud, so softly he hardly heard it himself. He coughed and swallowed some more blood. "Mister Julian . . ." he said feebly.

He rested for a while, thinking, or trying to think. He was shot full of holes, he thought. His chest must be raw meat. He ought to be dead, Marsh had been standing right by him, he ought to be dead. Only he wasn't. Sour Billy sniggered. *He* knew why he wasn't dead. Shotguns couldn't kill *him*. He was almost one of *them* now. It was like Julian had said. Sour Billy had felt it happening. Every time he looked in the mirror he thought he was a little whiter, and his eyes were getting more and more like Damon Julian's, he could see it hisself, and he thought maybe he could see better in the dark this last year or two. It was the blood had done it, he thought. If only it hadn't made him sick so much, he might be even further along. Sometimes it made him real sick, and he got bad cramps in his belly and threw up, but he kept on drinking it, like Julian said, and it was making him stronger. He could feel it sometimes, and this proved it, they'd shot him and he'd fallen and he wasn't dead, no sir, he wasn't dead. He was healing up, just like Damon Julian would. He was nearly one of them now. Sour Billy smiled, and thought that he would lie there until he was all healed, and then he would get up and go kill Abner Marsh. He could imagine how scared Marsh would be when he saw Billy coming, after the way he'd been shot.

If only he didn't hurt so much. Sour Billy wondered if it hurt Julian this way, the day that damn dandy of a clerk had stuck the sword through him. Mister Julian had sure showed him. Billy would show a few people, too. He thought about that for a while, about all the things he would do. He would walk down Gallatin Street whenever he liked, and they'd all get real respectful, and he'd have himself beautiful high yaller girls and Creole ladies instead of whores from the dance halls, and when he was through with them he'd have their blood too, and that way no one else would have them, and that way they'd never laugh at him, not like the whores used to laugh at him sometimes, in the old bad days.

Sour Billy Tipton liked thinking about the way it was going to be. But after a time—a few minutes, a few hours, he wasn't sure no more—he couldn't. He kept thinking about the pain instead, the way it hurt so bad whenever he tried to breathe. It ought to be hurting less, he thought. But it wasn't. And he was still bleeding bad, so bad he was starting to feel awful dizzy. If he was healing up, how come he was still bleeding? All of a sudden Sour Billy got afraid. Maybe he wasn't far enough along yet. Maybe he wasn't going to heal after all, and get up good as new, and go and get Abner Marsh. Maybe he was just going to bleed to death. He cried out, "Julian." He cried as loud as he could. Julian could finish the change, could make him better, make him strong. If he could only get Julian it would be all right. Julian would bring him blood to make him strong, Julian would take care of him. Sour Billy knew that. What would Julian ever do without him? He called out again, screaming so hard that his throat almost burst with the pain.

Nothing. Silence. He listened for footsteps, for Julian or one of the others coming to help him. Nothing. Except . . . he listened harder. Sour Billy thought he heard voices. And one of them was Damon Julian's! He could hear him! He felt weak with relief.

Only Julian couldn't hear Billy. And even if he could, he might not come, not out into the sun. The thought terrified Sour Billy. Julian would come when it got dark, would come and finish the change. But by dark it would be too late.

He would have to go to Julian, Sour Billy Tipton decided, as he laid there in his blood and pain. He would have to move and go to where Julian was, so Julian could help him.

Sour Billy bit his lip and gathered all his strength and tried to get up.

And he screamed.

The pain that shot through him when he tried to move was a burning knife, a sudden sharp agony that stabbed through his body and drove all thought and hope and fear out of him, until there was nothing but the pain itself. He shrieked and lay still, and his body throbbed. He could feel his heart thumping wildly, and the pain, the pain slowly fading. That was when Sour Billy Tipton realized that he couldn't feel his legs no more. He tried to wriggle his toes. He couldn't feel nothing at all down there.

He was dying. It wasn't fair, Sour Billy thought. He was so close. For thirteen years he had been drinking the blood and getting stronger, changing, and he was so *close*. He was going to live forever, and now they were taking it away from him, robbing him, they'd always robbed him, he'd never had nothing. It was a cheat. The world had cheated him again, the niggers and the Creoles and the rich dandies, they was always cheating him and laughing at him, and now they were cheating him of life, of his revenge, of everything.

He *had* to get to Julian. If only he could make that change, it would all be all right. Otherwise he'd die here, and they'd laugh at him, they'd say he was a fool, trash, all the things they had always said, they'd piss on his grave and laugh at him. He had to get to Mister Julian. Then he would be the one laughing, yes he would.

Sour Billy took a deep breath. He could feel his knife, still gripped in his hand. He moved his arm, took the knife between his teeth, trembling. There! That didn't hurt so much, he thought. His arms was still all right. His fingers spread and fought for purchase on the wet deck, slick with mold and blood. Then he pulled hard as he could, with his hands and his arms, dragged himself forward. His chest burned, and the knife blade came plunging into his back again, so he shuddered and bit down real hard on the steel between his teeth. He collapsed in exhaustion and agony. But when the hurt finally ebbed a bit, Sour Billy opened his eyes and smiled around his knife blade. He had moved! He had pulled himself forward a whole foot, he thought. Another five or six pulls, and he would be at the foot of the grand staircase. Then he could grab hold of the fancy banister posts and use them to haul himself upward. Them voices were coming from up there, he thought. He could get to them. He knew he could. He *had* to!

Sour Billy Tipton stretched out his arms, dug his long hard nails into the wood, and bit down on his knife.

CHAPTER THIRTY-FOUR

Aboard the Steamer FEVRE DREAM, May 1870

THE hours passed in silence, a silence laced with fear.

Abner Marsh sat close to Damon Julian, with his back against the black marble bar, nursing his broken arm and sweating. Julian had finally allowed him to get up off his belly, when the throbbing in his arm had gotten to be too much for Marsh, and he began to moan. In this position it didn't seem to hurt so much, but he knew the agony would come flooding back the instant he tried to move. So Marsh sat very still, and held his arm, and thought.

Marsh had never been much of a chess player, as Jonathon Jeffers had proved a half-dozen times. Sometimes he even forgot how the damned pieces moved from game to game. But even now he knew enough to recognize a stalemate when he saw one.

Joshua York was sitting stiffly in his chair, his eyes dark and unreadable at this distance, his whole body tense. The sunlight was beating down on him, searing the life from him, burning off his strength as it burned off the river mists every morning. He did not move. Because of Marsh. Because Joshua knew that if he attacked, Abner Marsh would be choking on his own blood before York could possibly reach Julian. Maybe Joshua could kill Damon Julian then, and maybe not, but either way it wouldn't make much difference to Marsh.

Julian was stalemated too. If he killed Marsh, he would lose his protection. Then Joshua would be free to come at him. Clearly Damon Julian feared that. Abner Marsh knew how it was. Defeat will do that to a man, even to such a thing as called itself Damon

Julian. Julian had broken Joshua York dozens of times, and bled him to seal the submission. York had triumphed only once. But that was enough. The certainty was gone from Julian. Fear lived inside him like a maggot in a corpse.

Marsh felt weak and helpless. His arm hurt like hell, and there was nothing he could do. When he was not studying York and Julian, his eyes returned to the shotgun. Too far, he told himself. Too far. When he sat up against the bar, it had put the gun even further away. Seven feet at least. It was impossible. Marsh knew he could never do it, even at the best of times. And with a broken arm . . . he gnawed his lip and tried to think of something else. If it was Jonathon Jeffers sitting where Marsh sat, maybe he would have been able to figure something out. Something clever and surprising and devious. But Jeffers was dead, and Marsh had only himself to rely on, and the only thing he could think to do was the simple, direct, stupid thing —make a grab for that goddamned shotgun. If he did that, Marsh knew, he would die.

"Does the light bother you, Joshua?" Julian asked once, after they had been seated a long time. "You really must get used to it if you are to become one of them. All the good cattle love the sunlight." He smiled. Then, quickly as it had come, the smile faded. Joshua York did not reply, and Julian did not speak again.

Watching him, Marsh thought how much Julian himself seemed to have decayed, just as the steamer and Sour Billy had gone to rot. He was different now, somehow, different and even more frightening. After that one, brief question, he had no more taunts. He had no words at all. He did not look at Joshua York or at Marsh or at anything in particular. His eyes stared off into nothingness, cold and black and dead as coals. They still had a lambent quality about them, and in the shadows where Julian was seated they sometimes seemed to burn with their own dim light beneath his pale, heavy brow. But they did not seem human. Nor did Julian. Marsh remembered the night that Julian had come aboard the *Fevre Dream*. When he had looked into his eyes then, it was as if he saw masks falling away, one after the other in endless succession, until at the bottom, beneath it all, the beast emerged. Now it was different. Now it was almost as if the masks had ceased to exist. Damon Julian had been as evil a man as Marsh had ever met, but part of his evil had been human evil: his malevolence, his lies, his terrible musical laugh, his cruel delight in torment, his love for beauty and its ruin. Now all that seemed to be gone. Now there was only the beast, hunched in the darkness with feral eyes, cornered and fearful, unreasoning. Now Julian did not ridicule Joshua, nor expound on good and evil and strength and weakness, nor fill Marsh with soft, rotten promises. Now he only sat and waited, shrouded in darkness, his ageless face devoid of all expression, his eyes ancient and empty.

Abner Marsh realized then that Joshua had been right. Julian was mad, or worse than mad. Julian was a ghost now, and the thing that lived inside that body was all but mindless.

Yet, Marsh thought bitterly, *it* would be the winner. Damon Julian might die, as all the other masks had died in turn, through the long centuries. But the beast would go on. Julian dreamed of dark and sleep, but the beast could never die. It was clever, and patient, and strong.

Abner Marsh eyed the shotgun again. If only he could reach it. If only he was as fast and strong as he had been forty years ago. If only Joshua could hold the beast's attention long enough. But it was no good. The beast would not meet Joshua's eyes. Marsh was neither fast nor strong, and his arm was broken and in agony. He could never lurch to his feet and reach the gun in time. The barrel was pointed in the wrong direction too. It had fallen so it pointed at Joshua. If it pointed the other way, maybe it would be worth the risk. Then he would just have to dive for the gun, raise it up quick, and pull the trigger. But the way it lay, he would have to grab it and turn all the way around to fire at the thing that had called itself Julian. With a broken arm. No. Marsh knew it would be futile. The beast was too fast.

A moan escaped Joshua's lips, a half-suppressed cry of pain. He put a hand to his brow, then leaned forward and buried his face in his hands. His skin was pinkish already. Before long it would be red. Then charred and black and burned. Abner Marsh could see the vitality ebbing from him. What will kept him in that burning circle of sun, Marsh could not know. Joshua had guts, though, damned if he didn't. All of a sudden Marsh had to say something. "Kill him," he called out loudly. "Joshua, get out of there and go for him, goddamn it. Never mind me."

Joshua York looked up and smiled weakly. "No."

"Goddamnit all to hell, you stubborn fool. Do like I tell you! I'm a goddamned old man, my life don't mean nothin'. Joshua, *do like I'm tellin' you!*"

Joshua shook his head and buried his face in his hands again.

The beast was staring at Marsh strangely, as if it could not comprehend his words, as if it had forgotten all the speech it ever knew. Marsh looked in its eyes and shivered. His arm hurt, and he had tears hiding in the back of his eyes. He cussed and swore until his face turned red. It was better than weeping like some damned woman. Then he called out, "You been one hell of a partner, Joshua. I ain't goin' to forget you as long as I live."

York smiled. Even the smile was pained, Marsh could see. Joshua was weakening visibly. The light was going to kill him, and then Marsh would be here alone.

They had hours and hours of daylight left. But hours passed. Night would come. Abner Marsh couldn't stop it coming no more'n he could reach that goddamned useless shotgun. The sun would set and darkness would come creeping over the *Fevre Dream*, and the beast would smile and rise from its chair. All along the grand saloon the doors would open, as the others stirred and woke, all the children of the night, the vampires, the sons and daughters and slaves of the beast. From behind the broken mirrors and the faded oil paintings they would come, silent, with their cold smiles and white faces and terrible eyes. Some of them were Joshua's friends and one bore his child but Marsh knew with a deadly certainty that it would make no difference. They belonged to the beast. Joshua had the words and the justice and the dream, but the beast had the power, and it would call out to the beasts that lived in all the others, it would wake their red thirst and bend them to its will. It had no thirst itself, but it remembered.

And when those doors began to open, Abner Marsh would die. Damon Julian had talked of sparing him, but the beast was not bound by Julian's fool promises, it knew how dangerous Marsh was. Ugly or not, Marsh would feed them tonight. And Joshua would die as well, or—worse—become like them. And his child would grow into another beast, and the killing would go on and on, the red thirst would flow down the centuries unquenched, the fevre dreams would turn to sickness and to rot.

How could it end any other way? The beast was greater than they were, a force of nature. The beast was like the river, eternal. It had no doubts, no thoughts, no dreams or plans. Joshua York might overwhelm Damon Julian, but when Julian fell the beast lay beneath: alive, implacable, strong. Joshua had drugged his own beast, had tamed it to his will, so he had only humanity to face the beast that lived in Julian. And humanity was not enough. He could not hope to win.

Abner Marsh frowned. Something in his thoughts nagged at him. He tried to figure out what it was, but it wriggled free of him. His arm throbbed. He wished he had some of Joshua's goddamned drink. It tasted like hell, but Joshua had said once it had laudanum in it, and that would help the pain. The alcohol wouldn't hurt none, neither.

The angle of the light pouring in through the shot-out skylight had changed. It was afternoon, Marsh figured. Afternoon and getting later. They would have a few hours more. Then the doors would start to open. He looked at Julian, at the shotgun. He squeezed his arm, as if that could lessen the pain somehow. What the hell was he thinking about? About wanting some of Joshua's damn drink for his arm . . . no, about the beast, about how Joshua couldn't never beat it, on account . . .

Abner Marsh's eyes narrowed, and he looked over to Joshua. He *had* beat him, Marsh thought. Once, he beat him once, beast or no. Why can't he do it again? Why? Marsh clutched at his arm, rocked slowly back and forth, and tried to drive off the pain so he could think clearer. Why, why, why?

And it came to him, like such things always did. Maybe he was slow, but Abner Marsh never forgot. It came to him. The drink, he thought. He could see how it had been. He'd poured the last of it down Joshua's damned gullet when he passed out in the sun. The final drop fell on his boot and he threw the bottle in the river. Joshua had left hours later, and it had taken him . . . how long? . . . days, it had taken him *days* to get back to the *Fevre Dream*. He'd been running, running to his damn bottles, running from the red thirst. Then he found the steamer, and all the dead, and started ripping loose them boards, and Julian had come . . . Marsh remembered Joshua's own words . . . *I was screaming at him, screaming incoherently. I wanted vengeance. I wanted to kill him as badly as I have ever wanted to kill anyone, wanted to rip open that pale throat of his, and taste his damnable blood! My anger* . . . No, thought Marsh, not just anger. Thirst. Joshua had been so mad he never even knew it, but he was in the first stage of the red thirst! He must have had a glass of his drink as soon as Julian stole off, so he never realized what it was, why that time had been different.

Marsh got a real cold feeling right then, wondering if Joshua had known the real reason he was ripping free those boards, wondering what would have happened if Julian hadn't intervened. No wonder Joshua had won then, and never again. His burns, his fears, the carnage all around him, no drinks for days . . . it *had* to have been the thirst. His beast was awake that night, and stronger than Julian's.

Briefly Abner Marsh was gripped by a great excitement. Then, rapidly, it dawned on him that his wild hope was misplaced. Maybe he had figured something out, but it wasn't doing them a goddamned bit of good. Joshua had taken a good supply of his drink on this last escape of his. He'd drunk a half-bottle in New Orleans before they set out for Julian's plantation. Marsh couldn't see no way to wake the fever in Joshua, the fever that was their only chance . . . his eyes went back to the shotgun, the damned useless shotgun. "Hell," he muttered. Forget the shotgun, he told himself, it ain't no good to you, think, think like Mister Jeffers would have, figure something out. Like in a steamboat race, Marsh thought. You couldn't just run her straight out against another fast boat, you had to be smart, you had to get a lightnin' pilot who knew all the cutoffs and how to shave them close, and maybe you bought up all the beech so the other boat couldn't get nothing but cottonwood, or maybe you had some lard in reserve. Tricks!

Marsh scowled and tugged at his whiskers with his good hand. He couldn't do nothing, he knew. It was up to Joshua. Only Joshua was burning up, Joshua was getting weaker by the minute, and he wasn't going to move so long as Marsh's life was at stake. If only there was some way to get Joshua moving . . . to wake the thirst . . . somehow. How did it come now? Every month, something like that, except it didn't come at all when you used the bottle. Wasn't there something else? Something else that might bring on the thirst? Marsh thought there might be, but he couldn't think of it. Maybe anger had something to do with it, but it wasn't enough. Beauty? Real beautiful things tempted him, even with his drink. He probably picked me as his partner cause they told him I was the ugliest man on the goddamned river, Marsh thought. But it still wasn't enough. Damned Damon Julian was pretty enough, and he got Joshua awful angry, but Joshua still lost, always lost, the drink made it so, it had to be . . . Marsh began to think back on all the stories that Joshua had ever told him, all the dark nights, the deaths, the terrible bitter times when his thirst had taken hold of him body and soul.

. . . caught me in the stomach, square, said Joshua, *and I bled badly . . . I got up. I must have been a terrible sight, pale-faced and covered with blood. And a strange feeling was on me . . .* Julian was sipping at his wine, smiling, saying *Did you truly fear I would harm you that night in August? Oh, perhaps I would have, in my pain and rage. But not before . . .* Marsh saw his face, twisted and bestial, as he pulled Jeffers's sword cane from his body . . . he remembered Valerie, burning, dying in the yawl, remembered the way she had screamed and gone for Karl Framm's throat . . . he heard Joshua talking, saying *the man hit me again, and I lashed out backhanded at him . . . he was on me again . . .*

It had to be right, Abner Marsh thought, it had to be, it was the only thing he could think of, the only thing he could figure. He peered up at the skylight. The angle was sharper now, and it seemed to Marsh that the light had grown just the tiniest bit red. Joshua was partly in shadow now. An hour ago, Marsh would have been relieved to see it. Now he wasn't so sure.

"*Help* me . . ." the voice said. It was a broken whisper, a ghastly pain-racked choking. But they heard it. In the darkened silence they all heard it.

Sour Billy Tipton had come crawling out of the dimness, leaving a trail of blood behind him on the carpet. He wasn't really crawling, Marsh saw. He was dragging himself, sticking his goddamned little knife into the deck and pulling himself forward with his arms, wriggling, his legs and whole lower half of his body scraping behind him. His spine was bent at an angle it shouldn't have bent at. Billy hardly looked human. He was covered with slime and filth, crusted over with dry blood, bleeding even as they watched. He pulled himself forward another foot. His chest looked caved-in, and pain had twisted his face into a hideous mask.

Joshua York rose slowly from his chair, like a man in a dream. His face was an awful red, Marsh saw. "Billy . . ." he began.

"Stay where you are, Joshua," said the beast.

York looked at him dully, and licked his dry, cracked lips. "I will not threaten you," he said. "Let me kill him. It would be a mercy."

Damon Julian smiled and shook his head. "Kill poor Billy," he said, "and I must kill Captain Marsh." It sounded almost like Julian again now; the liquid sophistication of the voice, the chill within the words, the air of vague amusement.

Sour Billy moved another painful foot and stopped, his body shaking. Blood dripped from his mouth and his nose. "Julian," he said.

"You'll have to speak up, Billy. We can't hear you very well."

Sour Billy clutched his knife and grimaced. He tried to raise his head as much as he could. "I'm . . . help me . . . hurt, I'm hurt. Bad. Inside . . . inside, Mister Julian."

Damon Julian rose from his chair. "I can see that, Billy. What do you want?"

Sour Billy's mouth began to tremble at the edges. "Help . . ." he whispered. "Change . . . finish the change . . . got to . . . I'm *dyin'* . . ."

Julian was watching Billy, and watching Joshua, too. Joshua was still standing. Abner Marsh tensed his muscles and looked at the shotgun. With Julian already on his feet, it wasn't possible. Not to turn it on him, and fire. But maybe . . . he looked at Billy, whose agony almost made Marsh forget his broken arm. Billy was begging. ". . . live forever . . . Julian . . . change me . . . one of you . . ."

"Ah," said Julian. "I'm afraid I have sad news for you, Billy. I can't change you. Did you really think a creature like you could become one of *us*?"

" . . . *promised*," Billy whispered shrilly. "You *promised*. I'm *dyin'*!"

Damon Julian smiled. "Whatever will I do without you?" he said. He laughed lightly, and that was when Marsh knew for a fact that it was Julian, that the beast had let him surface again. It was Julian's laughter, rich and musical and stupid. Marsh heard the laugh and watched Sour Billy's face and saw his hand shake as he wrenched the knife free of the deck.

"*The hell with you!*" Marsh roared at Julian, as he heaved himself to his feet. Julian looked over, startled. Marsh bit back the pain and went for the shotgun, diving across the room. Julian was a hundred times quicker than him. Marsh landed heavily on the gun, and almost blanked out from the pain that shot through him, but even as he felt the hardness of the barrel beneath his stomach, he felt Julian's cold white hands close round his neck.

And then they were gone, and Damon Julian was screaming. Abner Marsh rolled over. Julian was staggering backward, his hands up over his face. Sour Billy's knife was sticking out of his left eye, and blood was running down between his pale white fingers. "Die, goddamn you," Marsh yelled as he yanked the trigger. The shot blew Julian off his feet. The gun kicked back into Marsh's arm, and he screamed. For an instant he did black out. When the pain cleared enough so he could see, he had trouble climbing to his feet. But he did it. Just in time to hear a sharp crack, like a wet branch being broken.

Joshua York rose from Billy Tipton's body with blood on his hands. "There was no hope for him," York said.

Marsh sucked in air in great draughts, his heart pounding. "We did it, Joshua," he said. "We killed the goddamned—"

Someone laughed.

Marsh turned and backed away.

Julian smiled. He wasn't dead. He had lost an eye, but the knife hadn't gone deep enough, hadn't touched his brain. He was half-blind but he wasn't dead. Too late Marsh realized his mistake. He'd shot at Julian's chest, the goddamned chest, he ought to have blown off his head, but he'd taken the easy shot instead. Julian's dressing gown hung from him in bloody tatters, but he wasn't dead. "I am not so easy to kill as poor Billy," he said. Blood welled in his eye socket and dripped down his cheek. Already it was crusting, clotting. "Nor as easy as you will be." He came toward Marsh with languid inevitable slowness.

Marsh tried to hold the shotgun with his broken arm while he got two shells from his pocket. He pinned it under his arm against his body, stepping backward, but the pain made him weak and clumsy. His fingers slipped and one of the shells dropped to the floor. Marsh backed up hard against a column. Damon Julian laughed.

"No," said Joshua York. He stepped between them, his face raw and red. "I forbid it. I am bloodmaster. Stop, Julian."

"Ah," said Julian. "Again, dear Joshua? Again then. But this shall be the last time. Even Billy has learned his true nature. It is time for you to learn yours, dear Joshua." His left eye was crusted blood, his right a howling black abyss.

Joshua York stood unmoving.

"You can't beat him," Abner Marsh said. "The damn beast. Joshua, no." But Joshua York was past hearing. The shotgun fell from beneath Marsh's shattered arm. He bent, snatched it up with his good hand, slapped it down on the table behind him, and began to load it. With only one hand, it was slow work. His fingers were thick and clumsy. The shell kept squirting free. Finally he got it in, closed the gun, raised it up clumsily under his good arm.

Joshua York had turned around, slowly, the way the *Fevre Dream* had spun that night she came after the *Eli Reynolds*. He took a step toward Abner Marsh. "Joshua, no," Marsh said. "Stay away." Joshua moved closer. He was trembling, fighting it. "Get clear," Marsh said. "Let me get off a shot." Joshua didn't seem to hear. He had an awful dead look on his face. He belonged to the beast. His strong pale hands were raised. "Hell," said Marsh, "hell. Joshua, I got to do it. I got it figured. It's the only way."

Joshua York seized Abner Marsh around the throat, his gray eyes wide and demonic. Marsh shoved the shotgun up under Joshua's armpit and yanked the trigger. There was a terrible explosion, the scent of smoke and blood. York spun and fell heavily, crying out in pain, as Marsh stepped away from him.

Damon Julian smiled sardonically and moved like a rattlesnake, wrenching the smoking gun from Marsh's hand. "And now there are only the two of us," he said. "Only the two of us, dear Captain."

He was still smiling when Joshua made a sound that was half a snarl and half a scream, and threw himself on Julian from behind. Julian cried out in surprise. They rolled over and over, grappling with each other ferociously until they slammed up against the bar, and broke apart. Damon Julian rose first, Joshua soon after. York's shoulder was a bloody ruin, and his arm was limp at his side, but in his slitted gray eyes, through the haze of blood and pain, Abner Marsh could feel the rage of the fevered beast. York was in pain, Marsh thought triumphantly, and *pain* could wake the thirst.

Joshua advanced slowly; Julian moved back, smiling. "Not me, Joshua," he said. "It was the Captain who hurt you. The Captain." Joshua paused and glanced briefly at Marsh, and for a long moment Marsh waited to see which way the thirst would drive him, to see whether Joshua or his beast was the master.

Finally York smiled thinly at Damon Julian, and the quiet fight began.

Weak with relief, Marsh paused a moment to gather his strength before he stooped to pick up the shotgun from where Julian had dropped it. He deposited it on the table, broke it, reloaded it slowly and laboriously. When he picked it up and cradled it beneath his arm, Damon Julian was kneeling. He had reached into his eye socket with his fingers, and torn out his blind and bloody eye. He was holding it up, his hand cupped, while Joshua York bent to the bloody offering.

Abner Marsh stepped forward quickly, pushed the shotgun up to Julian's temple, against the fine black curls, and let fly with both barrels.

Joshua looked stunned, like he had been wrenched abruptly from some dream. Marsh grunted and tossed down the gun. "You didn't want that," he told Joshua. "Hold still. I got what you want." He walked heavily behind the bar, and found the dark unlabeled wine bottles. Marsh picked one up and blew away the dust. That was when he happened to look up and see all the open doors, all the pale faces, watching. The shots, he thought. The shots had brought them out.

One-handed, Marsh had trouble getting out the cork. He finally used his teeth. Joshua York drifted toward the bar, as if in a daze. In his eyes the fight went on. Marsh held out the bottle, and Joshua reached out and grabbed his arm. Marsh held very still. For a long moment he did not know which it would be, whether Joshua would take the bottle or tear open the veins in his wrist. "We all got to make our goddamned choices, Joshua," he said softly, in the grip of Joshua's strong fingers.

Joshua York stared at him for half of forever. Then he wrenched the bottle free of Marsh's hand, threw back his head, and upended it. The dark liquor came gurgling down, and ran all over his goddamned chin.

Marsh pulled out a second bottle of the noxious stuff, smashed its top off clean against the hard edge of the marble bar, and raised it up. "To the goddamned *Fevre Dream!*" he said.

They drank together.

Epilogue

THE graveyard is old and overgrown, and filled with the sounds of the river. It sits high on its bluff, and below it rolls the Mississippi, on and on, as it has rolled for thousands of years. You can sit on the edge of the bluff, feet dangling, and look out over the river, drinking in the peace, the beauty. The river has a thousand faces up here. Sometimes it's golden, and alive with ripples from insects skimming the surface and water flowing around some half-submerged branch. At sunset it turns bronze for a while, and then red, and the red spreads and makes you think of Moses and another river a long way away. On a clear night, the water flows dark and clean as black satin, and beneath its shimmering surface are stars, and a fairy moon that shifts and dances and is somehow larger and prettier than the one up in the sky. The river changes with the seasons, too. When the spring floods come, it is brown and muddy and creeps up to the high water marks on the trees and banks. In autumn, leaves of a thousand colors drift past lazily in its blue embrace. And in winter the river freezes hard, and the snow comes drifting down to cover it, and transforms it into a wild white road upon which no one may travel, so bright it hurts the eyes. Beneath the ice, the waters still flow, icy and turbulent, never resting. And finally the river shrugs, and the winter's ice shatters like thunder and breaks apart with terrible, rending cracks.

All of the river's moods can be seen from the graveyard. From there, the river looks like it did a thousand years ago. Even now the Iowa side is nothing but trees and high, rocky bluffs. The river itself is tranquil, empty, still. A thousand years ago you might watch for hours and see nothing but a solitary Indian in a birch bark canoe. Today you might watch for just as long, and see only one long procession of sealed barges, pushed by a single small diesel towboat.

In between then and now, there was a time when the river swarmed and lived, when smoke and steam and whistles and fires were everywhere. The steamboats are all gone now, though. The river is peaceful. The dead in the graveyard wouldn't like it much this way. Half of those buried here were rivermen.

The graveyard is peaceful, too. Most of the plots were filled a long, long time ago, and now even the grandchildren of those who lie here have died. Visitors are rare, and the few who come visit a single, unimpressive grave.

Some of the graves have large monuments. One has a statue on top of it, of a tall man dressed like a steamer pilot, holding a portion of a wheel and gazing out into the distance. Several have colorful accounts of life and death on the river inscribed on their tombstones, telling how they died in a boiler explosion, or the war, or by drowning. But the visitors come to none of these. The grave they seek out is relatively plain. The stone has seen a hundred years of weathering, but it has held up well. The words chiseled into it are plainly readable: a name, some dates, and two lines of poetry.

CAP'N ABNER MARSH
1805–1873

So we'll go no more a-roving
So late into the night.

Above the name, carved into the stone with great skill and great care, is a small decoration, raised and finely detailed, showing two great side-wheel steamers in a race. Time and weather have wreaked their damage, but you can still see the smoke streaming from their chimneys, and you can almost sense their speed. If you lean close enough and run your fingertips over the stone, you can even discern their names. The trailing boat is the *Eclipse*, a famous steamer in her day. The one in front is unknown to most river historians. She appears to be named the *Fevre Dream*.

The visitor who comes most often always touches her, as if for luck.

Oddly enough, he always comes by night.

George R. R. Martin was born in 1948 in New Jersey and went to university in Chicago. He published his first sf story, 'The Hero', in 1971 and he rapidly established himself as a writer of rare quality, winning three Hugos, two Nebulas and the Bram Stoker Award. He spent ten years in Hollywood, writing screenplays and serving as story editor on *The Twilight Zone* and as writer/producer on *Beauty and the Beast*, before beginning his majestic fantasy series *A Song of Ice and Fire*, which so far includes *A Game of Thrones*, *A Clash of Kings* and *A Storm of Swords*.